OFFICIAL PRIVILEGE

Also by P. T. Deutermann
Scorpion in the Sea
The Edge of Honor

OFFICIAL PRIVILEGE

P.T. DEUTERMANN

ST. MARTIN'S PRESS ✷ NEW YORK

This is a work of fiction. Characters, military organizations, ships, and places in this novel are either the product of the author's imagination, or, if real, or based on real entities, are used fictitiously without any intent to describe their actual conduct or character. Insofar as this book addresses military issues, policies, and history, the work represents the views of the author alone and does not necessarily represent the policies and views of the United States Department of Defense.

Design by *Basha Zapatka*

Library of Congress Cataloging-in-Publication Data

Deutermann, Peter T.
    Official privilege / P.T. Deutermann.
      p. cm.
    "A Tom Doherty Associates book."
    ISBN 0-312-11996-8
    I. Title.
    PS3554.E887035 1995
    813'.54—dc20   95-1829
                                              CIP

First Edition: June 1995

10 9 8 7 6 5 4 3 2 1

ACKNOWLEDGMENTS

I would like to thank my editors at St. Martin's. Thanks are also due to the lady at the Philadelphia Medical Examiner's office and a forensic scientist in the Georgia Bureau of Investigation who asked to remain anonymous; to Debby and Kathy and Aubrey for critical first readings; to Andy Fahy for help with the battleship layout; to the Naval History Division in the Washington Navy Yard; to the public affairs office of the Washington Metropolitan Police; and to two young army captains at Georgia Military College for help with some army organizational material. Special thanks as well to my agent, Nick Ellison, and his trusty sidekick, Liz, for their continuing encouragement.

This book is dedicated to those officers who attain flag or general officer rank in the armed forces and continue to exercise the hands-on, personally-involved style of leadership that got them their stars.

OFFICIAL PRIVILEGE

I

APRIL 1994

THE PHILADELPHIA NAVAL SHIPYARD

1

I'M NOT GONNA let those bastards scare me, Benny thought. I know what those dumb guineas are up to, a couple of 'em probably waiting down here in the dark for me, gonna jump outta one of these hatches and try to scare my ass. He stopped, then squinted through the scratched faceplate of the mask at the hull diagram, trying to shine his hard-hat helmet light down on the diagram and still keep an eye out in the darkened second-deck passageway. Sons a bitches, screwing off up there at the air lock while I go nitrogen diving down here, doing *their* damn job.

Benny was nineteen, a high school graduate, and he was trying like hell to convert an intern job in Production into a full-time job in the Philadelphia Naval Shipyard. That was probably why the ship's supe had told him to go to the battleship and do a no-shit sounding-and-security tour. Those goof-offs over in Shop 72 were reporting everything secure, but the supe had seen them up on the main deck, sitting around when they were supposed to be inside, going space by space through the Engineering Department. "You go do it, Benny," he said. "I know it's a little spooky in there, no lights and everything, but they'll set you up with the breathing rigs, and you go through the main holes in the *Wisconsin* and do the security tour right."

Benny was doing it right, but it was more than just a little spooky down here—cold black steel, some of it five, six inches thick, creating total darkness once you went through the air lock on the main deck. There had been a temporary lighting string hung in the overhead of the main deck's athwartships passageway, but once you went down to the second deck, it was like total darkness, man. He had a single air-tank rig on with a full facemask, because, below the main deck, the mothballed battlewagon had been backfilled with nitrogen gas to displace all the oxygen. No oxygen, no oxidation—nothing rusted. And no oxygen meant nobody else should be down here, either—except maybe a couple of wiseasses from Shop 72, waiting to scare the new kid.

He kept walking up the passageway, looking for the hatch down to Gasoline Alley and the main engineering spaces, flicking his helmet light from side to side, careful to step over the infamous knee-knockers, those steel reinforcement frames that stuck up out of the deck every twenty feet. He was cold—he should have worn the jacket, like that guy had said. But that was the same guy who'd been talking about ghosts and the souls of dead sailors wandering the passageways, rolling his eyes, and Benny wasn't having any of that stuff.

He finally came to an armored hatch; he stepped closer to read the brass plate on which the hatch number was engraved. Then he consulted the hull diagram again. Bingo. Down this sucker to the third deck, from which access to the fire rooms and engine rooms of the battleship could be gained. He pointed his light down the steep ladder, marveling at the four-inch-thick deck through which the hatch passed and the heavy hydraulic arms supporting the hatch. What the hell was that! He snapped his head around, but there was no peripheral vision in these damn masks. He'd had the sense that somebody might be following him in the darkness, but if there was, he knew it had to be one of those guys, come down after him to spook him. He'd seen other breathing rigs stashed up there by the air lock. Damn riggers—he wondered how long it had been since any of *them* had come down here to check the main spaces.

He stepped onto the first rung of the ladder and then reached up and snapped off the helmet light. He blinked at the total darkness. He had hoped to catch a flash of light behind him in case one of the guys was back there, but there was nothing—nothing but the blackness and the sound of his breathing in the mask. "The other place where the sun don't friggin' shine, man," the rigger chief had said. "It's a friggin' tomb down there, man, and you're gonna see why nobody in the shop wants to make the tour. Besides, they got all those electronic flooding alarms and shit—what do they need a guy to go down there for?"

But the ship's supe had laid it out: "Because they're supposed to do it once a month, go down there and physically inspect the main spaces, looking for the one thing that can spell disaster in a mothballed ship—water. The bilges are supposed to be bone-dry, so if there's water, there's a goddamn leak somewhere, and that's serious shit, because rising water can short out the flooding alarms, and then you get what the snipes call a no-shitter going, that big-ass battleship sitting there without one single swingin' dick on board and water rising in an engine room."

One of the mothballed heavy cruisers over in the west yard had settled right to the bottom over the period of a month, flooding out the opened steam turbines and eight boilers left opened under a dry layup. They had had to scrap the ship.

He checked the area behind him, but there was still only blackness. If there was somebody back there, they wouldn't be able to see him if he just stepped down the hatch, so that's what he did, going down carefully in the complete darkness, one step at a time, gently bumping his tank on the hatch coaming and then the individual treads of the ladder. When he felt his foot reach the solid-steel deck at the bottom of the ladder, he turned around and looked back up to where the top of the ladder should be. And he waited, watching for the telltale glow of another helmet light up there. But there was still nothing, and then he remembered he had eight main spaces to get through and about fifty minutes of air left in the tank.

Screw it, he thought. They wanna screw around, let 'em. He snapped his helmet light back on and consulted the diagram, his breathing again audible in the mask. Start from aft and work forward. Let's see . . . where the hell is aft? This way. First space to hit was the aftermost engine room, the hatch all the way aft, port side. Over the next half hour, he physically inspected each main engineering space, stepping through the hatch from Gasoline Alley, shining his flashlight down through the deck gratings three levels down to the bilge, checking for any glint of water. He worked his way toward the bow of the ship until he came to the last hatch, number one fire room, port side, all the way forward. The hatches had all looked much smaller than he had expected them to be. Be a bitch to get outta these places, some heavy shit went down in the middle of a sea battle, he thought as he worked his way forward. Probably why they made them that way— keep the guys from booking topside.

He undogged the final hatch and was surprised to see how loose the dogs were; every other compartment along Gasoline Alley had been dogged down all the way, damn near requiring three men and a small boy to move those lever arms. But this one was hand-tight. Weird. He started to open the hatch and then stopped. I wonder if one of the guys is in there, snuck in when I was in one of the other spaces. Gonna yell "Boo" when I open the hatch. He toyed with the idea of pushing the lever arm *down* instead of up, closing it, and then faking some noise to make it sound like he was slapping a lock on it. Whoever was in there'd shit a brick. But then he would not have looked in, checked for water in the bilges. He thought about it, his breath wheezing in the mask, looked at his watch, and once again thought, Screw it. He opened the hatch.

He stopped to initial the small green logbook with the time, date, and compartment number before stepping through. He tensed, expecting a sudden movement or a noise, but there was nothing. It was just another lifeless fire room, the huge shape of the boilers and all the piping flickering in his vision as he stood on the grating above the fire room and pointed the helmet light around the space.

The fire room was huge—nearly ninety feet wide and almost as long. The immense two-story bulk of the stainless steel–clad boilers glinted in the light, surrounded by a myriad of pumps and steam lines shrouded in their white asbestos lagging. He checked his watch again—twelve minutes left. "You don't have to go in and walk around," the supe had said. "Just shine your light down into the bilges. Something shines back at you, log it, then report back. You don't have to do anything else."

Benny shined the light straight down and saw only darkness, except— there. He saw something white, like flour—some kind of white powder in the bilges twenty feet below the platform he was standing on, over near the centerline, under 1B boiler. Shit, now what? Definitely not water, but definitely abnormal. Should he log it? He looked at his watch again. Ten minutes. Screw it. Go down there, see what this shit is, log it, and get out of here.

Taking one last quick look out into the passageway to make sure nobody was creeping up on him, he climbed down the ladder to the gratings of the upper level of the fire room, where he looked again, down through the deck gratings. Now he could see a white bag, shiny white powder all around it down in the bilges. Damn mask. Couldn't really see shit. His breathing sounded extra loud and raspy in the mask. Slow it down, man. Using too much air. He looked at his watch again. Nine minutes. Looked just like a big bag of flour had been dropped into the bilges under 1B boiler, where it had broken open. But no water. Okay. He pointed the helmet light around until he found the ladder to the lower level at the other end of the boiler-front aisleway, then went down one more level. He tramped across the steel deck plates to the front of 1B boiler, then got down on his hands and knees and pointed the helmet light at the remains of the bag. Even with all the scratches on the mask, he could read the printing on the bag now: POWDER, DESICCANT, NSTM 242-55-9010, Milspec 9710-1a. FOR USE IN WATERSIDES OF MARINE PROPULSION BOILERS DURING DRY LAYUPS ONLY. There was some smaller print that began with the word *Warning*, but he couldn't make it out through the mask. He sat back on his haunches and shivered. It was cold down here, really cold. The place felt like a burial chamber.

What the hell was a bag of desiccant powder doing in the bilges? He knew what desiccant was—he'd originally been assigned to the boilers shop before landing the intern position in Production. Desiccant powder was hygroscopic. It soaked up moisture, kept metal structures like the steam drums in a boiler bone-dry. He knew that desiccant powder bags belonged up in the steam drum. He looked up, but there wasn't enough light to make out the upper levels of the boiler front. Watch your time. Eight minutes. He went back up the ladder and walked over to 1B's boiler front. He examined the steam drum's manhole, which was visible because the big asbestos pad had been removed. He frowned. Dry layup—the steam drum should be open; each of the boilers in the other spaces had been open. He turned around and saw that 1A's steam drum was open, the manhole cover laid out on the gratings, with the two-inch-diameter bolts collected inside, the big pad hanging on a hook. He looked back at 1B's manhole cover and saw that the eight bolts were on. He felt one and found it was only hand-tight. Seriously weird. Why was this thing bolted up? He checked his watch again. Seven minutes. What the hell, I've supposedly got a fifteen-minute reserve on top of the normal stay time.

He took off his glove and began backing off all eight of the bolts. Once he had the bolts off, he pried the manhole cover, an elliptical-shaped one-inch-thick steel cover about thirty inches across and twenty-four inches high, back on its hinges. He dipped his head to shine the helmet light inside, then felt his stomach grab in shock.

"Oh Jesus. Oh Sweet Jesus," he moaned into the mask, which promptly fogged up from his sudden exhalation. He stumbled back away from the boiler, back away from those staring, wide eyes and the blackened, peeling features, one clawlike hand raised as if reaching for the manhole. Then he ran for the hatch, trying not to piss his pants. He took the ladder up to the entrance-grating platform two steps at a time and jumped over the knee-knocker, then nearly jumped out of his skin when there was a blaze of light and a shout as two figures waved their arms and made ghost noises at him through their masks. He knocked one of them flat on his ass and ran right for the hatch leading up to the second deck. He went up the steel ladder, through a second armored hatch, turned right, right again, down the passageway, up the ladder where the light was showing, through the athwartships passageway. He could hear the timer on his breathing rig ringing over his sobs as his pounding lungs fought for breath. He burst through the air lock and back into the blazing sunlight in a clatter.

He ripped his mask off and heard the laughter over his heaving sobs, all the old hand riggers standing around, yukking it up at the new kid getting the shit scared out of him by the foreman and his segundo, who were stepping through the air lock even now. He tried to tell them, but they were still roaring and carrying on. A fat, grinning face stuck itself right in front of him.

"Hey, kid, how ya like the grand tour now, hunh? Shit, look at him. He's—shit, lookit his face, Joey, you dipshit; you went an' scared this kid shitless!"

"Dead guy," Benny gasped. It was all he could get out. "Dead guy."

The rest of the guys roared anew as Joe and his helper stripped off their masks, but then the fat man saw the look in Benny's eyes and put up his hand. "Wait a minute, wait a goddamn minute, here—hey, guys, hold it, *hold it, awright?*" he yelled. "Benny, what's this shit about a dead guy? Hey, Benny, calm down. What is it, what is it, hey? Hey, Joey, the kid's hyperventilatin'. C'mere, c'mere."

The gang stopped laughing and crowded around Benny as he sank down on his knees, his lungs scraping for breath, his mask dangling across his thighs. Then he threw up over the edge of the teak quarterdeck. There was a sudden stunned silence as the men backed away from the mess.

"Hey, kid, what the hell . . . " said Joey, covering his own nose and mouth. "It was just a little joke, okay? Shit, you knew it was us, right?"

But Benny was shaking his head, trying to wipe his chin, his face ashen, miserable at the way his guts had betrayed him.

"Dead guy. In the boiler. Steam drum. One B boiler," he gasped. "I swear. Jesus Christ. Saw his face. A dead guy. A fucking mummy."

II

APRIL 1994

WASHINGTON, D.C

2

COMDR. DANIEL LANE COLLINS stood behind his desk chair and stared out through the grimy, rain-streaked windows of his fourth-floor Pentagon office. Facing him was the dreary space between the slab cement walls of the E-ring and the D-ring. The rain trickled down vertical ridges in the concrete, which still showed the imprint of the pine boards used to form the Pentagon's walls back in 1942. The sterile fluorescent lighting across the way showed the beginnings of another great Navy Monday as other Navy staff officers soundlessly shucked raincoats, made coffee, or began to sift through blooming in-boxes. He spotted that pretty, blond lieutenant commander who worked in OP-63 looking out her window, and he raised his coffee cup in a good-morning salute. But she didn't return the gesture. Didn't see him, or maybe was just ignoring him. Besides, his gesture probably constituted sexual harassment in the post-Tailhook era. He sighed.

His boss, Capt. Ronald K. Summerfield, USN, threaded his way through the cluster of gray desks to his private office in a bustle of wet plastic rain gear.

"You love it and you know it, Daniel," the captain announced cheerily as he shook out his raincoat. Captain Summerfield, a tall, ruddy-faced four-striper of some twenty-seven years service, was the 614 shop's branch head, in charge of Dan Collins and the one other staff officer of the NATO-Europe Plans and Policy Branch, Division of Politico-Military Policy, Directorate of Plans, Policy, and Operations, Office of the Chief of Naval Operations—or code OP-614 for short. It had taken Dan Collins several months to learn the Navy headquarter's arcane office-coding system, but, given the mouthful presented by the organizational titles, the OP codes were a practical necessity.

"It reminds me of Newport at sea detail, Captain," Dan replied, turning away from the window. "Only there's no ship and no sea. It is just a job, after all. That recruiter lied."

"They do that, recruiters," Summerfield said while hanging up his raincoat and hat. He then fished a raunchy-looking coffee mug out of his outbasket, turning it over to dislodge any overnight transients. "So, no more adventure, hunh? At least you still have a shot at getting back to sea. Me, now, I'm all done. All I get to do these days is make lots and lots of policy here at Fort Fumble by the Sea. Jackson—where's the goddamn coffee?"

Yeoman Second Class Jackson stuck his head around the corner of his anteroom by the front door. Jackson was the shop's admin clerk and general factotum.

"The element did a Three Mile Island when I plugged it in this morning, Cap'n. We're sharing with Six-sixteen next door."

Summerfield shook his head. "When I have to go to the bubbleheads to get my goddamn coffee, it *is* a shitty day," he grumbled.

Dan grinned as Summerfield, a dedicated surface-ship sailor, headed next door to bum some coffee from the submariners who ran the Navy's nuclear and ocean-policy shop. As Dan looked around the cramped office, with its four desks crammed into a space designed in World War II for one officer, the phone started ringing in Jackson's cubbyhole. The day beginneth, he thought, sitting down to his own in-basket, where a few hundred State Department overnight cables were piled for his personal reading enjoyment. But Jackson was calling his name.

"Yeah, who?"

"Front office, Commander. EA says that oh-six B requests the pleasure of your company, along with Six-fourteen himself when he gets back with his coffee."

"Roger that," muttered Collins. OP-06B. The Assistant Deputy Chief of Naval Operations for Plans, Policy, and Operations. The deputy dog: a senior aviator rear admiral whose main preoccupation seemed to be the fanging of various officers on the OP-06 staff for incomplete, tardy, or otherwise objectionable staff work. A summons from Rear Admiral Carson at 0735 was not a terrific way to start even a nice day, much less a gray one. As he slipped into his service dress blues jacket with its three gold stripes, he tried to remember which of his staffing packages might have made it up to the deputy presence. He grabbed his staff officer's notebook and went out the door, then turned right, heading up the polished tile corridor toward the front office. He stopped by the OP-616 shop to let his branch head know that he had been summoned by the deputy. Summerfield was standing in the doorway of Captain Ferring's office, but he waved him off like a friendly uncle.

"You're a big action officer now, Dan," he said. "Give his lordship a tug on your forelock and my sincerest respects. And be forthright: Admit right away that it's all your fault, whatever it is. It will save you lots of time."

"Even if you chopped it, Cap'n?"

"Especially if I chopped it, Dan. Oh-six B knows full well that the damage is done by the AOs and not us poor, overworked branch heads. The roaches leave any sugar in that box, John?"

Dan laughed and headed down the E-ring corridor. Summerfield had three years to go before mandatory retirement, unless he made flag. In general, though, he didn't appear to sweat 06B, or anyone else, for that matter. Dan was in a different boat: He had sixteen years in the Navy, which meant he had four to go even to qualify for his government pension. At thirty-seven, Dan Collins was beginning to show the lines and traces of his career as a line officer in the surface-ship Navy. He was an even six feet tall, slender of frame and face, with a shock of unruly black hair, bright blue eyes, an almost-too-long, straight nose, and prominent cheekbones. He had high, arching eyebrows that gave his face a perpetual expression of mild surprise, and he walked with a slightly stooping gait born of years of ducking through the low overheads in the destroyer force. His slender build was deceptive: His athletic passion was rowing an elderly George Pocock single along the middle reaches of the Potomac River just upstream of the Key Bridge. He could do the Navy's annual PT test and two-mile run without breaking a sweat.

The office of the Deputy Chief of Naval Operations for Plans, Policy, and Operations, otherwise known within the headquarters staff as OP-06, was a spacious corner E-ring suite befitting a three-star admiral. It was located on one corner of the five-sided building, of which the E-ring was the outer wall. The entire outside wall of the office was given over to a line of ten-foot-high windows that overlooked the Pentagon helipad area and Arlington National Cemetery across the nearby highway. The DCNO and ADCNO's offices were separated by a central reception area, wherein the executive assistant, Capt. J. Robinson Manning, held sway over a staff of two yeoman chief petty officers, two junior yeoman petty officers, and a lieutenant who was the DCNO's personal aide. The walls on either side of the reception area were covered with several rows of official Navy portraits of former DCNOs and ADCNOs. Near the front door, there were a large couch and two upholstered chairs, where miscreants summoned into the presence of either 06 or 06B could sit and perspire.

Manning, the EA, was an imperious officer whom many officers on the staff called J. R. behind his back. Well behind his back, Dan remembered. Manning sat stiffly erect behind the desk nearest to the office of Vice Admiral Layman, the DCNO. His desk looked like a command console, equipped with a standard multiline telephone, a STU-III encrypted telephone, and the preaddressed telephone system that networked all the other executive assistants on both the Navy headquarters staff and also in the office of the Chairman of the Joint Chiefs of Staff, who happened to be a navy admiral. Dan knew the EA network was routinely used to short-circuit the naval bureaucracy at the three) and four-star levels.

Manning peered briefly over a set of reading glasses as Dan came in.

"Ah. Commander Collins. Please have a seat."

"Morning, sir," Dan replied, but he remained standing, waiting by one of the chairs. He had discovered that it was too hard to get his lanky frame in and out of the ancient leather chairs. The door to the ADCNO's office was closed, which was a bad omen. Routine staff business between an action officer and 06B would have involved his knocking once, sticking his head through the open door, getting yelled at, saying, "Yes, sir" a few times, and withdrawing. A closed door meant that some serious thinking was being shared with somebody. That was 06B's favorite euphemism: Have Commander X come see me—I want to share my thinking with him. Dan also knew better than to ask the executive assistant why he had been summoned. Manning had a standard reply to that question: a long, rebuking look framed in silence that made it clear that when the admirals in their power and glory resplendent were ready to enlighten the summonee, they would do so.

While the clerical staff muttered through their paperwork and morning phone calls and Manning dealt with a crisis involving staff cars, Dan inspected the portrait gallery for the umpteenth time. This was his second tour of duty in Washington on the Navy headquarters, or OpNav, staff, and also his second tour of duty in OP-06, the Navy's political and diplomatic staff directorate. There were five divisions in OP-06: Strategy (OP-60), Politico-Military (OP-61), Technology Transfer (OP-62), Foreign Military Sales (OP-63), and Fleet Operations (OP-64). Dan's first tour as a junior staff officer in OP-60, from 1990 to 1991, had been professionally stimulating. This one in OP-61 had been less so, and now he was beginning to tire of it as he found himself plowing through some of the same old bureaucratic issues he had worked during his first tour. He was becoming convinced that Captain Summerfield had it right: Just resurrect your old point papers, change the date, and send them forward, because nothing ever really changes on the OpNav staff, especially the Navy's position on interservice policy issues. Summerfield had tacked up an old cheerleader's signboard from his Academy days over the entrance to his office. HOLD THAT LINE, it read, neatly summarizing the Navy headquarters' going-in position on just about any issue affecting Navy policy.

His two tours in OpNav had been separated by what now seemed an all-too-brief assignment as executive officer in USS *John King*, a guided-missile destroyer based down in Norfolk. His assignment as second in command of *John King* had been professionally demanding, often exhausting, and a huge education in just how many problems 285 sailors could get themselves into in the space of eighteen months. But he had been fortunate to have served under two very good commanding officers, and he had ended up his tour with selection to commander, USN, and screening for command on his first look. Sitting in the anteroom of the OP-06 front office on a rainy Monday morning made him yearn for the days when he could end the working day by pitching the wardroom softball team to victory against the engineers.

The promise of another tour of sea duty was his only lifeline to professional sanity. Screening for surface-ship command at the end of his XO tour was the first, albeit crucial, step. That was the good news. But now he was "in the bank" of commanders waiting for a ship to command. Since there were more commanders in the bank than there were ships to command, this could be a longish wait, especially with the Navy retiring so many ships. The bad news was that he would perforce remain in the Pentagon until his turn came up for command. These factors, coupled with the almost certain knowledge that when he had finished his command at sea tour he would be coming back to OP-06, did not improve his long-term attitude. Lately, it seemed that he had spent his professional life getting to the rank of commander, USN, and sea command. Now that a command assignment was glimmering on the horizon, he had begun to peer beyond it, and he was beginning to see himself in the image of Summerfield.

Living alone was also getting to be a depressing business, despite the tony surroundings of his town house in Old Town. It had taken him two tours of duty to recover, if that was the word, emotionally and spiritually from the death of his wife. But even after that long a time, he still could not muster the interest to return to the dating-and-mating game. His mind told him that living alone was probably the wrong thing to do, but the energy and effort to change his personal circumstances was simply not yet in him. It was still a pleasure to look at a beautiful woman from a distance, but, since Claire's death, his pleasure was directly proportional to the distance.

The intercom on Captain Manning's desk buzzed, and the EA picked up the handset, listened for a moment, and then looked over at Dan.

"Yes, sir. Very good, sir," Manning purred, pointing wordlessly at Dan and then to 06B's door. Dan walked over to the large white door, took a quiet breath, knocked twice, and went in.

The ADCNO's office was twenty feet square, with its own window wall, two couches and two upholstered chairs, a library table pushed up against the corridor-side wall, and a large mahogany desk centered against the back wall. The front wall was covered by pictures of Navy airplanes. Two curio cabinets filled with mementos from the admiral's own career rounded out the decor.

Rear Adm. Walter Carson sat behind the desk, a pair of bifocals pushed down on his scowling face. Carson was a florid-faced man whose portly figure and sometimes pettifogging manner belied a brilliant wartime record achieved during Vietnam as an A-6 pilot. His job as 06B was faintly analogous to that of the executive officer aboard ship—the final checkpoint for the quality and correctness of all the headquarters policy staff work headed up to 06 and on the Chief of Naval Operations himself. Carson was probably not going to advance to three stars, a fact that sometimes tended to color his attitude. He was the antithesis of the traditional naval aviator in that he was very formal, all business all the time, and a serious nitpicker—in short, a perfect deputy.

Dan saw that there was one other person in the room, a heavyset civilian who appeared to be in his fifties, dressed in a rumpled gray suit. The man was visibly upset; he shot Dan an angry look when he came into the office. But Dan was paying attention to the admiral, who was pointing wordlessly to the single empty chair in the room. The admiral remained at his desk.

"Okay," the admiral began brusquely, addressing the civilian. "Mr. Ames, this is Commander Collins. Commander, this is Mr. Roscoe Ames, who is a deputy director of the Naval Investigative Service."

Dan shook hands with Ames before sitting down, but Ames barely glanced at him. Dan felt a tingle of apprehension at Ames's palpable hostility. The NIS? Was he being investigated for something?

"Okay," the admiral said again. "Commander Collins, this is a verbal appointing letter. Hard copy to follow. You are hereby appointed to conduct a JAGMAN investigation into an incident that has taken place in the Philadelphia Naval Shipyard. The incident involves a death, which may be homicide. With me so far?"

"Uh, yes, sir, but—"

"But why is a politico-military specialist on the CNO's staff being tasked to investigate an incident that normally would be in NIS's bailiwick? First, because we say so, and that 'we' includes Admiral Torrance, the Vice Chief of Naval Operations. Second, I need a senior line officer to conduct a by-the-book, right-now, informal JAGMAN investigation, and since the NATO-Europe shop in OP-Sixty-one is not exactly a hotbed of diplomatic activity at the moment, you've been nominated. Mr. Ames here is going to appoint someone from the NIS to be your—what shall we call it, deputy? Yes, deputy . . . in the conduct of this investigation. But you are going to be in charge of it. Your 'deputy' will be there to marshal the investigative assets of the NIS as you require. Mr. Ames, are we clear on the relationships here?"

Ames did not speak for a moment. Dan now saw that the civilian was not just upset; he was furious. His mouth was drawn into a flat line and he was practically glaring at the admiral. Brave man, Dan thought.

"Yes, Admiral," he said finally. "We are clear on the relationships. But we—"

The admiral raised his hand. "Yes, I understand. The NIS protests most vigorously, which protests have been carefully noted. But this is coming directly from the office of the vice chief, as your boss, Admiral Keeler, is probably finding out this very moment through other channels, by the way. So let's not fart around anymore, okay? I have noted your objections, and I presume you have noted my instructions. Thank you for coming over at such short notice. That is all, Mr. Ames."

Ames rose from his chair. Dan could see that his hands were actually trembling as he took one last shot.

"Sir, I will advise Admiral Keeler to take this entire matter all the way up to the SecNav. This whole thing is out—"

"Fine, Mr. Ames," interrupted Carson, no longer looking at him. "That's fine. I'm sure that the director of NIS, who, as I recall, is a one-star, will listen very carefully to your advice, just like he'll probably attend to the good counsel of the vice chief, who, in case you've forgotten, is a four-star. Good day, sir."

Ames snapped his day-planner notebook shut and stalked out of the room, closing the door forcefully behind him. Dan was surprised to see that Carson was almost smiling as he got up and came over to the couch.

"I hate those NIS weenies," he muttered as he lowered himself onto the couch. "Ever since the *Iowa* turret explosion business, they've brought nothing but shit storms upon the Navy. Now let me tell you what this is all about—no, we don't want notes. Just listen."

The admiral sat down and leaned back in the couch, took off his glasses, closed his eyes, and rubbed the bridge of his nose for a moment before beginning. Dan closed his notebook. No notes, the admiral had said.

"What we've got here are two things: an investigation and a political power play. We've received a message from the shipyard in Philadelphia that a body has been discovered in one of the mothballed ships, the battleship *Wisconsin*. There's more in the report, but basically, they're treating it initially as a homicide. And since it's on a naval reservation, the local Philadelphia cops won't work it; it's a federal beef."

"Meaning the NIS."

"Yeah, normally that would be true. Except that since the *Iowa* mess, and more recently, the Tailhook debacle, the NIS is not entirely in good repute around the flag ranks in OpNav. Or in DOD, for that matter. I've heard the vice chief categorize them as a bunch of incompetent goons, but that's probably overkill, and flavored somewhat by OSD accusations that there was a lot of command influence imposed on the NIS by OpNav during Tailhook."

"They were pretty useful to me when I was an exec in Norfolk," Dan offered.

"I'm sure that, in the main, the majority of NIS people do a creditable job. But this is an incident involving a battleship. You will recall the last time NIS got involved in an incident on a battleship?"

"Ah, yes, sir. The *Iowa* turret explosion. All those conspiracy theories."

"Right." The admiral nodded. "You might want to read the official investigation report of that someday, especially the transcripts of the NIS interviews. You'd see what the problem is, and why the vice chief would probably disband the present NIS and start over if he had the chance. Which might also explain why one of the vice's crown princes, Rear Adm. Walker T. Keeler, is director of the NIS right now."

"Yes, sir. I guess we've all heard some NIS stories. But still, the Navy has homicides from time to time."

"Yeah, but this one is going to stir up the press. It sounds like a pretty bizarre case, but since you're going to investigate it, and since I'm the officer appointing you, I can't say any more about it. Command influence and all that."

"Aye, aye, sir," Dan said. The investigating officer was required to discover the facts for himself, with no overtones of command influence to taint his findings. "But Mr. Ames did seem to be really pissed off."

"To put it mildly." The admiral snorted. "But there's precedent—before there even was an NIS, incident investigations were always conducted by a line officer, although these were usually operational incidents. And we're not cutting NIS out—they've been tagged to cough up a deputy dog and give your investigation technical support—crime-scene work, forensics, and, best of all, I'm going to make them pay the travel and logistics costs for your investigation."

"A high-level lesson being administered. The sound of hammers on rice bowls. We can do without you."

The admiral nodded approvingly and got up.

"Summerfield said you were smart. It does have all the fingerprints of the vice chief on it. And you know what happens to people who attract the attention of the vice. But I wanted to make sure you know you'll be playing two games. Do the investigation, like I said, by the book. But require the full cooperation of the staff and resources of the NIS: OpNav is to be clearly in charge, Dan."

Dan stood up. "Aye, aye, sir. And I assume that OpNav's objectives vis-à-vis NIS do not take precedence over the investigation's objectives?"

The admiral gave him a direct look. "Absolutely," he said. "You find what you find. Facts, opinions, recommendations. By the book, Commander."

"Yes, sir. Will you want reports?"

"Not on the investigation—we stay at arm's length on that until you hand in your preliminary. But on the other matter, yeah. Be like E.T.: Call home occasionally. Talk to the EA. NIS is not just going to take this lying down, and you may need the occasional cudgel taken up. And since he did not care to come when he was called, you can use Captain Summerfield as your conduit to the EA or to me—if he would be so kind."

Dan walked back to OP-614 and reported the gist of what had happened to Captain Summerfield, including the tone of the admiral's last remark.

"Oh dear, maybe he'll transfer me out of OpNav," Summerfield said wistfully. But then his face grew serious. "I've heard of OpNav staffies being detailed into investigations, but never outside the building. The vice chief must really want to jerk NIS's chain."

"From the look on that guy Ames's face, we can consider said chain to have been well and truly pulled. I guess I need to go upstairs to JAG and get the latest gouge on doing a JAG investigation."

"Yeah, okay. And then go by the Oh-six travel office—you have to get rolling on this thing most-skosh. Although, actually, he said NIS had to pay the TAD costs? I love it. You know, I'd recommend you drive up to Philly. It's easier than doing all the airports, and you won't have to wait for the old ladies up on the fifth floor to do the TAD orders paperwork. Now, are there any actions you're leaving in the system?"

"Only two long-term actions: a nuke-submarine port visit to our beloved allies in Greece, and the NATO Portuguese frigate. The port-visit package is over in OP-Six-sixteen. And the frigate—"

Summerfield shook his head. "The NATO Portuguese frigate. Do you realize that that turkey's been kicking around the system now for about twelve years?"

"Yes, sir. I'm recognizing some of my old point papers."

Summerfield laughed. "I'll give it to Lieutenant Colonel Black of Her Majesty's ever-enthusiastic Marines. He will absolutely love the Portuguese NATO frigate issue."

Dan decided to get up to JAG before his Marine buddy found out what he was inheriting. Snapper Black was a Marine F-18 driver who was suffering manfully through every single day of a cross-training assignment to the Navy staff, albeit with a wicked sense of humor. He would need it when he inherited the Portuguese frigate issue, Dan thought. As a result of the unending budget cuts, the military service headquarters had been depopulated by about 40 percent. The cuts left the other two working staff billets in 614 vacant, so Snapper would necessarily inherit any currently working issues when Dan left to conduct the investigation.

When Dan got back to the office an hour later, he was carrying a large three-ring binder filled with the pertinent rules, regulations, and checklists of the *Navy Judge Advocate General (JAG) Manual* pertaining to the conduct of informal JAG investigations. Dan knew that the label "informal" was a bit of a misnomer. The actual investigation was plenty formal; it was just that courtroom rules of evidence did not apply until the investigation was used to make the decision to convene a "formal" military-justice proceeding, such as a board of inquiry or a court-martial. The use of an informal investigation gave the investigating officer the widest possible latitude in pursuing the facts of a case, and, at this stage, the facts of the case were the objective. He sat down at his desk and began to go through the check-off lists and forms. Snapper Black came in a few minutes later and walked directly over to Dan's desk.

"Greetings, comrade," he began. Snapper was built like a small tank, and he had a round, froglike face and a gravelly voice.

"Commander Collins isn't here," Dan said hopefully, keeping his head down.

"Commander Collins is a Communist, as the whole world knows. It's how he wants to die that's in question. The Portuguese frigate, for Chrissakes."

"You can't hurt me. The Vice Chief of all the Naval Operations has appointed me boy investigator. I've got a letter and everything." He waved his appointing letter in the air, on the theory that if Snapper was going to bite something, he might go for the letter.

"Death and destruction be rained upon you," Snapper intoned. "May your whiskey be perpetually watered. May the Communists suborn all your children. May—"

"Okay, Snapper," grumped Captain Summerfield from his inner office. "Go get your crayons and work us up a novel idea about the Portuguese frigate, you want to vent all that spleen."

Snapper cocked a theatrical eye in the direction of the inner office and then leaned closer to Dan. "That blonde you've been lusting after, over in

OP-Six-three? She's a he; Clinton rules. And has syphilis, which she got from your mother. Who—"

"*Snapper.*"

"Aye, aye, sir." Snapper backed away toward his desk, miming silent but graphic gestures in Dan's direction. Dan felt mildly sorry, but that was the code of the West: If somebody was lucky enough to escape from OpNav for some kind of temporary duty, the remaining inmates picked up the load. Yeoman Jackson was calling him.

"Guy on line two says he's from NIS, wants to talk to you. What'd you do, Commander?"

"He's been consorting with goats again," offered Snapper.

"Everyone's a comedian today," Dan said. "Patch him back here."

His phone rang once and he picked up.

"Commander Collins."

"Commander, this is Doug Englehardt over at NIS. I'm the case officer on the Philadelphia problem."

"You the guy's gonna be my deputy dog on this investigation?"

There was a moment's pause on the other end.

"Well, Commander, not exactly. That's actually the reason I was calling. I wonder if you can come over here to the Navy Yard for a little meeting. We'll introduce you to your, ah, deputy at that time. Can you make it this afternoon, say thirteen hundred?"

Dan thought quickly. Remembering the choleric Mr. Ames, Dan's political instincts told him that his first meeting with the NIS troops ought not to be on their home turf. One of him amidst all of them.

"Actually, Mr. Englehardt, I've got some policy issues to wrap up here in Six-fourteen." From out of the corner of his eye, he saw Summerfield and Snapper listening. Snapper was rolling his eyes. "Let's do this. I'll get the OP-Oh-six conference room at, say, sixteen hundred. We'll do the first organizational meeting then. And maybe you or your people can brief me at that time on the tech support services NIS can provide to this investigation, especially if it turns into a homicide case. And I intend to go to Philadelphia first thing tomorrow to get this thing under way. I have the appointing letter. Okay? See you here at the Puzzle Palace at Sixteen hundred? It's room—"

"I know where the Oh-six conference room is, Commander," Englehardt interrupted. His voice was decidedly less friendly. "We'll see what we can do."

"Great, Mr. Englehardt. Appreciate your cooperation. See you then." He hung up.

Summerfield was rocking back in his armchair and nodding in approval. "Very good. *Very* good. They come to you. They work for you. I like that."

"Those civilians are gonna hate life," Snapper observed. "Come to a meeting away from their offices at sixteen hundred? Those guys all go *home* at sixteen hundred."

"Everybody knows we OpNav weenies are dedicated," Dan said. "The hard part will be getting the conference room. Jackson."

"I'm talking to the secretariat right now, Commander. They say as long as you're out of there before OpsDep debrief at seventeen hundred, you're good to go."

"Jackson, you stop being efficient," ordered Snapper. "You're gonna scare the captain."

3

At 1610, Dan Collins and Captain Summerfield were waiting in the OP-06 conference room across the hall from Vice Admiral Layman's front office. The room was long, stuffy, and narrow, with paneled walls, behind which were banks of sliding wall-sized maps of the world. Although Dan, having called the meeting, was nominally in charge, he was glad Summerfield had come down. After two tours of duty in the Navy policy world, Dan felt reasonably confident about his Washington bureaucratic skills, but Ronald Summerfield was an acknowledged master within OP-06. He had spent years in the Washington arena, including a three-year tour in OLA, as the Navy's office of legislative liaison was known. Several of his Naval Academy classmates were already flag officers, including the vice chief himself. Being a classmate, Summerfield was reputed to have an unusual degree of access to the vice chief, access facilitated by the fact that he had also been the executive assistant to the previous vice chief. But Dan had noticed that, if all this was true, Summerfield was extremely circumspect about it. A branch-head captain who took advantage of such connections would be taking his chances with the one-, two-, and three-star admirals in the OpNav chain of command between Summerfield and the Vice Chief of Naval Operations. Dan did not know very much about his boss on a personal level, other than that he had an invalid wife and was a heavy-duty gun collector.

"From what you've told me," Summerfield was musing from his chair at the side of the table, "NIS has no real incentive to cooperate with you. They're also fully capable of running their own investigation behind your back to make you look bad. You know they have an office in Philly, just like they do at every other big naval installation."

"Yes, sir," Dan said, looking at his watch. "I've been thinking about that this afternoon. I was going to ask the office of the NIS Resident Agent–Philadelphia to fax down their preliminary incident report just as soon as I get a chain of command established here. I'm planning to go through this deputy for anything I want from NIS."

"Good. There are lots of potholes they can put in your way—lose your paperwork, misplace evidence, break the chain of custody on physical stuff, promise a report tonight but get it in after you leave town tomorrow, that sort of stuff. But you are correct in assuming that the cure is to put the NIS deputy on the hook to provide what you need. They derail him, they look bad, not you."

"Have you figured out why the vice chief might be doing this?" Dan asked.

The captain scratched the beginnings of a five o'clock shadow and looked away. "Well," he replied, "the current director of the NIS is one of the vice's protégés. His name is Walker T. Keeler, and he's a classmate of mine. Even back at the Academy, he always did think a lot of himself. What we may have here is a case of the protégé getting a little big for his britches and somehow managing to offend his patron saint. This might just be an attention-getting device of some kind. Ah, I think they're here."

The door was opening at the end of the conference room and four people filed through the door, shedding raincoats. There were three men and one very good-looking woman. The first man, who introduced himself as Doug Englehardt, was a well-fed and sleek-looking man of about fifty; he was wearing a dark blue suit and carrying an expensive leather briefcase. He introduced the second man, who was a young black civilian named Robby Booker. Booker was wearing a tan double-breasted suit and had a pronounced high-top fade-away hairdo. He immediately flopped into a chair at the table, put a bored expression on his face, and began to tap on the tabletop with the point of a pencil. The third man, named Smithson, was older, about sixty. He was wearing a shirt and tie but no suit coat. He carried a portable projector, which he positioned at one end of the table and then went looking for the screen. Obviously a briefer and not a participant, Dan thought.

Dan introduced himself and Captain Summerfield to the clutch of bureaucrats, then focused on the woman, whom Englehardt identified as Ms. Grace Ellen Snow. Only about one inch shorter than he was, she was dressed in an expensive-looking midcalf-length gray linen suit. Her dark hair was pulled back along the sides and top of her head to a barrette and then left to fall in a graceful cascade to her shoulders. She looked directly at him when they were introduced, and he was struck by her bright green eyes. She had a lovely, if somewhat aloof, face, he thought. As he tried to get his brain back on track for the meeting, he caught the beginnings of an amused expression on Summerfield's face. As everyone found seats around the table, Englehardt suggested they start, pointedly reminding the two naval officers that it was quite late in the day. He took a leather-bound notebook out of his briefcase.

"Not for OpNav, Mr. Englehardt," Captain Summerfield said with a patronizing smile. "We all still have the OpsDep debrief to do, and then our division director's meeting."

"I figure to be out of here by seventeen hundred at the latest," Dan said from his position at the head of the table. "First order of business is my appointing letter. I've made some copies for everyone."

He passed the copies down the table to the three NIS people, ignoring the slide pusher. Englehardt put his copy in his notebook without looking at it. The young black man left his copy facedown on the table and continued to play Gene Krupa with his pencil. Grace Ellen Snow scanned her copy, then nodded once.

"The second thing I want to do is set a schedule," Dan continued. "I plan to leave for Philadelphia early tomorrow morning, before rush hour. I plan to use my own POV as the quickest way to get going, given the normal delays we face here in OpNav making travel arrangements. I plan to spend a few days or so in Philly to see what we've got, and after that, we'll determine a formal schedule. Mr. Englehardt, that appointing order says you guys owe me a deputy."

Englehardt nodded, still not looking at the appointing order, as if to imply that its authority was of no consequence to him. He opened his notebook, looked down, and cleared his throat.

"Commander, the NIS will cooperate with this investigation to the maximum extent of its ability and authority under the law and the charter of the NIS," he began. Dan thought he sounded like a diplomat reading precise negotiating instructions. He looked over at Summerfield, who rolled his eyes. Grace Snow was watching Englehardt.

"We propose to appoint Ms. Snow here as your *operational liaison* from the NIS for the duration of this investigation, or until such time as the investigation is devolved back into more, um, conventional channels."

" 'Operational liaison'?"

"Yes, Commander. The assistant director of the NIS for criminal investigations thought that would be a more appropriate title, since Ms. Snow, who is a managerial employee of the NIS, necessarily must remain under the administrative control of the NIS." He paused and looked up at Dan.

"Okay. Continue."

"Right. Ms. Snow will accompany you during the field portion of the investigation and will then prepare a separate report to be appended to the report of your investigation required by the *JAG Manual*, based on all the evidence gathered by you and whatever might turn up from the efforts of our own field offices."

"Wrong."

Englehardt put down his piece of paper. "I beg your pardon?"

Dan could see that Summerfield was suddenly having trouble keeping a straight face. Dan sat back in his chair and smiled politely at Englehardt.

"I said, 'Wrong.' Or perhaps I should have said, Nice try. Look, I don't care what Miss Snow's title is. But there is only one investigation, and only one investigating officer, and there will be only one report. If you care to read that appointing letter, you will see that it has been signed by the JAG himself, Admiral Crutchfield, who works for the Secretary of the Navy, who is at the top of your food chain and mine. There had better not be any separate investigation activity going on at your NISRA offices that I have not set in motion. That would lead to a duplication of effort, confusion, people working at cross purposes, and probably a compromise of evidence in this case. I've been led to believe that these are the hallmarks of previous NIS investigations that lie behind my appointing letter in the first place."

Englehardt's face reddened. Grace Snow had begun to study the table; the young black man had stopped tapping his pencil and was looking at Dan with some interest. The older man at the other end of the table began to shuffle his slides, looking as if he wished he was elsewhere.

"If Ms. Snow is to be the operational liaison between my investigation and the NIS," Dan continued, "I propose to task NIS for all the support I need through Ms. Snow. It will be up to NIS to respond to Ms. Snow, and she to me. She will be, in effect, the investigation's expert on the capabilities of the NIS, and she will be the principal conduit of all information that the NIS now has or will obtain pertaining to this investigation. In that regard, my first tasking is to call for a summary report of whatever information NISRA Philadelphia has on this incident to be made available to me upon my arrival in Philadelphia, which should be at around ten hundred tomorrow morning."

"Our arrival."

Dan looked over at Grace Snow, who had spoken for the first time.

"Yes, precisely, our arrival," he amended, nodding in her direction.

Englehardt was shaking his head. "I cannot agree to that," he began.

"Easy fix," murmured Captain Summerfield.

"Sir?" said Englehardt, his voice strained.

"The Vice Chief of Naval Operation's office is twenty feet from here. He's a classmate of mine. I'm sure I can get us on his calendar at fairly short notice. Let's go see him, tell him about your problems. He can call Admiral Keeler, your boss's boss, and maybe help clarify the issue. The vice chief is really swell at clarifying things."

Englehardt pursed his lips. Dan thought he saw Snow shake her head fractionally while staring hard at Englehardt. The young black man spoke up.

"Mr. Englehardt. This sounds workable. I'm gonna be the dude at NIS workin' all this tasking. It's a nice clean line of communication, and you and Mr. Ames can get a copy of everything and anything. That'd be co-pacetic with you, right, Commander?"

"How you respond internally to tasking is NIS business, Mr. Booker. I don't want to try to deal with all the various branches of the NIS—I'll be looking to Ms. Snow."

"That's cool," said Booker. "She easy to look at."

In the moment of embarrassed silence that followed this remark, Engle-hardt tried one last time. "Commander, this case is a probable homicide.

There are established procedures for dealing with a homicide, with a crime scene, with evidentiary control. You know nothing—"

"But *I* do," interrupted Snow. Dan suddenly understood that there were more bureaucratic currents at play here than he had realized. Englehardt looked exasperated. Dan decided to step back in.

"Look, Mr. Englehardt. That's precisely right. I'm a line officer. I know how to run a Navy JAGMAN investigation. Presumably Miss Snow knows the NIS procedural drill. Mr. Booker here is the designated action officer at NIS. There's no reason we can't all work together at whatever the hell this is all about. But if the rice-bowl issue is going to be that big a stumbling block, then let's stop right now and do as Captin Summerfield suggests— go see the man across the hall. I understand he's nothing if not decisive."

Englehardt folded. "I will accept these arrangements on a pro tem basis, subject to the approval of the superiors. I—"

Dan cut him off. "Great," he said. "We have about thirty minutes left. How about your briefer giving us a down-and-dirty on the NIS's capabilities, and then we can get this thing under way. I—excuse me, we—have an early start tomorrow morning."

GRACE SNOW PULLED her coat tighter around her shoulders as the NIS group stood on the steps of the south parking entrance to the Pentagon after the meeting. Englehardt had pulled her aside while the others kept their eye out for the Navy Yard shuttle bus.

"You sure you know what you're doing here, Grace?" he asked.

Grace looked out over the sea of cars in south parking. It was just after 5:00 P.M., and the lot was still full.

"I think so, Doug. This assignment is crucial for me, and I think I also know what the game is here. But it's also obvious these people are serious."

"Their bosses are serious. I think the commander is switched in, but this JAGMAN investigation is just another temporary duty for him. When it's over, he goes back to his day job. But if it's true that the vice chief, Admiral Torrance, is behind this, we'll have to be very careful. He's slated to be the next CNO, and Ames is scared shitless that when this vice takes over, he might try to do away with NIS entirely."

"Ames is always scared," she said. "That's part of our problem at NIS— a big part."

Englehardt looked around to make sure the other two could not overhear them. "Your views are well known, Grace. Please remember that you're not in Career Services right now, due to your vast personnel experience."

"And I've been detailed to his little farce precisely because I'm in personnel, right, Doug? A little slap at the blue-suiters: You want a deputy, we'll give you a lawyer turned clerk?"

"So surprise them."

"Oh, I think I will, Doug. Trust me on this one."

Englehardt laughed. "Ames is a silly bastard who has no idea of what he's unleashed," he said. "But how about Collins? Can you handle this guy? I was hoping for some straight-stick line commander. Or better yet, an aviator. But this guy's had some Washington time. Witness where we did the meeting."

Grace looked over at him. " 'Handle'? I don't know if that's an appropriate word. I think first we do the investigation. Look, Doug, I still believe that our best chance to refurbish NIS's credibility—and perhaps our political lease on life—is by doing as good a job as we can on this investigation, despite its antecedents. We play this one straight, the OpNav admirals have no casus belli. We let Ames and the 'Gang of Two' play politics, we walk right into the vice's trap."

"In your humble opinion."

"Well, now—"

"Here's the shuttle, thank God. You drove over, right?"

"Right. And I have your private fax number."

"Yeah. Okay. Take care, Grace Ellen Snow. This might be some serious shit here."

"In your—"

He grinned. "Yeah. In my humble opinion."

Grace waved to the group as they boarded the Navy Yard shuttle bus, then walked down to retrieve her white BMW from the guest-parking row at the east end of the Pentagon parking lot. She drove out the south parking entrance and into the stream of traffic going past the Pentagon heliport toward Washington. She crossed the infamous X intersection just east of Memorial Bridge and dropped down onto the GW Parkway. She took the parkway along the river as far as the entrance to Roosevelt Island Park before remembering that there was no ramp to Key Bridge going into town from the northbound lanes of the parkway. She would have to go all the way up to Chain Bridge, cross the river, and drive back down into Georgetown.

"Damn it," she muttered to herself as she slowed down to creep through Rosslyn with the rest of the herd, once again cursing all the gentry of Georgetown for refusing to let the Metro system have a station there. "Well, if one has a driver, my dear, what does one care about the traffic?" Honestly, some of those people.

Grace Ellen Snow was thirty-five years old, a fact that had begun to intrude more frequently during her moments of personal reflection. Inching along under the high arches of the Key Bridge, the familiar assets-and-liabilities litany surfaced once again: You're reasonably good-looking; you have money and a nice town house in Georgetown; you come from a good family, have an economics undergrad degree from Brown, a law degree from Georgetown, an executive-level—correction, more like midlevel, isn't it?—civil-service job. And on the debit side, counselor? A nose that's slightly too long, breasts too small, the three-year-old emotional residue of a disastrous marriage, and a career history characterized most prominently by a penchant for irritating your superiors—irritating them to the point where

26

they applied the lateral arabesque for which the civil service is famous, or infamous, depending on whether or not it's happening to you. From NIS investigations policy as a GS-15 to the Career Services division. Still as a 15, but with zero managerial responsibilities and some fairly clear writing on the wall—and, oh, yes, while we're on the subject, the social life of a tree.

She was slowly, very slowly, and very grudgingly getting used to the idea that a traditional marriage, children, a family, and a Labrador in the fenced backyard were all becoming increasingly remote possibilities. Her parents had both passed on, so at least she did not have their expectations to deal with. But still, why the hell not me? she thought. Maybe it was all those advantages, and the dullards in government she had had to work with. There you go being an elitist again, still believing your ex-husband's line about people in government being automatically second-rate.

In a conversation after the meeting, she had told Collins she had eight years of field-investigation experience. But she had not told him that those eight years were in securities-fraud work for the Securities and Exchange Commission, with the "field" being the financial jungles of Manhattan. After her marriage to Rennie, the broker, had become a nightmare, compared with which, even divorce proceedings looked like a picnic, she had jumped at the offer of a political appointment in the Justice Department toward the end of the Bush administration. And, like many people who jump at things, she discovered that she had been extremely naïve. And then after not quite two years had come the arrival of the great unwashed hordes from the "other party," and suddenly she was just another low-level appointee scrambling to find a job. She had applied at the FBI, but anyone connected to the previous Justice Department had become persona non exista. Grace had just about given up on the idea of staying in government when a friend at Treasury had put her onto an opening at the Naval Investigative Service, in their white-collar-crime division. Since these were the people who chased down crooked military paymasters and inside jobs at the Navy exchanges, her resumé from SEC had been a pretty good fit. And, of course, being a female hire, it would help NIS meet the new and improved gender quotas. The NIS had been a comedown from being a principal deputy assistant U.S. attorney general, but, unwilling to admit to herself that she was too independent of mind to make a good bureaucrat, she had jumped at it—again.

In retrospect, she realized that the late-term appointment to Justice had been awfully convenient for two senior associate regional directors at SEC's New York Region offices. She now suspected that her departure had been gracefully engineered by one, if not both, of them. But the debacle of her four-year marriage to Rennie and the ensuing divorce had literally worn her out, making any appointment out of New York seem like a godsend. Poor Rennie. When the Reagan bubble had burst, with the subsequent economic corrections, life with Rennie, who definitely considered himself one of Tom

Wolfe's Masters of the Universe, had turned into an abusive nightmare, complete with girlfriends and finally a dependence on the shiny white powder. Leaving Rennie had been easy; owning up to her mistake in marrying him had not been quite so easy.

And even Justice had started off well, given her own emotional and physical state of exhaustion. But that familiar pattern had emerged during the first year. After only a few months at Justice, the signs had surfaced once again that Washington, like New York, was very much a man's world and that things were already getting a bit testy among her coworkers and supervisors. What had the deputy AG said one day after a two-day off-line management seminar? "Bureaucratically speaking, you're a difficult woman, Grace. You were never meant to work in an organization." He had initially come on like a paternal adviser, telling her how she would make a great litigator or even an independent counsel out there in private practice, but then he had spoiled it by making a remark about her legs. She'd thought she was doing well at SEC—until she was moved out. And the same thing at Justice, although there had not been time for a real test there, once the new administration had begun its purges. And now NIS: A GS-15 job in policy had turned into a nonjob in personnel—correction, Career Services. Her career path was once again looking more and more like a career trajectory.

After the Spout Run divergence, the traffic finally opened up on the parkway and she drove up to the Chain Bridge exit, cut across the swirling black waters of the Potomac, and turned right to go down Canal Road, back toward the city. When Canal became M Street at the Key Bridge, she turned up into Georgetown proper on 33rd Street. Out of the traffic mess along M and the Key Bridge, she made it home to her town house on P Street in three minutes. For a denizen of Georgetown, she lived in near luxury: She actually had a driveway, although no garage. The street parking along the narrow passage of P Street was, as usual, all taken, but at least her driveway wasn't blocked. She parked the car inside the wrought-iron fence, got out, closed the squealing gate, and went up the iron steps to the front door.

Fumbling in her purse for her keys, she reflected on the meeting. So now an actual field investigation, a criminal investigation, a homicide even. Right. An investigation to which she had been seconded in order to offer insult to the blue-suiters who thought they ran the Navy. Collins wouldn't stay fooled for very long—he seemed to be pretty smart. "Switched in," as Doug had said. She was going to ride up to Philly with him tomorrow, that would be the time to tell him. That way, there would still be a chance to make this thing go. Even if her bosses in NIS wanted the OpNav investigation to fall on its face, she needed to make it succeed. It was her only chance to—what? Make a name for herself? Make a fool of herself, more likely. She sighed. One of these days, she would have to get a grip, see where all this career stuff was going. It wasn't as if she had to work. But then, what

28

was the point of even living in Washington if you were not part of government, either in it or on the outside waiting to get back in it?

4

COMMANDER COLLINS WAS RIGHT on time the next morning. He had arranged to pick her up in front of the Pentagon's south parking entrance at 0600. She had agreed on the Pentagon after finding out that he lived in Old Town Alexandria. Halfway between Georgetown and Alexandria, the Pentagon parking lot turned out to be a good middle ground, an island in the midst of the morning rush-hour traffic. She was waiting in one of the covered bus kiosks when he pulled up in a large blue Chevrolet Suburban and activated the door locks.

She put her single bag on the floor of the backseat and got in on the passenger side. They exchanged brief good mornings and then she let him concentrate on getting onto the George Washington Parkway to retrace his journey through Old Town. It was still dark, and the streets were slick from a persistent all-night drizzle.

"You're going to use the Beltway, Commander?" she asked as they slowed down for the speed zone near Washington National Airport.

"Yeah. And the name's Dan, by the way. Save the 'Commander' bit for meetings. If we can get over the Wilson Bridge in one piece without falling through a pothole, we just follow I-Ninety-five up to just before the Delaware Memorial Bridge, and then up the river and into Philly."

"Please call me Grace. The Beltway scares me."

"It scares everybody. That's why I drive this big old hog. But New York Avenue is worse during rush hour, even outbound when everybody is coming in. Washington is hopeless where roads and traffic are concerned, or maybe just plain hopeless."

She remained silent as he threaded the big vehicle through the traffic along Old Town's main thoroughfare, Washington Street, wincing only once when they got to the jink in the street around the Confederate soldier statue and he swung the truck almost on top of a Honda in the right lane. He must have seen the wince.

"Laws of gross tonnage," he quipped. "Hondas mess with Suburbans at their peril."

"I wasn't sure you saw him."

"Oh, I saw him. It's just that there's nowhere to go around that damned statue, and he knew it. You get great visibility in one of these things."

"We are rather up in the air. But it must be difficult in most Washington traffic."

"Yeah, but I'm a rower. You know, crew? I keep a boat at the Potomac Boat Club, over there by Key Bridge. It's just a single, but I get out on the river each afternoon if I can get out of the Puzzle Palace in time. Sometimes I need to pull the boat to other rivers, or down to the Occoquan. This thing has a towing package."

"Ah. That must be beautiful," she said. She had often seen the crew teams practicing on the river below the bluffs when she took her walks in the precincts of Georgetown University. "I went to law school at Georgetown."

"You're a lawyer?"

She laughed. The way he had said "lawyer," he might have substituted the term *child molester*.

"Fond of lawyers, are we?" she said.

It was his turn to laugh. "If I tell a lawyer joke, will it spoil our working relationship?"

"Only if I've heard it. Actually, I'm not too sure what our working relationship is supposed to be."

"Oh, that's easy. Look at that *assh*—Excuse me. I'm used to driving by myself. The habits of living alone, I'm afraid—I talk to myself."

"You're not married?" she asked, then wondered where that question had come from.

"No. I was. My wife died several years ago. I've never—"

"I'm sorry," she said automatically when he didn't finish his sentence. "I didn't mean to pry. I really meant this business between OpNav and NIS." She was suddenly anxious for some reason to change the direction of the conversation. To her great relief, he went with it.

"Oh, that. I'm not entirely sure what's going on with all that. If this thing in Philadelphia is indeed a homicide, then I'd think it would be entirely in NIS's jurisdiction. But when the elephants dance, we mousies are well advised to just get off the floor, you know?"

She digested this in silence for a few miles. He was either part of it or he wasn't, but he was acting as if he wasn't.

"My bosses are pretty upset, actually," she said.

"That guy Ames certainly was. So what are your marching orders, then, Grace?"

She was taken somewhat aback by this direct question. " 'Marching orders'? I guess to act as your liaison with NIS, and to assist in the investigation."

"Okay, that's fair enough," he said. "Mine are to focus on the *JAG Manual* investigation. The Navy JAG—that's judge advocate general, head lawyer for the Navy Department—has some fairly clear guidelines about how a JAGMAN is supposed to be done, and I plan just to walk it down the checklist. I assume you're required to keep those angry bosses of yours informed as to what's going on, right?"

"Yes, of course."

"Okay, and so am I. Do you think they would like my investigation to fail in some way?"

"I . . . I don't know. Bureaucratically, I suppose they would. But I've seen no evidence that someone's waiting to sabotage it, if that's what you mean." He was being *very* direct.

"Right. Okay. So let's make a deal: Let's strive to keep the integrity of the investigation intact, and we take care of our respective bureaucracies on our own time. If there's a conflict between those two tasks, we talk about it, okay?"

"That sounds fair." This might be easier than I expected, she thought.

"Well, it's practical, because there probably will be conflicts. I think the way to look at this situation is that you and I are both sort of pawns in the larger rice-bowl game. Whatever the bigs are up to, on your side or mine, is above our pay grade, so if we play it straight, we give the elephants no excuse to trample us, if I can mix my metaphors. Ah, here's the Beltway. Shields up, everybody."

For the next hour, they talked only sporadically as Dan concentrated on surviving a trip around the Capital Beltway. She relaxed after awhile; he was easy to talk to, and he did not seem to have many pretensions. She told him about her years with SEC in Washington and New York, and the fact that she had been married to a stockbroker in New York and gotten divorced just before taking the appointment at Justice.

"So why NIS? Get run out of Justice by the new administration?"

"Yes, along with everyone else. I should have known better than to take a late-term appointment."

"Yeah. I guess that goes with the territory of political appointments. What does one do in Investigations Policy at NIS?"

Grace thought fast. Tell him, or play along? What if he already knows? Play it.

"I imagine it's like the OpNav Plans and Policy that you work in," she said. "We're supposed to develop organizational strategy, and we handle the Services's interdepartmental relations. NIS has an important counter-intelligence role, and, of course, there are lots of people in that game in this town."

"Amen, and all equally incompetent, apparently. The Navy had the Walker case, and now CIA has Brother Ames. We do much the same thing in OpNav, except we don't work counterspy, counterintelligence stuff. We do Navy strategy and long-range plans, budget support, and the staff work on a whole host of international treaties and agreements. The Navy does business around the world, so OpNav tends to do more of that than the other services. I'd call it quasi-important paper pushing."

She asked him where he lived, and he described his eighteenth-century house on Prince Street in Old Town, two blocks up the hill from the river.

"Prince is one of the streets with the original cobblestones. I thought they were really quaint when my folks passed it on to me, but my ankles know better now. But for a Navy guy, the price was very right."

She laughed. "My street has cobblestones *and* trolley tracks," she said. "My parents bought me the house when I went off to Georgetown Law. Father just assumed that the law school was on the campus, so I'm two blocks from there."

"It isn't?"

"No. Never has been. It's downtown. I didn't have the heart to tell him."

"I love it. I went to Gonzaga High School—supposedly a prep for Georgetown. But my parents were schoolteachers, and we couldn't afford Georgetown, so I went ROTC at GW instead."

He told her that he had grown up in the Washington, D.C., area. Born in 1957, the only child of two Fairfax County schoolteachers, he had lived in various suburbs of northern Virginia as his parents moved around in the school system. He had enjoyed a gentle upbringing, making his way through childhood with an easygoing, affable demeanor that allowed him to get along with just about anybody and to fit into whatever group seemed handy. Given his parents' profession—they were both history teachers—he developed a taste for learning, if not necessarily for achievement. He attended public schools up through junior high school, but by the time he reached the eighth grade, his laid-back, rather laissez-faire attitude about grades had prompted his parents, both attendant Catholics, to hand him over to the tender mercies of the Jesuits at the Gonzaga College High School in downtown Washington.

For a boy coming out of the public schools of northern Virginia, Dan had found his first year at Gonzaga to be an eye-opening experience, not so much from the point of view of his academic qualifications, but, rather, in terms of emphasis. Qualitatively, Fairfax County schools were above the national average, but for a popular and gregarious kid who was on the verge of puberty and whose focus had been happily coalescing toward those heretofore entirely ignorable aliens called girls, Gonzaga had provided a major course correction. There were no girls at Gonzaga, only Jesuits, lots of Jesuits who were seriously into academic and athletic competition, three hours of homework every night, daily Mass, unabashed physical discipline for miscreants, and an academic curriculum crammed with four years of mandatory Latin, mathematics, science, history, and English, all absorbed in a coat-and-tie atmosphere where all the adults were addressed as either Father or Mr. And above all, there was a heavy emphasis on personal achievement: There were daily grades, a First Honors roll, a Second Honors roll, academic and athletic prizes, lists in the hallways, and the constant pressure of the young black-robed Jesuit scholastics, called Mr. instead of Father, who taught most of the classes.

Dan had not been previously involved in organized sports, so the Jevvies drafted him for one of the freshman softball teams, where he surprised everybody, especially himself, by showing a distinct talent for being a pitcher. In the fall semester, the freshmen were organized into intramural teams, which allowed the athletic director a chance to inspect the talent for the coming spring season. Dan's selection to the spring team was his first major triumph at Gonzaga, as well as the beginning of his acceptance of the Jesuit system.

On the other end of the motivation spectrum, every classroom had a student beadle who recorded classroom infractions and demerits, and an after-hours detention hall called "jug," from the Latin *jugum*, where those individuals who had earned a notation in the beadle's book would be re-calibrated under the supervision of the enormous and ubiquitous prefect of discipline, one Father Shining. Jug would convene at 3:15, immediately after school, and that day's crop of miscreants would be instructed to write out things like the Nicene Creed one thousand times, after which they were graciously free to go.

The Jesuits' unalloyed academic zeal transformed Dan's first year at Gonzaga from just another school year with all his neighborhood buddies into the centerpiece of his existence. At first, the schoolwork at Gonzaga had been pell-mell, then totally unreasonable, then hard, and finally, interesting. The Jesuits taught on the principle of challenging young minds, and since there was a large variety of young minds, there was an equally large variety of challenges. Dan found out that the Jesuits took discipline seriously. Actually, the Jesuits took everything seriously, but this did not become evident to him until about the middle of his first year, when he had his first direct experience with the prefect of discipline. One of the toughest kids in his ninth-grade class had been named Marty Murphy, a graduate of Blessed Sacrament up in Chevy Chase and a stalwart of the CYO. Murphy made the grave mistake one day of talking back to one of the Jesuit teachers, to the secret delight of the whole class, although Dan failed to notice that there was a great deal of emphasis on the secret part. Dan went down on the beadle's pad as one of Murphy's accomplices—for laughing—and accompanied Murphy to the basement for jug. Upon arrival, Father Shining had come in and without further ceremony grabbed Murphy by the right arm. He took him down the hallway to the front door and out into the school's tiny front lawn, which faced Eye Street. The other inmates of jug watched through the windows as Father Shining dragged Murphy over to the aging white picket fence protecting the sparse lawn. Never relaxing his grip, the huge priest grabbed a single fence picket and in one nail-screeching movement tore it off the fence. Realizing the possibilities, Murphy stopped squirming and concentrated on the picket. Shining took his hand off Murphy's arm long enough to grab the picket in both hands and split it lengthwise with his bare hands right in front of Murphy's no-longer-insolent face. At this juncture, the by-now-wide-eyed spectators in jug did a down-periscope act at the windows and scrambled back to their desks, hoping against hope that all they would have to do would be to copy out the New Testament a few hundred times. Dan concluded that these people were indeed serious, and he began to pay attention, both to his studies and to how the game was played in his new school. Murphy never told whether or not Shining had actually used the fence picket, and no one had asked.

Graduating from Gonzaga with First Honors and as captain of the softball team in 1974, Dan had matriculated at George Washington University, again in downtown Washington, with a full Navy ROTC scholarship. Given his grades and his athletic ability, he had had a shot at the Naval Academy in Annapolis, but the competition in northern Virginia for political appointments was fierce, and besides, he was tired of being in an all-boys school. At GW, he majored in international affairs, which seemed to him an appropriate course of study for a budding naval officer, and graduated with a commission and an appointment into the surface line in 1978. His mother and father had been quite proud of him on commissioning day, although they seemed somewhat ill at ease among the many military parents in the audience, as well as with the elaborate military ceremony attending commissioning. The Vietnam War was over, but the social and political bruises created by that conflict were barely healed, and Dan's parents belonged to a profession that had made no secret of its animosities toward things military. They had swallowed hard when Dan opted for the Navy scholarship, but Dan was simply being practical: the NROTC scholarship had been a forty-thousand-dollar ticket to a college degree, and if he had to serve four years in the Navy afterward, well, it would let him see the world, just like the poster said, a need his parents probably would never understand. And, unlike some of his classmates, he had graduated with a job, the chance for a career if things went well, and a ticket out of Washington, D.C.

He told Grace a little bit about his subsequent career in the Navy, skirting over the dreadful year in Monterey when his wife had died. Grace let him ramble, not paying too much attention, while her mind focused on what would happen once they got to Philadelphia. She was especially concerned about how they would be treated by the NIS field office, which was known in Navy parlance as NISRA Philadelphia: NIS Resident Agent–Philadelphia. If the headquarters executives were going to throw a wrench into the workings of the OpNav investigation, the resident agent, one Mr. Carl Santini, would be their instrument. That would be a shame, because she really did want to know how on earth a body had come to be discovered in the bowels of a sleeping battleship.

III

APRIL 1992

WASHINGTON, D.C

5

FOR THE THIRD DAY in a row, Malachi Ward sat in the darkened Ford, watching the entrance to the apartment building perched above the E Street Expressway viaduct. With the viaduct on one side and an apartment complex on the other, the street was deserted. The windshield wipers, set on intermittent, groaned once as they swept away the mizzle that was descending all over Washington. He had watched the woman leave in the morning darkness, at the same time each morning. She was a daily commuter: a creature of habit. She returned home again between quarter to seven and seven each evening. Apparently, she was also dedicated.

He looked at his watch again: 6:45 P.M. Anytime now. The sounds of a diminishing rush hour echoed up from the viaduct, drifting in through the partly lowered window on the passenger side. He heard the voices of two women coming up the sidewalk, their features blurred in his misted-over right-side mirror. Fat, shapeless features. Not her. The one he was waiting for was definitely not fat. She was very pretty, in fact; into high leather heels and a snappy, staccato stride. She'd worn a stylish tan raincoat when she left that morning at 6:10. Out the front door, turning left onto the sidewalk and walking up to 23rd Street, then left again and up 23rd toward the Metro station near George Washington University. One quick jaywalk across 23rd to get a paper, a second jaywalk back to the left side of the street, and on to the Metro station. Considering that daylight saving time had just started and it was still dark at that hour, she wasn't very careful about it. Definitely a type A: out the door at zero-dark-thirty; first one into the office, probably the last one to leave. Go to work in the dark, come home in the dark: the Washington good life. Going to get ahead, our girl.

Heels. He swiveled his head around. Tan coat, fast stride. Here she comes and here we go. He picked up the stubby German binoculars from the seat of the car and focused in on the lobby. He had called her answering machine forty minutes ago, told her about the visit, depositing the message late enough so that she would not have checked it from the office. Special Agent Demarest, FBI. A security matter in the Pentagon, a possible classified-material compromise. He would need only twenty minutes or so. Strictly routine.

She clacked by his car, oblivious to the big man in the driver's seat, her head down against the wet mist. Up the steps, into the lobby. He leaned forward to watch her in the yellow light of the lobby. He focused the binoculars on the security door's keypad, conscious of her blurry image to one side as she busied herself with her mailbox, extracting the day's take. Closing it. Walking over to the door. Punching the keypad as he focused in: 4-4-7-8. Pushing open the door, and now she was gone. He waited. Give her time to get upstairs, take the coat off, kick off those heels, run the answering machine. He waited some more, then picked up the car phone and dialed her number.

"Hello?"

"Yes, Miss Hardin, this is Special Agent Demarest, FBI, calling. I left a message on your machine awhile ago. Did you get it?"

"Why yes. Yes, I just did. But—"

"Please don't be alarmed, Miss Hardin. This has nothing to do with you directly, but I do need to interview you regarding some classified-material control procedures having to do with an office you work with. And because of the details of the case, I didn't want to do that in your office. You know, the FBI is here to see you—people talk, right?"

"Well, yes, but—"

"Right. So I propose to come by this evening. Fifteen, twenty minutes and we're done."

"I just got home. I—"

"I understand, Miss Hardin. Actually, it's Lieutenant Hardin, isn't it? Look, I'm calling from a car phone. If I have the address right, I'm about five minutes away. You are in apartment four-twelve, the Kendall Apartments, correct? Is there parking nearby?"

"Well, Mr.—Demarest, was it? Parking's kinda tough. You'll have to use the street. The garage requires a magnetic card."

"Don't they all. I'll tell you—sometimes the cases are simple compared to finding a parking place in this town. Again, I apologize for the intrusion. I'll make it as quick as possible; then we can both call it a day."

"Okay," she said with a sigh. "Press the button for four-twelve in the lobby when you get here. I'll buzz the door open."

"Thanks so much, Miss Hardin. See you in a bit."

He hung up the phone and waited some more. Make it ten minutes. Time to get there, find parking. She had a nice voice—educated, but with a brassy overtone. The file said she was a public information officer, so she should be accustomed to dealing with all kinds of people on the phone.

He sat back in the seat and recalled the phone message that had led to his being here. From the captain, naturally; the principals never called directly. There was a little problem that needed his special talents. Please meet the captain in the Army-Navy Town Club library at eleven o'clock. He had been waiting on the third floor in the magazine reading room when the captain showed up. The captain had looked tired and annoyed; it had apparently been a long day, and it probably wasn't over. They had retired to the back reading room, where the problem had been explained, and it turned out to be a story very familiar to Malachi. It seemed that a certain senior officer had been indulging his tastes for younger women again, this time with a young lady on the Navy headquarters staff.

"Your 'great man' into uniforms now?" Malachi had asked.

The captain had just looked at him. They both knew the Washington rule about playing around in your own sandbox, but the captain was not there to discuss the right, wrong, or smarts of it. Malachi had waved his hand as if to say, Okay, go on.

"The young lady in question has decided that she does not want to continue the, um, relationship. My principal was not ready to, shall we say, acquiesce in that decision."

"He liked it; she didn't."

The captain shrugged. "Whatever. I think she simply got a little scared. What had seemed like a good idea at the time and all that. In any event, she said some intemperate things, according to my principal."

" 'Intemperate.' "

"His words."

Malachi had smiled from the depths of his armchair. He loved the way these executive assistant types talked. "Like back off or I'll do an Anita Hill number on you."

"Something like that. So now the principal wants the young lady warned off, or, at the very least, convinced to keep her mouth shut."

"Until some calls can be made and a suitable assignment can be found, preferably on the distant fringes of the empire."

"That does not concern you. What we want from you—"

"I know what you want from me. You want me to fix it. But what's so special about this one?"

The captain was silent for a moment, and then he produced an eight and one half-by-eleven manila envelope and handed it to Malachi.

"The subject," he announced gravely.

The subject, Malachi thought. Not the girl, or the woman, or her name, like she just might be human. The subject. Malachi opened the envelope and withdrew a glossy black-and-white official government photograph of an attractive woman naval officer, a full lieutenant, in blues. He stared at the picture for a minute. The woman was black.

"The principal is an idiot," he said finally.

The captain apparently decided to keep his own counsel. Malachi put the photograph back in the envelope.

"I presume the principal does not want to buy her silence?"

"The principal is not wealthy."

"At least not wealthy enough to pay both me and her. So then he wants the young lady scared into silence, right?"

"Well—"

"Well?"

"Well, no physical violence, of course. But you have succeeded in, um, delicate missions in the past. The principal, of course, doesn't really care or need to know—"

Malachi laughed. "Principals never do. Right. Got it. You have the retainer?"

The captain had passed over an envelope with Malachi's standard fee, in cash. He then pointed to the envelope containing the photograph.

"Her address and some particulars are in there."

Malachi had looked at his watch. "I'll take care of it. You look tired. You ought to come here more often, have a drink, read a good book. Relax a little."

The captain had simply looked at him, shaken his head, and left.

That had been last week. Malachi glanced at his watch again, nodded to himself, and got out of the car. He took a shiny leather briefcase and locked the car behind him. He wore a dark gray pinstripe suit, white shirt, and a conservative tie under an inexpensive but functional tan trench coat. J. Edgar would have approved. He carried the shield and photo ID of an FBI special agent in a credential case inside his breast pocket, and a 9-mm Beretta semiautomatic in a shoulder holster under his left arm. He looked both ways up and down the sidewalk to see if there were any spectators, or early muggers. Sometimes when he was bored, he sort of hoped for muggers, especially when he was carrying. Except that nowadays, the Washington muggers were likely to be sporting submachine guns. Still, it might beat watching *Jeopardy*. He stepped up to the doors of the lighted lobby and went inside.

Even at fifty-two, Malachi Ward was a visibly hard man. His large head was blocky, in a Teutonic cast, and he had a prominent, slightly hooked nose; deep-set and gleaming gray eyes under dark brows; wide, almost sensuous red lips; and sparse gray hair tonsured to an even quarter inch all over, and receding on his forehead behind a prominent widow's peak. His complexion was smooth except for crow's-feet around his eyes and two pronounced vertical creases framing his mouth. His face had ruddy patches on each cheek and an overall roseate flush that revealed a fondness for bourbon. If one looked closely, a network of scars could be seen just above his shirt collar. He was not especially tall, but he had a massive upper body, with trunklike forearms that were noticeable in the way his arms filled out the upper sleeves of the trench coat. He stood very straight when he walked, as if to keep all that upper-body muscle mass from getting ahead of him.

He looked the part of a cop, although he knew he had two features out of character for an FBI agent. The first was his overall size, especially his massive hands—workman's hands, all calloused and red around the edges from his toughening exercises, with blunt, spatulate fingers and square-cut yellow nails. In the Army, he had been self-conscious about his oversized hands until he'd made it into the Military Police corps and found that, sometimes, just the sight of his two enormous fists was enough to settle a lot of problems before they really got going. In his current line of work, Malachi would let people discover his hands as part of the process of intimidation. If the object of his attentions was at all observant, one good look tended to dissolve any doubts one might have about the aura of physical violence he projected. Where some men talked tough, Malachi could project tough with a steady stare and his physical presence.

The second uncharacteristic feature was his voice: a deep, hoarse, almost raspy voice, but one that had very little staying power, the result of an incident in Germany while he had been in the Army, which made him now a man of few words. But he had learned how to use that voice to add menace to his conversations whenever he needed to, a faculty that came in handy when he had to sit down with someone, as he was about to do.

He walked over to the keypad and, after looking around to make sure no one was watching, punched in the code. The door lock emitted a satisfying click. He nodded to himself. Always have two ways in and two ways out of every situation. Then he went back over to the communications pad, pressed the 412 button, and waited.

"Who is it?" asked a crackly voice from the speaker at the top of the panel.

"Special Agent Demarest, Federal Bureau of Investigation, to see Lt. Elizabeth Hardin," Malachi intoned. His reply echoed officially around the faux marble tiles of the lobby, but there was no one there to appreciate the act. He had to move quickly to catch the door when the buzzer sounded. He went inside, found the elevator, and rode it up to the fourth floor. Stepping out of the elevator, he looked around to find the exit stairs. He checked the stairwell door to make sure it was unlocked on the stairwell side, then took a look down the stairs to see if there was a fire block anywhere. Only then did he go looking for apartment 412, which was six doors down, to the right of the elevator. He knocked twice and produced his credentials, stepping back away from the door a little. Elizabeth Hardin cracked open the door on a chain and peered out.

"Lt. Elizabeth Hardin?" he asked formally.

"Yes."

"Special Agent Demarest of the FBI. My credentials, Miss Hardin." Malachi held up the two-sided leather folder. She flicked a glance from the picture to his face, then nodded. She closed the door, removed the chain, and stood aside to let him in. Malachi stepped in and took off his raincoat and hung it on a coat tree by the door. Elizabeth Hardin preceded him into a living room that was small and plain, with one large, curtained window overlooking an interior courtyard framed by the windows of several other apartments. There was a dining room table in one corner, an open kitchen area, and a door that presumably led to the bedroom and bath. Elizabeth Hardin indicated one of the two upholstered chairs in the room and asked if she could get him anything.

"Thank you, no, Miss Hardin. As I said, I apologize for the inconvenience, and I'll get this done as quickly as possible."

"It's your voice. Sounds like it needs a drink. Excuse me for a moment while I get my beer, then, Mr. Demarest. I just got home."

Malachi arranged his briefcase on his knees and opened it while he tracked her out of the corner of his eye. She went into the kitchen and opened some drawers and then the icebox. She returned with a frosty pewter mug and sat down across from him at one end of the couch. Malachi realized that she was indeed very pretty—about five foot six, maybe 120 pounds. Her face had an intensely black, smooth complexion, high, arching eyebrows, slightly slanted brown eyes, and features that Malachi would have called more white than African. Her hair had been straightened and pulled back in a glistening, tight bun. She wore a brightly patterned blouse and a long, flowing, shapeless skirt. He noticed that she was in her stockinged feet, and that she was watching him while he looked her over.

"I'm guess I expected you to be in uniform, Lieutenant," he began.

"I'm in CHINFO—that's Navy public relations. The media types seem to feel more comfortable talking to people in civvies, so we oblige." She sipped some beer. "So what's this all about, Mr. Demarest? We don't do classified where I work."

"The *possible* compromise of some classified material, Miss Hardin. But first let me verify some details about you."

He opened the briefcase, putting the raised lid between them, and rooted around for a leather folder containing a pad of yellow legal paper. He spread the folder and set it on the briefcase, out of her direct view, using the briefcase as a lap desk. He pretended to scan some notes for a moment, and then verified her social security number.

"You are Elizabeth Terry Hardin, born here in Washington, D.C. Date of birth: December 6, 1965?"

She smiled. "Your data banks are correct," she said.

"And you are a staff public affairs officer in the Navy headquarter's Chief of Information Office, as well as their computer information management specialist? And you've been assigned there for two years now?"

"Two years, that's right. I took a degree in computer science from GW. CHINFO is fully networked, but you know how computers are. Actually, we have good machines; it's the users who are defective. I'm the one they call when their machines defeat them. I'm also the CHINFO database administrator, and I do research for news organizations or with other offices in OpNav. Basically, I'm their data dink."

"OpNav, Dink?"

"OpNav." She sighed patiently. "The headquarters staff of the Navy. The executive staff of the Chief of Naval Operations. Operations, Naval; unit of issue, one each. OpNav. We also work for the office of the SecNav."

"The Secretary of the Navy."

"You're getting it. And *dink* is another word for *nerd*, Mr. Demarest."

"Right. I guess I don't associate a word like *dink* with a beautiful young woman, Miss Hardin."

He saw her stiffen. "And just what do my looks have to do with the classified-material problem here, Mr. Demarest?" she asked.

Malachi closed his notebook, lowered the briefcase lid, and sat back in his chair. The lady was on guard. Good. Now she would pay attention.

"Well, nothing at all, Miss Hardin," he said, smiling. "But your looks have everything to do with why I'm really here."

Alarmed, she put down the mug. He put up a hand. "No, no, don't get all upset. I'm just a messenger boy, all right?"

She shifted on the couch, putting her hands down as if ready to get up quickly.

"I want to see those credentials again, Mr. Demarest," she said. "And if you're—"

Again he put up his hand. "Those credentials are entirely authentic, Miss Hardin. I *am* a special agent with the FBI—by day. It's just that I'm moonlighting right now. I'm here to talk to you about your sexual involvement with a certain senior person in the Navy."

He heard her sharp intake of breath but continued before she could say anything.

"I've been sent here to give you some advice . . . some really good advice. You can either listen to what I have to say or you can say the magic word and I'll leave immediately. But before you do that, think about something. Think about the kind of power that can get an off-duty FBI agent to come calling about your love life."

"How *dare* you! Since when is my private life the business of the god-damned FBI!" Her hands were clenched and her eyes wide in anger.

"Exactly," he said gently, and waited for her to get it. She stared at him for a few more seconds, then slowly leaned back in the couch. He pressed on.

"I'll get straight to it. The background I have is that this senior guy got the hots for you, and you saw a chance maybe to get close to a powerful man. You did what lots of pretty girls do in this town, and then after the two of you got it on, you got cold feet about the whole thing, wanted to shut it off unless it could be put on the up-and-up. But he's senior, married, and wasn't ready for that, and he also wasn't ready just to say *sayonara*. He pressed to keep things as they were, you shut him off, he pushed harder, and you threatened to go public. That about sum it up?"

She was silent for almost a minute, glaring at him. He could see that she was really angry now; small round shadows flushed on her dusky cheeks. But she was also worried.

"No," she said finally. But then she looked down at the floor for a moment. "There was more to it than that. There *is* more to it than that."

"Not anymore," he said. Her head snapped up and she stared back at him. He realized in that instant that offering money would never have worked. The dummy was in love. The captain had had it backward. He decided to go straight at it. He leaned forward.

"Not anymore," he repeated softly. "Basically, you are going to forget about it and him. Just flat forget about it. That way, you keep your nice Navy career intact and everything works out for the best. But only if you keep your mouth shut and get used to the fact that it *is* now all over. Gone and down the road. In return, you get what you wanted: The great man keeps *his* mouth shut and doesn't bug you anymore. But no kiss-and-tell. No *Navy Times* scandals, no sexual harassment news conferences, no Anita Hill scene, no nothing. You are probably not the first pretty pasture he's plowed in his career, and you probably won't be the last. But you *are* going to keep your mouth shut."

"You really don't understand, do you?" she said. "I only threatened to expose him because he . . . he kept *after* me. I told him that a secret affair had been a mistake." She paused, looking down at the table. "The whole thing was a mistake. Bigger than he knows."

"You've got that precisely right," Malachi agreed. His voice was getting tired. "But then, twenty-something women who fool around with guys my age are always bound for grief—especially when you're mixing black and white."

She flared. "And just what the hell does that mean?" He realized he'd gone too far, but her snippy attitude was starting to offend him. Goddamn women were all alike.

"It means that whites and blacks shouldn't breed, that's what it means. It's against nature."

"You *bastard*! Against nature? *Against nature!* Who or what the hell *are* you?" she shouted.

Malachi felt his own temper surge. He put the briefcase down, stood up, and stepped closer to the couch. He was looming over her. *What are you? Impudent little bitch.* He narrowed his eyes and lowered his voice as she recoiled against the couch, her hands clutching the cushion, her face filling with fear.

"*What* am I? I told you. I'm the messenger," he whispered, putting his hand out to point a thick finger right into her face, letting her see those hands. "And the message is that you need to keep your head down and your mouth shut and your legs closed. And if you don't, you stand to lose a lot more than just your job."

But she wasn't getting it. There was still as much anger in her face as fear. He put his right hand in her face, his fingers clawing, advancing to grab her chin, when he glimpsed a flash of steel and felt a searing pain across the back of his fingers. He jumped back with a hiss of pain as she lunged sideways off the couch to face him, her body in a crouch, a long kitchen knife in her left hand. She had cut him across the backs of all the fingers on his right hand. There was blood welling up all over the back of his hand as he raised it to see how badly he was hurt.

"You get *out*—get out of here!" she was yelling. "Right now! Move!"

He stepped backward and straightened up, a white-hot rage framing his voice. Another goddamned woman with a knife—he could almost feel the other pain again, the sickening knowledge of what the German bitch had done. He thought about the gun for a moment but then regained control of himself. He took a deep breath and held his bleeding hand up in front of his face, turning it this way and that as if to inspect it, letting the blood run down his shirtsleeve and not on the carpet. Then he looked back at her. She was trembling but standing her ground.

"Right," he said calmly, his right arm still up in the air, turned so that she could see what she had done. "I will leave now. You've made a big mistake, bigger even than falling in lust with the wrong guy, as you will see in good time."

"You just get out," she said again, her courage rising when she realized he was going to leave. "You're the ones who've made the big mistake, buster, as you all are going to see first thing tomorrow. See and hear. I work in *public* relations, remember? Now you shag your white ass out of here."

She gestured toward him with the knife. He bent down and picked up the briefcase with his left hand and backed away toward the door, his right arm still held upright. Then he stopped, dropped the briefcase, and undid his suit coat, shucking it off awkwardly and then wrapping it around his bleeding hand. With the coat off, she could see the 9-mm gun in its shoulder rig, and he saw her eyes widen as she stopped in her tracks. He could feel without looking that the elbow of his shirtsleeve was soaked through, so he wrapped the rest of the suit coat around his forearm. He lifted his raincoat off the coat tree with his left hand and then opened the door carefully, glancing out into the hall to make sure no one was watching, deliberately smudging the metal of the door handle to wipe any prints. He picked up the briefcase and looked back at her.

"It's never nice to hurt the messenger, Lieutenant," he said with a cold smile as he backed into the hall. She moved quickly toward the door and kick-slammed it in his face.

Out in the hallway, Malachi tightened the suit coat around his forearm, wiggled his way into the raincoat, and headed for the stairway. He took the stairs down to the ground floor, cracked the fire door to see if the hallway was clear, but then chose to go out a fire exit that led to the parking garage's entrance area. His hand was beginning to really hurt, but he was more worried about being seen.

The parking garage was an unattended underground lot with a machine-operated door. The stairway door had come out on the first level, right next to the street doors. He walked quickly over to the out ramp and waved his left hand in front of the electric eye, which triggered the door opener. A minute later, he found himself out on the rainy street. He walked around the block containing the apartment complex before approaching his car. Bitch might have called the cops, and he did not want to walk into any traps. He kept the bloody bundle that was his right hand out of sight as best he could, but there was no one around. There was a flare of headlights as a car pulled into the apartment garage, the driver working his card key to open the door, but then the street was empty again. He walked quickly back to his car, unlocked it awkwardly with his left hand, threw the briefcase in, and got in. The material of the suit coat was beginning to feel wet and soppy. Hands and heads bleed the worst, he remembered from his Army first-aid courses. Another car came down the street, and he sank down in the front seat until it had gone by. Still no cops. He had an idea. He dialed her number again. Busy. So she *was* on the phone. Have to think about that; a possible loose end there.

When he was satisfied that the street was not going to fill up with flashing blue lights, he started the Ford, did a U-turn, and went back out to 23rd Street. He turned right and took 23rd down to Memorial Bridge and across the river to Arlington, struggling to keep the suit coat wrapped tightly around his right hand. He was being very careful to contain the blood. He was pretty certain he had dripped none in her apartment, although the knife might show traces if she hadn't washed it. He might have to go back there during the day to check on that. That would be easy enough. He had the keypad number, and those apartment door locks were a joke.

Once in Virginia, he took Arlington Boulevard over to the 10th Street exit, drove up Wilson to Quincy Street, turned right, and then turned left into the underground parking garage of the Randolph Towers apartment building. For several years, he had maintained a one-bedroom, Spartanly furnished safe-house apartment in the Randolph Towers, which was a twenty-four-story high-rise one block from the Ballston Metro station. With the apartment came secure underground parking. He rarely stayed in the apartment, but it was there as a bolt-hole if he ever needed one, another one of Monroney's recommendations. He could still hear his old Saigon mentor's hoarse voice and clipped New York accent: "If you're gonna get into the shadow-land business, you need to have at least one hidey-hole, Malachi, and at least two, maybe even three vehicles, with lots of different paperwork, the whole bit, for everything. Remember, you can buy any kind of vehicle paperwork you need from those scary-looking Haitians in the District, the ones who hang around the Traffic Division up on New York Avenue." Malachi had registered each of his three vehicles under assumed names and addresses, taking advantage of the District's rather porous tax-by-mail system. As long as he sent in the checks, the renewals came right back. He even had two driver's licenses—one from Virginia and one from the District—that matched the names and geographical registrations of each vehicle. In the age of computers, it wasn't a foolproof system, but it would withstand a street-side traffic check.

The Randolph Towers had good security at night after ten o'clock, but until then there were three entrances out of sight of the front desk, so he could come and go without attracting any attention. Several of the foreign embassies in town maintained blocks of apartments there, so transients and strange new faces were a way of life. The exits from the garage were also conveniently out of view of the security people at the front desk, and they were operated by automated access cards.

Malachi had taken Monroney's advice about vehicles to heart, and he maintained three for his operations: a pickup truck, a small van, and a Ford sedan. The Ford stayed at the Randolph Towers. He had purchased it at a police auction in Fairfax County. It was old, dented, painted black, with tinted windows and a small whip antenna on the trunk, as well as a chrome-plated, remotely-operated spotlight in front of the driver's side mirror. He kept two sets of plates for it: one from the District, when he operated in Virginia, and another from Virginia, when he was operating in the District, both sets arranged after a meeting in the parking lot of the District of Columbia's Traffic Division, just as Monroney had said. The Ford looked exactly like what it had been, an umarked cop car, which solved a lot of problems in certain neighborhoods and also made parking around Washington simpler. He could hit any empty space that said RESERVED FOR GOVERNMENT VEHICLES, of which there were hundreds in Washington.

He circled down two levels to the bottom level and parked. Keeping the coat bunched around his hand, he shucked the raincoat and rolled up the blood-soaked shirtsleeve. Making sure no one was watching, he retrieved the first-aid kit from the trunk of the car, dropped the suit coat, and bandaged his fingers by the light coming from the trunk. The cuts were deep and raw-looking; his entire hand already felt hot and tender, with swelling evident along the base of his fingers. Should have stitches, he thought, but there was no way he could go to an emergency room now. He put some antibacterial cream on the cuts, wincing at the stinging pain, and then used four butterfly bandages to pull the cuts together as best he could. He replaced the first-aid kit in the trunk and climbed back into the car. Making sure he had retrieved the FBI credentials from the suit jacket, he wiggled back into his raincoat, slipping his injured right hand into the raincoat pocket.

He waited while a sudden swarm of evening commuters sought their parking spaces in the garage, but when everyone had headed for the elevators, he got back out of the Ford, locked it, and walked up the ramp to the Randolph Street garage entrance, carrying the ruined suit coat. He triggered the door and walked out past the deli on the ground floor, pitching the bloody suit coat into one of the apartment building's Dumpsters as he walked by. He went across Randolph Street, into the parking lot behind the dentist's office, past the IHOP, across Stafford, and into the entrance of the Ramada Renaissance Hotel. With his right hand stuffed into the raincoat pocket, no one paid any attention to him as he went through the lobby area, past the concessions, out the glass doors of the hotel's back entrance, and directly down into the Ballston Metro station.

He took the first Washington-bound train that came through and dropped into an empty seat. It was a Blue Line train, going back into town at the end of rush hour, and therefore pretty much empty. He sat back in his seat and closed his eyes. He badly needed a drink and a cigarette. Hold that thought, he said to himself. Get home, wash this mess up, get proper bandages on it, maybe some sulfa powder, and then have a little session with Mr. Harper's hundred proof. He started to review the events in the woman's apartment, but the insistent, throbbing pain in his hand was too distracting. He must have dozed, because he was suddenly startled by a push of people boarding the train at the Metro Center station. When he looked around, he saw that he was now the only white man in the car. But he was used to that: The trains leaving Metro Center at night going to Virginia were mostly filled with whites; going east toward Capitol Hill and Northeast Washington, the crowd was predominantly black.

Malachi lived up on Capitol Hill, which by day was the province of the almost entirely white national legislature and its staffs and the Capitol Hill police. Once the working day was over, though, the area reverted back to what it had been before serious gentrification had set in during the eighties: a very black part of town. He had acquired the place in 1975, once again, courtesy of Monroney. The Army had stationed him at Fort McNair, the mostly ceremonial installation at the junction of the Potomac and Anacostia rivers, while he had been waiting for his discharge papers to come through after the incident in Germany. Monroney, retired by then and running his own consulting business in Washington, had introduced him to a middle-aged Realtor lady who had a passion for whiskey that was almost as large as Malachi's. Without telling her any more than absolutely necessary, he had revealed that he had saved some money and was looking for somewhere to live that might also be an investment he could make before getting out of the Army. Besides being a kindred soul in matters of good whiskey, she had steered him into buying a run-down brick duplex on 5th Street NE, three blocks back from the Supreme Court building, with the suggestion that he could restore the two houses himself. It had given him something to do during his final months in the Army, and now he lived in one and kept the second one, which he had eventually retitled under an assumed name, as a safe house for clients who needed a discreet place to hole up from time to time. The lady had given him some damn fine advice: The duplexes had appreciated many times in value since then, and having the spare house also brought in some nice retainer income from three congressional offices that seemed to have an occasional need for extremely discreet living quarters.

Two very large ladies were giving him a suspicious once-over as the train approached the Capitol South station, but he ignored them, pushing his throbbing hand deeper into the raincoat pocket. He focused hard on the help he could expect from Mr. Harper and on what he would do the next morning. Goddamned woman. Twelve years in the Army, and no man had ever really hurt him physically. Only a goddamned woman. He knew her commuting routine cold. He would up the ante in the morning.

6

AT QUARTER TO SIX the following morning, Malachi waited in his white Ford F-250 pickup truck on the southbound side of 23rd Street, just behind a bus loading zone. The truck had a yellow caution flasher mounted on the roof of the cab, a large steel push grate mounted on the front bumper, and magnetic signs displaying the logo of the Washington Metropolitan Transit Authority attached to both doors. Monroney had pointed out that in Washington, a Metro service vehicle could park damn near anywhere except in front of the White House. He sat there with the cabin light on and a large clipboard resting on the steering wheel. A Metro bus schedule checker, waiting for rush hour. Three cop cars had passed him without so much as a glance.

He wore a short-sleeved white shirt and a dark tie. From time to time, he would hold up his bandaged right hand to ease the aching pain. The little bitch. She had had that kitchen knife under the sofa cushions the whole time. Another hostess with the mostess. City dweller. Especially in this city, the murder capital of the free world. What was it—an average of two murders a night in the District for the past three weeks? Springtime in Washington. He looked at his hand again, the fingers buried now under a bulky white bandage. Four deep red cuts in a row right across the base segments of his fingers. Lucky she had slashed instead of jabbed. He was getting careless in his old age. Not expecting a woman to pull a knife: For Malachi, that was incredible. His mind shied away from a sudden vision of Inge, the German barfly who had put him down for the count in Frankfurt that night. Yes, he would have to pay much better attention.

He checked his watch again. Maybe thirty minutes now until she came out. There was little traffic in town as yet, although the surburban arteries were probably already swelling. A 17A bus with the words FOGGY BOTTOM illuminated on the signboards pulled in ahead of him, the driver waving casually in his mirror. Malachi waved back and pretended to write something on his clipboard. He had twice more tried her phone last night, but it had been busy both times. Telling somebody about her night visitor maybe. Definitely a possible problem there, depending on whom she had called. But probably not somebody at work—she would have had to explain the nature of the problem. A relative perhaps. The file said she had a brother, but he was away in the Navy somewhere. Her mother—he would have to check that out. The knife and the phone call—two loose ends.

He yawned and lit another cigarette, lowering the window some more. Getting a little old for this shit. Twelve years in the frigging Army, nine of those in the military police, and he was having trouble with a little early reveille. Maybe the booze hadn't been such a good idea. The whiskey hadn't helped like it used to. By the time he'd had enough to dull the pain in his hand, his head had begun to hurt. When he had rolled out at four thirty, his head and his hand were competing to see which could hurt the most.

He had bought the Metro signs four years ago from a guy who needed a little help, and the flasher unit was out of a catalog. With these two accessories mounted on a plain pickup truck, he had gained another vehicle that could go anywhere and park anywhere in the city without attracting attention. Before leaving his garage, he had taken the precaution of spraying WD-40 over the entire front end, lights, hood, bumper, and especially the heavy steel push grate, just in case he got too close. He had made two careful circuits of the local streets to check out his escape route before parking in the bus zone, making sure that the city's diggers and fillers hadn't placed a baby Grand Canyon in his way.

He looked at his watch again. Ten, fifteen more minutes and she should come clacking up the street on his side, cutting across about a hundred feet down 23rd Street for her paper. Commuters: absolute creatures of habit. They had to have their morning papers. Usually all he had to do was place one of his enormous hands on someone to convince them where the path of righteousness lay. So round one to the lady. Round two would involve a little escalation: This morning he would scare the living shit out of her with the truck. Power steering, bitch. Don't need two hands for that. Make sure she saw his ugly face at the moment of truth. Let her understand that she was extremely mortal, she wanted to press on with something. He waited, his head and his hand emanating pain in stereo. He gave up and fished in the glove compartment for his flask and took a hit, the whiskey immediately sanding down some of the rougher edges in his head.

Twelve minutes later, as another Metro bus pulled away in a roaring cloud of diesel smoke, he saw her at the far end of the block. He looked around, wincing at the movement. His mouth was dry and there was an aura of needlelike pain around the periphery of his eyes. But it looked pretty good: no other pedestrians around, still too early for serious commuter traffic on the street. He checked the mirror and saw the traffic lights up at Washington Circle behind him blink from yellow to red. Perfect. The street would be clear for another ninety seconds. He took a deep breath to steady his nerves, thought fleetingly of maybe one more little tug on the flask, and then put the big truck in gear, hearing the 460 V-8 engage the drive gear with a dull clank. He gently eased the nose of the big truck out into the street itself but then stopped before going more than a few feet. He kept the lights off. Down the block, the woman continued up the sidewalk. He could just make out the bottom of her face, her jaw outthrust in the glow of the streetlights as she strode determinedly, probably thinking about what she was going to do and say this morning, maybe an indignant confrontation with the great man, pumped by some deeper apprehensions that her career might suddenly be at risk. He saw her look briefly up 23rd Street and then step out to cross to the newspaper dispenser. He waited until she had taken three solid steps out into the street before mashing the accelerator, causing the truck to lunge out of its parking place and jerking his neck as it accelerated into the street with a clean surge of horsepower, passing forty by the time she finally saw it over her left shoulder, then fifty when she absorbed what was looming at her up the shadowy street. Malachi aimed right behind her, just to her left, intent on making it very close, leaning forward to put his face in the windshield so she could see it, see who it was. He assumed that she would jump clear, but she didn't. She froze instead, transfixed by the truck that was filling her vision, and then, instead of moving, she was focusing on his face, a flare of recognition visible in her eyes at the last critical instant when she finally did try to move. But her foot slipped on the damp asphalt and she lurched sideways and the left side of the push grate caught her, the eight-thousand-pound impact spinning her around and catapulting her deformed body seventy-some feet across the street, where it crashed in a heap of bloody clothes against the front stoop of a brownstone.

Malachi, his face frozen, had no time to look back. He knew a direct hit when he felt it. With the blood pounding in his head and a cold feeling spreading through his stomach, and suddenly very sober, he careened down 23rd for one more block, slowing down, braking on the gears as he went, and made the first available left, onto F Street. He crossed three more streets and then took a right onto 19th south.

The stupid bitch! The stupid, defiant little bitch! All she had to do was jump!

He flipped on the police scanner mounted under the dash as he took 19th down to Constitution, where he made a left and then turned on the yellow flasher unit as he headed up Constitution toward Capitol Hill at just over the speed limit. His headache was gone, he noticed. Nothing like a little adrenaline rush to clear the head. Her face—at the last moment, something had happened to her face. For an instant, she had become Inge. If he closed his eyes for even a fraction of a second, he could still see it—that same angry glare and then the shock. But, no: not like Inge's face at all. Inge had been white. *Damn it!*

He slowed down once again as he got into heavier traffic near the Russell Senate Office Building, then turned south on 2nd Street, intent on driving around for a while in the warren of side streets surrounding Capitol Hill, just part of the Metro fleet of supervisors, out monitoring the capital's daily morning madness. There was some chatter on the scanner now, some codes, and finally, a request for an ambulance, code eight. Twenty-third Street. Code eight—too late. The "don't hurry" code.

After driving down into Southeast Washington for a few minutes, he turned into an empty automated car wash. Normally, the place was filled with young men washing and waxing their rides, but at this hour he had the place to himself. Before running the truck through, he got out and took down the flasher unit and peeled the magnetic Metro decals off the sides of the truck. He drove the truck through the car wash twice, then headed back toward the duplex on Capitol Hill. After pulling into the garage, he shut the door, got out, and then carefully inspected the front of the truck with a flashlight. Nothing. The hard rubber on the push grate was still dripping water from the car wash, creating a small pool on the grimy concrete floor, but there were no visible dents, no broken glass, bits of fabric, scratches, or bloodstains on the truck. He stood up and closed his eyes for a moment, his mind's eye contrasting the sterile sheet-metal sides of the truck with the black-and-white image of her body deforming against the push grate, that black-white face twisting out of human shape as she was spun around and launched by the impact. He took a deep breath, shuddered, and then smiled. Ah well, at least the truck was clean. A clean machine. Cleanliness was next to godliness. And what the hell. An accident, that's all it was. And an unnecessary accident at that: All she had to do last night was say, Okay—I've got the message. I'll be good, and I'll be quiet. But no, she had to pull a goddamned knife on him, cut his hand, forcing him into having to try again. Another goddamned treacherous woman with cutting on her mind.

He put the flashlight back, shut off the light in the garage, and checked the locks on the electric door. Squeezing by the truck, he went through the backyard door and up the broken concrete walk toward the house, lighting a cigarette on the way, sending a huge puff of blue smoke into the dawn air. Hell, he had only meant to scare her; it was her fault she had chosen to look instead of leap. One of life's little choices, as Monroney used to say. Besides, Mr. I. W. Harper knew how to deal with unpleasant images. The only unsettling part of it was when his brain had flickered that overlay of Inge's face onto the lieutenant's face. Bad sign, seeing that face again. The girl had essentially killed herself by not getting out of the way. But where was the image of Inge coming from after all these years?

He walked up through the tiny, neglected backyard, up the wrought-iron back steps, and through the kitchen door of the left side of the duplex, hesitating for a moment in the kitchen to stare at the whiskey bottle but then continuing on through the house and grabbing his black windbreaker as he went out the front door. He walked the seven blocks over to the Eastern Market Metro station and caught an Orange Line train heading back into town. He got off at the Foggy Bottom station and surfaced on 23rd Street, across from the George Washington University Hospital complex. Something appeared to be causing a traffic jam down on 23rd, just a few blocks away. He stopped in at a 7-Eleven for coffee and a doughnut and asked the Korean proprietor what was going on down on 23rd.

"Hit-and-run. Some lady got killed by a car," the proprietor replied. "Got traffic all screwed up. You want a bag for that?"

THE FOLLOWING MORNING, Malachi went out early to get a morning paper and some cigarettes from the convenience store over on East Capitol Street. He walked across the street to the bakery and bought a coffee and a prune Danish, then walked the four blocks up to Capitol Hill. It was a pleasant spring morning, with a solid green haze showing among the tree branches and a hint of warmth in the air. A few commuters trying to avoid the major avenues sped through the quiet neighborhood streets, paying only very casual lip service to the stop signs. He felt the rumbling vibrations of a passing Metro bus on the uneven pavement as he crossed 2nd Street behind the Library of Congress. His head no longer hurt, because this time he hadn't made the mistake of interrupting his whiskey intake. He had not slept last night, or at least not for more than a half hour at a time. He had watched a series of increasingly boring night talk shows, smoked all his cigarettes, and killed a quart of Harpers. But he wasn't drunk, just pleasantly—stable, yeah, that was the word. The bourbon was warm in his veins and the lurking headache was being kept firmly at bay.

Reaching the small park behind the Supreme Court building, he found a bench that was upwind of the lumpy vagrants sleeping in the bushes, spread out his paper, and scanned the Metro section. He found it right away: A female Navy lieutenant had been the victim of an early-morning hit-and-run accident on 23rd Street. She had been DOA at George Washington University Hospital of multiple fractures and blunt-force trauma. She had been identified as Lieutenant Elizabeth T. Hardin, USN, age 27 attached to the Chief of Information (CHINFO) Office at the Navy headquarters in the Pentagon. She was survived by her mother, one Mrs. Agnes Hardin, of District Heights, in Southeast Washington, where the lieutenant had been born and raised, and a younger brother, who was a lieutenant (junior grade) supply corps officer stationed on a ship in the Navy. According to the paper, there had been no witnesses to the accident, nor were there any leads. Good, if true. The article closed with a police spokesman—correction, spokes*person*—making some remarks about the dangers of jaywalking, especially in the early-morning darkness. Two column inches. Ho hum. He spent the next half hour drinking his coffee, finishing the Danish and the paper, and watching the flow of women staffers clicking their way up the street to the various Hill office buildings. Every one of them was a looker. No wonder all those congressmen can't keep their pants zipped. Go ahead and look, Malachi: Looking's all you got left.

When he returned to the duplex, however, his answering machine was not ho-hum. There was a belligerent, almost hysterical message from the captain, directing him to call in at once on the private number. Treating him like a junior officer again. Malachi grinned and erased the tape. Let him stew for a while. The phone rang as he headed up the stairs. He stopped to listen to a second call from the captain, a repeat of the first message. The captain was trying to sound slightly more threatening, but came off sounding mostly frightened. Malachi gave the machine a mock salute and went upstairs to shower and shave.

He went back downstairs a little after 9:00 A.M., squeezed one last cup of last night's coffee out of the percolator, added a small—well, maybe a medium—whiskey helper, lit a cigarette, and called the captain's direct number, sipping the whiskey-flavored coffee. Gotta keep the levels right, he thought. A yeoman said the captain was not available and asked if he could take a message. Malachi left his number and the agreed-upon cover name. While he was waiting, he found the personnel file on Elizabeth Hardin and ran it through his shredder. The captain called back twenty minutes later, and Malachi let him talk to the machine again. Finally at around 10:00 A.M., the phone rang again, and this time Malachi picked up.

"Yes?" he said.

"What the hell have you done!" whispered the Captain.

"Can't talk?" Malachi asked innocently. "Got people around with their ears on fire?"

"You heard me, goddamn it!" A stage whisper now.

Malachi sat down on the bottom stair, his customary position when talking on the hall phone.

"Hell, I did what you wanted," he began. "I went to see her, got in right after she came home, told her I was an FBI guy. She bought the FBI bit, and once I was in, I brought up her love life and gave her the word. But she didn't want to play ball. She got all righteous and excited, threw me out. That's it. What's the problem with that?"

"The problem is that she's dead, for Chrissakes!"

Malachi feigned surprise. "Dead? *Dead?* She was damn well alive when I left her—calling me names, but very much alive and very pissed off. What do you mean dead?"

"Don't you read the goddamn papers? Watch the TV news?"

"Nope."

"Well, you should. She was run down on Twenty-third Street early yesterday morning, the morning after you paid your little call."

"No shit. So?"

"Well, I assumed you had something to do with that, Malachi."

Malachi put a little metal in his voice. "You assumed wrong. You specifically said not to hurt her, so I just did the monster-mash routine—gave her the word, just like you wanted, and then beat feet when she went hermantile. I figured you'd be on the receiving end next, shit she was saying. That's what I was going to report when I called, see what you wanted to do about it."

"What kinds of things was she saying?"

"Like she was gonna go see the great man and ream his ass out. Like she was gonna get extremely public. She reminded me that she worked in *public* relations, emphasis on that word *public*. I figured you were calling me this morning to tell me about a bitch kitty scene in the great man's outer office." Malachi was enjoying this.

There was a moment's silence on the line. Then: "He doesn't know about it yet."

"What, doesn't he read the damn papers? Watch the TV news?"

More silence.

"Ah," said Malachi. "I get it. You're elected to go tell him."

"Probably."

"Wonderful. Well hell, you're a big captain now, so go tell him. Or tell his wife, and let her tell him; that would be interesting. But get off my case. I *talked* to the little bitch. I did *not* do anything else. And like I said, she didn't scare so good. So you go tell your big guy. And here's a freebie: When he gets all teary-eyed and melancholy, point out to him that he's in the clear vis-à-vis any Anita Hill scenes, right? Silver lining sort of thing."

"Silver lining."

"One on every black cloud, Captain. See ya."

Malachi hung up and walked into his kitchen, whose rear windows overlooked the tiny backyard and the dilapidated fence running along the alley. He shook out another cigarette and then tore the filter off before lighting up. Every true addict knew that the tobacco they put in filter cigarettes had to be twice as strong as the unfiltered ones. The coffeepot was empty, so he got out the makings, eyeing the scant remains of the Harper hundred. Okay. Now, just those two little loose ends: the phone calls and the knife. The knife was simple. If the cops thought it was what the paper said it was—a hit-and-run and not a homicide—there'd be no detectives going to her apartment. So he ought to be able to just go over there, middle of the day, when everyone was at work, punch in the code, slip the locks, find the knife, clean it, and put it back under the couch, where she'd kept it. Where a friend or relative might *know* she'd kept it. But then he paused and thought about it. She'd probably already done that, and cleaned it off, too. But either way, the knife bit was simple if he moved right now.

He filled the percolator with water and plugged it in. The phone calls were more troubling. Depending on whom she had been talking to for nearly an hour, the cops might yet be coming around after all. Like if she'd called her mother, told her what was going down, and told her about the night visitor with the big hands. He held his right hand up and looked at his bandaged fingers again. Deep skin cuts. Hurt like hell. He'd had to change the bandages three times so far, but the sulfa powder was working its magic—there was no sign of general infection. If she *had* talked to her mother and the mother had told the cops, then he had better *not* go over there with his bandaged hand and walk into a stakeout. He sat back down at his kitchen table and thought about it as the coffeepot began making intestinal sounds.

Without knowing about the phone calls—whom she had called and what she had said—he really couldn't go take care of the knife. He conjured up a picture of the young woman in his mind. What would you do, Miss Navy Lieutenant, you cut some guy with a knife you kept under the couch pillows? A big guy with big hands who was scaring you? You'd run him out of the apartment, and now you're standing there in your living room with a bloody knife in your hand. That's right: you'd go into the kitchen, drop it into the sink, and then wash it off, and your hands with it. And probably put it back. You wouldn't be thinking forensics; you'd be slightly sick to your stomach at seeing a man's blood running down his arm after you slashed him. You'd wash it off and then wash your hands really good. So screw the knife—go find out what the cops were doing with the incident and who'd been talking to them about what. He got up and found a mug, poured the last of the Harper into it, sucked on his tattered cigarette while he waited for the percolator to finish.

When he was ready to make his calls, he went to his office, which had once been the dining room of the town house back when it had been a home. He sat down at his desk and activated the voice synthesizer. After what had happened to his voice in Germany, the machine had become a necessity. No one who heard his real voice would ever forget it, especially on the phone. And phones were his life. It was Monroney who had introduced him to the fact that you could find out almost anything in Washington simply by picking up the phone, Washington being as big a phone town as LA. That, plus the fact that every government organization published their phone book, which allowed you to find anyone who was connected with the government.

He chose voice program six, then made his first call to the *Washington Post*, asking for the reporter who had done the piece on the hit-and-run. While the operator was putting him through, he opened the Yellow Pages to "Attorneys." The phone rang four times and then he got voice mail. He hung up, then tried again a half hour later, and this time he got a human voice.

"Kit Freeman."

"Mr. Freeman, I'm calling about the piece in the Metro section today about the young Navy lieutenant who got run over."

"Yes? And your name?"

"My name is Farrell Greenberg, Mr. Freeman. I'm an attorney at Lyle, Spencer, Watkins and King, out here in Bladensburg." He closed the phone book.

"Oh, Jesus. I don't believe this, Greenberg. Let me guess, you're a personal injury liability guy, and —"

"No, no, Mr. Freeman. Not every attorney in this town is an ambulance chaser." Malachi wrote down the name Farrell Greenberg on a pad next to the synthesizer, and the number 6.

"Now that's news," Freeman said. "So what's your angle?"

"Our firm represents a client who is compiling statistics about the District of Columbia Police Department's solution rate on fatal traffic incidents—especially hit-and-runs. Your article today identified Lieutenant Hardin as being a black woman. My client believes that the police department relegates black traffic deaths to the back burner in terms of putting in the hours to find the perpetrators."

"The article didn't say she was black."

"It said she was from Washington, and her mother lived in Southeast, in District Heights. I concluded that she was black. Was I mistaken?"

"No."

"So, regarding what our client—"

"That's bullshit, and you know it."

"I said that our client believes that. Our—that is, my—instructions are to follow up on all such incidents in the city, such as the one that involved Lieutenant Hardin, to see what the police have done with it."

"So why are you calling me?"

"Because when I called the police hit-and-run division, I got stonewalled—investigation in progress, that sort of thing. I fully appreciate that it's been only one day, but most vehicular homicides are 'solved' about fifteen minutes after they happen. I'm calling you to find out if they know any more than they're telling, or perhaps to see if this incident is going to just dry up and blow away."

There was a moment's silence on the line. Malachi sat back in his chair. He was counting on the lawyer bit to distract the reporter from making any mental connections between the caller and the accident. It had been an accident, after all.

"Tell me, Mr. Greenberg," Freeman said. "What do your stats show so far?"

Malachi rustled the pages of his notebook, as if looking up the data. "In twenty-four cases of vehicular homicide or manslaughter in the past thirty months in the District, eighteen have involved black people, and sixteen of those are, quote unquote, 'solved.' That's eighty-eight percent. In two other cases, the witnesses told such convoluted stories, nobody could make sense of them. The remainder were either white people or other races, and about the same rate applies—eighty-five percent."

"So why doesn't your client just give it up?"

"My clients are not the kind of people who necessarily let facts distract them from their political agenda."

"Ah, an interest group. Right. That makes more sense, the way people act in this town. Okay: the Hardin case. The cops are stumped, literally stumped. Guy came out of his town house, on his way to work, found the girl's body draped across the trash cans next to his stairs. Deader than hell. No screech of brakes, no witnesses, no signs of robbery or any other crime than hit-and-run. Cops feel it's just what it looks like—a hit-and-run. They're going to work the usual guilt angle: Whoever you are out there, you know what you've done. Give yourself up—right now, it's an accident. We gotta come find you, it's manslaughter or even murder. That usually works, by the way."

Malachi went silent for a moment, then said, "Sorry, taking notes. So, there's nothing to indicate that they're sluffing it off."

"Nope. Although—"

"Yes?"

"The girl's mother. The detective on the case said the girl's mother was really strange about it. I mean, there was the expected grief reaction when a parent loses a child, even a grown child, but this was as if she had been expecting something to happen to her daughter. Not the normal reaction, whatever that is, but . . . Hell, I don't know."

"Oh dear. We never know how grief will manifest itself, do we?"

"You see a lot of grief in your business, counselor?"

"People rarely call their lawyers to celebrate one of life's little triumphs, Mr. Freeman. But I guess I need to put this one in the open column for now."

"Yeah, well, this being D.C., a hit-and-run can't compete with last night's umpteen drug shootings, so it isn't on the front burner, but it's not on the back burner, either. They just have nothing to go on so far. But as to that theory that the D.C. cops put black incidents—"

"I know, Mr. Freeman. I've got the statistics, remember? But thank you for your time and information. I'll pull the string with the police in about a week and see what they've got."

"Have a ball."

Malachi hung up and went back into the kitchen. So one phone call, assuming there had been more than one, may have been to mother dearest. He wondered if the girl's mother had known anything about her daughter's romantic entanglement with the great man—mothers often knew a lot more than their children ever gave them credit for, even their adult children. But the reporter could also be sandbagging him, or, more likely, he was just ignorant. Freeman had sounded like a kid. But one thing was clear: If the mother had told the cops that the daughter had called about being threatened the night before she was run down, the cops would have buried that little factoid deep indeed and opened a homicide file. He would have to find out what the mother actually knew, and if the cops were really working it.

MALACHI WAITED TWO DAYS before setting out to probe what the cops were doing with the case. He made one call to the police department, posing as a reporter, and, predictably, got nowhere. He then reset the synthesizer, called into Navy CHINFO, posing as a friend named Henry Bronson, and asked when and where the memorial service for Lieutenant Hardin would be. The young female petty officer who answered told him that it was a Baptist church up in District Heights—tomorrow afternoon. He thanked her and was about to hang up when he sensed she had something else to say. He probed. At first, she hesitated for a moment, and then she asked him if he was a white man. Momentarily taken aback, Malachi said yes.

"Well, Mr. Bronson, here's the thing: The CHINFO himself—that's Admiral Kenney—wanted to set up a memorial service over at Arlington— like at that chapel they got over there? She being active duty and all. So he had the deputy call Mrs. Hardin—that's Lieutenant Hardin's mother."

"Yes?"

"And, well, Mrs. Hardin, she got really, kind of, like, hostile about it. Told the deputy that she's had enough grief in her life from her daughter's involvement with the white man's Navy—her words, Mr. Bronson—and that there would be a *black* memorial service at their church for the *black* people who knew her daughter, that the service would be for her *black* family. Made it kind of clear that white people, and especially white Navy people, would not be welcome there. When the word got out in CHINFO, Admiral Kenney got us all together and said that people handle grief in different ways and that we should all kind of just, like, cool it. So I'm not sure just what to tell you. . . ."

"Right. I thank you for the heads-up. The last thing I'd want to do is crash a funeral, Petty Officer Berger. Appreciate the info, okay?"

"Yes, sir."

Malachi had briefly considered going up there, maybe sit outside the church and see what he could see, but he immediately thought better of it. He had never been to District Heights, but Southeast metropolitan D.C. was a no-go area. A white guy sitting in a car outside a black church, spying on a crowd of emotionally upset black people. Right. He would be as inconspicuous as a bunny in the tiger cage, with about the same prospects. Even if he made it look like he was in a cop car, the results would be the same. Maybe worse.

But what did the mother know? He wanted to probe the captain, but he had an inflexible rule in place there: The captain initiated any and all contact between them, never the other way around. In all probability, the captain and the great man had filed the whole thing away by now as a serendipitous happenstance—shame about the girl, but . . . The mother had already told off the Navy. Maybe if he just called her, acted as if he was another military guy trying to be nice, he might find out something, see whether her hate-on for Mr. Charley's Navy was personally specific or just general hostility. The funeral was tomorrow afternoon. He looked at his watch. No time like show time, he thought, and went to find his phone book.

There were seven Hardins in the directory, but only one with an address in District Heights. He gave it a shot, conjuring up an identity as one Major Carr, U.S. Army chaplains corps, Fort Myer. Using yet another voice program, he identified himself to the young female voice that answered the phone and was told to wait a minute. He logged the new name and the synthesizer channel. A much stronger woman's voice came on the line.

"I thought I told you people to leave us alone," she said.

"Is this Mrs. Hardin? This is Major Carr calling, from the Fort Myer's chaplain's office."

"The who?"

"The chaplain's office at Fort Myer. We provide the military ministry facilities for interments in the Arlington National Cemetery. We—"

"I told you people. I told that Navy man, that Chimpo or whatever, that we're all done with the Navy. My little girl got all the way through school, through George Washington University, got her computer degree, got her a commission in the ROTC, and what it'd get her? You tell me—what'd it get her! Dead on the streets, just like every other black child in this city. That's what—"

There was a moment of silence and then a young man's voice came on the line.

"Who is this, please?"

"This is Major Carr, from the Fort Myer chaplain's office, Mr.—"

"This is Lt. (jg) Wesley Hardin, Major. I'm 'Lizbeth's brother."

"Ah, yes, Lieutenant. I'm an Army chaplain. I was calling in to offer condolences and to see if the family needed anything in the way of assistance with services, that sort of thing. I spoke to Admiral Kenney's office, where I understand Eli—Lieutenant Hardin was stationed. They told me that the family had, uh, rebuffed the Navy's offer of a memorial service. They asked that we give it a try, since everything Navy seems to be on the family's, uh—"

"Shit list, Major?"

"Well, yes. If the military's done something wrong, we'd sure as heck like to rectify it."

He heard the young man sigh. There was considerable noise in the background—people talking, furniture being arranged, from the sounds of it.

"Well, Major, I'm down here on emergency leave from my ship, which is in the yards in Philadelphia. I'm the supply officer there. Hang on a minute." There was a sound of a door closing, and then Lieutenant Hardin was back on the line, the background noise much diminished.

"I'm not quite sure what to tell you, Major," he continued. "My mother doesn't want anything from the Navy or anyone else in the military. She's very upset. We all are. Elizabeth was something of a star hereabouts, and stars are kind of rare in our neighborhood—you know what I'm saying?"

"Yes."

"So, there's kind of a reaction going on here, okay? I'm the second of two kids, and right now I gotta tell you, I'm not going around reminding people that I'm in the Navy. But I'll tell you what, there's more to it than just that. My sister called me the night before she was—before she died. When this funeral's done, there're some things, some personal things, I plan to check out. I really don't want to say any more than that, and you don't, I believe, want to know any more than that. You follow me?"

"I'm not sure I do, Lieutenant, but I'll respect your wishes. Just be assured that if you or your mother change your mind—you need or want anything from us, just call the chaplain's office here at Fort Myer. Sometimes, after a few days go by, things pile up, you know? We can help a lot. That's what we're here for, okay? Can I give you the number?"

"We'll find it if we need it. Thank you, Major."

"And I'm sorry for your loss, Lieutenant."

Malachi hung up and reflected. Some personal things to check out. Maybe she hadn't told her mother after all. Maybe she had told her brother instead.

THREE DAYS AFTER his discussion with Lieutenant (jg) Hardin, Malachi's machine recorded a summons from the captain. The designated meeting place was the Arlington County central public library. Late that afternoon, Malachi caught the Metro to the Ballston station in Virginia, walked over to Quincy Street, giving the Randolph Towers a passing mental salute as he walked by, and entered the library. He found the captain, in full uniform, reading *The Wall Street Journal* in the magazine section up on the second floor. He sat down in an adjacent chair and waited for the captain to look up from his paper. The captain was in his early fifties and looked to Malachi like a middlingly prosperous banker, except for the blues and the stripes.

"Ah, you're here," the captain said, looking over the top of the paper.

"Indeed I am," Malachi responded, looking around. There was no one sitting very near.

"We have another problem with the Hardin case."

"The great man get over his loss, did he?"

The captain put the paper down on the floor next to his chair. "Yes, I think so. I wish you wouldn't call him that."

"You'd rather I use his name?"

"Well—"

"So what's the new problem? Something about her accident?"

"I don't think he's made any connections between your operations and the tragic, uh, incident on Twenty-third Street. At least he's made no mention of it."

"I thought you said that he didn't know anything about me," Malachi said.

"He knows that I engage contractors from time to time to take care of . . . special problems. He doesn't know who you are, specifically."

"That's good to hear."

"It's just normal procedure, Malachi. Air gaps are important when you want things sanitized—especially if they comprehend an accident like this."

Malachi nodded. He loved the way these guys talked—"air gaps . . . comprehend."

"Well," he replied. "There was no connection between my visit and the accident, except that she may have been preoccupied that morning."

"That's very good to hear. But this new problem *is* related, unfortunately. The young lady has a brother."

Malachi sat back in his chair, his fingers tented over the lower part of his face. He would reveal nothing to the captain about his own inquiries. "So?" he said.

The captain leaned forward and lowered his voice. "This brother—who also happens to be in the Navy, by the way—has requested an appointment with my principal."

"Ah."

"Yes. My principal demurred for the time being—heavy schedule, senior officials do not normally entertain calls from lieutenants junior grade, all that."

"But he persisted, didn't he? Maybe even got a little pushy."

"He bordered on being obstreperous, yes."

"And?"

"I'm not entirely sure what's going to happen. The principal, of course, wants him just to go away, which would usually be your province. But if he's coming in swinging, then any intervention on your part might be extremely provocative."

Malachi thought for a moment. An old man came over and asked the captain if he was done with the *Journal*. The captain picked the paper off the floor and handed it to him without a word.

"I think you're going to have to let the brother come in," Malachi said. "But maybe do it somewhere outside the great man's office. That way, if it develops into a scene of some kind, it's a private scene."

"Yes, that's what I'd thought—especially about the locus for the meeting. The girl must have said something to her brother, or there would be no reason for him to be calling my principal."

Malachi snorted. "Well, obviously," he said. "The question is whether or not the brother suspects there's a connection between her dustup with the great man and her flying lesson on Twenty-third Street."

The captain gave Malachi a pointed look. "And is there?" he said.

Malachi returned the look, saying nothing until the captain blinked. "All right. I won't bring it up again," he said.

"That's good to hear. I did not do that. For one thing, you didn't pay me enough."

The captain nodded slowly. "All right, I'll recommend that the principal meet with the lieutenant. Somewhere private."

"With both of you?"

"The usual setup—he'll meet with the principal; I will listen and record."

"Okay, then. What do you need from me?"

"We think—I want you to be nearby when we meet. Not present, but nearby. We want you to see the lieutenant, get a good look at him. We may need you to, uh, speak to him at some point in time."

Malachi smiled. "We." All these guys used the royal *we*.

"Where is this guy stationed? In case I have to go see him."

"In a ship. USS *Luce*—that's a guided-missile destroyer. The ship's in overhaul up in the yards in Philly."

Malachi remembered the kid saying something about Philadelphia. "Okay. Anything else?"

The captain gathered himself to leave. "No," he said. "Actually, yes. See if you can find out if there's any special police investigation going on with respect to Miss Hardin's accident. For obvious reasons, we can't make that call."

"I already did. There's nothing. Traffic Bureau knows an accident when they see one, and they've kicked it over to the hit-and-run division. They'll keep it as an open file. But I'll tell you what, that all might change if your young lieutenant decides to broaden his complaint, whatever it is."

The captain paused halfway out of his chair. He pursed his lips. "Right. We'll keep that in mind."

"You do that."

Malachi remained in the library after the captain had left. He strolled around the reading room right after the captain had disappeared down the circular stairway, then watched out the windows as the captain walked across the parking lot toward his car. No one in the parking lot appeared to be very interested. Satisfied that no one had followed the captain's car when he drove out onto 10th Street, Malachi busied himself with some magazines for a while.

There was little question in his mind that suggested this Hardin business wasn't over yet. She had spent a long time on the phone that night. The mother had turned down funeral service help from the Navy and harbored visible animosity for the service. Why? Had she known or suspected her daughter was having an affair with a senior government official? A married and white senior official? And yet it was the brother who was asking questions. Maybe the girl had confided in her brother, not the mother, and now he planned to brace up the great man, maybe even make some accusations: My sister said that some big guy had come around, sent by you, sir. Threatened her unless she agreed to keep her mouth shut. She had to cut on the bastard to get him to leave. Then she gets run down in the street the next morning. How convenient for you, sir. You have the connections to have goons come around, flashing FBI ID, why don't I just call the real FBI and tell them what she told me, hunh?

Malachi thought some more. The lieutenant might confront the great man, but he wondered about the police angle. The kid had sounded like this was something he might want to handle himself in some way. What was the current expression—"getting some get-back"? On the other hand, this guy was a naval officer. Hard to figure. He looked at his watch. Dinnertime. The Queen Bee was only six or eight blocks down Wilson Boulevard. He could take the Metro to Clarendon, or even walk it. Best North Vietnamese chow in town. He smiled. The North Vietnamese may have won the war, but now, twenty years after their "victory," the whole country was still on its ass. The North Vietnamese just never understood about money. But the South Vietnamese, now, they sure as hell understood about money. Hell, they'd even made him semirich back in those days. He went downstairs; he had decided to walk it.

Two DAYS LATER he paid a call on Capitol Hill at the request of the administrative assistant of a prominent Democratic congressman. Malachi had known the AA more than twenty years ago when the AA had been a captain on Westmoreland's staff in Saigon and Malachi had been a first lieutenant in the military police at Tan Son Nhut air base. For the past eight years, Malachi had done odd jobs for the AA when his boss took one of his not-infrequent walks on the wild side. The latest was typical: The congressman, loaded to the gills, had fallen in lust with one of Washington's more notorious drag queens at a bar. Given the reluctance of Washingtonians in general to tell one of the kings of the Hill that he had no clothes on, or the wrong kind of clothes in this instance, the congressman had gone blissfully back to the Willard Hotel with his prize. Upon discovering the error of his ways, the congressman had staged a colorful scene on the sixth floor of the hotel, the containment of which had required some muscle from the hotel security staff. A certain stringer for the *Washington Times* had gotten wind of it and had come sniffing around. Malachi had been asked to pay the reporter a call and convince him that the story was not based in fact.

"Appreciate the help, Mr. Ward," the AA had said. "My principal has asked that we increase your retainer. Just to show our continuing appreciation, you understand."

Malachi had pocketed the check and thanked him; the AA had been part of the sergeants' thing back in Saigon and understood how to encourage discretion. It was always a pleasure to do business in this town with people who knew how to act, and Capitol Hill was simply bursting with people who knew precisely how to act. He decided to walk back to the duplex.

Malachi had lived in Washington since his discharge from the Army in 1975. He had built himself a discreetly profitable client list over the years. His old mentor from the Saigon days, M. Sgt. Tommy Monroney, U.S.

Army, Retired, had already been in the business when Malachi got out of the Army, and he had showed him the ropes.

"You go for the horse-holders, Malachi—the executive assistants, executive secretaries, administrative aides—guys like that. These are the guys who take care of problems for the big guns. Sometimes the problems have to be worked off-line, if you know what I mean. Some of the problems don't smell so good, you get close to the situation. In Washington, people don't want problems, see? Shit, everybody's got enough problems, and the movers and the shakers in the government, they got the problems of the whole frigging world to deal with, see? That's where guys like you and me can do a nice little job of work."

Monroney had put him on his own payroll and showed him how things were handled.

"You don't want to do piecework, see—you wanna be on retainer. That's the secret to real money in this town. They pay you for the privilege of calling you when they need you. Now, you gotta understand something here: They call, you frigging well gotta come, see? But since they almost never get themselves in the shit all at the same time, you go get eight, ten, twelve permanent clients, and take a retainer from each one of them. It adds up, man."

And so it had. Because of his physical size, Malachi had specialized in what Monroney euphemistically called "off-line personal liaison work." Malachi thought Monroney was a hot shit, always using these two- and three-word phrases to describe what was a simple job of strong-arm. But his years in the military police had somewhat diluted his none-too-strong sense of right and wrong. He had done a good bit of strong-arm in the MPs, and the system on the outside was no different. Some guy is giving a great man gas pains, you go around and see the guy, share your thinking with him, convince him that there's another way to get ahead in life than the one he is currently pursuing. "Washington is the city of opportunity, the land of alternative choices," Monroney would say. "Alternative choices,"—Malachi loved it.

Malachi had been an Army brat himself; his father had been a sergeant all the way through World War II, rising to the rank of master sergeant. After the war, he had ended up assigned in Washington at the Arlington Hall station, an Army Intelligence organization. His mother had been a mousy little woman who kept her own counsel for the duration of her marriage to his father, who finally drank himself to death two years after retiring on thirty from the Army. Malachi later realized that the big war had probably been the highlight of his father's life. His old man had been an equal-opportunity hater: He had hated blacks, Jews, Catholics, foreigners, officers, lawyers, and just about any other recognizable ethnic or professional group. Malachi had soaked up more than a few of these notions along the way.

Life on a succession of Army posts as a kid had taught Malachi that there were two very clearly defined strata of people in the army: the officers and the enlisted. To hear his father talk about it over the sixth or seventh beer of the evening, the officers were the root of all the Army's problems. And while the adults had been clearly grounded in the differences, enlisted kids living on the base had to learn the hard way that officers' kids were better than the kids of the enlisted, just like officers' housing was much better than housing for the enlisted. The officers' club was a brick mansion at the end of the post's parade ground; it had a big fenced-in swimming pool that was reserved for officers and their dependents only. The enlisted club was a glorified beer hall, with a smaller, not so terrific pool, and something made it against the rules for the enlisted people's kids to use the officers' swimming pool. And about the only lesson his mother had taken the time to impart to him was that the underlying difference among all these people was what happened to them after high school: Officers' kids went to college and became officers, or lawyers, or bankers, and enlisted people's kids went into the Army and became troops.

After his father died at the Walter Reed Army Medical Center of liver failure, his mother decided to go back to Arkansas. Malachi, an only child, was given the option of moving in with an Army warrant's family to finish high school in Northwest Washington. The warrant, a crusty signals officer assigned to the Navy's security group command on Western Avenue, reinforced what Malachi's mother had told him: that a high school education would condemn him to second-rate status in just about anything he tried. With the warrant's help, he had plugged himself into the Army's enlisted education network and found out that there were college scholarships available to Army enlistees who had a high school diploma—scholarships that could lead to a commission. It involved taking a chance, because he would have to enlist first, then apply. If he didn't get it, he would do a four-year hitch in the barracks. But Malachi, with no other prospects, had enlisted in the Army Reserves one month after graduating from Wilson High in Northwest D.C., and he applied for the college-bound program after half a year of going to monthly Reserve meetings. He had gained a place at the University of Maryland three months later. Although not part of the ROTC program, he had been assigned to the Army ROTC unit for administrative purposes, and he surreptitiously competed with the more privileged cadets, even though he was technically an E-2 in the Army Reserves and they were already officer candidates.

Malachi had been a big, bruising kid when he went in, and he grew even bigger in the summers of basic and then midlevel infantry training required by the program. He found out that he was smart, or at least smarter than most of the cadets who were drinking their way through the ROTC program in the very early sixties. But in a way, it was the Army base all over again: There were a lot of officers' kids in the ROTC program. Unlike them, he had no money for fraternities or a car, and he worked two jobs all year long to pay his expenses, living with three other enlisted guys who were in similar straits. He majored in criminology after seeing a training film produced by the military police corps when they came on the campus recruiting, and he graduated in 1961 with a full bachelor's degree. After OCS, he had spent the obligatory eighteen months with the ground-pounders before being accepted for the military police corps in 1963.

Everything changed in 1965 when he was sent off to Vietnam and the brave new world of LBJ's counterinsurgency program, where the U.S. Army was bravely grappling with the mysteries of winning over the hearts and minds of unruly Asian Communists. As a first lieutenant, he had been assigned to run an MP shift out of the military police headquarters on the sprawling Tan Son Nhut air base outside of Saigon. Becoming bored with being a glorified police desk sergeant, he had taken to cruising the base in an MP jeep after dark, mostly to get out of the office and away from all the paperwork, and also to see what he might see. He had heard some interesting stories about a black market that was supposedly operating on the base, right beneath the Army's nose. None of the senior officers in the provost marshal office could understand how it could be going on when only the Americans had control and access to the goodies. Malachi, never having really graduated mentally from his enlisted background and upbringing, thought he might know how it was being done. One night he had apprehended three men who were loading up a deuce and a half with treasures from the back of the main exchange warehouse. One of them turned out to be a sergeant first class by the name of Monroney, a noncom Malachi had known back in the States when he was going through basic. Monroney had invited Malachi to take a little walk away from the warehouse, then had shown him five thousand American dollars in cash. Since the Army in Vietnam was using military scrip currency at the time, all that real cash was a mesmerizing sight.

"This is walking-around money for the guys who're playing the game right, Lieutenant," Monroney had said. "You want in, we can always find a use for a right-thinking provost marshal guy who knows the score."

Malachi had just stared at all that money.

"Who's 'we'?" he had asked finally.

"A buncha us sergeants. No slopes, okay? Just regular Army GIs, guys like you and me—grew up in the outfit all our lives—who've figured out this ain't no real war. So we're gonna make a buck or two out of it. Everybody knows this Vietnamese counterinsurgency stuff is all bullshit, so why the hell not? You been here awhile, you look around. The slope generals and colonels are all putting all that American AID money in their Swiss bank accounts. The American senior officers, the lifers, are all out here for the medals and the career shit. The only guys getting their asses kicked are the troops, as usual, hunh? But this is still Asia, see? Somebody's gonna run a black market. The big war, it was the civilians. Korea, there wasn't one until after the armistice. This time, it's gonna be the good guys, the sergeants."

Monroney had shuffled through the stack of bills and then invited Malachi to take a quick count, allowing him to discover what a wonderful sound money could make when it came in such quantities.

"Whaddaya say, Lieutenant?" Monroney purred. "Guy like you, inside the military police: You can name your price. And you don't hafta do bad-guy shit—you just hafta *not* do certain good-guy shit at the right time. You follow me?"

Malachi had made up his mind right there and then. His commission was not much more than skin-deep, anyway. He was a reserve, and all his superiors were regulars from West Point and the ROTC program. The ROTC guys had been given their commissions upon graduation; Malachi and his roommates had all had to go through OCS to get theirs. The real officers couldn't figure out who *had* to be running the black market scam right under their high-and-mighty noses. What this Monroney guy was offering was the first sensible proposition Malachi had seen since coming to this crazy country, and over the next two and a half years, Malachi made more money than he had ever dreamed of making in ten careers in the Army—in cash, nice, green, untaxable cash, complete with accommodating Chinese bankers in Cholon who could move things around a network of extremely discreet banks all over the world.

The sergeants' network had expanded to Germany as the Vietnam War dragged on, and Malachi, after two and half years in Saigon, had been part of it there, too. So it had been only natural that he migrated to Tommy's business when he got out, especially with Monroney right there in D.C. with yet another growing concern on his hands. Considering how Malachi's tour in Germany, and effectively his career in the Army, had ended, Malachi had been very fortunate indeed that Tommy Monroney was waiting outside the gates. And when Monroney had "retired" three years ago, Malachi had picked up some of his business, which gave him a sprinkling of clients across the spectrum of unofficial Washington. All of his business was on low-level monthly retainers, retainers that were sweetened from time to time when the great men and their horse-holders recognized that Malachi, given some of the things he knew about, had proved himself capable of exceptional discretion.

TWO NIGHTS LATER he was on the second floor of the Army and Navy Town Club, sitting in a chair in one corner of the bar. He was dressed in a subdued dark business suit. The captain had booked one of the suites on the third floor in his own name. The great man was supposedly attending a Defense intelligence association reception in the main dining room that evening. The plan was for the principal to break away from the reception to come upstairs to meet Lt. (jg) Hardin in the captain's suite for fifteen minutes. Once the great man had gone to the suite, the captain would come back downstairs, walk by the lounge, and give Malachi the signal, at which point he had been instructed to move from the lounge to the third-floor library and sit at the far end of the main library table, where he would have a clear view of the elevators. The idea was for Malachi to get a good look at this Lieutenant (jg) Hardin when the captain brought him up to the meeting. Once Malachi had had his look at Hardin, he was to return to the lounge on the second floor so that neither the principal nor Hardin would see him when they left the suite. After the meeting, the captain would back-brief him with new instructions, if any.

Sitting in an ancient leather chair that was beginning to hurt his legs, Malachi sipped a Harper hundred and watched the denizens of Geezer Gulch as they went through their martinis and cackled about the latest administration outrage. He was mildly amused at all the maneuvers laid out by the captain. It wasn't as if he didn't know who the captain's principal was. But maybe it was for the best—the old deniability rule: What you never saw, and so on.

The captain appeared from the second-floor elevators and walked by the entrance to the cocktail lounge. He looked in as if casually surveying the room, then turned around and headed for the double stairway that led back down to the main reception area. Malachi finished his drink, got up, and took the elevator to the third floor. He went into the library and did a quick tour. The offices were closed and there was no one in the library. He pulled a chair over to the end of the main table, the one farthest from the entrance, and then went over to the panel of light switches and turned off half the lights in the library, casting the main room into shadow. He settled back in his chair, popped out a book from the stack on the table, put it on his chest, folded his arms, and appeared to go to sleep. To anyone going by the double-door entrance to the library, he should look like all the rest of the old fuds who came up here to read the papers and fall asleep in their chairs.

Five minutes passed, and then the elevator doors chimed and the captain came out, leading a young black officer in uniform. The captain stopped near the entrance to the library to ask the lieutenant a question. Good moves, Captain, Malachi thought as he looked the kid over through slitted eyes; the kid was paying attention to the captain and never once looked into the library. He was young, very young—maybe twenty-three, twenty-four; not very tall, kind of thin, in fact, his double-breasted uniform coat with its one and a half stripes looked like it would wrap right around him. He had a narrow, intense face, close-cropped hair, and he was clearly agitated. His hands moved around a lot when he talked. Probably speaking in jive, Malachi thought unkindly. He doesn't look like an officer, Malachi thought. More like a kid in costume.

Finally, the captain led the lieutenant out of sight down the hall. Malachi listened for the sound of a door, waited another minute, and then got up and went down the hall. He had asked the front desk when he had arrived where the suites were on the third floor. There were two, all the way at the far end of the hall, overlooking 17th Street. He walked down the carpeted hall until he came to a pair of partially opened fire doors that led to the executive suite hallway. He could hear voices coming from one of the suites, and he crept closer to that door. But the voices remained indistinct; the club was an old building, and all these big oak doors were real. He listened for a few minutes, keeping one eye on the hallway, until he heard the voices starting to rise. Somebody was losing his temper. He still could not make out what they were saying, but the tone and the volume were pretty much self-explanatory. The lieutenant was not there for a social call—which meant he did know something.

Malachi backed away from the doors and went back to the elevators, taking one down to the second floor and returning to his corner seat in the lounge. His empty glass was still right where he had left it, sitting in a pool of condensation. Really alert service in here, he thought. The waitress saw him come in. She looked puzzled, but when he raised the glass, she smiled and went to get him a refill. While he waited for the captain to return, he considered the problem. He began to rummage around in his mind for contacts in Philadelphia while he waited for the captain to escort the kid out of there. Angelo Fiori, he thought. I'll bet old Angelo can help me out with this little problem. Angelo owes me one from our Saigon days.

The captain came back ten minutes after escorting the lieutenant downstairs. He found Malachi and pulled up a chair.

"Well, this thing gets more complicated by the hour."

"What does the kid want?"

"He came steaming in there, would not sit down, would not shake hands, big chip on his shoulder."

"What does he want?" Malachi repeated.

"He came right out with it—he confirmed that the girl had called him in Philadelphia, told him that she had been having an affair with the principal, that she had shut it off, and how things had started getting nasty. She told him about your little séance, and that you threatened her. She also told him she ran you out of there with a knife. Did that really happen, by the way?"

The captain was looking at Malachi's right hand with its four bandaged fingers. Malachi ignored the question and leaned toward the captain, his eyes intent, staring at him until the captain was forced to stop looking at his hand.

"Cut to the chase," Malachi said. "What does he *want?*"

"Want. Well, he wants . . . satisfaction. Unless my principal can *prove* that his sister's accident wasn't intentional, our lieutenant will go to the media and expose the story of this very senior, married white naval officer having an illicit affair with a black woman who also happened to be a junior officer."

Malachi sat back in his chair. "And what did your principal say to that?"

"He did the adulterer's dance. Denied everything. Denied that there had been an affair. He said that he had met the girl socially, in the course of official business, and had had drinks with her twice, both times in the context of official functions where they were both required to be. He made it out to be a father confessor sort of thing, that he'd been giving the girl career advice. Hinted that the girl had perhaps been indulging her imagination in thinking that there was more to it than that. Said that the notion of it being a sexual thing was ridiculous—he was more than twice her age, and he certainly knew better than to fool around with a junior officer. He added that she was a good-looking black woman who would necessarily prefer any attractive *black* male to some elderly white man—that seemed to hit home, by the way. It seemed to reinforce the kid's own notions of how things ought to be—I could see it in his face. Anyhow, he went on that he had never sent anyone around, because there was nothing going on in the first place. Said the girl had sought his advice because she had been having some problems adapting to a very white Navy headquarters staff job and had taken the opportunity to talk to someone about it, someone not directly in her own organization. He was good—very good. He's pretty smooth and convincing when he wants to be."

"That's probably what she thought at one time," Malachi observed. "Just before her Skivvies came off."

"Please. The girl's dead, for God's sake. Anyway, I actually think he talked the young man down. He said he would use all the resources at his command to confirm that it had been an accident."

"What'd the kid say to that?"

"He said that he'd give us—that's a good sign, by the way: He was depersonalizing it at the end—he'd give us a week. I had the impression that as my principal talked to him, the kid was beginning to realize whom he'd been talking to in a loud and disrespectful voice, and it was beginning to scare him a little. He's only a lieutenant junior grade."

"Okay." Malachi nodded. "I have no further information on what the Traffic Bureau is doing, if anything. My guess is they're going to stick with the old 'do the right thing' dodge. They'll issue a public statement: Whoever ran the girl down, turn yourself in and we'll discuss degrees of accident. If we gotta come find you, it becomes something ugly."

The captain was shaking his head in exasperation. "That doesn't do us any good. I'm going to have to think of something else."

"Can this kid find out what was really going on?"

"My principal says that he and Miss Hardin were extremely discreet. But as an active-duty officer, the lieutenant can, of course, get into the Pentagon building and into the CHINFO offices. But unless she had some close friends there in her own office whom he can get to, and they're people she confided in, *and* if they're willing to talk to him—a lot of *ifs* and *ands*. What I really

71

wish is that the son of a bitch would just disappear, go back to Philadelphia or wherever he came from, and butt the hell out of something that doesn't really concern him."

Malachi nodded and smiled. "I guess I can relate to that," he said, looking at his watch. He would definitely have to go see Angelo up in Philly.

9

ANGELO FIORI HAD GOTTEN really fat. He was moonfaced, triple-chinned, and his suit made him look like a shiny dark blue sausage. Malachi remembered that when he had first met Angelo in Saigon, he was already tending to fat, beginning to pop out of his wrinkled sergeant's uniform and always mopping perspiration in the punishing tropical heat. But now he was a miniature Pillsbury Doughboy. Malachi tried not to stare as they slid into a booth at Fiori's in South Philly. He felt the table move in his direction as Angelo squeezed in, puffing with the effort. Malachi had a headache after the flight up from Washington, and perhaps from the night before.

"So, Angelo, you ever hear from any of the boys?" Malachi asked, adjusting his dialect so as not to sound so much like Washington. He wondered if they had Harper hundred here. Probably not; probably all they had was goddamned wine.

Angelo was scratching the back of his neck. "Nah. One of my cousins, Salvatore, he's up in the Apple, but the rest of the guys, most of 'em are all retired, down south somewheres. How about you?"

"I see some guys from time to time in D.C. Gallagher, Monroney, Jackson—you remember, Jackson, that big guy, sergeant first class at the truck depot, heisted all those deuce and a halfs, then lost all the keys?"

"Who could forget. I thought goddamn Monroney was gonna kill him."

Malachi laughed. "He would have, too, 'cept Jackson got caught in a curfew violation and was in the stockade out there at Tan Son Nhut when Monroney came looking."

Angelo was toying with the bread sticks. "We did all right, those days. I gotta tell ya, these days it's tougher, lots tougher."

"The feds getting organized?"

"Yeah, that, and these fuckin' kids nowadays; they got no sense of organization, you know? It's all gangs this and gangs that, the blacks goin' totally crazy with all this disrespect warfare shit. You can't make no fuckin' sense outta territories or nothin'. It's a pisser. You wanna order? I'm starvin'."

Malachi nodded and Angelo signaled the maître d', who came trotting over, a waiter in tow. Stuffing a bread stick in his mouth, Angelo asked

Malachi what he wanted to eat. Malachi told him to order for both of them, it being his joint. Angelo rattled away in Italian to the maître d' and the waiter, who listened without writing anything down. The maître d' nodded, left, then returned with an opened bottle of Chianti and a bottle of cold mineral water before disappearing again. The restaurant was crowded, but their booth gave them quite a bit of privacy, which Malachi took to be a sign of Angelo's importance. In Saigon, Angelo had been considered long on cunning, if a bit short on brains. One night, Angelo had been caught up in a bar fight in which a Vietnamese woman had been knifed with what looked very much like an Army knife. Malachi had taken the incident call, then had managed to drop another knife at the scene, thereby clouding the evidence. Monroney had then paid off some white mice, the national police, and the issue had gone away, leaving Angelo firmly in Malachi's debt.

With the waiter gone, Angelo signaled with his eyebrows that he was ready to listen. Malachi lowered his voice.

"So," he said, "there's this guy, a Navy guy, over in the shipyard. I need him to get some religion. He's been messing around with a client of mine down in D.C., and I need him to get the message that it's time to butt out, get his nose out of other people's business."

"So what kinda guy is this? You said a Navy guy?"

"An officer—a black officer, a lieutenant junior grade. See, something happened down in D.C., and this lieutenant, he's making noises like my client had something to do with it. Which he didn't, okay? But this kid doesn't listen to reason. Believe me, we've talked to him. But all he comes back with are threats. So I was wondering if you had some guys down in that shipyard could maybe go see him, scare the living shit out of him, make him be quiet."

Angelo finished up the bread sticks without replying and poured himself some wine. He tipped the bottle in Malachi's direction, but Malachi shook his head. He hated wine. Angelo tried some wine, put the glass down, and wiped his mouth with his napkin.

"Yeah, we got some people who can do that. We in a hurry, or what?"

"Yeah, a little bit of a hurry. This guy's talking about going to the press, the little shit. So, this week, if it could be managed."

Angelo nodded solemnly. "In the shipyard, you say—this a yardbird?"

Malachi sighed mentally. Angelo wasn't paying very good attention. "No. A Navy guy. An officer—a young black lieutenant junior grade. He's assigned to a ship over there, the USS *Luce*. He's the assistant supply officer or something like that."

Angelo looked around the room casually and then nodded slowly. "Yeah, I think that can be managed. What's this all about, or do I wanna know?"

"I'm just taking care of a problem for a client. This client is an important guy down in D.C., and this guy, this lieutenant, is putting some heat on the client. Over the guy's love life, if you can believe it."

"So what's the message, exactly?"

"Keep your nose out of your sister's affairs; who she's been seeing is none of your business, and when you start talking about going to the papers, you might be shortening your life expectancy. Something like that."

Malachi declined to tell Angelo that the sister in question had just had her own life expectancy shortened. Angelo nodded again, drinking some more wine. "And that's what you do nowadays, you take care a shit like this for—whaddaya call 'em, clients? After all that money we made over there in the Nam?"

"Yeah. It's not the money—like you said, we made plenty, and I've still hung on to most of it. But yeah, that's what I do down there. I kind of like D.C., you know? It's sleazy, but they're sleaze with class most of the time. What I really like is when these picture-perfect Washington weenies, these great men with their thousand-dollar suits and their executive assistants and all that high-and-mighty shit, get their asses in a crack and then have to come to guys like me to unscrew it. And the money's pretty good besides. Anyway, this little deal—the client himself doesn't exactly know how his problem is going to be taken care of. And his people don't know about it, either."

"So, this ain't a contract deal—this is on your nickel?"

"Right. See, this lieutenant can maybe put me in the shit, too, he tries hard enough to do my client. That's why I'm up here, on my own, so to speak. This boy desperately needs to see the light."

Angelo, having finished off the bread sticks, was looking around the table to see what else could be eaten. He poured some more wine. "Yeah," he said over his glass. "I got it. I think we can work something out. We've definitely got some guys in the yard down there. We run some, you know, low-level shit down there, materials mostly, and of course we got the big unions, the metal benders, guys like that, and the scrap haulers. The unions keep some animals around to keep everything peaceful." He smiled for a moment at the image of peace on the labor front. "Some a those guys in Washington, they're pieces a work, am I right? I see those guys on the TV, those shiny shits, two-hundred-dollar hairdos, smooth as a baby's ass, and then you hear all this shit, congressmen humping the page boys in the bathrooms, that big chairman of some shit or other—guy's taking cash for stamps, for Chrissakes, fucking stamps! These are the guys pass the laws, tell us regular assholes how we're gonna live?"

"You don't know the half of it." Malachi snorted. "That's just the shit that comes out in the papers. Guys like me, we shovel a lot more than that down the sewer."

"Yeah, I can believe it. Look, there's something you gotta know here. These things, these deals where we send somebody around to talk to a guy, they can sometimes get outta hand, you know what I'm sayin'? Like, if it's a guy in the business, he'll know when to take good advice. We may still break his leg, but he knows as soon as he sees the guys what it's all about, what can happen, and what everybody expects. But a civilian . . . well, shit, you don't never know what a civilian's gonna do, right? So I gotta be up front with you. Sometimes what starts out as a little talk can turn into a big deal, the guy don't act right, okay? I gotta tell you that."

"I understand," Malachi said. "Believe me, I know how that shit can go down."

"Okay, because I gotta tell you, up front like, so's we don't have no surprises. You know, the kinds'a guys do this shit, we're not talkin' math majors here, okay?"

"I understand," Malachi repeated. "And I guess if something was to happen, then what I gotta have is that the problem, if there *is* a problem, and I'm not saying there *should* be a problem, okay, but if there is a problem, the problem's gotta totally goddamn disappear."

Angelo stared at him like a lizard for about ten seconds. Malachi wondered for a moment if they were talking past each other.

"Look," he explained. "I really don't want the guy whacked; this isn't like business between two families, where I need to reinforce some rules or anything. I just want him so scared that he stops even thinking about talking to anyone about what happened down in D.C., that's all. What I think you're talking about is a contingency, covering the bases, like, and I agree. But all I'm saying is that, if there's a real problem, I can't have a goddamn stiff popping up in the Delaware."

"Contingency," Angelo said blankly.

"Yeah. I mean, this is just good planning. But mostly I want him crapping a quart of loose prunes anytime the thought even occurs to him to go running his mouth. That's what I really need. Look, I brought some money—ten thousand."

"This is your money," Angelo said again, his little eyes unblinking.

"Yeah. And I know what you're going to say—that you'll do it as a favor, memory of old times and Saigon and everything. But I want you to take it; that way, you can lay some cash out, make things go smooth, especially since it's real short notice. It's the least I can do, okay?"

Angelo looked around the crowded dining room and then back at Malachi as he tried unsuccessfully to erase the glint of greed in his eyes. "Well, you're right," he said. "I would do it as a favor. We go back, you and me. You ran some slick shit in your day, and without your cover, our little thing there in Saigon wouldn'ta been so good. And I still owe you big time for that time in Cholon."

"Forget about it. We scratched each other's backs pretty good over there. I don't remember any debts. This is a favor, but the money . . . well, that's just a little grease, make things go smoother, you know?"

"Yeah, well, you know how to act. You always did."

Malachi handed over the envelope, keeping his hands below the level of the table. "Saigon was such a sweet deal," he said. "Here. Take the money. I appreciate the hell out of it, and you never know, some guy might get a little sideways, want a bunch of money just to do his job. This way—"

"Yeah. You're right about that. Some a these guys today . . . " Angelo rolled his piggy eyes.

"Right," Malachi said. "So, the mark's name is Hardin, Lt. (jg) Wesley Hardin, stationed on the USS *Luce*, which is a destroyer. I think it's a destroyer going through overhaul. There's a description in the envelope."

Angelo nodded thoughtfully, absorbing the information. The envelope had magically disappeared into the folds of his voluminous coat. "Hardin, yeah, okay, I got it. And he needs an attitude adjustment. Maybe get snatched, get wrapped head to toe in duct tape, maybe get folded into a dryer, down the laundromat, and go for a little spin, something like that. Give him a little Halloween, coupla six months early. I got some people who can do that. And you need it this week."

"If you can, yeah, this week. I'm guessing it can't be that hard. I mean, I've made some checks. He's living aboard the ship, probably has a car he parks in the yard somewhere. I'll bet they have a parking lot for officers, something like that. He's single, most likely goes out at night and howls at the moon like we used to do when we were that age. Maybe some guys could watch the parking lot at night, and—"

Malachi noticed that Angelo's body was jiggling like a plastic bag full of Jell-O. Angelo was laughing at him. "Pretty soon you gonna be telling me how to make good pasta, hey, Malachi? You want this spade to turn white for a night, he's gonna do it, okay?"

"Shit. Sorry, Angelo. Yeah, absolutely. He needs to forget all about what he was doing in D.C. The whole thing's gotta disappear right out of his mind. Poof. Like the magic dragon."

"Yeah. Hey, you remember those goddamn DC-threes—what'd they call 'em? Puff, yeah, Puff, the magic dragons. Like you just said. Had those GE electric cannons, shoot a gazillion rounds out the door. Looked like a horse pissin' fire down outta the sky at night, hose down a whole province at a time. Remember those guns?"

"Hell yes. Vulcans, they called 'em. And I remember when you guys boosted a shipment of those Vulcans down at the docks in Saigon."

"Yeah, and you had to come blow up the heist so's you could cool some CID heat that was sniffin' around the HQ."

"I picked on that one because you guys—I think it was even Monroney, said he couldn't figure out what to do with the guns after you heisted them."

"Yeah, we knew we couldn't go sellin' that shit to the VC."

"Right. Couldn't have the bad guys using electric twenties to zap our own guys. That wouldn't have been right."

"Absolutely."

They looked at each other for a second and then laughed as the waiter showed up with their food.

*   *   *

FIVE DAYS AFTER Malachi got back from Philadelphia, Angelo called. It was eleven o'clock at night, and Malachi was sitting in his kitchen, abusing some Harper and watching a M*A*S*H rerun. Angelo was apologetic.

"The deal went totally wrong, Malachi. Totally. Your guy went apeshit, is what my people are telling me. Absolutely apeshit."

"I know what you mean," Malachi said, remembering the knife in the apartment. "It must run in the goddamn family."

"What?"

"Nothing. So what happened?"

Angelo paused. It sounded to Malachi as if Angelo was eating something.

"Well, they snatched him up, just like you suggested. At night, in that officer's parking lot there, near Dry Dock Five. Put him in a van, sat him down between a coupla guys, work for a moving company, you know? They call 'em 'piano horses' in the business."

"Big guys."

"Yeah, really big guys. Anyways, they went somewheres and they did some shit, and they had a little talk with your guy. Went back to the shipyard, had another little talk, let him outta the van, back in the parking lot, musta been around one in the morning, real private like. Anyways, he wasn't doin' so good, is what my guys say. But he had a big mouth on him, they said; took some time to get that big mouth under control. So, anyways, he gets about fifty feet away from the van and then starts yellin', says he knows who sent them, gonna get that motherfuckin' somebody or other. Guys couldn't understand what he was sayin'—you know how it is, those people get to screamin' like that."

"So what'd they do?"

"They did a *French Connection* scene. Right outta the movies. Took after his ass with the van; guy ran around like a striped-assed ape, it's one a them cinder lots, so there's gravel and shit flyin' and this guy's runnin' in an' outta parked cars. Christ, I almost wish I'd been there, you know? But then the fuckin' guy does something really stupid: He picks up this fuckin' brick and throws it through the windshield of my guy's van. My guy's brand-new van."

"Wonderful."

"Yeah, wonderful is right. My guy gets pissed off now. I mean, up to here, it's been almost comical—it's one o'clock in the morning, they're chasin' this spook around this five acre parking lot in a van, the piano horses in the back of the van hangin' and bangin' around like a coupla hippos in a bumper car. But now, he runs the guy to the dry-dock wall in the van, jumps out, and, this guy, if you can fuckin' believe it—Mickey's two fifty, two seventy-five, six three, awright?—and this guy runs his mouth, calls him a honky motherfucker, the whole bit. Unbelievable."

"I can believe it."

"Well, my guy grabs his ass and throws him up against the sill wall, and

77

suddenly the guy's out cold, bleedin' all over the goddamned place, with his head kinda like stove in a little bit. Like I told you, these things can sometimes get outta hand, you know? You remember me tellin' you that?"

"Yup."

"I mean, nobody went out there to whack nobody or anything. It was just gonna be a little three-on-one social, and your guy up and goes apeshit."

"I believe it. So what did they do?"

"Well, now, Malachi, is that somethin' you really wanna know? Because if it is, I'll tell you. I mean, swear to God, it doesn't make a shit to me. But you oughta think about it. You know, shit you don't know is shit nobody can make you talk about, am I right?"

"Absolutely, Angelo. Forget I asked. I just hope that everything got put away like the kingdom of heaven. As in forever and ever."

"Oh yeah. Forever and ever. *Saecula, saeculorum*, like when I was an altar boy. I like that. But, yeah, absolutely. Where the sun ain't never gonna shine. I mean, hell, he's a Navy guy. Where he is now, he's gonna feel right at home."

"Well, okay. I guess that's that. Sounds like the problem is taken care of."

"Absolutely. I mean, if I told you where they put him, you'd never fuckin' believe it."

"I'd believe it."

"I feel like I oughta give you your money back," Angelo said.

Malachi smiled at the phone. Fat chance.

"Shit, no, Angelo," he said. "I wanted the kid to stop talking. Sounds to me like he's stopped talking. There'll probably be some heat down here from some guys, but as long as no bodies turn up, my problem and my client's problems are over."

"Well, okay, then," Angelo said. "Just so's you remember: I did tell you. Sometimes these things get a little fucked up."

10

THE VERY NEXT MORNING, the captain summoned Malachi to an urgent one o'clock meeting at a bar called the Black Crystal in the Crystal City underground. The Black Crystal was a well-known watering hole for the thousands of Navy types, military and civilian, who worked in the maze of high-rise office buildings near the airport called Crystal City. It had the advantage of offering very subdued lighting and private booths, amenities much appreciated by anyone looking for a discreet meeting place for business or pleasure, and especially pleasure. Malachi took the Metro over to Virginia to the Crystal City station, walked up the escalator, and turned left into the underground, which was a labyrinth of shops, bars, service stores, parking garages, and restaurants that spread underground from one end of Crystal City to the other.

He had to stand in the entrance foyer of the bar for a few minutes to adapt his vision; must be ladies' day, he thought. It being one o'clock, the bulk of the lunch crowd had gone back to their office cubicles or over to the Sheraton. But with the black carpets and black painted walls, he still could not see very well. He finally went to the bar, turned around, scanned the darkened room until he found the captain in an end booth. He walked over, slid into the booth, waved off a miniskirted waitress, and looked over at the captain, who looked, as usual, agitated.

"You called," Malachi said.

The captain gave him a speculative look. "Malachi," he began. "We've had another development in the Hardin business, and I'm beginning to think that you've not been entirely honest with me."

"I'm as honest as my clients," Malachi replied. "No more, no less. What happened? He do it? Your lieutenant go public on you?"

The captain continued to look at him. Malachi was surprised to see that he had a martini going. At the Black Crystal, martinis were taken seriously. Knowing what was coming, he suddenly wanted a Harper. But he didn't need whiskey to handle this guy—especially if the captain needed a martini to talk to him.

"The lieutenant," the captain said, sipping some of his drink and then staring at Malachi again over the rim of the oversized glass. "The lieutenant has disappeared. Vanished into the pollluted air of South Philadelphia. There's a message in from his ship."

"Vanished."

"Vanished. He's the ship's disbursing officer, so the first reaction has been to count the payroll. But there was nothing out of order. He's just . . . gone. The Navy has queried the immediate family, which apparently now consists of only his mother; she knows nothing."

Malachi tried to ignore the cold feeling that was spreading around his stomach, but he waited to see where the captain would take it. The captain continued to just sit there, looking across the table at Malachi, nursing his martini. Malachi knew this game. There were some people who could not stand a break in a conversation—any prolonged silence, pause, whatever, had to be filled. The captain was trying to manipulate him into saying something. He waited. At length, the captain gave it up and broke the silence.

"I need to know, Malachi. Did you have anything to do with this young man's disappearance?"

"Nope."

"Anything? Even indirectly?"

"The last time I heard the lieutenant's name and the word *disappear* in the same sentence, it was you doing the talking," Malachi said. "Maybe I should ask you: What have *you* done?"

The captain's face hardened. "Yes," he said, "I did say that. He was being a pain in the ass over something that did not concern him. He was capable of causing some real trouble, depending on who was ready to listen. But we were working on that. We had some pretty good damage control lined up. Now he's over the hill without a trace."

" '*Was being* a pain in the ass'? '*Was capable* of causing'? You're talking about the lieutenant in the past tense, Captain. There something you know that I don't?"

The captain leaned back in the booth. "Making people change their minds, influencing the directions they're taking, helping them to reconsider their positions—that's your game, Malachi. We, people like my principal and I, we have the need for such services sometimes, but you, you have the *means* to get them done. We have political agendas, career objectives, turf to protect, privileges to protect, reputations to polish. You have big hands for hire. I'm thinking if anyone could make the lieutenant disappear, you could. You even have something of a motive."

Malachi was suddenly tired of all the dancing around. He needed to calibrate this horse-holder. He leaned forward, put those big hands on the table, let the captain see those big hands, and put an edge in his voice.

"Seems to me, Captain," he said, "that I was *paid* by you and your principal to indulge in some less-than-legal coercion and intimidation. *Paid*. And it was not for the first time that I did some dirty work for you. I *know* what the lieutenant only suspected, remember? I know nothing about your lieutenant's disappearance, but if I did, *if* I did, I'd be recommending that you stop asking questions if you can't stand all the possible answers, understand? It seems to me that your principal's problems with the Hardins are really over now. He should be forever grateful to you, and you to me."

The captain was shaking his head. "I was willing to give you the benefit of the doubt when the girl had her 'accident.' My principal made no connection, but he was upset, visibly upset, when I told him what had happened. But now he's concerned on a different level. The girl has a fatal accident. Her brother comes around making accusations, and before we can deal with it, and I mean deal with it on a civilized level, he disappears. My principal is not stupid."

"He was when it came to pretty young girls. I think your principal is mostly frightened."

The captain said nothing for a moment. Malachi moved to shut it off. He was glad Angelo had called him.

"Here's the thing," Malachi said, leaning closer. "I know some things that could spoil your principal's whole day, yours, too, you want to get right down to it. But I've taken money to work out some of those things, which means if you go down, I could go down. I've got something on you; you've got something on me. In certain circles, that's known as a 'lock,' and locks are not all bad, see, because when there's a lock, there's no incentive for either side to run his mouth."

"That sounds like a threat."

"Wrong. That's a statement of fact. And there's some implicit advice in there, too."

"Advice."

"Yes, advice. Let me close with a little parable. It's set during Napoleon's retreat from Moscow, you know, dead of the Russian winter, cold as hell, snow and ice everywhere. This French corporal finds a little bird freezing to death in a snow-bank alongside the road. Stop me if you've heard this."

The captain just blinked. Malachi smiled, enjoying himself now. What the hell, the lieutenant was history; the problem really was over.

"This corporal finds this frozen little bird by the side of the road; thing's half-dead. But a big old ox comes by, dragging a cannon, and drops a big, fresh, steaming flop in the road. The corporal stuffs the bird in that hot cowpat, right up to his neck, to revive it. The bird soaks up the heat from the cowpat and it's so happy, it begins to sing. A big bad wolf out in the woods hears the singing, comes looking, finds the bird, and eats it. Now here's the moral—you listening to me? You need to tell this story to the great man. He needs to know this. Because it's not necessarily the bad guy who puts you in the shit, and it's not necessarily the good guy who gets you out, but whenever you're in the shit up to your neck, Captain, don't cheep."

IV

APRIL 1994

THE PHILADELPHIA NAVAL SHIPYARD

11

THEY MADE IT into the Philadelphia Naval Shipyard by ten that Tuesday morning and drove directly to the NISRA office on Broad Street. One of the desk officers gave them a copy of the preliminary report, then told them that base security was waiting to take them down to the waterfront to the crime scene. He then handed them each a pair of yard coveralls and showed them where the rest rooms were. They took a minute to skim through the report, then went to change. Ten minutes later, leaving their bags and street clothes in the Resident Agent's office, they went out front, where a Sergeant DeGiorgio of the shipyard police department picked them up in an ancient white Navy police car for the drive through the controlled industrial area. DeGiorgio was a pleasant individual whose overstuffed blue uniform bespoke a fondness for the excellent Italian restaurants outside the yard's main gates in South Philadelphia. He amiably pointed out the various yard shops—boilers, electrical, hull mechanical, propellers, the foundry, combat systems—as he threaded the cop car between the huge industrial buildings, avoiding rumbling yard cranes, smoke-belching yellow forklifts, clumps of shuffling hard hats carrying tool bags and lunch pails, and stacks of palletized materials that littered the sides of every street.

Dan sat on the right-hand side of the backseat, the customary position of an officer in an official car. Grace Snow sat on the right side of the front seat, a white plastic hard hat bobbing incongruously on her head. She held on to the armrest as the cop car bounced and bumped over cobblestones, potholes, and crane tracks. Their coveralls smelled in equal proportions of old grease and a very strong detergent. The grimy brick and stone buildings with their dirt-encrusted glass windows ranged along their upper walls made for a depressing sight, reminding Dan that the Philadelphia Naval Shipyard was over a hundred years old, accounting for its haphazard layout along the banks of the Delaware River. As a surface line officer, he also knew its reputation as one of the sloppiest yards on the East Coast—an installation where indifferent work and costly, impacted unions had prompted repeated, if futile, attempts by the Navy Department to shut it down.

"There," Sergeant DeGiorgio said, pointing through the dirty windshield. "That there's the *Wisconsin*. Ain't she something?"

Both Dan and Grace leaned forward as the car cleared the last of the big dry-dock sill walls and pointed down a long, flat pier that lay parallel to the river, where the dull gray bulk of the sleeping battleship filled the horizon. Across the river, the flares from two oil refineries seemed to frame the majestic silhouette of the sixty-thousand-ton ship, her sixteen-inch guns pointed flat along her teak-covered decks, her almost nine-hundred-foot-long hull rising in a graceful sheer of armored steel from waist to stem. As they drew nearer, however, they could see the hallmarks of the mothball fleet: gray paint that was fading and flecking, with several vertical lines of running rust smeared down her sides. The enormous white bow numerals proclaiming battleship number 64 had begun to fade into the background of the surrounding hull paint. The five-inch mounts ranged along her port side were covered in blister canopies, and the windows of the captain's and flag bridges were boarded over with sheets of plywood. The lifelines sagged along her decks and the signs of a flourishing pigeon colony desecrated the looming director towers. A large umbilical bundle of cables and steam lines rose from the pier amidships to the main deck, where there was a wooden guard shack mounted at the top of the cage-covered gangway. Dan could see that there was a small clump of men standing at the top of the gangway, four of whom were dressed out in coveralls and wearing yellow-colored plastic hard hats. Several of the men were wearing what appeared to be a harness rig that supported a single yellow air tank of a breathing-apparatus set. There were two other shipyard security police cars and an ambulance parked at the foot of the gangway.

As their car pulled up, Dan thanked DeGiorgio and reached for his own hard hat. They got out and Dan led Grace up to the gangway. She tried to stuff her hair underneath the hard hat with minimal success as they climbed the gangway up the sheer slab sides of the battleship. At the top of the gangway, they were met by the ship's superintendent for USS *Wisconsin*, Lieutenant Graveley, Civil Engineering Corps, USN, and the Philadelphia Naval Investigative Service resident agent, who introduced himself as a Mr. Carl Santini. Santini greeted Dan in a civil manner but appeared to be somewhat less pleased to see Grace Snow.

Dan found out that the four yellow hats were riggers who would escort them to the fire room in which the body had been discovered. The ship's superintendent, who was also dressed out in a breathing rig and coveralls, handed both of them a harness and a breathing-apparatus set. Dan saw that the riggers were ogling Grace; the coveralls, unlike her fasionable business suits, revealed that she was definitely a woman.

"Why do we need these?" asked Grace as Lieutenant Graveley showed her how to put on the harness.

"The ship has been deactivated for quite a while," Gravely said, as if this explained everything. Seeing Grace's blank expression, Dan cleared it up for her.

"When they long-term mothball a big ship like this, they seal her up hermetically below the main deck. Then they evacuate all the air and replace the atmosphere in the interior compartments with nitrogen. The nitrogen displaces all the oxygen, and without oxygen, nothing rusts. There's no breathable air anywhere inside there."

"Oh my goodness. Then how did the body get down there?"

"That's the main reason we're calling it a homicide," said Santini with an air of exaggerated patience. He was a middle-aged man with a completely bald head, and he was talking to Grace like an uncle who was less than thrilled that the nephews and nieces were here for the summer. "Somebody had to take him there, or at least put him in there. There's no sign of a mask on the body."

"Somebody wearing breathing equipment."

"Absolutely. If the dead guy was alive, say, maybe unconscious, when they took him in there, he would have been dead by the time they got to the fire room."

Grace looked at Dan. Pretty clearly a homicide, she thought.

"If we're ready to go in, I need to give you a quick safety briefing," Lieutenant Gravely said. He checked both of their harness rigs, blushing a little when he had to explain to Grace that those last two straps went between the legs. He then helped them hook on their air bottles and explained the mechanics of the masks and the lights that strapped onto their hard hats. He had them size their mask straps, then reviewed the main safety rules.

"I've got to emphasize there's no air down there—only nitrogen. That tank you're wearing is good for an hour of walking-around activity; we use forty-five minutes as a safe stay time, and that's what I'm going to set your timers for. The more strenuous the activity, the less time. We're going to walk into the ship, go down a couple of decks to Broadway, from which access to the fire rooms and engine rooms can be gained. We've had a set of temporary lights rigged along the route, but there's still not much lighting, so watch your step and watch your shins on the bulkhead dividers. There's a box of flashlights over there and everybody will carry one, and your hard hats have headlights, of course."

"What if we need more than forty-five minutes at the scene?" asked Dan. Santini, standing behind him, rolled his eyes as if to say, What for?

"Well, sir," Graveley replied, "we all come back out, change out air bottles, and go back in."

"We've done the crime-scene work," said Santini impatiently. "This is mostly for your benefit—to see the body in situ before we remove it for autopsy."

Dan got the message: This is a drill, for the benefit of the amateurs; the actual cops have already done the real work. But he kept his patience.

"I understand that, Mr. Santini. But we do have to go down there and see what we see."

Santini shrugged his shoulders and began attaching his mask to his face. The others followed suit, and once the lieutenant had checked their air systems, they entered the air lock mounted to the athwartship passageway hatch and went inside. Dan found that the atmosphere against his neck and hands was cold and palpably dry, and that the lieutenant had understated the lighting problem. Rigged to the overhead cableways was a thick industrial extension cord with a single caged bulb mounted every twenty feet. Through the slightly fogged and scratched visor of his breathing mask, the passageway looked like a steel mine-shaft tunnel with dull green sides. All of the bulkhead-mounted fittings—electrical junction boxes, hose reels, hatches and doors, ventilation diffusers, and fluorescent light fixtures—were in shadow, and his eyesight was further restricted by the limited peripheral vision caused by the mask. The probing white light from their helmets briefly illuminated brass fittings, the asphalt tiles on the deck, the dull gray cabling running along the overhead, and the brass ladder rails of the first main passageway ladder going down to the second deck.

They went down the double-wide ladder to the second deck. They passed through what appeared to be a berthing area, and Dan tried to imagine what it had been like when the ship was alive with its crew of over a thousand men. Now it was like being inside a pharaoh's tomb—literally, considering what they were going to see. They proceeded aft for about a hundred feet, and then turned right into a vestibule to go down through a second hatchway, ducking their heads and using their hands to deflect the hanging lightbulbs. Dan was reminded that they were in a battleship when he noticed that the deck through which this ladder descended was several inches thick. He shined his light on the hatch, which was held back by glistening hydraulic arms; five inches thick itself, it must have weighed a couple of tons. At the bottom of this ladder, they entered a longer and much narrower passageway, which was even darker than the one above. This passageway appeared to have a series of watertight hatches running down either side, each leading to one of the main propulsion machinery compartments arrayed in a line down the ship's centerline—hence its name, Gasoline Alley. This deck was lined with stainless-steel plates that had a raised herringbone pattern. Each of the side hatches was less than man-high and was surrounded by a battery of remote-operating steam-valve wheels, emergency fuel shutoff handles, and emergency communications ports.

Dan tried to remember the layout diagram he had seen that morning at the NIS office: The battleship had eight main machinery spaces, laid out in a boiler room/engine room, boiler room/engine room configuration, aligned along the centerline, with Gasoline Alley running longitudinally down the centerline, on top of the machinery spaces. In addition to the four boiler rooms, the ship had four main steam turbines, one per engine room, which together were capable of driving the armored behemoth at nearly thirty-eight miles per hour. The body had been found in number-one fire room, in the steam drum of the port-side boiler.

The lieutenant led them to the hatch leading into number-one fire room; it was marked by a cluster of lights suspended from the overhead around the hatch and, incongruously, considering the nitrogen atmosphere, by some yellow crime-scene tape. The hatch itself was open, and its six dogging handles were wrapped in what looked like clear plastic wrap. Lieutenant Gravely led the way through the hatch, stepping up over the knee-high hatch coaming and onto a steel platform just inside the fire room. He pointed down a steep ladder with his flashlight, then descended, followed by the others. The ladder rails, like the dogging handles, were also wrapped in plastic. At the bottom of the ladder, Dan found himself standing on deck grating between the two steam boilers, which stood side by side like two stainless-steel buildings. He was actually on the upper level of the fire room, standing one level above what was called the "firing alley." The steel gratings were closely spaced but allowed a clear view of the boiler-front area beneath them. There were six caged bulbs on a temporary string suspended between the boiler fronts. The steam drum on the port-side boiler was open, and a single portable floodlight was positioned to shine into the opening of the steam drum. The steam drum was a heavy steel cylinder at the top of the boiler; it looked to be about twelve feet long and about three feet in diameter. Access to the internals of the steam drum was through an oval manhole, whose cover and hold-down bolts had been removed and were lying on the deck gratings in front of the boiler. The lieutenant pointed soundlessly to the steam drum's opening and stepped back. The riggers stayed together over by the ladder leading up out of the space.

Dan and Grace approached the manhole and peered in, bumping their facemasks against the cold steel. The body was lying on its back, left hand at its side, right hand raised slightly, the head thrown back at an odd angle, feet toward the aperture of the manhole. It was dressed in what looked to Dan like Navy working khakis, and the single silver bar of a lieutenant junior grade glinted in the white spotlight. Dan could not see the entire face, but from what he could see of the neck and arms, the body had aparently mummified in the cold, dry, anaerobic atmosphere within the ship. The chest had lost definition, and the entire body seemed to have shrunk and flattened. The hands were clawlike, with dark, dry skin pulled over the bones like parchment. One of the body's shoes had a hole in the sole. Lumpy bags of desiccant powder surrounded the body like cement pillows. Dan backed away so that Grace could get a better look, and she put the one arm with her flashlight and then her whole head into the steam drum.

Dan found another ladder and went down one level to the lower level and looked around the boiler-front area. The fuel-oil valves, burner assemblies, and even the deck plates glinted in the light reflected from above. He touched a burner assembly and found it smooth, cold, and slightly oily. Perfectly preserved, like that guy in there. A black man, the NIS preliminary report had said. Age about twenty-something. A lieutenant junior grade. No identification in pockets, no rings, no watch, no wallet. Fingerprints taken but distorted. No signs of injury visible from the manhole, but an autopsy would tell the tale.

He looked around. The fire room looked like all naval boiler rooms: a maze of steam piping in the shadows of the overhead and suspended under the upper-level gratings; the silent, yawning maws of ventilation ducts pointed into the firing alley; two double-walled, two-storied, stainless-steel boilers sitting side by side. He recognized the M-type, recalling the design from engineering school, with separately fired superheaters producing 600 psi main steam. The burner assemblies for the four registers on the saturated side and the three on the superheated side stood in shining ranks on stands in front of each boiler, clean, lightly oiled, ready to go. The burner registers—large round holes with teethlike vanes fanned around their circumference to swirl the incoming combustion air with the fuel—were equally clean and shipshape. The face of the boiler-control console at one end of the firing alley gleamed in highlights of brass and stainless steel, its instruments airtight and all pointing to the far left. Mounted high on steel stanchions were the primary boiler gauges—main steam, auxiliary steam, fuel-oil pressure, feed-water pressure. He checked the expiration dates on the gauge-calibration stickers: December 1991; *Wisconsin* had been decommissioned in September 1991, after Desert Storm.

He admired the cleanliness and order, the solid paint, the absence of rust and dirt, the clean and oil-free lagging on the pumps and forced-draft blower turbines, and especially the little green notebooks hanging off the individual pieces of machinery, filled with notations as to each machine's quirks. Her engineers had laid her up properly, almost lovingly. One final ladder led below the lower-level deck plates, and there, in the bilge in front of 1B boiler, was the burst bag of desiccant powder that had attracted the sounding-and-security watch's attention in the first place. A bag moved out of the steam drum to make room for the body? How long had this guy been in there? Two years or so? At least—long enough to have mummified. Or had the ship's atmosphere not yet been evacuated when he was locked up in the steam drum? They would have to check the time sequence. He shuddered at the thought of waking up inside the internals of a ship's boiler, encased in a soundproof two-inch-thick steel cylinder in absolute darkness. If this guy had been a surface-ship guy, he would have probably figured out where he was . . . .

He climbed back up to the upper level just as Grace was withdrawing her masked face gingerly from the steam drum. Lieutenant Gravely was giving him a "Well?" sign with his hands. He then pointed to his watch and indicated they had about fifteen minutes. Santini was standing over to one side, arms folded, his body language expressing total boredom. The other shipyard workers were sitting on the upper-level railings, waiting, something they seemed to know how to do. Dan looked over at Grace, who indicated she wanted five more minutes to look around. He pointed down and then led her to the desiccant bag on the lower level, which she acknowledged with a nod of her head. She pointed back up, then led Dan back up the ladder to the upper level and over to the hatch that gave access to the fire room. She shined her light all around the hatch coaming. Dan did, too, but did not know what she was looking for. The lieutenant came over and pointed again to his watch, and Dan nodded. They filed out of the fire room, with Santini coming out last, pulling down the hatch dogs to seal the space. They retraced their steps up through the silent passageways to the air lock on the main deck. Once the group exited the air lock on the main deck and removed their masks, Santini took charge.

"If that's all the sight-seeing you plan to do, Commander, I'm ready to take a medical team down there to extract the body and wrap up the crime scene. I've made arrangements with the Philadelphia Police Department's medical examiner to get an autopsy done."

" 'Sight-seeing,' Mr. Santini?" Dan was rubbing his face where the hard rubber of the mask had left its mark. He put an edge in his voice. "Well, I—"

Grace Snow spoke up. "Mr. Santini," she said. "Commander Collins is in charge of this investigation. If you have a problem with that, I can make a quick call and probably get someone from headquarters up here who will be more accommodating."

Santini stared at her with all the hostility field-office people reserve for interfering Washington headquarters types, but then the Italian in him took over, and he threw up his hands.

"Okay, Okay, *Ms.* Snow, whatever you say. We've had enough parades through this scene—one more or a hundred more won't make a shit, I guess. So, Commander, what do you want us to do?"

"I want you to complete your examination of the area around number-one fire room, upper level, and then remove the body for autopsy. You keep calling it a crime scene. But I have to wonder if the murder, if that's what we have here, took place in or near the boiler. This whole thing looks like an effort to put a body where it would almost never be found. But I assume you're looking for forensic evidence that might identify who put that guy in there, right? Like maybe fingerprints on that bag of desiccant on the lower level?"

Santini gave Dan a patronizing look. "Yes, sir, something like that. And perhaps a few more sophisticated traces of evidence here and there."

"Which are described in your preliminary report?"

"Well . . . we're getting to that."

Dan began to fold up the harness on his breathing set. "No doubt, Mr. Santini. The sounding-and-security inspectors come through, what, monthly?"

"Supposed to be monthly. But Shop Seventy-two says it works out to be about every other month, the time they get around to it. They've got the flooding alarms to warn them if anything big gets going."

"So any residual dirt from shoes on the deck plates, or ladder backs— that could be from the watch making his rounds, right? For maybe as long as two years?"

Santini nodded again. "Absolutely. Anybody."

Dan looked at Grace Snow. "So," he said, "the best we're probably going to get from Forensics is who this guy is, or was, and how long he's been dead and down in the nitrogen."

"And how he died," interjected Grace, unstrapping her breathing-rig harness.

"Right. And how he died. Okay. Have the body removed. I'll need to see a shipyard functional organization chart—which shops do what—and get a tally of everybody involved in the baby-sitting of a sleeping battleship."

He looked at his watch: 12:30 P.M. "That O-club still open?" he asked.

Santini said yes, and Dan signaled Grace to come along. They went back down the gangway as the ambulance team came up, unfolding the straps of a Stokes litter. Santini changed his air bottle, as did the riggers, in preparation for going back in. Sergeant DeGiorgio was dozing in the car, but he woke up quickly enough and ran them over to the NIS offices to change back into their respective uniforms: blues for Dan and a business suit for Grace Snow. Fifteen minutes later, they walked into the dining room of the officers' club. By the time they were seated, the noon-hour rush had wound down. Dan ordered a beer and a Reuben; Grace had iced tea and a salad. To Dan's surprise, the food arrived very quickly. The Reuben was enormous. Her salad looked like it had been lightly microwaved.

"Eating trim," Dan observed.

Grace eyed the beer and the large sandwich. "How do you manage it?" she asked.

"I'm a rower, remember? I go out for an hour and a half every afternoon on the Potomac and work it off. I usually have a doughnut and coffee for breakfast most days, and a steak and salad at night. But I'm fortunate, I guess—this stuff doesn't stick."

"You are very fortunate. I'm gaining weight just looking at it."

"Not visibly."

Grace raised her eyebrows at him as if to say, Let's not go down that road, shall we? Dan put up his hands in mock surrender.

"I guess that wasn't very politically correct of me," he said. "But it was meant as a compliment."

"Thank you. But I think you and I are going to have to keep our relations on a strictly business footing. Remember, we're not exactly allies in this little venture."

Dan worked on his sandwich while he thought about that.

"Well," he said finally, "superficially, I agree about the allies bit, at least in terms of what our respective masters are up to. But, as we discussed, that game is beyond your pay grade and mine, I think. However the bureaucratic rice bowls make out, I do think we're supposed to find out what happened here."

"I agree. But if I were a man instead of being a woman, you would not be complimenting my figure."

"Yeah, I know. I'm sorry, but I'm not yet able to treat a woman like a man."

"You don't have to. But I think we'll get this thing done better and quicker if we keep it impersonal. Now, what's next?"

Dan finished his sandwich and sipped his beer. He noticed that Grace was toying manfully with her salad. Womanfully? He smiled.

"What?" she asked.

He shook his head. "Something my irreverent half thought of," he said. "So, what's next? We work on identifying this guy, I guess. The autopsy will reveal how he died. If he's been in that ship for a while, there should be a missing persons report in the system somewhere. He's a lieutenant junior grade in working uniform, which would indicate to me that whatever happened to him happened here in the shipyard."

"Go on."

"Well, if he simply disappeared, the Navy will have a UA report on him."

"UA?"

"Unauthorized absentee. AWOL. He had to have belonged to a command, either here in the yard or maybe on a ship undergoing overhaul. The command would have had to file a report when the guy vanished."

"Is UA the same as missing persons?"

"Well, not exactly. UA infers that the guy went over the hill, on his own steam. Missing persons—well, that means he went missing and that the command doesn't think it was of his own volition. An officer going UA is pretty rare, actually."

Grace sat back and pushed away the limp salad. "What I'm getting at is, if he was reported as a missing person, the NIS would have a file: the Bureau of Naval Personnel always cuts NIS in when there's a missing person."

Dan nodded thoughtfully. "So we can start right here, then. I assume the Philly field office can access your central data banks in D.C.?"

She smiled, and he suddenly realized that she could be really attractive whenever she shed that deadly serious expression.

"Don't assume, Commander Collins. Actually, it works the other way. The Washington headquarters can access the field office's computers. But Santini can give us a look. Although it may be archived."

"Okay, you run that trap, and I'll get on the horn to BuPers and see what we come up with regarding officers going astray in beautiful downtown Filthadelphia. Santini said we could have a desk and a phone."

12

THAT AFTERNOON, ENSCONCED in a temporarily empty cubicle of the NIS office, Dan consulted Santini's DOD phone book and called the Navy's Bureau of Naval Personnel in Washington. He reached the main operator and asked for the shop that handled long-term unauthorized absentees and deserters. A Master Chief Gonzalez answered the phone.

"Master Chief, this is Commander Dan Collins calling. I'm assigned to OP-Six-fourteen over in OpNav and I'm on TAD doing a JAGMAN investigation up here in the Philly shipyard. I've got a question for you."

"Shoot, Commander."

"Right. I want to know if you have any record of a lieutenant junior grade going UA up here in the yards anytime in the past two, three years."

"You gotta be shitting me, Commander."

"Yeah, I know. That's sorta broad—"

" 'Sorta broad'?" said the master chief. "Do you know how many officers and enlisted we have in the Navy today? Like right now?"

"Nope."

"Nor do we."

"Say what?"

"You heard me, Commander. We couldn't begin to tell you. And that's because of a thing we call the "float": transients, the sick, UA and deserters, and prisoners. We can tell you what the average float is on any given day— say, roughly speaking, around two thousand personnel, give or take a couple hundred. But that's as close as we can get. And you wanta find one guy?"

Dan changed the phone from his right ear to his left. "Not exactly, master chief. We've found the guy. We're trying to find out who he is—or was. See, he's dead. And it looks like a homicide."

"Whoa. Hang on a minute while I get a pen. Okay, where'd you say you worked, Commander?"

"Yeah, I know, it's complicated," Dan said, noting that Santini appeared to be eavesdropping from his office on the other side of the room. Grace was at another empty desk, on the phone with NIS in Washington. "But NIS is in it, too. I'm actually calling from the NIS office in Philly."

"How's about I call you back, Commander."

"Yeah, sure, Master Chief. You want the number?"

"I'll get it. I'll be right back to you."

Dan hung up and waited. The master chief was no dummy—anybody could call into BuPers and ask a question. He went to get a cup of coffee, and he heard the phone ring in the secretary's cubicle.

"Yeah," she said through a wad of chewing gum. "He's here."

Dan picked the phone back up. "Master Chief."

"Right. Okay, Commander. Just playing safe, you know. These days—"

"Right, Master Chief. So the guy I'm trying to ID is a lieutenant junior grade. And he's black. And that's all I got until we get the results of an autopsy."

"In the Philly shityard, hunh? Okay, lemme hit the cornpewter and see who we got on the run in Philly. I've got your number."

"Thanks, Master Chief."

Dan hung up at the same time Grace did.

"Any luck in D.C.?" he asked.

"Not yet. I've asked the question, but now I'm in the queue for an answer. Nobody works in real time in NIS."

"Man, ain't that the truth," volunteered Santini, now standing in his office doorway. "I'm surprised they gave you the time of day."

"I knew whom to call," smiled Grace.

"Wish I knew who the hell to call. I've got RFIs been down there for six weeks, some of them."

"RFI?" asked Dan.

"Requests for information. Like I said, NIS is not a real-time data bank. It's not like the FBI's NCIC. Those guys can come back in fifteen minutes for an office request, and within two for a cop calling from his car. That's an amazing system."

"Can't NIS just copy it? Or join it?"

Grace rubbed her thumb and forefinger together. "Money. OpNav submits our budget, and OpNav does not love us just now."

Dan sat back in his chair and nodded, then sat back up.

"Oh shit!" be exclaimed.

"What?"

"Where's that ambulance? You suppose they've left the shipyard yet?"

Santini looked at his watch. "Nah. I just got back myself. They're probably still strapping the body in on the pier. Why?"

Dan called out to the secretary. "Miss? Can you get the base cops' dispatcher on the horn? I want to know if they're still down on the pier. And if they are, I need them to do something."

Grace cocked her head to one side and looked at him. "Are you going to cut the rest of us in here?"

Dan put up his hand. The secretary had patched back the police dispatcher, who had one of the cop cars down at the battleship pier on the radio.

"Yeah, look, this is Commander Collins. I was down there earlier, with the NIS guys, looking at that body in the ship. Has the ambulance left yet?"

The dispatcher gave him a wait, then replied that the body was wrapped for transport and the guys were closing up the meat wagon. Santini was staring hard at him, obviously wondering what new interference the amateur was going to cause.

"Okay," Dan said. "Ask one of the ambulance attendants to open the bag and look at something for me."

The dispatcher consulted with the car on the scene and then came back.

"The NIS guy on the pier says those guys can't open the bag once it's sealed. Chain of evidence."

"All right. Hang on. Mr. Santini, I need you to tell your guy on the pier that it's okay to open the bag. I want them to look at something."

"Well, Commander, we did a prelim search of that body, best we could in that steam drum and everything, and there was no—"

"Yeah, sure. But the dead guy's in uniform. Navy working uniform. If he was ship's company, his name should be stenciled on the shirt collar and the waistband of his trousers—for the ship's laundry."

Santini's face began to turn red. "Shit. Gimme that goddamn phone," he said. Grace Snow busied herself with her notebook, taking care not to look at anyone in particular.

Five minutes later, they had it. According to his shirt collar, the dead officer was Lt. (jg) W. Hardin, and the insignia on his left collar indicated he was Supply Corps, USN. Dan called back to BuPers and talked to the master chief. The BuPers computer was down at the moment, but with the name and designator, the master chief promised a quick confirmation. Dan hung up.

"Okay," he announced. "Assuming this guy didn't borrow someone's uniform, now we have a name. BuPers will be back with a ship or station once their computer is back up. Mr. Santini, you sure your local files won't have anything on this guy?"

"With a name, yeah, we can maybe get a hit in the archives. Look, Commander, about the ID—"

Dan waved him off. "Forget it, Mr. Santini. I should have thought of it when I saw that the body was in a uniform. That's not something a civilian does, stencil his clothes."

"Yeah, well, okay, then. I was just, uh, kinda wo— concerned that we'd get a ration of shit from headquarters for not making the ID right away." He looked pointedly over at Grace Snow.

Dan nodded his head. "So in other words," he said, "I put in my report that an identification was made from the dead man's uniform, full stop. Not how and by whom. Or when."

Santini pursed his lips and nodded slowly. Two other NIS men in the office were listening while pretending to work.

"Yeah," Santini said. "Something like that. It would be appreciated."

"You got it. Now, assuming we get the command's name, we'll get closer to a date of the incident. We all agree, I think, that it's been awhile. And the forensic lab downtown will give us cause of death. After that—"

"After that, we'll probably not know very much," said Grace, leaning forward in her chair. "I mean motive or any other explanation for what happened to him."

"Don't be thinking we'll see the autopsy results in just a day or so—the city morgue is a busy place," said Santini.

Dan closed his notebook. "Even so, I think we'll have to wait for that autopsy before doing much more here—unless we can talk to some people in his previous command. But that's going to be tough—ships, assuming he was in a ship, have a turnover rate of nearly fifty percent a year. If it's been awhile, we're not likely to find many people who knew this guy or what he might have been mixed up in that got him killed. And the ship could be anywhere in the world. Motive will be real tough."

"Hey, Commander," Santini interjected, "this is South Philly you're talkin' about here; there's a gazillion things can get you whacked down here."

"Yeah, but in a shipyard?"

"Two gazillion," offered one of the other detectives.

"We don't know this happened in the shipyard," said Grace. "He could have been simply stashed in the shipyard."

Dan shook his head. "You're right. What we *know* is that we don't know anything."

Santini laughed. "Now you're starting to think like a cop," he said.

"We know that officer is dead and that someone probably killed him and put him in that boiler," Grace said. The laughter stopped.

13

SANTINI HAD BOOKED them two rooms at the Naval Station Philadelphia Bachelor Officers' Quarters, which was a run-down three-story World War II tempo building adjacent to the officers' club. The BOQ had been refurbished several times since its construction in 1942, but nothing could disguise its age and general decrepitude. The building was heated sporadically by clanking steam radiators, and the aging, lead-based paint was peeling in the hallways. The third floor was blocked off, its rooms having been deemed too far gone to be worth refurbishment. The rooms themselves were devoid of any decoration, with mottled ceramic washbasins sticking out of the wall, and a commode and shower crammed into what had once been a closet.

Individual air conditioners in each room blocked most of the sunlight, and the industrial grime on the windows blocked the rest.

Dan had apologized to Grace when he realized where they would be staying. But the alternatives were few: Either stay in the BOQ, on the base, where they could walk to the NIS office, or stay in an uptown hotel and face Philadelphia's exciting metropolitan commute across South Philly twice a day. Grace had taken it in good stride.

"I've always wanted to see how the brass lived," she remarked with a perfectly straight face.

They agreed to meet at the officers' club at 6:30 P.M. for a drink, and then they would figure out what to do about dinner. They would have to leave the base, as the O-club's dining room was open only at lunchtime. Dan was waiting for her in the side entrance to the club when she came out of the BOQ. He observed again that she would have been smashing if she would lighten up a little. But once again, she was wearing a severely cut, wholly unrevealing midcalf-length suit. She had her purse slung over her shoulder, and a light raincoat over one arm. He thought that the total effect—serious, businesslike expression, minimal makeup, painfully practical hairdo, plain shoes, and her alert, almost defensive posture—made her look just exactly like what she was: a cop. He wondered if she carried a gun in that purse.

Dan was dressed in gray slacks, a blue blazer, a plain tie and white shirt, and highly polished loafers. He carried a London Fog raincoat over one arm; it was April, but not yet warm in Philadelphia, and the sunset had promised wet weather before morning. They went into the gloomy bar of the O-club and took a table in the corner. The bar was almost empty, with only two crusty-looking warrant officers nursing beers and watching the evening news on the television. Grace ordered a white wine, Dan a gin and tonic. He noticed that she grimaced when she saw what the bartender was pouring for wine.

"This isn't exactly a high-rent, front-line operation here," he said. "This so-called officers' club wouldn't survive one week without the civilian shipyard clientele at lunch. This whole shipyard is one big armpit."

"You said that the Navy keeps trying to close it."

"Right. *Trying* is the operative word. The Pennsylvania congressional delegation must have some severely compromising photographs of some very senior Navy people, because the yard keeps going, year after year, no matter how lousy their work is."

"That's unbelievable." She tasted her wine and then looked at it. "*This* is unbelievable."

He laughed. "Don Carlo's finest, no doubt. Aged in the tank car at least one day. Part of the problem is the locale—this is South Philly, as Santini, he of the Irish heritage, said this afternoon. I was on a ship here once for six months; the yard is reportedly a major source of revenue for various racketeers, big and small. The rumor is that they do some big-league industrial-materials theft, contract fraud, union scams, phantom hours, world-class featherbedding, drugs. You name it, there's a local running it here."

She studied the darkened barroom, with its cheesy fake paneling, cheap brass light fixtures, the ancient, grainy television, and the threadbare, stained carpet, as if looking at something genuinely interesting. He thought he saw her wrinkle her nose in a little sniff.

"Could this killing," she asked finally, "could it have been mob-related—something to do with an officer, maybe a naïve young officer, who stuck his nose in where it didn't belong?"

Dan had to think about that one. "Maybe, but that's kind of remote. You mean, like exposing the scams? I don't think so. A lieutenant junior grade just doesn't draw enough water to worry a shop group superintendent or a union boss. They might have his tires slashed in the junior officers' parking lot, but kill him? No, I don't think so. There were easier, more effective ways to screw a junior officer up—lose his job orders, lose the materials for the jobs in his work center, vandalize his stateroom in the ship, that kind of stuff."

She nodded, sipped her wine, and then put the glass down firmly. She shivered. "That battleship, that was a spooky place. And that body—mummified. I felt like I was in the depths of an ancient tomb, with all that steel and that flattened brown—"

"Yeah. I guess, being from NIS, a battleship would make you feel uncomfortable."

She flared. "And what's that supposed to mean?"

He smiled. "Hey. I didn't mean to pull your chain. I just meant that the last time the NIS got into a battleship investigation, it turned into one of the biggest goat f— the biggest Chinese fire drills the Navy's seen for a few decades."

She studied the tabletop. "Well, I suppose you're talking about the *Iowa* thing; that was before my time. But from what I've heard, most of the old hands in NIS thought their theory was at least feasible. The problem was that some of the fieldwork, the interrogations, choice of witnesses, was pretty shoddy."

"Plus, they couldn't prove it."

"No. But I think the NIS has been made something of a whipping boy. Like in the Tailhook investigation: The main reason the Defense Department inspector general got into it was because they suspected there was a lot of command influence being exercised by OpNav."

"Maybe like this little deal," Dan said softly.

"Yes. You've been in the fleet—is NIS useful?"

"They came when I called, and I always thought they did a good job with our shipboard problems," Dan said. "But this is Washington we're dealing with. Once an incident or an issue breaks in Washington, everyone gets lots of management help from their superiors. Like in the *Iowa* thing."

"I've read some of the *Iowa* investigation materials—that was apparently a very loose ship, even if I say so."

Dan shook his head. "From what I've heard, she didn't start out that way when they first brought her back in commission. But I have to admit that I haven't read the actual investigation, although Captain Summerfield—he's my boss in OpNav; you met him at the meeting—recommended that I read it. He said it would explain why OpNav is gunning for the NIS."

"And *is* OpNav gunning for the NIS?"

"Beats me. Sometimes when things get nasty, organizations that report to OpNav get sacrificed on the altar of public relations. That's what the Tailhook affair looked like, down at the snuffy level. The admirals walked; the junior officers got nailed. But hell, I just work here. There. But you have to admit, the fact that I'm working this incident instead of the NIS system would indicate that *somebody* is gunning for the NIS, don't you think?"

She stared at her wine for a moment, her head down. He noticed for the first time that she had luxuriant almost blue-black hair, not brunette as he had first thought, and wide, squared-off shoulders. He wondered if she worked out. A swimmer perhaps. But then another voice: why do you care?

"I'm kind of in the same boat as you are," she said, looking up. "I said after our first meeting that I have several years of field-investigation experience. That's true, but not in criminal investigations. Remember I told you I worked for SEC? I did all my investigating for SEC in Manhattan—securities fraud, mostly."

He was surprised. Securities fraud? What the hell was she doing here? Reading his question, she continued.

"As I told you in the car coming up, I took a political appointment at the Justice Department in the last administration, toward the end, as it turned out. When all the hicks and tics showed up, I ended up in NIS as a civil servant in the Criminal Investigations Policy directorate. I guess I'm one of those political appointees they describe as burrowing in. But it was supposed to be investigative work, and it was criminal stuff, a change from strictly white-collar crime."

"And this was in Investigations Policy?"

"Yes. But I'm not there anymore. I'm now in the Career Services division."

Dan took time to stir the ice cubes in his drink. Curioser and curioser. "I see," he said finally.

"Do you?" She was looking right at him.

"Well, yes, and no. But probably yes. You pissed somebody off, and they executed what the civil serpents call the 'lateral arabesque.' When it happens in the Navy, the detailers call you up and tell you that you're going to get a professionally challenging reassignment."

She smiled. "I think I frustrated them more than made them angry. I wouldn't let the internal organizational politics interfere with a case. What

I didn't understand, initially at least, was how both internal and external political considerations colored everything we did, either at Justice or in the NIS. Let's go find dinner somewhere," she said. "I'll tell you about it."

They asked the bartender for a recommendation for dinner in the South Philadelphia area. He solemnly advised ordering a pizza delivered to the club bar instead. But one of the warrants named a restaurant that was two miles down from the main gate on Snyder as being truly outstanding. He also advised taking a taxi, as the locals were sensitive to out-of-town license plates, especially if they displayed a Washington, D.C., military decal. The bartender shook his head but did call them a taxi. Thirty minutes later, they were ensconced at a corner table at the Trattoria Firenzi and trying out a bottle of Antinori red Chianti, at Grace's suggestion. At Dan's suggestion, they ordered a series of dishes from the abundant appetizer listings instead of a main course.

"The warrant officer knew what he was talking about," observed Grace after the first of the dishes was presented.

"Warrants usually do; he also knew we were from Washington."

Grace laughed. "That's not a very big base, and one of those guys was from base security."

"How do you know that?"

"NIS trade secret: He was carrying a police-type beeper."

He smiled. "Well, see, you do know something about police work. Now, if you're willing, tell me why you think you were eased out of Investigations Policy and into Career Services at NIS."

She studied him for a moment, as if making up her mind. He looked back at her over his wineglass. Intelligent eyes, dusky green now. An almost severe face, faintly classical in bone structure and the fine planes of her cheeks and brows. Still no visible makeup. Something of a hard case perhaps. Except from what he had seen of her in coveralls, not that hard. And yet there had been zero coquettishness: strictly business. Maybe an undercurrent of insecurity. Why should she tell him anything? After all, they were working for opposing camps. But then he saw her decide.

She poured some more wine and then began to tell him about herself— her home and family in New England, mother and father both doctors, a comfortable upbringing for an only daughter, an economics degree from Brown University, a JD from Georgetown Law, and then the job at SEC, first in Washington, later in New York. She had graduated from law school in 1984. The following year, her parents had both died, which had crystallized her decision to stay put in Washington.

"My father had a heart attack, in the hospital, if you can believe it. One of the nurses said she looked up and he was suddenly standing there, right in front of her desk. She had said, 'Yes, Doctor?' And he had told her that his heart had just stopped, then keeled over. They had him in the CCU in one minute, but they couldn't . . . restart him. That was the word they used. Like he was a stalled old engine. He just . . . got away from them."

She sipped some wine for a moment, staring at the candle in the wax-covered fiasco on the table.

"That was in the spring of 1985. My mother willed herself to carry on, for a while, anyway. But at Christmastime that same year, I think she turned her head to the wall and just . . . died. She actually gave me some warning. There was one letter, although I didn't pick up on it. I was their only child, so I assumed the universe centered on me. I had no idea how close they were—no idea at all. I think now they felt that they had done a conscientious and loving job with me, then gone back to being totally involved with each other once I left the nest."

She paused to drink some wine, put down the glass, and drew her left palm slowly across her left cheek, reflecting.

"Mother was a psychiatrist in private practice with two other doctors. I don't think I've ever told anybody this, but I've often thought that she just took something—you know, being a doctor, they know how to check out if they want to. But I'm not sure. She was a very strong woman, and I also believe that she was capable of simply switching off. I think she just went to find Dad."

Dan saw her eyes mist over briefly, and he wished he had a handkerchief, but she dabbed her eyes with the corner of her napkin, took a deep breath, another sip of wine. The waiter came by with the next round of appetizers.

"Anyhow," she continued, "there was a startling amount of money that came out of that dreadful year—life insurance, his investments, their share of their practices, that sort of thing. It all came to me, and suddenly I didn't have to work. Not financially, anyway. But personally, I worked harder than ever. I just put my own head down and let the office take over my life. It was actually comforting for a while. And then I met Ren, my husband-to-be. He was testifying before the Senate Banking Committee on bond trading, and I was assigned to go monitor. I transferred to New York the following spring and we got married in early 1987."

He sipped his own wine and kept quiet. She seemed to want to talk, and there were some uncomfortable parallels in the story of their lives.

"The job and the marriage were wonderful, for a while. But then the go-go years on Wall Street began to unravel, and life got tough out there in the financial trenches. Rennie didn't handle it well, and then he got himself involved with cocaine and a couple of girlfriends, and a nasty habit of using me as a punching bag. I broke it off, but by then I was not a very comfortable person to be around. Which is why that appointment came along, I think."

"That was at the end of 1990?"

"It was 1991, actually. As I said, politically I wasn't very astute about it, or I might have waited to see who or what won the election."

"The 'whats' did."

"I think it was more of a case of the 'whos' losing it, but anyhow, by December, 1992, I was among the great Washington wave of the suddenly redundant. As I said, I didn't have to work, but I did, if you follow. What my mother did scared the hell out of me, and after my divorce, I was desperately afraid of being cut off from my life, which by then meant my work."

"And you've found nobody significant in Washington?" he asked, then blushed. "Excuse me; forget I asked that."

She smiled. "Why did you ask?"

It was his turn to scramble. "Well, your parents' passing, a divorce. I just figured that by now, maybe . . ."

She gave him an introspective look but appeared to ignore his embarrassment. "No. After Rennie, I've taken myself off the market, as it were. You have to remember, in SEC, I dealt professionally with government litigators and their antagonists—type A's, most of them, both the good guys and the bad guys. But kind of hard to warm up to, and, once you'd been through a twelve-hour day in that business, there wasn't much time or energy left for sex appeal, no matter what they tell you in the movies. Especially once the home front began to dissolve."

"I hear that."

"So now I live in Georgetown, in my own town house. It even has a driveway and a garden with nice high brick walls. High-rent solitude, the perfect refuge for the harried government executive, as the Realtor explained it. Do you know Georgetown?'

He laughed. "Out of my price range, I'm afraid. I've been a widower since . . . well, since 1988. I think I told you—my dad bought a listed eighteenth-century house in Old Town Alexandria twenty years ago as a rental investment and passed it on to me during my last shore tour here—in Washington, I mean. In theory, it's worth about ten times what he paid for it, but the remaining mortgage and the taxes are still pretty hefty."

"Old Town's pretty nice; I think it's what Georgetown used to be like," she observed.

"Georgetown looks like Armani country to me these days. Old Town's convenient to Fort Fumble, but the house itself isn't much. It's an old factor's building, two stories and an attic, a loading crane still hanging out one of the attic windows, but it's long and narrow rather than large, and not much of it is level or square anymore. I have a view of my neighbor's garden and the back walls of other town houses, and the river, if I want to step out my front door and stand on tiptoes and if it's wintertime. But there's no garage. All those damned cobblestones, and a wooden fence that's defying gravity better than it's defying the termites. Dad put in central air and heat a few years before I got it, which makes it bearable. Some of those old places are unlivable. But Georgetown always seemed to me to be reserved for either assistant secretaries of state or the serious disco crowd."

"There's a wider range of people than that, although I don't do much of the Georgetown social scene. I've been an extra at some dinner parties—neighbors, mostly, who need a fourth to fill out a table. After New York, though, I've been something of a recluse."

The waiter came back with the final round of appetizers, and Dan was approaching his limit. His daily workouts on the river or on his home rowing machine had left him very fit but without much capacity for restaurant food, especially after his noontime Reuben extravaganza. Grace seemed to be having the same problem.

"If I'm not intruding, what happened to your wife?" she asked.

Dan put down his wineglass and looked at the table, his eyes suddenly unfocused. After all these years, it was still surprisingly hard to talk about it; her question had ambushed him.

"Claire died in childbirth, or almost in childbirth. Something they called toxemia, came out of nowhere. We were at the PG school in Monterey—that's the Navy's graduate school. She'd had some problems with blood pressure on and off in her third trimester, but labor had been going normally, if you can call anything about labor normal. I left to go home to put the damn dog out, if you can believe it. Was back in thirty minutes, and when I got back, she wasn't there—in the labor room, I mean. A nurse intercepted me and took me into a doctor's office, and I waited there in a panic until a doctor came in with the chaplain and told me that Claire had had convulsions and what appeared to be a massive stroke. Lost her and the baby."

He ran out of breath for a moment, then said, "It happened so goddamned fast."

"I'm so sorry," she said, reaching across the table for his hand. In his sudden emotional state, her hand felt cool on his and almost strange. Grace appeared to sense his discomfort and withdrew her hand.

"Yeah, well. I'm kind of like you. Crawled into my cave and pulled the blankets up. I buried myself in my graduate work, finished a master's in mechanical engineering, and then asked for sea duty, something haze gray and under way and going way the hell out of the country. The Navy's exceptionally good about that, a guy loses his spouse. I was back at sea in a deployed cruiser in two weeks, and it was a godsend. Overseas, twenty-hour days, faraway places, as wet a shore liberty as your head could stand. Came to Washington for the first time in mid-1990. Shore duty's like civilian life—it goes a little slower."

"I know all about that slower," she said. Dan was getting uncomfortable with the conversation, and yet he sensed a kindred spirit. She was saying something about how weekends dragged.

"Oh, yes, weekends," he said. "Well, I've found the cure for them: I've become a Civil War–history buff. I drive out to the battlefields—there's a bunch within three hours of D.C.—and I read a lot of books. Some of those places are amazing, and the countryside is usually worth the trip."

The waiter asked if they wanted doggy bags; they declined and Dan asked for the check.

"I've begun a predoctoral program in political science at Georgetown," she said. "I don't really know what I'm going to do with it, but it fills those weekends with academic work."

She looked wistful as she said it, and Dan realized that they *were* kindred spirits. She was probably harboring some pretty serious emotional scar tissue, and, like him, she was careful to seek stable and predictable circumstances within which to make it through the days, and nights. As if she sensed his thoughts, she excused herself while Dan waited for the check.

His conversation with Grace made him wonder once again about his own prospects for a relationship with another woman. For the first few years, his widower status had protected him, but after his executive officer tour on *John King*, he had wondered if he should or even could start up again with someone new. None of the women he had met over the past few years had been able to breach that pungent aura of sadness that circled his vision whenever he thought about Claire and the family he had lost. He knew he would be better off with someone, but all the prospective someones had been either mildly desperate divorcées or other conjugal casualties. No longer knowing what he wanted, he had just let that part of life slide, focusing inward on his workdays in the Pentagon, his rowing, his weekend sojourns into the history-drenched Virginia countryside, the prospects for getting back to sea again, all the while politely rebuffing the occasional attempts of his professional contemporaries to set him up with a family friend. He watched Grace thread her way back through the crowded dining room—attractive, poised, aloof, not seeming to be aware of herself—and searched his feelings for some spark of real interest. Physically, she was definitely interesting, but his heart remained silent. He sighed. The waiter arrived at that moment with the check, and he returned to the business of the day, splitting the bill for their individual travel-expense reports.

14

At 8:30 A.M. on Wednesday morning, Master Chief Gonzalez called back from the BuPers with word that he had some information on the missing Lt. (jg) W. Hardin. Dan called the extension number over to Grace so she could pick up and listen.

"I can fax up the printout," Gonzalez said, "but it's not as much info as you might be expecting, 'cause the records all went off to that federal depository in St. Louis about a year and a half ago, after he was declared a deserter."

"So he was actually declared," asked Dan.

"Yes, sir. His ship, that's USS *Luce*, the DDG, she's been decommissioned since then. The ship initially filed an incident report when he went UA, like the manual requires, but then they declared him thirty days later. That part's all in here. And he was the assistant supply officer, not the chop. He was the DisBo."

"Uh-oh. Okay, Master Chief. Let me get you the fax number here. Oh, and can you get me his fitrep file?"

"I doubt it, Commander. Once the records go to St. Louis, we don't keep anything."

"How about those little old ladies up on the fourth deck—that place where officers can come in and review their records?"

"The microfiche should have gone out with the records, but, yeah, they might still have his package. I'll check it out. But I'm going to need some paper to get that released."

Dan thought about that for a moment. Getting access to another officer's fitness reports took a flag officer's signature.

"Lemme make a call back to my bosses in OpNav, Master Chief. Meanwhile, I'll fax you down my appointing letter so you can release the other admin. And I'm going to ask formally that the records be retrieved from St. Louis on a priority basis. This isn't a UA case; this is more than likely a homicide."

"No shit? You told his next of kin?"

Dan felt a wave of embarrassment. A next-of-kin notification should have been put in motion the moment they had the ID.

"No, I haven't," he replied. "Our ID is based only on laundry markings on his uniform. We presume that's accurate, but I need the records, especially the health and dental records, so the forensics guys can confirm. But the body is that of a black male, lieutenant junior grade, in uniform, Supply Corps insignia, and the uniform has his name on it."

"Well, that sure sounds like Hardin, just looking at the printout. Commander, lemme give you some advice. A body in a battleship—for journalists, that's going to be some sexy shit. It's gonna bring the press in pretty quick, somebody in the yard runs his mouth. Get a message sent down here to the bureau—to the Casualty Assistance Calls office—from ComNavBase Philly, probably, reporting what you've found, asking for the records, and asking for a CACO. That way, the CACO can go see the family—it says here they're right here in D.C.—and let them know something before they see it on the TV, okay?"

"Good advice, Master Chief. Message coming at you. Stand by for the fax number."

Dan switched off the speaker phone and looked at Grace Snow. "Nothing like a master chief to keep a commander off the rocks," he muttered. "I should have thought of that yesterday, soon as we had a name."

Grace was shaking her head as she looked at her notes. "I kind of got lost in the alphabet soup. CACO? FITREP? DISBO?"

"Right. Hang on a moment." He got up from his borrowed desk and went to find Santini, whom he asked to get the Commander Naval Base Philadelphia public affairs officer over to the NIS office right away.

"Can I tell her what it's about? The NavBase staffers don't just come because I call 'em," Santini said.

"Just tell him—her, did you say? Tell her there's a commander from OpNav in your office asking for the base PAO, and it's really urgent. If we're lucky, we're going to be just ahead of the curve here. And I need your fax number here for the guy in BuPers, and a copy of my appointing order faxed to him."

"You got it."

Santini buzzed the secretary, and Dan went back to explain the acronyms to Grace.

"A CACO is a casualty assistance calls officer. He's the guy who shows up in the black car to tell a family—the parents, or the spouse—that their service member has been injured or killed."

"Now there's a wonderful assignment."

"Right, but it's not a permanent specialty. Anybody can be tagged to go do the CACO job, just like I got tagged to do this JAG investigation. There's a BuPers manual section, procedures, specific instructions, all of that, on being a CACO. And typically, it's rank for rank: A commander dies, another commander is appointed CACO. Like that. And these days, if there's press interest, the CACO's main job is to beat the media to the prospective bereaved's door. After that, he helps any way he can. Interfaces with the whole Navy personnel infrastructure to arrange burial, deal with a mortuary, shipment of remains, notification to insurance and the VA, obtain a death certificate, all the admin stuff that a death stirs up. It's a good system."

"And we need one now?"

"Yeah, I think so. It's a judgment call—we don't have a positive ID, but I think we owe it to the Hardin family at least to alert them that we may have found their son. Especially since it was a civilian who read the name off the uniform."

"And FITREP?"

"Fitrep is an officer's fitness report. His ship filed an unauthorized-absence report when he went missing. Sounds like the command was assuming that Hardin went on his own steam, which might indicate a less-than-terrific officer. The fitness-report file—that's like your performance-appraisal reports—may reveal why they reacted that way. The problem is that all his records—service, pay, medical, dental, fitreps—should have been packaged up and sent to St. Louis to the federal records depository for microfilming by now. Getting things out of a federal archive center can take six to eight weeks."

"I can imagine. And this man in BuPers—he's going to try to expedite the retrieval?"

"Yeah. But I have to get ComNavBase to send a message to start the process."

Santini appeared. "Commander, the base PAO, Lieutenant Commander McGonagle, is on her way over. She sounded a little peevish."

"I'll handle that," Dan said. But as Santini withdrew, Grace suggested that *she* handle that. Dan thought for a few seconds before agreeing.

"Right. Good idea," he said. "You fill her in. I'm going to call the NavBase EA. This thing could get real big real quick."

"One thing—what's a PAO, again?"

"Public affairs officer—Navy spokesman, or spokeswoman, in this case. And DisBo means disbursing officer—Hardin was the paymaster. NIS field offices specialize in bent paymasters, which is why Santini here ought to have a record of this."

Dan got on the phone to the NavBase headquarters and asked for the admiral's executive assistant. While on hold, he tried to remember the organization. Back before World War II, the Navy's shore establishment had been divided into geographic districts, with the entire country and some of the overseas possessions being allocated to sixteen naval districts. The naval district commander had usually been a two-star rear admiral serving his swan-song tour just prior to retirement. The naval districts handled administrative matters within their territories: the pursuit and apprehension of deserters, trials and court-martials, formal and informal JAG investigations, the appointment and support of CACOs, administration of transient barracks and brigs, and the general personnel and administrative infrastructure support for all the Navy commands located within the district. In the years of base and flag officer billet consolidations since the war, the districts had been done away with and these duties apportioned to the largest base command located in what had been the respective districts. Dan knew that ComNavBase Philadelphia, now a one-star rear admiral, had a small staff of people who tried to cover the catchall functions of the old districts in addition to their normal duties.

"This is Lieutenant Commander VanSladen speaking," said a voice. Dan smiled. Even in a backwater like NavBase Philadelphia, the EA sounded impressed with himself. Dan identified himself and then brought the EA up to speed on what had happened so far.

"Commander," VanSladen said. "I'm a little distressed to be hearing about you and your investigation for the first time a day after you've arrived in our area."

"Well, Mr. VanSladen," Dan said, using the term appropriate to a junior officer's rank, "ComNavBase Philadelphia is listed as a 'copy to' on my appointing order from the Navy JAG. If you're surprised, you're not reading your mail." So much for your distress, bucko.

There was a moment of silence on the phone. Actually, Dan knew that the appointing order probably had not even physically reached Philadelphia yet, a fact that VanSladen also very likely recognized. But VanSladen was a lieutenant commander talking to a commander. Dan also knew that he should have touched base with the NavBase commander's office the moment he arrived. He decided to go smooth.

"Look," he said. "I'm having to move quickly here. Let me suggest that you call the EA down in OP-Oh-six; that's Captain Manning. Here's the number. Or better yet, maybe the admiral should call Admiral Carson; he's Oh-six B—the ADCNO Plans and Policy. That would be the quickest way for your boss to get the political slant on this situation, and a direct, flag-to-flag explanation for why I'm here instead of having the local NIS office running it. But more importantly, I've just sent for your base PAO, because I think there's going to be a pack of yapping journalists at the front gate, probably today. And I'm going to need a priority message to go out from ComNavBase requesting retrieval of some personnel records and assignment of a CACO."

There was a moment of silence, in which Dan thought he could hear scratching on paper. Then the EA spoke up. "I've got all that, Commander. What office are you operating out of?"

"I'm working out of the NIS office here; I think we're next door."

"We'll get back to you," the EA said, then hung up.

Dan grinned. EAs always talked like they had a mouse in their pockets. "We'll" get back to you, indeed. He quickly dialed up the OP-06 front office number in the Pentagon and told the yeoman chief to alert Captain Manning that ComNavBase Philadelphia might be calling 06B with a "what the hell" query. The chief took it in stride—06B was a senior two-star; ComNavBase Philadelphia was a one-star. But he did agree to alert the EA. Dan hung up and found Grace Snow standing in the doorway. Standing next to her was a tall, very Irish-looking redhead, who was wearing the service dress blues of a lieutenant commander.

"Commander Collins," Grace said, "this is Lt. Comdr. Helen McGonagle, the base PAO. I've briefed her on what we have so far. And here's the fax from that master whatever down at the bureau."

"That's master *chief*. Good morning, Miss McGonagle," Dan said, taking the fax from Grace. He was always somewhat at a loss as to how to address women officers—by their ranks, or Miss, or Ms. He had personally settled on using rank for lieutenants and below; Miss for lieutenant commanders, because of the two words in the rank; and the rank again—Commander, Captain—for the higher grades. Inevitably, the women would correct him. But McGonagle was all business, and indeed peevish.

"Commander Collins, your friendly PAO can be of much better service to my boss and yours if she gets cut in from the start."

"I agree, and I'm sorry I didn't call you sooner. I didn't expect this thing to move quite so quickly."

"Well, our dear shipyard commander should have been on to us the moment *they* found the body. We weren't even info on their incident-report message, but that's our little domestic problem, not yours. You're assigned to OpNav and directing a murder investigation in the field?"

"That's right."

"And not NIS. Why is that?"

Watch it, boyo; here's a staffie with her brain engaged, Dan thought. "I'll have to duck that one for now, Miss McGonagle."

"The name is Helen, and, no, you can't duck it. Look, think of me as your lawyer or your accountant—smart line officers always tell the PAO the whole truth so that their PAO can then efficiently keep the media jackals from holding a feeding frenzy on their collective haunches. Sir."

Dan laughed out loud. "Yes, ma'am. Ten thousand *gomenesais*. Come in and close that door, will you?"

With Grace listening, Dan reviewed the outlines of the story of the body in the battleship and also explained that the VCNO had decided to appoint a line officer to do the investigation to avoid any public association of the NIS with another battleship.

"Precisely because there might be media interest in the body in the battleship, and possibly invidious comparisons made with the *Iowa* flap," observed McGonagle.

"Um. Yes. Better make that a hundred thousand *gomens*."

"Accepted. But if that question comes up, we can point to Miss Snow here and say that the NIS is indeed involved in the investigation. And you're operating out of the NIS offices. Okay. That'll wash for the moment. Probably won't survive Washington media scrutiny, though."

"And what do we do then?" asked Grace.

"Washington heat is CHINFO's problem, isn't it?" muttered McGonagle. Dan liked this woman a lot all of a sudden. "Did you say you had identified the dead man?" she asked.

"Yes. A Lt. (jg) W. Hardin. He was a pork chop, the assistant chop in *Luce* when she was here a few years ago."

"Hardin? Hmmm."

"You recognize the name?"

"Well, yes—but not his. There was a Lt. Elizabeth Hardin who worked in CHINFO when I was down there two years ago, got killed in a hit-and-run accident over in Washington. As I remember, she had a brother in the Navy. But—" She was interrupted by the chirping of her beeper.

"Ah," she said, looking at the readout. "This is the CBS affiliate. We begin the beguine."

Using Dan's phone, Lieutenant Commander McGonagle called the reporter at the local CBS affiliate and found out that it was indeed a query about the body in the battleship. She told the reporter that the Navy would have a statement by three o'clock, in time for the evening news, and, no, they could not release a name, because the next of kin had not been notified. Yes, there would be more details at three. No comment on any homicide angle.

"I'll get a quick statement typed up and have the calls shunted over to my shop at the headquarters. I'm going to go back there and brief my boss.

I propose a meeting at the NavBase headquarters at fourteen hundred, so we can coordinate what we're going to tell the little dears."

"Will you fill in the CHINFO?"

"Yes, sir, I will. You let me know when BuPers has a CACO in the loop."

"Will do. And Helen, many thanks. This press stuff is scary to us ship drivers."

"Right. Just remember, I can't help you if you keep me in the mushroom mode."

When McGonagle had left the office, Dan called a quick meeting with Grace and Santini in Santini's office. He briefed Santini on what they had so far and on what was going on in the media loop.

"What I need now, until I get the records back from BuPers, is anything local that you—or maybe even the base cops—might have on the disappearance. I know it's nearly two years back, but surely there must have been at least routine paper on an officer supposedly going over the hill like that—especially if he was a disbursing officer."

Santini made notes. "I made a quick check yesterday," he said. "But lemme look some more. And maybe we ought to call the Navy supply system—I forget their acronym, but those guys who do audits on disbursing officers when somebody thinks something isn't kosher. We work with 'em when a DisBo goes wrong."

"Yeah, shit, I know who you mean. Gobbledygook name."

"How could you tell?" said Grace. Both men smiled.

"I'll find 'em," Santini said. "Jerry Watkins over there just worked a disbursing case. He'll know it."

"Grace," Dan said, "can you call downtown and see what's happening with the autopsy, maybe speed it along, federal case and all that. I'm going to check in with Oh-six and then with the NavBase EA."

The meeting broke up and Dan returned to his cubicle to call the Pentagon. Grace went to an empty desk out in the main office to make her calls. Dan's call was handed over to Captain Manning.

"Admiral Carson told me to call in from time to time, Captain. This case is going public this afternoon, so I thought now was a good time."

"Indeed. The admiral is down in JCS. Give me a precis of what you have and I'll relay it to the ADCNO and to the vice's EA."

"The vice chief?"

"Yes, Commander. He's the one who started this little food fight with NIS, remember?"

Dan glanced over at Grace Snow, who was busy on the phone.

"Yes, sir. Well. Here's what's happening." Dan gave the EA a three-minute recitation on where the case stood.

"And how are your relations with the NIS?"

"Actually, pretty good. I think. It started out testy up here in the field office, but now I'm apparently getting cooperation. The critical path time-wise is the autopsy to confirm that this was a homicide, and the records from BuPers so that we can positively identify Hardin, as well as some people in *Luce* who were there when he was there and can maybe shed some light on why this guy was murdered."

"I see. And the press interest?"

"Body in a battleship. There's at least one TV station that's on it; the base PAO is going to have a statement for the media at fifteen hundred."

"And you are not going to be part of that, correct?"

"Uh, I hadn't decided. They haven't—"

"I'd tell you to watch my lips, but that would be difficult. You will *not* be part of the press conference. The NavBase PAO can identify you as the officer conducting the investigation, if that's absolutely necessary, but otherwise we want you to keep a low profile."

"Yes, sir. But may I ask why?"

"You want to be a TV star, do you?"

"No, Captain. But the PAO will have a tough time fielding questions about the investigation if I'm not there."

"Precisely."

"Oh."

"Yes, oh. If your PAO is a professional, he'll have a lot less trouble than you think with questions."

"She. The PAO is a woman."

"How wonderful for you."

Dan thought for a moment. There was something else he had wanted to tell the EA. Then it came to him.

"Sir, one other thing. The PAO, Lieutenant Commander McGonagle, said something that might be relevant, especially if the press begins to dig."

"And that is?"

"That she knew another Lieutenant Hardin, a woman officer, down in CHINFO a couple years back. She remembered because the woman was killed in a traffic accident of some kind over in the District."

"And why is that germane?"

"I'm not sure it is. But if this lieutenant and that one were related, brother and sister, say, it would mean that the family had lost two children in the service in two years. If nothing else, the CACO ought to be told that."

"I see." Manning's voice softened a micron. "Yes. And it might be more effective for me to transmit that information to the bureau than for you to."

"Yes, sir, it might. I don't know that it's true, though. Hardin isn't that unusual a name."

"All right. Anything else?"

"No, sir. When we make some more progress, I'll phone in again."

"Very well." Manning hung up. Dan put the phone down and rubbed his face. He always felt uncomfortable talking to the EAs. They wore their bosses' stripes so arrogantly, most of them, and yet they certainly seemed to be in synch with their flags' way of thinking. Like the bit about not going to the press conference. Having not yet had command, Dan had had little direct experience with the media, but he had heard stories about innocent lamby-pie naval officers sticking both feet in their mouth under the skillful questioning of a reporter. The EA was probably entirely correct in telling him not to go. EA. He had to check in with NavBase. There was a base telephone list on the blotter at his desk, and he dialed the number for the NavBase commander's office and asked for the EA.

"Sir, the EA's in with the admiral and the PAO. May I take a message?"

"No, not really. Commander McGonagle will be bringing them up to speed with what's going on with my investigation. I'm Commander Collins. I was mostly checking in."

"Oh, yes, sir, you're *that* commander. Hold, please."

He was put on hold for a minute, then switched over to a speaker phone. The voice that came on identified itself as Rear Admiral Bostick.

"Commander Collins, this is the admiral. I've got my PAO and my EA in the room with me. Why am I finding out about all this secondhand and a day late?"

"Yes, sir, I apologize for that, Admiral. I assumed that since the initial message came out of Philly about the body being found that you at least knew about that, Admiral, which is why I went straight to the NIS field office. As to my heading up the investigation—"

"Yeah, what the hell, over? Since when does OpNav handle a murder investigation in one of the shipyards? You talked to the shipyard commander yet?"

"Uh, no, sir, I haven't."

"Well, you're a regular Lone Ranger, aren't you? I still don't understand why you are here instead of the NIS."

Dan was getting a little tired of all the fanging. He could just imagine the smug look on the NavBase EA's face about now.

"Well, sir, as Oh-six explained it, the Vice CNO wants it done that way. I guess all I can suggest at this juncture is that you call—"

"Don't be impertinent, Commander. You know damn well I'm not going to call a four-star and ask him anything of the sort. But if you want to succeed in this investigation, I suggest you don't come in here like some Washington hotshot and start throwing your weight around. I can make life very difficult for you, young man."

"Yes, sir. Aye, aye, sir," Dan intoned dutifully.

"That's better. That's the first correct thing I've heard you say. Now, I want you at that press conference this afternoon."

"Admiral, I can't do that."

There was a moment of silence, then he heard McGonagle's voice in the background ask why not.

"Because I've been ordered not to by . . ." He hesitated for a split second. Here was an admiral who wanted him at the press conference, but it was only a captain, the EA, who had told him not to go. But he'd used that royal *we*—did the EA speak for 06? 06B? And if ComNavBase pulled the string, would the EA back him up? "The DCNO, OP-Oh-six. Vice Admiral Layman," he finished.

There was silence on the other line, which he rushed to fill. "Apparently under the theory that if I'm identified but not actually there, the PAO can't tell them any more than the bare facts."

He thought he heard McGonagle say, "Thanks a heap, Commander" before the speakerphone was muted on the other end. Dan waited. Finally, the admiral came back on, his voice a little less angry.

"Okay. I think I'm beginning to get the picture here, and I guess I do need to make some calls. What's the EA's name in Oh-six?"

"Captain Manning, Admiral."

"All right. I want you to check in with my office at the end of each day that you're here. No more surprises."

"Aye, aye, sir," Dan said, and the connection was broken. Goddamned EAs, he thought. That little lieutenant commander had gone in there and told his mommy about the not-nice commander up from OpNav. He wondered if he ought to call Manning and tell him what he'd said about Admiral Layman ordering him away from the media. Screw it—he'd see what Manning did with it. Grace came back in.

"Any luck?" he asked.

"Only sort of. The medical examiner's office was underwhelmed with all my federal-case talk. They say that they work each homicide case in the order they come in, which probably means they'll get to it when they get to it. But they also said that the autopsies with a homicide tag are usually done within a day of receipt, so it won't be that long. The forensic investigator I talked to said that they had looked at the body and concluded that it will keep. I think that was a joke, by the way."

"Right, morgue humor. Okay, well, I just got my ass chewed by ComNavBase himself for operating on his turf without making the appropriate obeisances. Hopefully, the Oh-six EA will run top cover for me."

Grace pushed the door shut. "My headquarters may have had a hand in that. Robby Booker said something yesterday that didn't compute until just now, something about NIS Washington calling the base commander. If Roscoe Ames did that, your investigation would not have been presented in the best of lights."

"Wow. You mean they already knew? Turf *uber alles*, hunh? Do you get the feeling that the brass doesn't give a shit about who murdered this guy?"

Grace shrugged. "From what I've seen, the Washington right answer to that question is that there will always be murders to solve, but when an organization's power, authority, or budget is threatened, that takes first precedence. Always."

Dan leaned back in his chair. She was probably absolutely correct. There was a knock on the door, and Santini stuck his head in.

"Commander, there's some guy from Channel Six news on the horn. Wants to talk about you know what."

"How in the hell did he get this number?"

"He says ComNavBase public affairs office gave it to him." Santini was trying hard not to smile.

"Tell him that the Navy will have a statement to make at fifteen hundred today and that he should contact the base PAO for details. I'm not talking to any press weenies, period."

"You got it," Santini said, not bothering to hide his amusement now. He backed out and closed the door.

"Those sons a bitches," Dan began.

"The press?"

"No, the NavBase. They're mad at me for being here, so they sic the media on me."

"So, turn it around."

"Hunh?"

"Call the NavBase EA and tell him to knock it off or you *will* talk to the press and make NavBase look like a bunch of anally oriented individuals. Say you'll tell the next reporter who calls in the reason you're here is that NavBase is so screwed up, Washington had to send somebody in to unscrew it."

Dan looked at her with fresh admiration. "I like the way you think," he said. "But getting embroiled in turf fights won't do anything for the investigation—much as I'd love to do that."

"Okay." She sighed. "It was just a thought. So what do we do now?"

"We wait. Santini is supposedly developing background data on the kid's disappearance, if there is any. BuPers will have a CACO in motion pretty soon and is trying to dynamite the guy's records out of the St. Louis depository. The corpse rangers downtown will get to the autopsy when they get to it, apparently. The base PAO has a press conference set up for fifteen hundred. I need to sit down and write up what's gone on so far, but if you can think of something we ought to be doing—"

"Well, the only thing that's nagging at my mind is the battleship. Who would have access to the interior of that ship? I mean, not just anybody can go in there, right? They need access, breathing rigs, somebody who's aware that they're down inside that thing in a lethal atmosphere, in case they don't come back on time."

Dan was nodding his head. "Which would indicate that whoever planted the body knew how to do all that."

"Perhaps. Or a least they had some help from the people who do that on a regular basis."

"That's the shipyard. I guess we can go talk to someone in the yard, see how all that works. It'll get us out of here, at any rate."

"Maybe that ship's superintendent, Lieutenant Gravely, can help us out."

It took them an hour and a half to locate the ship's superintendent for

USS *Wisconsin*. The production shop's administrative staff had informed them that the lieutenant was ship's supe on three current overhauls in addition to his duties of supervising the caretaking of the battleship. They tracked him down finally aboard a wooden-hulled minesweeper in Dry Dock Four that was being prepared for decommissioning and layup. The ship's supe was not terribly informative. He told them that Shop 72, the riggers, had responsibility for monitoring the mothballed ships, especially the bigger ships on deep-nitrogen layup. Shop 72 had responsibility for pier-to-hull connections and for providing all rigging services within the yard—rigging meaning physical lifting, palletizing, crane service, forklifts, and gas-free engineering. It was the latter responsibility that was pertinent, in that Shop 72 maintained the breathing rigs for sounding-and-security personnel going inside the ships where there was no breathable atmosphere.

"So if you want to know about getting into *Wisconsin*, it would have to be the riggers, and I have to tell you, that's a pretty closed gang. They're like roustabouts or stevedores: They have a tough, physical, generally low-skilled job to do, so the kinds of guys they get tend to match that description. And you're talking about something that probably happened a couple of years ago. Most of the rigger crews have turned over a couple of times in that long a time."

Dan thanked him but decided to go talk to the Shop 72 foremen, anyway. If nothing else, he could put in his report that he had followed the lead as far as it went. They walked through the industrial area to the offices of Shop 72. When they arrived, it became obvious that someone had made a call, because the Shop 72 group superintendent, the boss of bosses, had nothing of substance to say to them. According to him, the security practices with respect to the mothballed ships were entirely adequate and there was no way somebody could just get aboard one of those ships, much less inside.

"But somebody did," Dan pointed out.

"I don't know anything about that, and I'm sure no one here does, either. It had to be somebody from the outside; my riggers wouldn't do that kind of thing. That's all I can tell you, Commander. And if you talk to any of the riggers, that's all they can tell you, too."

"In other words," Dan said to Grace as they left the office, "Don't go talking to my people, because I've told my people not to talk to you."

"That was a pretty good armadillo act," Grace agreed.

They stopped off at one of the shop canteens before going back to the NIS office. The canteen was squeezed into a questionably clean corner room of a warehouse. It had fly-specked screened windows, a single counter, a noisy, grease-covered exhaust fan, a respectable population of flies and bees patrolling two overflowing trash cans, and an extremely obese counterman decked out in catsup-stained whites. It was almost 2:30 P.M., and Dan was not anxious to return to the office, lest there be another summons from NavBase to attend the press conference. Figuring that if it came out of

116

boiling water, it ought not to make them too sick, they both ordered a hot dog.

They went outside to eat their hot dogs, batting away the swarming yellow jackets. As they were searching for napkins, a long-haired, pimply-faced young man sidled up to the canteen door. He was wearing the yellow hard hat of the rigger force, with a large X-72 stenciled on the front. He looked Grace over and then went inside and bought a hot dog with everything and a Coke. He came back out and stood next to an overflowing trash basket while he stuffed his face, giving Grace another once-over in the process. She was, as usual, wearing relatively shapeless clothing: loose wool slacks, a sweater, with a blouse underneath, and comfortable shoes. Dan had shifted from dress blues to working blues: black trousers and a long-sleeved black shirt with a black tie and his commander's silver oak leaves on the collar points. They both wore white plastic hard hats because they were in the industrial area.

When the rigger was finished, he crumpled up the debris into the trash basket and, after looking both ways, said something to Dan.

"What's that?" Dan asked, shaking a mustard-covered bee off his hand.

"I said, 'Yo.' You the guys wanna know somethin' 'bout the stiff in the Wo-Wo?"

Wo-Wo, Dan thought. Ah, *Wisconsin*. "That's right. I'm Commander Collins."

The boy sidled over to them, again staring at Grace as if trying to decide whether or not she was a woman who merited further attention. He looked around again, as if to see who might be watching, then turned back to Collins, ignoring Grace now.

"You guys need to talk to old Brannie Gutowski. He useta be a head rigger here, coupla years back. Hangs out over at McGurn's gin mill, over there on Fifteenth and Porter, near the Diablo Club. He's retired, on accounta his drinkin', but he's a guy. Anybody knows what went down with that dead guy got dug up in the Wo-Wo, Ski's your guy; check it out, man."

"I will. Thanks for the tip." Dan wanted to ask the boy some questions, but the boy again looked around one more time and then sauntered off.

"Feel like an adventure?" Dan asked. Grace grimaced but then nodded.

15

THEY CAME OUT of the industrial area right at 3:00 P.M. and walked up toward the main gate along the extension of Philadelphia's Broad Street on the naval station. Grace pointed out not one but two television vans parked in front of the administration building as they passed by, and they both quickened their step. Dan thought fleetingly about how McGonagle was doing in there. They found a cab out by the main gate and told the driver the destination. The driver turned around and looked at both of them, shook his head, and pulled away from the curb. Dan wondered what they were getting into but did not share his apprehensions with Grace. After a ten-block ride, they turned left onto Porter Street for three blocks, then did a midblock U-turn that elicited a small gasp from Grace. The cab pulled up in front of a seedy-looking place with a dirty neon sign proclaiming it as McGurn's Bar and Grill. The front window was tinted black and was so dirty, it did not even reflect the weak red neon sign above it. Dan paid the cabbie and they got out and went into the bar.

The interior was about what Dan expected: one long, narrow room with a bar and stools on the right and some dilapidated booths on the left. There was a row of low-wattage yellow light fixtures running down above the booths, and a single fan in the overhead stirring the stink of old beer and cigarette smoke. The floor appeared to be some kind of very old linoleum. Behind the bar were glass shelves containing the heavenly host of assorted rotguts stacked up against a large mirror. Mercifully, the place was empty, except for a surly-looking bartender and a solitary white man sitting on the last stool, closest to a television that was playing soundlessly above their heads.

"Almost heaven," muttered Grace.

"Bet that's our guy," Dan said, and walked down toward the end of the bar.

The bartender gave them a quick glance, then turned his back on them, picking up a glass and wiping it deliberately. He apparently knew heat when he saw it. Dan was suddenly conscious of his uniform as he focused on the lumpy man at the end of the bar. The man was in his sixties, pendulously fat, with a round red face, a fringe of white hair around an extensive bald spot, a bulbous red nose, and a vacant expression that he had focused somewhere about a half a mile into the mirror behind the bar. Dan concluded that he was indeed one of the fixtures, given his posture on the stool.

"Excuse me, are you Mr. Brannie Gutowski?" Dan asked.

The fat man did not acknowledge the question, except to hunch farther down on his bar stool, clutching the almost-empty glass of beer in his hands. When he did not reply, Grace stepped around Dan, flipped open her NIS credentials, and shoved them into the fat man's face.

"We're federal police officers," she announced. "Are you Brannie Gutowski?"

The bartender spat dramatically on the floor behind the bar but kept his back turned. The fat man finally acknowledged them.

"Yeah, so what if I am?"

Dan stepped in. "We'd like to ask you a few questions about something that happened in the yard a couple years back."

"I'm retired, for Chrissakes," Gutowski complained. "I don't rememer shit about the goddamned yard, so whyn't ya jist leave me the hell alone."

"We will," Dan said. "Just as soon as you answer a couple of questions for us. This won't be hard or even complicated. I'll even buy you a beer, how's that?"

There was a glint of interest in the fat man's eyes.

"Let's move over here to a booth; that way, we can keep it all nice and private. Bartender, give this man a refill."

The bartender turned around and gave them both a sullen look before taking Gutowski's glass. He refilled it from one of the taps and banged it down on the bar, slopping some foam. As Gutowski reached for the glass, Dan had an idea.

"Why don't you sweeten that brew up a little there, bartender. Looks kind of watery to me."

The bartender stared at him for a second and then reached for a bottle of gin and a shot glass. He filled the shot glass to the line and pushed it over toward Gutowski, who grabbed it greedily and slugged it down.

"One more for the road," Dan ordered while Grace picked up the glass of beer and moved it over to a booth. Gutowski slugged down the second hit, belched, looked around for the truant beer, and then unlimbered his sagging body off the stool and squeezed himself onto the bench seat of the nearest booth. Dan dropped a ten spot on the bar and sat down opposite the bleary-eyed ex-yardbird. Grace stood over Gutowski's shoulder, between the man and the bartender, who had moved away toward the other end of the bar. Dan lowered his voice.

"Okay, Mr. Gutowski. Here's the deal. We're conducting an investigation into the disappearance of an officer, a supply corps officer, in the shipyard about two years ago. A guy in the yard suggested we come talk to you."

Gutowski stared up at Dan, taking in the Navy uniform for the first time. "What the hell are you?" he asked.

"I'm Commander Collins, from the staff of the Chief of Naval Operations in Washington, D.C. Miss Snow here is from a federal criminal investigation service, the NIS. We're conducting an investigation into the discovery of a body aboard the battleship *Wisconsin* in the yard."

Dan thought he saw a flicker of recognition in the fat man's eyes. "This body," Gutowski said. "This the guy gone missin'? The black boy?"

"We think so, yes. He was an officer in the Navy."

"An' you guys think I done somethin'?"

Dan sat back. "No, we don't. But we understand that the riggers, the Shop Seventy-two guys, are the only ones who can get into a mothballed ship—because of the nitrogen atmosphere. You were a rigger boss then; we're wondering if you heard anything about this incident."

"Nope." Gutowski stared at Dan, and then there was a hint of a triumphant grin. "But thanks for the booze."

Dan stared back at him. Then Grace spoke up from behind Gutowski.

"Commander, there's an easier way."

Dan didn't know where she was going with it, but he followed her lead. "Yes?"

"We go downtown, talk to the FBI, get a couple of local Italian names. We go talk to them, let it drop that Mr. Body Beautiful here said some things implicating the family in our case." She paused to let it sink in. "Why don't you just leave Mr. Gutowski here a card. I think he's going to need to find us before we'll need to find him."

"Sounds like a plan," Dan said, moving to get up.

"Hey, wait a goddamned minute," Gutowski protested. "You can't do that! I didn't say shit to you guys!"

"But you will," Dan said, fishing for his business cards. "I'm glad you enjoyed that booze. Careful of where you walk next couple of days."

"Wait a minute, wait a goddamned minute here. Siddown. You guys fuckin' nuts, or what?"

"Your memory coming back, Mr. Gutowski?"

Gutowski looked around to see how far away the bartender was before answering. He hunched his shoulders and lowered his head, not looking directly at Dan anymore.

"I don't *know* nuthin', okay? I jist heard some shit, here'n there, around the yard. This is two years ago, awright? Shit's kinda fuzzy."

"I understand. So what was the word?"

"The black guy—the Navy said he was a paymaster. Word was that he shagged ass with the payroll from the ship."

"Was that the *Luce?*"

"I dunno. One a the ships in the yard. Whatever. They was all lookin' for him, but not in the yard. Word was he'd booked, see?"

"But he hadn't."

"Yeah, well, that's the funny thing, you talkin' about the guineas. A coupla months after this ni— black guy splits, the word goes around that the payroll story is all bullshit, that what really happened is that it was a hit—the guy got whacked. Reason I remember is that the guy who told me got his ass kicked by some a the goombahs from the inside machine shop, runnin' his mouth 'bout shit that didn't concern him, you know? They beat that guy up pretty good, and then there wasn't no more said about it, you follow me?"

"Nothing about stashing the guy in the battleship?"

"Hell no. I mean, shit, those goddamned battleships are spooky enough without no dead bodies in 'em. Word like that ever got out, nobody in the Seventy-two shop would ever go in one again. Everybody knows them things are haunted-up."

Dan sat back and looked at Grace, who shrugged. The front door opened and two men came in, both sporting shipyard hard hats. Grace gave Dan the high sign, and Dan got up out of the booth. He was about to thank

120

Gutowski, but something in Grace's expression stopped him. She stepped around Dan and looked down at Gutowski.

"Since you wouldn't cooperate with us, Mr. Gutowski, we're going to go get a bench warrant and bring you in for formal questioning," she announced in a loud voice. "So maybe you'd better rethink your story between now and then. Thanks for nothing. Commander."

They walked past the two staring newcomers and out of the bar. Dan remembered that Broad Street, the main drag, was back to the right, so they turned in that direction.

"You think Gutowski figured out you were doing him a favor?" Dan asked.

"I very much doubt it," she said. "His brain is so booze-soaked, he probably can't figure out his name most of the time. But that was an interesting story."

Dan nodded as he looked around for a cab. When they reached Broad, there was a heavy volume of traffic coming from the direction of the shipyard, but no cabs in sight on their side of the avenue. Some of the locals were staring curiously at his uniform.

"What the hell, you want to walk it? It's not raining, and I think it was only about ten blocks."

"I suppose we can," she said. "As long as it's daylight. That area around the stadium did not look too promising."

"Don't you carry a gun?" he asked as they started walking.

"Not normally, although I am licensed to, or was. Now that I think about it, being in Career Services, I'm not sure that the license is still valid. Only the field investigators go armed, and then not all the time."

"Pity. I'd bet a lot of these guys around here are carrying. What'd you think of Gutowski's story about this being a mob hit of some kind."

She concentrated on getting across the next street before replying. Dan found he had to shorten his stride so that she could walk without hurrying.

"Kind of far-fetched. I mean, really, if the supply officer had been embezzling money, then I could see some kind of involvement with the mob, you know, loan-sharking, gambling, a drug habit. But if that was true, we would have stumbled across a separate NIS investigation file about that in connection with his name by now."

"Your guys at NIS were going to look into that, weren't they? We really need to pull the string on that when we get back."

"I'll do that."

Dan paused at the next corner. "And," he said, "I kind of think we ought to keep this angle to ourselves for the moment."

The light changed and they crossed. On the other side, Grace walked on for a few strides before responding.

"Why do you say that?" she asked. "That almost sounds like you don't trust Santini, the NIS, or the people at NavBase, for that matter."

He stopped on the sidewalk to face her. "I'm not really sure I do trust Santini or anybody in the NavBase organization right now. They're angry that we're here, for different reasons, but they are perfectly capable of making common cause out of it. In their eyes, whatever we turn up is going to make NavBase and the NISRA look bad, so I'm not really expecting much help."

She looked at him. "That's going to make my working with you rather awkward. If you don't trust the NIS, then you implicitly can't trust me."

"I didn't say that, Grace."

"I work for them, Dan. You work for OpNav. OpNav has initiated a potentially lethal gambit against NIS by appointing you to head this investigation. And frankly, I'm not convinced that actually solving this case is as important to OpNav as torpedoing the NIS."

Dan resumed walking up the street toward the shipyard. Grace followed, waiting for an answer. He stopped again.

"Okay. I see your point. You may well be right," he said. "I suspect that, from the Washington perspective, the power struggle between OpNav and NIS *is* paramount, and the case incidental. But that's all the more reason for you and me to keep our findings to ourselves, at least for now. If we get tangled up in the power game, we're both going to get chewed up—this battle is being fought by people who are way above your pay grade and mine. I think the only safe thing for us to do is to focus on the investigation and go where it leads us. I mean, what the hell, a naval officer has been murdered here."

She resumed walking this time, while he walked alongside, waiting for her answer. He wondered if he had been wrong to assume they could be partners. She might have much more at stake careerwise than he had in this investigation. He could write his report and go on with his naval career. She was probably trying to salvage her career. Then he saw her nodding to herself.

"All right," she said. "That makes sense. But promise me this: We'll play the investigation absolutely straight, with nothing held back between us. And when OpNav does or asks something that's driven entirely by the rice-bowl issue, you have to let me know. And I'll do the same for you, okay?"

"But aren't you required to relay that kind of information back to NIS?"

"Aren't you required to do the same thing for your bosses at OpNav?"

He remembered Admiral Carson's instructions—"Be like E.T. He had been instructed to call home when he had something to tell about the NIS, but not about the investigation. "Of course," he replied.

"Well, then," she said. "If we both do it, we're square with each other and we maintain the integrity of the investigation. What the rice-bowl pooh-bah's do with our 'intelligence' is their problem."

He saw the logic of it. Maintaining the integrity of the investigation was their only protection, he as a line commander conducting a JAG investigation, she as a career investigator trying to reestablish her professional reputation.

"You're absolutely right. God, that's scary."

"What's scary?"

"A woman who makes perfectly logical sense."

"Up thine, as the Quakers are wont to say," she said, and he laughed out loud. She gave him a quick grin. They could see the main gates to the shipyard about five blocks ahead.

"I presume you're going to check right in with NavBase?" she asked sweetly.

Dan groaned above the noise of the traffic. "It's four o'clock," he said. "So, actually, I was hoping just to knock off ship's work and go out on liberty. But I suspect there may be a phone call or six waiting for me from my new friends at NavBase. McGonagle is probably really unhappy with me by now."

Santini was waiting for them when they got back to the NIS office. The rest of the NIS crew was wrapping up for the day. Santini indeed had a handful of yellow phone message slips in his hand for Dan, and one for Grace.

"Commander Popularity," he said, handing Dan the phone messages. "The NavBase EA especially wants you to check in. Apparently, the press conference was not such a wonderful time. Lieutenant Commander McGonagle is not a happy camper just now."

"I can just imagine," Dan said. "Grace, why don't you go over what Mr. Santini here has produced from his local files while I go make some phone calls."

Dan sat down in his borrowed chair and scanned the messages. The first one caught his eye immediately: from Captain Manning, the 06 EA. There was another "call me" message from the NavBase EA, and three from McGonagle. The rest were from journalists. He checked his watch and decided to take the EAs in order of importance. He tried the 06 EA first.

"Vice Admiral Layman's office, Senior Chief Preston speaking, sir."

"Senior Chief, this is Commander Collins calling from Philly. Is Captain Manning available?"

"Let me check, Commander," the chief said, putting Dan on hold. The chief came back a minute later. "He's attending the JCS debrief right now, Commander. He asked that you call back in thirty minutes."

"Right. Know what he called about, Senior Chief?"

"Uh, not exactly, sir. I think the VCNO's EA, Captain Randall, called him, but I don't know the subject."

"Right. Okay. I'll be back in thirty."

Dan hung up, took a deep breath, called the NavBase headquarters, and asked the yeoman who answered for the EA.

"He's in conference right now with the admiral and the PAO, Commander. But he did tell me that the admiral would *really* like to see you."

Dan grimaced. "I can just imagine, Yeoman Hardy. Let me see if I can arrange a root canal first, and then I'll run right over."

The yeoman laughed. "Between you and me, Commander, the admiral yells a lot, but he's a pretty good guy, actually."

"Okay, Hardy. I'm in the NIS field office. You guys are right next door, correct?"

"Yes, sir. Second deck. Executive offices at the end of the hall nearest the river."

Dan grabbed his commander's hat and found Grace huddled with Santini in his office. "ComNavBase requests the pleasure of my company on his very own scaffold," he told her. "Want to come along?"

"Not particularly, but I will," she said, gathering her purse. "We're done here. Carl, I guess we'll see you in the morning."

As they went down the stairs, Dan asked her what Santini had produced. Grace stopped in the lobby to consult her notebook. Dan realized that he needed a notebook of his own.

"Not much. The local NIS files did have a report of the assistant supply officer's disappearance, but, according to Carl, no indications of any other kind of investigation. The ship did an audit of the disbursing operation and found everything in order. The file contained the standard form for cross-bureau notifications after thirty days and a copy of the BuPers declaration of deserter status for one Lt. (jg) Wesley Hardin."

"Had NIS interviewed anybody in connection with the disappearance?"

"No, although there was a note taped to the declaration form that a Mrs. Hardin had called in and that the call had been returned by a Mr. Kent Friedman of the field office. But no info."

"Damn. Was Hardin married?"

"I don't know. Hope not."

16

THEY LEFT THE SHIPYARD administration building and walked next door to the NavBase headquarters, a three-story building made of brick that was almost black from industrial pollution. Dan wanted to ask Grace if she thought Santini was leveling with her, but he decided against it as they entered the admin building.

The main lobby was decked out like a ship's quarterdeck, complete with a large wooden steering wheel next to a brass engine-order telegraph, flags in wooden stands, pictures of all the previous NavBase commanders, and an entire picture wall of ships that had been built or overhauled in the

Philadelphia yards. There was a reception desk to one side, but no one present for duty. They went up the wide staircase to the second floor and walked down the dusty linoleum hallway, past a row of silent and darkened offices, to the admiral's office at the far end. Dan opened the glass-paneled door and stood aside for Grace to precede him into the clerical and reception area. There was a single yeoman working on an antique Wang word processor, two other empty desks, and a set of bat-wing wooden doors behind the yeoman's desk. The yeoman looked up, realizing who the visitors were.

"Commander Collins? I'm YN Three Hardy."

"This is Miss Snow from the NIS, Hardy. We're here to see the admiral. But before we go in, I need you to do me a favor. Call this number—that's the OP-Oh-six front office in the Pentagon—and leave a message for the EA that I'll call in right after I've seen Admiral Bostick."

"Can do, Commander. Let me tell them you're here."

But he did not have to; Lieutenant Commander VanSladen appeared at the bat-wing doors and motioned for them to come into the admiral's office. Dan was pleased to see that VanSladen looked just like he sounded: prissy, smug, and relatively small. Dan was surprised at how plush the inner office was—deep red carpet, mahogany desk and furniture, a window wall that gave an impressive view of the Delaware River, the shipyard, and the upper reaches of Philadelphia's waterfront. There was a long library table along one picture-covered wall, surrounded by conference chairs. The admiral, dressed in his service dress blues minus his jacket, sat at the head of the table, with a harassed-looking Lieutenant Commander McGonagle in a side chair. A large television was on but muted in the corner of the room. The admiral, an elderly, short man with white hair and a razor-thin mustache, peered at Collins and then Snow over half-lens glasses.

"You the Washington weenies?" he asked. He sounded exasperated.

"Yes, sir," Dan answered, preempting the EA's attempts to introduce them. "I'm Comdr. Dan Collins from OpNav, and this is Miss Grace Snow from NIS headquarters."

The admiral grunted but did not invite them to sit down. The EA resumed his seat, smirking officiously.

"Commander," the admiral began, taking off his glasses. "Why weren't you at the press conference as I asked you to be?"

"We were conducting interviews with people for the investigation, Admiral. By the time we were finished, the conference was over."

The admiral shook his head. "Let me tell you something, young man. As long as you are operating in my area of responsibility, if I want you to be somewhere, I expect you to be there or to tell me why not. In advance, understand?"

Dan had had enough. He thought this issue had been settled. "Admiral, have you spoken with Admiral Carson or Admiral Layman?"

"Nope. And I don't plan to just because you suggested to my EA here that I should."

Dan nodded. "Admiral, I'm conducting a JAGMAN investigation into what appears to be a homicide. I was designated as the investigating officer by direction of the VCNO. I didn't ask for this assignment. But, sir, if you propose to schedule my time and activities while I'm here, I will have to file a message report with the Navy JAG that my investigation is being manipulated by ComNavBase Philadelphia. I have had specific instructions from Op-Oh-six regarding command influence on this investigation."

The room went very quiet. Dan thought he heard Grace inhale sharply. The EA's jaw dropped and the admiral stared hard at Dan, who stared back. He knew he was out of line in terms of the respect due a rear admiral from a commander, but he also knew that if he did not stake out his own turf right now, the admiral and his staff would run him all over the place until he left. The admiral blinked first. He opened his mouth as if to say something but then clamped his jaw shut and looked down at the table for a moment.

"Okay," he said. "Point taken. The integrity of the investigation must of course be preserved." Dan felt the room relax fractionally. "What I *do* have to do," the admiral continued, "is to coordinate the public affairs response with Washington. With CHINFO. Do you wish to be a part of that co-ordination or not?"

Dan was about to say yes when Grace Snow spoke up. "We do not, Admiral. What we need is as complete a screening from the media as we can get. We would ask that Lieutenant Commander VanSladen not give out our names or phone numbers to any more members of the press."

The admiral glanced sideways at his EA and then back at Grace. Dan noted that the EA appeared to be embarrassed. Score one for Grace.

"And you are, again, Miss—"

"I'm Grace Ellen Snow, Admiral. I'm a GS-fifteen with the NIS. I'm the operational liaison between Commander Collins's investigation and the investigative resources of the NIS."

The admiral leaned back in his chair. "I'm confused," he said. "Is the NIS conducting this investigation or is OpNav?"

"It's an independent one-officer JAGMAN investigation, Admiral," Dan interjected. "The NIS is acting in support."

"Can I reveal that angle to the media?" asked McGonagle. "There was a question on that from CBS."

"No," said Dan after getting a confirmatory nod from Grace. "What I suggest we do here is to have Commander McGonagle check with me at fourteen hundred each day, for as long as we're here, anyway. I'll give her a fact sheet of what I think are releasable bits of information. She can coordinate that with CHINFO in D.C., and the Navy public affairs organization can decide what to release and what to hold. You, sir," he said, indicating the admiral, "would of course be privy to the facts proposed for release. And if we turn up anything that could be classified as, let's say, sensational, we will inform your office right away—through Commander McGonagle."

The admiral nodded, his indignation mollified somewhat by Dan's return to customary deference. Every officer in the room knew that face was being saved.

"So where do you stand now?" asked the admiral.

Dan reviewed the facts of the case to date, omitting their little discussion with Gutowski.

"We're kind of in a holding pattern until we get the official results of the autopsy from the medical examiner," he concluded. "We also need to study the victim's personal and professional records. We have what certainly must be a homicide, but we have nothing whatsoever on motive, or even means, for that matter. We think that somebody killed the lieutenant and then dumped his body in a ship with no atmosphere. It was only a fluke that he was found at all; the last time that ship was mothballed, it was for nearly forty years."

"So somebody meant not only to kill him but also to hide the body for goddamn ever."

"Yes, sir, that's what it looks like. But we're a long way from having our hands on the facts to support that or any other conclusions."

"So what's your plan?"

Before Dan could answer, the yeoman stuck his head in.

"Commander Collins, there's a call from the DCNO for Plans and Policy's office for you."

Dan excused himself from the inner office and took the call out front. Grace remained in the inner office; Dan could hear her talking as he picked up the phone.

"Commander Collins speaking, sir."

"This is Captain Manning. I've had a call from Captain Randall."

"The VCNO's EA?"

"That's correct. CHINFO's EA called the VCNO's office and told him that your investigation has gone public. He wanted to know what you have turned up so far."

Dan gave him a status report, again omitting anything about the ex-rigger's theories.

"The locals cooperating?"

"NIS isn't overtly throwing up obstacles, although their records seem to be pretty slim on this case. The NavBase tried to stick its nose in, but I think I have that under control."

"The *NavBase*? Does someone need to be stepped on?"

"No, sir, I don't think so, at least not right now. The main thing is to keep the press from getting directly to me or the investigation. I plan to hand in some facts that I think are releasable each day to NavBase PAO and let them coordinate with CHINFO so that there's a Navy press position instead of my getting into it."

"That sounds intelligent. But you're pretty sure this is a homicide case?"

"Yes, sir. Lieutenant Hardin didn't go into that battleship under his own power."

"How do you know that?"

"Because there's no air down there. The ship is under a nitrogen blanket from the main deck and below."

There was a moment of silence. "I see," the EA said. "Very well. Do you have anything else to tell me?"

"No, sir. BuPers is taking care of getting the records and the CACO—Hardin's family is there in D.C. We're working on the access issue and reviewing NIS files here while we wait for the forensics to come back."

"Very well," Manning said again, and then he simply broke the connection. Dan looked at the phone for a second. *And you have a nice day, too, Captain Cold Fish.* Every EA he'd ever met acted like that. The hell of it was that most of them at the three- and four-star staff level went from their EA jobs to flag selection and stars of their own, so their arrogance was based on credible expectations. His own boss, Captain Summerfield, was a notable exception—he had been EA to the vice chief who had preceded the current incumbent, Admiral Torrance. The rumor among the action officers was that Summerfield had not gone on to flag rank purportedly because of his wife's stroke during the second year of his assignment, which was also the reason he was now in the less demanding job of branch head of OP-614.

Dan looked at his watch. It was going on 6:00 P.M. He went back into the inner office. Everyone was watching the local evening news on the television, where the body in the battleship was receiving prominent coverage. McGonagle's prepared statement was terse and rigidly factual, and the station ran the tape through three of her "no comment" responses to questions before cutting back to the reporter for some breathless speculation. The admiral muted the set.

"I see we're not going to get just a passing reference to this mess," he said.

"I suggest that you forward all further inquiries directly to CHINFO in Washington," Grace said. "That way, you can feed them information but let them take the heat."

"Count on it," McGonagle said with feeling.

"Admiral, if we're done here . . ." Dan said.

"Yes, I think so. I don't know what else to say other than to ask that you keep me as informed as you can. It's the blind side that I'm trying to avoid, Commander."

"Understood, Admiral. We'll do our best. But we can't control all the sources of information in a place like this. I suspect it was the ambulance crew, for instance, who called the news guys in the first place."

"Right. Believe me, I know that problem better than you ever will, Commander. Until that time when perhaps you get a command of your own, that is."

17

AT GRACE'S SUGGESTION, they took Dan's car down South Broad Street to the nearest McDonald's for dinner, deciding not to talk about the case in that very public place. Dan wanted to go back to the O-club for a beer afterward; as usual, the club was nearly deserted except for a few stalwarts at the bar. They took a table in the corner. Dan asked her about the single message she had received back in the NIS office.

"It was my version of your E.T. message," she said. "Doug Englehardt wanted an update."

"I had a telephone audience with the Oh-six EA," he replied. "He apparently was being queried by the VCNO's EA."

"These EAs work the web, don't they?" she observed.

"I'm never sure whether I'm speaking to a Navy captain or a vice admiral's surrogate when I talk to Manning—he's the Oh-six EA. Guy's just a real bundle of personality."

Grace rotated her glass between her hands slowly. She knew another EA who was just like that. "Admiral Keeler—he's director of the NIS—has an executive assistant," she said. "A Captain Rennselaer. Not a very approachable sort, one of those people who is considerably better than thee or me. I think he had a claw in my internal reassignment. Anyway, Doug Englehardt didn't have anything special to report. Early days, I think."

Dan nodded. "I'm sure Santini's keeping them fully informed, in case you become corrupted by close association with an OpNav devil."

"What's more likely," she said. "is that they'll check what I tell them against what he tells them. I also talked to Robby Booker today, asking him to expedite our RFI. He implied that the data center was less than optimistic when he asked for an expedite on it."

"Booker a buddy of yours?"

"Sort of. Actually, yes. I took his side in a nasty little racial dispute. He lost, which was at least partly his fault, but that's when I was first tagged as a troublemaker. He's a product of the streets of Washington—very smart, cagey, and energetic. He spends almost all his time in the headquarters. He told me once that he couldn't believe he got a job there, and that there wasn't that much to go home to. When it comes to the workings of the NIS headquarters, though, he's a regular little ferret."

"And he can give you a sense of how the bigs are reacting to this investigation?"

"Yes. And that might become very helpful. But remember, I was somewhat suspect before I came out on this assignment."

"Makes me wonder if the various players on my side are telling me everything they know. Damn, it gets complicated."

She smiled at him and changed the subject. "Do you remember our talking about this Hardin incident being connected with the mob? And you said a junior lieutenant was too low level an officer to attract attention? Now we have someone saying it *was* a hit. Any second thoughts?"

Dan thought about her question for a moment. He had noticed that she had maneuvered the direction of the conversation away from their political relationship.

"What I said before," he replied, "was in the context of a junior officer discovering something that might inconvenience the mob, and jaygee's aren't likely to manage that. Now, an officer being involved personally in drugs or gambling—something that might take him to a loan shark—well, that's different. We'll need to explore that angle when we get confirmation that this is Hardin, and then maybe try to talk to shipmates who served with him in *Luce*."

"You said that's going to be hard to do."

"It might. The ship's been decommissioned, and crews and wardroom officers scatter in two years' time. We certainly won't find anybody here from *Luce*, for instance."

"And the records, the bureau, the Hardin family—they're all back in Washington, aren't they?"

"Yes. Ah, I see your point. Once we get the facts about the circumstances of his death, then the rest of this nut may have to be cracked back in D.C."

She nodded and then began to gather her things. "I agree that we'll need to exhume Lieutenant Hardin's character before we can approach motive and suspects. *What* happened to Hardin will probably be discoverable. Finding out *why* this happened will be the tough part."

She got up. "Now I'm tired. I thank you for the gourmet extravaganza tonight. I'll see you in the morning at the NIS field office, say eight o'clock?"

"Fine," he said. "I think I'm going to have another beer. I'm not ready to let go of all this atmosphere."

GRACE SMILED AS she left the club and walked across the parking lot between the club and the BOQ to her room. She undressed and decided to take her chances with the shower. The water pipes clanked and ran some rust initially, but at least there was hot water. She had not told Dan the entire truth about their RFI's status at headquarters. Robby had informed her that the data center had flat out stonewalled him. The lady who ran the place had pointed dramatically down the hall toward the admiral's office and told him that she had her instructions from Rennselaer himself.

"Oh, for God's sake," Grace had erupted. "If that pill's getting into it, we'll never get any information."

"It's cool," Robby had replied. "Latonya has the night shift in the data center. Me'n her, we tight. I'll get it."

As she dried off, she thought about Dan Collins. She was faintly embarrassed at having been positively voluble the other night about her personal background. She had told him more than she needed to, and she wondered why. Perhaps it was that aura of vulnerability about him. He was smart enough to recognize the general outlines of the turf battle, but perhaps a bit naïve as to exactly how nasty and even personal it could get. Maybe it was different for the officer corps. She had met other naval officers like that; they all seemed to believe that there were certain thresholds of personal honor and integrity, below which one did not go for something as trivial as bureaucratic power. She well knew that government civilians took these things much more seriously, and she sensed that the NIS headquarters mavens were circling the wagons over this one. Even Doug Englehardt, who was as close to a rabbi as she would have in the NIS organization, was not to be trusted entirely, especially since he was as interested in her personally as professionally. She had rebuffed a few subtle advances, and now, much as she needed a friend in upper management, she sensed that if it came to making a choice between keeping his job and saving hers, Englehardt would drop her over the Anacostia River seawall in a heartbeat. Wasn't government fun.

DAN AWOKE EARLY Thursday morning. Checking out what looked like the beginnings of a nice day outside, he decided to go for a short run around the grounds of the base. As he went out the BOQ doors to the parking lot, he encountered Grace Snow, who apparently had had the same idea. She was dressed out in a gray jersey tank top, some flimsy running shorts, and expensive-looking running shoes, and she was performing some interesting stretching exercises. Definitely a woman. He enjoyed the view for a minute before she noticed him and straightened back up, her face slightly flushed.

"Morning," he called. "Didn't figure you for a runner."

"Why, do I look that soft?" she asked, gathering her hair up into a barrette.

"Not at all. Well, maybe. I mean—" He stopped in some confusion when he realized she was laughing at him. "Aw hell, you want some company?"

"Sure." He did his own warmup and then they took off at a brisk pace, jogging down a perimeter road that went out along the abandoned runways of a now-defunct naval airfield and down to the Delaware River itself, where they encountered several other runners out enjoying the promising April morning. She kept up with him easily, challenging his casual assumption that she wouldn't be able to stay up with a man who ran five miles as easily as most men walked one block. They rounded the perimeter of the airfield and doubled back, enjoying the sunrise appearing over the gleaming steel stacks of the refineries across the river. When they finally got back to the main base area and dropped down into a walk, he had to work at it to keep from staring at her body, which in the flush of exertion was stirring some urges he hadn't felt in several years. He found himself imagining that this was how her face might look if they were making love. The thought surprised him. If she was aware of his interest, she gave no sign of it.

They agreed to meet in the NIS field office at 0730. Once there, Santini told them that the medical examiner's office had called. They had a preliminary report. He asked if Dan wanted to go over to the ME's office to talk to them or whether he should have them just fax it. He added that the ME needed those medical and dental records from the Navy. Dan had no desire to visit the city morgue, so he told Santini to get the prelim faxed over to them. He then called the master chief down in BuPers to get a status on the records.

"No status is what we've got, Commander. St. Louis says they're working on it."

"Is it possible to put a priority push on the dental records—we need them for a positive ID."

"I know, but with that outfit, I'd recommend them pressing ahead for the whole shebang. Now, you want a positive ID, you do have another alternative."

"What's that?"

"Get the CACO to get a family member up to Philly."

"Wow," Dan said. "I'd have to think about that. The body is . . . well, it's not mangled or anything, but it is . . . well, mummified. Looks like something out of the British Museum. That might be nightmare territory for a close relative."

"I don't know, Commander. I've talked to the CACO—she's a Lieutenant Shea out of NavSea, over in Crystal City. There's only one close relative, and that's Hardin's mother. I get the impression that knowing what happened to her missing son might be more important than what she's gonna see. You wanna talk to the CACO?"

"Yeah, I guess I'd better."

The master chief gave him Lieutenant Shea's phone number, and he was dialing it as Grace came into his cubicle with two coffees. He told her whom he was calling as the phone was ringing at the other end, then indicated for her to pick up the extension at another desk. He got Lieutenant Shea, identified himself, and asked her what she thought about having the mother come up to Philly to make an ID. To his surprise, she approved right away.

"I think we ought to do that, Commander. But I have to warn you, she's a pretty tough lady, and she's displaying a whole lot of animosity toward the Navy."

"Any idea why?"

"Well, sir, for starters, she had two children, a son and a daughter. Both went into the Navy."

"Yes, so?"

"And both are dead."

"Say again?" He saw Grace taking notes, and an elusive memory began to twitch somewhere in his head.

"That's right. The daughter was a lieutenant at CHINFO; she died in a traffic accident over in the District—a hit-and-run thing. Nobody was ever picked up for it. Two years ago. And then about two weeks after that happened, her son, also in the Navy, disappears. A master chief over in the bureau alerted me to check into this before I called on the family, and that's the story."

Then Dan remembered: Lieutenant Commander McGonagle had mentioned that she remembered the name. He had even told Manning. He shook his head. Better start writing this stuff down.

"Right," he said. "The base PAO up here knew something about that. I'd forgotten."

"Yes, sir. Well, I've visited the mother, Mrs. Hardin, twice. She was unfriendly, and I initially thought it was a black-white thing, but now I don't think so. I get the impression—and that's all this is, Commander, an impression, okay? I have no facts here. But I think she thinks the Navy somehow had something to do with her daughter's death and is maybe now covering up—or perhaps never properly investigated—her son's disappearance."

"Covering up a traffic accident? But why? And what was her reaction to the news that we might have found her son?"

"Sort of a suspicions-confirmed thing. Some nasty talk about how long we, the Navy, have been covering this thing up, that sort of thing. She's very angry and very distrustful."

"You have my sympathy, Lieutenant. Being a CACO is tough enough without this kind of stuff."

"The manual says that the bereaved react in different ways, and this is one of them, I suppose. What do you want me to do, Commander? I'd like to move this little assignment right along, if you know what I'm saying."

"Yeah, well, we're at the point where we really need a positive ID. Let me talk to my, uh, people up here. I'll get back to you shortly."

Dan hung up and looked over at Grace. He had almost said "partner," but then, realizing she was listening, changed his mind at the last second. When she walked back over to his cubicle, he told her that the Philadelphia ME's office was faxing out a prelim on the cause of death but that without the dental records, they could not make a positive identification.

"Which is why you're proposing the mother come up here?"

"Yes. But you heard the CACO—that's apparently going to be even more awkward than it would normally be. I'm a little worried about the press angle—some news ghoul finds out she's here to make the ID, and then she gets on the air with all sorts of wild accusations about a Navy cover-up, you know?"

Grace nodded. "But what the investigation needs is a positive ID. The Navy has a whole press corps to deal with the other problem."

Dan shook his head. "McGonagle's gonna really hate us now. Okay, I'll set it up. I'll call the master chief at BuPers and the CACO back; how about you getting back to the Philadelphia medical examiner's office and tell them what we're planning, and see how one does this sort of thing. It's early; maybe we can get this thing in motion today."

An hour later, the secretary brought Dan the fax of the forensics report. He asked her to tell Miss Snow that it was in, and then he scanned the report.

> Preliminary report only; full anatomical and toxicological studies to follow. Black male, early to mid-twenties. Time of death not capable of estimation, but the victim had been dead for more than a year. Body desiccated but reasonably well preserved. Cause of death attributed to suffocation, preceded by a blow to the back of the head. Some signs of ligatures on arms and legs. The head injury was adjudged to have been capable of causing unconsciousness but not death.

Dan frowned when he read that the fingers on both hands were remarkable in that they were severely abraded, with broken nails and badly torn skin. Elbows and knees showed signs of contusions before death. The degree of desiccation was not entirely consistent with immersion in a nitrogen atmosphere. In the opinion of the pathologist, the body was emaciated as well as desiccated.

He put the fax down and thought about it, then sat bolt upright when he realized what that final comment implied. Emaciated? He had *starved* to death?

"Jesus H. Christ!" he exclaimed.

"What?" asked Grace as she stepped into his cubicle.

"You read this. But I think the pathologist is saying that Hardin was alive when he was shut up in that steam drum."

"Alive? Oh my God," Grace said, her face going white as she sank down into a chair. Dan handed her the report and picked up the telephone. He called the shipyard operator and asked for the shipyard Production office. A civilian secretary answered the phone. Dan identified himself and then posed his question.

"Can someone there tell me when the *Wisconsin* was actually deactivated?"

"Hold on."

After a minute's wait, an older man's voice came on the line.

"This is George Warren, Commander. I work for the Production superintendent. You have a question about the *Wisconsin* deactivation?"

"Yes, Mr. Warren. Can you tell me precisely when she was deactivated?"

"Sure—it was September of 1991. I remember it because *Wisconsin* had been the last one of the battlewagons to be reactivated, and yet it was the first one to go back into mothballs after Desert Storm. Everybody thought it was pretty dumb."

"I'm a surface-ship guy, Mr. Warren. You won't get an argument from me about that," Dan said. "But what I really need to know is when the ship filled with nitrogen? Did that happen when she was deactivated?"

"Oh, no, sir, not hardly. Deactivation takes awhile. They do the ceremony and all that, but that's nothing. We have to empty, clean, and then gas-free all the tanks and voids in the ship, and there's several hundred of those on a sixty-thousand-ton ship. And then we have to seal the systems up all throughout the engineering spaces and in the sixteen-inch and five-inch gun turrets. Then we have to install all the space alarms and string some temporary lighting throughout the ship, and we're talking about a mile's worth of cables and lights in all those passageways. You must remember, she's nearly three football fields long and over thirty yards wide, okay? Then we button up all the compartments, one by one. Close and seal the hatches. The whole deal takes nearly six months to actually put her to sleep. The nitrogen backfill comes last, and that takes about two weeks to do the atmosphere exchange below the main deck."

"I get the picture, Mr. Warren," Dan said.

"Say, is this about that body they found?"

"Yes. I'm the investigating officer. And I guess what I really need are the precise dates for the start and completion of the nitrogen backfill. Will your records show that?"

"Sure, but I'll have to access some archives. What's your number?"

Dan gave him the NIS office number and hung up. He looked at Grace. "Well?" he asked.

"I think you're right. We've been assuming that he was put in the ship *after* the atmosphere had been removed. This thing suggests he was alive when they sealed him up in there." She shivered at the thought.

"Well, we'll know shortly. If Production's records show that the nitrogen backfill happened after Hardin was declared missing. . . ."

"How awful. Buried alive!" She shivered again, apparently unable to dislodge the image of the lieutenant regaining consciousness in the steely blackness of a boiler steam drum, three decks down in the armored bowels of a deserted battleship.

Dan spent the rest of the morning bringing his report up to date, while Grace chased down the details of USS *Luce*'s overhaul to nail down dates and circumstances around the time of the alleged murder. The CACO called back at noon to report that she would have Mrs. Hardin in Philadelphia late that afternoon. They went to lunch at the club, then conferred with Santini's investigators to transcribe their crime-scene findings into the investigation report.

18

BY FIVE O'CLOCK, Grace and Dan were waiting in the reception area of the Philadelphia County Medical Examiner's Office on University Avenue, which was across the Schuylkill river from downtown Philadelphia. Because Mrs. Hardin was coming, Dan was dressed in service dress blues, and Grace was looking almost formal in a dark three-piece suit with a straight skirt, a four-button vest, and a hip-length jacket. The CACO, Lieutenant Shea, had called in from the airport that they were on their way, but the receptionist on duty at the desk had suggested that they not hold their breath, the traffic around the airport being a bear in the late afternoon.

The receptionist had reviewed the morgue viewing procedure with both of them, notified the duty examiner that a viewing was in the works, and then went back to her desk. There was a television set in the corner of the reception room, and Dan was watching the early-evening news while Grace reread the ME's report.

Warren at Production had confirmed that the nitrogen backfill had begun seven days after Hardin's disappearance. Dan sighed as he thought about that again. Christ. The poor bastard. And the sleazoid press would have a field day if this got out. But so far, there had been only a sixty-second spot on the body in the battleship on the early news. Lieutenant Commander McGonagle arrived a few minutes later, looking worried.

"Somehow, they've found out the mother's coming in," she announced without preamble—"they" obviously meaning the media. "There's a Channel Ten press van setting up shop outside, as we speak."

"Wonderful. Somebody here, probably," grunted Dan, eyeing the receptionist. "I had to tell them all earlier that she was coming, because it was going to be near closing time."

McGonagle nodded, getting out her notebook. "I'll try to give her a briefing, accompany her through the door when it's time. Maybe keep it down to a discreet mob scene. If we're lucky, there'll be only the one station."

Dan stood up and went over to mute the television.

"I don't know about that," he said. "Apparently, she is not too friendly toward things Navy. She may *want* to go out there and throw some gasoline on the fire. And we've got some unsettling feedback from the ME's office."

McGonagle looked at his expression and then opened her notebook expectantly. Dan could see that the receptionist at the front desk was trying hard to eavesdrop, so he lowered his voice and back-briefed McGonagle on his conversations with the CACO, then concluded with the disturbing implications of the ME's report. McGonagle swore softly when she heard the part about the lieutenant being entombed alive. Grace intervened as he finished up.

"We're not going to tell her that, are we? His mother?"

"No," Dan said. "I'd like to keep that under wraps for as long as we can. Maybe we can use the ploy that it's inside information—only the killers would have known that, so please don't release it."

"Nice try," said McGonagle. "But there'll be a Freedom of Information Act request coming the moment you try to sequester that report. I have to call CHINFO with this. Right now."

Grace said, "Dan, we need to remember that this is a mother coming to see the remains of her son. I know we all have to worry about the media angle, but I suggest Commander McGonagle handle that while you and I concentrate on breaking down whatever barriers she has erected against the Navy. Her cooperation may be crucial to our investigation."

Dan nodded even as McGonagle scowled. But Grace was right—again. Focus on the investigation. McGonagle went to the window in the reception room and then turned around hurriedly.

"I suggest you two find an office to hide out in; the lady vampire from Channel Ten is headed in."

The receptionist reluctantly found them an empty office two doors down the hall and then went back to call her supervisor in the medical examiner's office about the press interest. Dan sat on the edge of a desk; Grace took the chair while they waited. They had argued earlier about whether or not to introduce themselves to Mrs. Hardin as investigators right away or to let the CACO take her through the viewing first. Dan had been against trying to talk to her.

"She's already mad at us, or the Navy, anyway. She's going to be in shock at seeing her son, assuming this is her son. I think it would be a lousy time for us to start with the questions," he had argued.

Grace had disagreed. "All of that is true, but I think we must at least identify ourselves as the Navy's investigation team. I think the right tack is simply to introduce ourselves and tell her we are trying to find out what happened. If I understand it, she's mad at the Navy because she thinks no one cares about what happened—to both of her children."

"Don't you think we'll just poison the well?"

"No. If it's just the CACO with her, she's going to feel like she's being shepherded but that no one cares. And because we're in the city morgue, it's even worse—in the morgue, no one really does care. This is just another body."

"I guess I'm just not eager to get a tongue-lashing from a bereaved parent."

"We're going to need this woman if this is indeed Lieutenant Hardin. Let's just introduce ourselves. That's all—no questions, nothing about— you know, unless it's unavoidable. No hassle. Just let her see that someone,

someone fairly senior-looking in the person of a full commander, USN, is working the case. Later, when we have to ask her questions, at least she will know who we are."

He had appreciated the sense of it but was still apprehensive. The fact that the lieutenant had been buried alive was still bothering him. Maybe a week, a couple hundred hours before the nitrogen had come seeping in through the boiler tubes to end it. In the end, he had agreed to let McGonagle and the CACO escort Mrs. Hardin through the press, which, so far, consisted of one TV news team. The receptionist would then have to keep the hounds at bay, and he and Grace would meet Mrs. Hardin, explain who they were, and then accompany her to the identification room. The receptionist was supposed to call them when the CACO arrived. Dan was fidgeting with his uniform buttons when the phone rang.

"I think they're here, Commander," the receptionist said. "A female Navy type and an older woman are getting out of a taxi out front. The other Navy lady is on her way out front."

Dan thanked her, straightened out his uniform, and cracked open the office door. A minute later, he and Grace stepped out to intercept Mrs. Hardin, escorted by Lieutenant Shea, the duty forensics investigator, and a woman from the Grief Assistance Program in the hallway. The receptionist had closed off the hallway doors to prevent the TV news reporter and her cameraman from filming them. Dan introduced himself and Grace Snow while continuing to walk with her down the hall to the identification room. The forensics investigator from the morgue led the way, his face a professionally blank mask. Lieutenant Shea brought up the rear.

Mrs. Hardin was a short, trim woman in her mid-fifties, with gray hair, an alert round face, mahogany-hued skin, and weary, intelligent eyes. She appeared to be composed, with no outward signs of nervousness or apprehension. Like she already knows, Dan thought.

"Mrs. Hardin," Dan said, "I'm Comdr. Dan Collins from the Department of the Navy, and this is Miss Grace Snow from the Naval Investigative Service. We've been assigned by Washington headquarters to investigate the circumstances surrounding the discovery of a body in the mothballed ship USS *Wisconsin*. We have reason to believe that this might be your son, Lt. (jg) Wesley Hardin. We very much appreciate your coming up here to Philadelphia."

Mrs. Hardin looked up at him. When she spoke, her voice was surprisingly husky, hinting perhaps of a lifetime of cigarette smoking.

"Lieutenant Shea told me you would be here, Commander Collins. Is this my son these people have in here?"

As the investigator turned a corner, Dan stopped, now that they were out of range of the newspeople. "We think so, Mrs. Hardin," he replied. "But our identification is based only on two distinguishing features: Your son's name was on the uniform pants and shirt, and that uniform is that of a lieutenant junior grade in the Navy Supply Corps. And second, the person is—was—black."

Mrs. Hardin looked at Grace and then back at Dan. "If this city is anything like Washington, a body in the morgue being black would hardly be a distinguishing feature," she said.

"Yes, ma'am, that's probably true." Dan tried to think of something intelligent to say while Mrs. Hardin watched him, waiting. He decided to move it along.

"I think the procedure here is that we go to the identification room, where they will take down some information for the death certificate."

"Will I get to see him?" she asked.

"Not in person, Mrs. Hardin," the investigator interjected. He was a youngish white man dressed in khaki slacks, with a white medical jacket over his white shirt and tie. "The way it works, we have a television monitor in the identification room. We'll dim the lights and then turn on the monitor, which will give you a facial view of the deceased. We'll ask for your identification at that time."

"I can't touch him, see him up close?"

"No, ma'am. We don't do it that way anymore. If this is your son, your funeral director can help you with that. It's this way, please, ma'am."

The woman from the Grief Assistance Program took Mrs. Hardin's arm and spoke quietly to her, finally eliciting a nod. "Let's get it done," Mrs. Hardin said to the investigator, who nodded and walked ahead to the identification room.

Dan and Grace followed her down the hall, through two turns into different hallways, and then into the viewing room itself. The viewing room was an austere space with four blank white walls, a carpeted floor, and three chairs set in front of a large, darkened television monitor mounted on a TV cart. The forensics investigator motioned for Mrs. Hardin to sit in the center chair, then brought over a clipboard and sat down next to her to take down the information for the death certificate. When he was finished, he made a phone call. Dan and Grace Snow stood behind the chairs, as did the rest of the group.

The young man came back over to Mrs. Hardin. "If you're ready, Mrs. Hardin," he said.

"All right," she replied.

The man reached up behind the monitor and operated a dimmer switch, which brought the lights in the room down to low power. He then reached up to the side of the monitor and turned it on; after a few seconds, an image appeared, showing the head and face of the body in close-up. Mrs. Hardin stared for several seconds, sighed, and then seemed to slump in the chair. Finally, she nodded and stretched out her right hand as if to touch the image, but then she dropped it.

"Yes. That's my son, Wesley Hardin. God rest his soul."

The investigator thanked her and turned off the television, nodded at the woman from Grief Assistance Program, and left the room. They then retired to the Grief Assistance Program's counseling office next door, where Mrs. Hardin was asked if she wanted anything, some coffee, or whatever. She shook her head and sat down carefully on a couch. Grace sat down on the couch next to her, and Dan sat in one of the chairs. Lieutenant Shea remained standing in the middle of the room, staring at the floor. Dan described the general circumstances of the body's discovery and then his own tasking with regards to the investigation. Mrs. Hardin sat silently, and Dan could not tell if she was taking it in or was still in shock from seeing her son.

"Mrs. Hardin," he finished, "we're all very sorry for what you've had to go through today. I can't promise you that we're going to be able to find out what happened, but I *can* promise you that we're going to try very hard to find out."

Mrs. Hardin finally looked over at him, and then she began shaking her head slowly, as if to deny what he had just said.

"No, sir," she said quietly. Then louder: "No, sir. You were doing all right until you said that. I know. I *know* that isn't true. It wasn't true when Elizabeth died, and it won't be true now; this I *know*. My 'Lizbeth, she was a lieutenant in the Navy, too. Did you know that?"

"Yes, ma'am. We just found that out today. I guess your family hasn't had much luck with the Navy." Even as he said it, he realized how fatuous he must sound.

Mrs. Hardin snorted and tossed her head. She fished around in her purse for a handkerchief, which she used to dab at her eyes. When Dan saw that she was crying, he looked over at Grace as if to say, Now what?

"Mrs. Hardin," Grace said, "we are sorry for your loss, for both your losses. We're new to this case. We know very little at this point. But Commander Collins here has been appointed by the most senior officers in the Navy to find out what happened here. And if something happened to your daughter that hasn't been explained, and if it's related to this case, we will broaden our investigation if we have to."

Dan was alarmed at Grace's promise to broaden the investigation. The daughter had died in a traffic accident. If the D.C. cops hadn't been able to solve that, there was no way in hell they could do it. But Grace was continuing.

"Mrs. Hardin, your son's body has been in that ship for nearly two years. We are going to have to reconstruct the last days of his life here in the shipyard to see if we can find out why he was murdered."

Mrs. Hardin sat up. "Murdered? You say murdered?"

Grace looked up as Dan flushed. He thought someone would have told her. We just did, dummy.

"Yes, ma'am," Grace said, her voice steady. "The medical examiner's report indicates he was hit over the head. We're surmising that he was then put down in the ship so that his body would never be found. But, yes, someone killed your son. That is why we are not just going to file this case away as another unexplained disappearance."

Mrs. Hardin stared across the room, her eyes unfocused, her upper body rocking ever so slightly back and forth. It was obvious to Dan that it had never occurred to her that her son had been murdered. He leaned forward in his chair.

"This isn't the time or place for us to ask you questions, Mrs. Hardin. Lieutenant Shea here will help you make arrangements to take your son's body home. But later, after you've had some time, we will need to come see you."

But Mrs. Hardin was shaking her head again. "No," she said. "No. Lord God knows I've had enough of the Navy. Look what it's done to my children. Done to me. No. You want to go play detective, you go do it. But you leave me alone. I've had enough pain with the Navy."

Grace gave Dan a "let's leave it right there" look, then got up.

"Mrs. Hardin," she said, "we are very sorry for your loss. Lieutenant Shea and this office will help you with the paperwork. Thank you for taking the time to talk to us."

Mrs. Hardin would not look at them. Dan rose from his chair and followed Grace out of the room, pulling the door to close behind him. Lieutenant Shea, the CACO, came out a moment later.

"What do I do about the reporters, Commander?" she asked.

"Duck 'em if you can. Maybe see if there's another exit you can take. Have the cab meet you in back or something . . . I don't know. Commander McGonagle is up there now. You might contact the receptionist, see if she can tell you what's going on. Do whatever Command McGonagle recommends. We're going to find a back door."

"Aye, aye, sir," Shea said, giving him a less-than-respectful look before going back inside. The investigator was coming back down the hall, bearing a folder.

"If you have a moment, Commander?" he said.

"Yes, what is it?"

"Normally, we have to have two people to make a formal identification. I understand that this lady is the young man's mother, but is there anyone else?"

"She flew up from Washington for this," Dan said. "I don't think there's anyone else, certainly not here in Philadelphia, anyway."

"Can you offer any identification, Commander?"

"Only that he matches the description of an officer who disappeared in the shipyard two years ago, and the name and rank stenciled into his uniform matches Wesley Hardin. We'll have medical and dental records coming up from the federal archives pretty soon. Can you use those?"

"Yes indeed. We'd appreciate it if you'd make sure we get those. But I think we have enough to release. I'll go tell Grief Assistance and Mrs. Hardin's escort. Thanks."

"Is there a way out of the building that avoids the front reception area? There are reporters up there we don't want to talk to."

"Yes, sir—go that way, down that hall to the end, then turn right out the door marked FIRE EXIT. But call the receptionist up front first so she doesn't get an alarm on the door. Just dial three-three on any phone."

They followed his instructions and found themselves in the parking lot behind the medical examiner's building. Dan let out a loud exhalation after they were outside.

"Gosh, that was just wonderful," he said.

Grace looked at the ground. "Thank God they have that Grief Assistance Program; that woman told me Philadelphia is the only city that has one."

"I feel like a rat, running out like that," Dan said. "But I really wanted out of there."

"That poor woman," Grace said. "I'm not sure I can blame her."

"Yeah, I know what you mean. Both of her children, for Christ's sake."

"Do you suppose there's a connection?"

"Grace, c'mon."

"I suppose you're right," she said with a sigh. The high-rise buildings of downtown Philadelphia were barely visible in the smog haze across the river. "If we're through here, I think I need a drink."

19

ON FRIDAY MORNING, Dan called a meeting with Grace, Santini, and Lieutenant Commanders McGonagle and VanSladen in the NIS field office conference room.

"Time to recapitulate, I think," he said. "We now have a reasonably positive ID on the body in the battleship. We have a preliminary medical examiner's report that indicates a homicide, with evidence that the victim was hit on the head and otherwise beaten up prior to being taken to the boiler room on the battleship. We also have a forensic opinion that suggests the victim was alive when bolted into that steam drum. The shipyard records indicate that the cold nitrogen atmosphere that actually killed him was injected around seven days after he went missing."

"Jesus Christ," VanSladen said. He had obviously not known about the time lag.

"Yeah," Dan continued. "We are assuming that the incident happened around two years ago, when the victim was first reported UA. We know that the victim was assigned as the disbursing officer in USS *Luce*. There is local press interest, and the potential for national media interest. What we do not have is a motive, or any suspects."

"And a very cold trail," offered Santini.

"Very cold indeed," Dan agreed. "But, to paraphrase John Paul Jones, we've just begun to look. Miss McGonagle, what's the state of play in the press?"

"We've had two nights of local news coverage, but no national coverage—yet. So far, they've played it pretty straight: facts about the discovery, and today an ID on the body now that next of kin has been notified. No mention of homicide, and no speculation on the fact that a Washington Navy headquarters officer is conducting the investigation. But it's only a matter of time."

Dan nodded and turned to Grace Snow.

"Miss Snow, I request that you initiate tasking via NIS headquarters to have the Philadelphia NIS field office explore the issue of access to the battleship. I want everyone in Shop Seventy-two who could have had access to that ship interviewed. I want to find out specifically if anyone still working here in the shipyard also had access in 1992 when we think this incident took place. In these interviews, I specifically want their *opinions* as to how hard it would be for unauthorized personnel to gain access. Mr. Santini, you're familiar with the facts-versus-opinion methodology of a JAGMAN investigation?"

"Yes," Santini said. He did not appear to be overjoyed to hear that tasking was inbound, but Dan was pleased to see that he was taking notes.

"I want you to interview all current riggers, and if you develop leads to former riggers who reasonably can be reached, I want them interviewed, as well. I'm not optimistic we'll dig up anything, but these are the guys who should have had access to the ship. Some of them were either involved or made it possible for others to put that man in there. The fact that it might have happened before the nitrogen blanket went on actually widens the possible suspect list—no breathing apparatus would have been needed."

"Current and former employees?" protested Santini. "That could go on forever."

"Why don't we limit it to the time frame of the incident, then," Grace suggested. Dan assented and then continued.

"And I need the written procedures and requirements for the sounding-and-security watches for the inactive ships—what they are supposed to do and how often. The written procedures will be facts. I also want opinions as to how the system really works—whether or not they do the job, or if they just gun-deck the logs and screw off for a few hours rather than actually go into those ships."

Santini nodded. "That I can predict—they gun-deck the hell out of it if they're anything like the rest of the yardbirds here."

"Yeah, but we would like to have some hard evidence of that," Dan said.

"That's a different story," Santini said. "These guys don't believe in ratting out."

"I understand. What I'm hoping for is that a pattern will emerge after you've talked to enough of them. For example, it took two years before anyone noticed that a boiler steam drum was buttoned up when it should have been opened. But I don't want to direct your inquiries into any given right answer."

"Got it. Miss Snow, what's the priority on this tasking vis-à-vis the rest of the things we're working up here?"

Grace hesitated. She had no idea of how much backing she would really get from NIS headquarters. "Make it your first priority, Mr. Santini. I'll confirm that with Mr. Ames back in Washington."

"What are your near-term intentions for the investigation, Commander?" VanSladen asked. "The admiral asked me to find out."

" 'Near-term,' Mr. VanSladen? The investigation is moving to Washington."

DAN BEGAN TO RELAX as he finally exited the construction zones around the airport and pushed the big Suburban southeast along Interstate 95. To his left, the Delaware River glinted in the midmorning sunlight, the flat surface cut into chevrons of rippling V's as a big tanker plowed her way down to the sea from the oil refineries upstream.

"That's better," he said to Grace. "We're relatively safe until we get down to the big bridge; then it's shields-up time again."

Grace smiled at the *Star Trek* allusion. "I don't know why, but I was awfully glad to leave that shipyard," she said. "It was a pretty depressing place."

Dan nodded. He knew firsthand the dismay that accompanied taking a ship from the clean ocean to the dismal industrial warrens of South Philadelphia and then having to be a willing accomplice while a bunch of union goons happily tore the ship up under the guise of an overhaul. It was enough to break any sailor's heart. Going there to investigate a murder had been even more depressing.

"I can't stop thinking about Lieutenant Hardin," she said. "Buried alive inside all that steel."

"We don't know that," Dan said. "That's still an opinion."

"Right. One of your famous JAGMAN opinions."

Dan set the cruise control for sixty-five before replying, conscious that the locals were breezing past him on either side.

"Rightly famous, because it keeps all us boy investigators honest. You can't go riding your favorite hobbyhorse if the facts aren't there. And given that there are some fairly serious political games going down on the margins of this investigation, you and I have to be doubly careful to adhere to JAGMAN rules. Triply careful if this thing really hits the media."

Grace shook her head. "When, not if. And I'm not sure I understand the political issue anymore."

"Which one—OpNav versus NIS?"

"Yes. Suppose we do untangle this thing, as unlikely as that sounds right now. But suppose we actually find the murderer and can indict: How does that really bear on NIS? Or OpNav? The CNO's Washington headquarters staff is not going to go into the business of homicide investigations, is it?"

"I shouldn't think so," Dan said. "But really senior, permanent civil serpent guys like Ames who run NIS are going to see their independence threatened if outside line officers end up being *in charge* of high-profile investigations. The civilians in NIS would end up with lofty-sounding titles but no power, and all the rest of the civil serpents would know it. And the line officers wouldn't have to come from OpNav, you know. In the JAG-MAN system, any damn line officer can be put in charge of an investigation. Even me."

"All right, but how does that bear on what we do?"

"Damn! Look at that idiot. Right when I thought we were safe. Because as we start pulling this onion apart and getting closer to a solution—that is, the OpNav weenie looks like he's going to pull it off—you might start getting direction from NIS to put diamond dust in the Vaseline."

Grace was silent for a few minutes. Dan let her think about it. What he hadn't said was that the same pressures might be laid on him: If they approached success, he was going to be told to ensure that his report made the NIS input look insignificant.

"I won't do that," she said finally.

"Do what?"

"Sabotage the investigation. I want to know who did this."

"Hell, so do I. But *sabotage* is too strong a word. They wouldn't be that overt. They'll simply start throwing obstacles in the way. Avenues of exploration will be closed off. Field officers like Santini will go armadillo on us. Reports will get lost, or sanitized. Priorities will change—remember what you told Santini, about top priority? Ames or Englehardt could tell him to forget that. That kind of stuff."

"I won't allow it."

Dan laughed. "Love your spirit," he said. "But people at our level in government don't have 'allow it' privileges. If some guy at the 'assistant secretary of' level drops a hint to the organization, be it NIS, the Navy Department, or even OpNav, to stonewall, you can believe that the permanent civil serpents and all the EAs will damn well do it. And be very clever and circumspect about it, too."

"I'm a GS-fifteen, for Christ's sake! And stop saying *serpent*."

"Sorry about that. Yes, you're a GS-fifteen—in the career-development business now, as I recall."

She glared at him for a moment, then turned her head to stare out the window.

"And," he said more gently, "you're an ex-political appointee who burrowed in. Grace, the same system that eased you out of SEC and into a late-term political appointment also allowed you to burrow in when everyone else was scrambling to find a job. Somebody did somebody a favor, that's all. When you turned out not to be brain-dead, the entrenched system quickly got you out of policy and into personnel. In my experience, when the old-timers go to work on you, it's like getting a sunburn: It feels nice and warm all day, but by sundown you're dying."

Grace treated him to ten minutes of silence before finally sighing out loud.

"Shit," she said.

"Shit, aye," he agreed.

"And will OpNav indulge in the same kind of games?"

Knew she was smart, he thought. "Absolutely," he said. "Especially if we start making sense out of this thing. But I'll tell you what: I'm with you. The thought of that kid being stuffed into a boiler and left to starve to death in the dark is sticking in my craw. I'd like to propose that we stick to our deal back there on Broad Street. You and I play this thing straight— the investigation and what we tell each other—no matter what."

She nodded. "Yes, no matter what. Although from what you've been telling me, I may not appreciate the extent of that 'what.' "

"I may not, either." He sighed. "We've got three hours to go. Let's talk about where to take it from here."

They reviewed what they knew and what they did not know. Dan thought the next step was obvious: get Hardin's records, see what the fitrep file told them, and then find people who had served with Hardin in *Luce*—his skipper, his exec, his department head, other officers. Maybe some chiefs in the Supply Department.

"That's going to be a big telephone drill," he said. "We need a home."

"I can probably get us an office down in the Washington Navy Yard."

Dan shook his head. "My bosses won't allow that."

"Too close to the enemy, hunh?"

"Yup. NIS subversives would bombard my poor brain with super-secret Q-waves and turn me into a double agent. OpNav would be betrayed and all would be lost."

She laughed. "No Q-waves in OpNav?"

"Hell no. OpNav just got electricity a few years back. Before that, it was whale-oil lamps, hemp rigging, bells, signal flags, and lots of ship pictures. It's rumored that they have a computer trapped in a room up on the fifth floor. Most of the admirals feel that if they don't feed it, maybe it'll just die. No, an OpNav office is perfect. We'll hang out in OP-Six-fourteen and you can get to see firsthand how little NIS or anybody else has to fear from OpNav."

They arrived in the Washington area at 2:30, coming onto the I-495 Beltway from the north. They were able to travel exactly one mile before all traffic southbound began to congeal. Dan managed to maneuver to an off ramp, where he went up and over, heading back westbound around the Beltway in the counterclockwise direction toward Virginia. With rush hour impending, he suggested to Grace that he simply take her home.

"There's no point in your trying to get down to the Navy Yard at this time of day," he said. "I can drop you off, go by the Pentagon and get us set up for Monday, and then get down to Old Town before the serious traffic begins."

They agreed to meet at the south parking entrance to the Pentagon on Monday morning at 8:30. He drove her into Georgetown, made sure that she got safely into her house, and then zipped across the Key Bridge to Rosslyn, from where he took 110 down to the Pentagon and found a parking place close to the building, in north parking.

20

GRACE WATCHED THE BIG Suburban thread its way carefully through the two lines of parked cars crowded along P Street and then went to her study. The brick town house had a fairly simple floor plan: a small front hall that led to stairs on one side and a living room to the right. There were four rooms on the ground floor: living room, powder room, dining room, and a spacious eat-in kitchen. Upstairs were two bedrooms and two baths, as well as a room the Realtor had quaintly referred to as a "sewing room," which Grace used for storage. The master bedroom door was at the top of the stairs, with the second bedroom down a hall, and a guest bathroom separating the two. The sewing room was on the street side of the house.

Grace had converted the dining room to her home study, since it had a beautiful view through a bay window of the back walled garden. The previous owners had added a small pantry combined with an enclosed back stoop off the kitchen, which meant that Grace tended to live in the kitchen and study area, going upstairs at night when she was ready for bed. The guest bedroom was kept ready for company—which never came. There was a basement, but it was damp and moldy, with old earth showing between some of the foundation bricks. The furnace, hot-water heater, and a central air conditioner were down there, but Grace, suspecting monsters, avoided going down there, and she even had a small bookshelf placed in front of the basement door in the kitchen. She had a maid in every other week, and an ancient gardener who took excellent care of all the patio gardens in that block, albeit on a somewhat random schedule.

When her parents had died, Grace had selected a few pieces of furniture from the large house in Beacon Hill to bring down to Georgetown, including a Queen Anne cherry dining room table that now served as her desk, not that one could see it under all the clutter. She made some space in front of one of the armchairs and checked her answering machine—one indignant message from the maid, whom she'd forgotten to tell that she would be going to Philadelphia. Who's working for whom? she wondered absently. Silly question. The second message was from Englehardt. It was short and of the E.T. variety: "Grace please call my office in the NIS headquarters downtown in the Washington Navy Yard." She got up, picked up the phone, and moved to the huge high-backed leather chair her father had brought back from Harrod's and dialed the number.

"Mr. Englehardt's office."

"This is Grace Snow. Returning his call."

"He's out of the office, Miss Snow. I'll tell him you called back. Are you home?"

Grace said yes, thanked her, and hung up, then went upstairs to take a shower and change into casual clothes. She daydreamed about Dan Collins while she was in the shower, and then she laughingly wondered what significance her mother, the shrink, would have made of that. The phone was ringing by the time she got back downstairs. As per her habit when she was in the house and the phone rang, she let the machine pick up and listened to the caller identify himself. It was Doug Englehardt. She picked up.

"Hi, Doug. I'm back, as you can see."

"Hi, Grace. Ames said you were returning to D.C. today. How was Philadelphia?"

"Pretty awful. W. C. Fields was right. But then, of course, we had this grisly crime to brighten up our stay there."

"So I've heard."

Grace hesitated for a moment. "Santini keeping the home front fully informed?"

"Of course. Ames has him reporting directly to him. He's still pretty annoyed over this OpNav gambit. He badgered Admiral Keeler to go to the Secretary of the Navy with it, but the vice chief had apparently offered Keeler some friendly advice, and nothing came of it. For now, anyway, we've lost that round. Ames said Keeler didn't appear to have his heart in it, for some odd reason."

"This vice whatever seems to get around."

Englehardt laughed. "Admiral Torrance is going to be the next Chief of Naval Operations, and he's a very powerful and ambitious flag officer. The way it works traditionally, the vice chief runs day-to-day Navy policy, while the Chief of Naval Operations spends most of his energy with the Joint Chiefs of Staff at the national policy level. The vice has usually been the man with the hammer, around with whom one does not mess, if I can paraphrase Sir Winston."

"I left tasking for Santini. Is that going to be supported?"

This time, it was Englehardt who seemed to hesitate, and Grace found herself holding her breath.

"I'm not sure, Grace," he said. "I think Ames knows that I'm kind of your rabbi here, and he was a little coy about that when I asked the same question. How vital is what you wanted them to do?"

"It's part of a homicide investigation, Doug. This young officer was not only murdered; he was also mewed up in the steam drum of a ship's boiler for something like a week *before* they flooded the ship with cold nitrogen gas. Basically, the forensic evidence, such as it is, indicates he was alive in there for some time."

"Jesus Christ. I hadn't heard that."

"Well, it renders the rice-bowl issues more than a little trivial in my book," she said. She felt herself getting angry and had to remind herself that this was supposedly her ally she was talking to.

He must have read her mind. "Calm down, Grace. I'm one of the good guys, remember?"

"I'm sorry, Doug. You are one of the good guys."

"How's this guy Collins? Present for duty?"

"Yes. Rather self-effacing, actually. Makes mistakes and owns up to them. Pretends not to be very smart but then says things that prove otherwise."

"Is he committed to what the OpNav elephants are up to?"

"I think not. I have the sense that if they took the invesitgation and gave it to someone else, he would take it perfectly in stride. Until then, he's working it."

"Where is he now?"

"On his way home, I would guess. He was going by the Pentagon to arrange some office space for us next week. He said it wasn't worth my going into the office by the time we got back. Why do you ask?"

"He's right. You two getting along all right?"

She hesitated for a second or two, then said, "We've sort of reached an understanding that he and I will work the investigation aboveboard, without respect to the NIS-OpNav 'food fight,' as he called it. I think I can trust him."

"Maybe, maybe not. Trust but verify, as Reagan used to say. And now that you're back in town, keep in touch. I'll keep my ear to the ground for you."

Grace laughed, thanked him, and said good-bye. She suspected that Doug Englehardt was still more than a little smitten with her. He was married and by all appearances reasonably serious about it, and he had never really overstepped the bounds of propriety. She wasn't so sure about what might happen if she encouraged him, however. If she had any chance of getting back into the policy world, Doug's help was going to be the key. But his comment about Ames reminded her that he was also a survivor: If he had to choose between supporting Grace and saving his own hide, there was little question in Grace's mind as to how that would come out. Fortunately, she had Robby Booker to fall back on. He couldn't do anything for her career, but he got around and could keep her informed. She suddenly realized how few friends she had in this town.

* * *

DAN MADE IT UP to the fourth floor and OP-614 by 4:45, where he met with Summerfield. The office was otherwise empty. Having to come in at 0600 to sort the diplomatic traffic for the officers, Yeoman Jackson normally went home at four, and Snapper was attending a meeting at State on the Portuguese frigate. Summerfield was having his last cup of coffee for the day and reading a *Wall Street Journal* exposé on the administration's most recent pecadillo, a daily ritual he truly relished. He eyed his watch as Dan came into the office.

"The boy investigator is back," he said. "At sixteen forty-five on a Friday. I thought I trained you better than that, Daniel."

"Yes, sir, you did," Dan said, dropping his briefcase on his desk and eyeing his own bulging in-box. "But I needed to get some stuff set up for Monday. Grace Snow and I will need to operate out of Six-fourteen for the next couple of weeks, if that's okay with you. We have the empty desks here, and the alternative is that I go to the Navy Yard."

" 'Grace Snow and I'—that sounds cozy. Okay, no problem. You'll have to keep Snapper from drooling at the estimable Ms. Snow, but otherwise that should be workable."

Dan nodded. "We can get a bib for Snapper," he said. "Let me bring you up to speed on where we are with this thing."

When he had finished, Summerfield rotated in his armchair and stared out the window for a minute. The windows of the D-ring stared back.

"Wow," he said finally, turning around. "I think you're right to come back to town. With a two-year-old datum, neither you nor NIS will find out anything more of any significance in Philly. Those yardbirds can stonewall better than a tax assessor. Politically, the first thing you need to do is to get on Oh-six B's calendar Monday and give him a data dump."

"I've been keeping Manning informed."

"Yeah, good. But remember, you're not allowed to brief the appointing officer on the investigation, per se, but you can go down there and tell him how things are going with NIS. But let him ask the questions. Don't volunteer, and don't tell him as much as you've told me. I suspect his focus will be on his marching orders from the vice chief, whatever those are."

"His focus, and the Navy's, may change," Dan said. "If the national press gets ahold of the buried-alive angle, we're all going to be fending off offers from *Hard Copy* around here."

"No, the Navy's Chief of Information will. And that's an important distinction: the 'Grace and I' team should keep a very low profile. I think you've got the right plan—talk to people who knew Hardin in *Luce*. I also think maybe we'd better do some furniture moving in here: You and Ms. Snow take the back room and you control the keys and access. Snapper can have your desk. I can't get you any more phone lines anytime short of Christmas, but we already have four—you guys can have two dedicated to your project. Tell me about Ms. Snow."

Dan briefed his boss on Grace's professional background and their relationship to date in the investigation. The telephone in the outer office began to ring, but Summerfield shook his head when Dan reached for it.

"Too late in the week to answer phones. So she's not one of these bra-burning, politically correct bitch kitties."

"No, sir, I don't think so. She's smart—Brown, Georgetown Law, a Wall Street financial-crimes investigator. And she's focused. She seems to be willing to work the investigation in a straightforward manner and let the mandarins handle the rice-bowl issues."

Summerfield nodded reflectively. "Where is she now?"

"I dropped her off at her house in Georgetown. It was too late in the day to try for the Navy Yard."

"Georgetown. How nice for her. So in your opinion, she's playing it straight for now."

"Yes, sir, I think so."

"That'll change if you guys begin to home in on a solution."

"Yes, sir, that's what I felt. She does, too, actually. We even talked about it. That's when I expect NIS to start dropping sand in the reduction gears."

"Yeah, okay. We'll handle that problem when and if it comes on the screen. You get to tell Snapper he has to move."

"Wonderful," Dan said.

"I've got to leave," Summerfield said. "I've got a meeting of my gun club."

"Going shooting this weekend?"

"No, just our weekly get-together to look at the new toys. We're collectors. We like to show off."

"Gun collectors are becoming an endangered species in America."

"All the more reason to be armed, don't you think?" Summerfield asked with a wicked smile.

21

At 8:30 on Monday morning, Dan met Grace in the small anteroom just inside the doors of the Pentagon's south parking lot entrance. She was dressed in a two-piece charcoal gray suit with a closed collar and low-heeled shoes. She carried a black leather purse over one shoulder and a Compaq portable computer in a black fabric carrying case. He shepherded her through the metal detectors and package scanners, then took her down to the concourse to get her a temporary building pass. En route, he stopped at a building map to give her a brief explanation of the Pentagon layout.

"I'll escort you out this evening or whenever you leave," he said.

"Is that really necessary? Now that I have my own pass?"

"Yup. This is still the largest office building in the world, in terms of miles of corridors. Seventeen miles, to be exact. Five concentric buildings—or rings, as they're called—five floors above ground, two or maybe more below ground, depending on the color of your badge, and about twenty-three thousand inmates during the working day. You have to know the layout to get around this place."

"It seems logical enough," she said, looking at one of the framed building diagrams.

"Yeah, but you'll notice that there's one of these diagrams every fifty feet. Basically, think of the building as a spoked wheel. Each office has a number, like four-E-four-eight-seven. First number is the floor, the letter is the ring, and the final number is the number on the door. The quickest way to get to any office is to go down a spoke to the hub, go up or down stairs to the appropriate floor, then walk around the hub—that's the A-ring—to the appropriate corridor—that's another spoke—and back out that corridor to the ring where your objective lives and around that segment of the ring to find it."

"Clear as mud," she observed, looking around at the steady stream of people walking by, all of whom looked like they knew where they were going.

"That room number I gave you is OP-Six-fourteen. Want to try it?"

Fifteen minutes later, she admitted defeat, and then Dan, by now carrying the computer case, showed her the system.

"It really is pretty logical," he said lightly as they walked down the E-ring toward OP-614. She gave him a sideways look but said nothing.

In the office, Dan introduced her to the 614 crew. The resident Marine was a model of decorum and politeness. Snapper had not reacted well to Summerfield's comments about a bib that morning, and he had given Dan a meaningful look that foretold unspeakable acts of retaliation. Dan was rescued when Grace said how much she admired the Marine Corps. They set to work creating the investigation's base camp, and by lunchtime they had Snapper moved and their command cell up and running.

At lunchtime, Dan took her down to the center-court snack bar for a hamburger. The center court was actually a beautiful botanical garden planted in the hollow five-sided center of the building, encompassing about five acres of grounds. He pointed out a quaint tradition held over from the Cold War, which was that the snack bar in the center of the courtyard was known to the Pengaton inhabitants as "Ground Zero."

"Just to remind you that, while the Pentagon is an architecturally interesting office building, it's also the nerve center for the most powerful military machine on the planet, for better or for 'worser.' "

"I'm kind of amazed at how dilapidated it is. I mean, this garden is beautiful, but the offices are—"

"Grungy. Yeah. This building was literally poured into a five-sided mold in about sixteen months during World War Two. It's built on the remains of an old airfield, which itself was built on landfill—basically, a swamp. The building foundations are all on pilings. Forty-one thousand pilings, if I remember my tour book. In the basement offices, you can tell the state of the tide in the Potomac—the walls sweat at high tide. The flag and general officers' offices are nice, and the major command centers are pretty high-tech. The rest of it is a dump."

She looked around at the groomed lawns and exotic trees in the center court, which was filled with a good-sized lunchtime crowd enjoying some sunlight. Recalling the bleak air-shaft view from OP-614, she could appreciate the sunlight herself. When they returned to the office, Grace sat down at her desk and began pulling small cables out of the carrying case for her computer. Once she had had time to set up her machine, he brought her up to speed on what he had been doing.

"I've called BuPers, and they tell me Hardin's records will take another week to get out of St. Louis. So in the meantime, I'm going to try something else. I've asked the bureau to give me a printout of the names of the wardroom officers in *Luce* at the time Hardin served, starting with the captain. I've asked for the printout to include present duty stations."

"So we'll be starting a big telephone exercise, then."

"Yeah. I guess we'd better figure out exactly what we'll be asking these people."

Snapper stuck his head in the door and pointed an imaginary gun at Dan.

"His eminence the EA requests the pleasure of your company in the front office," he announced.

"Now?"

"Anytime in the next eleven seconds would be entirely satisfactory. Yes, now would be nice. Excuse us, Miss Snow. Commander Collins is the Op-Six-one pet rock, as well as being a well-known subversive. It's always difficult to get his attention, and even then he whines."

Grace smiled as Dan put on his jacket. "I'll work up a list of questions," she said.

Dan walked up to the 06 front office, greeting some fellow action officers in the hallway. They congratulated him on his detail to the investigation; any escape from OpNav, even temporary, was cause for congratulations. When he arrived in the front office, he found Captain Manning engaged in a muted conversation with Capt. Eldon Randall, senior aide and executive assistant to the Vice Chief of Naval Operations. Randall was a tall, dark-haired, and impeccably turned out naval captain, who wore the four gold aiguillettes of his station as senior aide and executive assistant on his left shoulder like the mantle of a crown prince, which in a sense he was. He had been selected for flag rank on the previous December's promotion list and was now reportedly awaiting an assignment as a cruiser-destroyer group commander. Randall maintained an aloof, distant expression, even when talking to other EAs. He had bright black eyes, heavy brows, a wide, shiny forehead in front of a receding hairline, a dramatically hooked nose, and thin, almost bloodless lips. He was tall enough to look down at most officers on the staff. In many respects, Randall looked a lot like his boss, the Vice Chief of Naval Operations himself, Admiral William H. Torrance.

Dan had never seen Randall without his coat on, even at his desk, as if he could not stand to be without those gold loops in full view. As an action officer, Dan had not had any direct dealings with the vice chief's EA: Manning was as high as any of the 06 action officers were allowed to go. But he knew his reputation: a fiercely protective palace guard, fully invested with the power of the vice chief's office, and direct to the point of being rude to any officer not an admiral. In the surface-ship community, he had earned a reputation as a commanding officer who indulged in the time-honored surface Navy tradition of eating his young. If an officer did not measure up to his own high standards, Randall would write him the kind of fitness report that would wilt a budding career to the point where the officer would be advised by the bureau to try civilian life. Among the more senior OpNav staff officers at the working level, Randall's reputation was equally menacing. He seemed to enjoy taking a staff briefer apart, cleverly provoking mistakes at the podium and then calling everyone's attention to them.

Dan literally hesitated in the doorway when he saw Randall, but the two EAs ignored him. Dan gave the high sign to the chief yeoman, who nodded, indicating that he would get him in to see 06B when the admiral was available. Dan turned his back on the two EAs and tried to make himself inconspicuous by once again staring at the picture gallery. A helicopter droned by the window from the Pentagon heliport outside, suspending all conversation for a moment.

"You are Commander Collins?" an imperious voice wanted to know. Dan realized Randall was talking to him, and he turned around but did not walk over to Manning's desk.

"Yes, sir, I am," he said.

Randall gave him a three-second inspection and then turned his back to talk to Manning, dismissing Dan without further word. And a pleasure to meet you, too, Your Friendliness, Dan thought. He turned away again, not wanting to look as if he was trying to eavesdrop on the EAs. Dan realized that some of Randall's demeanor arose from the fact that his admiral, the vice chief, was almost certainly going to be the next Chief of Naval Operations, the senior officer in the entire Navy. If visibility was indeed the key to promotion in the Navy, one could not be better positioned than to be the senior aide and executive assistant to the next CNO. But Summerfield had made some interesting observations about Randall during one of their late-afternoon talks.

According to Summerfield, one of the main reasons Randall and the other EAs acted the way they did was because they *were* so visible. They had to serve in their EA billets for sometimes two or even three years literally without ever making a mistake. Typically, they came in to work at 5:30

A.M., sometimes earlier, six days a week, in order to know everything that was going on by the time their principal arrived at seven. Then they stayed in the office until their principal went home at night, however late that might be. Dan had been astonished one night when he had the duty to observe Manning performing the EA's final chore for the night, known as "desk mapping." When Vice Admiral Layman was through for the day, he would simply get up and walk out of the office to his official car. Manning was then expected to go into the DCNO's office, draw a quick map of where every folder, letter, or staff paper physically lay on the large desk, stack everything away in a safe for the night, and then reconstitute the desk the next morning, using the map, putting every paper right back where the great man had left it the night before.

"Being an EA is kind of a rite of passage," Summerfield had observed, "and the admirals are pretty ruthless about it: You want to be an admiral like me, see if you can cut it as my EA. And you better be very damn good at it. If you are, then we'll *think* about making you one of us." Some captains wanted no part of it, preferring to stay down on the naval bases or at shore staffs after their captain sea commands, avoiding the rarified air of the three-and four-star front offices throughout the Navy. And since Summerfield had been an EA himself and was a classmate of admirals, Dan felt that he knew what he was talking about.

"Commander Collins, the admiral will see you now, sir," announced the chief yeoman, and Dan headed for 06B's closed door. The two EAs stopped talking as he walked by, with Randall giving him another studied look.

"Close the door," Admiral Carson said as Dan entered. "Sit down. I'll be right with you."

Carson was reading a staff paper clipped to a brown manila folder, a red felt-tip pen in hand. Dan knew all about that red pen. Finally, Carson put the folder down and looked over his reading glasses at Dan from his desk.

"You've moved your operations back to Washington. Why?"

"I felt there was nothing more I could do in Philly, Admiral. I have the NIS field officer working on extensive interviews with shipyard workers who could have had access to the battleship, but that's going to take some time—if in fact they do it. I thought I'd be more productive trying to develop a possible motive or reason for Lieutenant Hardin's death."

"And that motive is in Washington?"

"We don't know that, sir. But all the records are or will be here, and it's a better place to locate Hardin's shipmates from two years ago than in Philly."

"I see. You said *if* they do it—is NIS not cooperating?"

"Ostensibly, yes, sir. We'll have a test pretty soon, though. Miss Snow, the liaison with NIS Washington, told the Philadelphia field office guy that these interviews were his first priority. If that stands, then I've got no complaints."

Carson nodded. "Director NIS is Rear Admiral Keeler. We understood that his deputy, Mr. Ames, was pushing to take this matter up to the Secretary of the Navy, but it didn't happen. So I suppose you're still in business."

"Yes, sir."

"I'm not going to inquire about the details of what happened up there, but the CHINFO got up at the CNO's morning briefing today and said that it had the potential to be rather sensational."

"Yes, sir, I think it does."

"If it does, you may start to get some stick and rudder from all sorts of helpful Harrys. Remember the JAGMAN rules: You are the investigating officer, and you call it the way you see it. And if somebody senior really interferes, then you recuse yourself and hand it over to him and then it becomes *his* investigation. Kind of like when the captain walks out on the bridge and gives a maneuvering order: The captain then has the conn, right?"

"Yes, sir. But how senior does that advice go, Admiral?"

Admiral Carson's face showed the ghost of a smile.

"You'll probably find that out. That's all, Commander. You have a wonderful day."

When Dan got back to 614, he was surprised to find a courier package from BuPers on his desk. Grace told him that it had come over five minutes ago. Dan opened the package and to his surprise extracted a tan personnel folder, a white fitrep folder, and two green medical records, one health, one dental. The records had a transmittal letter from the federal records depository stating that these records had not yet been archived and must be returned. He sat down with Grace and showed her what kinds of records were in each, then asked her to see if the medical examiner's officer in Philly still wanted the dental records. He began to study the fitness reports, but he soon found that they were not going to be of much help.

"Damn," he muttered.

Grace hung up the phone. "Philadelphia does want the dental records; they're satisfied with the ID, but they took impressions, and the records will close their files. What's the matter?"

"The fitness reports: They're all plain vanilla—nothing superlative, nothing adverse. Ranking one of one, because the only other supply corps officer in the ship was the department head. These are going to tell us nothing."

"Do they identify who the captain was?"

"Oh, yes. And I've got the wardroom list and locating info coming. But I was hoping there'd be some indication here, something pointing to a professional or personal problem, or even a personality trait."

Grace sat back in her chair. "Why do you expect there to be a problem—just because he was black?"

"No, of course not. Because he was killed. My sense is that these things don't happen out of the blue: He was involved in something that led to his being murdered."

"Based on what evidence?"

It was Dan's turn to think for a moment, but Grace pressed him.

"You see what I'm saying? That's the wrong way to approach an investigation, making assumptions like that. I think it's time for a case board."

"Case board?"

"Yes, like the British police use. They set up a situation room, like this one, and then they list all the facts as they become available on a big white board. Each fact has a date or time associated with it. Then they list the names of anyone tied to the case in any way, again with dates of association. Then they set up a master board with a chronological timeline on it and place the facts and the people on that line. If there's a pattern or connections, it typically shows up on the master board. We should do that now. You've got these three white boards here already."

They spent the next hour setting up the boards. Both Summerfield and Snapper looked in occasionally while they worked, but neither man said anything. When they had finished, Dan sat back down and stared at the boards.

"If there's a pattern here, it's eluding me," he said with a sigh.

"We've just begun the investigation," Grace said. "But I see one pattern already."

Dan looked hard but did not see it, but Snapper, who had reappeared in the doorway, did.

"Two deaths," he said, pointing at the left side of the master chronology board. "Hardin's sister dies in a traffic accident in D.C. on the twelfth of April 1992. Her brother gets killed around two weeks later, only nobody knew it at the time. Brother and sister, both Navy, both dead in less than a month. What are the chances of that happening in an unconnected manner?"

Grace was nodding. "And the only reason more wasn't made of it was that, at the time, it was one death and one disappearance. We only find out about the second death two years later."

"The question is, then," mused Dan, "are they in fact related: Is Hardin's murder related to his sister's accident? Maybe we should go talk to the D.C. cops."

Captain Summerfield appeared in the doorway next to Snapper. He had exhumed his pipe and was pretending to puff on it in deference to all the new antismoking rules.

"Seems to me," he said, "that's pretty unlikely. You're not going to get much from the D.C. police on a hit-and-run that's two years cold. I think you need to talk to Lieutenant Hardin's CO, XO—people like that. I agree with Dan: Whatever got him into trouble is probably something they knew about."

"The fitreps are plain vanilla, Captain," Dan said.

"Yeah, but that's not atypical of jaygee reports. He hadn't been in the Navy long enough to warrant very elaborate fitness reports and all the promotion board code words. Promotion to full lieutenant isn't automatic, but damn near so. I recommend you talk to the guy who was CO of *Luce* when she was in the yards. There has to be some reason, something about this guy, that brought this on his head. And I'll wager, since he was the DisBo, that it had something to do with money. Even if the skipper won't really talk about it, that will tell you something. There's my phone."

Summerfield and Snapper left the back room. Dan looked at Grace, who shrugged. Dan got up and closed the door.

"Captain Summerfield is probably right," Dan said. "We have to talk to the senior officers on his ship."

"I've got a better idea," she said. "You talk to them. They'll be more likely to talk to another naval officer than to a woman from the NIS."

"Hey," Dan protested. "We're not all that bad."

"I'll give you the benefit of the doubt. But you must admit, mention of the NIS typically brings the shields up pretty quick, to use your expression. A commander calling from OpNav is likely to produce better results. I've got a list of questions ready."

"And you?"

"I think I'm going to give the D.C. police a call."

22

ON TUESDAY, MALACHI WARD returned to his town house on Capitol Hill and screened his answering machine. There was a message from the captain to call in. He had to consult his Wizard for the number; he hadn't heard from the captain for nearly two years. His beloved principal must have had an attack of chastity and learned to keep his zipper shut for a while. It was nearly 6:00 P.M., but he knew the captain would still be at the office. The captain was nothing if not dedicated. He dialed the number.

Malachi was tired after the four-hour drive back from Norfolk. He had accompanied the chief of staff of a House subcommittee down to the Tide-water area to have a little heart-to-heart with the head of a maritime-trade lobby group. It seemed that the lobbyist had crossed the subcommittee chairman during hearings in the middle of an important power play on the Hill, this after promising to support a quota issue of interest to the chairman. The merits of the bill itself had not been in question: The political issue had been about the prerogatives of the chairman to control a bill. Malachi was hired to go along as an attention-getting device.

They had driven down to the Tidewater area, timed to arrive at the man's home in the early evening, where the chief of staff had shared his thinking with the trade rep. Malachi, whose instructions were to say nothing, simply stood at the side of the patio and looked meaningfully at the man, his home, and his pretty wife and children visible through the kitchen windows. The message seemed to have penetrated. The following morning, the chief of staff met with the lobbyist and his entire staff to ensure that everyone was properly calibrated. Malachi had revisited the house in time to catch the lobbyist's wife on her way to morning tennis, all pert and perky in her little white tennis outfit. Again he had said and done nothing: He had just pulled up in front of their house and waited. When she came out the front door and saw him looking at her, she turned right around and went back in. He had given her time to get on the phone to her husband before slowly driving away.

When a voice he didn't recognize answered the phone, Malachi left the code name and number and then went to make a drink. He had been good last night—traveling with a client. The chief of staff had a dinner invite somewhere, so Malachi had contented himself with the microwaved mystery d'jour at the Holiday Inn dining room and one double Harper before going up to his room. He had taken a quart of bourbon with him but decided to test his willpower. He had put the bottle out on the motel room dresser, unopened, and then watched television and smoked cigarettes until finally falling asleep. The still-unopened bottle sitting there the next morning was a vivid testimonial to his self-control. But that had been last night. This was tonight. He poured his usual and went to watch the evening news. The phone rang as the local broadcaster was reviewing last night's body count in some of the more socially dynamic neighborhoods of the District. He picked up the phone.

"Yes?"

"Greetings."

The captain.

"Greetings indeed. You called," Malachi said.

"Yes, I did. Remember the Hardin boy? Went missing a few years ago, up in Philadelphia? Guess what?"

Malachi didn't answer. He did not like guess-what games.

"He's no longer missing," the captain said.

Malachi sat up straight and muted the television. Not possible, he thought. But watch what you say.

"Where? And what's he done?" he asked, trying to lodge the impression that, as far as he knew, the boy might still be alive.

"What he's done is turn up very dead in the boiler room of a mothballed battleship in the Philadelphia Naval Shipyard. And now there's going to be an investigation."

"Dead?"

"Very dead. So dead, he's even mummified. It seems he'd been confined in one of the battleship *Wisconsin*'s boilers ever since he went missing. You see, there's no air below the main decks in a mothballed capital ship—they replace it with nitrogen gas. It was something of a shrinking experience. I'm sure you'll be hearing about it pretty soon on the news."

Malachi sipped some whiskey and tried to think. "Well," he said, "I guess the operative question is, So what? If he's dead, he's not going to be telling any interesting tales to anyone. You can remind your principal of the pirate's first rule."

"It's the investigation that concerns us, not Lieutenant Hardin. But we are hoping that two years will leave such a cold trail that nothing will come of it."

"Sounds reasonable to me. Most homicides are solved in the first seventy-two hours or not at all."

"Is this a homicide, Malachi?" The captain's voice was silky. Malachi grinned into the phone.

"You tell me, Captain—it's your guys' investigation, right?"

"Yes, exactly. And like all investigations, we'll have to see where it leads us. There's actually a political dimension to this issue that may give me the opportunity to influence the course of the investigation. In a way that can help us all. But—"

"Yeah, I hear that 'but.' What do you want from me?"

"Just wanted you to hear it from us first, Malachi. We may be in touch. Stay tuned, as it were."

"Okay. You know where to find me. But remember that it's your investigation. Hold that thought, as it were."

Malachi hung up and stared at the muted television and worked on his bourbon while the color images of a commercial flickered across the screen. A sexy young woman in a short flip skirt was bending over a store shelf, with the camera behind her, while supposedly focusing the keen minds of the viewers on the decision of which spray cleaner was best for her and the rest of mankind. Women's liberation at work, Malachi mused. The voyeuristic shot of the woman's thighs was undoubtedly supposed to titillate, but Malachi felt nothing—not now and not since that night in Frankfurt, when a routine bar roust had gone horribly wrong. Malachi and an MP sergeant named Terry Eastman had been sent down to the Sachsenhausen district to pick up an AWOL Air Force warrant officer who was reportedly holed up in a bar on a three-day toot. Malachi and Eastman had gone into the bar. It should have been ho-hum: "a no big deal, roust the drunk, pour him into the MP van, and then make the long drive back to Rhein-Main" evolution. Eastman could have done it in his sleep, but Malachi had gone along with an eye toward maybe doing a little forty-eight himself in Frankfurt afterward, if things worked out.

Things did not work out. A barfly got into it—Inge. He hadn't known her name then, just that there was this plumpish hooker sitting at the bar when they went in after the warrant officer. As Sergeant Eastman was breaking the news to the warrant, who was so drunk he couldn't even lift his head, the blowsy barfly with the too-red lipstick and the big floppy front had swiveled around on her bar stool and started yelling at Malachi in

German. Malachi had been surprised—there was no big deal going down, no fight, no real problem at all. He was the officer, not the MP, and he was in uniform. He had put up a hand to tell her to shut up and stay out of it, the other customers starting to look up, when Inge had reached behind her, grabbed a beer bottle, smashed the top off, and in one smooth swinging motion shoved the jagged edges into Malachi's crotch. The pain had been so incredible that Malachi couldn't even scream as he sank down into a crouch by her bar stool, his hands clutching at his sodden trousers, his mouth open but nothing coming out, and then the bitch had jabbed the bottle into his throat. Malachi had remembered only one thing after that, one thing besides the wetness that was flooding his pants and pumping down his arms, all over his shirtfront, and that was Terry, good ole Sergeant Terry, eyes wide as white dinner plates, unlimbering that big .45 and opening fire at the whore, emptying that cannon and all the shelves behind the bar with five thundering blasts, the sounds of the bullets buzzing by Malachi's head in counterpoint to the red muzzle flashes, the thunking noises as two slugs hit Inge, one in the chest, the other tearing her right arm, the bottle-wielding arm, right off at the elbow, the rest blasting big holes in the wood of the bar and shattering everything behind it in a noisy cascade of glass and schnapps. Malachi and Inge had ended up on the floor together, Malachi bent in half, eye-to-eye with the whore, his eyes seeing, but barely, her eyes glassy and seeing nothing, the echoes of a glass avalanche behind them somewhere, and Sergeant Terry screaming his name, and the smell of blood, gunpowder, and urine.

Malachi had ended up spending four months convalescing in the Army hospital at Wiesbaden, fighting off a huge infection and then learning how to form sounds in his mangled voice box again. They hadn't told him of his castration until the end of the third week.

He stared at the television screen, unseeing, for a long time, reliving that night for the millionth time, and then came back to the present. He discovered that his hands were shaking, and his shirt felt too tight. Shit. Where the hell had that come from? He took a deep breath, got up, and went out into the kitchen to get some more whiskey and a cigarette. It was amazing what brought it all back sometimes—seeing a woman on the Metro who looked like Inge, seeing something on the TV, like tonight. He often wondered if he might not be just a little crazy. Her face sometimes materialized on the faces of women he passed in the street, or when some woman at a desk gave him a hard time. It always disoriented him when it happened. Like the morning he had taken out that black girl—what, two years ago?— her face, her angry, distorted face, had triggered the image just before he hit her. Which was maybe *why* he had hit her.

And living on Capitol Hill didn't help: It seemed like all the little basement flats around the neighborhood had one or more beautiful young women living in them, women who came strutting by his windows every morning, headed for the Hill, dressed like Parisian call girls, every one of them with a "my shit doesn't stink" expression on her face. Hundreds of them. For all the good it did him. Malachi had no use for women.

He came back into the living room and sat down again. So the Hardin kid had turned up, after all. In the boiler of a battleship, for God's sake. Nice try, Angelo. Nothing if not original. He closed his eyes and waited for Mr. Harper's elixir to infuse his brain with some new capital. He had worked for a master sergeant once who was full of little homilies about getting by in the Army. One seemed to apply now: Don't waste your time and energy on things you cannot do anything about. Killing the girl had been an accident, a bothersome accident, but there you are. After what a woman had done to him, he felt that womankind in general owed him a whole shitpot full of opportunities for—what? Revenge? Retaliation? Call it justice. Maybe she hadn't slipped out there on the street. Maybe he had seen Inge's face and had simply touched the wheel a tad, just enough to alter the balance, just like that German whore had altered his balance, and his voice, and his sex life—forever.

Taking her brother off the boards had also been something of an accident. Like brother, like sister, apparently: They had been a pair of shit-magnets. Angelo had warned him, and, just like with the girl in Foggy Bottom that morning, things got away from them. Shit happens in the big city. But now the body had been found and the Navy was going to do an investigation. Can't do anything about the body being found, and Angelo wasn't the kind of guy to hand him his money back; the *paisans* were not into warranties.

He considered the implications of an investigation. A Navy homicide investigation—that would be the Naval Investigative Service. He snorted. The Navy's lame attempt to emulate the Army's CID, only dumber. In his Germany days, he had had some experience with an NIS crew up from their Naples office when he had been setting up a Marine corporal for a drug fall to protect some friends. He had wired the thing so tight that all the NIS weenies had to do was be there, but, no, they wanted to dick around, talk to some people, almost queering the deal. They were just a bunch of ex-sailors running around in polyester suits from Sears and trying to use three-syllable words in their reports. He had not been stunned to read that the NIS had had a heavy hand in the Navy's recent PR problems with the Tailhook scandal. But none the less, they would start snooping around and talking to people. And while it was better having the NIS on it than, say, the FBI, it still meant that a federal police outfit was going to be poking around. That was going to make the captain and his principal nervous sooner rather than later. Already had, in fact.

He went back into the kitchen and refreshed his drink. When he came back to the living room, an especially homely car dealer was screaming silently at the screen. Why did car dealers and furniture salesmen always have to scream? He was convinced that the mute switch on TV remote controls had been invented because of car dealers and furniture salesmen.

He sat down again. Even the NIS might eventually connect the girl and her brother, both dying within a two-week time frame. But over and above that regrettable coincidence, there was nothing to connect *him* to the girl or her brother. Oh, Angelo, maybe, but Angelo was about as safe as anyone could be. Safer, actually. You might not admire their business, but the Guidos observed their own rules and regulations a lot better than most elements of American society.

And the captain. He thought about that. If the NIS weenies did stumble across something, the weakest spot in Malachi's own personal-security perimeter was the captain—the guy who had handed him the money to scare off the girl two years ago, and the guy who had invited him in the Army-Navy Town Club to see what her brother looked like. "What I really wish is that the son of a bitch would just disappear," the captain had said to him. The captain was the only guy in this whole Hardin deal who could finger *him*.

Malachi drained his glass, savoring the familiar expanding ball of comfort in his stomach and the certainty that his brain was computing at top end. This whole mess had started with an honest, straight-forward job: to go see some twist, warn her off some great man's very busy, very important life in the big city. Little scare didn't work, so he'd set up a medium scare, only the bitch had messed it up for everybody. Any way you looked at it, that one had been just an accident. Then the not-such-an-accident to her mouthy younger brother.

How had his master sergeant put it? "If you're gonna get into it, get into it." Maybe, just maybe, and depending on what the captain decided to do, he'd have to take one more pass at the Hardin case. The girl had been a shit-happens deal. Her brother . . . well, her brother had run his mouth in front of the wrong honkies. Now he might have to take one more guy off the boards to cover his own ass. That would leave the principal, the great man, out there all alone if the NIS somehow happened to wander down the right road. Malachi decided he could get his arms around that picture. He liked it; liked it a lot, in fact. Damn near as much as this fine bourbon. He also realized that he was thinking in circles, and perhaps that he was medium drunk. What a surprise.

23

ON TUESDAY MORNING, Grace walked into the District Municipal Center on Indiana Avenue and consulted the directory listing mounted over the unmanned information desk. The lobby was spacious and rather dark, with streams of people moving through it. There were citizens coming in to deal with automobile paperwork, jackbooted motorcycle cops, plainclothes cops, and many other people milling around whom Grace could not readily identify. The terrazzo floors amplified the noise of people talking, asking for directions, or just coming in and out. The sign above the information desk told her that the Homicide Division was on the third floor, so she went to the elevator bank and pushed a button, joining a small crowd of people who were waiting. Every so often, the request light would go out, and then someone would push it again, with no visible effect. Just like the District, she thought.

She fished in her purse for the name of her point of contact: a Captain Goldsmith. She had called yesterday afternoon for an appointment. She had called again this morning before taking the Metro over to the District, and Goldsmith's secretary had confirmed the appointment. When the elevator finally came, she had to move quickly to get in. At the third floor, she went left, read a door number, turned around, and walked all the way to the end of the corridor to the next-to-the-last office, whose door was open. The room numbers were missing from most of the doors.

Inside the office were two desks, a secretary standing by a coffee maker, and a doorway that led into a larger and better-furnished inner office. A well-dressed black man in a charcoal gray suit was talking to the secretary when Grace walked in. He immediately asked if he could help her.

"I have an appointment to see Captain Goldsmith," she said. "Can you tell me where his office is?"

"I'm Captain Vann," the man said. "Captain Goldsmith is the head of the Homicide Division; that's next door. Lemme show you."

He took her next door, where there was another secretary guarding the corner office. Vann stuck his head into the inner office, showed Grace in, and left. Wendell Goldsmith was a white man in his mid-fifties, who looked more like a prosperous lobbyist than the chief of Homicide in a city like Washington, D.C. He was florid-faced and showed the beginnings of a double chin, and he filled out his expensive suit with what looked like the lifetime result of feeding well and often in the city's finer restaurants. He had the careful eyes of a long-term bureaucrat, and he was polite but reserved in his greeting when Grace presented her credentials. Goldsmith glanced briefly at her badge and ID while motioning her to a chair. Grace noticed that he made sure the door between his office and the secretarial area remained open.

"Well, Miss Snow, what can I do for the NIS today?" He had a pleasant voice, devoid of any particular emotion. Grace wondered if he was a political appointee or if he had ever been a working police detective.

"Captain Goldsmith, thank you for seeing me on such short notice. As I told your secretary, I'm working on an investigation for the Navy, and it involves the apparent homicide two years ago of a lieutenant in the Philadelphia Naval Shipyard."

He just looked at her, not voicing the obvious question.

"The reason I'm coming to see the D.C. police is that this individual's sister, who was also in the Navy, was the victim of a fatal hit-and-run accident here in the District about two weeks before the lieutenant was murdered. Apparently, the case was never solved."

"Has your investigation established some kind of link between the two deaths, Miss Snow?"

"No, not on a factual basis. But it does seem a bit too coincidental to us: a brother and a sister, both in the Navy, dying within two weeks of each other."

"I see," Goldsmith said politely. I doubt it, thought Grace, but she pressed ahead.

"I'd like to be able to sit down with the people who did the investigation of the hit-and-run incident. The victim's name was Elizabeth Hardin."

Goldsmith wrote the name down on a pad and appeared to consider it.

"If it was a hit-and-run," he said finally, "or so classified by the department, it would have gone to the hit-and-run division in the Traffic Bureau. They're actually over on New York Avenue. If the case was resolved, the case files will be stored here, in central records—that's down on the ground floor, where you came in."

"And if it was not resolved?"

Goldsmith shrugged. "It would be an open case; they'd have the original records downstairs, and a duplicate set over in Traffic. The chances of resolution at this late date . . ." He shrugged his shoulders and looked at his watch.

"I understand, Captain. Can you refer me to someone in the Traffic Bureau?"

"I can, but we have a standard procedure for letting other law-enforcement agencies look at police records. You'll have to go through that drill first. Your agency has to make a formal request—a fax will do it, though. Want to make a call?"

She had to wait almost an hour down in the records center before Robby Booker was able to get a fax sent over from NIS with the approved records request. Finally, a very thin, elderly black lady produced an equally thin police file. She had Grace sign an access sheet, then indicated a combination chair-desk of the type that Grace had not seen since high school over in one corner of the records area's lobby. Grace thanked her and squeezed into the chair-desk to review the file. It was a thin file indeed. The old refrain from the Jack Webb TV show of the fifties flitted through her mind: "Just the facts, ma'am. Just the facts."

Facts were all that was in the file. The preliminary report stated that, on April 12, 1992, a citizen had called 911 to report finding a young woman, apparently deceased, on his front steps on 23rd Street at 6:35 A.M. Emergency services were dispatched at 6:37, and arrived on the scene at 6:45 A.M. They confirmed that the victim, a black female, had expired at the scene due to what appeared to be multiple blunt-force trauma injuries indicative of the subject being hit by a vehicle. There was evidence in the street (two shoes, blood spots, and a woman's handbag) of an impact with a vehicle or vehicles unknown. There were no skid marks or other visible signs of avoidance maneuvers. The distance between point of impact in the street and the final position of the body was seventy-three feet, eight inches. No witnesses heard or saw anything.

Seventy-three feet, she thought. The vehicle had been moving right along. Figure something big, like a van or a Suburban like Dan's: eight, nine thousand pounds going forty, fifty miles an hour. What was that old inertia equation: $mv = mv$? Eight thousand pounds times fifty miles an hour versus 125 pounds going one mile an hour. The difference in the energy equation had to be absorbed by the smaller participant, hence the distance. She shivered.

The poorly typed report of the follow-up investigation, conducted by one Detective (second grade) William Marshal, was not much more informative. Appropriate news releases had been filed, including an appeal to the hypothetical driver and to the public at large for any information, all without further results. Bulletins to local area auto-body shops had produced no reports. Victim's clothes had been sent to Forensics for collection of paint samples, but none had been found. Interview with the girl's mother had produced no adverse or incriminating information that would indicate this had been anything but an accident. Investigating officer's conclusions: hit-and-run; perpetrators unknown; vehicle type, make, and color unknown; case status: open. A handwritten note on the bottom in the "Contributing Factors" block indicated that the woman had been a black woman, jaywalking in the early-morning darkness, wearing dark clothes.

The third page was a report from the medical examiner's office as to extent of injuries and cause of death, which conformed to the previously described consequences of the human body going one-on-one with a large steel mass moving at high speed. There were some notes in a cramped, difficult-to-read doctor scribble at the bottom of the page, probably from the ME, which she skipped over. She turned the page. The fourth page of the report was the report of the examining physician who had declared the young woman dead on arrival at George Washington University Hospital emergency room. The litany of blunt-force trauma, multiple internal injuries, and massive shock was repeated: "High likelihood of near-instantaneous death, based on extent and severity of injuries. Next of kin, one Mrs. Angela Hardin, notified in accordance with instructions in victim's wallet. Body released to the ME."

Grace turned back to the ME's report, scanned the unfamiliar form with its anatomical and laboratory findings, and then tried to decipher his handwritten notes. The ME's handwriting was just about unintelligible, but one word did leap out. Elizabeth Hardin had been in the very early stages of pregnancy at the time she died. Grace closed the file.

Well, now. That might be important. Pregnancy indicated a relationship with a man, a man who might be able to shed some light on Elizabeth Hardin the woman, the person, as opposed to Elizabeth Hardin the hit-and-run victim. Possibly, through Elizabeth, they might learn something about her brother. Grace was ready to concede that the young woman's death was just what it looked like: an accident. The cops usually had a pretty good sense of these things, and the investigation looked to have been by the book, but no more than that. But she was still bothered by the coincidence of the two deaths—first the sister, then the brother, within a two-week time frame. She needed a human contact to explore that coincidence.

"Excuse me, Miss Snow?" a voice at her elbow interrupted her thoughts. Startled, she nearly dropped the file in surprise and looked up. Standing to her side was the captain who had taken her into Goldsmith's office. Vann, that was the name. There was no graceful way to get out of the chair-desk, so she continued just to stare up at him. Vann was of medium height, slender build, and had a thin-looking face that Grace found vaguely familiar.

"Yes," she said. With her neck at an odd angle, there was a squeak in her voice.

"I'm Moses Vann. I'm the executive assistant to the Deputy Chief of Police for Criminal Investigations. Used to be chief of the Homicide Division. I understand you've come in asking about the Hardin case?"

"You've spoken to Captain Goldsmith?"

He looked away for a second, as if impatient or annoyed with her answering a question with a question. "Why are you here, Miss Snow? Why is the Navy Department suddenly interested in Elizabeth Hardin's death?"

Grace was becoming uncomfortable looking up at him from the chair. She slid sideways out of the chair and put the file back on the counter before replying. The clerk dutifully signed it back in and disappeared with it.

"I'm conducting an investigation into the death, and apparent homicide, of her brother, Lt. Wesley Hardin, in Philadelphia. He was—"

"Yeah, I heard about it. See, I know Angela Hardin. What's the connection?"

"I—we—that is, I have a partner, actually he's in charge of the investigation—he's in OpNav, and, uh—"

"What's the connection, Miss Snow? Is there a basis in fact for your being here? Or are we Easter-egging here?"

Grace resented the tone and substance of his question. This man almost seemed to be angry with her. "I'm a federal investigator," she replied. "I'm with the NIS—that's the Naval Investigative Service. I represent the federal government, Captain Vann. Is there some special sensitivity to this case behind your tone of voice?"

Vann stared at her and then laughed a nasty laugh.

"Naw," he said. "That's just my usual sparkling personality comin' through, dig? Us local cops jes naturally likes to jone on pretty white women. Especially when they feds, you know what I'm sayin'? Specially when they feds."

Grace gave him an arch look. "That was truly special, Captain Vann. Can you do Bill Cosby, too?"

Vann tried to glare at her but then began to have trouble controlling his face. He finally grinned. "All right, Miss Federal Government Snow. I guess I had that coming. How's about I buy you a cup of coffee and let's start over."

She hesitated, but then she agreed and began gathering her things. He led her down the hallway that led to the building's entrance lobby. They walked out into the bright sunlight of the plaza in front of the Center, where the same crowd she had seen when she arrived still seemed to be milling around. There was an ongoing traffic jam as a few cars tried to creep through all the people, and two harassed-looking women police officers were in the street, contributing to the disorder as they tried in vain to direct pedestrians and traffic. Several of the cops greeted Vann as he shepherded Grace across the crowded street to a corner café called Barista, which was next to the entrance to the Judiciary Square Metro station. Vann pointed Grace to a table outside, asked her what kind of coffee she liked, and stepped inside to get their orders. He returned with two coffees and a prune Danish, which had been cut in half.

"Prune Danish is my downfall," he said, sitting down. "But this time it's okay, because I had 'em cut it in half; now you gotta eat half so's my conscience doesn't hurt."

Grace smiled and obliged. Vann took the other half and consumed it in two eager bites. She noticed that he was never still, shifting around in his chair and looking around all the time.

"The coffee's just an excuse to get the Danish," he said, licking his fingers. His coat had flopped open and she saw a shoulder rig with what looked like a miniature cannon hanging upside down in it. He saw her looking.

"That's a Ruger Blackhawk forty-four Mag," he said. "I can't hit anything with it smaller than a building, but when it goes off, every guilty bastard within a block usually puts his hands up. We solve a lot of cases that way."

Grace smiled. "They gave me a three fifty-seven Magnum for a side arm at NIS," she said. "As kind of a new-girl joke, I think. I was afraid to pull the trigger after I'd fired it once. It hurt my hand."

Vann laughed. "Know what you mean. We got a little lady here on one of the detective squads—Tamassa Green, her name is. Little bitty thing. She showed up on the qualification range first time with a Colt Woodsman— that's one of those high-priced twenty-two semiautos. The mob likes 'em. Instructor said she wasn't gonna stop anything with that thing. She said yes, she would, since she favored putting the first round through an eye and the second round between the mutt's legs. I remember how it got quiet when she said that, how all the macho dudes started to ease sideways a little bit, sorta tryin' to make room without bein' caught at it. That's what she's carryin' to this day, and when she does her quals, she finishes up with an extra two shots, one high, one low, if you follow. She's something else. But enough of this. You came over here from the Pentagon on a hunch, right? You're looking for something, don't know what it is?"

Grace nodded and then recounted where they were with the investigation. Vann seemed almost to solidify and settle into place as she talked. His body stopped jiggling around and he focused his eyes on hers. She got the impression that every word she said was sticking in his memory like insects to flypaper.

"You used the term *basis in fact* a little while ago," she concluded. "We have precious few facts to go on right now, and a very cold trail. We only picked up the pattern of the two deaths today using a case board."

He nodded, indicating he knew what a case board was all about. Then he took out a pack of cigarettes, shook one out, and gave her an inquiring "do you mind?" look.

"Go ahead," she said. She didn't mind it as long as she was outside.

"Can't smoke damn near anywhere these days," he grumped, lighting up and taking a deep drag. He was careful to blow the smoke away from her. "Appreciate it. So what exactly were you looking for over here?"

"I was hoping to come over here and talk to the people who did the hit-and-run investigation. Goldsmith felt that the file would tell me as much as they could, given the time that's gone by."

"And?"

"The report seems open-and-shut. I guess we'll press on with what Commander Collins is doing—talking to Lieutenant Hardin's ex-supervisors in that ship to see what they might tell us. We're operating under the theory that something he did or was doing got him killed. My guess is that it was probably something here in Washington."

"So you found nothing of interest in that Traffic file?"

She thought he might be testing her. "Well," she said hesitatingly. "One thing—Elizabeth Hardin was pregnant."

"Ah," he said, taking a second enormous drag on the cigarette. "Yes. Why is that significant?"

"It would indicate a boyfriend, a fiancé or a lover—someone close to her, someone who might know something about her brother. Again, what, exactly, I don't know."

He nodded approvingly, mashed the cigarette out, and then sipped some coffee. She felt a sudden need to keep talking, to fill the silence between them, but then decided to see what he would do if she shut up. At length, he spoke.

"I know Angela Hardin—that's Elizabeth and Wesley's mother."

"So you said. We met her in Philadelphia, when she came up to ID the body."

"I know about that, too. How did she react to you and your partner, the—what, commander? Yes, Commander Collins. How did she react to you?"

"She seemed hostile. We put it down to grief reaction. Except—"

"Yes?"

"I had the sense she came up there knowing that it was going to be her son she saw in that morgue. Like she was resigned to his being dead, and that the trip to Philadelphia was simply a formality, a confirmation of something she had known in her heart. Again, we put it down to grief reaction. To lose both of her children—"

"This is Washington, D.C., Miss Snow," Vann said grimly. "There are many, many black families here who have lost more than one child. Sometimes all their children."

"Yes, I know," Grace said. "But tell me why you sought me out today. You obviously have a special interest in the first Hardin case. Is there something you can tell me?"

He hesitated before replying, and he began to move around again in his chair. He frowned, sighed, looked across the street, down at the floor, and then back at her. Finally, he spoke.

"No," he said. "I have nothing to tell you that you can put up on a case board. I just happen to know the family. I knew about Wesley's disappearance, and I heard on the news about the Navy finding a guy dead in the shipyard—in that ship. I wondered if it just might be Wesley. But, no, I have no insights to give you." He paused. "At least not at this time. But we'd appreciate it very much—very much—if you would let me know what you find out about Wesley's death."

"We?"

"The department. The chief takes murders in this city very seriously, despite the image you may have of us from the papers. And if you need stuff from us, call me first."

Grace nodded. "Of course," she said. "And we'd appreciate it very much if when we do that, you might share with us any insights that you develop. Here's my card."

Vann went fishing in his pocket for one of his own cards. Grace picked up her purse and stood up. "As best we can tell, Captain, Wesley was buried *alive* in that ship. Bolted into a boiler when he was probably unconscious after getting beaten up and hit on the head. He would have awakened in the dark, inside that boiler. Dan Collins says he would have figured out what he was in. He was probably in there for a week or so. Then the shipyard filled the ship with nitrogen gas. 'To put her to sleep,' as the shipyard calls it."

She looked at him for a moment. He was holding one of his own cards in midair but had gone motionless, the card suspended over the table, his face registering a sick shock while he just stared at her. Then he swallowed.

"You get something, you call me," he said in a strangled voice, handing her his card. "Please."

24

THAT SAME MORNING, Dan made his first call at 9:30 A.M. to a Capt. Martin Fletcher, ex–commanding officer of *Luce*, now serving on the staff of the Commander in Chief, U.S. Atlantic Fleet, in Norfolk, Virginia. Captain Fletcher was in a meeting; the yeoman asked if he could take a message.

"Yes. Tell him Commander Collins called from OpNav regarding a JAG investigation. I need to talk to him about a Lt. (jg) Wesley Hardin. I also need you to work up a Freedom of Information form for him to sign and fax so I can use his Social Security number on an interview form."

Dan gave the yeoman his phone and fax numbers and hung up. He had to wait until 10:30 A.M. to make a second, similar call to San Diego, this time in search of a Comdr. William Brownell, formerly the executive officer in *Luce*, who was now the skipper of a destroyer in San Diego. The phone call to the ship's number was shunted over to the base operator, who said that ship was out at sea. He then called the Naval Surface Forces Pacific Fleet scheduler on his secure phone and found out that the ship would be back in port in three weeks. Dan thanked the scheduler and hung up. Zip for two.

The third name on his list was a Lt. Francis Baler, Supply Corps, USN, who had been Hardin's department head, and thus Hardin's direct supervisor, in *Luce*. The locator listed Baler as being assigned to the Shore-Based Intermediate Maintenance Activity, or SIMA, at Mayport, Florida. After three calls, he got a hit.

"Lieutenant Baler speaking, sir."

"Lieutenant, I'm Comdr. Dan Collins, Division of Politico-Military Policy, on the CNO's staff in Washington. I'm conducting a JAG investigation into the disappearance of Lt. (jg) Wesley Hardin two years ago. I understand that you were the chop in *Luce* prior to your present assignment."

"Yes, sir."

Dan informed him that this was a formal interview and that he would need some forms signed when they were done. He also told him that he was taping the interview so that he could keep accurate notes. Baler understood the drill and they went through the name, rank, and serial number motions to establish Baler's identity for the tape.

"And Lieutenant Hardin was the disbursing officer and your assistant when you were the supply officer in *Luce*, correct?"

"Yes, sir. He was the DisBo and the supply division officer. Has he finally turned up?"

Dan was struck by the supply officer's choice of words. He had used the phrase "turned up" in a way that implied that a runaway had finally returned to the fold.

"Yes, in a manner of speaking, he has, Mr. Baler," Dan said. "It appears that he didn't go UA back there in 1992. It appears that he was murdered and his body hidden in one of the main engineering spaces of the *Wisconsin*."

"Holy shit! I heard about that. You mean that was Wes Hardin?"

"Yeah. I'm talking to you in hopes of finding out anything about Mr. Hardin's performance of duty or personality traits that might have a bearing on why such a thing might have happened. I also have calls in to your former CO and the XO."

"Holy shit," Baler said again. "Although I don't know what I can add to the first investigation, Commander."

"What first investigation?"

"Well, we had to do one when he went missing. Standard procedure, you know, a JAGMAN. I was the designated investigator, but the Philly NIS office actually ran it because Hardin was the DisBo. But that part of it was clean. There were no funds missing or anything out of order other than some admin nits and hits. He didn't book with bucks."

Dan felt a warm flush rising on his neck. There *had* been an investigation at the time of Hardin's disappearance, and the NIS knew about it? Hell, they'd conducted it! Santini had never mentioned this. He was doubly embarrassed, because, as a prior executive officer himself, he should have known that there would have been an investigation done. Hell's bells.

"We've talked to the NIS," Dan said. "But they failed to mention that *Luce* had done a JAG investigation. Do you remember the NIS guy in Philly who participated?"

"Yes, sir, a guy named Santini. He was the number-two guy at the NISRA, the field office. I don't remember who the head guy was then."

Santini. Wonderful. "But to your knowledge, there was no obvious, substantive reason for Hardin to have just disappeared like that."

There was a pause on the other end. "I didn't actually say that, Commander. Not then, not now. But your question kinda touches a sensitive nerve."

"This have to do with race?"

"Yes, sir." Another pause. "What the hell, I said this before, so I'll say it again, although the CO and the XO won't back this up, in all probability. But it goes to the heart of the problems I had with Hardin. He did his job, he was a competent disbursing officer—the admin discrepancies they found after he disappeared consisted of pretty standard little shit. But as an officer, he did as much harm as good, because I think he had a real problem dealing with white people. Plain and simple, I think he was more than a little racist."

"That's usually not a plain and simple attribute, Mr. Baler."

Baler sighed. "Yes, sir. But as far as I'm concerned, it's the truth. Not that a white guy can say anything like that out loud or in a fitrep. Especially today. But I figured at the time that Hardin skipped out because he'd had it up to here with conforming to Mr. Charley's Navy rules. Look, I have two black officers in my department here at SIMA, and there's none of that shit. They're both very damn good at their jobs and in how they get along. Everybody respects them as officers, and also as mature, black men. But Hardin had an attitude and he made no effort to keep it a secret."

Dan reflected while he jotted down some notes.

"Did this attitude color *everything* he did? I mean, was his racial animosity visible enough that he would have done or said something that in turn could have gotten him killed?"

"Wow. You really want me to speculate here, Commander."

"Yeah, well, this is an informal JAGMAN. We're not doing rules of evidence, and you're not a suspect or a prospective party to the investigation or anything like that. I'm trying to dig out facts and opinions, and you were not only somebody who knew this guy professionally but you're apparently willing to talk about it."

"Then the answer to your question, in my *opinion*, is no. He was smart. Angry, but smart. But he certainly knew the limits to the racial angle. He was from the inner city of Washington, D.C., so presumably he knew the code of the streets, in the sense that he knew where not to go and what not to say. So if he got himself killed, I doubt very seriously it was over a black-white racial issue."

"What, then? Was he a big-time womanizer? A gambler?"

"Not that I ever saw, and we kind of watch our disbursing officers for those traits. Philly's an expensive town for junior officers to go on liberty in, so most of the bachelors, including Wes, hung around the base—the O-club, the base pool, wardroom parties, that sort of thing."

"What, then?" Dan could not tell if Baler was avoiding the question, or sincerely did not know anything.

"Commander, I think, and this is without knowing what's going on here . . . I think . . . well, shit, I don't know what to think. I guess I'd have to say that whatever it was, it probably arose from something in Washington. Either something in his past, when he was a kid, or something that he did or said to someone in D.C. that pissed them off enough to come get him. He used to go down there a lot on weekends. He had a sister down there—she was killed in a car crash or something, as I recall. Right before he disappeared, now that I think about it. Like I said, Wes was street smart, but from what I read, sometimes you can trip a disrespect mine without even knowing you've done it, you know what I mean?"

"But bottom line, there was nothing he did or said professionally or personally in the wardroom social setting that would indicate to you that he might have had a serious problem in Philadelphia."

"Sir, that's correct. But it's also purely speculative: Nobody really got that close to Wes in that wardroom."

"No white officers, you mean. Was he the only black officer?"

"Yes, sir."

Dan thought for a moment. He couldn't think of anything else to ask at the moment. He looked at Grace's questionnaire, but Baler had covered the ground pretty well.

"Okay, Mr. Baler. Thanks for the input, and double thanks for your candor. I'm going to write this up as a statement and send it down for you to sign. I'll use, uh . . . discretion in how I write this; I understand that even talking about race issues these days can get you in trouble. And triple thanks for telling me about the first investigation."

"Yes, sir. And I'm sorry to hear about Wes. He could have . . . well . . ." He paused. "Well, I don't know if that's true. I didn't have any answers for a Wes Hardin then and I don't have any now."

Dan thanked him again and hung up. He popped the tape, called in Yeoman Jackson, and asked him to transcribe it. "But keep the tape intact; I have to save all the tapes until my witnesses sign their interview sheets. And do it in rough draft—I'll want to edit that interview."

Jackson grumbled about having to do JAG stuff in addition to his regular duties, but he left with the tape. Dan checked to see if his call to Norfolk had produced a reply, but there was nothing. He wanted to call Santini in Philadelphia and raise hell about that prior investigation, but he decided to wait until Grace came back and let her beat up on NIS.

He reflected on what the supply officer had said. As an executive officer in a ship, Dan had some experience with racial attitudes of both complexions, as well as the problems they produced in the close confines of warships. The frictions generated were very real and often made people acutely sensitive. But had that kind of thing led to murder? He walked over to the case board.

Grace had keyed on the two deaths, brother and sister, so close together in time. If only statistically, that had to be significant. Baler had said that whatever it was, it wasn't in Philly, it was in Washington. He got out a dry erase marker, went to the names board, and wrote Hardin's name at the top, under which he synthesized Baler's comments about Hardin's attitude problem and a possible Washington connection to his death. He put the marker down. He knew what was bothering him: Now they would *have* to go back to see Mrs. Hardin. He was sitting there looking at the board when Grace walked back in just before noon.

"How'd it go with the D.C. cops?" he asked as she shucked her coat and purse and sat down.

"Nothing on the hit-and-run," she replied. "The case file is still open and they have nothing in the way of suspects, vehicle ID, or witnesses. I was all ready to believe that it was what it looked like: a hit-and-run accident where the driver got clean away."

"Was?"

"Yes. While I was there, a police captain, ex-chief of the Homicide Division, heard I was there and sought me out."

Dan suggested they go down to the corner snack bar and get a sandwich while she filled him in on the conversation with Captain Vann and on the undercurrents of that conversation, including the bit about Elizabeth Hardin being pregnant. Dan whistled at that news, he was intrigued, but then felt compelled to ask the pertinent question.

"How much of this can go on the fact board?"

Grace acknowledged his question with a frown. "Just the police incident report itself," she said. "But the fact that she was pregnant tells me we are going to have to go back to Mrs. Hardin."

Dan nodded and told her he had come to the same conclusion. They took their sandwiches back to 614 and he reviewed for her his conversation with Lieutenant Baler, including the news about the prior joint NIS-USS *Luce* investigation in which, by the way, one Mr. Carl Santini had been involved. Grace's face tightened in anger.

"Damn that man Santini. He walked me through what he said were his files, but he never mentioned a prior investigation."

"He'd probably counter that you asked about prior NIS investigations but never asked him for a ship's investigation."

"Robby was right," she said softly.

"It's partly my fault," he said. Her anger seemed genuine, so Dan elected to ameliorate the issue. "I should have asked the JAG guys upstairs if there had been a prior investigation," he said. "An officer disappears, there usually is. Santini told us about the disbursing audit, but not an actual investigation. I should have thought of that. I'm going to go upstairs and request an archive copy. But right now, I'm waiting for a call back from the ex-CO. You need to transcribe your findings at the police department while it's still fresh in your mind. Did you bring back a copy of the Traffic Division report?"

"Oh damn! No, I did not. What was I thinking about!"

"Okay, call 'em up and see if you can have a copy of that Hardin file. When I get back from Navy JAG, I'm going to call the ex-CO again. Navy meetings don't go on that long."

While Grace made her calls, Dan went upstairs to the JAG corridor and filled out an archive request for the ship's initial investigation into Lt. (jg) Wesley Hardin. Then he returned to 614 and tried the captain in Norfolk again. The same yeoman said the same thing about a meeting.

"Same meeting there, yeoman?"

There was a slight hesitation. "Uh, yes, sir, I guess so. I took him your message earlier, but I think he said he was gonna be in meetings most of the day, sir."

"Okay, thanks," Dan said, and hung up. He went to see Summerfield and explained his problem.

"Sounds like a captain who isn't too interested in returning a commander's call," Dan complained.

"Especially on this subject, I suspect," replied Summerfield. "Let me go whisper in the EA's ear."

Thirty minutes later, Grace reported that yes, she could have a copy of the police report, but only if she went over and signed for it in person.

"So it looks like I'm getting back on the Metro," she said.

"Won't they fax it?"

"They probably would, but Robby sent in a copy request, so that means someone has to go get it. Ve haff our rules, you see."

Dan grinned and then Yeoman Jackson reported a Captain Fletcher on the line for Commander Collins. Dan was tempted to have Jackson take a message, but then remembered what the call was about and who had started the telephone tag. He indicated that Grace should listen in and switched on the recorder before picking up.

"Captain Fletcher?" he said. "Thank you for returning my call, sir."

"Don't be a wiseass, Commander," a gruff voice said. "You got somebody to call the CincLantFleet EA, who 'encouraged' me to return your call. What do you want?"

"I'm investigating—"

"The deserter, Hardin. I know that. And I assume we're on tape. What do you want?"

"I wanted to ask you if there was anything you could tell me about Lieutenant Hardin's performance of duty or personal situation that might shed some light on why he was murdered in the shipyard."

"Murdered? Did you say murdered? He went UA."

"No, actually, he didn't, Captain," Dan said. "You'll probably be seeing it shortly on the evening news. Now, is there anything you can recall about him personally or professionally that would lead to murder?

"No, I can't. Anything else?"

Startled, Dan tried again. "Do you have any opinions as to why such a thing might happen?"

"Nope."

"Was Lieutenant Hardin one of your better officers, Captain?"

"No comment." Dan couldn't believe it. No comment?

"Excuse me, Captain, but I'm not the press here. I have read your two fitness reports on Mr. Hardin, and they seem to me to say very little of substance. He did his job; he should be promoted to full lieutenant. Full stop."

There was a moment of silence. "You a surface guy, Commander?"

"Yes, sir."

"Had your command yet?"

"No, sir. Going from here."

"Well, I haven't done my major command yet, so maybe I'll see you in the fleet one day. But before you get to command, you'll hopefully learn a couple of things about fitness reports."

"What's that mean, sir?"

"Fundamentally, it means that if you've read my fitness reports on Hardin, you shouldn't have to ask any dumb questions, like, Was he one of my better officers? What I have to say about him is on the record. Hardin was the perfect product of his environment. And that's all I'm going to say about Mr. Hardin. You're doing an informal JAGMAN, right?"

"Yes, sir."

"Then we're done. End of interview. I'll do a Freedom of Information Act down here; you send me a transcript of this conversation and I'll sign it. But I have nothing more to say about Mr. Hardin. Good-bye."

Dan sat there with the dial tone humming in his ear for a few seconds before replacing the phone. He became aware that Grace was watching him. He switched off the tape.

"Was that normal?" she asked.

"Stone wall, more like it. That was Hardin's ex-CO. And as you heard, he had nothing to say. Fully stands behind the investigation—way behind it. He actually said, 'No comment.' "

"But is that what you would call a normal reaction of a ship's captain to the news that one of his officers had been murdered?"

"No way," Dan said, standing up. "No way."

Grace got up and walked over to the case board that listed names. She wrote "*Luce* captain" on the board, then looked back at Dan.

"Fletcher," he said. "Capt. Martin Fletcher."

She wrote the name down and then put "No comment" below his name. Then she listed the executive officer's and the supply officer's names, leaving the XO's line blank while annotating the supply officer's line with Dan's notes. She then erased what Dan had written.

"You list the names you have talked to and what they say, not the victim's name. You never talked to Hardin."

"Got it. How about that detective?"

Grace wrote his name down on the board and then hesitated. Then she wrote "Knows something" below Vann's name as an opinion. She closed the door to their room and sat down again.

"See a pattern?" she asked.

"The supply officer saying bad things, and the politically more astute CO being careful to say nothing at all?"

"Yes. By saying nothing, the CO unwittingly is confirming what the supply officer said. I'm ready to write an opinion about Hardin."

They discussed it for a while before agreeing to list some short descriptors under Hardin's name on the opinion board: "competent, a loner in the wardroom, had a racial chip on his shoulder, visited Washington often."

"It will be interesting to see what the executive officer has to say—or not say," Grace mused.

"If we get him—they're at sea for the next couple of weeks. I'm seeing another pattern," Dan said. "The supply officer thinks that whatever was going on in Hardin's life wasn't happening in Philly, but in Washington. And the captain's comment—'Hardin was the perfect product of his environment'—again referring to Washington, D.C."

Grace studied the board. "That's a stone wall, all right. We'll have to go see his mother."

"How do we do that? The last time we saw her, she made it pretty clear that she wanted nothing to do with us."

Grace thought for a moment. "I've still got to go over to the District police headquarters. I think I'll call Captain Vann. He told me he knows Mrs. Hardin, knew her son and daughter. Let's see if he can get us on at least neutral ground with that lady."

After Grace left the office to go back into town, Dan began bringing his notes up to date, filling out some of the checklists provided by the JAG office. Captain Summerfield wandered in after an hour or so.

"Where's your ace partner?" he asked.

"She had to go back into D.C. to get a copy of the police report on Elizabeth Hardin," Dan replied. "She read the thing but then didn't bring back a copy."

"You two seem to be operating as a team," Summerfield observed, sucking on the cold pipe again. "You still think she's playing it straight?"

"She is, yes, sir." He told Summerfield about the previous investigation that the ship had conducted and what she had turned up at the Municipal Center. "On the prior investigation, I really think she was sandbagged, too—that NIS guy, up in Philly, Santini, acted polite, but I think he might be taking his marching orders from someone else. Grace has a buddy in NIS headquarters who kind of confirms that. Anyway, I've asked Navy JAG for a copy."

Summerfield stood in the doorway, leaning against one side, while he thought about that.

"Sometime when she's not here," he said at length, "you might want to pull the string on all that. Tell her to get you a copy of that first investigation from the NIS archives. See how long it takes. And then *you* call this Captain Vann and see what kind of a reading you get from him as to what he knows or doesn't know. Make sure he understands who's running this investigation. And another thing—didn't she give this Santini guy some instructions before you left Philly?"

"Yes, she did. I wanted the entire Shop Seventy-two rigger force interviewed. She told him it was a matter of first priority."

"So call the Shop Seventy-two people; see if the NIS has been around. It's been a couple of days. You can do this right now. See if Santini is sloughing it off or actually doing it. Let me know what you find, and maybe we'll go see Oh-six B or the EA, give him a data dump on the progress of our little alliance with the NIS."

After Summerfield had gone back in his office, Dan hesitated. He really did not want to go checking on Grace Snow, especially behind her back like this. He certainly could not call over to the police headquarters and talk to this Vann guy until she had completed her mission over there. But if the captain was right . . . He decided he would pull the string on the

Shop 72 interviews. He got the shipyard operator on the phone and asked for the Shop 72 foreman's office. The foreman was not available. He asked the secretary if the local NIS office had come in with a request to interview the people in Shop 72 in the matter of the Hardin case.

"Hardin case?"

"You know, the guy they found in the battleship."

"Oh yeah, I heard about that. The dead guy. The riggers are all freaked about it. Ghosts and stuff in the battleship. But there's been nobody interviewing anybody here."

He thanked her and hung up. He was once again tempted to call Santini himself, then decided against it. Grace had to do that. If the NIS headquarters weenies were stonewalling things, let Grace unearth that fact; then he'd see what she did with it. She seemed to be too sincere to be part of it, no matter what Summerfield thought. And, he decided suddenly, he did not want to make an enemy of Grace Snow, no matter what game the mandarins wanted to play. Hell, he liked her.

25

AFTER HAVING TO TAKE a number and wait in line for nearly an hour, Grace finally managed to get a copy of the Hardin file. She had called Vann's office before leaving 614, but the secretary had said the captain was not available. But as she was leaving the building with the report, she ran into Vann as he was headed back into the Municipal Center. He stopped short when he caught sight of her coming out of the building.

"Miss Snow," he said. "Back already?"

"I tried to call you, Captain," she said. She indicated the folder under her arm. "I forgot to take a copy of the Hardin report back to the Pentagon with me. But I did want to ask you something."

"What's that, Miss Snow?" he said, looking around at the four o'clock crowd on the steps. "And should we go inside?"

"I don't think that's necessary, Captain. We need to speak to Mrs. Hardin, formally. We wondered if you could help us with that?"

"You got a mouse in your pocket, Miss Snow? Who's this 'we'?"

"I told you. NIS and OpNav—that's the Navy headquarters staff—are cooperating on this investigation. 'We' means Commander Collins and I."

"Hold it, Miss Snow. I guess I wasn't paying attention about how this deal is set up. In my experience, the feds don't usually team up to work a homicide investigation with another agency. Homicide cops don't share, Miss Snow—they either work it or shop it."

Grace thought for a moment. "How about this, then: Let me set up a meeting with you and Commander Collins and myself, at the Pentagon. We'll brief you on the arrangements and what we have so far, which admittedly isn't much. But I think you'll see why we need to go back to Mrs. Hardin."

Vann shrugged. "Okay, talk to my secretary." Grace thanked him and then said she had to hurry to catch the Metro; she walked off before he could change his mind. When she looked back toward the Municipal Center, he was nowhere in sight.

When she arrived back at the 614 office, she nearly ran into Snapper, who was standing just inside the door, by the yeoman's desk.

"Miss Snow," he announced. "You're just in time to go up to the front office. I'll show you where it is. You can leave that folder if you want. I've gotta double-lock the door—the safes are still open and I'm the last guy out. The Commies, you know."

He waited for her to step back out of the office, and then he disabled the cipher lock and key-locked the door. He filled her in on the way up the hall.

"There's a genuine flap in the making. Apparently, the Hardin case is going to be featured on the national network news tonight, and the EAs severally want to know, What's happenin' now, comma, baby? Young Commander Collins, the famous detective and Communist sympathizer, awaits your presence."

"I can hardly wait," Grace said. She followed Snapper up the E-ring hallway. He was humming the Marine Corps hymn and marching to the beat of an inaudible drummer. Grace had to hurry to keep up. They arrived at the front office to find a cluster of captains in the reception area. Snapper handed Grace over to Dan, who introduced her to the executive assistants, Captains Manning and Randall, who greeted her cooly. Summerfield was there, as well as another captain from CHINFO. She noticed that the two EAs, distinctive in the gold aiguillettes draped over their left shoulders, stood apart from the others and indulged in a subdued conversation. Summerfield stood next to Dan, who was asking her if she had obtained the report.

"Yes, I did," she replied. "And I saw Captain Vann. Goodness, so many captains."

"He agreed to help us?" Dan was keeping an eye on Admiral Carson's door.

"Not exactly. He wants a meeting."

"Why?" asked Summerfield, speaking for the first time.

"He doesn't understand why NIS and OpNav are doing a joint investigation. And I think he wants to be put into the picture. He knows the Hardin family personally, and he's probably the only way we're going to be able to get anywhere near the mother, Angela Hardin."

Dan was about to say something when Admiral Carson's door opened and a tall, distinguished-looking officer stepped out. He was wearing service dress blues, with the single broad stripe with two gold stripes above that of a three-star admiral on each sleeve. Grace had never seen so much gold on one uniform; the admiral who ran NIS was a one-star. She detected a sudden squeeze of tension clamp down over the room. All the clerical staff shot to their feet and the officers went silent in midsentence as the DCNO looked around, nodded absently to everyone in general, and went into his office, closing the door behind him. Grace felt the officers in the room relaxing slightly. They acted as if they were a bunch of small-town parish priests admitted momentarily to the presence of a cardinal of the Roman Curia.

"*That* was Vice Admiral Layman, the DCNO Plans and Policy," Dan whispered. "Exceedingly large Kahuna."

"Why are we whispering?" Grace asked innocently.

Summerfield chuckled as Dan groped for an answer, but then Admiral Carson, in his shirtsleeves, appeared in his doorway, waving everyone into his office. The two EAs went first, followed by Summerfield and the CHINFO captain. Dan brought Grace in with him and introduced her to Admiral Carson, who gave her a friendly handshake and then asked everyone to sit down. The admiral returned to his desk.

"Okay, everybody," he said. "Subject is the escalation of press interest in the Hardin case. Captain Smythe here from CHINFO will bring us up to date."

Smythe opened his folder and announced that CBS News was going to feature the story at the national level this evening. To Smythe's knowledge, the story had been reported already, but not featured. CHINFO assumed the other two networks would follow suit.

"What's been released?" interrupted Randall, speaking out loud for the first time. Grace realized that it was a measure of the EA's power that he could question peremptorily the CHINFO briefer when an admiral had established that he was running the meeting. Smythe looked over at Randall and went into his spokesperson routine.

"The Navy Department is conducting an investigation into the matter; the Navy Department does not ordinarily comment on investigations in progress. We can confirm that a body was discovered in the engineering spaces of USS *Wisconsin*, that the victim has been identified as Lt. (jg) Wesley Hardin, formerly of Washington, D.C., and that the Navy Department is treating the matter as a homicide. That's it."

"Did you have to say he was from Washington?" Randall persisted.

"Yes. You have to understand, Captain Randall, our statements at this level are often determined by what the media already knows. They had Hardin's name, the fact that he was from Washington, D.C., and even that his body was found in a mummified state. If they already have it, we often give it back to them in our own statement; makes us look more forthcoming."

"Okay," said Admiral Carson. "Commander Collins, any ideas of where their information is coming from?"

"Several possible sources, Admiral," Dan replied. "Every bit of what the captain just said could have come from the ambulance crew, except maybe the bit about his being from Washington."

"Excuse me, Admiral," Randall interrupted again. "Miss Snow, you are the appointed operational liaison from NIS?"

Startled, Grace looked over at the EA. "Yes, Captain, I am."

"Admiral, I request that Miss Snow be excused from the meeting at this time."

Grace was stunned. Admiral Carson's eyebrows shot up. She could see that he was perplexed, but this was the vice chief's EA speaking.

"Miss Snow," Carson said. "I'm sorry, but if you would be so kind . . ."

Grace tried to control the flush on her face. She got up and went to the door. She paused for a second, trying to think of a way to object, but then let herself out.

DAN FELT ACUTELY embarrassed, and he was on the verge of speaking up when Randall cut him off.

"Commander Collins, I've been informed that you believe this Miss Snow is being fully cooperative in the course of this invesitgation."

Been informed? By whom? he wondered. "Yes, sir, I do believe that," he said. But the problem of the prior investigation, and what the secretary at Shop Seventy-two had revealed about follow-up interviews, suddenly intruded on his mind. Randall caught his expression.

"Yes?" he said, his eyebrows raised.

"Well, sir, I'm pretty sure I can vouch for Miss Snow, but not for the NIS. I found out today that there had been a prior investigation done on Hardin's disappearance, by his own command, USS *Luce*, in cooperation with NISRA Philadelphia, something the NIS office in Philly did not choose to share with me. And Miss Snow had directed NISRA Philadelphia to interview all the riggers, as a matter of first priority. I called the riggers shop today—there have been no interviews."

"Surprise, surprise," Randall said. "Frankly, I'm willing to bet that it's NIS that's been leaking to CBS."

"Two can play that game," Manning offered. "We can always leak the fact that OpNav is in it because we want to ensure that NIS doesn't screw it up."

"That's a two-edged sword," Admiral Carson countered. "We can make NIS look bad, but that in turn makes the Navy look bad."

"I can fix that," Randall said. "My principal can call in NIS himself and share his thinking with him on the subject of leaks."

"Let's table that for an off-line discussion, shall we," Carson said, eyeing Dan. "Commander, where are you with the investigation?"

Dan had been expecting this question. If it had been Carson alone asking for his own information, he might have gone along with it. But it was obviously the VCNO's EA who had called this meeting, and he owed Randall nothing. He hesitated, then made up his mind.

"Admiral, as the investigating officer, I can report that my investigation is not yet completed. I would prefer to withhold my report until such time as it is completed. That way, there can be no possibility that anyone can infer that there was undue command influence on the course of the investigation."

Randall sat up straight in his chair. "Don't be an ass," he snapped. "This isn't some 'destroyer bumping the pier' case we're talking about here. This is a very serious matter that has the attention of the Vice Chief of Naval Operations himself."

"I understand its importance, Captain. But I must insist."

"You must *what!*" Randall was almost shouting.

"Captain Randall," the admiral interrupted, giving Dan a wry look. "Commander Collins, we'll of course respect your position. And excuse you now, if you please."

"Aye, aye, sir," Dan said stiffly, and left the room. He closed Carson's door carefully and found Grace sitting in the outer office in one of the wretched upholstered chairs, looking less than pleased.

"Well, I've been thrown out of better bars than that," he announced. The chief yeoman looked up for a moment as Dan dropped into the other chair, but then he went back to his typing.

"You, too?" Grace asked.

"Yeah. I'm afraid I sassed the VCNO's EA when I invoked the command-influence rule. They wanted to know what I had found so far. When Randall started to get really pissed, Oh-sixB invited me to the egress."

"Well, I'm not sure what I did."

"You didn't *do* anything. You're one of *them.*"

"Oh. Right. So are we done here?"

Dan grinned. "Not hardly. Or at least I'm not. I was excused, but not dismissed. Either Randall or Carson is going to come out of there and fang me before I get to slink back to Six-fourteen. I trampled on some serious EA toes in there. And I apologize for your being asked to leave like that. But there is something I need to tell you, relating to the NIS-OpNav food fight. I called on Shop Seventy-two's foreman this morning; his secretary confirmed that nobody from Santini's office had been around. Summerfield asked me to make the call."

"Ah. So these people think NIS is trying to derail the investigation, and that I'm part of that program."

"Some of them probably do; I can't read Admiral Carson, but I would bet the EAs feel that way. Randall seems to be the point man on the anti-NIS crusade."

"And he's the vice chief's executive assistant?"

"Right. And a powerful guy hereabouts. Already selected for admiral, and not timid about throwing around Daddy's four stars."

"Have you made me an enemy?"

Dan laughed. "I'm not significant enough to become an enemy of a guy at that level. He'll probably step on my neck, but that's about it. Tell you what: If the vice chief wants to assign another boy investigator, he's more than welcome to it."

Grace was silent for a few minutes. Dan realized that they would have to have a heart-to-heart talk when they were able to get away from the front office and all the horse-holders. Then the door to Carson's office opened, and the parade of captains appeared, in reverse order of their going in. The CHINFO captain, Summerfield, Manning, and Randall. Summerfield walked right by Dan, shooting him a surreptitious wink as he left the office. The chief yeoman told Manning that Vice Admiral Layman wanted to see him, and Manning grabbed a notebook, knocked on the DCNO's door, and went in. Randall strolled over to where Dan, standing now, was waiting. He glanced at Grace dismissively before focusing on Dan.

"You like to live dangerously, Commander?"

"Did I do something wrong, Captain?"

"You did something worse than wrong; you did something dumb."

"On instructions, Captain."

"Oh, really? Whose, might I ask?"

"Admiral Carson. He specifically directed me to permit no intrusion into the investigation that could be construed as command influence. Sir."

Randall smiled down at Dan. Dan concluded that Randall smiling was not a pleasant sight.

"It was Carson who asked you the question, Commander. Don't play sea lawyer with me. You're out of your league."

Dan felt a flare of anger. "As a sea lawyer, Captain?"

The icy smile disappeared as Randall's face tightened, and then he drew back and looked down at Dan the way a snake might inspect a frog. "Dumber and dumber, Commander," he said softly. "You had your command tour yet?"

Second time today he had been asked that question. "No, sir."

"Fancy that," Randall said, and then walked around Dan into the E-ring corridor, turning left to go to the vice chief's office.

"Sounds like an enemy to me," Grace observed from her chair. "Really good resemblance, in fact."

They went back down to 614, passing a series of now-darkened offices. For most of the Pentagon, the day was over. The rattling engine sounds of a propane tractor hauling a wagon train of office trash to the pulping rooms could be heard echoing through the corridors. There was no light showing through the opaque windowpane in 614's front door, but the door was unlocked. When they went in, they walked into an aromatic cloud of pipe tobacco.

"Aha! Serious crimes and misdemeanors going down here," Dan announced in a stage whisper.

"Shut the damn door before the tobacco police come around," Summerfield said. Dan and Grace walked around the cluster of desks in the outer office and stood in Summerfield's doorway. Summerfield was sitting in his chair, beneath a layer of blue smoke. The captain had only his desk light on, and on the desk was one of the captain's many gun catalogs. Dan saw that he had his windows open just in case.

"Well, Daniel, did you have a nice day?" Summerfield asked innocently.

"It was a little rough around the edges, Captain," Dan replied. "Grace here thinks that possibly I irritated the vice chief's grand vizier."

"If you're gonna piss somebody off, you might as well do it to a four-star's EA and flag selectee," Summerfield said. "More points that way."

"Yes, sir. He made an unhappy reference to my command tour."

"The one in Argentia, no doubt. Well, you probably did the right thing up there. Miss Snow, I apologize for your getting hove out of the meeting, but it's probably for the best that neither of you were there, given what they ended up talking about."

"How's that, Captain?" Grace asked.

But the captain shook his head. "No. You two just proceed. What you don't know can't hurt you, at least not for a while. It will depend upon what the press does with this. But Dan, if I were you, I'd do a memorandum for the record on the meeting today. Miss Snow, you, too. Write down your version of what happened, then bury it in your files. What time is it? Oh, almost eighteen hundred. Now, if you'd close my door so I can fumigate in peace. Oh, and Dan?"

"Yes, sir?"

"Take the rest of the day off, if you please."

"Aye, aye, sir," Dan replied with a straight face. He closed Summerfield's office door, and they went over to the back room. Grace fired up her portable while Dan sat down to one of the PCs to construct his MFR. Grace was finished first, having been the first to be ejected from the meeting. Dan was a bit more verbose. When he was done, he looked up, to find Grace watching him. He thought he caught a speculative look in her eyes, and for a moment, he did some speculating of his own about what she might be like in bed. The thought surprised him.

"So what do we do now, Mr. Holmes?" she was saying.

"We call it a day, I think, Dr. Watson. The powers that be are gonna power around for a while, covering their stern sheets and their principals' position. Tomorrow, I'd suggest you call into NIS and smoke out their copy of that original investigation, and then call Santini and get a progress report on his purported interviews with Shop Seventy-two. After that, we'll meet with your Detective Captain Vann."

"And you?"

"I'm going to start building my final report, getting the paperwork in order. I have this funny feeling that they, whoever they might be, may come down here soon and instruct me to turn over all investigation materials to a new, more politically pliable boy investigator—one who has the confidence of his executiveship, my lord Captain Randall."

"Can they just do that?"

"Sure. If they really want to mess around, they could, for instance, write me a set of orders and then, regrettably, due to the exigencies of my unexpected transfer, appoint a new guy to run the JAGMAN."

She sat back in her chair, being somewhat careless about her skirts. Well, my goodness, Dan thought, trying to keep his eyes in the boat. If she saw him looking, she gave no visible sign of it.

"I guess I'm a little naïve," she reflected. "If somebody tried that in NIS, there'd be hell to pay."

"Would there? It wouldn't stun me to find out that the passive resistance going on at NIS, *if* that's what's going on, isn't the result of some fairly high-level guidance—or even collusion with someone high up in OpNav. Remember, this thing's gone public, and the Navy hates public."

She slumped a little at that.

"What would you do" she asked, "if they took you off the investigation, gave you orders?"

"Truth? I'd take those orders, clutch them to my heaving bosom, and run, not walk, right out the door. I'm due for sea duty and a command of my own. Throw me in that briar patch, Br'er detailer."

"And what about the Lieutenants Hardin?"

Dan took his time with that one. "The Lieutenants Hardin are dead. From what I can see at this juncture, there's not a snowball's chance that I—that we—can somehow achieve justice for the one who was murdered. It's been two years. Any trail in Philadelphia is stone-cold. Any trail here in D.C. probably leads into a part of town where you and I would be neither welcome nor effective. I'm beginning to think that some reasonably big bosses would like this thing to go down-scope for a while. If I had to wager, I'd say that's what Summerfield's talking about. They're going to kill it."

"And now?"

"For now, I follow my last legal order: Captain Summerfield said to proceed. That's what we'll do: proceed until something changes. But not tonight. Tonight, I have a date with a rowing machine, since daylight on the river has long gone. See you tomorrow, Miss Snow."

26

MALACHI EASED HIMSELF into an upright position in his bed and tried unsuccessfully to get the room to stop moving. It wasn't exactly spinning, but there were suspicious indications of movement in his peripheral vision whenever he cracked open either of his eyes. It was still dark outside, and his head felt like a lumpy sponge that had soaked up a few gallons of pulsing pain. His stomach was queasy, and his mouth gave new meaning to the words *whiskey sour*. He tried to concentrate, trying to remember how much he had had to drink last night. Or was it the past two nights? And maybe a day in between? What the hell day was this? With his eyes still pretty much closed, he reached for his cigarettes. He found only one left. He felt both ends of the cigarette, pinched off the filter, and then lit up, wincing at all the noise the lighter made. He started to shake his head to clear his mind, but pain central got wind of it just in time and threatened to take his head right off. Might be a blessing, he thought as he gingerly swung one leg at a time over the edge of the bed and tried to get approximately vertical before staggering into the bathroom. So what happened to all that self-control, Ward? Was there some reason behind our going through a couple of quarts of hundred-proof? What little worm is squirming in your mind, you have to drown it like that?

He sat down heavily on the throne in the darkened bathroom, closed his eyes, and let his chin settle down on to his chest one degree at a time. Each degree hurt. His insides felt as if they were settling, too, perhaps all the way into the toilet. A tiny flick of hot cigarette ash landed on his chest. He ignored it and took another drag. The Hardin thing—that's what this was. He had seen the evening network news—when, last night? Must have been. Body in the battleship. Officer missing for two years. Government investigation. "Just wanted you to hear it from us first," the captain had said. Fucking wonderful. He had wanted to call the captain, ring the number, say the code name, find out what was really happening, but of course he couldn't do that. They would think he was getting scared.

And the call from Angelo hadn't helped. Apologizing for the body being found. Thought a sealed-up, nitrogen-filled, inactivated battleship was a pretty secure place. Reassurances of what a stand-up guy he was, nothing to worry about; likewise for the hard hats who had been involved. No problem whatsoever. Except for maybe one thing. About the need for Malachi to start watching his own back, because the people who had hired him might be getting antsy now, and they could, of course, always hire somebody else. "Way I see it, Malachi, you're the guy who can finger your client. This federal beef grows some hair and teeth, your client might be tempted to eliminate the connection between the 'body in the battleship' story and himself, which is namely you, am I right? Feel like I own a piece of all this shit, so I thought I'd better call, and say: watch your ass, *paisan*. You need some help, let me know. We have some guys in D.C., can arrange some shit, you need it."

Thank you, Angelo. Make my fucking day, Angelo. He remained perched on the john like a stone gargoyle, listening to his heart beat and his lungs breathe, waiting until the light coming in from the bedroom grew stronger and the day became unavoidable. He finally heaved himself up, washed his face and hands, and then decided to take a shower, after which he went out to the kitchen to get a Coke to settle his stomach. With maybe the slightest dollop of Harper to really settle it. He looked around inside the icebox, but what little food there was revolted him. Aspirin, that's what drunks have for breakfast. Aspirin, a Coke to get some caffeine running, and a little hair of the dog to take the edges off the Coke. He sat down gingerly in a kitchen chair and reached for the sugar bowl, which he kept full of aspirin tablets.

Thanks a heap, Angelo, that was just what I needed to think about. Of course the captain could hire somebody else, although he wasn't too sure that the captain would know that many guys in the business. On the other hand, he'd hired him, hadn't he? And there were certainly other contractors in the business in this town; Malachi even knew a few of them. Hell, everybody was a contractor of some kind or another in Washington—contractor or a consultant. Same difference: talent for hire. But it was so damn simple: If everybody just kept their damn cool, sat still, kept their mouths shut, the feds would be stymied. There just wasn't any trail. It was a no-brainer, as all the modish bureaucrats liked to say.

He swished the Coca-Cola around in his mouth to get rid of the sour taste of the aspirin tablets, the noise sounding like a wave breaking in his ears. Maybe the thing to do was to hit the road, just disappear. Retire. He had a nice fat cash stash from the sergeants' Mafia days in Vietnam and Germany, and another couple of hundred grand in bank accounts and safe-deposit boxes around town after all these years of shoveling shit for the bigs. He thought about it as he waited for the caffeine to work. Go down south somewhere, get a little farm or something, and settle into the weeds, drinking bourbon under a willow tree somewhere. What damn near every sergeant he had ever known had talked about doing when the big three-oh came along. Except that not that many had actually done it. Health problems, a wife who was settled finally into a good job and tired of moving, grown kids who were still hanging around, the fear of being too far away from the almighty exchange and the commissary and the Army hospital. Basically, the habits of three decades of Army life. That's probably what would keep him here, too—habit.

He finished half the Coke, found some bourbon, topped the can back off, and then deliberately drank it down. Screw these people. He was not going to get run out of town because of some rinky-dink investigation, and if the bigs tried to take him out, he just might throw some shit in the game in reply. Shit, he was in the business, wasn't he?

HE LEFT CAPITOL HILL that morning on the Metro to check on his bolt-hole apartment in the Randolph Towers and also on the Ford. He came out of the Ballston Metro, walked through the Ramada Renaissance lobby, across two streets, and into the Randolph Towers building by way of the deli, where he topped off his cigarette supply, grousing at the Lebanese proprietor over his prices. Once in the building proper, he took the elevator directly down to the third level of the garage and walked to the corner where his Ford was parked. Finding a small pool of what looked like power-steering fluid under the car, he decided to run it down to the nearest Ford dealer, which was on Wilson Boulevard. As he pulled the sedan out onto Quincy Street and turned right, he thought he saw a car swing into traffic from a street parking place a half a block behind him, next to an abandoned car dealership.

He had begun watching his back, just like Angelo had recommended, even doing a little fancy stuff on the Metro trains, ducking in and out of newspaper shops and convenience stores to see what might be going on behind him or even ahead of him, but there had been nothing. Just the stone-faced commuters and the first of the spring tourist hordes on the Metro, and all the politicians, bureaucrats, and other great men whizzing down the avenues in their official cars. But as he bounced along the potholes by which Arlington County controlled speeding on Wilson Boulevard, he noticed that the dark-colored car seemed to be staying with him, three, maybe four cars back. Single driver, but he couldn't see much in the vibrating mirror, and he didn't want to turn around and look. So he drove past the dealership and went one more block, accelerating into a left turn and going through a yellow light that went red as he made the turn. He circled the block, coming back out on Wilson, headed back toward the dealership. He drove down the next three blocks slowly, staying in the right lane as if looking for a parking place, his turn signal blinking, scanning the ranks of parked cars and the aprons of two gas stations, looking for a dark sedan. But there was nothing. He'd either lost the guy or spooked him. Or maybe there'd never been a guy in the first place.

He turned around in a gas station and drove back on down to the Ford dealership, where they told him it would be a three-hour wait, he wanted to wait for it. He told them he'd leave it, be back tomorrow, but then he stood for a while in the corner of the front showroom, looking out the big tinted windows on Wilson, waiting to see what might show up. Nothing did. After thirty minutes, he walked out of the dealership and headed down the street toward the Clarendon Metro station, stopping briefly in the entrance of a Vietnamese grocery to scan the street again, keeping his eyes open. Still nothing. He decided to go back to Capitol Hill.

He thought about it during the subway ride home. If a guy had been following him, and thought maybe Malachi had made him, he'd break it off, wouldn't he? Just drive on down the line. Your target speeds up and turns off the main drag, he's made you, right? On the other hand, there was no way a guy could know where he had been bound that morning, certainly not in advance, and no way the guy could have had a car waiting out there on Quincy, because Malachi had taken the subway. Unless they knew about the apartment in the Randolph Towers. But even then, the garage had two exists. Two watchers? Shit, he was getting paranoid. Well, yeah, but even paranoids have enemies.

He stared at the darkened train window as they rolled through the tunnels under Pennsylvania Avenue. Jesus Christ, you're working yourself up over jackshit, he told himself. He hadn't heard from the captain since the last call, and he was determined not to call in like some panicked teenager. There had been nothing else in the Washington papers about the case. You're spooking yourself, man, he thought. But when he got back to the town house, there was a message on the machine from the captain: "We're taking steps to neutralize the investigation. Two years is a long time. One of the principal investigators has been ours all along. You can relax."

That was it, no instructions to call in, get in touch, "we need to meet" stuff. Malachi quickly saved the message and then replayed it a couple of times, listening to the captain's voice carefully, trying to strain any nuances from the mechanical words. "Neutralize the investigation"—what the hell did that mean? "Two years is a long time." Right, we're all counting on that. "One of the principal investigators has been ours all along." Was he no longer on the case? "You can relax." Yeah, relax. Let down your guard. Forget about it, so our guy, our *new* guy, can maybe solve our *new* little problem for us.

He left the message on the tape, lit a cigarette, and walked around the ground floor of the town house as he thought about it. He needed to do something, not just stay hunkered down inside the perimeter. Anyone who'd done time in Nam knew that rule. Only targets stayed inside the wire. Survivors got out there in the weeds in onesies and twosies and did unto Chuck what Chuck was trying to do unto them. But he needed a face, some names. Okay, so he'd start by finding out who'd been doing this investigation that was now going to get "neutralized." He went to his desk and got out a yellow legal pad, took it back into the kitchen, and fixed up some coffee. He sat down at his kitchen table.

The news had said the Navy was conducting the investigation. That meant that bunch of clowns at NIS. So he had to find a way into NIS to ferret out who had the Hardin case. What was the worst thing the NIS could find out? That there was a connection between the Hardin sister's little accident and the Hardin brother's killing. So where would they start working on that? In the D.C. Metropolitan Police Department. So he'd call them, maybe dig out who from NIS had been pulling on that string. He sipped some coffee, thought about maybe slipping a little whiskey sweetener into it, then shook his head. Mr. Harper could wait—but not too long.

He walked to his desk in the dining room. So who would he be today? The lawyer. Cops wouldn't give a journalist the time of day, but a lawyer, they had to sweat a lawyer just a little bit. But they'd check him out first. So he wouldn't talk to cops; he'd talk to their clerks. Go after the paper— that's what the NIS would have to do. He looked up the number, set up voice program six for Lawyer Greenberg, called the main police department's number, and asked which division would handle a hit-and-run. Hit-and-run division, in the Traffic Bureau. Well, no shit. But how about the records? The records office at Municipal Center. The sullen operator made him call back on a different number, but he scored on the first call when a little-old-lady voice answered the phone. She's old. Be polite, he thought.

"My name is Farrell Greenberg, ma'am. I'm an attorney at Lyle, Spencer, Watkins and King, out here in Bladensburg. I have a question, but I'm not quite sure where to go with it, so I'm taking a wild shot and calling the records office. Perhaps you can assist me."

"What you lookin' for?"

"Our firm has been retained by the Naval Investigative Service down at the Navy Yard to do a large-scale records search on hit-and-run accidents in the District of Columbia. The Navy's had some people attempting veterans claims fraud based on what the Navy thinks are an exceptional number of hit-and-run cases here in Washington, D.C. What we need—"

"Well, why don't you just ax the lady?"

Lady? "I beg your pardon, ma'am, I don't follow."

"That lady, she workin' for the same folks you workin' for, that Navy investigation service, what's her name, Miss Snow, yeah, I remember it, 'cause she come over here, lookin' at a file, and then she have to come on back, get her a copy of it, on account she forgot to get her a copy the first time. Everybody looks at a file here, they usually takes a copy, you know what I'm sayin'? She done forgot it, had to come all the way back from the Pentagon, she said. Nice lady, didn't hassle me about it none, like mos' folks."

"Do you remember which file that was, ma'am? If I had a name, I can find out if we're duplicating our efforts here."

"It was some hit-and-run, I remember that. Old one—two years back. Don't remember no names, though. Too many names down here."

"Well, thank you, ma'am. I think I better stop right here and go back to the NIS and talk to Miss Snow. No point in both of us bothering you, is there?"

"Yeah, that's true. Maybe they just be checkin' up on you, see if you get 'em all, you doin' your survey. Folks is always checkin' up on folks around here."

"Thank you, ma'am. I'm going to go see what's going on here. Appreciate your help, though."

He hung up. Miss Snow, from the NIS. Pulling a two-year-old hit-and-run file. *Miss* Snow. The captain had said the investigator had been "our man." No; wait—go listen to the tape again. He got up, went into the hall, and ran the tape. *One* of the principal investigators has been ours all along. So they had two people working it. One from NIS—Miss Snow. Another one from—where? Who was the second guy? He went back to the kitchen, drank some more coffee. Couldn't just call NIS. They might have little old ladies out there, every Washington agency had them, but the NIS variety would be trained not to talk to outsiders. And he couldn't just call some Pentagon number in the sky. If the captain found out, it might spook him and his principal. So where else? Philadelphia. The news story had broken in Philadelphia. A Navy spokesperson had been quoted. What was Navy up there? Well, that shipyard, of course.

He called long-distance information and got the main number for the shipyard. He selected another voice program and an identity as a new staffer on the House Armed Services Committee. The shipyard operator put him through to the shipyard commander's office, where he identified himself and asked to speak to the spokesperson for the shipyard. He was switched over to another number, then a third before a civilian secretary told him he had to talk to the NavBase PAO.

"NavBase?"

"Yes, sir, Commander Naval Base Philadelphia. ComNavBase. They have a CHINFO type on their staff; she's the spokesperson for all the Navy activities up here. That's probably who you're looking for."

CHINFO. He remembered that word from his seance with Elizabeth Hardin. The secretary gave him two numbers: one for the public affairs office at NavBase, and a second for the commander's office. He chose the PAO, again using the identity of the committee staffer. The PAO was not available. "Could she call back?" he was asked. Malachi hesitated. As a rule, he never left his own phone number for a callback. He said no, he was out of his office, away from his desk, but it was urgent, the chairman needed to know something. He asked when the PAO would be back in. The secretary did not know. Malachi said he would try again, then hung up.

He sat there, chewing on his lower lip. From his Army days, he knew that calls from a congressional office had to be reported up the chain of command—especially if they came from one of the Armed Services committees. That could possibly get back to the captain, too, and one phone call to the HASC might expose him. No. Somewhere else in Philadelphia. The cops? The Philadelphia media? Too hard to sustain the cover story. He needed someone low level, a worker bee. "Always be a snake," Monroney had said, "stay down in the grass." They had found Hardin's body on the base—where would they take it? Maybe there was a naval hospital up there; a naval base usually had a Navy hospital.

He called the base operator again, but she told him the naval hospital had been closed down two years ago. Thank you very much. So where would they take the body? They'd want an autopsy, so maybe the city morgue. It took him four more calls to get a number for the Philadelphia County Medical Examiner's Office, but there he ran into a cop, one Officer Wykowski. Damn. He walked through his House committee staffer routine again. Wykowski listened politely and asked him for his number—standard procedure: "We gotta call you back, make sure you are who you say you are." Malachi almost did it, but then he hung up. From a pay phone, maybe, but pay phones didn't come with a voice synthesizer. He could imagine the cop laughing at him on the other end, and he hoped the guy didn't have caller ID. But they probably got calls from reporters all the time trying to disguise who they were. So who you gonna call, there, Ghostbuster?

The Navy spokesperson had been from the naval base headquarters. Maybe the congressional angle wasn't such a good idea. How about just a reporter? He selected another voice program and called back, this time to the commander's office. He identified himself to the Yeoman Third Class Hardy who answered as a reporter with the *Washington Times*. He had a quick question: What were the names of the Navy investigators working the Hardin case, the body in the battleship?

"You'll have to call the PAO, sir," Hardy said.

"I called them; they referred me to your office. Look, I know one of the names. It's a Miss Snow from the NIS. But my sources indicate that there are two." He decided to take a long shot. "I need the name of the other one, that captain they sent up with Miss Snow."

"He was a commander, sir, but I can't give out their names."

"Okay, Yeoman Hardy, I understand. Thanks."

He now had Miss Snow and Commander X. Back to the PAO. The newspaper had said that Hardin's mother had gone up to Philadelphia to ID the body. Snow and the commander would have been there for that, he was sure of it. He switched voice programs as the PAO's office picked up, and this time he was Officer Wykowski from the Philadelphia city morgue, needing a name to finish his monthly report.

"Those two Navy people who were here on the Hardin case, that guy they found in the battleship? I got two names, one's a Miss Snow; the other's a Commander somebody, but some jerk spilled coffee on his name."

"You mean Commander Collins."

"Yeah, okay, that works. It starts with a *C*. Looked like Cowin or something. I just couldn't read the rest of it. 'Preciate it, lady."

Malachi smiled and hung up. Commander Collins and Miss Snow. He pulled out a Department of Defense phone book and went to the back. Collins. Bunch of them: two on the Navy headquarters staff, one on the Army staff, one on the Joint Chiefs—two captains, one commander, one lieutenant commander. The lone commander was Collins, Daniel L., in the Division of Politico-Military Policy, Office of the Chief of Naval Operations, office code 614C. He went back to the Navy index, looked up the NIS, and then tried to find Snow, but there was no listing for her at NIS. He toyed with the idea of calling there, too, but let it go. He had two names; now he would go wrap up some other business and then go scare up some faces to put with those names.

27

ON WEDNESDAY MORNING, Dan asked Grace to call Captain Vann at the Municipal Center and arrange for Vann to come to the Pentagon at 1100. In the privacy of the back room, they had kicked around how much or how little to tell Vann about the bureaucratic warfare dimensions of their working together. Dan had been leaning toward a fairly restricted data dump, but Grace argued for full disclosure.

"He'll see through any smoke screen we put up to explain why I'm here, and why you are not at NIS," she had pointed out. "Cops are some of the best bureaucrats there are. And he's probably our only hope to get to Mrs. Hardin."

"I'm just concerned about folding outsiders into this investigation; it's a Navy deal."

"But it's a homicide, not a collision at sea. We've already established that Hardin's killing is probably not related to his job as a Navy paymaster, so whatever's behind the murder is buried in his personal world, maybe the civilian world of Washington. That's Vann's turf."

And yours, Dan had thought, but he had been persuaded. Grace was good at that, he noticed; must be that Jesuit training at Georgetown. As agreed, Dan went to meet Vann, who was waiting on the sidewalk in front of the south parking entrance, looking somewhat conspicuous among the stream of uniforms entering and leaving the building. Dan cleared Vann and his oversized side arm through the guard station, after much admiring comment about the weapon from the two Federal Protective Service cops, and then took him up to 614.

"First time in the Pentagon, Captain?" Dan asked as they worked their way through the maze of rings and corridors.

"Came over here for a shooting in the parking lot few years back," Vann replied. "Some weird Harold shot a Navy officer at random. But I've never been inside the building, no."

Dan made introductions when they got to 614, then closed the door to the back room when they were ready to begin. Grace had been making some phone calls while Dan had been picking up the detective. She looked glum.

"Suspicions confirmed on Santini," she reported. "They've done nothing. A 'change in priorities' is the excuse of the day. And NIS is 'researching' the USS *Luce*'s previous investigation. They hope to get me a copy by the end of next week."

"Next week? Yeah, that's definitely in the suspicions-confirmed regime. I've got Navy JAG digging up a copy; we'll see who gets us one first. Let's fill our guest detective in on what's going on. You want some coffee, Captain?"

It took an hour. Vann had said he could give them forty-five minutes, but he sat impassively in an elderly desk chair as Dan ran over the time limit. Dan gave him the political background behind the investigation's organization, replayed what they had seen and heard in Philadelphia, including their meetings with the retired rigger and Mrs. Hardin, and then walked him through the case boards. When it was over, Vann shook his head slowly.

"What you've got," he said, "is jackshit. Two-year-old, two-year-cold jackshit."

Dan nodded, looking at the sparsely populated fact board. "We know."

"Less than jackshit," Vann continued. "If Hardin was killed in Philly and dumped in that battleship, it was probably done by a squad of eye-talians who were following orders—like your rummy rigger said. And you said yourself that only the riggers could get inside that ship. The chances of finding out who was giving those orders, in South Philly, are zero. You habeas one corpus, but have no visible motive. You have nobody who gained, unless there was a big insurance policy out there somewhere. Was there? Surely you've checked? Uh-huh. Like I said, you got shit. Old, cold shit."

"We've done a lot of hypothesizing and speculating about a connection between the two deaths," Grace said. "The salient feature is that it's just too coincidental, both of them dying that close together. But that's all we have—speculation. Which is why we want to talk to Mrs. Hardin."

"She won't want to talk to you," Vann warned. "Far as she's concerned, she handed over two pretty good kids to the U.S. Navy and they both ended up dead."

"I should think she'd be desperate to know why this happened," Dan said.

Vann shook his head. "You should think? Pardon me, but you talkin' like a Martian. You simply have no idea of what it means to have two out of two black kids, in one family, coming up from the District, make it out of the streets and into the white man's professional world. Black kids in this town, half of 'em are s'posed to end up dead before they're twenty-one. That's what a lot of parents *and* their kids have come to believe these days. That there's some law of averages working to thin out the black-kid population. So when it turns out that way, it's just life in the black lane, see? That woman is beyond anger, but mostly she's resigned to her fate."

"But how about you, Captain?" Grace asked quietly. "You resigned to just letting this thing go by? Surely you can see that there's too much coincidence here."

Vann was silent for a moment, staring at the middle distance between them, his thin face working. Then he looked down at his watch.

"I gotta boogie," he said. "I saw the Hardin thing on the national news last night. What's the Navy gonna do?"

"Do?" asked Dan.

"Don't shit a bullshitter, Commander. This thing gets media heat, the Navy's gonna damp it down, put it on a slow track until the heat goes elsewhere. Lemme ask you something: Can you assure me that you'll still be running this investigation by next week?"

Dan looked at Grace before answering. Vann caught the look.

"Uh-huh. I tell you what. You still in business by the beginning of next week, you call me. But I'm not putting Angela Hardin through the wringer of a federal investigation unless there's a future in it, you dig?"

"I suppose we could do it without you," Grace said.

"Bet you can't," Vann said, staring at her. "She'll tell you to go away. And then what you gonna do? Subpoena her? Take her into the back room?"

"Oh c'mon," Dan interjected. "We wouldn't do anything like that, Captain, and you know that—she's lost both her children, for Chrissakes. But neither one of us is willing to just let this thing go, even if the politics do start to get in the way."

Vann snorted. "Here's the thing," he said. "This is the only unsolved homicide you got. Over there in town, we've got the world's supply of unsolved homicides, mostly because people won't talk to us, and mosta them 'cause they're scared of getting whacked themselves. *This* thing is hopeless."

"Well, will you think about it?" Dan asked. "Just don't shut your mind to it, until we see what else we can develop. Will you do that?"

"I'll think about it. Now, who's gonna get me out of this place?"

When Dan returned to the office after escorting Vann out of the building, Grace was on the phone, having an animated discussion with someone, and there was a message on his desk directing him to go see the 06 EA, Captain Manning. He reread the message while trying not to eavesdrop on Grace's conversation, but it was difficult.

"What do you mean, 'a coincidence of interests'?" she said, her voice rising. "What kind of gobbledygook is that? A week ago, you were trying like hell to get this investigation away from OpNav and back to NIS. And now you and OpNav are getting in bed at the policy level? What for, to kill it? A homicide, Doug?"

Grace looked over the phone at Dan and then averted her eyes, but he could see from the flush around her throat that she was genuinely angry. Doug. That had to be Englehardt. She hadn't used his first name at that initial meeting, so maybe Doug really was her rabbi at NIS. And they're talking about killing off the investigation? He looked at the yellow phone message: "See EA." He put the message form down where Grace could see it, mimed that he was going up to the front office, and left. Summerfield intercepted him as he came out of the back room.

"Jackson said the EA wants to see you," he said. "What's up?"

"Don't know, Captain, but it sounds like Grace is in there talking to her boss at NIS. She mentioned killing off the investigation. Sounds to me like some serious circling of the wagons has been going on."

Summerfield walked up the hall with him. "You see the *Washington Post* this morning?"

"No, sir. I don't usually read the paper until lunchtime."

"There's a little piece in there about the Hardin case, and it makes the connection with the family here. There's also a sidebar on how interesting it is that OpNav is running the investigation instead of NIS. No reasons offered, but there is some speculation about Tailhook and the USS *Iowa* case. The usual NIS bashing. It's in the Metro section."

"Wonderful. That sidebar—somebody up front lift a leg?"

"I wouldn't be surprised."

Dan stopped in the corridor just before they reached the 06 front office. "But how can they kill it off now?" he asked. "With all this publicity, 'inquiring minds' will want to know."

"They probably won't kill it off, exactly. But go see the EA. He might be ready to enlighten you."

Dan walked into the front office and reported to the EA, who was on the phone. Manning waved him imperiously toward one of the chairs while he continued his conversation. Dan walked to his familiar waiting position at the picture gallery. There were three other staff officers waiting to see one of the flags, and the yeomen were all busy at their word processors. The DCNO's personal aide, an extremely presentable young lieutenant, was on the phone making a big deal over room reservations in London for the DCNO. Dan could hear the drone of a large helicopter turning up on the helipad outside. Just another normal day at the office, Dan thought.

A part of him was hoping against hope that the investigation would go elsewhere, perhaps back to NIS, where it belonged. The Hardin case itself looked hopeless in terms of finding whoever had killed the lieutenant, especially if the murder had its roots on the streets of Washington, D.C. "You talkin' like a Martian," Vann had said. As far as Dan was concerned, inner-city Washington *was* another planet. He had been startled by Vann's almost casual statement about the expectations black parents in the District had for their children. And, he realized, there was something else: If the investigation was shelved, Grace Snow would be leaving.

"Commander Collins." Manning was looking at him. Dan walked back over to stand in front of the EA's desk.

"There have been some decisions made about the Hardin investigation," Manning announced, consulting his notebook.

"Made by whom, may I ask?" Dan said.

"You may ask," Manning replied. "Let's just say that, as far as you are concerned, they were made by competent authority. You are hereby directed to suspend your investigatory efforts and to compile your findings into a summary preliminary report, which you shall transmit under memorandum to the Assistant Deputy Chief of Naval Operations for Plans and Policy, Rear Admiral Carson, the convening authority. You are then to resume your regular duties in Op-Six-fourteen. I will have this to you in writing as an amendment to your convening order directly, but Oh-six B will expect that report by the close of business today."

"Copy to JAG?" Dan asked.

"Copies to no one. This office will handle the distribution of your preliminary report."

No copy to JAG? That meant that the heavies were going to massage this one themselves. "So they're just going to drop it?" he asked. "Kill off the investigation because of the media interest?"

Manning pretended surprise. "Drop it? Kill it off? Absolutely not. The investigation is being remanded to the NIS with instructions to bring the person or persons responsible to justice. We are absolutely not going to drop it. Any further questions, Commander?"

Dan had about a hundred, but he decided that talking to Manning was futile, a decision visibly encouraged by Manning's expression.

"No, sir," Dan said. "I'll get the paperwork going. What do I do with Miss Snow?"

"She should probably call home. I'm fairly sure that NIS will find a prominent role in the continuing investigation for her, don't you think?" Manning's smirk made it obvious that he believed no such thing.

"Right, Captain. I'll get on it."

"You do that, Commander. Oh, and Captain Randall sends his regards. He's apparently looking forward to serving with you in an operational environment one day. Or so he says."

Dan managed a weak smile and left the front office. With his luck, he would get a ship in soon-to-be Rear Admiral Randall's destroyer group, thereby ensuring a positively wonderful command tour.

Summerfield had been half-right, he reflected, as he walked back to the office. When he got back to 614, he realized it was almost one o'clock and that he was hungry. He found Grace busy making notes in her PC when he entered the back room.

"Want to go grab a sandwich?" he asked. "One last time."

She stopped typing and looked up at him. "It's official?"

"Yup. We're to wrap this thing up and hand over all the paperwork to Oh-six B, the flag officer who appointed me. From there, it's purportedly going back to NIS, as are you."

Grace shook her head. "They won," she said. "They're going to kill it."

"Oh, no, on the contrary, the EA promised me that NIS is going to pursue the matter most vigorously, until all the bad guys are caught and—

get this—brought to justice—his words. He even forecast a prominent role for you in the new and improved investigation."

Grace laughed, but it was not a pretty sound. "What they're really going to do," she said, "is call a press conference, announce that they are *expanding* the investigation, adding more resources, and centralizing the investigation effort at the NIS precisely because of the increased emphasis being placed on it by the highest levels of the Navy Department."

"So they're not going to kill it?"

"Oh yes. They'll fragment the whole effort into a dozen different shops, making sure everybody gets a piece of it, and that way, the bureaucracy can quietly envelop it. The press will get tired, and life will move on. That's how it's done."

Dan sat down.

"I've gotta tell you," he said, "I don't know whether to feel bad or good about that. I haven't really been too comfortable about this game since it started. I don't have your insider's knowledge about the NIS, but personally, I felt pretty uneasy about my role as a homicide investigator, even with you along. A collision, a grounding, a fire at sea—these are calamities within my professional competence. Murder belongs to the cops, and for better or for worser, NIS is the cops."

Grace shook her head. "That's not the point," she said. "The point is that one person has been murdered, and another one has died in mysterious circumstances. Brother and sister, both Navy, and the Navy brass is opting to let some nebulous political and bureaucratic factors drive what it does with the investigation. I smell a rat."

Dan sat back in his chair. "I guess I can't help you with that, Grace. The Navy *is* a bureaucracy, just like every other government agency in this town. It's a fact of life that bureaucratic factors in Washington are extraordinarily important. I mean, Six-fourteen is in the *political* division of the Navy staff, and bureaucratic factors drive everything we do. All I can surmise is that the bosses, the flags, have their reasons. They had their reasons when they first pulled NIS's chain, and now they have their reasons for patting NIS on the head. I don't know what those reasons are, but I guarantee they aren't going to tell me. We gave it a fair shot, and now—"

"And now it's going to atrophy behind a smoke screen of sincere publicity. Shame on us. Hell, even Vann saw it coming."

Dan didn't know what else to say. "So, how's about lunch?" he said weakly.

Despite the surrounding beauty of the center-court arboretum on a spring day, it was a dismal lunch. The heaviest part of the noontime crowd had thinned out by 1:30, leaving them a wide choice of benches and their very own flock of mendicant pigeons. Dan tried to put the best face on what had happened, but Grace was not having any of that. She was visibly angry. "Shame on us," she had said, and he could understand that sentiment. He finally asked if she was going to go back over to NIS headquarters in the Navy Yard that afternoon.

"I'll have to call them first," she said, folding her unfinished sandwich into a tight little ball in the wax paper that came with it. The pigeons looked offended. "I'm not sure if I should go back over there today. I think I'd make something of a scene."

"Grace, you're taking this thing too personally," he replied. "I mean, you *think* that they'll tank the investigation, but you don't *know* that. And the flags have every right to direct how this thing goes. It belonged in NIS in the first place."

"I know that. It's the admirals and these damned EAs I'm mad at. They brought the investigation over here to the Pentagon for some awfully petty reasons, and it looks to me like they're dumping it just because the press might make a hot potato out of it."

"I guess I'm at a disadvantage here," Dan said. "On the operational side, we're trained to follow orders in our business. Our whole system would fall apart if everybody started questioning orders. And, you never know when your boss knows something you don't know, something that might explain the whole thing."

"I think they count on that, some of these glorified file clerks masquerading as senior military officers," she said. "All that little admiral up in Philadelphia wanted to hear from you was 'Aye, aye, sir.' Not because he had some overwhelming reason to exercise a role in the investigation—he was just mad because you failed to kowtow when you came on his turf. Honestly."

Dan didn't know what to say to that; she was uncomfortably accurate about ComNavBase Philadelphia. But he was not as convinced when it came to what was going on with this investigation. In his mind, what was more likely was that the OpNav flags and the EAs had realized how hopeless a case this was and wanted to land it back on NIS's plate before it became an unequivocal disaster. But he was not quite willing to say that to Grace Snow, who might yet have to work the case. He looked at his watch. It was almost two o'clock. The shutters on the center-court snack bar were being rolled down, and an old man in a white cook's outfit had begun to hose down the area around the snack bar.

"I guess we better go back," he said. "I've got some paperwork to hand in by close of business. And you—"

"Yes. I have to call home, don't I."

28

GRACE FELT LIKE an interloper when she returned to the OP-614 offices after lunch. Captain Summerfield and Snapper were both polite, but she had the distinct impression that she was expected to leave now that the investigation had been transferred back to NIS. Dan was being solicitous, acting almost as if she alone had been visited with the bad news about the investigation. On the one hand, she was grateful for his concern, but on the other, she was angry with him for giving up the investigation so easily. The problem, she decided, was that she was starting to like him. *I'm not mad at him; I'm disappointed in his precious Navy.* While he began finalizing his summary report, she sat down and called Doug Englehardt.

"Mr. Englehardt's in a meeting," his secretary, Brenda, said. "Can I take a message?"

"This is Grace Snow. No message. I—"

"Oh, he left one for you, in case you called in, Miss Snow. He said to report back to headquarters first thing tomorrow morning. Said there was no point in coming in this afternoon."

"No point?"

"That's what he said."

"I see. Do you know who will be working the Hardin case now?"

"I don't know anything about the case assignments, Miss Snow. I do know Mr. Englehardt and Mr. Ames are in a meeting with the admiral and the EA, Captain Rennselaer. I think it's about the body in the battleship— is that the Hardin case?"

"Yes, it is. Tell me, Brenda, what's Mr. Englehardt's calendar look like for first thing in the morning?"

The secretary put her on hold and then came back.

"He's got the policy division staff meeting at eight-thirty, then a teleconference with East Coast NISRAs at nine-thirty."

"How about penciling me in for eight o'clock, would you? I'd like to talk to him off-line before the staff meeting. I need about fifteen minutes."

The secretary agreed, with the understanding that there was no appointment until Englehardt confirmed it. Grace gave her the home number in Georgetown, then hung up. Dan, who appeared not to have been listening, was banging away on his keyboard. He looked up when he sensed that she was looking at him.

"Get through?"

"Yes, and no," she said. "My mentor said not to bother coming in this afternoon, that tomorrow would be fine. And he's attending a meeting with the director of the NIS on the Hardin case."

"So they're getting right on it; that doesn't sound like they're going just to tank it."

Grace looked out the window at the concrete walls of the D-ring across the air shaft.

"If they were starting to work it," she said, "don't you think they would include the one person from the NIS organization who has been intimately involved with it so far? Or be waiting for a copy of your summary report? No, I suspect this is a strategy session, one that they very much do *not* want me to attend. Englehardt as much as said so: He told the secretary to tell me that there was no point in my coming in this afternoon."

He put his pen down. "So they're going to freeze you out?"

"I'd guess so. I suspect I'll be told to get back to my overflowing in-basket down in Career Services."

It was Dan's turn to hesitate. "I don't know if I should be saying this to you," he said, "but it sounds to me like there were two messages in that."

"Oh, yes. I think there were. We'll handle the Hardin case. And when are you, Miss Snow, going to take the hint and exit gracefully?"

Dan got up and closed the door.

"Hell," he said, "if that's the game, why not make a deal? Tell them you'll quit the organization without a fuss as long as they make it look good on your resumé. They obliterate the record of your being shunted down to the personnel office. Then they write a departure evaluation that says you were a valuable member of the policy staff, they sincerely regret your decision to leave, et cetera, et cetera."

"You've become cynical in your old age, Dan."

He grinned. "Yeah, but practical. You haven't done anything that constitutes high crimes and misdemeanors, and somebody has to be whispering in the deputy's ear that you *could*, if you wanted to, launch a sexual-harassment or equal-opportunity suit that would tie them up in very public knots. Make a deal: They reinstate you temporarily to the policy staff, give you a fancy title, wait sixty days, and you'll exit quietly, no fuss, no muss, with a glowing letter, top evals, maybe even a nice commendation. That way, you could give them your input on the Hardin case even if you're not going to work it. Hell, if you've got a rabbi, use him."

Grace turned to look at the Hardin case boards. Dan was probably right. She made about twice as much a year from her trust funds as she did from her GS-fifteen government salary: it wasn't as if the collection agencies would be coming around. She could go full-time on the Ph.D., take a year or so on sabbatical, and then go back into government . . . if she still felt like it. She was more than a little soured on government service just now. But the Hardin case still rankled.

"You're right, I suppose," she said. "I'm fortunate in that I have more alternatives than most people. It just bothers me about this case. I have no faith that the system is going to press on with it."

Dan shrugged. "We can't know that, as I said before. But you have to admit, without Mrs. Hardin's cooperation, it's going to be a bear to get much further with this thing."

"I think Vann was ready to help," she said.

"But conditionally—only if the Navy kept the thing going. Like you said, he saw the potential for the hot-potato treatment. And now—"

"Yes. And now what? There was a pretty heavy-duty subtext in what he had to say: the official white world dealing with just another black homicide."

Dan was shaking his head. "I'll grant you that the big guys may be taking a pass until the media interest cools down, but I don't subscribe to a racial angle. For one practical reason, if not for an ethical one."

"And what's that?"

"If they ever got caught, everyone involved would lose their stars and bars. And besides, the Navy is a recruit-dependent organization. It simply can't afford to discriminate against blacks or any other minorities. We need people to run this outfit, and we have to compete with all the other services and industry for a shrinking national pool of physically and mentally qualified talent."

Grace had no answer for that. She had thought before of just giving up on government service, and Dan's advice about making a deal seemed eminently practical, if a bit distasteful. But maybe that's why she wanted out: Working for the government was distasteful.

"I don't know what I'm going to do," she said finally. "Do you need any help tying off your interim report?"

"No, I'm about done. We don't have that much, really, when you start trying to reduce it to the almighty facts and opinions. There are some Privacy Act forms outstanding, but the little we have is all here."

"May I have a copy when you're done?" She surprised herself by asking.

"Sure," he said. "I'll go Xerox what I have now; my instructions are to make no copies once it's actually completed. The EAs are going to handle distribution."

He left to go to the Xerox room. She wondered why the EAs were going to handle distribution. Probably because there wasn't going to be any distribution. She sat still for a moment, wondering what to do next. It's time to go, she thought then. Time to go. She got her things together and was waiting, PC and coat in hand, when Dan came back.

"Here's your copy. I'll escort you down," he said, getting his coat.

"I can probably find my way," she said. Except that she did want him to walk her to the south parking exit. She suddenly realized that she wasn't ready just to walk away from Dan Collins. But he was all business.

"I have to," he said. "We need to turn your badge back in, and you can't get through security without a pass or an escort. They catch you, they give you orders to a three-year tour here."

They walked together, saying nothing. He took her the long way around the E-ring and then down a narrow stairway that miraculously came out one door away from the south parking exit security area. He walked her through security, depositing her building pass with the guards, and then stopped on the steps outside. She didn't know what to say.

"Do you want me to let you know when I find out what they're doing with this thing?" she asked. She assumed he would want to know.

"If you'd like," he said, implying by the way he said it that he didn't really expect that she would.

"Very well," she said. "Then I guess this is good-bye."

He seemed to hesitate. "You gave me your home phone number," he said finally. "Would you mind if I call you sometime?"

For some reason, she felt suddenly a lot better. She looked directly at him, and he smiled.

"Please do," she said. "I'd like that."

He smiled again, an almost embarrassed, boyish grin, gave her a mock salute, and went back inside the Pentagon. Grace went to find her car.

29

At 7:45 on Thursday morning, Grace pulled her car into the 3rd Street gate at the Washington Navy Yard in Southeast Washington. The Navy Yard, sometimes also called the Old Gun Factory, was situated on the banks of the Anacostia River. It was the Navy's oldest shore establishment, having been authorized in 1799. Many of the industrial buildings dated from the 1850s, when the yard had begun to specialize in the design and production of naval ship ordnance, culminating in the production of sixteen-inch guns for the Navy's battleships, hence the name Gun Factory. When the Navy stopped making battleship guns in the early sixties, the huge foundries and gun works were abandoned and fell into ruin. The largest industrial-works buildings were later stripped of all their equipment and converted into office buildings in the Defense Department's eternal search for more office space. New office buildings were erected within the hollowed-out brick shells of the nineteenth-century originals. The NIS headquarters was in one of these, called the Forge Building.

Grace drove into a part of the Navy Yard that had been the final assembly area for the battleship guns. She drove through a guard station to get into the military side of the Navy Yard, drove four blocks down to the Anacostia riverfront, and, since she would probably not be staying, parked in one of the visitor spots in front of the Forge Building. Behind her was a small grass park in which a collection of ship guns were displayed, including a sixteen-inch battleship gun. On the river side of the gun park was moored the USS *Barry*, a destroyer now part of the naval history museum. The ship was open to public tours after ten in the morning.

She walked into the main entrance, past the Navy Judge Advocate offices on the ground floor, and up the stairs to the NIS reception lobby. Showing her pass to the desk guards, she went down a long hallway to Englehardt's office and sat down to wait. She was scanning the *Washington Post* in Englehardt's outer office when he came through the door at just before eight o'clock. She had come early in hopes of getting more time to talk than the ten minutes he had promised her on her answering machine the night before. She had been flipping through the pages but not really seeing much of the news, her mind preoccupied with the decision she was close to making.

"Well, good morning, sunshine," Englehardt said breezily. "Give me a minute to start the coffee machine and then we can talk inside. Brenda doesn't get in until eight-fifteen. I assume you want to talk about the Hardin matter."

"Yes, I do. And the future of my illustrious government career."

"The lady wants free advice," he said cheerily as he rigged the coffee machine and flipped on the lights in his inner office. "I've got the world's supply of that. Worth what it'll cost you, too. Okay, we'll let the evil brew perk up. Come on in."

Englehardt's office was on one corner of the second floor of the Forge Building. The office was a long rectangle, about twenty feet by twelve, with high ceilings, in deference to the old building's 1850s architecture. A long row of exterior windows gave a Spartan view of the sides of a building called the Quadrangle Building, which was across the street, and of the ten-story-high blank brick walls of the abandoned Turret Lathe Building. Englehardt's cluttered desk was positioned so that he could just see a small wedge of the river visible around one corner of the Turret Lathe Building. There was a library table pushed up along the window wall, covered in even more paperwork and notebooks. The back wall was filled with bookcases, a television console built into the middle. There were two armchairs in front of his desk, and a much larger, leather chair nearer the windows. He pointed Grace to the leather chair, quickly leafed through a small stack of yellow phone messages, and then took one of the armchairs for himself.

Grace sat down and arranged her skirts. She was wearing a one-piece dark green calf-length dress and she had taken some care with makeup for a change. The smell of coffee brewing began to fill the air, and she could hear the sounds of nearby offices coming to life and people walking down the hallways. Englehardt bounced up and checked the coffee one last time, then closed the door to the secretary's area.

"I believe it's your nickel," he said, giving her outfit a quick once-over. "You look terrific, as usual, Miss Snow."

"Thank you, Doug. But I don't feel terrific about this Hardin case. I know . . . I know that my involvement in the case was meant to be something of a studied insult to the brass right from the beginning. But I am a trained investigator, even if not in criminal work, and this is a nasty business we've uncovered."

"Yes, it is," he agreed. "We've had a fairly good briefing from NISRA Philadelphia, including the bit about this young man probably being buried alive in that ship. And I know what you're thinking, Grace. At least I think I do."

"And what's that, Doug?"

"That because there's media interest, we're going to put this thing on a back burner and let it wither on the vine for a while, if I can mix my metaphors. We're not going to do that."

"So who's going to work it from headquarters?" she asked.

The intercom phone buzzed at that moment, and Englehardt got up to take it. As Grace waited, she could see that the top button on the left of the intercom console was lighted, which meant that the call was from Admiral Keeler's EA, Captain Rennselaer. Everyone in NIS who had an intercom knew that button. Englehardt mostly listened for a minute, said, "Yes, sir" a few times, and then hung up. He returned to his chair.

"Button zero-zero; have to take those calls," he said.

"The dreaded EA," she replied.

"He who must be listened to, at any rate. Now, the Hardin case. Specifically who will take it hasn't been decided yet. The DCIC will be in charge, of course, and they haven't named an action officer yet. But it won't be you. You do understand that, don't you?"

Somehow she had known that fact without being told, but hearing it was still disappointing. "I suppose so," she replied. She had been tossing and turning over that little fact for most of the night. "I can't say that I entirely agree, but I would at least expect to be debriefed."

"Of course, although we're supposed to get a summary report out of OpNav today from the investigating officer. I have to tell you that the admiral and the deputy are not unhappy with how this turned out."

"I can well imagine. What changed the OpNav admirals' minds; or do we know?

Before answering, Englehardt got up and checked on the coffeemaker again. Grace was quickly gaining the impression that Englehardt was uncomfortable with this meeting and wishing it was over. She wondered if the EA's call had anything to do with that. He rattled around in a cabinet out near Brenda's desk and then returned to the office with two cups of coffee, handing one to Grace before sitting down again. He glanced at his watch and then sipped some coffee.

"You want my opinion or the official reason?"

"Your opinion will be closer to the truth; what did they actually say?"

Englehardt put on an official announcer's face and voice. "Their lordships said," he intoned, "that since this matter was now confirmed to be a homicide, and since cooperation with external law-enforcement agencies would probably be required, it had been determined, upon extensive review at the appropriate levels, that the NIS was the logical management focus within the Navy Department for the case, after all. That's what their lordships said."

"And your take on the real reason?"

"They see a bizarre two-year-old homicide case that probably can't be solved, with media involvement that has a strong tabloid future, with a probable no-win outcome in the public's eye. So give it to NIS."

"Wow. It's too hard, so let someone else fall on his face."

"Precisely. I mean, it's not like it was hard to put two and two together—the EA figured it out pretty quick."

"Which EA was that? I've been surrounded by EAs this week," Grace said.

"Our very own Captain Rennselaer. He who was so exercised when this thing started out in the first place. He who spun Ames up to go convince the admiral to try to see the Secretary of the Navy even after the vice chief had sunk a fang or six in his side."

"And NIS will actually work it?"

"We will work it. Of course we'll work it. Along with all the other unsolved homicides, fratricides, patricides, and any other kind of 'cides' presently in our backlog."

"Ah."

"Yeah, I know. From your point of view, that's tanking it. But be practical, Grace. What's the urgency? This isn't about some slavering serial killer who's working himself into a lather in his basement lair to go out and slaughter another nun. It's a two-year-old black male homicide on a federal reservation. We have damn near an unlimited supply of aging homicides involving black males. And white males. And Filipino and Hispanic males. Domestic violence and murder in the armed forces is an equal-opportunity business, and there's been a lot more of it with all these cutbacks. Besides, there's no statute of limitations on federal homicide. We find the perp, he goes to jail. Later rather than sooner, maybe, but he goes to jail. The wheels of justice grind slowly, et cetera."

Grace nodded and looked out the window, trying to keep the disappointment from showing on her face. It was promising to be a beautiful day outside, but the looming nineteenth-century brick walls of the abandoned Turret Lathe Building across the street cast a pall on her spirits. She had wondered all along if Lieutenant Hardin's being black might have a bearing on how the case was eventually disposed. Englehardt was looking at his watch again.

"And what was your other question, Grace—the one about career?"

She took a deep breath before answering, but the revelation that they really were going to let the thing subside into the bureaucratic ooze had just crystallized the decision in her mind.

"I'm aware that the powers that be would not be heartbroken if I was to leave NIS," she said.

Sensing what was coming, he started to mouth a protest, but she put up a hand to silence him.

"They've made it pretty obvious without actually saying it," she continued, "even to the point of making what could be construed in certain politically correct circles as an improper internal reassignment."

"Now, Grace—"

"No, Doug. Let me finish. I'm saying this to you because you've been . . . you've been very honest throughout my tenure here at NIS. Now I would like to ask you to carry a message."

"A message. Which is?"

"I have a deal to offer: In return for a temporary transfer back to Investigations Policy, say for sixty days, I will tender my resignation from the civil service for the ostensible purpose of pursuing my Ph.D. When I leave, it's with a commendatory final evaluation, and a terminal, nonmonetary award of some kind. In return, I'll agree to go sweetly into the night, and will further agree not to employ my law degree from Georgetown in pursuit of a sexual-harassment lawsuit or any other drawn-out unpleasantness."

Englehardt put his coffee cup down and looked at her for a moment. "Jesus. Whom have you been talking to?" he asked softly.

"You let me loose in the Pentagon," she said sweetly. "As you pointed out at the time, they are not unused to political maneuvering in that building."

"Wow. Okay. And you'd like me to bear these tidings up the chain of command?"

"As your final rabbinical act, yes, I would very much appreciate it. The sixty-day number is key, by the way. That's the limit on temporary appointments within an agency without having to notify the Civil Service Commission or the GSA. This is Thursday. I've told the director of Career Services that I need to take today and tomorrow as regular annual leave. I'll be back Monday morning. I'll expect a call by close of business tomorrow, Friday, with the director's decision."

Englehardt nodded, evidently considering it. He finished his coffee and then got up. "But fundamentally, if we do all this, you will resign?" he asked.

"Yes."

"Then I don't see a problem, Grace," he said. "None at all, actually."

She realized then that NIS management had probably been waiting for her to initiate some kind of proposal along these lines. She got up, feeling as if a load had been lifted from her shoulders. Dan had been right. She felt relieved. Even Englehardt looked positively relieved.

"For what it's worth, Doug, I think upper management here is going to rue the day they dropped the Hardin case into the routine box."

Englehardt escorted her to the door. "Grace, criminal work is different from the white-collar stuff. There are just too many cases for us to get excited about any one of them. We've got finite resources, and we have to apply those to the cases where we stand a chance of getting a conviction. The Hardin case doesn't qualify. So, I'll be in touch on that other business. Speaking personally, I'll hate to see you leave us, but it's probably for the best."

THE CAPTAIN CALLED MALACHI late Thursday afternoon and left a message. The message had been short, just to inform him that the investigation had been moved to even more controllable channels, with the original investigating team broken up. "Just to keep you advised, Malachi." A couple more weeks and the Hardin case would simply blow over. Malachi had again saved and replayed the message a few times, but it seemed to be just what it sounded like: an update. He dialed the number, left the coded name, and waited. The captain was back to him in an hour.

"You called."

"Yes, I did. I want to know a little bit more about how this Hardin thing is going to be buried."

"Actually, you don't. Suffice it to say that the less you know, the better off you are. The investigation was originally being run out of OpNav, due to a, um, political misunderstanding within the Navy. That's been straightened out, and now it's back where it belonged in the first place, at NIS. And, as you may or may not know, my principal has some influence with NIS."

"And they can just bury it?"

"Not exactly bury it. But it can be added to an existing caseload, and given a priority commensurate with the likelihood of solution."

"Which hopefully is slim to none."

"Exactly. The media is the wild card, as always, but we've been proactive on that front, and they seem to be satisfied that the Navy is indeed working it. It's just going to be really hard to work. But, now that you've called, we probably ought to cool our relationship for the time being."

"Meaning?"

"Meaning that my principal wants no connections being made between any contractors and himself. Meaning that I don't call you, and you don't call here, unless something really urgent comes up, or until we are positive that the Hardin grass fire has died out."

Malachi laughed. "So I'm being fired?"

"Not exactly, Malachi. You are being unretained—for the moment. You know this is the smart thing to do, for both of us, right? If no current connection exists, there's less likelihood that someone will stumble over any previous connections."

Malachi treated the captain to a silence on the line.

"You disagree, Malachi?"

"No. But I do want to know when and if there's a development in the Hardin case. I want to hear about it from the inside, not from the *Post*. Because you don't want me getting surprised, do you?"

"Absolutely not. But what I've been trying to tell you is that there won't *be* any developments in the Hardin case. Believe me, I'm in a very strong position to make that guarantee. You simply need to do what you do best: stay low. I've got to go. We probably won't speak again for some time, Malachi. That's the safe and smart way for us to handle this now. Agreed?"

Malachi said nothing, and after a few seconds, the captain simply hung up. Malachi put the phone down and went out to the kitchen and stood by the sink, looking out the back window.

"Unretained," the man said. Cut loose. On one hand, the captain was making perfect sense: Malachi was the only connection, and it would be stupid to keep that connection alive, only to have some NIS stumblebum trip over it by accident. But suppose they were setting him up? What's the first thing they would do? Cut off all contact. Isolate him from what was going on. Lull him into a sense of false security. And then ice his ass. So what to do? What the smart soldier would do: keep his eyes and ears open. Assume the worst: They were lining somebody up to come after him, maybe even take him off the boards. Okay, run that theory out. What would he do if he did find some guy on his tail, or some other concrete indication that he was being hunted? Well, first he would take out the contractor who was on his ass. Then he'd go over to the offensive himself, maybe introduce the good captain to a little terror, or maybe even his sacred principal. It wasn't as if he didn't know where to find them. He nodded to himself, then wondered if it was too early for a little pop. He decided it wasn't.

ON THURSDAY EVENING, Dan walked up the uneven sidewalk of Prince Street from the corner of Union Street, after a better-than-usual dinner at Landini's, one block over on King. Dinner in one of the King Street restaurants was a weekly extravagance he usually enjoyed at midweek to avoid the touristy crowds of the weekends, and Landini's took good care of their regulars. The waiter had recommended the fresh mussels steamed in white wine sauce, and Dan, repeating the experience of the Italian restaurant in Philadelphia, had settled for two appetizers: the mussels and an order of the fried calamari, plus an entire bottle of chilled Lacrima Christi and a basket of their excellent bread. His leg muscles were aching after his rowing session against the spring currents on the Potomac that afternoon, but the wine had helped, or at least his slightly fuzzy brain thought so. The evening twilight was perfect, a clear, humidity-free April atmosphere gently burnished by the gaslight street-lamps on Prince. There was a slight breeze out of the north, into which the big jets descending on National Airport three miles upriver whooshed as they swept by the 250-year-old waterfront of Alexandria. A large Mercedes descended the cobblestoned segment of Prince Street in a red flare of brake lights and teeth-jarring tire bumping. The driver, a platinum blonde with too much lipstick, gave him a fleeting once-over as they passed in the night.

As he approached his house at number 128, he thought of Grace Snow, she of never too much lipstick. He fished the antique key out of the geranium pot next to the wrought-iron gate, unlocked the garden gate, went in, re-locked it, and slipped the key through a crack in the fence back into its high-security pot. He went down the wobbly brick walk along the side of his house to the garden. Some previous renters had begun an ambitious program of flowering plants and boxwood, to which Dan was totally indifferent. He enjoyed the greenery but did not do anything to maintain it, which in the lush Washington summers had produced a pretty good imitation of a jungle. The resulting riot of flowering plants, shrubs, weeds, and vines greatly distressed the judge's wife next door, who was something of a fanatic gardener. The doctor's wife on the other side called her a bush Nazi.

There was an octagonal brick patio in the center of the garden just big enough to contain a small, circular wrought-iron table and four chairs whose cushions undoubtedly harbored an interesting ecology all of their own. Two ancient but wonderfully high brick walls running down each side of the twenty-eight-foot-wide lot provided a sense of real privacy. There was a back wall that ran parallel to an alley between the row of houses on Prince Street and the rest of the block. His neighbors on either side had much larger houses and gardens, complete with some massive old oaks whose overhanging shade and company Dan could share without losing any space, at a cost of dealing with cubic yards of leaves in the fall. His dad had installed two real gaslights in the corners of the garden area, which Dan used to attract the hordes of summer bugs on those evenings he wanted to sit outside. But the Washington springtime was wonderfully free of insects, and the cool, lambent air in the garden was conducive to the digestion. He decided to aid and abet said digestion with a glass of Courvoisier from a decanter secreted in a stone hibachi on the edge of the patio.

As he sat in the gathering darkness, he thought about Grace Snow. He conjured up her face, and some fleeting images of expensive-looking clothes and shoes. Other than that one night at the restaurant, she had operated behind a facade of intelligent reserve—strictly business. She was undoubtedly frustrated with her status at NIS but strangely unaware of how much resentment her socioeconomic status must have generated in the ranks of the workaday civil service. A house in Georgetown, a late-model BMW, those clothes, and degrees from two prestigious private universities were the attributes of an upper-level political appointee at State, not a GS-14 or even 15 down in the trenches of the federal bureaucracy. Dan had been around midlevel civil servants for most of his naval career. He knew that many of the Washington bureaucrats did not have a college degree, and that they were more likely to live in Dale City or Herndon than in Georgetown, along with a working wife and a mountain of debt.

So why the hell did she stay? She did not get along with the ways of the bureaucracy and was vocally impatient with turf fights and all the other elements of internecine warfare civil serpents found to be perfectly normal and even interesting. Given her education, she was theoretically capable of contributing a lot more to society in civilian life than she ever could as a government worker.

As he sipped the cognac, he considered an even more interesting question. Grace Ellen Snow was a very attractive woman. Why was he reluctant to do what any normal guy would have done by now—that is, call her for a date? He had been almost ambivalent about his intentions to call her during yesterday's parting on the Pentagon steps. Could it be that, after six years, he still had not recovered from the loss of his wife, Claire? And did that mean he preferred wallowing in his comfortable pond of self-pity to engaging an attractive, intelligent, hell, even wealthy young woman?

Something slithered along the margins of the shrubbery and he smiled into the darkness. The bush Nazi would be skipping up the brick walk at the speed of heat over such a sound. But maybe his unkempt garden was a fitting metaphor for his personal life, his outside-the-Navy life: a ragged, unattended, almost random sprawl of not very interesting shrubbery, somewhat gone to seed, alive with the seasons, asleep in the winter, and going nowhere in particular, but nonetheless contented in its existence. It wasn't as if he was completely dead inside when it came to women: He still appreciated the passage of an attractive woman going down the E-ring corridor, and Grace stretching in her running togs had been cause for a second look. But whenever he contemplated the effort of going back into the dating-and-mating game, his inner self immediately said to hell with it.

His marriage to Claire had been entirely joyous. He was beginning to understand as he looked around at the marriages of many of his contemporaries in the Navy, that the unalloyed happiness he remembered with Claire was due at least in part to the fact that it had been tragically brief, unburdened by the pressures and strains of children, mediocre Navy pay, and the long separations caused by sea duty. He also understood that, at his age, the women with whom he would normally associate were typically focused on a single purpose: collaring a mate. After what had happened to his wife, Dan was not that anxious to try it again. And the Navy, with its extended terms of sea duty and soon, command, offered the perfect excuse to maintain his present course. Because it guaranteed that every two or three years, just as he was getting bored with his current assignment, he would move on to the next. Maybe he was just getting lazy in his old age. Grace Ellen Snow was perhaps a complication he did not need. And yet, now that the Hardin thing was subsiding, he might just call her. Was she worth the trouble? Probably. Was *he* worth her trouble? Ah, now there was a question. So call her. *I will.* But not tonight. Next week.

On that note, he finished his cognac and went inside.

AT NOON ON Friday, Dan was finishing a sandwich at his desk when the yeoman told him the 06 EA wanted to see him. Dan groaned. Captain Manning had already called down twice complaining about a staff package that Snapper had sent up during Dan's absence. Snapper had made the basic error of writing down the simple, military truth about one of State's proposals regarding foreign military sales, which truth was at odds with current Navy policy, as directed by current Defense Department policy. Since the issue had originally been Dan's before he had gone off to Philadelphia, Snapper had quietly neglected to change the name at the top of the staff paper before sending it up the line, and the EA now wanted to share his thinking with said name.

Dan wolfed down the rest of his sandwich and got his uniform jacket. He sought some sympathy from Captain Summerfield, but the captain was less than interested. He walked up the E-ring to the front office, where Manning treated him to a three-minute wait while he went through the elaborate drill of placing a phone call for the DCNO to another admiral. Since it was a three-star calling a two-star, protocol demanded that the three-star's EA call the two-star's EA, ask if his great man was available to speak to the other's great man. The two-star's EA would get the junior admiral on the phone, and then the three-star's EA would put him on hold, and go in and get the senior admiral to pick up his phone. After he had orchestrated what seemed to Dan like an interplanetary connection, Manning listened for a few seconds on his muted handset to make sure that the great men were indeed speaking and that there was nothing juicy to record, then hung up and handed Dan the offending staff package.

"This is unacceptable; you know full well we can't send anything so . . . so declarative up to the CNO. I've already talked to the CNO's EA and he told me not to bother. So rework it, and conform it to policy, please. By the way, did you actually write this?"

"My name's on it."

"So it is, although that's not an answer, is it, Commander? Oh, well, you're an owner, if not an author. There's another thing."

"Sir?"

"Rear Admiral–select Randall would like to see you. On the Hardin matter, I believe."

"I'll go right up."

Dan left the front office, carrying the staffing folder under his arm as if it were a miscreant child. He would have a word or three with 614's resident jungle bunny when he got back. He could just imagine Snapper trembling at the thought. He walked up the E-ring corridor past OP-04, the office of the DCNO for Logistics on the left, and the Visiting Flag Officer suites on the right. He waved at Captain McCarthy, the OP-04 EA, who was the only friendly executive assistant up on Elephant's Row. Probably because he was an aviator.

The Vice Chief of Naval Operations's outer office seemed to be actually smaller than 06's, with much more space being devoted to clerical operations than visitors. Both Randall and the VCNO's personal aide sat at their desks like mannequins in full uniform, coats on and buttoned. The ornate mahogany door to Admiral Torrance's inner office was closed. Dan noticed that the clerical staff were all women petty officers, and all very good-looking women at that. He also noticed that no one greeted him as he came into the front office.

He approached Randall's desk, where the EA sat reading through a staffing package. Randall ignored him for a full minute, and Dan was careful not to look over at the aide as if asking for help. The aide was a supercilious lieutenant well known among OpNav staffers as being promising raw material for the national penile-implant program. Dan did not want to give him the satisfaction of acknowledging that he was being treated like a truant schoolboy by the EA. More than one commander on the staff looked forward to seeing that lieutenant in the fleet one day. After another full minute, Randall put down the staffing folder and looked up at Dan.

"Yes, Commander?"

"Captain Manning said you wanted to see me, Captain?"

"Do I? Do you have a name?"

"I'm Commander Dan Collins, Op-Six-fourteen, sir."

Randall stared at him for a few seconds. Dan knew damn well that Randall knew who he was. This was just part of the game: I'm a terribly important EA, very busy, couldn't possibly know everyone's name, have to deal with so-o-o many people, you see. Dan had been about to prompt him, to mention the Hardin case, but he kept his silence. If his lordship here couldn't remember, Dan would happily go back to 614 and do something useful, like jump in Snapper's shit.

"Ah, yes," Randall said finally. "Commander Dan. You worked on that murder investigation, the what's-his-name case."

Dan noticed that some of the petty officers had stopped their fierce concentration on their work at the word *murder*.

"The Hardin case, yes, sir," Dan said. "But I understand that's gone back over to NIS. I've turned in the summary report to Captain Manning."

"Yes, I know that," Randall said, leaning back in his chair, which was when Dan saw his investigation folder on Randall's desk. He saw the barest hint of a smile cross Randall's face, but it was quickly erased. "That's what I wanted to talk to you about. There's not very much real substance in this report. What do you think actually happened to Hardin, and why?"

"We didn't get that far, Captain Randall. We suspect that he didn't end up in the battleship under his own volition, and that he was alive for a while after he had been bolted into that boiler. Why he was killed, or by whom? We have no idea."

"And few prospects for finding out, it would seem to me."

"Yes, sir. The incident is two years cold, and there was nothing immediately visible in his record to indicate a reason for murder. But I think we barely scratched the surface."

"You keep saying 'we.'"

"Yes, sir, Miss Snow of the NIS and I. I assume you remember Miss Snow? From the meeting—"

"Yes, of course I remember Miss Snow. And the NIS's objections to having OpNav involved in the first place. We are fully briefed up here, despite what the staff might think. I just was wondering if there was anyone else involved in the investigation effort besides you and this Miss Snow."

Dan's mind conjured up the image of Captain Vann, but for some reason he did not want to bring Vann into this conversation. The yeomen were listening hard now, but Randall put them back to work with a quick glare in their direction.

"No, sir, just the people we interviewed," Dan said. Which was partially true. The notion that Grace might keep on with the Hardin case was also something Dan instinctively did not want to share with this man.

"Very well," Randall said. "NIS has an advance copy of this. We will now forward it formally to them. They've assured me that they will pursue the matter with all deliberate speed. You may go."

As Dan started to leave, Randall raised his left hand, index finger poised in the air. "One more thing, Commander."

"Yes, sir?"

"As far as you are concerned, this matter is concluded, understood?" Randall lowered his finger, pointing it at Dan like a gun.

"Yes, sir."

"And a matter that deserves the exercise of your complete discretion. Admiral Torrance is someone who really appreciates discretion, and the converse is also true, understood?"

"Yes, sir. Understood."

"Very well, Commander. That's all."

Dan got out of there, aware of a dampness around his collar as he headed back down the corridor to 614 with the staff package under his arm. The matter is concluded. Stay away from the Hardin case. The vice chief expects the exercise of your complete discretion, so keep your frigging mouth shut or we will severally squash you. Yes, sir, clear as a bell, sir. What the hell do I tell Grace, sir? And why does this guy want this case under such tight wraps? He decided he better back-brief Summerfield on this conversation.

32

ON FRIDAY AFTERNOON, Grace returned to her house from her weekly run to Neam's, the local posh grocery store over on Wisconsin Avenue. She put away the groceries and then checked her answering machine, which was flashing. She looked at her watch: It was just past 4:15. They hadn't missed close of business by much, she thought. She called up the message, expecting Doug Englehardt's voice. But it wasn't.

"Miss Snow, this is Captain Rennselaer, executive assistant to Admiral Keeler, Director NIS. We've been apprised by Mr. Englehardt of the Policy Division that you wish to resign from your position with the NIS. The admiral has authorized me to accept your resignation, effective this afternoon. Since you are on leave, I have instructed the director of Career Services to clean out your desk and personal effects. These will be shipped to you at your home address on Monday morning. We request that you return your NIS credentials and weapons permit by traceable means as soon as possible. You do, of course, have the option of seeking another appointment within the civil service at your current grade, and you may contact the appropriate civil service office to begin that process. Your performance records and other administrative data will be forwarded for disposition. I've directed Career Services to confirm all of this in writing, of course, which you should receive at the beginning of next week. We thank you for your loyal and dedicated service at the Naval Investigative Service. Good-bye."

Stunned, Grace sank slowly into her desk chair. What in the hell had happened? Had Doug not transmitted her offer? Had he really just gone up there and said Grace Snow was ready to resign? Or had Doug played it straight and this was Rennselaer playing hardball? By not submitting anything in writing, and by relying on a back-channel approach through Englehardt, she may have walked into a trap. And she knew that she was vulnerable, having burrowed in from a political appointment to a GS position. But as her emotions tilted from initial shock through apprehension to bewilderment, she also experienced a growing sense of anger. Okay, people, you want to play hardball, I'll go to the Merit Service Board and toss a grenade into the civil service grievance system and show you some hardball of my own. But as quickly as the anger came, it melted away as soon as she allowed the cold light of reality to illuminate her situation. The deal she had offered was not something she could hold them to, because it would have circumvented civil service regulations. She had acknowledged that she would resign, albeit in sixty days. They had simply pocketed her willingness to leave and advanced the date. She certainly couldn't claim to be desperately happy there—shunted off to a nonjob after a series of acrimonious arguments with her boss in Policy, where she had been dead right on the issue but politically off base. In the context of Washington bureaucracies, such behavior made one extremely vulnerable. And her appointment at NIS had been through the good offices of a friend at Justice. If someone wanted to get nasty, the case could be made that her job was the result of improper influence, that the "competition" for the job in the first place had been a farce. The fact that most civil service job competes were a farce was beside the point: If someone wanted to make the case, she would lose. Face it, kiddo: If they want you out in this town, they can squeeze you out, especially if someone jiggered the system to get you in in the first place.

She picked up the phone to call Englehardt but then put it down after only a few rings, realizing that is was after 4:30 on a Friday. No one in this town would answer a government phone after 4:30 on a Friday, except maybe those poor fools over at the Pentagon, in their zeal to demonstrate their dedication to duty. That gave her an idea: Call Dan. She picked up the phone again. And tell him what? That you followed his suggestion and walked into a trap?

That goddamned Rennselaer had lived up to his reputation. She had often visualized the EA sitting like a spider up there outside the admiral's office, with strands of his web reaching into every nook and cranny of the NIS headquarters. He must have felt the vibrations of vulnerability as soon as she made the pitch to Englehardt, then lifted the essential kernel out of what Englehardt was saying—that she's willing to go. Discarding all the rest, he told the admiral that the problematical Ms. Snow has finally seen the light and was willing to resign. Yes, sir, I'd recommend we pocket this, sir. Today, sir. Fine, sir. I'll make it happen, sir. The dial tone erupted into a series of angry beeps in her hand and she put the phone down again.

She looked out the window. It was a lovely afternoon out there. And it was positively depressing afternoon in here. She decided that she needed to get out of the house and go for a walk. Fifteen minutes later, she found herself at the top of the stone steps that led down to Canal Road from Prospect. The steep stairway, made famous by the concluding scene in the movie *The Exorcist*, descended almost seventy feet. Below was the smoky grunt and grind of rush-hour traffic headed for Virginia via the Key Bridge, and below the vehicular tangle were the deceptively placid waters of the Potomac River. And the boathouses. She wondered, then decided to go check it out.

She walked carefully down the steps, crossed M Street on the Washington side of the busy Key bridge intersection, and walked down a small brick lane to an arched footpath bridge over the historic Chesapeake and Ohio Canal. After some very careful steps down to the gravel and clay of the towpath on the other side, she could see further steps leading down to Water Street, which ran parallel to the river banks underneath the elevated Whitehurst Freeway. Water Street, with its row of warehouses, truck-loading zones, and derelict buildings presented an unattractive prospect for a woman walking alone, but there were students out on the towpath, and it was still broad daylight. She decided to try it, so she went down the steps to Water Street, turned right under the steel beams supporting the freeway overhead, and headed for the Potomac Boat Club buildings visible about a third of a mile up the street. The area underneath Key Bridge was littered with broken whiskey bottles, and smelled of vagrants and the pungent aroma of leaking sewage. An abandoned off-ramp leading down from the Key Bridge was littered with broken glass, trash, and thick weeds. She hurried along, hoping that the club would be open. Walking down here had not been a terrific idea, after all, she decided.

The Potomac Boat Club was a ramshackle wooden building of approximately three stories that squatted between the extension of Water Street and the banks of the Potomac. The green-and-white walls of the building along Water Street bulged and curved as the result of flooding over the years. A small plaque indicated that the club had been going for almost 130 years, so it probably had been drowned more than once. She pushed open the front door and looked around, but the place seemed to be abandoned. The door at the river end of the entrance hallway was open, and she could see that there were rowers already out on the river. A sweating young man in shorts and a sleeveless T-shirt came into the hallway from what looked to Grace to be a boat loft to her right. He was carrying a set of oars and what seemed to be an outrigger of some kind.

"Excuse me, but has Commander Collins been down today?" she asked.

The young man looked her over for a second, blatantly sizing her up.

"Who's asking?" he replied.

"My name is Grace Snow. I'm just a friend. We did an assignment together in Philadelphia last week, and he told me he rows a single—a scull, is it?—that he keeps here."

The man smiled then, and pointed with his chin toward the front door. "You're in luck, Grace Snow. That's his Suburban coming in now."

Grace turned around and saw Dan's Suburban bump its way through the potholes on Water Street and pull into a parking place in front of the building. She watched as Dan got out, still dressed in his blues. When he turned around and saw Grace standing in the entrance to the boathouse, he waved and smiled, and, for some reason, she felt better than she had during her entire walk down to the river. Out of the Pentagon, he had a boyish grin that took years off his age. She walked over to the car as he opened the back of the Suburban to get his gear.

"Well, fancy meeting you here," he said. "I didn't realize you were this close to the river. Tell me you didn't walk down here."

"Well . . . actually, yes; I needed to take a walk and ended up at the *Exorcist* steps and decided to—"

She ran out of words, and he rescued her. "I walked back up that way once on a Saturday morning; you're in for a climb and a half on the way back. Come on in; let me park you somewhere while I get changed."

He walked her back through the main hallway and straight out to the sunlit boatyard behind the club building.

"So you've come to see the intrepid rower battling the treacherous torrents," he said, leading her to a decrepit-looking folding chair close to the riverbank.

She looked over at the river, which, from this closer vantage point, did indeed look treacherous, with large silver gray swirls appearing and disappearing everywhere on the surface under the pressure of the spring currents. A large gray rock fifty yards offshore had a visible bow wave, and the river made a soft hissing sound as it scoured the boat ramp and tugged at the pontoon pier fifty feet away.

"Is that safe? It looks so . . . disturbed."

"Yeah, well, we crew types are exceptionally brave; not too bright, maybe, but certainly brave. But no, that's not especially safe right now. But if you know the channels and where *not* to go, it's a pretty good physical challenge. Most of us row upstream against that current for the workout, and then it's an exercise in control getting back downstream without hitting anything and then getting across the current somewhere near the landing. It's a perfect antidote for a day at Fort Fumble, though."

"That I can appreciate. I almost called you this afternoon; I've had some news."

He put his bag down while she related her conversation with Englehardt on Thursday and then told him about the EA's nasty little surprise this afternoon.

"Damn," he said. "They were laying for you. It also sounds like your rabbi cut you loose. I'm sorry to hear this. Look, daylight is limited. There's a Coke machine over there. Why don't you grab a Coke and one of those lawn chairs out by the river. This whole evolution takes a little less than an hour, and then we can go get a drink somewhere. Those sons of bitches. Just like that?"

"I'm afraid so. In a way, I'm really angry about it, and yet, in another way, I feel a bit relieved to be out of it."

"Hold that thought," he said. "And when I get back, don't watch my landing too closely."

Twenty minutes later, he launched the scull into the river and headed out across the currents. Grace took his advice and sat in one of the dilapidated lawn chairs and watched the river go by. Out on the river, one of the Georgetown eights came sliding upstream, the boat seeming to move in a jerking motion with each stroke, losing a little way to the current each time the rowers reached for the next stroke. A small boat appeared to be chasing the shell, with a man shouting something at them through a megaphone. A pair of rowers came out of the boathouse carrying a slick-looking two-man shell and entertained her with their efforts to drop the boat into the water and board it before the current could take it downstream. She had never seen one launched before, and it seemed a miracle that they even managed it. Forty minutes later, Dan came sculling at what looked like an alarming speed across the currents, did a pinwheel turn downstream of the dock, and then maneuvered the scull alongside the pontoon pier. She went down and held on to the side of the shell while he extricated his feet from the shoe straps, stepped onto the pier, removed the oars, and then reached down and picked the entire boat up out of the water. Holding the boat over his head, he walked it back up the ramp area to the boathouse while Grace went back to her chair. He said he would be back in five minutes. Grace watched him go up the hill, conscious that she was appraising his lithe body, the way the muscles in his back corded effortlessly as he carried the boat. She turned away abruptly when she realized that another man was watching her watch Dan.

He was back in five minutes, as promised, still in his sweaty tank top, grubby, stringless sneakers, and a pair of khaki shorts.

"What I usually do at this point is drive home like this and then make myself presentable again. If you can stand it, why don't you ride back to Old Town with me. I'll get cleaned up and we can go over to one of the gin mills and have that drink."

Grace hesitated for just the fraction of a second but then agreed, the thought of climbing back up to Georgetown from the riverbed facilitating her decision. They walked over to the Suburban and he let her in, pitching his gear bag into the back. She was amused when he rolled down the rear windows to improve the ventilation, and yet, as they drove out of the boathouse parking lot, the smell of manly sweat brought back some disturbing memories of sex with Rennie before her marriage turned sour. Rennie had also had a good body, maintained by daily sessions at an expensive Wall Street athletic club. As she stole a glance at Dan, she realized that it had been a very long time since she had been with a man. For once, she did not find the speculation discomforting.

Dan had to swerve as he rounded the curve just at the point where Water Street went under the Key Bridge to avoid a large white Ford pickup truck that was parked half in, half out in a driveway on their side of the street. Grace caught a glimpse of a large man inside, who appeared to be studying a map as they went around him.

33

MALACHI FOUGHT THE URGE to look up from the map as the Suburban drove past on Water Street. He was pretty sure that the woman had noticed him, but he had had his face partially obscured by the map. Still. He started up the truck and waited for the Suburban to turn up the hill toward the city. He had not expected her.

He had followed the Suburban over from the Pentagon's north parking lot. Locating the vehicle had been a piece of cake: He had looked Collins's name up in the Virginia suburban phone book and found the address in Old Town. He had known to look in the Virginia book because these Navy officers were snooty: They generally considered it beneath them to live in Maryland or, worse, the District. Then all he had to do was go take a look. The Prince Street address signified Old Town; the guy either came from money or had gotten lucky with some real estate. Old Town was for rich people.

He had taken the metro over to Ballston the previous evening and retrieved the Ford sedan from the Randolph Towers. He had then driven down into Old Town at 10:30. He had cruised down through all the four-way stops on Prince until he reached the block with the cobblestones, and then had bumped his way past number 128 on the left as he pointed downhill towards the river. It being late Thursday night, he had found a parking space on Union Street, near the old InterArms warehouse, and walked back up the diamond-patterned brick sidewalks to the block where Collins lived. He noted that all the curb parking was by District 1 permit only, and it didn't take him long to find the Suburban with its Naval District Washington base decal on the bumper and the strange-looking racks on the roof. None of the other vehicles on the street had a military sticker. Out of habit, he memorized the license plate, wrote down the serial number on the navy decal, and then returned to his car to drive back to the Randolph Towers. The following noon, as a Colonel Smith, he called into the Pentagon Parking Control office to complain about a car parked in his reserved space in south parking, then gave the woman the Suburban's Navy decal number. She told him that decal belonged in north parking and asked if he wanted to file a formal complaint. He said no, the week was nearly over, and he was leaving, anyway; he'd just leave the guy a nasty note. He then drove the pickup truck, this time without its Metro decorations, over to the Pentagon, cruised up and down the north parking lanes until he found the Suburban, and then parked three rows away and waited. Collins had come out at 5:15, and Malachi had followed him over to Water Street. When Collins had continued under the Key Bridge to the boathouse, Malachi had swerved into an alley next to a deserted building three blocks back, then backed out once he figured Collins had had time to go inside.

Now as he turned left onto the extension of Wisconsin Avenue that led back to M Street, he decided not to try to follow Collins back to Old Town. He was pretty confident that Collins was going back home after his preppy little outing on the Potomac, with his swell little boat and undoubtedly admiring little girlfriend. He wondered if the woman might be Miss Snow from the NIS. He had tried Snow in the phone book and found a couple of candidates, but none in Georgetown. Collins had been alone when he drove to the boathouse, so the girl presumably had walked there to meet him. He decided to go back to Old Town himself and see what he could see.

It took him nearly an hour to get back downtown to the Memorial Bridge, across the river, and onto the GW Parkway southbound. Then he had to sit through the Friday-afternoon rush-hour creep-and-crawl routine once the parkway hit Old Town itself, stop and go through all those wonderful traffic lights on Washington, until he came to Prince Street. He turned down toward the river again but found that every single parking place in the entire town seemed to be taken. After some driving around, he finally spotted a small commercial lot practically on the riverfront, on Strand Street, and only a half block off of Prince. He pulled in, but there was a LOT FULL sign already in the entrance. A dark-skinned man was lazily waving him away from inside a wooden hut. Malachi fished in his wallet and flashed two twenties out the window, and the man stopped waving. Two minutes later, Malachi, now afoot, walked back up Prince to the intersection with Union Street, where he had noticed a small bistro nested up against the InterArms warehouse buildings.

As a rule, Malachi didn't use commercial lots when he was tracking someone: Too many things could go wrong, and the process of retrieving a car in a hurry could be problematical at the damnedest times. But it was a Friday night in Old Town, at the beginning of tourist season on a lovely spring evening, so he really had little choice. He turned right to walk along Union to King, then turned left up the hill into the chichi shopping district, joining the throngs of people who had begun the evening promenade on both sides of King. Malachi was dressed in casual khaki slacks, a short-sleeved yellow knit polo shirt, and a khaki windbreaker. Even in his flat tennis shoes, he stood a head taller than almost all of the people around him—all of whom were decked out in a wide variety of Friday night sport coats, ties, and even cocktail dresses. The smell of garlic and seafood spread over the street from all the restaurants along the lower blocks of King, intermingled with exhaust from the line of creeping cars trying to get through the crowds. Malachi walked slowly, letting people either get around him or out of his way, depending on which way they were going. He was of a size that caused the crowd on the sidewalk to part around him like a stream around a big midchannel rock. He was careful not to make eye contact: He didn't want anyone remembering him.

He walked slowly as he circled the block where Collins lived. The Suburban was in residence, three doors away from number 128, and there were lights on in the house. He kept walking, circling the block again, where he discovered that there were two alleys cutting into the block containing Collins's house. The first ran behind the stores and restaurants on King. The next one up gave access to garages and off-street parking for the houses on Prince. On either side of the alley was a staggered line of brick walls, some high, some not so high, some with iron gates, others with wooden gates. There were some green plastic trash bins behind some of the houses, apparently in preparation for the Saturday-morning pickup. He could see the second story of most of the town houses behind the walls, but they were beginning to be obscured by springtime greenery on several large trees. At the far end of the alley, he could see the furtive shadows of cats darting in and out of the lights behind what looked like some abandoned garages. The sounds of kitchen exhaust fans from the other alley were barely audible over the middle row of houses. As he was looking into the alley, there was a flare of headlights at the other end as what looked like a cop car turned around slowly at the end of the alley, prompting Malachi to resume his walk toward Prince Street on the uneven brick pavement.

He kept walking, making another large circle along the river that brought him back to the second alley entrance after fifteen minutes. For Malachi, there was nothing like actually walking the ground around a surveillance target; you could pick up things that you would never see from a car. He looked into the alley again, but this time the car was gone, so he strolled into the alley and walked downhill until he came to a green plastic trash bin with the number 128 on it, parked next to a solid wooden gate set into one of the higher brick walls. There was a garage wall jutting out three feet into the alley by the gate, and it provided some shadow.

It was approaching full darkness, but he still looked around the alley carefully to make sure no one was watching, and then he gently tried the gate handle. It was locked, but the wood was old and he could see through the cracks if he put his face right up against it, which he did. Behind the wall was a garden and a patio, overhung by drooping tree branches from the yards on either side. He could see Collins and the woman sitting in some chairs, but they were too far away for him to overhear their conversation over the general noise of a Friday night in Old Town. There was a sudden clatter of trash cans behind him and he drew back into the shadows while a man emptied a bag of garbage into the Dumpster behind his house, which was about fifty feet away. When the man went back inside, Malachi returned to his peephole, trying to make out details of the woman's face in the twilight, but it was too hard. Feeling that he was pushing it in an area that was probably well patrolled, he walked back out of the alley and over to King, then went down the hill again to Union and the waterfront, turning right along the river, past the parking lot. His truck sat right up front, pointed at the street; he had paid the attendant another twenty to keep it unencumbered and ready to go. He retraced his steps to the bistro at the intersection of Union and Prince.

The small café on the corner had umbrella-covered alfresco tables along the sidewalk, diagonally across from the intersection of Union and Prince streets. Malachi walked over and sat down at the end table on the sidewalk, farthest away from the restaurant's door. The rest of the sidewalk tables were empty. It was a relatively pleasant evening, but most of the people having dinner in the café were dressed for inside restaurants; the men in their coats and ties would have been comfortable, but most of the women would have found it too chilly to be out on the sidewalk. But it was a perfect place to keep watch on number 128, almost a full block up the hill from the café, and that big blue Suburban. Malachi wasn't entirely sure why he was keeping a watch on Collins and the woman, but if the woman was the mysterious Miss Snow, and if she went home tonight, he might be able to find out where they both lived—if that *was* Snow in there.

After a half hour, a pimply-faced waiter inside the very busy café finally saw him out at the table and came hustling out, trying manfully to disguise his irritation at finally having to service the sidewalk tables, and yet obviously prepared to catch hell for taking so long.

"Relax," Malachi said to him. "Bring me a double I. W. Harper hundred proof on the rocks, water back, and your dinner menu. And take your time, hey? I'm mostly out here tonight to people-watch."

The waiter nodded and hurried away to get his drink, and Malachi settled back into the chair. Upon reflection, he doubted very much that the woman with Collins was Miss Snow from the NIS. Probably just one of those female officers that had sprung up all over the military in the past few years, although she looked a little expensive for the Pentagon. He would wait for two, maybe three hours. If it looked like Collins was going to score, he would give it up for Lent and just go home. If not, and he took her home, he would follow the Suburban to see if it led him to where the woman lived. Just in case. In any event, one thing was perfectly clear: If the captain had hired some new talent to come after Malachi, this pretty boy with the big car and the little boat was probably not it.

34

DAN REFILLED GRACE'S wineglass and his own, then read aloud some of the wine babble off the back label.

" 'A hint of violets, a soft edge on the palate'—who thinks this drivel up, do you suppose?" He snorted.

"Short, little, round men who wear bow ties and odd glasses." She laughed. "I wish they'd just say it's a nice wine. It *is* a nice wine."

"Yes, I thought so. They have this evil establishment over here in Old Town called the Sutton Place Gourmet. Hungry-Yuppie heaven. I go in there once in awhile and do serous damage to my entire physiology: Everything they have there is first-class, but a health-food store it is not. Got the vino and this pâté there."

She nodded and looked around the garden, giving Dan a nudge of momentary regret about not keeping it up better. He supposed the neighbors would have had him up on charges if this were Georgetown.

"I like the . . . natural look," she said at last, managing an almost straight face.

Dan laughed out loud. "Yeah, it's natural all right. I call it a Darwin garden: The fittest species are going to make it. I amputate anything that encroaches on the patio or the walkway back to the alley; otherwise, they're all on their own."

She laughed, but then her expression grew more serious.

"Tell me," she said, "do you think the racial aspect has something to do with what's happened with this case?" she asked.

Dan was almost annoyed that she had come back to the Hardin case. He had been enjoying her company, and the chance to have a drink with an attractive woman without having to maneuver through all the quivering thornbushes of the mating game. But the Hardin case is really why she's here, right? She didn't come down to the boathouse to watch you row, did she? He did not give her a direct answer.

"Did Englehardt say anything to indicate that race was a factor in how they'd handle the case?" he asked.

She put her glass down. "He didn't mean to, but yes, he did. He said it was just another unsolved black homicide, one among too many. And then he tried to cover his tracks by citing the backlog of Hispanic, Filipino, and even unsolved white homicides. But I think he revealed how he felt with his first words. The gist was, This is probably some black thing. Another young black male ending up getting killed over a pair of tennis shoes. That's hardly front-page news. His sister was also killed, although that appears to be an accident. Well, that's Washington. We get three of those a night in this town. Next. Like that."

Dan nodded and stared down at the table. Grace sounded bitter about what had happened. He didn't know what to say to her. Having seen the body, the murder of Lieutenant Hardin was a lot more personal than daily newspaper stories of life and death in the inner city. He could not trivialize the hideous fact that the lieutenant had been literally entombed alive in that ship. Grace had seen it, too, which maybe was why she wouldn't let it go.

"What do you plan to do?" he asked.

"About . . . ?"

"Well, first, about getting the shaft from your erstwhile rabbi, Engle-whatever, and the NIS. And about the Hardin case."

"Ah. You think something should be done about the Hardin case?"

He had surprised himself, and maybe her, as well. But it was true: Something should be done. "Regrettably, yes, I do."

"Why regrettably?"

He had to think about it for a moment, figure out how to explain his situation. "Because," he replied, "it's politically risky, careerwise. I have this instinctive feeling that if I continue to poke around in this, I'm going to step on a land mine with those EAs."

Grace was surprised. "How could the Hardin case make you professionally vulnerable?"

"Easy. I'm in a Washington headquarters staff job, and in the bank for command. I stick my nose where it doesn't belong, piss somebody off, especially one of these EAs, they can derail all of that if they want to. Delay giving me a ship; extend me in the staff job. Or give me a ship that's being decommissioned: You spend a year and half putting her to sleep in some armpit like the Philadelphia shipyard. Dismantling the armed forces seems to be a priority of this administration, you know."

He leaned back in his chair and stared out into the darkness of the garden. "Or, if somebody like that guy Randall wanted to do some damage, they can descreen me: He exercises poor judgment; perhaps not in the Navy's best interests that he go to command. Remember, there are a lot more commanders than commands available—that's why we have a bank. They could always tell me to ride my desk to my twenty and get out. Unless, of course, I got SERBed, and then I could get out right now."

"Serbed?"

"Selective Early Retirement Board. All the services are doing it now, in celebration of the fact that the Cold War is over and American is finally safe. They convene a special board to screen the inventory of oh-fives and oh-sixes each year, the commanders and the captains, the lieutenant colonels and the colonels, and send about twenty percent of them a Dear John letter. Thank you for your x-teen years of loyal service, but we have decided that we don't need you anymore. Report to the personnel office in ninety days and they'll make you a civilian."

"I've never heard of this. What exactly happens?"

"Just what I said. It's the civilian equivalent of downsizing, only the Navy calls it 'right-sizing' . . . do you love it? Orwell would have approved. They convene a formal selection board around Thanksgiving and then several hundred lucky souls get a very sincere Christmas card from the Chief of Naval Personnel telling them that the Navy wasn't serious about that twenty-year career stuff, and, regrettably, they will be civilians in ninety days. Good frigging luck."

She shrugged. "You guys get ninety days. Most civilians get two weeks. I got one day."

He sighed and refreshed their wineglasses. "I know. But when I signed up, we were promised at least a twenty-year career. They promised the twenty years because we were signing up to put our lives on the line for Uncle Sam. Civilians always lived with the two-week notice clause in their contract, because civilians were mostly signing up for just a job—nine to five, home every night, every weekend. No six-month deployments to the Indian Ocean, no firefights in the back alleys of Mogadishu, no station-keeping blockades off Haiti."

"But the military is all volunteers, isn't it?"

"Yup. I'm not knocking the cruises, going to sea, or standing up on the firing line. But part of that deal is a twenty-year run and then a secure pension for everyone who survives the twenty years. Cops and firemen are in an analogous situation, which is why most of them get retirement on twenty if they want it, and if they survive that long. That's the promise that's being broken."

"Well, it's not all nine to five out there in the civilian world," Grace observed. "Civil servants, yes, but many civilians in the business world put in overtime hours without pay just to *keep* a job."

"I know," he said, beginning to feel a little bit annoyed. "But I still can't equate what I do to what a civilian who's in the business of selling soap does."

"The soap salesman would point out that he pays your salary. I think maybe you've been a bit insulated in the armed services. Even as a civil servant, I still got only one day's notice."

"Yeah. Unfortunately, you told them you would resign."

"At your suggestion."

That made him suddenly angry. He put his wineglass down on the glass-topped table with an audible crack. I knew it. Trust your instincts, he thought. You were right the other night. Suddenly, he wanted her to go home and to take her little crusade about the Hardin murder with her. He wanted to recoup the solitude of his garden, to scuttle back to his pleasantly encapsulated life. She read his expression.

"I guess I'd better go," she said softly. "And I apologize for saying that.

Your idea should have worked; with anybody but that Rennselaer snake, it would have. The truth is, I didn't belong there. I never belonged there. I should have just bowed out when the administrations changed. Can you call me a cab?"

Now he felt a tinge of embarrassment. How the hell had they run the evening right off the tracks like this, and so fast? And why do you care? I don't. I guess.

"I can run you back," he offered. "I did promise—"

"It's no bother. Besides, you don't want to try driving into Georgetown on a Friday night; it's a real madhouse. A cab's fine, really."

Once again, he didn't know what to say. Part of him wanted to try to retrieve the evening, but another part was whispering in his mind, What are you waiting for? Go call the goddamn cab.

"I'll go call a cab," he said.

He left her in the garden and went up into the kitchen to use the phone. "Twenty minutes, buddy," the dispatcher said. "It's Friday night and everything." He hung up and stood there in the kitchen, looking out the window into the garden. He could see the pale oval of her face, but not her features. He didn't really want her to go just yet. He had projected a nice Friday night with her: a drink in the garden, maybe wander down to King Street for dinner, walk around after dinner through all the stores in their eighteenth-century buildings. She was beautiful, smart, even sexy, and he couldn't pretend that he hadn't noticed. He sensed that he had somehow screwed the thing up. Or she had, or maybe they both had. Neither one of us knows how to act anymore. Too late now. He sighed. He went back out to the garden.

"Twenty minutes," he announced.

"Thank you," was all she said.

They sat there in the darkness for a while. He wanted to say something, do something, and he wondered if she did, too. Not necessarily to keep her there, but to end it better.

"What will you do about the way they terminated you?" he asked finally.

She looked away into the garden. "I don't know. The lawyer in me wants to sue them, to go to war. Another part of me isn't ready for the ugliness and the hassle of all that. I may make some noises as if I'm going to sue them, maybe extort some professionally appealing paper out of them for my resumé. But I think, on balance," she said, smiling at her own use of such a bureaucratic term, "I'm mostly relieved it's over."

"I guess I'd say that's a sane approach. As you can tell, I'm not as secure in my own profession as I expected to be at this stage. Being in the bank for command should protect me from the SERB. But not if somebody decides to single me out."

"So if I do follow up on the Hardin case, you're not in a position to help, are you?"

He avoided answering her question. "How would you do that, if you're not in the NIS anymore? How could you find out what was going on?"

"I think Robby Booker would help me. My guess is that he'll be pretty upset if the NIS just buries the case. He'll see the bias angle pretty quickly."

"I see. Well, in today's Navy, the bureau is looking for ways to invite people at my pay grade to leave the party. You attract the wrong kind of attention and then some EA hisses to another one, and suddenly you're out in the cold with all the other middle-aged white males, pounding the pavement, looking for a job. When I joined the Navy, a commander was something special—a guy who had made it to scrambled eggs on his cap and had a shot at being the captain of a ship. Nowadays, a commander in the Navy is middle management, the new national endangered species in America."

"Won't you have to face that prospect, anyway? I mean, after your command tour?" she asked.

He resented the implication, but she had a point. Look at Summerfield. "Guys who get through their command tour without running their ship aground go on to make captain," he said. "Your career gets a new lease on life. Twenty years can become thirty."

"So the career is the objective."

"In a way, I guess it is, yes."

"I guess that's the part I never digested. And probably why I no longer have one in government."

"That's because you have money, which means security. Most people who work for the government really do it for the security. That's why something like the SERB seems like such a betrayal. And it's not like the policymakers don't know that."

"But the policymakers aren't career, are they?" she mused. "They're appointees."

"You got it."

They sat there for a while until a horn honked out front. Dan reluctantly led her along the garden walk to the front gate. He unlocked and opened the gate, stepped through, and held it open for her. A Yellow Cab was double-parked in front of the house; it was facing downhill, it's interior light on. The driver was a hugely fat man who made no move to open the door. Dan opened the left-rear door for her.

"Well," she said, "thanks for the wine. And good luck with your career. I had no idea life in the Navy had become so precarious."

"I suspect it's life everywhere," he said. "It was a pleasure to see you. Sorry I wasn't better company."

She smiled—a little sadly, he thought—said good night, and got into the cab. The cabbie turned off the interior light and drove down the hill. Dan watched the cab for a few seconds as it rattled down the cobblestones to Union Street, exhaled aloud, and then went back into the garden. As he closed and locked the gate, he thought he heard a large vehicle take a turn much too fast down the block. He walked back to the table, sat down, and poured himself some more wine. Well, Casanova, here's to you. You sure impressed that lady all to hell. She'd been effectively fired with one hour's notice after running a gambit that was indeed your suggestion, and you spend the evening complaining about how exposed you are to the current round of reductions in force. Yeah, but she's got tons of money and doesn't *have* to work; you do. She's working for the psychic satisfaction of working; you're working for the chance of getting your own command at sea one day and, let's face it, for your twenty and the security of a Navy pension.

Neither of which would be worth sacrificing for the sake of finding out who iced the lieutenant two years ago in beautiful downtown Philadelphia. Especially not after the VCNO's EA had taken some pains to warn him off the case. He could just see Captain Randall's smiling face if he found out that young Commander Collins had not quite let go of the Hardin investigation. Lovely thought, that. Americans had supposedly always been afraid of the dreaded Man on Horseback; they ought to be taking a real hard look at the Man's horse-holders.

He sighed and corked the wine bottle. If Grace Ellen Snow wants to pursue the Hardin case, more power to her. She is literally a free agent now. But he could predict what would happen: The NIS would discover that she was still playing detective and warn her off in a hell of a hurry. For the sake of his career, he did not want to be around when that happened. He decided to go around the corner to McDonald's, grab some grease, and then go home for some cognac. Maybe the cognac would help him forget about the Hardins and Grace Ellen Snow.

But as he walked down the block toward King Street, he realized that forgetting about Grace Snow and the Hardin case was not really possible. Captain Randall had made it clear that the Hardin affair was clearly a no-go area, but his own sense of right and wrong was sulking in a corner of his mind and giving him dirty looks. The murder of the young lieutenant was bad enough, but if the Navy tubed the investigation just because it might expose some sensitive nerves at high levels, that was doubling the wrong. Sure, he could let Grace do it, but the fact of the matter was that she would be on the outside of whatever was going on in the Navy. He stopped as he reached the crowds and the bright lights on King Street. He knew that he wasn't going to be able just to turn his back on the Hardin case. And there was also no way he could just turn his back on her. Damn it.

35

MALACHI NEARLY LOST the cab in the stop-and-go maze of the back streets of Old Town. The cabbie had elected wisely not to go out onto Washington Street on a Friday night, and he was shooting through the back streets between Washington Street and the river until he could merge back into the GW Parkway up near the power station. Malachi had to run one stop sign near the public housing projects, then douse his lights to cover the next two blocks without attracting the cabbie's attention. Once on the parkway itself, the tail was a lot easier. He assumed they were headed for town, maybe even for Georgetown, since that's where the lady had first appeared. As they headed north up the parkway past the airport, Malachi tried to remember the possible approaches into Georgetown.

He had spotted the cab about a block away from his vantage point at the bottom of Prince. It had proceeded slowly down Prince, the driver obviously reading house numbers. He had relaxed when it passed 128, but then it had stopped and backed up, causing him to jump up, his dinner unfinished, drop two twenties on the table, and sprint for the car park. He started up the F-250 before the attendant even knew he was there and drove back to the corner of Prince and Union, scattering some tourists as he came out of the lot. He had stopped at the corner before he realized that he was pointed the wrong way on a one-way street. Out of the corner of his eye, he could see the waiter counting his money at the table and looking around. Up the street, the cab was still there, waiting. A car honked at him from across the street, but he ignored it. The car honked again, the driver pointing to the one-way sign, but he concentrated on watching as Collins and the woman came out of a small side gate, the woman getting in the cab and Collins going back in through the gate. Solly, Cholly, he thought; you're in a nooky-free zone. Boy wonder strikes out. The cabbie had come down Prince, stopping almost face-to-face with Malachi's truck, and then turned in front of Malachi to head north on Union toward the airport and the Potomac River bridges.

After following them up the parkway past the Pentagon, it became clear that the cabbie had opted for the Key Bridge, which would be direct, although jammed with traffic on a Friday night. Malachi settled in for the ride, staying three cars back and making sure he matched the cab's lane once they got on the Key Bridge. There were two choices at the Washington end of the bridge. He knew that the tough part would be if she lived in one of those small blocks between Wisconsin and the university—it would be impossible to follow the cab into that rabbit warren without being noticed. At the end of the bridge, the cab turned right onto M Street, then really slowed down amid the world-class congestion of a Friday night in Georgetown. It took them ten minutes to make the two blocks to 33rd Street, and then another ten to make the left turn onto 33rd, which Malachi did through a red light, to the accompaniment of a lot of horns. But he got stuck behind a bus at that juncture and could only watch as the cab disappeared around the bus. But the cabbie had his left turn signal on, so they were close. Three minutes later, he took a shot and made a turn onto N Street off 33rd, but there were no cabs up ahead, just quiet residential streets packed with parked cars. Cursing, he drove all the way to 37th Street and the edge of Georgetown University, looking down into each of the side streets, but there was no cab. Trapped in the labyrinth of alternating one-way streets of the Cloisters area, he decided to spend a few minutes driving down each one, crisscrossing the neighborhood, looking for any sign of the cab. But after twenty minutes, he realized that she had to be out of the cab and in her house by now, so he gave it up and turned for home. He still did not know for sure whether the woman with Collins tonight had been Snow, but he would have liked to have found out. Back to the trusty telephone, he thought as he turned off M onto Pennsylvania Avenue.

THE CABBIE GRUNTED in appreciation at the tip she gave him. Grace was used to taking cabs in this city, where they were relatively inexpensive, and she tipped well as long as the driver did not try to fiddle the city's curious fare-zone system. The driver turned around as she was preparing to get out, or at least he turned his head; his body appeared to be much too big to move without a small crane.

"That guy you was with tonight, over in Old Town—that dude married?"

Grace held the right-rear door open and looked at him in surprise. "Why, no," she replied. "He was married once, but his wife died. Why on earth do you ask?"

" 'Cause we picked up a tail when we was leavin'. Guy stayed on us all the way to M Street, when I ditched his ass behind that bus. White guy in a big ole white pickup. Figured maybe some jealous wife, gone an' hired one a them private eyes, you know?"

Grace shook her head. "No, it's nothing like that. We worked together on a . . . project, for the past two weeks. Are you sure someone was following us?"

"Yeah, I am. No fool gonna bring a F-two fifty pickup truck into Georgetown on a Friday night, less'n he has to. You be careful, now. That dude was follerin' you, sure enough."

Grace got out of the cab and automatically looked up and down the street, but there was no traffic, nor any darkened cars parked suspiciously in alleys or driveways. The cab took off in a cloud of smelly exhaust, listing visibly to port, as she went up to her door. Looking through the narrow windows on one side of the door, nothing seemed out of the ordinary, but when she went inside and closed the door, she did not turn on any more lights; instead she stood beside the curtained living room window and watched the street for a few minutes. Two cars came by during her vigil. One she recognized as a neighbor's, and the other was a cop car, cruising the neighborhood. That driver must have been dreaming; why would anyone follow her back to Georgetown? In a pickup truck? Feeling foolish, she went back into the dining room and checked her answering machine. There were no calls.

She went into the kitchen and poked around in the refrigerator for something to eat, then decided to have some ice cream and call it a day. She took her ice cream to the desk, pushed aside some papers, and sat down. She had thought that perhaps Dan Collins might have called; she had had the sense that he was disappointed in the way the evening ended. But perhaps that was just wishful thinking. He's a very nice man, and I'm comfortable in his company, she thought. At times, Dan seemed interested in her as a woman, and yet at other times he seemed to revert back to his role of widower, more or less permanently detached from life with women. So why did she care? She didn't know if she really did, and after the trauma of marriage to Rennie, she had some empathy for Dan's attitude.

She finished her ice cream, checked all the locks, put out the downstairs lights, and was about to go upstairs for an evening with a good book when she heard a vehicle coming slowly up her street. The engine did not sound like the usual purring motors one would associate with her neighborhood. Standing in the darkened hallway, she peeked through the window curtains at the door and saw a very large white pickup truck moving slowly up the street toward the university campus. She caught only a glimpse of the shape and color of the driver's face as the truck passed under a cone of streetlight, barely enough to make out his features. For just a second, she thought she had seen that face before. The truck cruised past her house, the driver looking straight ahead, stopped at the stop sign on 35th Street, and continued on out of sight into the next block.

Grace stood there wondering. The cabbie had said they were followed by a white pickup truck, and here was a white pickup truck cruising the narrow streets of the Cloisters neighborhood in the early evening. Going slow, so he was looking for—what? Or whom? And where had she seen that face? Then she remembered: She had seen the truck today, when they had come out of the boathouse onto Water Street: the pickup truck with the big, fearsome-looking man in it, parked under Key Bridge, scanning a map. She remembered that Dan had swerved to avoid it. She walked back to the study and picked up the phone to call Dan. She got his answering machine and left a message asking him to call, preferably before 11:00 P.M. Then she checked all the locks again and went upstairs.

Dan called at 10:45, apologizing for the late hour.

"I went down to McDonald's for a greaseburger. What's up? You sounded worried."

She told him about the pickup truck.

"And you think this guy followed you from Old Town?"

"I never saw him, but the cabdriver says he did. He even described it as a white F-two fifty, whatever that is. You do remember that truck you had to steer around at the boathouse when we came out?"

"No. Oh, yes, I do. So maybe this guy was on your tail even before Old Town? I wonder—"

"What?"

"Well, right after you left, and while I was still up by the garden gate, I heard what sounded like a fairly large vehicle screech through a turn down the block. But I never actually saw it."

"He could have been parked somewhere, then hurried to catch up with my cab," she said.

"Yeah, if you admit the possibility you were being followed. Any ideas as to why?"

"No. That's what kind of scares me. I mean, the cabbie says he lost the truck behind a Metro bus, and I know there was no one on the street when I got out of the cab or for some time afterward—I sort of watched. But then I did see a white pickup truck coming up my street a short while later, and I think it was the same man that was at the boathouse."

Dan was silent on the other end for a moment. "I just don't know what to tell you, unless it's connected to NIS in some fashion, and that doesn't make much sense. They wouldn't be following someone that . . . that didn't even work there anymore."

She smiled at the way he phrased it. "And not in a pickup truck, I shouldn't think. NIS tends to dark four-door sedans with aerials on the trunk that no one in a million years would suspect are cop cars."

"Yeah, right." He laughed. "I think cops use them to avoid parking tickets more than anything else. Which brings up the logical next question: You call the cops?"

"And tell them what, that I think I'm being followed?"

"Well, you *do* think you're being followed. The tough part will come when they ask for possible reasons or suspects, and then it comes out that you've just resigned from NIS. This being Washington, they're automatically going to assume there's some problem there, and they probably won't be very helpful."

"I guess you're right," she said with a sigh.

"Just what you want to find out at eleven o'clock at night, isn't it? Some guy in a pickup is starting to follow you around. By the way, I'm sorry our evening together ended so abruptly."

That had come out of nowhere, but she felt a flash of —what, relief?

"I am, too," she said carefully. "Perhaps I need to sort this NIS business out, and then we can try again. After my divorce in New York, I haven't . . . well, dated, or really seen anyone. I'm afraid I've lost my touch, if I ever had one."

"Well, I know I've lost mine. Since Claire's death, I've lived in a kind of emotional Thermos bottle for a long time, and I'm afraid I've gotten used to it. It's more comfortable than people might imagine."

"Cocoons do have some advantages," she said.

"And there are drawbacks: You can't see out of them very well. So when something valuable comes by, you might miss it."

She was silent for a moment. He apparently felt compelled to fill the silence.

"Which is why I guess I didn't want just to shake hands and say good-bye. And despite my concerns about stepping in something over the Hardin case, I have to admit that I'm not comfortable with just saying forget about that, either. It's just that I'm a straight-stick, tin-can sailor and I don't know the first thing about how you would proceed."

"I don't know, either. First I'm going to try to get clear of NIS with my resumé intact. But then I think I'll go back and see Detective Captain Vann. I have the impression that he might have a personal stake in the Hardin business beyond just knowing the family. Maybe he can point me somewhere that I can do some good, especially when I tell him NIS is going to put it in the too-hard basket."

"Okay. And on reflection, you probably *should* make that call to the cops. Get this thing on record; that way, if any more pickup trucks show up, you're not starting from scratch. They have these stalker laws now, too, so I don't think they can just brush you off."

"I'll think about it."

"Okay. And I'll call you Tuesday evening."

"Good."

They said good-bye and Grace put the phone down gently. Better, she thought. Much better.

ON MONDAY, GRACE talked to her father's attorney in Philadelphia, Robert Fishbein, about the way she had been terminated at NIS. The lawyer quickly brought it down to a case of balance: "First, how much pain are you willing to endure to get back at them, and, second, do you really want to get that job back?" She knew the answer even before he was finished. This wasn't about getting the job back; this was about the way they had gone about it. The way that damned EA, Rennselaer, had gone about it.

"Let's do this, Bob," she said. "Make a call for me. Identify yourself as my lawyer and then ask for the full and correct spelling of three names: an Admiral Keeler, a Mr. Ames, and a Mr. Englehardt. That's the director, the deputy for Policy, and the principal assistant deputy for Policy, respectively. They may or may not give them to you, but I want to smoke out a phone call. At the very least, I want a decent piece of paper from them."

She gave him Ames's office phone number and hung up. She had called the District police to report the guy in the pickup. The police had been politely underwhelmed but did say that they would open a file on it. Grace had the impression that it would not be a very big file, but the detective's clerk had taken her name, address, and some of the particulars. She quickly discovered that the police liked to deal in facts: description of the man, description of the car, precise times when she was followed, and the exact route, only parts of which she could provide with very much accuracy. And, no, she didn't have any idea of who might have a reason to follow her: no jealous wives, no ex-boyfriends, no panting coworkers. There had been no phone calls, no prowlers, no hate mail, or love mail, for that matter. And just the one instance. "Right. Okay, call us if it happens again; we'll keep a file on it. Here's the file number. Good-bye." Grace had put the phone down with the feeling that she'd been told to take two aspirin and call the doctor in the morning. But she couldn't really blame them.

She tackled the mess on her desk until noon, when Doug Englehardt called in. She picked up as he was identifying himself on the machine.

"Well, Doug. Fancy hearing from you on a Monday morning."

"Don't start, Grace. I only heard about it at the morning staff meeting. I carried the message just the way you phrased it, and the damned EA said he would take care of it. I'm calling to apologize for the way they've behaved, and for failing in what I thought was a no-brainer, win-win for everyone. That Rennselaer guy is a piece of work."

"And what would you suggest I do now, Doug, or are you out of the advice business?"

Englehardt paused before replying, but then he came out with it. "I think maybe you've already done it. I just got a medium-frantic phone call from Ames's office, saying your lawyers in Philadelphia had called in asking for the correct spelling of some prominent names here."

"The *Post* called yet?" she asked sweetly.

"The *Post!* Jesus Christ, Grace, what are you doing?"

"Just taking a leaf from your clever little EA's book, Doug, and indulging in a little hardball. It strikes me that a very public discrimination lawsuit is just what the doctor ordered for the likes of Captain Rennselaer. And we both know how much the NIS admires publicity. I would think that there are some people over in OpNav who might enjoy it, too, don't you think?"

"Grace, for God's sake—"

"No. For my sake, Doug. NIS has besmirched my record of government service with a no-notice termination disguised as an acceptance of a putative resignation. I'm think I'm going to deny I ever talked to you, in case you want to pursue the logic."

"Grace, Grace, we can fix all that. We can—"

"Don't say 'we,' Doug. You don't speak for anyone in authority at NIS, as we've both found out, haven't we? I'll tell you what: I'll entertain one phone call, just one, from the admiral, and it needs to be really constructive, and made by close of business tomorrow, okay? And if that Rennselaer reptile so much as disturbs my answering machine, it's war. 'Bye now."

Grace hung up and then laughed out loud. She could just imagine the phone call that had come down to Englehardt's office from the choleric Roscoe Ames. She made a note to be home at around four the next afternoon, then went to make a sandwich. After lunch, she would call Captain Vann.

On Monday, Malachi made some calls to the NIS. Since he might end up going down there, he used his own voice. The Defense Department phone book had given him the number of the Criminal Investigations Division, where he told the lady answering the phone that he needed to speak to someone about the Hardin case. The woman passed him off to another woman, who in turn gave him yet another number. He played this game for twenty minutes before getting an actual NIS agent on the line. Malachi described himself as a private investigator by the name of Costas who needed a couple of minutes of face time with the agent working the Wesley Hardin case. The agent told him that, per NIS policy, investigating officers did not discuss their cases with outside civilians. Malachi told him that he understood perfectly, that he was a retired Army MP, and that he wouldn't dream of asking questions about the case. He simply needed to get face-to-face with the investigating officer to confirm that the Hardin who had been in the news was indeed Lt. (jg) Wesley Hardin, of Washington, D.C., and that he was indeed deceased.

"I have to be able to record that with attribution, see—my client is somebody that Hardin owed money to, and now he wants to confirm that the guy is no-shit dead. Won't take five minutes, and since I know this can't be done on the phone, I wanted to come down and talk to the investigating officer, somebody who could make that statement authoritatively, to my face and then I'm outta there."

"Well, shit, if that's all it is," the agent said. "We had a woman on the

Hardin case, but I heard in the hallway this morning that she got canned. But you could come in and talk to one of the policy people—they've been involved and can probably solve your problem for you pretty quick."

"Got a name I should ask for?"

"Oh, I don't know. Try Mr. Englehardt."

Malachi went next door to the apartment, turned on the answering machine, and recorded a voice message for the Costas Detective Agency. He then connected a caller ID box and activated the monitor feature so that it would record numbers coming into the answering machine. Putting on a suit and tie, he took the Metro over to Arlington to get the Ford sedan.

He made sure the Virginia plates were still in place from his last trip into D.C., shuffled the registration and driver's license so that everything matched, and fired it up. He went up two internal ramps and out onto Randolph Street, then headed for the Navy Yard over in town. Twenty-five minutes later, he pulled up at the main gate and showed the guard his retired military ID card. The guard eyed the wheels.

"Workin' for the county now, hunh, Cap?"

"You know how it is," Malachi said. "That retired check don't cover a whole lotta ground these days."

"Tell me about it," the guard said. "I'm a retired chief, and now lookit me—a freakin' rent-a-cop. Where ya bound?"

"I gotta find some outfit called NIS. They're supposed to be down here somewhere."

"Yeah, they're in the old Forge Building, down on the waterfront. You go down there and take your first left, then take your first right at the navy museum, and it's the next building. There's a buncha ship guns in a park in front of the building." The guard waved him through the gates and went back to his paper.

Malachi patted the Ford's dashboard as if it were an old dog as he pulled past the gatehouse. Amazing what assumptions people would make when they thought they were looking at a cop car. He had come over to the Navy yard a few times when he had been stationed at Fort McNair just before getting out of the Army. The Navy Yard was situated in the southeastern quadrant of Washington, which was still a sufficiently rough part of town to warrant the twenty-foot-high brick wall that surrounded the old industrial area. He remembered the oppressive one-mile shuttle-bus trip from Fort McNair to the Navy Yard, through the run-down and torn-down shambles of Southwest and Southeast D.C., with its burned-out buildings abandoned since the 1968 riots and the chain link–fortified liquor stores surrounded by clumps of glaring men. He remembered that McNair also had a very high brick wall around it.

He drove down the main-entrance avenue and tried to take a left on Parsons Avenue, but the Navy Yard's diggers and fillers had the street torn up, which forced him to take a long detour through the looming, blackened brick facades of the old gun factory buildings. The buildings were big enough to block out the sunlight as he drove through the abandoned complex, bumping over old train tracks and even some thinly asphalted cobblestoned sections. He drove down along the waterfront, circled a couple of blocks, and then turned right, going by the only surviving remnant of the actual gun factory, the giant Turret Lathe building, where the battleship gun barrels had been bored and turned. Almost by accident, his final turn brought him out on the waterfront, where five piers pointed slantwise downstream into the Anacostia River, including one at which an elderly destroyer was tied up for public visiting.

Across from the ship was the Forge Building. Sure enough, there were no available parking spaces, except for three vacant slots reserved for government vehicles right in front of the building. He pulled the old cop car into one of them, shut it down, and got out. A Federal Protective Service police truck came by, but the officer inside ignored the Ford. Malachi smiled to himself and went into the Forge Building. Inside the 1850s brick shell was a modern office hallway, with glass doors proclaiming the offices of the Judge Advocate General Appeals Board on either side. He asked a lady lawyer in Navy whites where NIS was, and she pointed him up a set of stairs.

The NIS reception area was surprisingly small, a holdover from the Desert Storm security panic, when hordes of wild-eyed Iraqis had been expected to charge their way into American government buildings seeking Muhammadan heaven. There were two female FPS cops leaning on the counter, and a third security officer was reading a paper in a glassed-in enclosure behind them that was filled with TV monitors. Malachi dragged out his PI license for the desk guards.

"I need to see a Mr. Englehardt in Investigations Policy."

"You knowin' his extension?" the larger of the two female cops asked.

"Nope."

The woman wearily looked up Englehardt in the NIS phone roster, gave Malachi the extension, and pointed him to a wall phone at the end of the counter. Malachi dialed the number and got a secretary. He could see office hallways and people going back and forth beyond the glass doors.

"Investigations Policy. This is Brenda," a voice said.

"This is Mr. Costas. I'm down at the front desk. I called in earlier this morning and was advised I needed to see a Mr. Englehardt. I need about two minutes of his time."

"Do you have an appointment with Mr. Englehardt?"

"No, I don't." Using the PI cover, he explained what he was looking for, a certification from someone who could vouch personally for the fact that one Wesley Hardin was in fact deceased. He asked if he could speak to Miss Snow.

"Miss Snow? I thought you wanted to speak to Mr. Englehardt?" The woman was starting to sound suspicious.

"The people at the Philadelphia County Medical Examiner's Office said the NIS agent of record was a Miss Snow," Malachi replied patiently, "and that she was from the Washington office. She viewed the remains, is all. I don't really care—all I need is a live human being that I can cite as the source. You want to, you can give me Miss Snow's phone number. I'll go see her direct if Englehardt is unavailable."

"Just a minute, Mr. . . ."

"Costas."

"Just a minute," she said again, then put him on hold. The desk cop looked over at him, and Malachi rolled his eyes. She went back to her newspaper. Then a new, male voice came on the line.

"Mr. Costas, I understand you have some questions about the Hardin case? This is Douglas Englehardt."

"No, not really, Mr. Englehardt. I'm a P.I.; I'm also a retired Army MP. You got a homicide investigation going, you don't answer questions about it, not if you run it like we did in CID. All I really need is a face-to-face statement that Wesley Hardin is officially deceased—from somebody who actually saw the body. Then I can tell my client that I *know* for a fact that Wes Hardin is dead and that he's probably not going to get his money."

"What money is that, Mr. Costas?"

"My client came to me when the news stories broke. Apparently, this Hardin guy owed him three thousand dollars, or so he says. He hired me to confirm that this is the same Hardin and that he is indeed dead."

"Well, we don't know anything about a money angle, but I can tell you that Lieutenant Hardin is very much deceased."

"Did you view the body?"

"No, but—"

"Well, here's the thing," Malachi pressed. Another man had arrived and was waiting to use the desk phone, and the desk cops were starting to look annoyed. "My client insisted that I talk to someone official who has *seen* the body. I know it sounds weird, but there it is. I was told that a Miss Snow—"

"Miss Snow doesn't work here anymore," Englehardt interrupted. This momentarily threw Malachi for a loop. Then he remembered the other guy saying she got canned.

"She doesn't? Well, can you give me a number I can—"

"No. That's not possible, Mr. Costas. Listen, as a matter of policy, we don't—"

"Wait," Malachi interrupted before Englehardt could dig his heels in too deep. The desk cop was pointing at the phone and indicating his time was up. He ignored her.

"How's about passing her a message, then, okay? All she has to do is call my office, confirm over the phone that she saw what she saw, and then I'm done. I mean, I've driven all the way down here and everything. How about that—can you at least pass on a message to this Miss Snow? One lousy phone call solves my problem, okay? I don't need to bother anyone here.

It's nothing that hasn't already been in the papers—I just need it official like. Clients. You know how it is. Please?"

Englehardt hesitated but then agreed, although he sounded annoyed. Malachi gave him the number for the safe house on Capitol Hill. Then he thanked him profusely, relinquished the desk phone, and left the building. He knew that Englehardt might just throw the number away and get on with his Monday; he sounded like a prick. Except that Malachi had made it pretty clear that he could be persistent. We'll see, he thought; it's worth a shot. As he came outside, he noted with relief that his car was still there and not under tow to some federal impound lot. He looked at his watch. He had time to get over to McNair and visit the package store, refresh his supply of I. W. Harper and cigarettes, get some stuff at the commissary there. He really did not have to hurry home at all: The caller ID box would record the number if Snow called him, and with a phone number, any average asshole could get an address in this city. He backed out of the parking spot and headed for Fort McNair.

GRACE SNOW TRIED Captain Vann's office after lunch, but the secretary said he was in a meeting. Grace asked for a callback and left her number. She thought about calling Dan, but he had said he would check in with her Tuesday evening, and this was just Monday. She called her bank to check her balances, then decided to go over to the branch office to arrange some periodic transfers from savings, now that she no longer had a paycheck coming in. The bank branch was only six blocks away on Wisconsin and N Street, and it appeared to be a pleasant April day, so she decided to walk over.

When she came back, the answering machine was flashing at her. Expecting Vann, she got Englehardt's voice instead. He gave her a brief background of what someone called Costas needed, a phone number to call, and advised her that she could forget about it if she wanted to, Costas being some itinerant civilian PI. He also passed on the fact that he had relayed her message to the NIS front office, to Rennselaer himself. He made no comment on how Rennselaer had reacted. She replayed the message once to assess his tone of voice, but it all seemed pretty matter-of-fact. There was no message from Vann.

She decided to dispatch the Costas problem. She pulled the phone over and dialed the number. She got an answering machine that announced the offices of the Costas Detective Agency. As Englehardt had suggested, she left a brief message that she had been the NIS investigating officer in the Hardin case and had personally viewed the remains of Lt. Wesley Hardin, and that he was in fact deceased. She also said that she no longer worked for the NIS and therefore could provide no further information on the matter. She did not leave her number.

After hanging up, she sat at the desk, thinking about what to say to Vann. I've been fired from the NIS, they're going to tube the investigation, and I want to press on with it on my own. She almost knew what he would say: You're a civilian now, it's a federal homicide, and there's nothing we can do about the case as long as the feds are working it, however slowly. Not like it's a fresh kill. She shuddered at the image that term conjured up. But Vann, being a cop, would tell her to do what she already knew: Stay out of it.

Maybe a different approach: I've resigned from the NIS *because* they are putting the Hardin case in a too-hard box. I'm going to put my thinking cap on, see if I can come up with some possible ties between the death of Elizabeth Hardin and her brother's murder. If I can, I'd like to be able to kick it around with you—informally, of course. Entirely off-line.

Better, much better. He's a bureaucrat. The second approach doesn't ask him to do anything, and it doesn't imply that I'm actually sticking my nose where it doesn't belong. Just thinking about it. Much better. She waited for his call.

39

When Malachi got back to the town house from Fort McNair on Monday afternoon, he found two messages waiting. One was on the answering machine programmed for Costas, along with Snow's phone number registered in the caller ID window, which he promptly wrote down. The other was on his house machine and it surprised him: It was from the captain, asking for a callback. He called the captain's number first and left the coded message. He then went to unload groceries and the case of Harper hundred, carrying everything in from the alley, where he had parked the Ford crosswise in front of the garage door, and through the garage. He chided himself for feeling so much better that another dozen hundred-proof soldiers were securely on watch in the cupboard. First things first, his old man had always said, except that his old man had never said any such thing. His old man had been too drunk to say much of anything. Like father, like son, hey? Well, it sounded good. The phone rang and he picked it up in the hallway. He had left the back door open, so he could keep the Ford in sight through the open garage doors.

"Yes?" he said.

"Greetings. I just wanted to update you on the Hardin thing."

"Didn't expect to hear from you so soon. But I'm all ears."

"You'll notice that it hasn't been in the press anymore."

"I've noticed."

"Well, we've put it back in its box, I think. The OpNav element has been withdrawn from the investigation, and the officer involved returned to his regular duties with appropriate instructions about keeping his mouth shut. The whole business is now back in the capable hands of the NIS."

Malachi snorted. "Capable? Last time I saw the NIS in action was when I was still in the army; it was like six monkeys trying to screw a football."

"Well, they're part of government: They're supposed to screw something or someone every day. The point is, whether NIS buries it or actually works it, I think we're all reasonably safe."

"Most criminals are when NIS is involved."

"Well, NIS sometimes gets lots of high-level advice. You think we're criminals now, Malachi?"

"Unindicted co-conspirators is the term of art, Captain. And that's the way we want to keep it. Especially the *unindicted* part. You can keep tabs on what NIS is doing with it, correct?"

"To a certain extent, yes."

"I'll keep an ear to the ground on the metropolitan police side," Malachi said. "I've got some contacts downtown. As long as the first Hardin case stays in its box, this other Hardin case ought to go nowhere."

"Very well. Anything for me?"

Malachi hesitated. What did that mean? Were they aware that he had been exploring a little bit?

"No," he replied. "Your principal is keeping his wick dry?"

The captain actually laughed. "My principal is mostly trying to keep his flag-rank billet intact, what with all the budget cuts. Relax, Malachi; as far as the Navy is concerned, this Hardin thing's back in the weeds, where it belongs."

"Nasty things sometimes come out of the weeds," Malachi replied. "I suggest we both keep our eyes open."

"Count on it, Malachi. I know that I said we would not be in touch for a while. This time, I think I mean it."

"Except for emergencies, right?"

"Absolutely. Except for emergencies."

The captain hung up, and Malachi did likewise. He sat on the steps, thinking about what the captain had said. The OpNav element was out, so Commander Collins of Old Town and the Potomac Boat Club should now be out of the game. And Miss Snow of somewhere in Georgetown no longer worked for NIS, which should take her out of the game. The captain had some serious pull: He or his influential friends had managed to get the investigation moved back into the exclusive hands of NIS and, apparently, handed off to entirely new people. "Relax," the man had said. For the third time, he'd told Malachi to relax, that everything was going to be just fine.

But then that quiet, insistent whisper in his mind: What was the only loose end the great man and company had remaining? Malachi Ward. Angelo was no math major, but he had to have pretty damn good street sense to survive in his line of work. Relax? No fucking way. He decided to finish putting away the stuff from the commissary and then to make a call to his little friend in the Billing Department at C&P Telephone, the one who could turn a hundred bucks into an address if you had a phone number. Then he had to get the Ford back over to Arlington before some Capitol Hill cop car came prowling down the alley—and, more importantly, before the frigging rush hour started.

40

Moses Vann called Grace back just before four o'clock on Monday. He sounded tired.

"Been a damn Monday all day," he said. "I don't recognize this number."

"It's my unlisted home number."

"And why are we at home at four o'clock on a Monday? Last week, you were stayin' late and bein' a big-time G-woman. Lemme guess. The Navy's pulled the plug."

"In a manner of speaking," she said. She told him what had happened with the investigation, sticking more or less to the version that she had resigned over the handling of the Hardin case and was now wondering what to do, saying she didn't want it to just languish in the too-hard basket.

"You let them do it," he said immediately. "You can't be messin' with a federal homicide investigation. That's double OJ one. You remember: obstruction of justice?"

"I didn't intend to interfere," she said. "I only—"

"You just want to freelance. Nobody likes a freelancer, Miss Snow. Just about the time the squad is setting up the collar, along comes the freelancer and blows the case, every damn time. You gotta remember, there're three parts to a homicide: there's the killing, there's finding the perp, and there's building the case that puts the perp away. First part's always free: The perp hands you the killing. And there's lots of cases where we know who the perp is. The hard part is building the case, 'cause these DAs aren't gonna waste their time, you can't build the case. That's the part the freelancers usually screw up. Nobody needs an extra player."

This wasn't going at all the way she wanted it to. But then she had an idea.

"I appreciate all that, Captain. I've been in the investigations business, remember? But I may not have a choice."

"Meaning what?"

She told him about being followed on Friday night from Collins's house, and also about seeing the same man and vehicle on Water Street near the boathouse.

"You report this?"

"I did. To the District police."

"Uh-huh. You report it to the NIS?"

"No. I don't know what's behind it, and I have no way to make a connection—"

"Ah-ha-ha, Miss Snow. We tryin' to have it both ways, aren't we? First you're tellin' me that you may already be involved in the Hardin case—because you think you were followed when you were with this Collins guy. But then you say you didn't tell the NIS because there ain't no facts connecting the man in the truck with the Hardin case? C'mon, you want to freelance. Right?"

Grace was getting angry. "I don't care what it's called, Captain Vann. The Policy director at NIS said he had been instructed by the admiral's executive assistant to put the Hardin case in the routine hopper along with all the other unsolved black homicides. I rather think that stinks. My other problem is that I *saw* Wesley Hardin down in that boiler. I'm having a hard time getting that image to fit nicely in the routine hopper."

Vann went silent. Grace let him think about it. She could hear his desk chair protesting as he fidgeted around. When he finally spoke, he sounded even more tired.

"Damn, I hate Mondays. All the other unsolved *black* homicides? Man actually say that?"

"He did. Then he realized what he'd said, so he tried to muddy the waters. Look, I don't know what, if anything, I can do, and I know all about helpful outsiders fouling up official investigations. But first there has to *be* an investigation. I don't think there's going to be one, beyond a lot of eye-rolling bureaucrats going through the motions. But I'm convinced that the key to this case is the fact that his sister died shortly before he did, and that his death has something to do with something or someone here in Washington."

"And what do you want from me, Miss Snow? A papal dispensation?"

"I want to speak to Mrs. Hardin. With a little preliminary softening up having been done by you. With you there, if at all possible."

"Hmmpf. That's what I was afraid was comin'. Tell me somethin'. Where's that Navy guy, Collins, stand in the game?"

"He's been returned to his regular duties in the Pentagon."

"He in the game or out?"

"I have to assume he's out. He told me Friday that he could get into a lot of trouble if he stuck his nose back into the Hardin case. He implied that some powerful people had warned him off."

"Smart boy."

"Well, I've already given up my job, so I have nothing to lose in that regard, do I? Will you help me? Or even just think about it?"

He was silent again for about thirty seconds. Then he surprised her.

"Miss Snow," he said in a very official voice, "you're implying that there is a conspiracy of silence surrounding the Hardin case. That maybe some high-level executive assistants at NIS and in the Pentagon are manipulating this case so as to neutralize its effective prosecution. Have you forgotten something? I'm the executive assistant to the Deputy Chief of Police for Criminal Investigations. How do you know I'm not part of it, Miss Snow?"

It was Grace's turn to be silent for a few seconds. She had not missed the sudden change in his speech: the precision of his syntax and the cold, political essence of his question. She thought about it, then saw through it.

"Because if you were, Captain," she replied evenly, "you would have agreed to help me right from the beginning of this conversation. That way you could control or manipulate what I was doing and thus protect your principals. In my experience, EAs are not singular spiders; they like to work the web with all the other EAs, and they rarely work just for their own benefit. Besides, you're still talking like a human."

Vann chuckled. "A human. Ouch," he said. "Okay, I guess you got me, Miss Snow. My guile is getting like my nostalgia: It ain't what it used to be. I'll tell you what: I'll talk to Angela Hardin, sort of feel her out. I'm not promising anything, hear? There's . . . well, there's history to deal with there. I'm gonna have to ask her to look into her heart, and that thing's in pieces, you know? And in the meantime, don't you go *doing* anything. Thinking is okay. I always admire people who think. But don't *do* anything until I say it's okay, understood?"

"All right. I promise."

"Okay. I'll get back to you."

She thanked him and hung up. It was a start.

41

"C&P Telephone Customer Service. This is Wanda. How may I direct your call?"

"I need to speak to Loretta, in Billing," Malachi said.

"Loretta's line is busy, sir. She's assisting other customers," the voice said. "I can put you through to the next available billing adviser."

"No, let me hold, please. Loretta has been helping me and I don't want to have to explain the whole deal again."

"Thank you, sir. Please hold, sir."

Malachi waited, the yellow gummy with Snow's phone number in his hand. After four minutes of breathless telephone company advertising, a new voice came on the line.

"Billing. Loretta speaking. How may I help you?"

"Loretta, this is Mr. Wizard."

"Hey, Wiz baby. What's happenin' in the wonderful world of science? And what's our number today?"

He gave her the number. "And our name might be Snow, and we may even be unlisted."

"Oooh. Unlisted. We're important. And expensive, like the address I'm seein' right here. And, Miss Grace E. Snow, can we confirm that our address is two-one-three-five P Street Northwest?"

Malachi wrote down the street address. "Absolutely. Your computer does good work, Loretta. It's two hundred times better than mine."

"Aw, baby, you too kind."

"Thanks, Loretta. Keep your bills dry."

He hung up and went into his study, where he fished two hundred-dollar bills out of the desk safe and folded them into an envelope, which he addressed to Ms. Loretta Smith, care of C&P Telephone's Washington offices, Billing Department. He marked personal on the envelope. Loretta was part of the old Monroney empire. As part of the Chesapeake and Potomac Telephone Company's Billing Department, she could call up any customer's account as long as he could provide the phone number. One hundred for info on a listed number; two hundred for unlisted. As long as she did no manipulation of the screen data, the phone company's security systems would not pick up on it—people called in all the time to ask questions about bills, and the operators always asked for the phone number, which doubled as the account number. They also always checked the address to confirm; Loretta simply asked it out loud.

He went back out to the kitchen and fixed himself the first of the day, a short one, because he still had to drive back to Virginia. He took his drink back to the study and sat down. So the lady in the garden *had* been Grace E. Snow. He wondered if they called her Gracie. Probably not—she didn't look like a Gracie. More like a Grace Kelly with dark hair. And she lived in Georgetown, so there was money there. He tried to remember how a woman who looked like that—polished, trim, expensively dressed—used to make him feel, but there was nothing there anymore. That's because you're a fucking eunuch, Malachi. Since your evening with Inge, Inge of the broken bottle, Inge of the perfect aim, the only thing you feel for women is the urge to improve their traffic-safety consciousness with an F-250.

He closed his eyes and tried to get a hold of himself. Think rationally, logically. What was it about the Snow woman? She was not the normal fit for the NIS, that was for damn sure. Then he remembered what Englehardt had said: "Miss Snow doesn't work here anymore." And she had confirmed that. So why had she been visiting Collins? It hadn't looked like a date, not with her going home in a taxi early in the evening. But maybe that was how the Navy boys did it. It used to be a standing joke among his buddies in the sergeants' mess that an officer took two weeks to get from a woman what any sergeant could get in thirty minutes. Officers had to talk about it beforehand; sergeants talked about it afterward. Collins the rowboat man, Snow the Yuppie princess from Georgetown. But had the visit been work or pleasure? And could these two powder puffs *possibly* be contractors set in motion by the captain and his crowd to take care of the one remaining loose end?

He shook his head. He couldn't see it. Not those two. Snow was a remote possibility; as he knew only too well, women were capable of any fucking thing at all. He had met a fifty-year-old woman hitter once who had scared the hell out of him with her ice-cold intensity. She purportedly did wet work for the Agency, although lots of people out on the edge in this town claimed to work for the Agency. But Malachi remembered thinking that if he had known there was some kind of contract out on him, just the sight of that woman would have had him diving behind a wall. She *looked* like a killer. This Grace Snow looked like nothing of the sort. And the Navy guy. Again, no way, no matter if James Bond had been a commander. That would imply a degree of deep cover that the Agency might be capable of, but never the Navy.

He downed the whiskey and sighed. It was time to get the Ford back to its hidey-hole. If there was somebody in motion in his backfield, it wasn't these two, which meant that he had to increase his vigilance. He decided to dismiss Collins and Snow; sometimes it was just as useful to know who wasn't coming after you.

He closed up the house and set out to drive the Ford back to Arlington, but then he had an idea. Maybe he'd go by and actually see where the mysterious Miss Snow lived. He decided to circle around the Capitol grounds and take Pennsylvania Avenue all the way over to Georgetown. It would not be quick, but, it being a Monday night, most of the commuter traffic would be clearing out by now. He took Pennsylvania all the way to its junction with M Street, got off M as soon as he could, and zigzagged his way over to P Street. Once past Wisconsin, he had to go slowly on P with its cobblestones and old trolley tracks, but he was able to drive right by 2135 P Street Northwest. There was a 500 series BMW locked in behind wrought-iron gates; he automatically memorized the license number. He went around the block one time, noting that there was an alley off the next street north, Volta Place. The alley actually had a name, but the street sign was partially obscured by the low branches of a tree. The alley was almost directly behind Snow's house. He caught a glimpse of some construction equipment at the end of the alley. Satisfied that he had seen enough, he headed back down toward the Key Bridge and Virginia.

42

DAN FOUGHT A strong urge to close his eyes as he stroked up the river. The current was uncompromisingly hard and fast, but there was too much flotsam sheeting downstream for eyes-closed concentration. He wore one of those bicycle helmets with a small round mirror on an extension arm to watch for problems. He was in the burn phase of his workout, his muscles complaining, but doing so in unison, as he made tiny adjustments in oar strength to maneuver the scull between branches and other debris careening down the river. The water smelled of mud and wet greenery, and the sound of the spring current was audible, its echoes reflecting off the sheer stone palisades of the Virginia side as he approached Chain Bridge. The chair had developed an annoying squeak, which finally broke his concentration, and he eased off to a bare headway pace. Another single came steaming by, its occupant shooting Dan a knowing look as Dan eased up and prepared to come about. There were usually more rowers out, but this current was on the verge of meanness. The only advantage other than the intensity of exercise was that the river was deeper, allowing a wider area in which to row. The big eights and fours from the university had all headed downstream to the more placid reaches of the river, trading off the malodorous vapors of the Blue Plains sewage-treatment plant for calm water. No, thank you very much, Dan thought. He scanned the upstream water briefly before beginning a sculling turn, then settled back into a slow, come-down rhythm that would take him the two miles back down to the boathouse.

He wondered briefly if Grace would be there again. He had found himself thinking about her ever since the phone call late Friday night. And try as he might, it had little to do with the Hardin case. He backed the starboard oar slightly to avoid a wicked-looking whirlpool that had surfaced in front of him, but then he relaxed as the knifelike shell responded, scooting easily around the outer tangents of the disturbance. He looked on either side and found himself momentarily in formation with two largish tree branches. Must have been a hell of thunderstorm up on the Shenandoah to bring all this stuff down.

So why don't you call her tonight? Because it's Monday and you said you would call her Tuesday. So? You want to see the woman, you don't play by teenage rules. Hell, you could call her from the boathouse. It can't be more than ten minutes to her house. Yeah, but it's rush hour.

He grinned then, recognizing the wiggling of a semihooked fish. He shipped his oars and just let the current take him. An older man with a British accent had caught up with him at the river landing one evening and asked him why he felt compelled to row all the way back downstream. Returning to the real world that enticing, old boy? The trick is to go like hell upstream, then soak up some of the serenity of the river on the way back down. Enjoy it up while you can; pandemonium awaits at the boathouse driveway. The river *was* beautiful, even when it was feeling its oats. And she is, too, he thought. Claire was prettier. Claire is gone. Claire was more fun, not so serious, not so damn New Englandish. And yet, Grace is elegant, quick, even sexy. Claire was sexy. Claire is gone. A wave of sadness overtook him like one of those sudden squalls that could dash down the river all the way from the cataracts at Great Falls. Heretofore, a summons to the ghost of Claire was all that it took to extinguish any sparks of interest in another woman. But Claire is gone. Grace is ten minutes from the boathouse.

Maybe fifteen.

Maybe she's not there.

Maybe she is.

He landed the boat without doing any significant damage and toted it up to the boathouse. He called her from the lobby after hanging up the boat, and he got the answering machine. He started to hang up, but then he said to hell with it and identified himself. She picked up, startling him.

"Sorry about that," she said. "One of the defenses of women who live alone, I'm afraid."

"Yeah, well, I was still trying to figure out what to say to your machine when you picked up. But basically, I'm down here at the boathouse, and I was wondering, uh . . ."

"Would you like to come by, Dan?"

"Uh, yeah, I would, actually. I'll even take a shower."

"That's nice to hear."

Dan felt his face redden. Want to tell her you'll use soap and everything? Wash behind your ears?

"What's the best route from down here?" he asked quickly.

She gave him succinct instructions, and he said he'd be there in twenty minutes. It was more like half an hour, what with a fender bender on M Street and a broken-down Metro bus on 33rd. Dan remembered her house, but he missed her driveway the first time past. After much backing and filling, he was able to maneuver the Suburban into the space across her driveway, which was really only two ribbons of brick leading into the tiny yard. The Suburban looked like a beached blue whale against the diminutive front yard. He surveyed his makeshift outfit: slacks and sport shirt he happened to have in the car from the cleaners, his uniform shoes, and a black leather Navy-uniform belt. Oh well, he thought, beats cutoffs, a sleeveless sweatshirt, and a pair of canvas sneakers that qualified as EPA violations.

The front door of the house opened and Grace stepped out. She was wearing gray wool slacks, a long-sleeved ivory-colored blouse, and some flat leather shoes. She wore a slim gold bracelet on her right wrist, and Dan thought he could detect a hint of makeup. He caught himself staring when he should have been getting out of the car, and then he scrambled to get the door open. If she thought his outfit peculiar when he walked up the steps, she contained it well. She took him through the living room and the study and then into the kitchen, where she had laid out some white wine and a tray of crackers and cheese.

"If you'll bring the wine, we can try *my* garden this time," she said over her shoulder. "But first we have to put this permit in your car window. Otherwise, you'll get a ticket for blocking my driveway."

He took the permit back out to the car and then went back through the house and out to the garden, picking up the wine along the way.

"This is very pretty," he said as they walked down the brick walk to a patio table and chairs. "Makes my garden look medium scruffy."

"I have a man who comes in periodically and gives it a haircut. Yes, put that there; that's fine. But I forgot the glasses. I'll be right back."

She went back to the house while Dan looked around. The garden and yard were not as long as his, but the trees were more stately, the lawn trimmed, and the flowers identifiable as such. Two whitewashed brick walls on either side led down to a third wall and gate, probably into an alley behind. A building visible over the top of the back wall had scaffolding all the way up to its roof.

Georgetown even felt different from Old Town. Probably the absence of tourists, he decided. He had read that although it was now the province of the rich and famous in Washington, much of Georgetown had originally been a slum, something Old Town had never been. What tourists there were in Georgetown stayed down around the bars and restaurants along M Street, while in Old Town, they were everywhere, often peering right into peoples' living room windows because the house fronts were often right on the street. He watched Grace come back down the steps with two wine-glasses and an ice bucket. She was appropriately named, he thought, and her outfit reinforced the notion that she was indeed a woman—a long-legged one at that. She put an ice bucket and glasses on the glass-topped wrought-iron table, swept a few acorns off her chair, and sat down.

"There. You can tell I entertain a lot. But I did get the wine bottle open. If you would do the honors, kind sir."

Dan poured the wine, gave her a glass, and then tipped a *salut*. She responded and their eyes met for a fraction of a second longer than necessary. She looked down first.

"So, Commander," she said, a hint of a smile on her face.

"So, indeed, Miss Grace Ellen Snow. This is a nice wine."

She laughed at the allusion to their previous discussion about wine critics.

"So it is; I wasn't expecting your call until tomorrow night."

Dan nodded. "I was out on the river," he said. "I thought of you and decided to call."

"Just like that?" Her voice was softer now.

He looked away, recalling the serenity of the river, even when it was up and running. "No, not just like that," he said. "I usually have a ghost to wrestle with whenever I consider speaking to a woman who . . . who—"

"Who is not your wife."

"Yes. Well, see, my wife is . . . gone. That was the funny thing out there on the river this afternoon, and the reason I decided to go through with it. Calling you, I mean. My mind kept making comparisons, kept saying— well, all sorts of things. But there was this refrain that kept invading: Claire is gone." His throat had become annoyingly dry. "Claire is gone," he whispered, softer. "Oh hell."

His eyes suddenly misted over and he put down his glass. He was aware of his surroundings at the periphery of his vision, but straight ahead he could see nothing. He was afraid to look at Grace, afraid even to breathe. He felt like he had just made a cosmic discovery: Claire was gone, gone for good, gone away, gone so damn far away that even now, as he tried to capture her face, her figure, to recall anything at all about her, he discovered that all the loving images had escaped from his mind's eye in one great rush while he wasn't looking. He stared, blinking, unseeing, at the green lawn and the blurred pattern of the brick wall, trying hard to reconstruct her outline in the soft evening light, but failing. For two or three minutes, he sat there, lost in this sudden onslaught of emotions, emotions he couldn't define, except that they were tinged with a little shame. Finally, he took a deep breath and came back to the garden.

"Sorry about that," he whispered, and then cleared his throat and took a gulp of wine, nearly choking on it. "I didn't mean to—I'm not sure what just happened there. Maybe I'd better go."

But Grace was shaking her head. "I don't think so," she said. "Listen, I'm glad you called. You should have seen me, Dan, running around the house like a chicken with its head cut off. Look at me, I even put on makeup. Look at me."

He finally looked at her, and he saw something soft in her face he hadn't seen before—luminescent softness in her eyes. Green eyes, he realized. She has green eyes. I knew that. He suddenly realized that she understood what had just happened.

"Sometimes," she said, "sometimes I think life has to turn our heads before we see clearly. You've been at the back of my mind since last Friday night."

He nodded a silent "me, too," but said nothing, not quite willing to trust his voice.

"I'm not really sure how to act, Dan. I had all the flirt burned out of me after the fifth or sixth time Rennie beat me up. And yet, I'm a middle-aged female who knows damned well that time is short. Oh, shit, this *is* hard. What should we do?"

"Well," he said finally, finding his voice, "we could drink some of this wine, this nice wine."

She laughed again, a clear exhalation of relief and humor and shared enjoyment. He laughed with her, shaking his head as if to chase back the treacherous emotional shadows. They spent the next two hours talking about themselves, working on the wine, and beginning to explore the edges of a relationship, both of them being very careful to probe neither too deeply nor too soon. After dark, they walked down Wisconsin Avenue to one of the few small bistros that was open on a Monday night for dinner, where they continued the exploration, checking the fit of their interests, touching tentatively on politics and religion, doing better on his love of history and her fascination with unraveling complex crimes, his expectations of what his command tour would be like, and his recent realization that his time in the Navy after his long-sought command tour would look a lot like the time leading up to it.

She tried to explain some of her reasons for going to work for the government, based in part on her having been handed all the advantages of money along with a first-class education. He tried to put a better face on the reasons he had stayed in the Navy. They paced themselves, becoming surer that the feeling was worth pursuing, but being very careful to make small moves. After dinner, they walked back through the quiet streets of the neighborhood to her house, admiring the rich variety of architecture and means on display in the genteel rows of mostly brick houses. They walked the last block to her house in silence, content that they had talked enough for a while. When they reached her front steps, he felt a tinge of uncertainty while she unlocked the door, but he then took her hand in both of his.

"Hey, hand," he said, not looking at her face, "this is the moment when the boy usually tries to kiss the girl, but the boy's still not sure of what he's doing, and he desperately doesn't want to make any mistakes, so he's gonna just say good night and run home to figure out when he can see you again, okay? Will you pass all that on to your owner for me?"

She smiled in the soft glow of the porch lights and then took hold of his hand.

"Hey, hand," she said, "make it very soon, all right?"

He grinned at her and walked to his car, waved once as she went inside, and then addressed himself to the difficult business of getting the Suburban out of the driveway without hitting any of the densely parked cars. As he drove out of Georgetown, he realized that they had spent an entire evening together without once mentioning the Hardin thing. Maybe the EAs were right: Maybe that mess *was* better off in the moldering bureaucratic backwaters of the Washington Navy Yard. And—he had her parking permit.

43

MALACHI AWOKE TUESDAY morning with another world-class hangover. Driving back over to Virginia the night before had turned into a traffic nightmare when two carloads of Arlington Vietnamese had sideswiped each other on the Virginia side of the Teddy Roosevelt Bridge and then proceeded to stage a gunfight. The ensuing Olympic-size traffic jam had taken ninety minutes to clear out. By the time he returned to Capitol Hill on the Metro, he was in a decidedly foul humor. Coming out of the Eastern Market Metro station, he had seen three young men sizing him up as a possible mark in the early-evening darkness. He had crossed the street and walked right at them, hands open at his sides, daring them with a belligerent, flat-eyed stare to start something. Then he bowled right through them on the sidewalk, eliciting a chorus of "Hey, man" from the startled men.

He had gone right to the bourbon when he got in and proceeded to drink himself insensible right there in the kitchen. He woke up on the floor of the second-story hallway, his head on fire and his stomach tied up in a bilious knot. He spent the first five minutes wondering how he had managed those stairs without breaking his neck, and the second five minutes trying to organize a sufficient number of muscles and nerves to make it to the bathroom. It was nearly two more hours before he could do much more than sit up straight, and even then he needed some whiskey in his coffee to get color vision back. He sat at the kitchen table, his eyes mostly closed, nursing the coffee, a cigarette smoking in a saucer, his head resenting the noise the refrigerator made, waiting for the whiskey to do something. He could feel each heartbeat in his temples.

Curiously, he remembered a lecture on alcoholism he had been forced to attend by the battalion commander during his last year in the Army. This surprisingly tough-looking chaplain had given a talk on the stages of alcoholism, and Malachi, along with the other dozen or so troops in the audience, had been able to fix himself with quick accuracy on the slippery slope the chaplain was describing. He also remembered that the sergeants had all retired to the club for a drink while they talked about the lecture. Malachi had gone with them. He was an officer, but he was far closer to the sergeants than he was to the other officers, especially after Vietnam, where the sergeants had made him very nearly a rich man. But what he really remembered was what the chaplain had said about the root causes of alcoholism: The booze is addictive, and it will eventually overwhelm your life, but there is usually something profoundly wrong in your life that the addiction for booze itself feeds on. Well hell, he thought as he sat with his head on his arms on the kitchen table, we all know what that problem is, don't we? I got castrated by a German whore, who also threw in a wonderful new voice and some scars that scare children and make dogs bark at me.

But instinctively he knew it was deeper than that, that his entire life after falling in with Monroney and Angelo and the other guys in Saigon had been an increasingly empty experience, despite all the money. By the time he'd spent his first year in Germany, he had become aware that the CID had been onto him and some of the scams going down there, and maybe even before, in Nam. But the sergeants' mafia was slick and wise in the ways of the Army, and there were just too many insiders at work for the CID ever to put a case together, especially against a captain in the Military Police Corps. His assignment to McNair after the incident in Germany had been a deliberate warehousing job, under the guise of a humane convalescent assignment. He had been in titular charge of the gate guard details that protected generals' row and all those bright-faced up-and-comers who drove through the gates every morning on their way to the National War College. Yeah, he got some disability retirement, and yeah, he never got caught. But they knew. During those last months, he had begun to hear the whispering behind his back: There's more to that guy than just the horrible incident in the bar. Where most Vietnam vets got respect when, leather-faced and bedecked with ribbons, they walked into the club, Malachi got furtive, curious looks. He had been vastly relieved to get his disability discharge papers, and he had even opted out of having any sort of traditional retirement ceremony. The battalion commander had seemed vastly relieved.

Since then, his life in Washington, first working with Monroney and then for himself, had been profitable and occasionally even interesting. Living entirely alone, he had absorbed himself in the mechanics of being a shadow-land contractor, adapting readily to the mechanics of his trade even as he struggled to fashion a life after hours, increasingly with the help of I. W. Harper. But where was the future? He knew in his heart what kind of future that empty Harper bottle promised: His own father had dissolved in a bottle, leaving the boy Malachi to finish high school as a teenaged foster child. Now he had a small retirement pension and enough money stashed here and there never to have to work again, but what was he going to do with it? Having shoveled shit for some of the great men of Washington for almost twenty years, he was still little better than an enlisted man, the eternal snuffy, paid to take out the garbage, thrown a couple of bills by the fat cats in their thousand-dollar suits. She was a great piece of ass, Malachi, but go back up there and see if I left a rubber on the floor, okay? It's a no-fingerprint sort of thing, Malachi; you know how it is.

Before the Hardin problem, the quality of his life had been measured in degrees of emptiness and loneliness; he did what he did because there was a demand for his services and because that's what he did for a living. He could appreciate the circular nature of his rut, but it was a rut that seemed made for him, especially after Germany.

But now, for the first time, he was feeling a sense of threat, a tingling of unease along the ratlike nerve bundle he had developed since throwing in with the sergeants in Saigon, that over-the-shoulder sixth sense Monroney was always talking about. Up to this point, everything he had done since leaving the Army had been on instructions. Anyone wanted to come after him, there was always a principal or a high-priced assistant to offer up. But this time, with this Hardin thing, he had the sense that the principal and his horse-holder might be working on offering *him* up, maybe before somebody started closing in. It didn't help that this was murder. Okay, yeah, they said they had the investigation bottled up. And yeah, there was no direct connection to be made between Malachi and the Hardin killing in Philadelphia—except for the accident on 23rd Street. Well, mostly an accident—he hadn't really meant to kill her, not until she had shown him that glittering, man-hating stare, that stare Inge had as she drove the broken bottle into his groin. Always cutting, these women. He looked down at the puckered, still-red scars across the back of his right hand.

Try as he might, even the Harper couldn't get Angelo's warning out of his mind, and he realized that there were going to be some more of these binges until he took care of it. That little voice was still whispering in his ear, telling him to get out of it: Get out of town, use your fake IDs and your contacts in the shadow world to chuck it, get clear of it, before these goddamned officers get their shit together and think of something. But he knew he wouldn't do it; he'd been doing these bastards' bidding for his entire life, even when he was supposedly one of them, but this time he wasn't going to just salute and hop right to it, backing deferentially out the door, saying, Yes, sir, no, sir, three bags full, sir. Just once, he wanted to kick *their* asses, and he wanted them to know he had kicked their asses. Then maybe he would beat feet, fold his tents, and steal away into the desert night.

He got up and went to the refrigerator, got out some ice cubes and cracked them into bits using a heavy steel mess-hall soup spoon and the palm of his hand. He filled a glass with cracked ice and then turned it amber with bourbon from a fresh bottle of Harper. He lit a cigarette and sat back down again and sipped the icy liquor. Maybe he ought to preempt the bastards. Maybe put an anonymous call into the D.C. cops, tell 'em that they needed to go talk to the great man, because, here's the thing: He had been doing Lieutenant Hardin's sister. So what? All right, try this: Lieutenant Hardin was iced because he was going to blow the whistle, going to embarrass the great man for porking his sister. What could the captain do about that? He couldn't point to Malachi without admitting they had hired him. And even if they did that, there was no evidence. Malachi could simply do the armadillo, deny everything. And Angelo sure as hell wouldn't talk, even supposing the cops could walk it back all the way to the Guidos in South

Philly. But they couldn't even do that, because nothing had been done directly. Everything had been done through intermediaries, contractors, untraceable cash, untraceable phone calls, and discussions over dinner in a place where retirement-minded cops did not venture—the Washington way. The cops might eventually put together the whole story, but without evidence or a confession, they could not indict or convict.

Or maybe do the Washington thing—expose the whole sorry story to the cold light of day. Give it the *Washington Post* test. Leak a little. Malachi had been around Washington long enough to know that if even the outlines of the story got out in town, the great man wouldn't remain a great man for very long, because the Navy, embarrassed by the charges and the inevitable calls for an investigation, would deep-six his ass, and maybe the captain along with him. And if Malachi could separate them from their official privilege and federal power, then they would no longer be in a position to make some calls and maybe line up another contractor to come take care of their Malachi problem. They'd be distracted, tainted with a whiff of scandal, retired, but not so honorably, and definitely not invited to serve on all those fancy Beltway bandit boards or to become consultants. Then they'd be down on the rug with him and the other fleas, just another pair of retired military stiffs in Washington, grasping for whatever crumbs might come their way from the government's table. Hell, once they were down on his level, he might even have some fun with them.

Malachi mulled over that engaging prospect but then rejected it. He could hear Monroney: Even that's too direct, Malachi; that's not how you do shit in this town. The better way was to drop a dime all right, only play the real Washington game, just call the cops and simply ask a rhetorical question: What was the connection between a certain Washington admiral's illicit affair with Lt. Elizabeth Hardin and her brother's getting snuffed right after the sister died? Don't name any names; let the cops dig for it. Because once the cops came asking questions, the word would get out on the EA network pretty quick, and then the great man and his captain would have other things to think about than sending someone after Malachi. Yeah, that's how to do it—not once removed, but twice removed. And now is when to do it. He got up to refresh his glass of ice. He needed to get his brain in high gear so he could figure out precisely whom to call. Hell, he was already feeling better.

44

On TUESDAY AFTERNOON, Grace was filing her 1993 tax returns in the upstairs file cabinet when she heard the phone ringing downstairs. Since her mother had died, she kept only the downstairs telephone ringer activated, as she had developed something of a dread of phone calls in the night. She walked to the head of the stairs, where she could hear the answering machine, and listened. When she recognized the voice of Moses Vann, she quickly went into the bedroom and picked up the portable bedside phone.

"Captain Vann, I'm here," she said as the machine made an offensive noise and clicked off abruptly, as if annoyed.

"Miss Snow. I'm glad I caught you."

"Coming from a policeman, that sounds ominous, Captain."

"Yeah, well." He laughed. "I say 'got you' and people get really scared, you know? But something interesting's come up on the Hardin case. The department got a phone call."

The Hardin case. Grace sat down abruptly on the edge of her bed. She had not thought about the Hardin case since . . . well, since seeing Dan last night.

"An anonymous tip of some kind?"

"You must be psychic. That's exactly what it was. Somebody dropped a dime."

"What did they say?"

"Well, it was kind of a thin dime, but basically, the caller asked a question. I'm calling to find out if you might be interested in coming in, tomorrow morning, say around eleven o'clock. And maybe bring your Navy friend with you, that Commander Collins."

"Well, I can make it. I'll have to call Dan to see if he can. As I think I told you, he doesn't have as much freedom of action as I do right now."

"You think you can talk him into it?"

"I can try."

"Yeah. Because this call may be doubly interesting to him. How's about asking him, anyway. He says no, it ain't the end of the world. But make sure he understands that we'll be off the record, what you feds call a non-meeting meeting."

"Ex-feds. But, yes, we had those all the time in SEC. I'll call him. Please don't misunderstand, Captain Vann: The Hardin case bothers him as much as it bothers me. It's just that he can pay a price if some of your captain counterparts over in the Pentagon find out about it."

"Like I said, that makes the call even more interesting. Give it a shot, Miss Snow. But either way, I'll see you in my office at eleven. Just come on up to the third floor, like you did last time."

Vann hung up and Grace did likewise. She lay back across the bed and stared up at the ceiling. Damn it, she thought. She didn't want her next phone call to Dan Collins to be about the Hardin case. She didn't want him to think her only interest in him was the murder. She sat up and went downstairs to get her phone book. It was almost five o'clock. Dan should still be at the Pentagon. As she was flipping through the book, the phone rang again. Now who could this be? Maybe Dan. She listened as the machine went through its spiel, and then she heard a young man's voice.

"Miss Snow, this is Lieutenant Garrison calling from Naval Investigative Service headquarters. As you may remember, I'm the naval aide to the director. I was calling to see if you were available to speak with Admiral Keeler. My number—"

Her phone call from NIS—she had forgotten all about that, too. Feeling a flare of irritation, Grace picked up and hit the machine's record button as she lifted the handset. "I'm here, Lieutenant Garrison. But before you put the admiral on, I want to make sure this is a private conversation. I don't want any EAs or other undersirables hanging on the extension, is that understood? Otherwise, there will be no conversation."

She waited while the lieutenant digested this bit of news. She knew that she had no way to keep Rennselaer off a muted extension phone, but she also wanted to put these guys on notice that this was not a social call.

"Uh, I'll see what I can do about that, Miss Snow. Stand by one, please."

She went on hold. She peered into the little window of the answering machine to make sure the reel was turning. The machine could record up to one hour of conversation on its microcassette. It was a holdover from her days with SEC, when she sometimes took calls after work from informants or prospective witnesses who were in the perspiration stage.

"Miss Snow, the admiral's coming on."

Good for him, she thought as she waited. There was a clicking noise and then the smooth voice of Admiral Keeler filled the earpiece. Grace had seen the admiral several times, although she had spoken to him only once. He was a handsome man, in his late forties, and he looked to Grace as if he would make a good con man or politician. She had seen many men who looked like him running some very pretty schemes on Wall Street.

"Miss Snow. I'm sorry we're having to communicate under these awkward circumstances. I'm afraid we haven't handled the matter of your departure from our ranks all that well on our end."

"You certainly haven't, Admiral. You had the chance to arrange for my departure in a much more gracious manner. But, apparently, your executive assassin decided to put your stripes on and try a little hardball instead. Or was this your idea, Admiral?"

"No, no, Miss Snow, it wasn't. I always prefer a discreet maneuver to a head-on collision. Captain Rennselaer thought he was acting according to my wishes. These misunderstandings sometimes happen, you know."

Grace understood full well that the EA was being used in one of his most important roles, that of lightning rod in case one of the admiral's decisions went off the rails. The principals would let the EA make or announce the move; if it began to draw an adverse reaction, the principal could always step forward, disassociate himself from the offending idea, and blame the EA. It was a game that principals and EAs all understood well and used often.

"Well, now you have a final chance to rectify your EA's little misstep, Admiral," she said. "Let me tell you my terms: I want a fulsome good-bye letter, signed by you, saying that you accept my resignation from the NIS and government service with the deepest regret. You will declare in the purplest prose how much I contributed to the success of the organization's mission, how much you will miss my services, and how wonderful our professional association was during my tenure in the Policy Division at NIS, et cetera, et cetera. Clear so far, Admiral?"

"Exceptionally so, Miss Snow. And I presume that your final performance appraisal should be similarly incandescent."

"Yes. I wouldn't want NIS to be inconsistent in its treatment of a departing and much-valued employee. I think Captain Rennselaer ought to sign it, too. Maybe one of those arrangements where he signs it and then you countersign your approval. And we'll have no mention of Career Services, shall we?"

"Absolutely, Miss Snow. Investigations Policy Division all the way. Tell me, do you plan to work in government again, Miss Snow?"

"If I do, Admiral, it will be as a political appointee, only this time I'll come in at the beginning of an administration. Perhaps we'll have the pleasure of crossing paths in the investigations business again some day."

"That would be interesting, I'm sure, Miss Snow. And now, for your part—"

"For my part, Admiral, I await your paperwork. When I've seen it *and* deemed it satisfactory, I will then call off my family's legal staff in Philadelphia."

"I see." There was a pause. "And how will we know that this, um, little contretemps is actually over, Miss Snow?"

"When you move on to your next star and your next assignment without having undergone a very public and personally costly lawsuit, Admiral. It's what I *don't* do that you hope and pray for, Admiral. And the people I don't talk to. But don't worry—we'll have a lock, won't we?"

"A lock, Miss Snow? I'm not quite—"

"A lock, Admiral. It's an underworld term—from my days when I worked on real criminal investigations for a real live government agency. There are probably some people on your staff who know what the term means. Ask Captain Rennselaer. I'm sure he knows what a lock is. But basically, once you have signed out all this pretty paper, I would have a fairly difficult time asserting in court that you terminated me unfairly and without due process, right?"

"Ah. I see, Miss Snow."

"I knew you would, Admiral. So, I await the official correspondence. Which is coming soon, is it not?"

"Very soon, Miss Snow."

"Good-bye, Admiral. And you, too, Rennselaer."

She hung up and exhaled a deep breath. That had been as nasty as she could make it. Hopefully, they would see the sense of a paper solution, because she had little stomach for the other route. And besides, she had been the odd duck in the NIS pond, not them. But still, she had been around the government long enough to know that there were civilized ways to handle these situations. And she also knew that glowing departure appraisals could become pivotal in the future if she ever did want to go back into government, especially as an appointee. All those security checks would certainly involve a look into her civil service files. And most of all, in her opinion, these executive-whatevers needed to learn that when they lunged out from under their rocks at someone, there was always the possibility of being trampled upon. She opened the answering machine and popped out the microcassette, sealed it into an envelope, and marked it *SD box.*

She retrieved the phone number for OP-614 and dialed it, looking at her watch. It was nearly 5:30. The phone rang several times, but no one picked up. He's already out on the river, she thought. She hung up, called Dan's home phone number, and asked his machine to have him call her at home.

45

BY SOME MIRACLE, Dan found a parking spot for the Suburban directly in front of his house. He sat in the car for a moment to survey his unexpected good fortune. It was a balmy evening, with most of the large trees lining the street in full bloom. And full pollen, he noticed. The windshields of adjacent cars were covered in a light yellow-green dust. He decided to go down to the little bistro at the foot of Prince Street for a quick dinner. Since Monday night, he had been packing civvies over to the boat club after work instead of coming back to the house in malodorous sweats. He got out, locked up the car, and walked down the hill, crossing Union after waiting for a parade of tourists to go by. Thankfully, they kept on going, walking right past the little restaurant.

There was a positively smashing young blonde sitting at one of the sidewalk tables—which prompted Dan to take an outside table. She gave him a brief smile but then looked pointedly at her watch, making it clear that she was waiting for someone. Dan sat so as to be able to see her, and immediately he compared her with Grace. The blonde was younger, much younger, with more color in her face and flashing a lot of leg in her abbreviated skirt. She was very pretty, he decided, but hot-pretty. Grace was more of a cool beauty, infinitely more elegant, probably a hell of a lot smarter, and possessed of a faintly mysterious air. Most of what he would want to know about the blonde was there for the world to see, but there was a lot he did not know about Grace Ellen Snow, and that intrigued him. The fact that she was closer to his own age than the young beauty across the way also made a difference. Although he had been out of the market since Claire's death, he had discovered that women with thirty-five years of life's experience were far easier to talk to than the ones who were ten years younger. The extra decade of living allowed an immediate mutual recognition that most of life's little traumas were not something unique to one's own experience. It also helped that Grace was not obviously hunting, as most of the middle-aged women he had met since California were.

The waiter appeared, checked briefly with the blonde, and then came over to his table with a friendly greeting; Dan was a regular.

"Commander Collins, good evening, sir. A glass of KJ chardonnay? And I recommend the mussels tonight. Maybe with a little angel-hair pasta in a fresh tomato and basil sauce."

"Sounds great, Mario. A small side salad with that and I'll be set."

"You got it, sir." The waiter hustled back inside, returned with his wine, and refilled the blonde's ice water. When he left, Dan raised his glass in a small *salut* to the young lady, who gave him a much better smile this time.

"If he stands you up, he's a Communist," he declared across the tables.

"He's a lawyer," she said lightly. "A junior associate. I'm getting used to it."

Dan almost said that if he was a lawyer, he was already a Communist, then decided to hold his peace when she turned her face away. See how mature I'm getting, he thought. Learning to keep my trap shut. Make a wiseass remark about lawyers and find out that she's a lawyer, too. That was more his usual style. Grace is a lawyer. Damn, that's right. But not one of those jackal ambulance chasers or auto-accident specialists. Just that afternoon, he had seen a great bumper sticker that read SUPPORT A LAWYER: BE A DOCTOR. No, Grace was a specialist in white-collar crimes—a hunter who pursued her prey through drawers of paper, intricate networks of bank accounts, tax forms, and computer files. It was a sterile sort of policing, where the bad guys were primarily guilty of making too much money.

Mario returned, bearing a large bowl of steaming-hot mussels, a side dish of pasta, and the small salad, all of which he set down with a flourish. He knew that Dan came for dinner, not for contrived delays between several courses.

"Here you are, sir. Everything all together, just the way you like it. I'll get you a plate for those shells. And here's your bill. I apologize for that, but after Friday night, the manager told me to bring the sidewalk bills out early."

"That looks great, Mario. What happened Friday night?"

"Some older guy was having dinner here—kind of a strange dude. Big guy, funny voice, sort of ugly, kind of a mean look to him. He ordered dinner, and right in the middle of it he jumped up and ran outta here like his pants were on fire. I was inside and saw him booking out."

"He stiff you?" Dan asked, reaching for his wine.

"No, he left some money—more than enough, actually. But it was seriously weird."

"Where'd the guy go?"

"Don't know. He disappeared by the time I got out here. I was picking stuff up here—it was this table, actually—and then this enormous pickup truck comes around the corner and goes down Union, going like hell, you know? I didn't get a good look at the driver, though. Don't know if it was him or not. Weird shit. Lemme get you that shell plate."

Dan was halfway through the mussels before he made the connection. A white pickup truck had followed Grace home. And from behind his gate, he had heard what sounded like a big vehicle making a hard turn onto Union. He put his fork down and looked up the street. He could see the Suburban out in front of his house. Through the trees, yeah, that works. Some guy wants to watch my house, he can do it from here. Can't cover the back gate, of course, but if he wanted to see me come and go, or someone who's visiting me come and go, yeah, this works fine. But why? And was he watching me or Grace?

The missing lawyer finally showed up in a bustle of briefcases, a portable flip phone, and apologies to the blonde. To Dan's disappointment, the guy was handsome, well dressed, and, based on the smile on the blonde's face, worth waiting for. Definitely a Communist, Dan concluded. He finished dinner, left cash to cover the bill and the tip, waved through the window at Mario, who waved back, and headed up Prince Street. He stopped by the Suburban to retrieve his exercise clothes and his briefcase, then went into the house, where he found the answering machine blinking at him. He listened to the message and immediately called her. He had to wait for her machine to do its thing. He announced himself and then paused. She picked up.

"Hi," she said. Her voice sounded bright.

"Hi yourself. Sorry to be delayed in getting back to you. I was restoring my blood-garlic levels down at one of the local bistros. Keeps away vampires, you know."

"Got a big problem with vampires in Old Town?" she asked.

"Only at the Tax Board. What's up?"

"It's the Hardin thing," she said.

"Oh."

"Yes, oh. It seems someone has made an anonymous phone call into the District police department. Captain Vann called me this afternoon. He wants to meet, and he asked me to convince you to come with me."

Dan thought about it for a second. "When?" he asked, stalling for time.

"Tomorrow at eleven. At the Municipal Center. It's right next to the Judiciary Square Metro. Dan, I told him that you might not be able to do this. I explained that people can make life difficult for you if you stick your nose back in; that I'm a free agent and you're not."

"Did you hear back from the NIS people? The admiral make his manners?"

She laughed. "Yes, he did call, and I was not terribly polite. But I think they'll give me my piece of paper. He played the stupid EA gambit."

"I've met some sneaky EAs," Dan said, "but never a stupid one. Let me see what I can do about this meeting. I've got a JCS paper due at morning briefing—that's seven-forty—but I'll talk to Summerfield. Vann didn't say what the phone call was about?"

"Only that he needed to talk to both of us—you especially, I think. He thought the fact that the EAs had warned you off the Hardin case made the tip doubly interesting."

"Curiouser and curiouser."

She appeared to hesitate. "I didn't want the Hardin case to be the only reason to call you," she said finally. "I'm glad you called me yesterday afternoon."

He laughed. "I want you to know I took civvies to the boathouse this afternoon. I was going to call you again, but I chickened out. How's about we do lunch tomorrow, after seeing Vann? That would also give me good cover as to why I'm out of the building in the middle of the day."

"Sounds fine. Although I'll bet you hear about it from Snapper. I'll wait for your call tomorrow."

Dan groaned as he hung up. He would undoubtedly hear about it from Snapper, probably for days. The question was what to tell Summerfield.

As it turned out, Summerfield did not seem to care. Dan told him he needed a couple hours off in the middle of the day to take a lady to lunch.

"Tell Miss Snow hello for us," was all he said as Dan stood in the doorway to Summerfield's private office, with Snapper eavesdropping dramatically, a hand cupped to his ear.

Snapper's reaction was suspiciously muted: He looked at Dan over the top of a Marine field manual and gave out a series of *heh-heh's*, showing a lot of teeth. Dan knew that the real harassment would come later, when there was a bigger audience. But he finished his Wednesday-morning staff drills and then called Grace to let her know he was coming. Summerfield and Snapper had to go to a meeting at ten o'clock, so Dan was able to leave the Pentagon and catch the Metro at ten-thirty without attracting undue attention.

Grace was waiting for him in the lobby of the Municipal Center. Dan was wearing his service dress blues, and Grace had on another one of those simple but expensive-looking suits of which she seemed to have an infinite supply. They took the elevator up to the third floor, and Grace remembered the way to Vann's office. Vann himself was waiting in the reception area.

"Miss Snow. Commander. Thanks for coming in. Coffee? No? Okay, let's go into my office."

Dan followed Grace as she followed Vann, closing the door behind him. Vann went behind his desk and Dan and Grace sat down in the chairs.

"First," Vann said, "lemme say that this is an official policy matter and is not to be discussed with anyone outside of the metropolitan police department. I trust you both to be discreet, but I'm required to say that. And, second, what I'm about to reveal to you is for the purpose of obtaining unofficial input. In other words, this is a nonmeeting. It also means I don't know what to do with this little chili pepper, okay?"

Dan grinned and nodded. He ran into at least one of those a day back in the Pentagon.

"Okay. What we got was an anonymous phone call from a pay phone at Metro Center; nice private place. We have this crime-solver's hot line; there're posters with the number all over town and the Metro cars. Crime-prevention sort of thing. We caller-ID each call, or course, but most peo-ple've seen enough TV to know that. Like this . . . person."

" 'Person'?" Grace asked.

"Yeah, person," Vann replied. "On accounta because I can't tell if it's a he or a she makin' the call. It almost sounds like someone placed the call and then turned on a tape recorder to play the actual message. Anyway, what he says is this, and I'm going to read it to you word for word:

" 'This is about the body in the battleship. What's the connection between a certain very senior naval officer's secret affair with Elizabeth Hardin and her brother's murder?' "

Dan listened carefully while Vann reread the question.

"That's it?" he asked.

"That's a lot," Grace interjected. "It shows that our theory was correct—that what's behind his murder had something to do with his sister's accident."

"Whose theory?" Vann asked.

"Well, mine, actually," Grace said. "We've talked about this, remember? When we did a case board, we both noticed the seeming coincidence of Elizabeth Hardin's death by accident and then her brother's death by hom-icide about two weeks later. Only at the time, no one knew it was a homicide, he'd just disappeared."

Vann nodded. "So you're thinking that maybe Elizabeth Hardin's death wasn't an accident?"

"I saw no evidence that it was anything but an accident. But the sister's death could still be related to the lieutenant's murder, if there's any truth behind this phone call."

"Uh-huh," Vann said, looking at Dan. "And how would someone go about finding out who this certain high-ranking naval officer might be who had something going with Elizabeth Hardin?"

This case is getting crazier by the minute, Dan thought. "Beats the shit out of me," he said. "Grace, didn't you tell me that Elizabeth Hardin's postmortem showed that she was pregnant?"

"Yes, it did," Grace said excitedly. "Which at least would prove that she was on intimate terms with someone."

Vann was shaking his head. "Prove, hell. Slow down, everybody. It's not like we got evidence, here. This could be someone just throwing some shit in the game, or some loony tune makin' a phone call. We get all kinds of shit on that hot line."

"What will you do with this?" Dan asked.

"I'm probably gonna have to give it to the Navy," Vann replied. "It's their case, It's just that . . . " He paused, looking at Dan, who understood at once.

"I'd have to assume that very senior naval officer is an admiral. And if this is an admiral we're talking about here, then giving it to the Navy might be the same as giving it to the bad guys, whoever they are. And let me guess. You'd like me to sniff around, see if I can find out who was having it on with Elizabeth Hardin before she got hit by that car, right?"

"You were all wrong, Miss Snow," Vann said with a grin. "This guy *is* smart."

But Grace had a worried look on her face. "Dan," she began, "I—"

"It's okay, Grace. I know this wasn't your idea. And I wish I could help, Captain Vann, but I doubt there's any way in hell I could find that out. First of all, she worked in CHINFO a couple of years ago. There's not likely to be anyone there now who was assigned there then. And if she was having an affair with a flag officer, she would want to keep it very damned secret. For one thing, it's illegal fraternization. They would *both* want to keep it very damn quiet."

"And they'd have another damn good reason to keep it quiet—especially him," said Vann.

"What's that?" Grace asked.

"If he was a *white* flag officer."

"Wow," Dan said. "I see what you're saying." And then he felt a bit embarrassed at having said it. But Vann did not seem to take offense. He got up and stared out the window behind his desk, thinking. Dan looked over at Grace, who raised her eyebrows at him as if to say, Now what?

"Suppose we could find out who it was," Vann said, his back still turned toward them. "Suppose we *could* find that out—the boyfriend. What would we have, Miss Snow?"

Grace tilted her head and looked at Vann's back. Then she put her hand up in front of her mouth.

"Oh," she said. "My God. Yes. We might have a suspect."

"You mean because Lieutenant Hardin found out that his sister was dating some senior officer, a white guy?" Dan asked.

"No," Grace said as Vann turned around. "Because Lieutenant Hardin found out or suspected there was a connection between Elizabeth's death and her senior officer lover."

"Holy shit!"

"Yeah," Vann said. "A threat to expose the affair might be grounds for retaliation, but probably not for murder. I knew Wesley Hardin—he would be upset with the situation, but he would raise hell with his sister, not the boyfriend, specially if he was some senior white dude in the Navy. But if he thought 'Lizbeth's accident wasn't an accident, well that would be something else again. Wesley'd be on that like a snake on a rat."

"Which would tie in with your suspicions about all the coincidence," Dan said to Grace.

"That's right." Vann nodded. "Although they're probably not directly related, in the sense that there probably weren't two murders. But if Wesley *thought* her death wasn't accidental, he'd do something, even something stupid," Vann said.

"So either way, the two deaths *are* connected."

"Well, they might be. Let's not run too fast down this road," Vann said, sitting back down. "We got some slick-sounding theories and zero proof or evidence. But you see, Commander, why I was in no big hurry to hand this phone call back to the Navy just yet."

Dan nodded. "I surely do. But can you just sit on it? Eventually, you'll have to give it to them."

Vann grinned. "Oh, I can sit on it. This is the District, remember? We have no active cases involving either Hardin, just one open but aging hit-and-run. I guarantee you nobody would be surprised if we sat on it, or even lost it."

"How did it get to you?" Grace asked.

"The only reason it didn't go into the unknown pending card file was that the hot-line dispatcher put it on internal E-mail," Vann said, patting his computer monitor. "Anything they can't correlate with existing cases, they circulate for a day or two on the E-mail in what they call the 'jeopardy' file: Here's an answer—anybody working a related question?"

It was Dan's turn to get up and stretch. These chairs must be for prisoners and suspects, he thought. "Suppose this does go over to NIS," he said. "You realize there might be another problem with that."

"Why's that?" Vann asked.

"Because you're talking about a flag officer involved in at least a scandalous situation, and maybe in murder," Grace interjected. "I was there long enough to realize that flag officers receive very special treatment when it comes to being investigated by the NIS."

"They get very special treatment throughout the whole Navy," Dan said. "It's part of their official privilege. Hell, these guys run the Navy. And they protect one another—there's even a term for it: the 'flag protection' circuit."

"Does that extend to murder?" Vann asked, his face in a scowl.

"No," Dan said emphatically. "No, I think if there's evidence of a serious crime on the part of a flag officer, the other flags would swallow hard but do what they have to do."

"Ah, the *E* word," Vann said, and they all went silent.

Grace stood up. "Let's think about it," she said. "Let's all just think about it and see if we can come up with a course of action. I know I need time to think."

"So do I," Dan said. "I can still see the poor bastard stuffed into a boiler. And now, well, now I don't know what to think. But I do want to help. I just don't know how, right at the moment."

"Okay," Vann said. "Thinking always helps a case. I want to run this by some of my people, see if we're out to lunch or what. And I need to talk to some folks in the community."

"Meaning, I hope, Mrs. Hardin," Grace said.

"Let's do a teleconference," Vann said, ignoring Grace's remark. "I'll call you both when I'm ready. Commander, you got a card?"

Dan left one of his OpNav business cards, and then he and Grace took the elevator downstairs. By mutual consent, and since they were already on the Metro's Red Line, they decided to have lunch at the American Café in Union Station. It being the beginning of tourist season, they had to wait fifteen minutes for a table. After the waitress had left with their orders, Dan looked around the crowded court.

"This Hardin thing won't let go, will it?" he said, thinking of what he had said to Vann.

"I'm sorry," she began. "I—"

"No, it's not you. I'm glad you called me. What I didn't tell Vann up there was that one of the reasons the EAs might have folded in their little turf fight with NIS was because somehow, somewhere, one of 'em knows about this boyfriend angle. That might be why they shut us off."

"Wow. Do you *know* that?"

"Well, no, I can't prove it, if that's what you mean. But the EAs are a network; that's where that flag protection circuit I mentioned operates. If they smell a scandal, they work together to protect the sanctity of *all* flag officers and thereby the Navy's good name."

"But not for murder."

"No, of course not, but, you see, they're not thinking of murder; they're thinking about a white flag officer, probably married, having an affair with a black woman officer who's also a junior officer. That's a medium-sensitive nerve these days in the USN. They're thinking Tailhook and *National Enquirer* or *Hard Copy*, and they're thinking damage control, the good of the Navy, the image of flag officers everywhere. Hell, that's their job."

Grace toyed with her iced tea. "So if that's going on, what are the chances of penetrating the smoke screen?"

"For me, slim to none. But I think I need to talk to Captain Summerfield. He used to be an EA until his wife had her stroke. He knows the system, and he's good buddies with a lot of flags. He might be able to sniff out what's going on."

"Vann said we shouldn't talk to anyone about this."

"He also said he wanted my help. He needs somebody inside the flag EA system for this, and Summerfield has at least been there and done that. I know I can't do it, but somebody like Summerfield might be able to. What do you suppose Vann's game is, anyway?"

She hesitated. "I still have the impression that it's personal. I would imagine the D.C. police have their hands entirely full, and no homicide bureau looks for more cases to work, so he's being cautious. But he's an ex–chief of detectives, and I think his interest is amplified by whatever this personal relationship with the Hardin family is."

"And that's probably why he's being so protective of Mrs. Hardin. Yeah, that computes. Here's lunch."

They spent the next half hour enjoying their lunch and the pleasant surroundings of the grand gallery of the train station, which had been elegantly refurbished into a first-class tourist attraction. The dominant feature was an enormous polished marble central hall, around which there were dozens of small restaurants, café's, shops, and bars. With Metro access, it was a very popular place for lunch for both tourists and government workers, while also offering first-class intercity train station services.

When their table had been cleared away and coffee brought, Grace looked pensive.

"A penny," Dan said.

"You know, you asked what Vann's game was," she replied. "I've been wondering a little bit what my game is, staying involved in this Hardin mess."

"Investigator's instincts, I suppose."

"Well, partly, but this is murder. I've been dealing with intricate fraud schemes, manipulations of securities rules and procedures, so-called white-collar crime. Nice and clean. No wide-eyed, mummified bodies staring at the innards of a ship's boiler."

Two women at an adjacent table looked away suddenly, and Dan and Grace smiled as they realized the tourists had been eavesdropping.

"When we would make a case in SEC," Grace continued, "we usually ended up around a big mahogany table in some executive conference room, making yet another deal: how big a fine, who would or would not admit wrongdoing, who would be sanctioned or banned from the trading business, that sort of thing. Then the so-called criminals would be whisked off in their big black limo to lunch at the Four Seasons. For an investment banker or a bond trader, getting caught usually turned out to be just another business expense."

"You make twenty million a year, a one-million-dollar fine is just that," Dan offered.

"Exactly. But my point is that those cases were almost an intellectual exercise: Could the government's lawyers and experts outfox the insider traders' lawyers and experts. It was about taxes and protecting small investors, and at least making a pretense about keeping the playing field level. But I never took a case home with me in the sense that I lost sleep over it. But this—"

"Yeah. I see where you're going: Are we sticking our noses into this because we might get some kind of vicarious thrill?"

"Well, partly. Or because it offends us. But maybe we ought to just butt out, like the EAs, this NIS, and even Vann says."

"Like Vann *said*. But not anymore. He called you, remember? Look, let me take a giant step. If I land on your toes, say so."

She smiled. "And what's that?"

"The main reason I came today was because you asked me to. I'll play in this game, whatever it is, but not if it screws up the chance to . . . to . . . Hell's bells, I don't know how to say this."

She reached across the table and put her hand on his. "You mean if we can get something going between us, let's try not do anything or say anything that messes that up. How's that?"

"Damn lawyer."

She laughed, then grew serious. "I hope that's possible. I could always hand off a SEC case to another lawyer or investigator. I sense that a murder case is very different: It's a game that once you're in, it's not so easy just to up and leave it. I feel like this one's becoming a threat of some kind, like that guy following me."

"Glad you mentioned that. I talked to a waiter I know down at the corner bistro. He told me that some guy ran out of the place without finishing his dinner the night you took the taxi home. And then he saw a big pickup truck make a wild turn onto Union."

"He see the driver?" she asked.

"No. But it kind of ties together."

She thought about that for a minute.

"Let's play it this way," he said finally. "You and I do what we can to help the real detectives; but when it comes down to knocking on doors in the night, that's for the cops, the real cops. The trick is for us to stay in deep background, so that the bad guy or guys don't see us—they only see the real cops. Bad guys don't usually go after the cops."

"Amen to that. So what will you do?"

"I'll have a talk with Summerfield. Let him pulse his contacts in the EA network and maybe some of his classmates who are already flag officers. Wait for Vann to call—he said he was taking that hot-line call up his tape. Figure out where we're going to go to dinner tonight. You know, important stuff."

46

DAN GOT IN to see Summerfield at five o'clock Wednesday afternoon while they were waiting for the staff call to the JCS debrief. The Joints Chiefs of Staff, the four-star officers who were the heads of the Army, Navy, Air Force, and Marines, met every Wednesday afternoon in the JCS conference room, called the "Tank," at two o'clock, accompanied by their operations deputies. The Navy's operations deputy was Vice Admiral Layman, OP-06. He would come back to the 06 offices in the late afternoon after the Tank session and debrief the staff officers on all the issues that were discussed and on any decisions made. Any staff officer who had an issue working in the Tank was on call until the JCS meeting broke up and the debrief was conducted. Many issues fell into what the staff called the kick-the-can mode: The chiefs would talk about it and then decide nothing, so the JCS debriefs were rarely about brand-new issues. But no one could go home until Admiral Layman came back.

Dan closed the door and plopped down on Summerfield's couch. The walls in Summerfield's office were covered in ship pictures and mementos: Summerfield had been in OpNav for almost four years. The captain was longingly fondling his pipe, but he knew it was too early.

"So, Daniel. Got a personal problem?"

"Yes, and no, sir," Dan said. He proceeded to debrief Summerfield on what he and Grace had been up to, what Vann was asking, and what help he, Dan, needed from Summerfield. When he was done, Summerfield said nothing; instead he went ahead and loaded his pipe and stoked it up, filling the room with a pungent blue cloud.

"This is a dangerous game you're playing, Daniel," he said finally.

"Because of the EAs?"

"Yes, although you have to assume that they were indeed speaking for their principals when they wanted this thing handed back to NIS. Now perhaps we know why. On the other hand, they might just have wanted to work it back-channel because there was potential for embarrassment to the flag community, short of murder, or course. But, either way, they find out that you got out of your box, against orders, they could find you a new box, somewhere wet and very warm, or dry and very cold, you follow?"

"Yes, sir. I keep reminding myself that I'm just a mark one, mod zero tin-can sailor. But in a sense, this cat's already out of the bag, isn't it?"

"How do you mean?"

"Well, first, there's Captain Vann. He's a honcho in the police department, ex–chief of detectives, now the EA to the deputy chief of police. If he gets the idea the Navy's covering up a murder, especially of somebody he knew, a family he knows, wouldn't it be best if the Navy got to the bad guy first, even if a flag might be involved?"

"Yeah, that computes," Summerfield said. "And there's Miss Snow, isn't there?"

Dan shrugged. "Yes, sir. She's fully aware of the implications of the hotline call. But she's not in government anymore."

"Meaning?"

"She's a private citizen. A free agent, if you will."

Summerfield nodded. "Free to do any goddamn thing. In other words, a potential loose cannon."

Dan remained silent. He was suddenly wondering whether Summerfield was worried or angry, or both. Perhaps confiding in him had not been such a good idea, because Summerfield appeared to be viewing this problem from the point of view of protecting the Navy, not finding a murderer. On the other hand, he had to admit that, for a Navy captain on the OpNav staff, this would not be an unreasonable reaction on Summerfield's part, especially for an ex-EA.

"Okay," Summerfield said at last through a cloud of blue smoke. "Let me ruminate on it. There are lots of points of entry into the EA and flag officer networks. I can start at the top—go see my classmate, the vice chief. If there's a flag officer involved in a murder, the vice is just the guy to flush him out fast. Or I can schmooze some of the EAs." He put his pipe down for a moment before continuing.

"But you should understand one thing, Daniel: Yes, there is a flag protection circuit, but that's mostly about saving face *after* a bureaucratic or operational bungle. The flag selection system isn't foolproof, or we wouldn't retire sixty percent of each year's selectees as one-stars after only two tours of duty. On the other hand, the flag protection circuit is also about protecting the Navy from its bureaucratic enemies, like the Air Force or certain career politicians who hate the Navy. It is not about protecting incompetent or evil individuals."

He stopped for a moment to draw on his pipe. "Well, maybe incompetence falls into the sphere of something that might be protected, given some of the people I've seen get two and three stars. But I can guarantee that every flag officer would want a murderer nailed. But preferably by our own investigatory system, see?"

"Yes, sir, I roger that," Dan said. "My only problem is that if you happened to tell the wrong guy in that system, you could be telling the bad guy."

"I think I can take that chance, Commander. Because if the network ends up alerting the bad guy, he'll start to wiggle and squirm. And the flag network, with all those EAs tuned in, can sense a squirm like a spider can sense a bug on the web—with about the same results. But my advice to you is to back out, and to tell your girlfriend to back out, too. This could get real nasty real fast."

"She's not exactly my girlfriend, Captain."

"Yeah, I hear you. And how was lunch? And have you considered this: If there's a flag involved in murder, he'll have a guy or three working for him—principals don't get their hands dirty, remember? That's why they have EAs. These guys can go in motion if the principal starts to squirm, sometimes without the principal's knowledge, you follow? Because if the principal goes down, his EA goes down. Miss Snow seems like a nice young woman, but she's not a real cop, is she? And neither are you."

"Yes, sir, but we've only been talking about it, we haven't really done anything."

"The bad guy might not appreciate that nuance. Tell your Captain Vann we're working on it, but you and Miss Snow go play house somewhere and leave this game to the cops—the real cops."

GRACE LET HERSELF back into the house and locked the front door. It had been a lovely evening, with dinner at L'Auberge Provençal out in Great Falls, Virginia—on her nickel; naval officers could not afford that restaurant. Then back into town for a leisurely walking tour of the Lincoln Memorial after dark, which had been surprisingly full of people. From the steps of the Lincoln, they had been able to enjoy the shimmering reflection of the entire Washington Monument in the long reflecting pool.

She had been more than a little ready for Dan to come in tonight. The chemistry between them was ripening well, without artifice or any apparent effort. But she had sensed his unease as they drove back to Georgetown, and she had contrived a small excuse to end the evening. She had kissed him affectionately on the cheek before saying good night, and he hadn't really known what to say or do. He was such a nice man, handsome, amusing, unpretentious, and yet emotionally still a bit fragile; the lady Claire must have been something indeed. She parked her purse in the hall and went to the answering machine, which was blinking impatiently at her. She turned on the overhead light and sat down to listen. It was Captain Vann.

"Miss Snow, hello. This is Moses Vann. I've talked to a few people here. I can confirm that this Hardin thing is a bit of a hot potato. I've been directed by my bosses to turn over the tape and the transcript to the Navy, like ASAP. In fact, I've already done it—a guy from the NIS named Englehardt sent someone for it late this afternoon. Give me a call, please. There's more. Thanks."

Grace replayed the message once, her good mood evaporating. Even Vann had sounded a little disappointed. Give it to NIS. Throw it into the Grand Canyon with the rest of the Navy's investigation. She looked at her watch and thought about calling Dan's machine; he wouldn't have made it home yet. But she didn't want to end the evening on the Hardin case. She called it anyway and left a brief message about how nice the evening had been and that she just wanted to say good night. Time enough for the Hardins and Moses Vann in the morning. She rechecked the house locks and went off to bed.

DAN HAD TO CIRCLE his neighborhood streets before finding a parking spot on Lee, one full block away from his house. He locked up, checked his parking permit, and walked back to the house. It was a lovely night, cool, almost zero humidity, with the night air appearing to generate a light of its own in the soft glow of the gas lamps. When he got in, he listened to Grace's message on the machine and smiled. He had acted like a damn virgin teenager on the way back from the Lincoln Memorial. He wondered if she had noticed the sheen of perspiration on his forehead as he piloted the Suburban down her street. Everything had been so damn pleasant, without a single false note the whole evening. He *had* wanted to go in with her. Hell, he wanted to go to bed with her, and he sensed she felt the same. But at the last minute, a whirl of nameless emotions had seized him and he had backed away. From what? he wondered as he went around securing the house. Grace wasn't some piece of fluff, some one-night stand. It was understood between them that they were working on something, maybe even falling in love. He could make her laugh, and she made him feel like a human again, conscious of needs that had been too long suppressed. He knew that someday they would have to talk about Claire, and he was comforted by the knowledge that Claire's death was something he could talk about to Grace.

He went out to the kitchen and fixed himself a small cognac. He turned out the lights and stared out the kitchen windows into the shadows of the garden. The darkened windows of the houses across the alley looked like caves in an irregular, moonlit cliff. He had spent a lot of time doing just this: staring out the kitchen window at everything and nothing, seeing the familiar, if mundane, details of the garden and the back wall and the buildings beyond, listening to the sounds and currents of life passing him by, and suspending himself halfway between acceptance of that fact and doing something about it.

Grace had rekindled an impetus in his life that had been missing for a long time: something besides his career, getting to his almighty ship command, and all the other trappings of his Navy-centered life. Life after Claire, and before Grace. Since Monterey, all he had had was the Navy, which offered the advantage of being able to fill up his every waking hour if he cared to let it. Meeting Grace had exposed the fact that his personal life was supremely contrived, designed to minimize time alone, time to think about the future and face his prospects, time to stare out this kitchen window. Seeing to it that by Tuesday at the latest he had something lined up for the weekend, a trip, a stay with friends, a day's domestic project, anything to fill up those empty weekend hours, when the streets filled with people bustling about doing all the mundane things people did; when they had a life. And Sundays. Saturdays could be consumed by errands, laundry, housecleaning, washing the car. But Sundays lay in wait; Sundays in an empty house accentuated the noise of clocks, the sounds of voices outside on the sidewalk, the sense that living alone could be downright lethal. Meeting Grace had forced him to rediscover how the quality of a man's life could end up being defined by the presence or absence of a woman. Above all, he now wanted to be very careful, because he sensed that, with Grace, he had come into the orbit of a valuable woman.

He finished his cognac, washed out the glass, and headed upstairs. As he climbed the narrow stairs, the Hardin case intruded, provoking a flare of irritation. He hadn't cared for the warning note in Summerfield's voice during their little séance that afternoon. His boss had focused almost automatically on protecting the Navy, to the apparent exclusion of finding out who had done this thing, and why. And what was it that Summerfield had said about principals not getting their hands dirty? He had a nagging sense that he had missed something, something important, but for the life of him he couldn't remember. The captain was probably right in one respect: They really ought to let the cops handle this. Let the NIS get wrapped around the axle with the flags and the EAs—serve 'em both right. Right now, you've got something more valuable to attend to, don't you? He stopped again at the top of the stairs, a nagging thought evading him, but then went off to bed.

48

GRACE CALLED CAPTAIN VANN'S office at 9:00 A.M. on Thursday morning, but he was once again in a meeting. The secretary told her that Vann wanted to do a teleconference at 10:30 with Grace and Commander Collins. Could she make that? Grace could, and the secretary said that Vann would initiate the conference calls. Grace hung up and wondered if she should call Dan, but he would know by now, so she let it go and went to attend to household chores. At 10:30, she was sitting by the phone with a notepad ready. At 10:35, the phone rang and she picked up. It was Vann, with Dan Collins already on the line.

"Good morning, Miss Snow, this is Moses Vann. I have Commander Collins on the line. This connection okay?"

"It's fine, Captain Vann. Hi, Dan."

"Morning, Grace. And, everybody, let me start by saying that I'm in an empty office for right now, but that can change. If I start talking about car repairs and shut this off, that's why, okay?"

"Got it, Commander," Vann said. "I'll be quick. We caught another tip on the Hardin case last night, by fax this time—to the Traffic Division. Lemme read it to you. Says: 'If you want to know how Elizabeth Hardin really died, call this number,' and it gives a metro D.C. phone number."

There was a moment of silence common to conference calls, and then Dan said, "What in the hell is going on here?"

"Good question, Commander. This message was forwarded into the hotline center, and since I'd snatched up the last Hardin-related information, they flagged it to me. I've had the phone number checked out, and it belongs to one Captain Malachi Ward, U.S. Army, Retired, in a house up on Capitol Hill."

"Capitol Hill? That's hardly an Army captain's country," Dan said. "An army captain is an Oh-three."

"Ain't no tellin' with those places: Lots of 'em were abandoned dumps in the late sixties; you could pick 'em up for a song if you agreed to fix 'em up. I own three as rental units myself."

"Where did the fax come from?" Dan asked.

"A phone booth in a hotel that had a data plug; somebody probably used a portable PC. Effectively anonymous."

"Did you call him? Ward?" Grace asked.

"No, no," Vann said. "That's not how it works. First we check a guy out, especially when someone else is putting him in for some heat. We've only done a preliminary screen—nothing in depth. But this guy Ward is interesting. He's a sort of a contractor, got a business license as a PI and as a 'security consultant' in the District. He owns half of a duplex on the Hill outright. Now we'll have to check around to see what he consults about and who he works for, but we'll need probable cause, a warrant, all that stuff, before we can go much farther down that road. But there're a couple of things that interest me. Like the fact that he has no driver's license or vehicle in any of the metro-area jurisdictions, and, get this, no credit history or even a credit rating."

"What's bad credit got to do with anything?" Dan asked.

"Not bad credit—*no* credit rating. Not with any of the three major credit-reporting systems. Nowadays, everybody's got a credit rating. For a guy *not* to be in the national credit-rating databases takes some doing—a lot of doing, in fact. This is a guy who wants to be invisible. And he damn near is."

"Captain?"

"Yes, Miss Snow?"

"What *is* going on here? You've had one anonymous tip alleging that an unidentified senior naval officer was having an affair with Elizabeth Hardin and that her love life was somehow connected to her brother's murder. Now a second tip involving this Captain Ward in Elizabeth Hardin's death."

"Yeah, it's gettin' a little crazy. But this being Washington, it's beginning to sound like a conspiracy of some kind starting to unravel: The players begin leaking information, usually to the press, trying to put the blame on someone else. Only these guys are leaking to the cops—who, I gotta tell you, don't have a damn clue as to what this is really all about, unfortunately. Commander Collins, who've you talked to?"

"To my boss in Op-Six-fourteen—you met him, Captain Summerfield. Remember, he's plugged in to the flag officer EA network in the Pentagon in a way that I am not."

"Okay, that's reasonable. And I was ordered to pass the first tip over to the NIS. So maybe this second tip makes sense."

"How so?" Grace asked.

"Because between what you've done and what I've done, we may have lit two separate fuses in the Navy admirals' network inquiring about a tie-in between the Hardin murder and a senior officer's love life, presumably an admiral's."

"Two channels?" Grace asked.

"Yeah—NIS and the commander's boss, Summerfield. This second tip might just be a reaction from said admiral: If this guy Ward is what I think he is—and we don't know that yet—this second call might be a shot at putting somebody's hired hand in the shit, in retaliation for the hired hand putting that somebody in the shit."

There was another pause while Grace and Dan digested this theory.

"Well, if that's true," Grace said, "it means this guy Ward made the first phone call. Why didn't he just give you a name? And how did you get Ward's name?"

"That's two questions. Question one: That isn't how it's done in this town. You want to get somebody in trouble in Washington, you launch an interesting question, not an accusation. You make an accusation, the accusee denies it, it's over. You ask a question, somebody besides the accusee gets into the game of answering. Much more effective. Second question: We backtraced the phone number to Ward and the address on Capitol Hill. I've also spoken to a friend in our Frauds Division. He's got a stakeout going on another matter up near the Capitol building. I've asked him to shift some assets over to Ward's street, just a couple of hours each night, for the next three nights, see if we get a reaction. If this guy Ward is a player, he'll tumble to the stakeout, and then maybe we can spook him into doing something."

"Like what?" Dan asked.

"Shit, I don't know. Something. Way I see it, something's come unglued among those involved with the Hardin killing. Probably because someone found the body. But we got what looks like the players starting to snipe at one another. We got jackshit for evidence that there was even a crime in Elizabeth's death, and similarly jackshit for leads in her brother's death. So when you got nothin', you shake the bushes, see what scuttles out, right? Hell, I'm open to any bright ideas. Anyone?"

Grace didn't know what to say, and Dan was silent on his end.

"Okay, then, that's where I'm at, too. I'm going to target this guy, run the standard traps, see what else we can come up with. I'm doing that on my own hook, remember—I was kind of told to drop this thing. Getting tips in helps, but . . ."

"Is there anything you'd like us to do?" asked Grace. "Or, actually, me to do? You and Dan are in similar boats."

"No," Vann said emphatically. "Not until I know lots more about this guy Malachi Ward. Again, if he's what I think he is, he's not somebody you want to meet; some of these guys play very rough. Commander, you get any feedback from your end, let me know, okay?"

"You got it, Captain."

"All right. That's it for now. And, folks, I appreciate the help. I think you've both figured out that this is more personal than official business for me right now, okay? I just want you to know I really appreciate it. Be cool. And lock your doors."

49

ON FRIDAY NOON, Malachi sat in his kitchen, staring down the hallway. Two days. He had called the captain's contact number Wednesday afternoon, and there had been no reply. The captain had said they were going to break off communications unless something important came up. Malachi had nothing important to report, but he had wanted to see if the captain would call back. Two days of silence had confirmed that his little phone call from the Metro Center had probably had the desired effect. But the question now was, What were *they* up to? He got up again and walked around the ground floor of the house, checking the deserted noonday street through the curtained windows, looking for anything different. His antennae were prickling, but that was only natural. He'd thrown some shit in the game, and now there was a reaction, or at least what looked like one. The captain wasn't returning his calls. There was probably some heat building up in the Navy, and the captain didn't want to be in touch with his hired hand just now. He went back to the kitchen and eyed the whiskey bottle.

Nope, not now. His head still hurt from what he had done Wednesday night, and that was thirty-six hours ago. If there was something stirring, he couldn't afford to be screwed up. Might have to move here; might have to move fast. He suddenly felt an irresistible, instinctive urge to get out of the house. He got up and checked the locks all around, then went out the back door to the garage, carrying his windbreaker and a pair of dark glasses. Walk or drive? Walk. In a city, a car was a trap. On foot, he could disappear into any alley, building, backyard, or, best yet, into any Metro station. He squeezed between the F-250 and the garage wall and peered through the line of dirty windowpanes across the electric garage door. Looked like an alley. Maybe he was being stupid, panicking over a phone that didn't ring, getting the d.t.'s from too much Harper. Maybe. Maybe not. He went back through the garage and around to the gate in the back fence, slipping on the windbreaker and the glasses. He cracked the back gate and looked out. Nothing. Still looked like an alley, with its collection of trash containers and the line of tilting, weed-bordered wooden fences. Looked perfectly normal. He could see down two blocks' worth of alley in either direction. Nothing unusual. The sounds of light traffic from Constitution and East Capitol Street. A trash truck grinding through its urban delicacies somewhere nearby. A dog barking.

He stepped out and turned towards A Street, went down one more block through its alley, and then left when he got to Constitution, which in his neighborhood was just a two-lane street, albeit one with reversible lane controls for rush hour. He walked up Constitution Avenue toward Capitol Hill and then turned left onto Second Street behind the Supreme Court building. He turned left again onto East Capitol and finally ended up on his own street. There was little traffic in this neighborhood at noon; it was not a kids and moms area, with most of the gentrified town houses being owned or rented by professional associations, independent lobbyists, and staffers on the Hill or at the Library of Congress. Only thing moving on Capitol Hill at noon are congressmen and criminals, he thought, sensing a distinction without a difference. And lovers. As he neared his own block, he saw a distinguished-looking older man and a very pretty young woman coming down the other side of the street, so engrossed in each other that Malachi could have been naked, for all they would have noticed. A congressman hard at work, or working on getting hard, he mused as the couple turned down some steps to a basement flat in a town house.

At the intersection leading into his own block, he crossed the street and walked past his own duplex on the opposite side of the street, looking for anything unusual, strange cars, telephone trucks, vans, any signs of a surveillance. Nothing. Wall-to-wall cars, of course—parking was a constant war up on the Hill. But not a damn thing out of place: The birds were singing, the trees were blooming, the politicians were in rut, the streets were empty, and the captain wasn't returning his calls. He kept walking, down to the end of the block, turned left, then left again into his alley, where he reentered his house via the back gate. He was actually sweating a little. Goddamn booze. Summer coming, hateful summer in Washington, D.C., which was nothing but a damn swamp, anyway. That little voice intruded again as he unlocked the kitchen door: Get clear, Malachi; get outta Dodge. This Hardin thing is bad news, definitely not business as usual, and you're starting to play in a game that's out of your league. That last thought made him pause on the back steps: Up to now, he'd been content to be the hired hand, letting the principals and their EAs call the shots— if things got screwed up, he simply waited for new instructions. But making that phone call had been something new: He had made a move all on his own, and now the big guys were meeting behind closed doors.

He went inside and checked the machine. Ah, the light was blinking. He pressed the play button and listened to the machine record the sound of a telephone being hung up, followed by a dial tone. That was all. Somebody doesn't like answering machines. Or somebody was checking to see if he was in the house. A call like that was often the precursor to a burglary in this city. The difference was that, in Washington, it wasn't always a crook checking out the house. He canvassed the windows again, but the streets were still empty. But the phone call had solidified a decision he had been kicking around all morning: Arlington. For years, he had kept the essentials prepositioned in the apartment: money, a couple of weapons, clothes, some elementary first-aid stuff, as well as two telephone lines. Okay. He'd spend the afternoon sanitizing his side of the house; the duplex next door didn't need it. He would load the truck up with some odds and ends, some bottles of Harpers mostly, and bail out after dark, after rush hour. He'd have to get an additional parking spot at the Randolph Towers for the truck, but they were always accommodating.

He began to prowl through the house, examining it from a cop's point of view, doing a preliminary search. He gathered up papers, tax records, his phone logs, mail, checkbooks, laundry slips—all the day-to-day minutiae that would flesh out a police report if they came in to search the place. The longer he worked, the more certain he became that going to ground was the right move. Maybe it was just that he was doing something instead of just sitting around. But the next trick would be to find out what exactly was going on.

50

LATE FRIDAY AFTERNOON, Dan was walking down the fifth corridor on his way back from a two-hour long, tailbone paralyzing, brain-desiccating action-officer meeting in JCS. He had stayed conscious only by daydreaming about the pleasure of Grace's company last night. They had done a movie and pizza, and had enjoyed themselves thoroughly. He was thinking about her when he ran into Yeoman Jackson bopping down the passageway. Jackson stopped him.

"Yo. Commander Collins. Captain Summerfield said that the VCNO's EA is lookin' for you. But he say you gotta talk to him first, before you go see the man."

"Wonderful," Dan said. He looked at his watch: 4:45. There went his river time. "How long ago was this?"

"Oh, 'bout half hour, maybe less."

"Okay. You shoving off for the day?"

"Yes, sir. It's Friday, which means it's *fly* day. I'm gone. Say, it true what Colonel Snapper been sayin'? That you goin' to Egypt?"

"Egypt?"

"Yeah. Colonel Snapper, he hear about you havin' to go see the VCNO's main man, he say you gettin' orders to east Egypt. We got bases in Egypt?"

"No, Jackson. What the colonel is implying is that I'm about to be sent far away for pissing off the VCNO's EA."

Jackson considered this for a few seconds, then shook his head. "He wasn't implyin' nothin'," he declared. "He was just flat sayin' it, you know? Well, I gotta split. I'll see you Monday, you still here."

"Thanks a heap, Jackson," Dan said, but Jackson was already headed down the hall. Dan threaded his way through the departing stream of civil servants as he turned left into the E-ring corridor. After 4:30, it was mostly uniforms left in the building; civil servants had to be paid overtime if they stayed late. He got to Op-614 and found the door locked. He punched in the cipher code and went in, where he found the office empty, although not secured for the day. The sign-out board above Jackson's desk was, as usual, several days out of date.

He went back to his desk and put the JCS staffing papers into his safe. There was a yellow message impaled on the pen of his desk set: "See RADM-sel Randall when you get back, but talk to 614 first." The message was initialed by Snapper at time 1620, so this had been written just twenty-five minutes ago. The captain and Snapper must have been called out. Without knowing where they had gone or for how long, he had to decide: Should he wait for Summerfield to get back or answer the summons from Randall?

The phone rang. He debated answering it. It might be the VCNO's office, or it might be Summerfield trying to catch him. So what's it gonna be, Commander, he thought, the lady or the tiger? He picked up the phone.

"OP-Six-fourteen, Commander Collins speaking, sir."

"Commander this is Senior Chief Batzel in the VCNO's office. Did you get the message that Rear Admiral–select Randall wants to see you, sir?"

Shit. The tiger. "I just walked back into the office from JCS, Chief. I have the message in my hand."

"Yes, sir. Now might be a real good time to respond, Commander."

"This gonna be one of those horizon-expanding sessions, Senior Chief?"

There was a pause on the other end. "Well, sir," the chief said, as if he were giving the matter great thought, "*expanding* is probably a good word. But maybe not your horizon. Sir."

Dan laughed. "Okay, Senior Chief. I'll go get my asbestos Skivvies. Tell the EA I'm on my way."

"Aye, aye, Commander."

Dan hung up the phone and locked up his safe. He checked around the office to make sure there were no egregious security violations in full view, then left a note for Summerfield that he had zigged when he should have zagged. He checked to see that the door was locked behind him and headed up the E-ring. He stopped by the OP-06 front office to see if Summerfield might be there, but the chiefs there had not seen him. Captain Manning was not in evidence, and it looked like the DCNO and the ADCNO were also out of the office. He remembered that the DCNO would probably be with the CNO down at the JCS meeting in the Tank. A minute later, he walked into the VCNO's front office. The aide was there, but Randall was not in evidence. The VCNO's inner office door was, as usual, closed. Dan walked over to the aide's desk.

"I'm Commander Collins. I got a message to come see Captain Randall," he said.

"*Rear Admiral–select* Randall is in conference with the VCNO," the aide replied without looking up from the staff paper he was marking up. "He'll be with you shortly, Commander."

"Thanks a bunch," Dan said. From the other side of the office, the senior chief rolled his eyes and indicated the lone chair by the front door. Dan sat down to wait, but he had barely crossed his legs when the VCNO's inner office door opened and Captains Randall and Manning came out. Randall saw Dan and stopped.

"About time, Collins. Senior Chief, give me the keys to the visiting flag office."

The senior chief fished out a set of keys as Dan stood up. Manning was giving him the fish eye but said nothing. Randall walked out the front door, across the corridor, and unlocked a plain glass-fronted door across from the VCNO's office. He went in and turned on the lights, followed by Manning, who indicated over his shoulder that Dan should follow. Dan closed the door behind him and stood in a small vestibule office. Beyond was a much larger office equipped with a desk, a small conference table, a sofa and some chairs, and a bank of telephones on the desk. Dan knew that these offices were used when flag officers were summoned from around the world to come see the senior admirals in OpNav. Randall sat down behind the desk, while Manning stood to one side.

"Commander Collins," Randall began in a voice about one decibel below a controlled shout, "I thought I made myself fairly clear the last time we talked about the Hardin case. Now I'm finding out that you don't listen so well."

"Sir?" Dan said. He wanted to see what the beef was before saying anything, especially with the way Randall's face was getting red.

"Sir, indeed," Randall yelled. "Goddamnit, why are you still involving yourself in the Hardin investigation?"

"I'm not, Captain." With the shades drawn across the windows, the harsh fluorescent lighting made the room look like an interrogation room, despite all the fancy furniture.

"Oh, but we have reason to believe that you are, Commander," Randall said, leaning back in the armchair. "Admiral Torrance himself told me so. You wouldn't dispute the word of the vice chief, now would you?"

Summerfield. He said he might go see his classmate, Dan thought.

"I handed the Hardin investigation over to you, Captain," Dan replied, trying to keep his own voice calm. "You purportedly gave it back to NIS. I've not been involved in the investigation, per se, since that time. I was asked by the Washington D.C. Police to make a recommendation as to what they should do with a tip received on the other Hardin case."

"What other Hardin case?" Manning asked, speaking for the first time. Randall looked annoyed at the interruption but held his tongue.

"The lieutenant's sister," Dan replied. "She was also a Navy lieutenant, a PAO type. She was killed in a traffic accident in Washington about two weeks before Lieutenant Hardin disappeared. That was two years ago. To my knowledge, it was nothing directly to do with the homicide case."

Manning looked at Randall, who was staring at Dan.

"And what did you tell the D.C. police?" asked Randall.

"I told them they had to give it to NIS, who has the investigation now. Except—"

"Yes? Except what?" Randall leaned forward, concentrating. Dan felt himself beginning to perspire; this man focused on you like a snake.

"Well, sir, the nature of the tip. It was an anonymous phone call that implied that Lt. Elizabeth Hardin—that's the sister—was having an affair or was otherwise involved with an admiral and that their relationship was connected somehow to Lieutenant Hardin's murder."

"And you don't think that has a bearing on a murder case?" Manning asked.

"I'm not working on a murder case anymore, Captain," Dan said innocently. "I have no way of telling if it's related. Before we handed over the case—"

" 'We'? Who's we?" Randall interrupted.

"Miss Snow, from NIS, and I. We examined the Traffic Bureau report of the hit-and-run accident, but there were no indications it was anything but an accident."

"What else did the police ask you to do?"

"Nothing," Dan lied. "I told them there was nothing else I could do, that they should hand the tip over to the Navy. I did come back and tell Captain Summerfield."

"Yes, we know about that," Randall said, his voice coming down a notch. "It's a damned good thing you did, too. Now tell me why you did."

"I guess it's because it sounded like a flag officer might be involved in a potentially embarrassing situation. And with all the media interest in the brother's murder, I thought perhaps it was a good idea to prevent the flag officer or the Navy from being blindsided."

"And which flag officer might that be, Commander?" Randall asked softly.

Careful, careful, Dan thought. "I have no idea, sir. I assumed that, like the Hardin investigation, that issue is above my pay grade."

Randall stared at him for a long moment, then swiveled around in the armchair to look out the window, where it was getting dark. Manning was studying the pictures of sailing ships on the wall, waiting to follow Randall's lead. Dan wondered if either of them had talked to the D.C. police and knew anything about the second tip. He decided that this was no time to volunteer anything. Randall swung back around to face him.

"Very well, Commander." Commander, not Collins, Dan thought. Randall seemed to be a lot less excited. "If the D.C. police have anything more to say to you, you make sure that Captain Summerfield is informed. He will make sure that I am informed. I hereby reiterate my instructions to you, which are to steer clear of this Hardin matter. By the way, what role does this Miss Snow play in all this? I understand from Captain Rennselaer at NIS that she no longer works there."

"Again, nothing direct, Captain," Dan said. "Captain Vann of the D.C. police called her when he called me. She was the one who initially interviewed him about Elizabeth Hardin's accident."

"This Captain Vann understands that neither of you is officially empowered anymore in the Hardin case?"

"Yes, sir." Dan said. "He also knows that the NIS has the case for action. My guess is that we're done with it, now that he has an official point of contact to deal with."

"See to it that you are, Commander," Randall said. "If there is some kind of scandal lurking in the background of the Hardin case that involves a flag officer, the vice chief has sole jurisdiction. It's his official privilege to take care of problems like that, assuming they exist. Commanders who stick their noses into an issue at this level do so at their great personal and professional peril. I think I've said this before."

"Yes, sir."

"And the fact that you are personally involved with this Miss Snow, while none of our business, had better not lead you back into the Hardin case, assuming that she persists in involving herself."

Dan saw red. "You're absolutely right, sir," he said in a clipped voice.

"I beg your pardon, Commander?"

"My personal relationship with Miss Snow is none of your business."

Manning let out a theatrical sigh while Randall's face settled into a blank, cold mask. He stood up.

"If Miss Snow interferes in an official U.S. Navy homicide investigation, Commander Collins, you had better be several thousand yards away from it, or I will see to it that the obstruction of justice charges brought against her include you. Now get out of here before I lose my temper."

"Aye, aye, sir," Dan said through tight lips, then headed for the door. Manning was looking at him as if he were a dog that had made a mess on the carpet. Dan paused for a fraction of a second as he walked by, and shot Manning a look that made the EA blink. Dan went on through the door and closed it forcefully. He stomped down the passageway towards OP-614, his heart pounding. Those sons of bitches, who the hell do they think they are? Rear admiral–*select*. A select-grade asshole. Goddamnit, he had done the right thing in telling Summerfield. And Summerfield had done the right thing by transmitting a warning to the flag network, and now they responded by threatening him, and Grace. He could suddenly understand how Pearl Harbor had happened.

He steamed down the polished E-ring corridor, nearly bowling over two yeomen who were coming the other way. But at the intersection of the fifth corridor and the E-ring, he stopped. A sudden, chilling thought had just struck him. Jesus H. Christ, do you suppose those goddamned EAs already know who it is? He suddenly felt like an ocean swimmer who has just discovered that the beach, all by itself, is getting farther away. Snapper, in a serious mode for a change, had even warned him this morning: "Summerfield is getting concerned about you—you're starting to piss off some powerful people."

He continued back to OP-614, walking slower, where he found the office as he had left it. It was now 5:45. He wondered where the hell Summerfield and Snapper were. These were pretty late hours for a Friday, even in OpNav. He scribbled a note to Summerfield on the original telephone message about seeing the VCNO's EA, left it on the captain's desk, and then went around securing the office's desks and safes. The duty officer would be making his rounds at 6:00 P.M., and open safes, even behind an alarmed cipher lock, would be a security violation. Normally, he would have stayed and waited for the branch head to return, but tonight he was suddenly sick of OpNav and all its bullshit.

He realized he wanted to talk to Grace, needed to talk to Grace. He called her number, got the machine, waited for her to pick up, and when she didn't, he left a message for her to call him at home. Then he called the OP-61 front office and told the duty officer that he was wrapping up 614 but leaving the lights on, as Summerfield and Snapper were still out. The duty officer promised not to write them up for leaving lights on.

Dan drove home in the Friday-evening rush hour with his mind barely registering the heavily congested traffic. He had long ago learned not to be in any hurry, and he knew how to avoid all the lights on Washington Street once he got into Old Town. The light was blinking on his answering machine when he got in, and he felt a surge of elation.

"Hi, Dan, this is Grace, playing telephone tag. I'm home; call me back."

He picked up the phone and called her. To his surprise, she picked up without waiting for him to identify himself, and for an instant he almost didn't know what to say.

"Hey, Grace. You startled me. What are you doing picking up?"

"Thought it might be you. I don't get that many calls these days, remember?"

"Oh, yeah, telephone woes of the unemployed. I might be joining you in those ranks."

"Oh my God, what happened?"

"Can you come over? We'll catch a bite somewhere and I'll tell you about it. It was kind of bizarre, actually."

"Oh dear, the Hardin mess, right? All right, you find me a parking place and I'll be there in a little bit."

"Take your time. I've got to shovel this place out, and the tourists will have all the tables for the next hour or so, anyway."

"I'll call you from the car when I'm about five minutes away."

They hung up and Dan scurried around the house, picking up the detritus of his bachelor existence. He slipped a bottle of wine into the refrigerator, examined three blocks of cheese and rejected two for exhibiting excessive hair, and tentatively crunched a cracker. When Grace called, he went out front and stood by the Suburban. When she showed up, he pulled it out and waved her into his parking place, then went around the block until he found a spot for the Suburban.

"The joys of upscale street parking," he said once they were ensconced in the garden after playing musical cars and trading parking permits.

"And I thought Georgetown was bad," she replied. "It's still a nice wine."

"I'm almost in the mood for something stronger," he said, then told her about his session with the EAs. She was shaking her head by the time he was finished.

"I'm beginning to wonder the same thing you are," she said. "These guys are awfully worried about this investigation."

"Especially Randall."

"Captain Vann said to give him word about any feedback either of us might get," she reminded him. "This sounds like feedback."

"Yup." He looked over at her, saw how pretty she was, and suddenly didn't want to deal with the Hardin business anymore. She caught his look and smiled. He had been working up to something, and now he decided to plunge ahead.

"If you don't have the weekend all booked up, I was sort of thinking about going to Harpers Ferry tomorrow," he said. "It's really pretty in the spring, and there's a lot of history there. There's also a great inn overlooking the river. For lunch."

She grinned. "Sounds delightful, and, no, my weekend is not booked up."

"Super. Let's finish our vino and go find someplace for dinner, and then I'll tell you about it. Maybe we can swing through Sharpsburg and I can show you the Antietam battlefield. I'll call the good Captain Vann Monday about these frigging EAs and their threats. But right now, I want to concentrate on the Grace and Dan show, if that's okay with you, ma'am. Besides, I think it's trying to rain."

"I can handle that," she said, smiling at him again over the rim of her wineglass. "I can definitely handle that."

51

By 8:00 P.M. Friday night, Malachi was ready to go. The pickup truck was loaded with two suitcases, all of his telephone equipment, and four large plastic boxes of papers and records, all covered with a brown plastic tarp against a light rain that had developed. He had been through the house several times, executing room-by-room searches, looking in and under the furniture, into every drawer, in the basement and in the attic, trying to see what a cop would see, looking especially for any evidence that might tie him to the Hardin case. He left one unprogrammed telephone in the house but took his answering machine and the synthesizer. He cleared the memory in the fax machine and then turned it off. He had thought about disassembling and taking the computer but then decided that was too hard. He packed his backup tapes, dumped the data files, and then locked out the hard drive. He wanted to leave enough stuff in the house to make it look like he might come back. He did not want them to think he had fled the country, just that he wasn't there, although the absence of any household paperwork might give it away.

The doorway connecting his house with the duplex next door was concealed in the downstairs coat closet, behind what looked like a floor-to-ceiling ventilation recirculation screen. If they seriously tossed the house, they would find it, but it wouldn't prove anything: The duplex was seventy years old. He had stashed ten thousand dollars in cash in a hidden floor safe next door, along with a Browning .380 automatic. There were no records or papers of any kind next door, although it was otherwise ready for occupancy. Let them try to figure out what that was all about, or where the owner was. As a final measure, he had loaded up two miniature voice-activated tape recorders, concealing one in the living room air-conditioning duct of each house. Cops searching a supposedly empty house tended to talk about what they were doing and why; the tapes might reveal how much they knew or suspected. He would physically have to get back into one or the other of the houses to lift the tapes, but that was doable, especially if they didn't realize he had access to both houses.

He locked up the house, turning out all the lights, and headed for the garage. He got into the truck and then hesitated. Maybe one more surveillance sweep, just to make sure he wasn't about to drive into their loving arms with all his stuff in the truck. Right. He got out, fished behind the seat for a lightweight trench coat and hat, and then let himself out into the alley. With the dripping overcast, the only light came from an alley street-light positioned right in the middle of the block; each end of the alley was conveniently in the shadows. The mizzle formed a cone of precipitation around the streetlights. He walked quickly to East Capitol Street, turned left, away from his own street, and went around the block, walking rapidly. People who walked these streets slowly after dark were usually morally challenged individuals looking for someone to rob; the potential victims tended to move right along. He ignored the domestic scenes visible through lighted windows of the houses and kept his eyes open for shapes and figures among the rows of parked cars. It occurred to him that he should have brought a piece with him. After walking one more block parallel to his own street, he started back, taking two left turns and crossing his own street once again to be on the side opposite his own house. He stopped on the corner in a shadow of a large tree and stared down his block, carefully scanning each parked can and van. Van. Well, now. There was a van, parked on the same side of the street he was on, five doors down from his house. He smiled in the darkness. There were no people with vans living on this block.

He moved slightly around the tree so that he had a good look at the sidewalk side of the van and waited. The sounds of traffic up on Second were muffled by the wet trees along the crowded blocks of houses. He saw a couple walking hand in hand across the street at the other end of the block, two fleeting figures appearing in a cone of streetlight and then disappearing again. Someone opened a kitchen door and called in a dog or a cat—he couldn't tell which. One of the houses had a radio going with a heavy, thumping rock beat. Over all these sounds of urban domesticity came the whir of tree frogs and the rustling and cheeping of small birds settling in for the night in the row of trees. Drops of rain collecting on the new leaves spatted occasionally onto the sidewalk around him. There. The flare of a lighter glinted for a second in the rain-streaked, right side mirror of the van. All right, he thought. All fucking right.

He fought a sudden urge just to walk down there, down the sidewalk, while the guy was still night-blind from lighting his cigarette, and yank the damn door open and pull the bastard out onto the sidewalk. Yeah, and then what? His partner shoots your ass while you're stomping his buddy? He assumed that there had to be somebody in the driver's seat; maybe not, but that lighter had looked to be very close to the right side window. He examined the van again, looking for an aerial or other signs of police gear, but there was nothing. D.C. plates, a standard car radio antenna on the right side forward, no windows except up front and two dirty squares of glass in the back doors. Could be cops; could be anybody.

He exhaled and stepped back closer to the tree, looking around to make sure no pedestrians were inbound. So, somebody was under surveillance. He had to assume it was his house, although in Washington, it could be anybody's house. For all he knew, the neighbors three doors down from him could be the Serbian Liberation Army, plotting to blow up Congress. Go Serbs, he thought.

He looked around to make sure there were no cars coming down his street or Constitution, and then, keeping the tree between him and the van, he backed across the intersection to the next corner, turned, and walked rapidly away into the darkness. He circled the next block and then slipped back into his alley. He stopped in the shadows at the entrance to the alley to let his night vision readjust. Depending on how serious they were, they might have the alley staked out, too. Except no one had been there when he had come out. No one he'd seen, anyway. He stood there for ten minutes, getting warm and sweaty in the raincoat, oblivious to the thin mist falling, absorbing the sounds coming from kitchen windows and backyards. He nearly jumped out of his skin when a cat brushed up against his leg, and again he had to fight down a powerful urge to stomp the cat into the cracked concrete. He realized he wanted very badly to lash out at something or someone.

He had no way of knowing if the captain's refusal to return his call and the watchers in the van out front were related, but he had to assume they were. The game had changed, and it was no longer Malachi's game. As he had suspected. It had to be about the Hardin case, but why, why would they finger *him*? He was the one guy who could finger them! He hadn't given the cops enough to get a name when he made his call—only a hint that Elizabeth Hardin had had a boyfriend in the Navy. But that had been enough to send a tremor up the EAs' web, apparently. But what the hell was the captain doing—and how had the cops made the connection? The captain had said that the Hardin investigation was in the someday box. So unless the captain had called the cops himself and given them Malachi's name, which would be tantamount to suicide, there had to be another reason the cops were in on it. But the Navy had no one working with the cops or even talking to them. He closed his eyes and concentrated; there was something he was missing—something from the phone call he had made. Ah, yes they did: the mysterious Miss Snow—who supposedly no longer worked for the NIS. Son of a bitch. Maybe she was an independent. And the captain probably thought that Malachi would never be watching for a woman. Son of a *bitch!*

He scanned the alley again but then concluded that there were no cars or other signs of surveillance. He was about to move when there was movement behind the gate right in front of him, and then the gate latch tripped. The gate opened, throwing a wedge of light into the alley from a back porch light. A fat man came out, dressed in shapeless Bermudas and a slack T-shirt and carrying an armload of trash. The man popped the top off a green plastic trash can with his elbow and dumped the garbage into it, totally oblivious to the big man standing in the shadows, not ten feet away, staring at him. Malachi could hear the man's wheezy breath as he bent down to retrieve the wet lid. The man slapped the lid back on and then went back in through the gate, latching it forcefully before tromping back to his kitchen door. Great situational awareness, man, Malachi thought. Really aware of your surroundings. No wonder so many people got mugged up here on Capitol Hill—they deserved it. He moved out of the shadows and walked down to his garage, suddenly confident that he could get out of there without being seen.

He went through the fence gate and entered the garage through the backyard door. He cracked open the truck's driver side door, which turned on the cabin light, and turned the headlight switch to the left, turning on a small white light over the truck bed. He went around and climbed up into the bed of the pickup and unscrewed the garage door's lightbulb so it would not come on when he activated the electric door opener. He then lifted the Metro yellow flasher unit down from the rafters of the garage. He mounted the flasher unit on its magnetic base and draped the wire down to the opening in the rear window. He reached back up into the rafters and pulled down the magnetic signs for the doors, the ones displaying the logo of the Washington Metropolitan Transit Authority on them. He got down again and slapped on the Metro signs, then threaded the flasher wire through the back window but did not plug it in. He then turned off the bed light, started the truck, and hit the remote switch to open the electric door. He backed cautiously out into the alley, took one last look around, commanded the garage door to shut, and drove down the alley to East Capitol Street. He crossed East Capitol and went down to Independence, then turned right. Once on Independence, it was a straight shot downtown to the Fourteenth Street Bridge approaches and the safety of Arlington.

*   *   *

AN HOUR LATER, Malachi stood at the balcony glass doors of the one-bedroom apartment, sipping on some high-octane shaved ice. The apartment had a truly stupendous view of the darkened office building across Ninth Street, but that suited him just fine. This place was a bolt-hole, not a home. Not that he had ever really had a home. The apartment management had assigned him a two-week temporary parking permit for the F-250. After that, he would have to figure something else out, because the duty manager reminded him that in Arlington, apartment buildings had to report vehicles garaged to the county tax office. But hell, in two weeks . . .

He thought about Miss Snow, his brain running very smooth with the help of the Harper. He'd seen a movie once where you knew that someone was trying to kill the good guy, but you never suspected that it was the beautiful actress that the guy falls in love with. She was entirely too sweet and too beautiful for the thought to even cross your mind. Until she pulled out this goddamn .22 automatic with a long barrel. He remembered the whole audience groaning out loud when they saw the piece. He was having the same problem getting his brain around the idea that the captain had maybe hired somebody, and that the somebody might be this Snow woman. Admittedly, discovering the surveillance out on his street had helped to concentrate his mind, but that still didn't necessarily mean that there was a contractor out there. And yet Malachi had fired a round into the cave to see what might be stirring in there, and now there were cops, or other people, sitting in a van across his street. That round could really have spooked the captain and the great man, so who knows what they might resort to. They had a lot to lose, both of them.

So go see. Go do a little surveillance of your own, see if this Snow woman is a player. And also go see if her boyfriend, the Navy guy, is in the game. By God, that would be a pretty play, the captain using a Navy guy and an ex-NIS agent to clean up the trail. Who the hell would ever suspect that? I would, he thought grimly. But, yeah, tomorrow he would go see what Miss Snow and company were up to. Go on over to Yuppieville tomorrow morning, check things out. No, it would be Saturday. Tomorrow night, then. First go to Old Town, see if she was with Collins, *then* ease over to Georgetown, maybe get into that alley. For that, he would need the truck. No: For Georgetown, he would use the telephone company van. Miss Snow, he thought, as he chewed on a piece of fiery ice. Miss Gracie Snow. I know where you live. I wonder if your phones are working.

291

52

AFTER SPENDING SATURDAY touring the historical town of Harpers Ferry and the haunting grounds of the Antietam battlefield park, Grace and Dan had driven up the Shenandoah Valley to Berryville and then through the rolling Virginia countryside to the Ashby Gap, where Route 50 cut through the Blue Ridge range as it headed east toward Middleburg and, eventually, Washington. After topping Ashby Gap, Dan pulled off into the booming metropolis of Paris, Virginia, population about eighty-six. Paris was a one-street village whose most famous landmark was the renowned Ashby Inn, located at the eastern end of the street.

Dan parked the Suburban in the lot behind the inn while Grace went in to see about their reservations and to use the powder room to change into something more suitable for dinner than her slacks and sweater outfit. Dan put a tie on in the car, felt the stubble of an emerging five o'clock shadow, got out, and slipped on a blue blazer. The day had been—what were the right words—increasingly exhilarating. Grace had started out being relatively serious about the sight-seeing, but then, after lunch, he had detected a change and the beginning of some subtle flirtation—subliminal looks, several occasions where they ended up standing well within each other's personal space, and a growing consciousness on his part that she was acting much differently from the all-business Ms. Snow of the NIS. He walked around the gravel parking lot for a few more minutes, kicking absently at small stones, before going inside. He was beginning to wish that he had tried for a room.

He waited for Grace in the reading room to the right of the front door, along with four other people waiting for a table. After fifteen minutes, Grace came in and lit up the room with her smile. Most of the men he had seen coming in for dinner were dressed in suits, and Dan had begun to feel somewhat out of place in his corduroy slacks, gray shirt, and plain blazer. But Grace more than made up for him: She was decked out in a beautifully tailored cream-colored sand-washed silk crepe de chine suit, the skirt of which was cut just above her knees. She wore the flowing jacket over a white silk knit blouse, without jewelry, and she had done some magic with cosmetics that he was sure rendered him happily invisible.

The waitress led them downstairs to the lower dining room. The Ashby Inn was an eighteenth-century restoration that advertised itself as a bed-and-breakfast, but it was much closer to the French concept of an auberge than a simple bed-and-breakfast. There were several small suites upstairs and an outstanding full-service restaurant downstairs. The lower dining room was done in stone, with low-hanging hand-hewn beams, and had two fireplaces. There were eight tables in the lower dining area, which looked like it had originally been part of a bank barn a few hundred years ago. Dan and Grace were ensconced in a corner table by one of the fireplaces. A lone bartender was all flying arms and glasses in the corner. It being a Saturday night, there was a good crowd, and the staff was bustling about at high speed.

"I think I've read about this place," Dan said, looking around. Every man in the place had been stealing surreptitious looks at Grace across the room since they had been seated.

"It's been voted one of the ten best inns in America," Grace said. "More than once. I've never eaten here, but the food's supposed to be exceptional."

"Hopefully not that minced cuisine," Dan muttered, examining the menu suspiciously. Grace laughed at him.

"I don't think so, and I believe that's *cuisine minceur* you're worried about. The great big plates and the little bitty portions laid out as flowers?" Her green eyes were sparkling, and he was having trouble concentrating on the details of ordering dinner.

"That's the one. Commie chow," he growled.

"Now you sound like Snapper."

"Snapper eats out of a dog bowl. Mostly, I'm hungry. I mean, Harpers Ferry, Sharpsburg, the Antietam battlefield all in one day?"

"You're perhaps forgetting the little snack at the inn in Harpers Ferry?"

"Details, woman," he replied. "Hey, this looks good. And smells good. Just like you."

She smiled back at him with another brilliant flash of her green eyes; the lawyerish-looking man at the next table put his wineglass down in his butter plate, a move not unnoticed by his wife.

"Wine, innkeeper," Dan commanded in a stage whisper. The bartender, ten feet away, picked right up on it. "Aye, your worship," he said in his best tavern accent as he tugged at an imaginary forelock. "Wine 'tis, an' a plague on yon feckless wenches."

Dan grinned as a mildly red-faced waitress came right over with a wine list. Dan selected an Australian chardonnay, which was brought to the table by the bartender in short order. The waitress returned and took their dinner orders. When she had left, Dan raised his glass in a toast.

"To the first good weekend in a long, long time," he announced.

"Yes, I'll drink to that," she said, looking at him over her glass. "I'd forgotten how beautiful the Virginia countryside is at this time of year. Especially up here in the Blue Ridge Mountains. I'd often thought of getting a country place up here, except—"

"Except that the commute would be horrible, and the Blue Ridge Mountains are no place to be if you're alone. Too many ghosts up here."

"I felt them at Antietam," she said "It reminded me of one of the Bruce Catton Civil War books—the one that had a title with the word *stillness* in it."

"*Stillness at Appomattox*," he prompted.

"Yes. There *was* such a stillness there. Did you notice how even the tourists spoke softly?"

"Nearly twenty-five thousand were killed or wounded on that field; I've always thought their ghosts are sleeping lightly just beneath all that tall grass. I keep going back, and I can't really tell you why. You ought to see it on a fall Sunday afternoon; there's a mist that comes off Antietam Creek that'll raise the hair on your neck."

"I can well believe it," she said as the waitress brought bread and topped up their wineglasses. "Still, there's a certain charm to this area of Virginia— all the history, the Washington scene, this countryside: I could never go back to Boston. But I don't know what I'm going to do next."

"Go work for a think tank. Wait for a change in administrations," he said.

"Where will you go next?"

"I have no idea—literally. We get to submit a preference card, which allows us to specify which is the most important thing on our wish list: the kind of ship, the coast, or the job. Since I'm slated for command, I've chosen the type of ship—a destroyer type—as the priority. I could end up Atlantic or Pacific, or even overseas."

"And then?"

"Ah. That's the question. I'll be very close to my twenty-year mark. I've always thought it would just go on forever. But now—"

"What would you want to do if you got out at twenty?"

"You mean when I grow up?" he said. She laughed. The waitress returned with dinner, and they broke off speculating about the future to enjoy the Ashby's first-class cookery. Dan ordered a second bottle of wine, and they lingered over crepes suzette after the main course. Dan was grateful there was no band lined up; the warmth and coziness of the dining room, the fireplaces, and a congenial crowd all made for a delightful ambience that did not need, in his opinion, to be spoiled by some aspiring singer. Besides, just the sight of Grace in war paint and an extremely alluring dress was distraction enough.

He watched her as the evening subsided into a comfortable buzz amid the wine and good food. She was almost radiant, her cheeks the slightest bit flushed, her eyes dancing, her hands animated. The day had been so pleasant: They had been interested in the same things, admired or commented on the same aspects of everything they had seen, and laughed at the same foibles of other people or places. He realized that his answer to her earlier question about the future had been a bit disingenuous: He simply could not quite figure out how to put her into the picture. But he realized that he had become entirely entranced by this woman, felt like he had known her for a very long time, and wanted her in any of his possible futures. He put his wineglass down and almost upset it.

"I guess I better eighty-six on the vino," he said, eyeing the treacherous glass. "We have a long drive back to town."

She gave him a speculative look across the table, then put her own wineglass down and took his hand across the table.

"Not necessarily," she said quietly, giving him a very direct look.

"Oh?" he replied, trying not to squeak.

"I may have booked a room here. It is a *bed*-and-breakfast, or so they advertise."

He grinned in spite of himself. "When the hell did you manage that?"

"At Harpers Ferry. While you were working on that *minceur* of apple pie à la mode. I took a shot, and they had a cancellation—she said they're normally booked here weeks ahead."

"Wahoo," he said, looking around for the waitress. She was not in evidence at the moment, but the bartender, who might have been watching them, raised his eyebrows at him.

"Innkeeper," Dan declared, "be there cognac?"

They went up to the room an hour later, Dan trying very hard not to grin from ear to ear as he followed Grace up the stairs from the dining room, fully aware of the envious stares from the remaining male patrons. Their room was on the second floor, in the back of the building, and their bedroom windows overlooked a spectacular panorama of open mountain meadows interlaced with a series of cattle ponds stretching down the side of Ashby Gap, seemingly for miles and miles. A full moon was suspended over the Blue Ridge Mountains, painting each of the ponds a bright, glimmering silver. By unspoken consent, they did not turn on any lights, just sat down on the bed, hand in hand, absorbing the view. When she finally turned to him, the sweetness of her kiss took his breath away, and then they began the glorious exploration, fingertips, hands, and lips, the momentary awkwardness of tugging and undoing of clothes, until they finally stretched out next to each other in the moonlight. He ran his fingertips over her whole body as she relaxed on the covers, wondering at the satiny feel of her skin and his own tumbling emotions as he held back just to look at her. Then he moved, pushing her gently down onto her back and sliding his body between her legs, suspending his weight so that he covered her but barely touched her. He kissed her again and she held his face against her lips, first searching and then demanding. He kissed her lips and then her face and then her throat as she guided his head lower, onto her breasts, her hardened nipples, and then back to her lips again. They both had an enormous reservoir of pent-up need to control, and they could both experience the luxuriant sensation of satisfying their hunger, pacing the need, knowing instinctively that when they eventually lost all that control, it was going to be sweet and good. He shifted his body to lay one muscular thigh directly between her legs, and she gripped with her own thighs and began to move, moaning softly now, hands down at her sides, her head thrown back. He let her feel his strength and then started all over again, kissing her throat, her breasts, and then working lower, sliding his thigh away and replacing it with his mouth, focusing every ounce of his energy on her until she arched her back and cried aloud. Before she really had time to come down or even catch her breath, he pushed back up and entered her, holding her knees up with his hands and going as deep as he could while she groaned with the feel of it. He held her that way for almost a minute, until she began to move, and then it went hard and fast, a rising frenzy of powerful thrusting, her legs slipping behind his hips, locking him in while they fed their individual needs, so long deprived. When he came, she didn't stop, but gripped him tighter and drew a great gasp from him before letting him subside, first on top and then alongside of her, his head on her breast, her fingers in his hair and her lips on his forehead with soft murmurs of love, comfort, and the certain knowledge that the entire night lay before them.

After a few minutes, when he thought she had gone to sleep, she pulled him up so that they were face-to-face. Eyes wide, she looked expectantly at him. She seemed to be waiting for him to say something. He hesitated for just a fraction of a second as the name Claire spirited across his mind, but then he said the words, realizing that as he said them he wanted to say them, wanted to tell her.

"I've fallen in love with you, Grace Ellen Snow."

She sat up then and gently pushed him back down onto the covers, then slid her body on top of his. She took his face between her hands, her eyes lustrous in the moonlight, her perfumed hair framing her face.

"I know how hard that was to say," she whispered.

"No it wasn't. Well, a little. But not because of you."

"If you loved her, you can't just throw away all those memories and feelings. I guess what I'm saying is that there's time enough to share, and I don't ever expect you to forget her memory or the love you had. That's part of you, and that's one of the reasons I've fallen in love with you." She bent down to kiss him, then melted down on top of him, her face buried in his shoulder, her breathing softening into sleep. He lay awake for nearly an hour, reveling in the glorious treasure life had just handed him, too happy to sleep.

53

AT JUST BEFORE midnight on Saturday, Malachi took one of the last Metro trains going into the city. He got off one station later at Clarendon. He was wearing khaki slacks, a short-sleeved shirt, a dark windbreaker, and a pair of high-topped tan leather boots. The train was practically empty at this time of night, and Malachi was alone in the car except for six teenaged girls, who burst into fits of giggling interspersed with furtive looks in his direction. It would have been fun to produce a chain saw, he thought. At the Clarendon station, he rode the escalator up to the concrete island between Wilson and Clarendon boulevards. Crossing the street, he walked back up along the row of Vietnamese shops and restaurants and turned right on Hudson Street. He walked down one block to a small run-down-looking house nestled in an alley next to an apartment building. Behind the house was a single-car garage with a sagging roof and a visible port list, whose door opened onto the alley. A single streetlight, which was hanging at an odd angle from a heavily wired telephone pole, left the front of the garage in shadow. He paused to look down the alley but saw nothing moving in the light. He checked the street and the sidewalks, but no one was visible. This neighborhood was not necessarily an area where Caucasian strangers were welcome after about ten o'clock at night, the Vietnamese having several interesting operations of their own going. He could hear a small dog yapping away somewhere nearby, and the smell of Oriental food hung in the air. A brave dog, he thought, to bark so long and loud near an entire block of Vietnamese restaurants.

Checking again to see that there were no lights on in the house, he walked down the alley to the garage, fished out a set of keys, unlocked a padlock, and swung back the two graffiti-sprayed wooden doors, whose windows had been long since painted over. Nearly filling the garage was the telephone van. Leaving the doors open, he went around to the back of the van and unlocked the back doors. He extracted a set of coveralls emblazoned with the logo of the Chesapeake and Potomac Telephone Company, took off the windbreaker, and put the coveralls on over his street clothes. He fished a white hard hat out of the van, closed the back doors, and opened up the driver's side.

The side doors of the van were painted with C & P logos, and there were three radio antennas on the roof. The interior of the van behind the front seat was filled with cabinets and shelves, holding nearly all the tools and equipment of a genuine telephone repair truck. Interspersed among all the legitimate telephone company equipment were some interesting devices for gaining access to houses, a long-range video camera, two handguns, a pair of Army FM radios, a receiving unit and tape recorder for inside bug installations, and a flasher unit like the one he had for his Metro truck. He set up the flasher unit on the roof, plugged it in for a quick op test, and then unplugged it. He started the van, drove out into the alley, and stopped. He got back out, looked around one more time to make sure he was not being watched, and closed and locked the garage doors. He then got back in and headed for Wilson Boulevard, where he turned right and then did a U-turn back onto Clarendon, which took him back down toward Rosslyn.

He checked the glove compartment as he drove down Clarendon Boulevard and found an envelope with about an eighth of an inch of cash wrapped in a rubber band inside. He smiled. He had acquired the van three years ago from another security consultant, who said that he had acquired it from yet another contractor who had been on the Iran-Contra project, working for persons unspecified. Malachi had paid fifteen thousand dollars cash for it and all the equipment, with the understanding that, from time to time, certain parties whose names would remain anonymous might need to use the van. If these certain parties did use the van, they would leave a rental fee, in cash, in the glove compartment. So far, he had collected three envelopes in the past three years.

The van came complete with telephone company registration, which was good enough to withstand a streetside examination. The radio was tuned to the dispatch frequencies of the C & P Operations Center, so it could lend some audio credence if a cop was to stop him. Completing the outfit was a clip-on badge with an expert forgery of a C & P telephone company identification, complete with picture, which he attached to his coveralls pocket as he drove. And if all that failed and the van was ever picked up, there were two four-inch-diameter PVC pipes buried in the shelving structure. They contained rotary motion fuses and enough thermite to seriously disrupt a truly intrusive search.

His major vulnerability would be if another C & P crew was to stop when Malachi was working a project, but so far, that had never happened. He used the van sparingly, usually at night, and was careful to park it out of sight and off any main streets. But it had been an invaluable base of operations for break-ins, surveillance, or monitoring operations, all of which were services he offered to his retainer clients, especially some of the larger lobbying firms. It was amazing how many individuals these people were interested in putting under surveillance, and doubly amazing what some of those surveillances had produced. He had one videotape of a State Department official in drag making out in the front seat of a Fiat with a man from the Hungarian embassy. He had considered sending that one into the "funniest home video" show on the TV.

Earlier that day, he had made a swing down Prince Street in Old Town and confirmed that the woman's car was parked out in front of Collins's house. So he should be clear. He drove down Clarendon Boulevard to the high-rise district of Rosslyn and then worked his way down to Key Bridge, crossed the Potomac, and wound his way up through the still-crowded bar, disco, and pub scene of lower Georgetown to Grace Snow's street. Two cops parked along M Street actually waved at him as he went by, and he dutifully waved back. By 12:40, he was cruising by her house to confirm that her car was not there. Her house was dark, except for a front porch light. Slowing down, he circled the block and came to the alley he had noticed before. Now he could read the sign; it was named Pomander Walk. He slowed way down and turned into the alley, which was lined with diminutive carriage houses and garages converted to living quarters and apartments. The alley ended in a turnaround area right in the middle of the block between P Street and Volta Place, where there was a garage presently being converted into living quarters. Keeping the engine quiet, he pulled the van into the turnaround area, backed it up against the scaffolding on an almost-complete brick wall, and shut it down. Putting on his hard hat, he turned on the interior light, rolled down the driver's side window, turned up the dispatch radio volume a little, and listened for a couple of minutes while he pretended to scribble something on a clipboard. All the windows of the houses along Pomander were dark, although almost every house had a porch or security light shining into the alley itself. Malachi sniffed contemptuously at all the lights: To anyone looking into the alley, all those lights shining at one another had the effect of throwing the lower portions of all the houses into deep shadow.

He had a cover story all set: There was a telephone pole at the very back of the turnaround area, right next to the green wooden gate and the brick wall that, by his calculations, bounded Miss Snow's backyard. Her address was 2135 P Street. The green plastic trash receptacle right next to the gate had the number 2135 painted on it. For the first ten minutes or so, he would open the back doors of the truck, turn on the lights in the back of the van, and lay out some equipment. He would take some test equipment over to the amplifier box at the base of the pole and pretend to analyze some kind of a problem. He had to do that long enough to convince anyone who had gotten up to see who was out there that he was legitimate and that he was going to be out there for a while. He wanted any watchers to get bored and go back to bed. There was no sign that anyone was watching, but Malachi had to assume that there was at least one little old lady who was even now peeking out her window at him. He did not want a cop car coming back in here to check him out. If someone did come out to talk to him, he had some electronics mumbo jumbo ready about a sector circuit fault, and he would say that he'd eventually have to climb the pole to find it.

After twenty minutes of pretending to chase down the sector circuit problem, he put on a climbing harness at the back of the truck, strapped some side spikes to his boots, clipped a satchel of equipment to the harness, and went up the pole. He had done this more than once during surveillance operations, and he knew it was no big deal once you reached the installed climbing spikes about ten feet off the ground. He clung to the pole for about five minutes in front of an equipment panel, casually examining the windows that fronted the turnaround area for faces or other signs of movement. From his vantage point, he could also see into the windows of the houses behind the line of brick walls surrounding the turnaround area. Everything seemed pretty normal, and there were no dogs, thank God. Taking one last look around, he descended the pole to the top of the wall, stepped out onto the wall, and then dropped behind it into the backyard of 2135 P Street. He immediately unclipped the satchel and dropped it behind the gate, then opened the alley gate and walked back to the truck. If anyone was watching, the drop into the yard would have been suspicious, but not if he came right back out. They'd think the problem must be in that house or yard. He made two more trips through the gate, reappearing each time within a minute. On the first trip, he left a second satchel. On the second trip, a bag of tools went into the yard. He then returned to the front seat of the van and pretended to talk on the radio before getting back out and going back through the gate, this time leaving it ajar behind him.

Now he had to move fast. Clutching the three bags, he trotted up to the back door and checked for alarm systems, finding none. Leaving the bags on the porch, he went around to the side of the house and examined the telephone line where it came down from the overhead wire insulator. Normal wire, no signs of anti-intrusion cladding; no disturbance pads on the window glass. From the back porch, he could see into what looked like the kitchen pantry, but there were no red LED lights. He opened the equipment bag and took out a pair of thin leather gloves and a roll of duct tape. The back door had a window divided into six panes. He bent over the back door and taped over the small square of glass nearest the lock, then broke it with his fist. He extracted the sheet of tape with the shards of glass stuck to it and put it in the bag. Reaching through the broken window, he opened the dead bolt and let himself into the house. He found himself in the pantry, with the kitchen three feet away. He paused to listen, but the house felt empty. He looked back out into the yard, but all was quiet out there, too.

He figured he had about ten minutes' stay time in the house. Keeping all the lights off, he made a fast walking tour, using the light from the streetlights out front. He inspected the front and back, upstairs and downstairs, noting the layout of the rooms, where the telephones were, verifying that there were no alarm-system control panels. He moved a small bookcase aside and opened the door to the basement steps, although he did not go down. The stairway was cluttered and obviously not used. He took in the tasteful furniture, the thick rugs, and the polished floors. Using a tiny black Maglite, he searched the kitchen for the key rack, finally finding what looked like the spare house key, which he tested in the front and back door locks. He pocketed this key and what looked like the key to the back gate.

Retrieving the second equipment bag, he went back upstairs to what looked like a spare bedroom, which was being used mostly for storage. Getting down on his hands and knees, he shone the flashlight around the baseboards until he found a phone jack. From the bag, he extracted a small white box that had a male telephone connector sticking out of the center. He snapped the connector into the phone jack, felt with his fingernail for a dip switch, and moved the switch. Then he placed two cardboard boxes of what felt like books in front of the wall jack, retrieved the bag, and left the room.

He stopped in the study area and, again using the tiny flashlight, scanned the paperwork scattered all over the table, taking care to keep the light shielded from the windows. There was a picture of a distinguished-looking older man in what looked like a doctor's coat, and another picture of a very impressive town house. The answering machine's red light was blinking, but he had learned not to touch answering machines after one demanded a code and then sent an alarm signal to a monitoring company when he couldn't produce the code. He touched none of the papers, but he looked through everything that was faceup, which is where he found the notepad with his name on it. He stopped breathing for a moment, but there it was: Malachi Ward, followed by the abbreviation *Capt.* and the word *Army.* There were some mostly illegible notes and some doodles on the page, and below them was the word *invisible*, underlined, followed by the words *credit system.* But it was the final line of three words that got his immediate attention: *Captain. Target. Ward.*

Son of a bitch! he muttered out loud, then quickly looked around as if to see if anyone had heard him. He looked at his watch and then snapped the light off. He went back to the kitchen and checked the backyard windows, but there was still nothing moving. Time to go. He went to the pantry and retrieved the third bag, which made a gurgling noise when he picked it up. He placed it on the basement stairway among all the clutter. Then he walked out the back door and all the way to the van, where he went through the talk-on-the-radio drill. Then he returned to the back door. He knelt down, opened a bag, and took out a measuring tape and a screwdriver-sized wood pry. He pried off the four segments of molding of the broken window and quickly measured the broken pane. Then he went back out to the truck in the alley. He slid into the front seat and pretended once more to talk on the radio for the benefit of any spectators, then returned to the back porch, where he opened the bag containing a taped bundle of windowpanes of various sizes. He fished in it for a pane of approximately the right size. None of the glass was new, so there would be no bright shiny pane among all the older ones. Working by the light of the streetlight from the alley, he found one that was pretty close, cut it to size with a glass cutter and wide-mouthed pliers, and installed it with four glass points, using a rubber-tipped screwdriver to set the points. Then he used a tack hammer to renail the molding. He rubbed the edges with a swipe of dust from the pantry shelves so that it would blend right in.

He put the tools back, made sure he still had the keys, and then closed and locked the back door. He was feeling pretty good now, his breathing strong and deep, and adrenaline running through him like the whiskey did, amplified by a slow fuse of fury in his stomach at what he'd found on that notepad. *Captain. Target. Ward.* Trust your instincts, Monroney always said. And his instincts had been right the fuck on. Except that now he knew about it. Forewarned, Brother Malachi was not going to be some sitting duck behind the wire. Brother Malachi was going to be out there, beyond the perimeter, in the weeds, ass in the grass, on the move. He had the key, he knew the layout, knew where the phone systems were, and had everything he would need already stashed in the house.

He walked quickly through the garden to the back gate, where he tested the gate key while still in the shadows of the backyard. It was a latch lock on the inside and a key lock on the outside. Bingo. He went through the gate, closed it, and walked casually to the truck: No utility workmen ever walked fast. He did the talk-on-the-radio drama one last time and then took his time wrapping things up, pretending to check the box at the base of the pole one more time with a repairman's handset cradled on his shoulder before closing up the truck and driving out of Po-faggoty Walk.

He started feeling really good as he headed down Volta toward Wisconsin Avenue. He had been right about all that "relax" shit from the captain, right about the surveillance, and right about their being another player. So now she's probably on a weekend with her pretty-boy officer friend, he mused. A little forty-eight before she gets down to business. She'd be back, probably Sunday night. So would he. Then we'll find out who's the fucking target, missy. See, I've been down your spider hole, Miss Snow. You're good-looking and you've got money, Miss Snow, but you sure as shit are no pro, Miss Snow. Hell, it even had rhythm. He was actually looking forward to it. He smiled a feral smile in the darkness.

DAN DROVE GRACE back to Old Town in midafternoon after a late rising at the Ashby Inn and an indulgence in the Ashby's lush Sunday brunch. They had tried to walk off some of the damage by doing an hour's worth of window-shopping in Middleburg on the way back, but it had still been a battle to stay awake through the rolling green countryside. From Middleburg, Dan took Route 50 through Aldie before settling reluctantly into the traffic of the northern Virginia suburbs of Washington. Dan opted for the GW Parkway rather than the Beltway to get back to Old Town, and the scenic Sunday-afternoon descent along the Potomac palisades provided a perfect cap to a perfect weekend. They did not speak very much as he drove down along the river; instead, they held hands across the front seat of the Suburban.

Grace did not come in when they got to his house on Prince Street. She gave him a quick kiss and then moved the BMW out to make room for the Suburban before driving away with a wave. Dan went in to change to casual clothes and do last week's laundry. He was considering a stint on the river to make amends for the weekend's gluttony when the phone rang. It was Grace.

"There's a message from Captain Vann."

Dan's heart sank a little. The Hardin case had not even crossed his mind since Saturday morning. She picked up on his silence.

"I know," she said. "It's like welcome back to the world, isn't it? But he's set us up to talk to Mrs. Hardin—tonight. Both of us, he said. In District Heights, wherever that is. I think it's Maryland."

"Well, sort of," Dan said. "It's kind of an extension of Southeast Washington."

"Oh."

"Yeah, that's Injun country. We better take my Suburban."

"Then you'll go?"

"I think we have to. We asked him to set this up. And you're not going into District Heights at night by yourself, that's for damn sure. What time?"

"At seven-thirty. I have the address, and it's in the street-map book. It doesn't look complicated."

He thought about it for a moment. District Heights. He realized that he had never even been into the southeastern part of Washington, that area between the actual District line in Anacostia and the Capitol Beltway. "And Vann will be there, right?" he asked.

"Yes. Look, after what happened Friday, I can—"

"To hell with them," Dan interrupted. "I'm getting suspicious about those guys. I sort of understood the political play when this all started, but now that there's a flag officer involved, there seem to be an awful lot of draw-bridges going up all of a sudden. If Elizabeth Hardin confided in her mother, we may actually learn something pretty interesting."

"If she'll really talk to us."

"Yeah. Big *if*. I'll be over there in an hour."

55

Malachi had queried the line monitor in Snow's house three times that Sunday afternoon. He had a set routine to query the monitor: As soon as the phone started to ring, he would press the pound key. This activated the monitor, which would swallow the ring signal so that the target phone would remain silent. After the second ring signal went out, Malachi punched in a three-digit code, at which point the monitor would respond: one beep for nothing on the tap, two beeps if there was. If the box had something, Malachi would enter a different three-digit code, at which time the monitor would play back what it had on the tape. On the second try, he intercepted Vann's call to her machine. On his fourth try, he listened to Grace's call to Dan.

Vann's message had revealed that he wanted all three of them to meet with a Mrs. Hardin in District Heights. Malachi knew that had to be Lieutenant Hardin's mother, but that wasn't what interested him. This Captain Vann, whoever he was, had also said he had more information on Ward for them. The mention of his name confirmed his suspicions that Snow might be a hitter. He wondered if this Captain Vann was an EA, some new player in the Navy system. It was also bad luck that Snow had made a call out after this captain had called in: The monitor had a callback feature that would dial the last number it had monitored, but Grace's call had deleted the incoming phone number. But whoever Vann was, he was passing them information on him, targeting information no doubt. But it was also clear they were assuming Malachi didn't know anything about them, which gave him an enormous advantage.

He made his move right after sunset. They would probably allow an hour to get out to District Heights from Georgetown, which meant a 6:30 departure. District Heights—he doubted that either of those two had ever set foot in that part of Washington. He almost prayed they would have a flat tire, so that they might get to enjoy a unique intercultural experience. Dressing in dark clothes and wearing his black windbreaker, dark leather gloves, and a dark gray fedora, he took the Metro down to Rosslyn and then walked down past the Key Bridge Marriott and across the Key Bridge into Georgetown. It was shaping up to be a dark, moonless night, and the lights from the ornate streetlamps on the Key Bridge completely obscured the waters of the Potomac River beneath the high arches of the bridge.

Everything he would need tonight was already stashed inside Snow's house, which allowed him to enter the Cloisters neighborhood without any satchels or otherwise suspicious-looking bags. He walked purposefully, as if he belonged there, and when he got to Snow's house, he let himself in through the wrought-iron gate, ignored the car parked on the apron, walked right up to the front door, and let himself in with the key. He closed the door, pulled the curtains on the front windows, and turned on a table lamp, then he went into the kitchen to see if she kept any decent whiskey in the house. He would have to remember to retrieve that monitor; he wouldn't need it after tonight, and the damn things were actually hard to get.

56

DAN TOOK PENNSYLVANIA Avenue all the way through town until he could see the Capitol building, at which point he cut down on 7th Street to Independence Avenue to get around the Capitol. Turning left on Independence, he was able to rejoin Pennsylvania behind the Library of Congress and proceed into Southeast Washington. Neither of them spoke much as he piloted the big Suburban through increasingly more dangerous-looking neighborhoods, both of them keenly aware of the openly hostile stares they were getting from the street corners every time they had to stop for a red light. This was one of the times Dan wished he had owned a gun, because a lot of the people out on these streets looked like they did. When they finally hit the District line, Pennsylvania Avenue widened out into the four-lanes of Maryland Route 4.

"We're looking for Silver Hill Road now," Grace said. "We'll go left."

With Grace reading from a three-by-five card with Vann's directions, Dan got them to the Hardin's house ten minutes early. He found a parking place big enough for the Suburban in front of what looked like an unmarked cop car. He pulled in and shut down. The address they were looking for, number 1117, was the third house in a row of four two-story brownstones joined together. There was a wrought-iron fence running in front of all four units, with a banked front yard that required two sets of steps to get to the front porch of each house. There were lights on in the downstairs of number 1117, and the front porch light was also on. Only one of the other four had any lights showing. There did not seem to be any people or even very much traffic on this street. They looked at each other and then got out of the car.

Dan had decided to wear his service dress blues. While it was true he was no longer officially on the case, Mrs. Hardin would remember him in uniform from Philadelphia. He left his cap in the car, however. Grace was wearing a subdued gray wool ankle-length jumper over a deep V-neckline, long-sleeved white blouse. He almost took her arm as they went through the squeaky gate and up the steps, but he didn't. She caught his hesitation and smiled at him, and he suddenly felt a lot better about being here. When they arrived at the front door, Moses Vann, dressed in a three-piece charcoal gray suit, opened it for them and invited them in. He took them into the living room, which was to the right of the front door.

The house was warm and smelled of fresh coffee and flowers, of which were was a great abundance stationed in vases and glass pitchers all around the room. The living room was larger than Dan expected, with a piano in one corner, a couch with end tables, three upholstered chairs, and a small fireplace with flowers in it at one end. On the mantel above the fireplace, there were two eight-by-ten black-and-white photographs, one a full-figure picture of a very pretty young woman in a Navy ensign's service dress whites. She was standing with a beaming Mrs. Hardin. The other photo was of a bright-looking young man dressed in what Dan thought was the shirt, tie, and coat of navy service dress blues. He swallowed as he recognized who that was.

Mrs. Hardin was seated in the chair nearest the fireplace, and Vann showed them to the couch before sitting down in one of the other chairs. There was a dining room off the living room, and a swinging door led to what Dan figured was the kitchen. It sounded like there was someone in the kitchen. Mrs. Hardin gave them each a reserved greeting but did not get up, and it was obvious that she was looking to Vann to steer the conversation. Before he could begin, a very pretty teenaged girl came out of the kitchen with a small tray that contained three cups of coffee, spoons, and cream and sugar in silver serving pieces. The girl brought the tray over to the couch, put it down on the coffee table, and left without a word or without looking either one of them in the eye. Dan thanked her retreating back.

"You find it okay?" Vann began, shucking his jacket.

"No problem, Captain," Dan said. "We took Pennsylvania all the way from Georgetown."

"Ah," Vann said. "The scenic route. Have some coffee. You probably need it." He helped himself to a cup.

Mrs. Hardin looked into the middle distance, her face set in a motionless mask, as Dan and Grace leaned forward to fix their coffee. Grace was closer and took over, then had to ask Dan what he liked in his coffee, making him realize for an instant that they still had a lot to learn about each other. Grace passed him a cup as the silence in the room built, but as soon as she had fixed her own, Vann started.

"Angela here," he said, speaking almost as if Mrs. Hardin was not in the room, "she's agreed to talk to us tonight. It's not something she wants to do. But I've told her it's important, that there's a chance that one or both of you might be able to find out who's responsible for what happened to her children."

Dan looked at Vann. "Does she understand that both of us are working unofficially at the moment?" he asked.

Vann nodded. "All three of us are working unofficially. That's why she agreed to talk to us. I told her about the heat you've been getting, and the fact that Miss Snow here lost her job because of this case." He glanced over at Grace to make sure that she wouldn't contradict him, but Grace apparently understood the gambit. She nodded and looked down at the floor. "I've shared with her informally some of the aspects of the case as we know it so far. So what I'd suggest is that you go ahead and ask your questions, Commander."

Dan put his coffee cup down and looked directly at Mrs. Hardin for the first time. She continued to stare straight ahead.

"Mrs. Hardin, again I want to extend my condolences. I won't sit here and try to tell you that I can appreciate your losses, because I lost my wife before we ever got the chance to have and raise some kids."

Mrs. Hardin looked over at him with a flicker of interest. Dan pressed ahead.

"My questions center on your daughter."

"My 'Lizbeth."

"Yes, ma'am."

"She was a good girl, the best girl," Mrs. Hardin said.

"Yes, ma'am," Dan said. "But did she ever reveal to you that she might be seeing someone, someone fairly senior, or important, in the Navy? Dating him even?"

Mrs. Hardin shot a look at Vann but then shook her head.

"No," she said defiantly. "Never did."

Vann leaned forward. "Angela," he said with a hint of exasperation.

Mrs. Hardin looked down at the floor for a long minute and then sighed. " 'Lizbeth never did," she repeated. "But Wesley, he told me somethin'. Right after the funeral, he told me somethin'."

"Mrs. Hardin, did he tell you who it was?" Grace asked, speaking for the first time. "Did he tell you a name?"

Mrs. Hardin shook her head slowly. "Only that he knew who it was and that he was gonna go see the man, find out some things. He was hot on it."

"Why was he hot about it?" Dan asked.

Mrs. Hardin looked over at Vann, who nodded. For the first time, she looked right at Dan.

" 'Cause he was white," she declared. "Wesley thought that was about the wrongest thing she could do, be seein' some white guy." She paused, took a deep breath, apparently somewhat embarrassed by her outburst. "I'm sorry, but that's what it was."

"I can understand that, Mrs. Hardin," Dan said. "But did he suspect or did he say anything that would make you think he suspected that Elizabeth's accident might be related to her relationship with this white man?" Dan asked.

"What do you mean?" she asked, looking first at Dan and then again to Vann for guidance.

"Did he say anything that would lead you to believe that what happened to your daughter might not have been an accident?" Grace asked.

Mrs. Hardin's expression changed to one of alarm. "Moses?" she cried. "Moses, what's this girl sayin'? What's she sayin' here about 'Lizbeth?"

Vann bit his lip and looked fixedly at the floor. Dan realized that the two of them must have talked long and hard before they arrived but that Vann had not raised this possibility.

"Angela," Vann said finally, "the police have no concrete evidence that what happened to Elizabeth was anything but an accident. But we're trying to figure out why someone would want to kill Wesley. Because of some tips we've had, it's possible, just possible, now, that Wesley *thought* her death was not an accident and that maybe he braced somebody up about it. That somebody might have had something to do with what happened to Wesley."

"The connection is Navy, Mrs. Hardin," Grace said. "Wesley was probably killed on a Navy installation. Elizabeth was seeing someone senior in the Navy. Both of them were in the Navy themselves."

"And what's the Navy doing about all of this?" Mrs. Hardin asked, looking directly at Dan.

Dan glanced over at Grace before replying. "That's part of it, Mrs. Hardin. We—and we're on the outside now, remember—we think some people in the Navy don't want anything done about it. We were the original investigation team, and now Miss Snow here is no longer with the NIS, and I've been told to stay out of it by some pretty powerful people in the Navy Department. That's why we need your help, because if there's anything at all you can tell us that would identify Elizabeth's . . . friend, we can give that to Captain Vann here, and he can come at it from *outside* the Navy. Once that happens, I think the rest of the Navy, the people who aren't involved in this, will do the right thing."

"Do the right thing?" She sniffed. "Tell me something: You get caught messing around with this thing, you gonna get in trouble?"

"That's what they tell me," Dan said.

"So why you doin' this?"

"Because I want to know who killed your son. Especially if it was someone in the Navy."

"Seems to me, your Navy isn't doin' too good these days, tellin' right from wrong."

"Yes, ma'am. But the Navy's a big outfit. A lot of the bad things seem to have happened here in Washington, but there's a whole hell of a lot of Navy out there around the world, thousands of men and women serving their country and doing it honorably. That's the real Navy, not the Washington Navy, and I guarantee they have a clearer picture of what's right and what's wrong than a lot of folks in this town seem to."

Mrs. Hardin stared at him and then looked over one more time at Captain Vann. Then she got up. "I got one thing. Maybe it's something; maybe it's nothing."

When she had left the room, Dan looked over at Captain Vann. "How much have you told her?" he asked. Vann shrugged.

"Enough," he said. "She's felt all along that there was a cover-up of some kind, but there was nothing to go on. The past two years have been exceedingly . . . difficult."

Mrs. Hardin came back into the room, carrying a small white envelope. She gave it to Dan.

"That was in her things, her personal things. You can see the date—it's about a week before . . . before what happened over there in town."

Grace moved closer as Dan opened the envelope and drew out what appeared to be a Valentine card. There was a large red heart on the front panel, with the words *Be My Valentine* in silver writing across the bottom. Inside there was a message: "Don't shut me out—I love you too much to just stop now," it read, written in longhand in the black felt-tip pen. It was signed with the initials W.T. Dan turned the envelope over and noted the postmark: Foggy Bottom. The envelope had been mailed in her own neighborhood. He handed it over to Captain Vann, who studied it carefully before putting it down on a side table.

"And we have no idea who W.T. is?" Dan asked.

Mrs. Hardin shook her head. "That's the only thing, the only personal item in her papers. The rest were bills and a bunch of Navy paperwork about leave, and some forms."

She went back over to her chair and sat down, then seemed to sag. Dan saw a look of concern in Vann's face, so he nudged Grace.

"Mrs. Hardin, we thank you very much for seeing us. We're going to keep working it, see if we can find out who this is. I hope we don't have to bother you again."

The look in Mrs. Hardin's eyes was bleak, but she didn't say anything, just gave them a small wave and turned in her chair to stare at the wall. Vann got up as Dan and Grace did and walked with them out the front door to the porch. He pulled the front door to but did not close it. Inside, Dan saw Mrs. Hardin walk slowly into the kitchen.

"I told you," Vann said. "Way I see it, she's been trying to erase all of this stuff from her mind so that she can just get on with what's left of her life. That's why I didn't want to do this. You saw her."

Dan nodded and Grace pulled her jacket around her shoulders. It was considerably cooler and there was a hint of rain in the air. Two teenagers strolled by, slowing to give the Suburban the once-over. Then they recognized the cop car, looked up at the porch, and sauntered away.

"Had you known about the Valentine card?" Dan asked.

Vann shook his head. "Not until tonight. It wouldn't have meant anything until now—if it does mean anything."

"It does to me," Dan said. "The one guy in the Pentagon giving me the most heat about staying away from all this is the VCNO's executive assistant, one Captain, soon-to-be Rear Admiral, Randall."

"Yeah, so?"

"So his boss, the Vice Chief of Naval Operations, a four-star admiral and the number-two guy in the whole Navy, and soon to be number-one guy, his name is Torrance. William H. Torrance, Admiral, USN."

Vann stared at him. "As in W.T.," he said softly.

"Yeah, as in W.T."

Vann looked out over the front yard, chewing on his lip again as a car went by. Grace stood there quietly, watching Vann.

"I suggest we do some more thinking," Dan said, turning to go down the steps, taking Grace's arm this time. Vann came with them. "It's a big jump from tips about admirals to making some accusations. Oh—your message said you had some more on this guy Ward?"

Vann nodded and fished a notebook out of his vest pocket. They stopped next to the Suburban.

"This guy is apparently one of those security consultants or contractors—take your choice—who specialize in doing trash hauling for important clients in this town."

"Trash hauling?" asked Grace.

"Yeah, well, a combination of strong-arm, discreet muscle for hire, surveillance work, bodyguard, some PI stuff, bagman—all the not-so-polite scut work that goes on behind the thousand-dollar-a-day guys in the silk suits. I talked to a buddy at the IRS who 'lent' me a ten-ninety-nine printout—shows who wrote him or his PI agency some checks, those who bothered to file. Then I talked to some of those people. They all knew him, but they got real vague real fast when I asked what he did for them. They all said he was a big motherfu— guy, so if he's the dude was following you, Miss Snow, you need to take care. Some of these guys are medium bent."

"Any connection to the Navy?" Dan asked.

"Nope. His clients are mostly political types: committee staffers, lobbyists, one lawyer whom we love to hate downtown, one company that's supposedly a front for the CIA, and an import-export licensing firm—people like that."

"Are these activities legal?" Dan asked.

"What *they* do is legal; what they have him do probably is a mixture. These guys operate almost entirely in the shadows; the last time you got to see lots of them was Watergate."

"I think I was in high school," Dan said with a smile.

Vann grinned. "Sorry to hear it, sonny."

"Thank you for arranging this, Captain," Grace said. "That poor woman in there deserves better than having this thing just fade away."

Vann's face became entirely serious. "For her, none of this is going to fade away. Or for me." He looked at her steadily. "You've figured it out, haven't you Miss Snow? I saw you looking at that picture and then at me in there."

"He was your son, wasn't he, Captain?" Grace said softly. Dan was startled. He had never considered that possibility. He watched Vann's face work its way through several expressions. Finally, he spoke.

"Yeah. It's a complicated story. Things here . . . well, they just didn't work out. Wesley never forgave me for leaving. When I came to Elizabeth's funeral—she was Angela's child by her first husband—Wesley wouldn't speak to me. He was so damn torn up by the whole thing. But I didn't figure it was anything other than her getting killed that way, so damn . . . wastefully. Neither one of them told me anything about this. That's why when you came along—"

"I think I understand," Grace said.

"I doubt it, Miss Snow," Vann said after a few seconds. "But thanks for the sympathetic tone of voice. Commander, you know your way back to town from here? This can be an interesting neighborhood at night."

"I think so," Dan said, looking around.

Vann nodded and looked as if he was going to say something else, but then he shook his head. "Let's all talk tomorrow, shall we? I think I need to go back inside for a while."

"We'll be in touch, Captain," Grace said.

Vann nodded, shook hands with both of them, and went back up the steps. Dan took off his uniform coat as Vann went into the house, and then he unlocked the doors, holding the curb door open for Grace to get in. He hung his uniform jacket up on the hook above the backseat and walked around to get in. Neither of them spoke until they were back out on Pennsylvania Avenue, headed back into the city. The dome of the Capitol gleamed faintly in the distance through the growing mist.

"How the hell did you glom on to that little secret?" he asked her finally as they went over the Sousa Bridge.

"Like he said, the pictures. And I've never been able to put a finger on why he was in the game—if he thought they had a homicide to work, he's enough of a pro to have turned it over to one of the Homicide squads. But the pictures, and the way she kept looking over to him for guidance—it had to be something like that."

Dan nodded. The trained investigator at work, he mused. But she had been right on the mark. He gunned it to get through a yellow light; he was not comfortable stopping on these streets.

"It will complicate things, I think," he said.

"Why?"

"Because he's freelancing, and he may not be able to confront the people I think we'll have to confront with this."

"Freelancing? That's funny," she said, going on to explain why. He smiled, but it didn't relieve the problem.

"I've got to talk to Summerfield," he said. "He'll know how to do this. I'm way the hell out of my league."

As he drove the rest of the way, they talked about the Hardin family and speculated on what the relationships had been. By the time they reached Georgetown, it was close to 9:30. It being a Sunday night, even the Georgetown traffic had thinned out, and there was even a double parking space in front of Grace's house. Dan pulled in, partially across the driveway. Her front porch light was on.

"You turn that light on?" he asked.

"No, it has an electric eye. Comes on after dark. Otherwise, I'd forget the darn thing all the time. Why don't you come in for a little while."

"Yeah, that's a plan."

HE LOCKED UP the Suburban and walked her through the iron gate. She stopped to make sure the BMW was locked, then remembered that Dan's car had to show a parking permit. Finally, they went up to the front door. She fumbled for keys and then unlocked the door and stepped through, with Dan right behind her. As he turned to close the door behind him, he heard her inhale sharply.

"Comdr. Daniel Collins, U.S. Navy?" a harsh voice demanded, practically in his ear. Dan whirled around from the door and saw a huge man, all in black, standing right in front of him, a head taller than he was, a ferocious expression on his face.

"What—" he began, but then the big man poleaxed him in the stomach and his head and chest snapped forward as all the breath whooshed out of his lungs, his entire middle a blaze of pain. He was unable to straighten up, to raise his arms, to do anything, and then what felt like a tree fell on his neck and he pitched over into a black roaring canyon.

AFTER DROPPING DAN, the man turned to face Grace Snow, who was frozen in her tracks, her mouth open but nothing coming out, her eyes wide. Before she could move, he stepped in very close to her, grabbed the front of her blouse with one enormous, gloved paw, and lifted her up on her toes. His face was something out of a nightmare, big, rawboned, with terrible scars all over his throat. There was a strong smell of whiskey on his breath.

"And you, you must be Miss Snow of the NIS, right?" the man growled in her face. His breath really stank. "Formerly of the NIS, I think is more accurate, right, Miss Snow?"

Grace, flailing, raised her right hand and tried to push him away, but he caught her wrist in his left hand and squeezed; he was so strong that it felt like a car was running over her wrist, and she cried out reflexively, her left side turning to him as if in some grotesque jitterbug move. Desperate now, she tried to knee him in the groin, achieving a solid hit with her left knee. To her horror, he just laughed at her again, then kneed *her* in the groin. She yelled and crumpled forward with the lancing pain, wrenching her neck as he held her up, now completely off the floor, like a rag doll. Then he dropped her, letting her hit the wooden floor on her hands and knees, and kicked her arms out from under her before kneeling down with one rock-hard knee into her back. As she fell, she knocked over a card table by the front door, shattering the small glass lamp in the process. He ignored the broken glass and pinned her arms behind her hard enough to make her cry out again. The pain from her groin was awful; she thought she would be sick. Then she heard a ripping noise and felt some kind of tape being wrapped around her wrists. When her arms were bound behind her, he lifted her head, again wrenching her neck. He was looking into her terrified eyes, his own eyes blazing with hate, and then out of nowhere he slapped her so hard, she literally saw stars and fainted.

Malachi stood up and surveyed the scene. Navy was rolled up in a fetal ball, his head almost between his knees, his head twisted sideways, out cold. Yo, Navy boy. Now you know what Pearl Harbor felt like. The woman was bent in the middle like a hairpin, the left side of her face bright red from where he'd slapped her, and her arms secured behind her with duct tape. Her dress had rucked up in their struggle, and her left leg was exposed all the way up to her white panties. He looked at her for a moment and then lifted the rest of her dress with the tip of his shoe, staring at her nakedness. But there was nothing in it for him. She was just meat. He prodded her breast with his foot and she moaned. Welcome to the NFL, honey bunch, he thought.

He turned away and bent down over Collins. He took the roll of duct tape and began pulling off a continuous strip of tape and wrapping it around Collins's head, from his hairline all the way down to under his jaw, leaving only the barest slit in front of his nose. Using his elbow, he hit Collins on the left side of his nose, starting an immediate nosebleed. There, he thought. Now he'll have to be real careful with his breathing when he wakes up. He took some more duct tape and wrapped it around Collins's left wrist, then pulled his left arm and wrist between his legs, forced his right arm under his right buttock, and then taped the two together, forearm to forearm, leaving Collins totally immobilized. The final step was to tape Collins's fingers together so he couldn't get a hold on anything when he came to. He considered taping his feet together but then decided to leave them free. If he struggled when he came to, he'd soon find out that he had to choose between drowning from that nosebleed or staying perfectly still.

He took a quick look around. He had rigged the house in case he had to get out quickly: The back door was unlocked and partially open, as was the back gate. The phone line was cut. The gasoline was also ready. He looked out the front windows, listened for a moment, and then nodded with satisfaction. It had been a perfect surprise attack. He had especially loved the expression on her face, just like the country song said, that "deer in the high beams" look, when she saw what happened to her boyfriend. Standard procedure: Hit the woman first, you have an enraged guy on your hands; take out the guy first, the woman will stand there in shock every time. He turned back to the woman, got behind her, grabbed her under her armpits, and pulled her up the stairs, her heels thumping up each step, and toward the bedroom, which was all prepared for her coming interview.

BACK DOWNSTAIRS, DAN came to in a haze of pain, almost totally disoriented. He could neither see nor hear, and it felt as if he was trying to breathe through a wet cotton plug stuffed into his nose. He tried to open his eyes, but they were literally stuck together. Then he realized that his head was wrapped in something sticky, his whole face, ears, mouth, eyes, most of his nose, lips, all covered up and seemingly solidified, like a mummy. An image of Wesley Hardin flooded his forebrain, and for a moment he panicked, his heart racing out of control, until he remembered what had happened. Grace. What had the bastard done with Grace! He tried to call out for her, but suddenly he could not breathe anymore, his nose filling with a warm, sticky fluid, causing him to swallow and then sneeze violently. With his mouth taped shut, the sneeze made things a lot worse, and he ended up gargling uncontrollably, a drowning sensation sweeping over him before he fought it back and regained control of himself. He took a painfully slow breath, inhaling in little tiny bites of air past the obstruction in his nose, then exhaled forcefully, feeling the spray on his shirtfront, but he could breathe now, and he did, twice, three times, getting a grip on himself, repeating the process, and then discovering that part of the problem was that he could not straighten out.

His forearms were taped together between his legs, and his hands felt like big sticky paws. His first effort to pull his forearms apart sent a spear of pain into his groin, so he gave that up right away. Worse, his neck felt all mushy from the bottom of his head to the top of his spine, especially on the left side, and there was a core of pain in his stomach where that guy had hit him in the first place. He tried to think of who this guy could be and what this was all about, but there was a red haze in front of his taped-shut eyes. He knew he had to move, get out of all this tape before that guy came back, or he was dead meat. The front door. Maybe he could get to the front door, attract some attention from the street. How? Where is the front door? he thought. I don't know, but gotta move, gotta move. Scrunching like an inchworm on its side, he started across the floor, not knowing if he was headed for the door or the kitchen or the bottom of the stairs or into a wall. No sight, no sound, not even any feel from the skin on his face. He could move a couple of inches, snort his nose clear, move again, snort again. This is hopeless, he thought. I could be going in a circle down here. He forgot to snort, and a small river of blood welled into his throat, almost causing him to lose it again.

He tried to move his hands and his arms; maybe he could pull that leg through—he was pretty limber from all the rowing, but there was simply no room. He inched again, then one more time. Snort, clear that nose. Inch. Snort. Carpet's gonna be a mess; they'll never let us in that rug store again. And then something sharp pricked the balls of two fingers on his right hand. He froze, his fingers stinging with pain. Glass. Broken glass. Broken glass can cut the tape. But not without fingers. Nothing to hold the glass with. *Shit!* The bastard really had him. He almost cried in frustration, except that his eyes were taped shut. And then he realized that the tips of his fingers were bleeding. And moving. Moving! The damn blood was dissolving the tape mastic. That's right— if this is duct tape, water turns it into a sticky, soggy mass. Blood. Gotta have more blood.

He wiggled around on the floor, searching for more glass, finally finding it when a shard punctured his knee and then the back of his right arm. Focusing furiously, he tracked the shard of glass with his skin, positioning it and himself so that he could touch it with the tips of his fingers, then jabbing at it, exulting in the sharp little stings and then the greasy, sticky feel of blood. He rolled sideways, trying to force his bound hands into the air so that the blood would flow back into the tape, then straining with his fingers and his hands, pulling his hands back and forth until finally, after what seemed like forever, he could feel the tape moving slightly along his fingers.

MALACHI HAD DRAGGED Grace up the stairs and into her bedroom at the back of the house. He pitched her up on the bed, her hands still bound behind her back, and then closed the door. He turned on her bedside lamps and then picked up a large, sharp kitchen knife and cut the tape on her wrists. He rolled her onto her back, pulled her arms up to the headboard, and retaped her wrists to the bedposts; then he pulled her legs apart and taped her ankles with several straplike segments of tape to the footboard. She whimpered, her eyes still shut, as he pulled her body into a spread-eagled position. He took another short hank of duct tape and smacked it down over her mouth. He would let her see and let her breathe. It didn't matter if she saw him, he thought, because if these two were what he thought they were, neither one of them was going to survive the night. She whimpered again and turned her head, keeping her eyes closed tight.

While she was coming around, he pulled her makeup table over to the side of the bed, where she would be able to see it. He pulled a large black bundle out of his equipment bag and opened the Velcro straps that held it rolled up. Inside were several surgical instruments, a stainless-steel handsaw, a cranium drill, a mixed set of scalpels, forceps, hemostats, rib spreaders, and a variety of clamps, their stainless- and chromium-steel surfaces gleaming in the light of the bedside-table lamps. He positioned the implements on the table so that she would be able to see all of them clearly. He reached into the bag and brought out a small mason jar of alcohol, which he opened and set next to the implements. She coughed once and then groaned, but she still did not open her eyes.

He went into the bathroom and found a pitcher she used to water the houseplants that were set under the bedroom windows. He filled it with cold water, came back into the bedroom, walked over to the head of the bed, and poured the entire contents into her face. She jumped, straining at the tape, coughed, spluttered through her nose, and opened her eyes.

"Reveille, reveille, reveille," he intoned. "Welcome back to the world, Miss Snow. At least for a little while."

She looked frantically around the room, refusing to meet his gaze, and he laughed at her.

"Looking for Navy? Navy's downstairs. He's a bit wrapped up at the moment, but he's doing fine, as long as he doesn't try to move. Or breathe very much."

He sat down on the edge of the bed and ran his hand over her face to check the tape. She flinched at the feel of his hand.

"What's the matter, Miss Snow? Don't care for a man's hands on you? Or is it just on your face? Is that it? How about here—is that better? Or here, yeah, that's better, isn't it? No?"

He touched every part of her, gently and then harder, massaging her breasts and then her belly and then between her legs with his gloved hand, watching her face all the while. So much meat, that's all it was. Too bad, she was very pretty. Maybe a little thin for his taste, but what the hell. Once upon a time, he would have had a hard-on by now, but now there was nothing left down there. Thanks to a woman. Which was why when she kicked him, he had laughed at her. He laughed at her now, sliding his hand up under that long dress, between her legs, his gloved thumb probing the softness of her sex. She was starting to cry.

"This game is called hearts and minds, Miss Snow," he said. "When we were in Vietnam, we were supposed to be fighting for the slopes' hearts and minds. McNamara's counterinsurgency bullshit. What the sergeants all knew was that if you grabbed them by the balls, their hearts and minds would follow you anywhere. And that's what I want from you Miss Snow—I want your heart and mind to follow me through some questions here, okay? *Okay?*"

She jumped when he raised his voice with the second "*okay?*" and then she nodded.

"Very good, Miss Snow." He withdrew his hand from under her dress. "That's much better. Hearts and minds, yes, ma'am, that's how we did it in Nam, hearts and minds, and then maybe some of these little numbers, over here, Miss Snow, yeah, over here, what do you think?"

He watched her face as she focused on the surgical implements, watched her eyes widen, that "deer in the bright lights" look appearing again. Shit, this was no pro. She was too soft, too easily frightened. A pro would have shown fear but would have been looking around, calculating how to get out of this fix. But what the hell—she was the bird in hand, so to speak. He started picking up the implements, one by one, naming them, telling her what they were for, embellishing the details of how they worked. When he was finished, she was visibly trembling, and he leaned forward and placed the bone saw on her chest, just under her chin. He jostled the bottle of alcohol, spilling a little, filling the room with the smell. He patted her cheek, laughing when she flinched behind the duct tape again, and he then got off the bed.

"Scrub time," he announced over his shoulder, heading for the bathroom. "Cleanliness is next to godliness, I always say. How about you, Miss Snow? Don't go away."

He went into the bathroom and turned on the faucets. Give her time to let her imagination run a little bit. He had no intention of really using any of that stuff except maybe the scissors, but a guy who had been fired from the CIA had taught him that nothing you could do or say was as scary as what they could think up using their own fervid imaginations. Properly stimulated, of course. He took off the black leather gloves and then looked at his face in the mirror. Should probably go down and check on Navy. Fuck it, he wasn't going anywhere. Might even have choked to death by now. That was okay, too. But still . . .

He left the water running and came back out of the bathroom. Ignoring the woman tethered on the bed, he went to the bedroom door and opened it up and listened. There were no sounds from downstairs. He closed the door again. Nothing happening downstairs. He went back into the bathroom and started washing his hands.

He stared at his face in the mirror. You've really done it now, Malachi, he thought. Kidnap appetizer, murder for two coming up. The Hardin girl was murder, dummy. No it wasn't—that was manslaughter. Woman-slaughter, to be politically correct. The bitch went the wrong damn way, just like most of them did when they were driving. And her brother? Well, that wasn't supposed to have happened either. The Guidos screwed that one up. Neither of them supposed to be whacked. Screwups, both of them. Not deliberate. But the whole thing had come apart, just like so many things in this goddamn town. How many really big messes in this town had begun over nothing more than a series of screwups? He took a deep breath through his nose, filling his chest while he watched his face in the mirror. He had found her liquor supply while prepping the house, and the bourbon hadn't been half bad—a little weak, not like the Harper hundred, but good enough. He could feel that familiar core of warmth in his stomach, all his nerve ends nicely pacified and his mind running at top end. Amazing what a little jolt or six could do for you.

But this here business tonight, this was going to be clear-cut. He was going to confirm that the captain had sent them, and then he was going to immobilize them both and set the house afire. Two quarts of high-test gasoline were waiting on the kitchen table. Keeping it indirect, of course. He wouldn't kill them—but the fire might. Yeah, might. And then he was going to seek out his former employer, the good captain, and break his back. That one, he would do directly. And if the captain's almighty principal came over the horizon, showed up at the right place at the wrong time, he'd ice him, too. About time one of the great men paid the piper, instead of just all the snuffies. Then he was going to disappear right out of this town. The only thing he couldn't change about his appearance was his size and his voice, but he had enough vehicles and papers and money to disappear with ease. He searched his conscience, but, like his sexual drive, it was long gone. So, hey, let's get to it.

The water from the sink had begun to steam up the mirror, so he shut it off and dried his hands. He pulled the automatic from his right-front waistband and stuffed it into his pants at the middle of his back. In the sudden silence, he fished out the pair of rubber gloves from his pocket and snapped them on, making lots of noise for the benefit of the "patient" in the bedroom. He had thought about wearing a mask but then had discarded the idea. His face probably lent a certain something to the proceedings. Holding his gloved hands dramatically up in the air in front of him, he went back into the bedroom.

By WEDGING HIS right hand between the hard floor and his left forearm, Dan had managed to start the wad of blood-soaked tape moving. After several tugs, he got two fingers of his right hand free. Now, where's that shard of glass? Gone. He felt all around the floor for it, but it was gone. Gotta move around, find another piece of glass. He bumped his head against something and grunted, and then he thought he heard a door open somewhere. He froze. Upstairs. The sound was coming from the second floor. Don't make noise. Don't make that bastard come back down here and kick your head in. Grace's only chance is if you get out of this. He heard the door close again, definitely upstairs, and started his blind inchworm act again. Find it. Find it. Find it. Don't think about what's happening up there, just get free. His nose started bleeding in earnest again, and he had to snort it clear several times while he did his blind crawl. Finally, the back of his right hand landed on something sharp. He froze, then carefully, carefully rotated his hand, having to twist his whole body because of all the tape, until he got the piece of glass between his thumb and forefinger. Twisting his hand, he started sawing on the band of tape that bound his wrist to his other forearm. It was very hard to do. The same blood that had dissolved the mastic now made it almost impossible to hold on to the glass. He dropped it several times, freezing each time so that he could find it again. After an eternity of effort, he was able to twist his right wrist and feel the wonderful sound of tape tearing. The more the tape tore, the more he could move his hands, and the more he could cut. Within a minute, he had freed his arms; he could finally sprawl on the floor in something besides the fetal position, the shard of glass gripped tightly in his right hand.

He recovered his breathing for a moment and then went to work on the face tape, cutting straight up from the nose slip, slicing his cheek in the process but not stopping, cutting until he reached his hairline. He took a deep breath and then ripped the tape off his face in both directions, gulping great drafts of air through his mouth now that he was free. Free. Using his teeth, he tore the rest of the tape off his hands. Gotta get up there, get Grace out of there.

But how? The guy was a monster. He needed a weapon. Dumb shit, What you need is help. Call the cops. Call 911. Then go after the bastard. He rolled over onto his hands and knees, then made the mistake of trying to stand up. There was a loud buzzing noise in his ears as he raised his head to get up, and then a great sheet of purple pain flowed from the back of his neck and across his eyes. He collapsed onto the floor, his neck on fire.

He lay there for a minute, trying to get his bearings and swallow down the waves of nausea roaring through his body. The guy had rabbit-punched him, and now his neck didn't work. Tough to walk with no neck. How the hell did those guys in the movies manage it? His neck felt like it was broken. Okay, so crawl. But get to a phone. He crawled like a baby, elbows down, hips scrunching forward, elbows moving, then hips again. He was unable to really lift his head, his chin bumping along the carpet in the living room and on through to the dining room. He could see the white phone cord coming out of the wall. But how to reach the phone. It was way the hell up there, on the table. Pull it down. It'll make noise. He'll hear it. He rolled over on his back and began pulling on the cord. Slowly. You're gonna catch it when it falls. No noise. No noise. His nose had started bleeding again. Won't wear this shirt again, will we? Flat on his back now, he kept pulling, his eyes locked on the edge of the dining room table until the phone appeared.

Now. Sit up. Maybe you can reach it. But his head was buzzing again, and his vision was fading in and out. Lots of pretty colors, though. The buzzing grew louder.

MALACHI WALKED OVER to the bed. The woman was all eyes, staring at him, her mouth trying to work under the tape; she was making a sort of mewing sound. He stood over her for a minute, picked up the bone saw and examined it before putting it back down on the table, and then began to rearrange the surgical implements on the table, as if trying to decide. He sloshed a little more alcohol out onto the table to heighten the atmosphere.

"What I've got to know, Miss Snow," he began, "is why you have my name down there on that pad of paper. My name and two little words with it: *Captain* and *Target*."

He looked over at her to see if she was watching. She was. Good girl. He picked through the instruments while he talked to her, picking each one up, turning each of them over and over. Letting her watch. Letting the light make them gleam.

"See," he continued, "when I was here the other night, I sort of read your mail. Yeah, that's right, I've been here before. And that's when I knew that you and I were destined to meet. Here's my theory, okay? I think the captain has hired you to come after me because of the Hardin problem. You remember the Hardin problem, don't you? Just nod your head. That's right. Okay. So that's what I need to know."

He stopped and looked down at her.

"You know, you don't look very comfortable. Why don't we make you a little more comfortable, okay? Let's start with all these clothes."

He picked up the large pair of surgical scissors and, starting at the hem of her dress, began cutting straight up, right alongside the line of buttons, cutting the slip and the dress together, all the way up to the shirttails of her blouse, and then cutting that, too, until he reached the V of her blouse. He pulled all the fabric aside and then he cut down either arm, baring her shoulders as he flattened the remains of the dress and the blouse and the slip. Her bra and panties were bright white in the light of the table lamp as he cut them off, snipping all the elastic and straps until he was able to brush everything aside. He put the scissors back on the table and then folded the cut clothing away from her body, pulling it out from under her and leaving her totally exposed on the bed. He sat back and admired his handiwork. Damn the German whore again for the thousandth time. What a waste.

She was crying again, her eyes squeezing shut, her mouth working under the gray duct tape. She didn't know it, but there was nothing sexual about this part: Naked and pinioned on her back, she was totally, inescapably helpless. He reached up and ripped the tape off her lips in a single pull. She cried out but then went silent, tears welling in her eyes.

"Don't cry," he said. "You think I'm going to rape you. I'm not going to rape you. You kicked me, remember? I mean, after all, what kind of a guy can do a good rape after a kick in the balls, hunh? Have to be a really special guy, don't you think? But you know what? I am special. *Look at me, bitch!*"

She jumped when he yelled at her, her eyes getting wide again. She mumbled something, her voice unintelligible.

"That's right, Miss Snow, I'm a really special guy," he said, getting up off the bed and moving up to stand next to her head. "Really special. Here, take a look. *I said: take a look!*"

He undid his belt and pulled his trousers down over his hips. The gun dropped out on the carpet with a clunk, but he ignored it. He wanted her to look. He wanted her to understand that she was going to be a part of paying off an old debt. Standing no more than two feet from her face, he pulled down his underwear. She gasped at the sight of his mutilated groin, at the web of pale white belt-sized scars crisscrossing where his sex should have been.

"See, Miss Snow?" he hissed, leaning over her. "I can't fuck anybody. I can't even piss like a guy anymore. I have to squat, just like you girls, Miss Snow."

He continued, his voice rising, the fury returning as he yanked his clothes back together. "A goddamned woman did this to me, Miss Snow. And I swore that I would never, never, ever let another woman hurt me again. So when I found my name and that word *Target* on your little notepad down there, Miss Snow, I decided to come back here and take care of business. So that's why I'm here and why you're there, and now you're going to answer my questions. Because if you don't, I'm going to select one of these little toys and maybe do unto you what that woman did unto me. I'm not a doctor, of course, but I can make a stab at it, so to speak. Understand? *Understand?*"

She swallowed hard, nodded her head mutely, and finally got a single word out. "Yes."

He smiled then, an unlovely smile, and shook his head in mock wonderment. "God love a woman with no clothes on who says yes, Miss Snow."

58

DAN CAME BACK around after a minute or so, to find himself facedown on the floor, his head throbbing, breathing rapidly, and sweating like a pig. He tried to figure out where he was, and then the realization of precisely where he was and why jolted him fully awake. The phone. He turned over very slowly, careful not to invoke that buzzing noise again. He had to be very careful; he must have a concussion. He started tugging on the phone line again, until the instrument was teetering on the edge of the table, and then down it came in a cascade of instrument and handset, the phone hitting him in the stomach and the handset bouncing off his cheekbone—but noiselessly. Grab it, grab it and make the call. 911—three easy numbers. Just wait for the dial tone—there was no dial tone. The phone was stone-dead. He put it down on the floor. The bastard must have killed the phones while he was waiting for them. Of course he would have.

Upstairs. The sounds of the door opening and closing had come from upstairs. Gotta get up there. Right fucking now.

He rolled over again, tried to collect himself on his hands and knees, and it was okay, not terrific, but okay, the buzzing noise coiling at the edges of the room, the room not moving around too much. The kitchen. Get a weapon of some sort out of the kitchen and get up there before . . . before . . . He didn't want to think about what was going on up there. He crawled into the kitchen, still on his hands and knees. The door. The back door was open. Fuck the back door. Go out the front door, get to the street, and maybe crawl next door. Get help. And leave Grace? No way. He pulled a drawer open. Towels. He pulled another one out. Knives. Maybe he should get a knife. No way. Guy was too big; he would have to get real close to use a knife, and he could barely move. The next drawer came out and emptied itself on the floor. Baking equipment: sifters, cake pans. Wait. There was one of those straight rolling pins, the ones without the handles. A club. Shit. But a club, a club he could throw. He'd have one chance, surprise the fucker, step through the door with it in his hands, and when the guy came at him, he'd try to throw it underhand and hit him between the eyes. You're a pitcher. This would be the ultimate slow pitch. David and Goliath. Right. Move your ass.

Clutching the rolling pin in his left hand, still on his hands and knees, he scuttled across the linoleum floor to the dining room and then back into the living room—which was when he heard Grace scream.

MALACHI HAD SLAPPED her when she screamed. He'd asked her a simple question—"Did the captain send you after me? Yes or no?"—and she had tried to lie. She'd said no, no one had sent her, asked which captain he was talking about, there were so many, and then he'd picked up a hemostat and clamped it onto her right nipple, and the bitch had screamed. His slap shut her right up, though. She wasn't entirely stupid.

"Don't lie to me, bitch. I've taped your phones. I know all about Captain Vann. The one you met with tonight. With Mrs. Hardin. Don't tell me you're not working for him, because when he calls, you go. And you got Navy down there to go with you. On the Hardin case. So I *know* what this is about, okay? But here's what I have to know: Is this Captain Vann working for the vice-chief's flunky, Captain—"

At that instant, the bedroom door burst open, and Malachi whirled around. He was stunned to see Dan in the doorway, but then he almost laughed. Navy was in the doorway all right, Navy with his swollen face, blood all over his face and shirt, patches of hair missing from his forehead, Navy wobbling around in the doorway as if his head wasn't screwed on right, and holding a fucking *rolling pin!*

"Oh shit, oh dear," Malachi said, straightening up. He felt for the gun but then remembered it had fallen on the floor. Not a problem, he thought, looking at Dan. Not a problem at all. Look at this bozo. Check it out, friends and neighbors.

"Well, if it isn't Julia Child," he sneered. "Is she gonna bop me with that big bad rolling pin? Gonna run me right outta her kitchen?"

He laughed again, and then, hunching his shoulders, he lunged across the room, but Navy did something with his arm—he couldn't follow it, really—a whirl of motion, like a softball pitch, and then something hit him directly in his right eye, like a cannonball. He screamed and grabbed his face, unable to stop his forward momentum, dimly aware that Navy had fallen down in the doorway. Get you, you motherfucker, get you. Bending forward to get—but then he was hit in the right shin by another cannonball, and his leg gave way, pitching him right over the flailing figure on the floor and out into the hallway, to the top of the stairs, where he just stopped himself from going over by grabbing the balustrade. Jesus Christ, his leg was broken; he'd heard it crack. And his eye, his fucking eye—but then the crazy bastard was on him, screaming at him, hitting him with something. Have to get away. Let go. And then he was sliding down the stairs, the guy screaming something about knowing who he was, saying they were going to get him, that they knew everything. And then he went crashing onto the first-floor landing, by the front door, knocking a leg on the over-turned card table and picking up a handful of broken glass as he tried to break his fall.

There was an instant of silence when the lunatic stopped screaming at him from the top of the stairs. He rolled over and got up on his hands and knees, the movement almost making him throw up, his leg hurt so bad. His right eyeball felt like red-hot jelly, and then there was a noise. He looked up the stairs and damn near fainted: Navy had his gun and was firing at him. The 9-mm was bucking in the guy's bloody hands with that unmistakable blamming sound; he could hear the bullets blasting holes in the front door and the floor and the window and the wall, just like goddamn Frankfurt again, except that that wasn't Terry Eastman and he wasn't Inge. He rolled once, twice, out of the line of fire, not sure he'd been hit, but scrambling to get clear, his leg and his eye screaming at him, a hot gush of nausea surging up his throat.

He picked himself up in the sudden silence, holding on to the sofa to steady himself, his right leg dangling underneath him. *Motherfucker!* How the hell had he gotten loose? Go get your other goddamn gun and go back up there and waste both of them. Right now. But he knew he couldn't: His eye felt like mush and he was afraid even to touch it. He was having trouble seeing out of the other eye now, and the pain in his leg was so intense that he was seeing stars every time he moved. He checked himself over but found no bullet holes. Five rounds, missed every damn one of them. Typical fucking amateur.

Get out. Get out now while you can. She may have a gun stashed somewhere up there that you didn't find. Get out. You can't see for shit, and that leg is really going to slow you down. No. Do what you were going to do originally: Salt the place with gas, torch it, and then roll. He staggered back into the kitchen, where the two mason jars were waiting.

Limping awkwardly, he brought one back out into the front hall, opened it, and slopped a quart of high-test up the carpeted stairs, smashing the bottle against the stairway wall when it was almost empty. Then he took the other one and stumbled through the living room and study, slopping gasoline on the furniture and the drapery, maintaining a trail back to the front hall and the stairs. He had to keep taking deep breaths to keep from vomiting, his leg and eye pulsing with bright spears of pain every time he moved. He smashed the second jar against the kitchen wall in a fury and then fully opened the back doors to the pantry and the garden. He limped back in to light it and saw the gas stove. Even better, he thought. He lurched over to the stove, grabbed the cooktop with both hands, pulled it off the stove body, and dumped it onto the kitchen floor in a crash, exposing the corrugated natural-gas-supply pigtail. He grabbed a big kitchen knife from an open drawer and chopped through the thin metal, releasing a steady hiss of natural gas into the kitchen. Then he got out his cigarette lighter and went back to the gasoline trail in the study and lit it. There was a satisfying whooming noise, and the fire trail streaked around the downstairs like some malevolent spirit. He watched for a few seconds and then dragged himself out the back door and down to the garden gate, propping open the back door as he went. When he got to the garden gate, he looked back. He could see the flickering patterns of the flames beginning to grow in the downstairs area of the house. He took a moment to collect himself and then lurched through the gate, closing it behind him.

WHEN THE GUY landed in a heap at the bottom of the stairs, Dan staggered back into the bedroom and saw the gun on the floor. He grabbed it and careened back out the bedroom door. He was wildly unsteady, his balance shot to hell, but he had done it: He had nailed the bastard—a direct hit with the rolling pin. Now he stood at the top of the steps, pointing the gun at the scrambling figure below, trying to get his eyes focused, pulling the trigger. But nothing was happening. The slide. Pull back the goddamned slide. He did and then pointed again, and this time there was a satisfying explosion and a kick that raised his hand. He kept the trigger held back and emptied the gun down the stairs, only dimly aware that the guy was rolling out of the line of fire. When the gun stopped firing, he backed into the bedroom, slammed the door, and slid down to the floor with a jolt to his neck that made his head swim. He was having trouble seeing.

He was pretty sure he had actually blacked out for a moment when the guy had tripped over the top of him and fallen on the floor at the top of the stairs. He'd been aiming for the man's forehead and missed, but the underhanded shot to the eye had done the trick, even though the effort of the throw had caused Dan to collapse like a stringless puppet. But the big man had been stunned long enough for Dan to grab the rolling pin again as Ward tripped over him, and the fact that he was down on the floor had enabled him to hit the bastard a second time, this time in the shin.

He heard a sound from the bed. Grace. He turned around and stared. Her eyes were wide with terror, her body was stretched obscenely across the bed, a glinting surgical clamp of some kind clipped to her breast like Cleopatra's asp.

"Oh Jesus," he said, getting up, wanting to avert his eyes. He heard what sounded like a bottle breaking out in the stairwell. He froze in place. Bastard's coming back. Block the door. Block the door. He turned around and tried to lift her dresser bureau in front of the door, but he lacked the strength and almost collapsed again. His neck felt like it was connected to his spine by a tube of soft, hot sand. He tried a second time. Slide it; don't lift it. He got the damn thing to move sideways a little, and then a little more, until it partially blocked the door. Then he staggered over to the bed, telling her it was okay, it was going to be okay, removed the clamp, and used one of the scalpels to cut her loose, rolling her into the bedspread to cover her, then holding her from behind when she started into a heaving, sobbing fit. He was comforting her, cupping his hands in front of her face as she began to hyperventilate, when he felt rather than heard the compression wave of the gasoline igniting in the stairwell.

He stopped breathing. He knew what that sound was: He'd felt that thumping pressure wave before, in Navy fire-fighting school, at the moment when the instructor tossed gasoline on the pool of diesel fuel and then followed it with an ignition torch.

He rolled off the bed and looked around for the phone. No good—the phone was dead. Grace, wrapped up in the bedspread, called his name when he rolled off the bed. Then there was a crackling noise outside the bedroom door, and the house felt like it was beginning to vibrate.

"What—" she said.

"He's set the house on fire. We've gotta get out of here. Are you hurt?"

"N-no," she said. "He was going to . . . going to—"

"It's okay now. I hurt him. But my neck isn't working. I can barely stand up. You're going to have to help me. He's cut the phones. Which side is closest to the ground?"

She was trying to sit up, struggling with the bedspread, disoriented, trying to understand his question. "I don't . . . I don't know," she mumbled, looking uncertainly at the windows.

He lurched over to the window on the right side of the house, looked two stories down, to some bushes and a brick wall. He thought he could see an orange glow reflecting on the brick wall from the downstairs windows, but the wall was too far away from the side of the house to get to. He went to the other side, conscious that there was smoke coming in under the bureau in front of the door.

"Grace," he said, "you have to get up. Get some clothes stuffed under that door."

She stared at the bureau and the first tendrils of smoke coiling up into the room for a moment before finally comprehending, and then she moved, rolling out of the bedcovers and scrambling naked across the room to the bureau.

He looked out the other side window. Same deal. If the wall had been only about three feet closer to the house, they could make it, but there was a good eight feet between the house wall and the brick wall. Grace was stuffing some clothes under the bureau, stopping some of the smoke, and then she was hurriedly pulling on some clothes. Good, he thought, she's back in battery. He went to the back window of the bedroom, saw immediately that they could get onto the roof of the back porch.

"Okay!" he shouted. "Here's our way out."

He tried to open the window, but it was stuck, probably painted shut. He tried again, but the effort sent his head spinning. He slumped down for a moment to cradle his head in his hands—which is when he found out the carpet was warm, very warm.

"Grace," he yelled, "we gotta move—the whole downstairs is going. Help me open this window!"

Grace ran back over to the window, barefoot, but with shorts and a sweater on. She grunted and heaved against the window, and Dan tried to help, but they couldn't budge it. While they were trying, Grace stepped on the hardwood floor and yelled when it burned her feet. The floor was clearly vibrating now as the fire in the kitchen, amplified by an unlimited supply of natural gas and fresh air, was turning the downstairs into a combustion chamber. There was an arcing noise from the wall and the lights flickered out. The air in the room was suddenly getting very hot. He realized that they had only seconds.

"Throw something through it!" he yelled, realizing that he was having to yell because of the rumbling noise that was filling the house. There was a loud crash from the front of the house, and the rumbling noise got heavier, really shaking the floor now. Grace picked up the bench from her makeup table and attacked the window until she had knocked most of the glass out. Dan dragged the bedspread over and padded the bottom of the window, conscious of the sounds of exploding windows downstairs and then the shouting outside. He pushed Grace through the window, helping her to turn around so that she was able to hang on to the edge of the windowsill and the bedspread for a moment before dropping down onto the porch roof and then sliding all the way off the roof into the shrubbery below. Behind him, the bedroom door began to rattle in its frame as if a banshee from hell was on the other side, howling to get in. As he looked over his shoulder, all the paint on the door suddenly bubbled up into large and viscous black blisters. The door started to warp outward, revealing a bright yellow rectangle of firelight. He could hear air being sucked out into the hallway as the drapes on either side of the window billowed in toward the disintegrating door. He had planned to tie the spread off and let himself down on it, but he knew that there was no more time. He threw the spread through the window and onto the porch roof and climbed through the window, his neck almost failing him when he turned around and tried to hang for a moment, his hands stinging from glass cuts.

"Drop, Dan, drop," Grace was screaming from the backyard. There was a noise like a giant jet engine intake practically under his feet, coming from the back door to the house. He let go and dropped in a heap onto the slanting roof of the back porch, landing mostly on the bedspread, skinning knees and elbows, and then tumbling off the roof into the same clump of boxwood Grace had landed in. Grace was there in an instant, dragging him and the bedspread away from the house just as a vicious gout of flame howled out through the upstairs bedroom window, as if searching for them. Then there were people around him and the sounds of sirens. Safe from the fire, he surrendered himself to the irresistibly cool comfort of the damp grass.

59

MALACHI, HIS LUNGS BURSTING, had to stop when he reached the shadows at the top of the *Exorcist* steps. His leg was killing him, and his right eye had closed up entirely. He had grabbed a rake on the way out of Snow's backyard, snapped off the tines in the doorjamb of the gate, and used the handle as a makeshift crutch in his escape through the back streets of the Cloisters. His leg was obviously not broken, or he would not have been able to get this far, but his shin felt like a bundle of twigs and the pain was incredible. Instinctively, he knew the eye was more serious. He no longer had stereo vision, and the socket was so puffy and swollen that every involuntary blink sent a shot of white-hot pain jabbing back into his skull. Even worse, the eye was leaking what felt like a clear fluid down his cheek; if that was what he thought it was, he would have almost preferred that it be bleeding.

He stood at the top of the steps, catching his breath, trying to will the pain in his eye to subside. His view down the steep steps to M Street was disturbing, the lack of one eye making it look even steeper than it already was. Better down than up, he thought gamely, and forced himself to start down the steps, having to turn sideways for each one, leaning on the stick and putting his left leg down, then pivoting to drag his right leg over the next step. The real bitch was that he hadn't gotten his question answered. But maybe he had. He'd seen the look in her eyes when he told her he knew all about Captain Vann. She had seemed to wilt a little, as if she realized what was going to happen now that he knew she'd been hired to take him out.

But it bothered him that she had been such a pushover. He had found no weapons in the house or on her person. Nothing hidden in her clothes, which had been the main reason he had taken her clothes off—God knew, her naked body couldn't do anything for him. The hitter woman who had frightened him several years ago had told him she carried two guns on her body and another in her purse, as well as having some razor blades sewn into the panels of her bra and a six-inch surgical-steel hatpin in her hair. Snow should have mobilized her fear into anger, screamed at him, fought back when he had her tied up on the bed, but she had been thoroughly cowed, almost in shock. That bothered him. Something not fitting together here. He stumbled on a step and very nearly lost his balance, crying out in pain when he had to land on his injured leg. He had to stop for a full minute to get his breath back and to control the nausea.

And the hell of it was that now he didn't know if they survived the fire. He had heard the sirens, and Navy had been upstairs, so he could have untied her and gotten her out. But Navy had been fucked up, that was clear—his rabbit punch had been expertly delivered; people tended to forget that its name came from the blow designed to kill a rabbit. But he nailed you, didn't he? He got lucky, that's all. He winced as he remembered laughing at the ridiculous rolling pin. Thank God the guy couldn't shoot for shit.

Reaching the bottom of the steps, he hobbled over to the closed gas station on M Street and sat down heavily on a bench outside the men's room. Damn, he needed a drink right about now. He looked across the busy street at Key Bridge, at the steady flow of cars passing through the orange glow of the streetlights. He was going to have to get across M Street, then cross the bridge, make it up the hill to the Rosslyn Metro station before it closed for the night, and get back up to Ballston and the Randolph Towers. No cabs. No rides.

And hopefully, no cops. With any luck, Navy and his girlfriend would have their hands full with the fire long enough for him to get out of the neighborhood. The bridge would present the greatest exposure if the cops were out looking. So, hump time, Malachi. He took a deep breath and launched himself off the bench and back onto his feet. His eye felt as if it was going to fall out when he stood up, and he had to grit his teeth against the searing pain in his leg. Tomorrow. Concentrate on tomorrow. Time enough then to figure out what to do. But it was clearly going to involve the captain.

DAN WOKE UP in a corner of the emergency room at Georgetown University Hospital. Blinking his eyes, he was able to recognize where he was because the fabric curtains were stenciled with the hospital's name and the initials ER in several places. Must be popular curtains, he thought. His neck was in some kind of brace, his stomach hurt, and there were bandages on his cheek, fingers, and left elbow. There were some people standing right outside the curtains, talking softly. He tentatively called Grace's name.

Grace came around the curtain and took his left hand in hers. She was still wearing the ridiculous-looking shorts and a torn sweater, and she had grass stains on her knees. Her face was pale on one side and red on the other but the look in her eyes made him feel considerably better.

"Welcome back," she said as Captain Vann came into view behind her left shoulder.

"Hey, man, what'd I tell you guys about freelancin', hunh?" he said with a grin.

"Damn, Officer, all I did was take the girl home. Early, even. But there was this bad dream waiting for us in the house."

Vann's face sobered. "Yeah, we're figuring that was Mr. Malachi Ward, lately of Capitol Hill."

"Lately?"

"Yeah, he's booked. But Grace here, she says you dinged him pretty good."

Dan tried to shake his head, but the brace had him confined. "I don't know—I threw a goddamned rolling pin at him, trying to knock him out, but I got his eye instead. And I got him once in the leg, I think. Then I emptied a nine-millimeter at him."

"You hit him?"

"Probably not. Mostly made a lot of noise, but it moved him along. It happened kinda fast, and I didn't feel up to hot pursuit."

Vann looked at the neck brace. "He gave you a karate chop of some kind on the neck. Doc says you're lucky he didn't break it."

"Feels like he did," Dan said with a sigh. "And the house?"

"All gone," Vann said. "Sucker used some gasoline, and then the city gas company got into it. Nasty, hot, quick fire. You two were extremely lucky."

Dan tried to massage the back of his neck. The brace felt awkward and ugly, but it definitely helped—as long as he kept very still. Grace squeezed his hand. "Severe sprain," she announced. "They've x-rayed it and braced it. The doctor said it'll heal fairly fast but hurt for a long time. They want to keep you here for the night."

He tried to shake his head, forgetting once again about the brace. "I can't afford Georgetown—they need to get me to the Bethesda Naval Hospital," he said.

She smiled at him and told him she had already taken care of the hospital's paperwork witch. He focused on her face then, especially the side that was all red. He could almost see fingerprints—and that hemostat.

"How—" he began, but she shushed him.

"I'm fine. He slapped me around, but that was all." Her eyes were telling him not to bring up the rest in front of Vann. There was still a hint of panic in her face.

"We need to get a statement," Vann said. "And sooner is better than later. We've gotta find this guy. I don't think it was in his plan that you two were gonna get away."

"The cops check around the neighborhood?"

"Yeah, but he vanished. He may have gone over the Key Bridge to

Virginia. By the time our guys talked to their guys . . ." He shrugged.

"I'll bet," Dan said. "Let's do this. They've got my neck braced. At these prices, I'd sleep better in my own tree. Can you maybe give us a ride over to my house in Alexandria? Grace is going to need somewhere to stay, and I can talk to your guys there as well as here. Or even in the car."

Vann pursed his lips. "You'd be safer here than at home; remember, Ward also got away."

"My guess is we're okay, at least for tonight. He wasn't in any shape to mount another attack," Dan replied, watching Grace's face. Her mouth was working, and her eyes jumped every time there was a loud noise outside the curtains.

Vann finally nodded. "Yeah, okay. The docs are gonna hassle you some; man said he wanted to check you in, get some more pictures on that neck tomorrow. But what the hell. I hate hospitals, too."

It took a full hour to get discharged, but finally they were on their way back to Old Town in Vann's cop car. Another unmarked car was behind them, with two Homicide detectives from the District on board. Dan was able to salvage his uniform trousers and shoes and socks, but he had to wear a hospital pajama shirt when he left the ER. His bloody shirt had been cut away when he had been brought into the ER, in the mistaken belief that he had been shot. Grace had had to acquire a pair of hospital slippers, having climbed out of the window barefoot.

After they arrived at Dan's house, the two cops debriefed both of them for an hour on tape, and then Vann, seeing that they were starting to droop, shut it off. It was close to midnight when the Homicide cops gathered up their taping equipment and went out front. Vann, Grace, and Dan remained behind in the kitchen for a few minutes. Dan's neck hurt with a steady, throbbing pain, but he was running on caffeine for the moment, and some industrial-strength painkillers.

"We'll talk some more tomorrow," Vann said, taking his cup to the sink. "Now that this has happened, we have an active case. Kidnap and attempted homicide, not to mention a little first-grade arson. I've had people tossing Ward's house on Capitol Hill tonight. We'll see what we get. But we mostly have to figure out why he came after you two."

Grace shook her head. Dan could see that her face was gray around the edges, and she sounded exhausted. She had refused coffee, and now she was slumping in her chair. "I told you," she said wearily. "He was trying to find out if we'd been hired by someone, someone he thinks is you. There's something else going on, but I don't know what it is."

"But hired to do what?"

"Come after him. That's what he said. . . . Dan, I think I better go lie down now."

"Right," Vann said, getting up quickly, looking over at Dan. "Gimme a call in the morning, okay? And we'll ask the Arlington County cops to cruise by tonight. Can't hurt."

Dan thanked him and Vann let himself out. Dan put his mug in the sink and pulled Grace close.

"Nifty date, Miss Snow. But I don't think your old man likes me."

But she didn't smile. She was shaking, and her breathing was getting ragged. He hurried her upstairs to his bedroom, but she recoiled when she saw the bed, starting to cry and holding on to him, her face buried awkwardly between the neck brace and his shoulder. He sat her down on the edge of the bed, stroked her hair, and tried to calm her, but she was keening, speaking incoherently, shaking almost uncontrollably, and then suddenly she sat up straight.

"Bathroom," she gulped, her face ashen.

He steered her into the bathroom, where she became violently ill, vomiting into the toilet bowl with great retching heaves, crying the whole time, and finally hyperventilating again. Dan could only kneel at her side and hold her, awkwardly because of the neck brace. When her convulsive heaves had stopped, he got a wet towel to clean her face, making a mask out of it to stop her roaring inhalations as she fought to recover her breath. When she finally subsided onto the floor, it became obvious that she had lost control at both ends, and when she realized that, she began crying again, but this time with less hysteria and more anguish at what had just happened. Dan reached over and turned on the shower, adjusting the temperature until it was just past the warm stage, and then he took her clothes off and eased her into the shower. He slowly raised the temperature while he held her, standing at the side of the tub, letting the water wash away the horrors of the night. He used a hand towel and soap to scrub her body. At first, she recoiled again when he touched her, but he kept murmuring, "It's me, Grace. It's just me. It's all right. "We're safe now; we're safe." Then she started to calm down. The nipple of her right breast was swollen and bruised. She stood in the shower until the house's elderly hot-water heater began to lose the fight, and then he shut the water off, sat her down on the toilet seat, and went to fetch towels from the linen closet across the hallway, his neck brace dripping all over the floor.

After drying her off, he gave her one of his ancient flannel nightshirts and a pair of wool socks, after she complained in a small voice that her feet were cold, then put her in bed. Ever since the shower, she had kept her eyes closed, as if she could keep the night at bay as long as she did not open her eyes. He pulled the covers up to her neck and pushed her damp hair away from her face. He undressed and found a second nightshirt for himself, then went downstairs with the soiled clothes and threw everything in the trash. He saw his Courvoisier bottle on the sideboard, and he went to find two snifters. He double-checked the door locks and then turned on every light on the ground floor before going back upstairs with the two glasses of cognac. He left the hall light and bathroom light on, with both the bedroom and bathroom doors cracked to let some light into the bedroom. He turned off the bedroom light and carefully sat down beside her in the bed, staying on top of the covers. She was almost completely under the covers, nothing but the top of her head showing. He gently touched her hair.

"I've got some cognac," he said softly, in case she was sleeping. He got a definite "Unh-unh" from somewhere down in the covers. Okay, be that way. He tried some of the cognac and found that it tasted wrong. Probably the pills, he thought. He decided to get rid of the neck brace for the night, putting it over on the night table, from which it promptly rolled onto the floor. He wondered fleetingly about his car, and what the hell he would tell Summerfield in the morning about all this.

Then he noticed Grace's arm was out of the covers, tugging on the edge of the blanket and the top sheet up by the pillow.

"What?" he asked.

"Get in here," she said, her voice still muffled by the covers. "Hurry. I'm freezing."

AT MIDNIGHT, MALACHI lay on his back on the couch in the darkness of the Randolph Towers apartment. His right leg was propped up on a chair in front of the couch, with an ice pack covering the golf ball–sized knot on his shin. His head was thrown back on the arm of the couch, with another ice pack covering the whole right side of his face. He held the bottle of Harper between his legs, his right hand clamped onto the neck of the bottle, his functioning left eye closed, and his brain focused on getting the next breath in and out of his chest. He could hear the sounds of a television laugh track coming from the next apartment; another insomniac in his box. A faint smell of cumin invaded the night breeze that was blowing gently through the curtains covering the partially opened balcony door.

The trek across the Key Bridge and up the hill to the Metro station had been hell on wheels—defective wheels, at that. There had been a moment out on the bridge when the cold black waters of the Potomac had beckoned. He had been furious at his body's incapacity to handle pain from what should have been two fairly low-level hits: a crack on the shin and a smack in the eye. And, although he sensed that the eye injury was serious, the pain from his shin had been incredible. The diciest part had come when the Rosslyn Metro station manager had come down onto the lower platform to see if he was all right after one of the people waiting for a train had said something.

"Jesus, mister, you get mugged? You want a cop or a paramedic?"

Malachi, sitting on one of the concrete benches in a fog of pain, had had to think fast when he heard the word *cop*, despite his throbbing shin.

"My boyfriend caught me with another guy," he said. "I'd just like to be left alone right now, if that's all right."

The station manager, an elderly black man, had retreated with a peculiar look on his face. Malachi, thankful that prejudice against gays was alive and well in America, was counting on the probability that a spat between homosexuals was not worth a call to the cops. The deskman at the Randolph Towers, an elderly Pakistani gentleman, had also reacted to his appearance, but Malachi told him he'd been mugged and had been down at the police station for hours and just wanted to get to bed. The deskman was appropriately sympathetic, then went back to his television.

He had taken a handful of aspirin when he got in, washed down by two quick jolts of the Harper. He had had to cut part of his trousers leg off his right shin—there had been bleeding and swelling down there that he hadn't known about, and the fabric had matted into the cut. The eye was a more serious problem. He had tried to examine it in the bathroom mirror with his good eye, and the image staring back at him almost made him ill. He had been very lucky the Metro station manager had not called 911. Where his eye had been, there was this puffy black, red, and blue mass the size and texture of a large ripe plum. The eye was still leaking a clear fluid out of both sides. There was a sympathetic black-and-blue ring starting around his other eye, as well.

When he went to doctor his eye, he discovered that his hand was stinging from several small glass cuts, and he had to spend twenty minutes picking out bits of glass before building an ice pack for his eye and getting a cigarette. Now he wanted a shower—his clothes stank and he stank, and he was a goddamned mess. He would have to remember to bundle up everything he had worn tonight into a plastic bag and put it in the garbage chute down the hall. Although that wouldn't matter much if those two had made it out of the fire. The papers would tell him, or, actually, the early-morning TV news.

He took another hit of the bourbon and sighed out loud as the cacophony of the nearby Arlington fire engine squad echoed through the high-rise canyons behind the building, probably on their way to a problem out on I-66. It was amazing how loud they were. He had heard fire engines on their way into Georgetown when he was about three blocks away from her house, but there would have been nothing left for them to do, not with both gasoline and natural gas in the game.

He'd done only one house fire before, that one with the connivance of the owner, a married lawyer who had fallen in lust and wanted to disappear. The lawyer's girlfriend worked at the D.C. General Hospital, and she had smuggled body parts out of the labs for six months, with the lawyer storing them in his basement freezer. With the wife out of town, they had put together the greater part of a corpus for the night of the fire, arranging the parts in the lawyer's bedroom. Malachi had rigged a hose made out of the cylindrical cardboard cores of paper towel rolls to pipe natural gas from a stove burner in the kitchen up to the second floor. It being Christmastime, he had set a yule candle burning on the mantelpiece downstairs, cracked open three windows for good oxygen flow, and then everyone had cleared out. The resulting gas explosion had dismantled the house and incinerated everything in it, leaving only some charred bits of bone and human tissue burned into the frame of the mattress to lead the investigators to the conclusion that another esquire had gone to his just reward.

If the two of them had made it out of that little deal tonight, they could tell their tale, but usable corroborative forensic evidence was going to be really tough to come by—except maybe those medical instruments. Well, screw it, he thought, sipping some more whiskey. He was pretty close to endgame here.

So now what? The time line depended on whether or not they had gotten out and talked to the cops. If they'd become toasts, he would have time to develop a pretty clear shot at the captain and then blow town. But for practical purposes, he had to assume Collins and Snow had survived, and that the captain would be alerted that Malachi was now an active threat. Navy was going to have to watch how quickly he turned his head for a while. And the woman . . . well, she wasn't going to be anxious to tangle with Malachi anytime soon. Not after being treated to hearts and minds.

So, options. First, get gone, right now. Get down the road. The cops know who you are, and you talked about Hardin in front of the woman, so they're gonna put it together. There will be federal records on you from the Army, and probably even some old CID stuff to complete the picture. Anonymity was what you've had to offer all these years, big hands and a face with no name. That cover's blown. So the smart thing to do is to get yourself gone. You could do it. You could leave tonight. The cop car was excellent cover, and in two hours you could be into West Virginia, a state filled with people who understood all about anonymity. The pickup truck would be even better.

He took another hit from the bottle, thinking exceptionally well now, the pain beginning to retreat to the margins of his consciousness. He acknowledged the logic of making his creep and forgetting about the captain. So his employers had cut him adrift at the first sign of real heat—big deal: It's what anyone in Washington would do. The captain was just playing by the rules. But something about this Hardin thing had begun to really piss him off. Both of the Hardins would still be alive and kicking if His Eminence there had been able to keep his pecker in his pants. None of this shit had been Malachi's fault. And now these pretty boys were trying to put *him* in the shit, after he had clearly taken care of business for them—twice. If the captain had dumped him like Nixon's aides had dumped the Watergate boys, that would be one thing. He remembered reading that unlovely metaphor in the *Washington Post:* "twisting"—"twisting in the wind." But to send someone in, even an inept like Snow . . . well, that made it personal.

He took another hit of Harper and coughed violently when some of the hundred proof went down the wrong way. His right eye felt like it was sloshing around in its socket when he coughed. Terrific. He wondered what he would do if it fell out. Probably feel better. He lit up another cigarette. He sat up to take the ice pack off his face, which felt like it was beginning to freeze. The towel on his leg, mostly water now, slid off onto the floor. He took another hit of whiskey, corked the bottle, put it down on the floor, and lay back again to think some more.

Was it really necessary to chuck the whole thing? What did the cops or the NIS really *know?* All they'd have would be some hysterical noise from the woman and some trembling, whiny stuff from rowboat man. He had not been face-to-face with the Navy guy for more than three seconds all night, and even Navy would have to admit that he had been preoccupied at the time. The woman had probably memorized his face, but he'd provided some distractions for her, too. Hearts and minds. He closed his eyes. Had the cops been to his house on Capitol Hill yet? Probably, if the woman had survived the fire and talked. They'd have probable cause after the fireworks in Georgetown.

Hell, let's go see, he thought. Wait until it's two, three in the morning, then drive over there. Scope it out. Nobody there, get into the house and pull those tapes. He could get in and out of the garage from the alley, and he could use the cop car to get into the neighborhood—there were always lots of cop cars prowling D.C. at that hour of the morning.

So, option two. Go see what the cops were up to, and then, he decided, what he really wanted to do was have one last little séance with his dear friend and client the captain. Then he would bail out, get himself down the road and gone. Meantime, let the ice do its thing. He put the remains of the ice pack back on his throbbing face. The ice and the Harper, his old friends in need. He set the alarm on his watch for 0200, squinting hard with his one good eye to see it, stabbed his cigarette out on an ice cube, and dozed.

AT AROUND TWO in the morning, Grace awoke with a shout and started a frantic bout of kicking at the covers, startling Dan out of a deep sleep and causing him to wrench his neck again as he sat up in the bed. When he realized what was happening, he grabbed her, trying to pin her flailing arms, shouting at her to wake up. At first, she struggled harder, babbling incoherently, but then she did wake up. She sat up in one violent motion, nearly knocking Dan back out of the bed. When she realized where she was and recalled the dream, she started crying again, filling the bedroom with great heaving wails that nearly broke his heart. He held her and comforted her as best he could, his neck on fire again, a fact she finally recognized when her own misery subsided. She turned in the bed, saw the mask of pain on his face, and reached to comfort him. They lay entwined in each other's arms, making small noises and holding each other until they both fell asleep again.

AT 3:30 MONDAY morning, Malachi slid back into the driver's side of the sedan and locked all the doors, puffing from the exertion but buoyed by the excitement of getting in and out of the house without being caught. The car's windows were covered with enough condensation to prevent anyone from seeing that the car was even occupied. He took a deep breath and then laughed. He'd made it into the duplex from the alley in two minutes, after spending nearly forty minutes watching the alley from the next block to see if there was anyone waiting for him near the darkened house. He had originally parked one block away on his own street and phoned both phones in the houses to see what would happen, but there had been no reaction— no lights, no machines, no nothing. There had been no strange vehicles parked out on the street, either.

Once he decided to make his move, he had not wasted time; after retrieving the one tape, he hit the safe and removed his money stash and the extra gun, and then he'd gone from the duplex apartment into his own via the door in the closet, which did not appear to have been discovered. But the cops had definitely been there. There were signs of a search in every room. He'd retrieved the second tape and backed right out, going out the kitchen door and into the alley, getting back to the car as quickly as his throbbing leg would allow. As he sat there now, fondling the two cassettes, he smelled a peculiar smell. From his feet; something on the car's carpet. He looked down. There was a grayish powder on the rubber mat. Those sons a bitches—they'd left some Carpet Fresh on the rugs in his house. Shit, he'd forgotten that old trick. Now there would be footprints in the powder— which would tell them he'd been back. He realized now that he had smelled it in the house but hadn't paid any attention. Well, what the hell. So they'd know he was still around. They would want to know what he had been after. Too late, suckers, he thought. If you ran your mouths, I'm gonna be ahead of you, and I only need one day to get done what I need to get done.

He cranked up the car and mashed the defrost button for the windshield. He waited for a minute for the windshield to clear, then drove out of the alley and took Pennsylvania down into town, wanting to merge into the anonymity of the city's wide boulevards as quickly as possible. Below the Capitol, the streetlights along the majestic concourse of government buildings cast a dignified roseate glow on all the ornate facades, barely illuminating the shadowy lumps of the homeless littering the Metro system's exhaust grates. A District cop car passed him on Pennsylvania, and he dutifully exchanged waves. He worked his way over to Constitution, and from there, he drove across the Teddy Roosevelt Bridge into Virginia. The whiskey and the aspirin were wearing off, and the throbbing in his eye was beginning to overtake the pain in his leg and occasionally make all the streetlights blur together. The right side of his face felt leaden, as if it were starting to sag off the bones like the makeup in some horror movie. The pain in his leg was throbbing in perfect time to the beat of his heart. Careful, he thought as he swerved out of his lane going up Wilson. Can't get picked up on a stupid DUI at this stage. He turned off the main drag as soon as he was out of Rosslyn, then worked his way back toward Ballston by using the side streets; the Randolph Towers was tall enough to be seen above the trees and houses along the sleeping residential streets, giving him a landmark.

He did not relax until back in the apartment, where he had to lie down right away to get the pain back under control. The eye in particular was generating waves of pain that became pulses of red light in his brain, and his left eye was not operating very well, either. He turned off all the lights. Gonna be a blind son of a bitch pretty quick, this keeps up, he thought, flopping on the couch, his head thrown back and his right leg elevated. He looked at his watch. It was almost five o'clock. Daylight pretty soon.

He forced himself to get up off the couch and stagger into the kitchen. The ice maker in the small refrigerator was nearly empty, exhausted by his earlier demands. He opened another bottle of Harper, took a small shot, and lit a cigarette. The deli would be open in an hour or so; they'd have ice. But he would need a patch over that eye before he went back out in public. Assuming the worst, that one or both of them had made it out of the fire, he also had to assume the cops would be looking for someone with an injured eye. But maybe not by the morning news—he might have a day of grace before his description made it to the television. Doesn't matter, 'cause once the composite gets out on TV, people will remember seeing you—the Metro guy, the desk people. So make a patch. He lay down again on the couch, with the whiskey bottle on the floor. Maybe get an hour of shut-eye. Shut-eye, right. He started to laugh, but it hurt too much. Something he had to do, to listen to. The tapes. Right. In just a minute.

64

DAN LOOKED AT his watch and almost bolted from the bed—it was 7:30 on a Monday morning, the time at which he was normally at his desk and sorting through his weekend message traffic in 614. But then the events of the night flooded back into his mind, and he lay back and turned to find Grace, who was still submerged in the covers. Her hair was inches from his face, and he could hear her breathing slowly. His neck did not hurt quite so much, but he moved very slowly as he explored its limits of motion. After a few minutes, he disentangled himself from Grace, eliciting a small noise from under the covers. He stroked her head until she went back to sleep. Then he got out of the bed—and very nearly fell down. He had to sink to his knees to regain his balance, and he remained in the duckwalk position, one hand grabbing a handful of covers, for almost a minute before the room stopped spinning. He tried again, much slower, and this time succeeded in staggering into the bathroom.

He sat on the throne and fought down a thin wave of nausea and dizziness. His neck bones felt like a series of overlapping plates, each one protesting when he tried to move his head. The nausea must be from that damn painkiller they'd given him. He did not want to consider what the hell his neck would feel like if he had not taken the painkiller. Gotta call Summerfield, tell him why I'm not there, tell him what's happened, he thought. Have to get my car back, assuming it survived the fire. When he closed his eyes, he could still hear that jet-engine roar of the fire and see that monster standing over Grace, her defenseless body spread-eagled obscenely across the bed with all those shiny— He shook the image out of his mind, trading it for a wave of pain for his efforts. Better put that goddamn brace back on.

After using the bathroom and checking on Grace again, he put on some shorts and a rugby T-shirt and mounted the brace around his neck. Leaving his bathrobe on the foot of the bed for Grace, he went downstairs and then began looking out each of the windows on the ground floor, bending awkwardly because of the brace. But everything outside appeared to be normal. He went to the kitchen and fixed a pot of coffee, preceding that with a glass of milk and a piece of bread to overcome the metallic medicinal taste in his throat. Once he had a mug of coffee safely in hand, he sat down and called the office, reaching Yeoman Jackson.

"Jackson, let me talk to the captain," he said.

"Hey, Commander. They been talkin' 'bout you," Jackson said. "Colonel Snapper, he sayin' you takin' this hot romance—"

"The captain, please, Jackson."

Jackson sniffed and put him on hold for a minute, and then Summerfield picked up.

"Well, Daniel, are you two all right?"

"You've heard about it?"

"It was on the six A.M. news—house fire in Georgetown, house belonging to a Miss Grace Ellen Snow. Miss Snow and a friend surprised an intruder in the house; the intruder threw gasoline, burned the place down. They said you both got out but that the intruder got away."

Dan paused for a few seconds. "Where in the hell did they get all that?" he asked.

"Officials reported. Snapper says you're taking the concept of a hot date to extremes, even for a sailor."

Dan smiled. "Tell Snapper that at least I date girls. His sheep are still safe."

"You tell him; Snapper takes his barnyard seriously. I assume you need a couple of days' leave to help Miss Snow get her life put back together?"

"Well," Dan said, pausing, trying to think fast. How much could he tell Summerfield? He understood now that anything he told Summerfield would get to the EAs. He had to talk to Vann before he said anything more. "Yes, sir, I'd appreciate that. My Suburban's over there, and Grace is over here. I'm assuming we won't be able to salvage much out of the house."

"House? There is no house. There's nothing there but a hole. She drive a sedan?"

"Yes, sir."

"Well, that's gone, too. I didn't see your Suburban, but there were still fire engines there this morning."

"Damn. I'm going to have to get her some clothes, and she's going to have to get to her bank and her insurance company. A couple of days would be very useful. And I've injured my neck—getting out of the house. They've got me in a brace, and I've gotta tell you, I'm definitely operating on one shaft right now."

Summerfield's voice lost its bantering tone. "Okay. From the looks of that house, you've been through a bad night. I'll open a leave chit for you for the rest of the week; you can come in whenever you're up to it. Take care of your lady friend and be religious about that damned brace. If you need wheels today, I can have Jackson meet you in the parking lot with my keys and you can borrow my car. Anything else we can do for you here, make sure you call me. And Dan—does this fire have anything to do with the Hardin case?"

Got me, the old fox, Dan thought. He couldn't lie to Summerfield. But he did not have to tell him everything he suspected.

"Yes, sir, I think it does."

There was a pregnant pause, as if Summerfield was waiting for more. "Okay, Dan, I think I understand," Summerfield said finally. "But promise you'll tell me what's going on when you get Miss Snow sorted out."

"Yes, sir. It's just that right now, there are some things you may not want to know."

Summerfield laughed softly. "Call us if you need help," he said before hanging up.

Dan thanked him and hung up. When he turned around, Grace was standing in the kitchen doorway. She was wearing his bathrobe, and one side of her pale face was still somewhat red and puffy where the guy had slapped her. Her hair was mussed and she was having trouble keeping her eyes open, but she was still beautiful. Dan felt a sudden wave of affection sweep through him, and he went over to her and took her in his arms. She bumped her face on the neck brace and they both laughed. But she did not let go.

"Sorry about last night," she said in a soft voice.

"A date with you is nothing if not interesting, Miss Snow," he said.

"I meant—"

"Yeah, yeah. You'd think I'd learn. I ply my wenches with demon rum, and do they get all hot and ready for romance? They do not. They get sick in my car, is what they do. Happens time after time. Like I said, you'd think I'd learn."

She hugged him tighter, and they stood that way in the middle of the kitchen for a few minutes while he rubbed her back and felt her trying to control her breathing. Finally, he moved her over to a chair and poured her a cup of coffee. He partially refilled his own mug and sat down across the kitchen table from her.

"This is going to be an all-day, never-ending, no-shit, original-bitch Monday," he said, and she smiled finally, stirring some sugar into her coffee.

"Has it been on the news?"

"Yes. Summerfield saw it this morning. Grace, the house is totaled, and I'm afraid the Beamer is gone, too."

She slumped a little in her chair. He took her hand across the table before continuing.

"And while I'm making your day, we have some other problems. I called Summerfield to get some leave so I can help you with this disaster. I suspect we'll spend the whole week getting you off the reef and back into the channel again."

"I can hardly wait. But—"

"The problem is that Summerfield asked if this was connected to the Hardin case. And I told him yes, but I didn't tell him any more than that, because I think everything I've been telling him has been piped straight into the headquarters EA system."

"Dan, they can hardly blame you for what happened last night."

He got up to dump and wash out his coffee mug. The coffee was not sitting well. "Yeah, well, maybe they can and maybe they can't, but that's not my real concern. What I'm worried about is that Vann obviously believes that the bad dream we ran into last night was a hired hand. He wasn't some itinerant burglar—that badass was sent. Grace, I don't think either one of us was supposed to survive his little interrogation last night. Someone sent that guy in to kill us."

She put her coffee down as the color drained out of her face and he came around the table quickly to take her hands. She leaned her head into his stomach as he stood next to her.

"I might be wrong, but obviously that guy was waiting for us. And you said he said he'd been in the house before. He obviously believed that you and I were involved in the Hardin investigation. I think he was sent to find out what we knew and then to eliminate us, in a house fire. He brought gasoline, remember?"

She moved her head against his stomach in a nodded yes.

"And based on what he said last night, this might be the guy who did the Hardin killing—but not on his own. There's somebody paying this guy, and I've got this terrible feeling that the somebody is a Navy flag officer."

She pulled her head back and looked up at him. "Except . . ." she said.

"Except what?" he had trouble looking down at her because of the brace.

"He kept asking me if 'the captain' had sent me. He was acting as if *I* was somebody hired to get *him*. If he had been hired to get us, why would he care?"

Dan stared out the kitchen window. Why indeed. Why the interrogation scene with Grace, not with him, but with Grace? If he had been hired to kill them, he could have knocked them both over the head, put them in a bedroom upstairs, and torched the house. Grace had a valid point, but he was still convinced that the guy had meant to kill them—but only *after* he found something out.

"Dan," she said, putting a hand to her mouth, "I just remembered something."

"What?"

"He was about to say a name last night . . . when you came through the door. He wanted to know about Captain Vann. He wanted to know if Captain Vann was working for Captain somebody. He didn't say the name, just called him the 'vice-chief's flunky.' "

Dan stared down at her in horror. "The vice-chief's 'flunky'? He said that?"

"Yes. Something like that. And I think that's what he was really after. He assumed that I was working for Captain Vann and that Captain Vann was working for this other captain."

Dan pulled a chair under him and sank into it.

"Jesus H. Christ. The vice-chief's flunky. Captain Randall. Now it all makes sense. That's why Randall has been so all fired up about the Hardin case. Hell, this explains why OpNav took the investigation away from NIS in the first place. At the vice chief's orders, remember? Son of a bitch! Don't you see it? Elizabeth Hardin was having an affair with the Vice Chief of Naval Operations! No goddamn wonder he needed to cover it up. Son of a *bitch*!"

Grace was staring at him. "And you've been briefing Summerfield," she said.

"Yes. And he's been feeding it all back to his dear friend and classmate, the vice chief."

"Do you suppose Summerfield knows?"

Dan shook his head. "I can't believe he does. He was just keeping the vice chief informed to keep the Navy from getting blindsided. Summerfield, the ex-EA. No, Summerfield wouldn't be a party to murder. But he might as well have been. Grace, this is awful. After all the scandals in the Navy these past few years, this is going to kill us."

She got up, and this time she came to hold his head against her body. "Poor Dan," she said softly. "Some bastard tries to kill us both, he's probably killed one if not two other people already, you think the second-most-senior admiral in the Navy hired him to do it, and you're worried about what this will do to the *Navy*?" Her voice was rising hysterically at the end.

"The Navy is my life," he said, his voice muffled. He tried to look up at her, but the brace was in the way. "Especially after I lost Claire. And before I found you. The Navy is special to us, Grace. The ships, the crews, going to sea, all the history and tradition. You understand after a while that you are allowed to be a part of it, a part of something bigger and more important than any individual. And you're supposed to do an honorable job of it."

He stood up. "And this son of a bitch has dishonored his uniform, not to mention instigating a murder and almost getting away with two more. No wonder Mrs. Hardin didn't want to talk. Especially if she knew whom her daughter was seeing. She'd think it's hopeless."

"You don't suppose Wesley Hardin went to see him, do you? A lieutenant confronting a four-star admiral?"

"You heard Vann. He said Wesley would jump on it, whether or not it was the smart thing to do. We've gotta talk to Vann. Right now."

"Can we get me some clothes first?" she asked in a small voice.

He smiled at her, but then the smile disappeared. "Yes, but then we've gotta move. As soon as the hired gun watches the news and finds out we got away, we're targets again—high-priority targets. Right now, Vann is our only protection, but only if he knows what we know."

Dan went back upstairs to retrieve his wallet. He felt like a freak in the brace, but to his dismay, the brace helped a lot. His neck still hurt, but the brace kept him from adding to the problem with sudden moves of his head. He found his wallet, retrieved Vann's card, and went back downstairs. Grace was stirring some sugar into a second mug of coffee and staring out the back window. Almost automatically, he went to her.

"You'll stay here, won't you?" he said, putting his hands on her shoulders.

"And what will the bush Nazi next door have to say about that arrangement?" she asked.

"Probably that it's about time," he replied. "But I don't want you out of my sight until we know these people have been taken off the boards. Depending on what Vann can do, we may be going up against some seriously big guns."

"What can Vann do? He can't just arrest them."

"I know that, Grace. The Hardin case is a federal matter, remember? Vann's bosses told him to turn loose of it. He can get something going after the fire last night, but he has to find the bad guy before he can possibly move on the flags. Right now, the people with jurisdiction are the NIS, and, as we know, the vice chief can make them do whatever he wants."

"It *was* a federal case, until last night," she snapped. "Vann can make that into attempted murder and arson, to name just a couple of charges. Making the case and proving it might be tougher, but Vann can surely get their attention."

"Let's find out."

He called Vann's number, but, as usual, the captain was in a meeting. Dan left his home number and asked the secretary to have Vann get back to them as soon as possible. He hung up and told Grace to start making a list.

"A list?"

"Of what you need for a set of clothes—sizes, brands. There are some shops around the corner where I think we can put at least one outfit together. After that, if we still haven't heard from Vann, I think we have to go to Georgetown."

Two HOURS LATER they were in a cab heading for Georgetown. Dan had taken Grace's list and done his duty, even the part where he had to stand somewhat red-faced at the lingerie counter giving monosyllabic answers to the salesgirl's helpful questions about what style of panties he was interested in, much to the amusement of two women waiting behind him. Grace had looked into the packages, given him an arch look, and gone upstairs without comment. Dan had changed into some wash khaki trousers, a long-sleeved white uniform shirt that had been retired from naval service, and a khaki windbreaker. Grace was wearing a mid-length gray skirt, a white blouse, and a dark red jacket. A brand-new lightweight London Fog raincoat was on her lap.

They talked in the cab about how she would get into her safe-deposit box at the bank without keys—both sets of keys had been, of course, in the house. The local television news had given them a glimpse of what they were going to see when they arrived, but even that did not prepare them for the absolute devastation they found when the cab pulled up on P Street. A single fire truck was still there, its two-man crew probing through a blackened mound of debris with occasional shots from a hose. A small crowd of students from the university stood around gawking at the smoldering hole where the house had been. Half the street and the entire perimeter of her property was circled by fluttering bands of yellow police tape. Of the house, only the bricks of the side walls were recognizable. The heat from the blaze had been intense enough to burn all the leaves off the nearby trees and blacken the paint on both adjoining houses. They could see all the way to the back garden gate from the street; the garden looked somehow inde-cently exposed without the house. Grace's car was squatting on its tire rims in a bed of broken glass. The body had been burned down to its metal shell, parts of which were already showing a rusty brown patina after being drowned in fire-fighting water. Dan's Suburban was still parked across her driveway, and they could see that some of the paint on its hood had been blistered. Grace stared at the steaming mound that had been her home and fought back tears as Dan paid the taxi bill.

A uniformed cop got out of an unmarked car across the street and came over as they got out.

"You the owners?" he asked.

"I am," Grace said, her voice not entirely in control.

"Okay, lady. The arson squad's on the way out. I've got some forms we gotta get filled out."

"Have you spoken with Captain Vann?" Grace asked. Dan had walked over to his car and was now on hands and knees, checking out the Suburban.

"Vann? No. What's Captain Vann got to do with a house fire?" The cop, a pudgy Hispanic-looking individual who needed a shave, looked faintly annoyed. The brass tag on his shirt said his name was Lopez.

"There's some background to what happened here, Officer Lopez," Grace said patiently. "The arson people should talk to Captain Vann before they start here."

"Okay, I'll tell 'em. But I still hafta get this paperwork done. You wanna come over to my car or what?"

Grace accompanied the officer to the cop car and they sat together in the front seat. The stink of burned insulation, water-soaked, charred wood, and melted plastics permeated the entire street. Some of her neighbors were out on their front porches, and two of them waved tentatively to her as she got into the cop car. After twenty minutes of filling out police report forms, Grace saw what she presumed to be the arson squad pulling up in a police van. Four men dressed in dark blue overalls got out of the van and began to assemble their equipment. A middle-aged white man with sandy red hair and an enormous handlebar mustache came over to the cop car and intro-duced himself as Detective Sergeant Cowans. It turned out that he had already been contacted by Vann and knew what had started the fire. He had a message from Vann for Grace.

"He said he'd like to see you and Commander Collins downtown around three-thirty, four o'clock."

"We tried to call him this morning," Grace said.

"Yeah, well," the sergeant said, looking faintly embarrassed, "he's got a whole day of department-wide sexual-harrassment seminars to go to, and they're not letting anybody skip out, not even the captains. It's been scheduled for weeks."

Life goes on, Grace thought, looking over at the small knot of college students. "We'll be there," she said. "I've got a lot to do this morning. That's four o'clock at the Municipal Center, right?"

"Yes, ma'am. Sorry about your house. Was there anything of especially high value in there? Like jewelry, and particularly diamonds? Sometimes we find them."

Grace held up her hand, where she still wore Rennie's engagement ring as a buffer against single men on the prowl. "This is the only diamond, Sergeant Cowans. The rest of my jewelry was gold, and I suppose that's all melted."

"We'll keep an eye out, Miss Snow. Sometimes we get lucky. But usually—"

"I understand, Sergeant. Thank you."

The sergeant asked her a few more questions about the layout of the house and whether or not there had been any guns or ammunition in it and then he went back to the van. The uniformed cop tagged along, leaving Grace sitting in the passenger seat of his car, trying to take stock. The house and furnishings had been insured, but she had lost every one of her possessions in the fire: furniture and heirlooms from her parents' house in Boston, the only pictures she had of them, all of her clothes, her favorite books, childhood mementos. It was as if her past had simply disappeared. She looked around for her purse to get a tissue, but of course her purse had gone, too—wallet, checkbook, credit cards, driver's license, everything. She wiped her eyes with the back of her hand as a wave of dread seized her then, as the image of that horrible man bent over her in the bedroom came back, the total helplessness she had felt when he had cut her clothes off, the nightmare sight of his maimed body. That man was still out there. Maybe not that far away, maybe out there watching them even now. She knew that Dan had been lucky to have even made it up the stairs after that karate chop in the front hallway, and even more fortunate to have been able to drive the man off. Dan was right: That man had planned to kill them both. She began to tremble again, her mouth working, her vision blurring as her eyes concentrated on Dan, who was only twenty feet away, half in, half out of his car, rooting around for the hidden spare ignition key, his movements made clumsy because of the neck brace. She called his name, but no sound came out. And yet he turned around, as if he had heard her anyway, from all the way across the street. He closed his car door and came over to her, opening the door of the cop car and taking her hands. She sagged against him, trying not to cry.

"Hey," he said. "Hey, it's gonna be all right. The Suburban's okay. Let's get out of here. Let's go back to my place. You can contact the insurance company and everyone else by phone. Come on."

He helped her out of the car and into the Suburban, both of them stepping through a slushy mat of burned leaves and standing water at the curb. Dan checked out with Officer Lopez, who seemed indifferent, and then drove back to Old Town. The paint of the Suburban's right side had been blistered, and the air in the car had a faint smell of char to it. Dan ran the air conditioner to try to get the smell out of the car. Grace concentrated on looking at the familiar scenery along the GW Parkway to keep her mind on an even keel. Then she remembered what the sergeant had said.

"Vann wants to see us this afternoon," she said. "Four o'clock at the Municipal Center."

"Not until then?" Dan said. He seemed to be annoyed. Grace realized then that, in her misery over the house, she had shut the Hardin case out of her mind. She sat up straight in her seat. Pull yourself together, she thought. We both got out with our skins intact. Her mind shied from the thought of what it would have been like if she had survived and Dan had not. But then her Yankee practicality asserted itself. You can't do anything about the house. But you better start thinking about the possibility that Malachi Ward might try again.

"Are you going to tell him what you suspect?" she asked as they drove into Old Town.

"Hell yes," Dan replied. "Vann's the only outside guy who can confront the Navy on this. But he'll need my help. And your testimony—that bastard didn't seem to want to talk to me last night. But it will take both of us, because the NIS sure as hell isn't going to do anything. That's why I'm worried about time—if the vice chief and his ace EA, Captain Randall, put two and two together, they can move against me. They could probably stiff the District police if they could neutralize me."

"If they did that, could Vann do it with my help?"

He laughed, then recited: " 'Disgruntled former employee of the NIS levels accusations against the number-two officer in the Navy. Charges two-year-old hit-and-run accident linked to admiral's love life. Accuser resigned under pressure from NIS top management. Questions surface about how she got the appointment in the first place.' No, I think they could taint any testimony you gave claiming it was the result of a grudge. I'm the one who can testify about being pressured to stay out of the Hardin case *after* they gave it back to NIS. But if they send me to a weather station in Patagonia, working the case gets real tough."

"They wouldn't be that stupid," Grace said.

"Wouldn't they? You'd think that really senior officers wouldn't be caught within a hundred miles of a three-day flyboy orgy in Las Vegas, where junior officers traditionally tear the clothes off of young women in public hotel hallways, all in the name of a professional seminar, mind you. And it looks like this guy, who's married by the way, was dumb enough to have a sexual relationship with an Oh-three right there on the Navy staff. If they thought they could keep this under wraps by shipping me out, you better believe they'll put my ass on Antarctic ice in a heartbeat. The only way we can stop it is to confront them first—Randall and his boss. But we need Vann for that."

When they returned to Dan's house, there were two messages waiting. The first was from Vann's office, confirming what Sergeant Cowans had told them. The second was from Summerfield.

"Dan, this is Ron Summerfield. I think we have a serious problem here—the vice chief's office wants a meeting with you and me at seventeen-thirty in the vice's office. I told them you were on leave because of the fire, but Randall was, shall we say, less than sympathetic. So I'd recommend you come back to the building, say around seventeen hundred. I'm afraid some shit's about to hit a fairly large fan."

Dan sat down in a chair as the machine beeped off and rewound itself. "Well, oh shit, oh dear," he said. "Looks like my dance card is filling up, Miss Grace Ellen Snow."

"Fortunately, we'll see Vann before you have to go do this. You will let me go with you, yes?"

Dan thought for a moment. "That's not going to be a very friendly session, Grace. On the other hand—"

"Screw that," Grace swore. "That was *my* house that was destroyed last night, and, if you're right about Randall, by *his* hired hand, who, by the way, was probably going to kill us in the process. I think we need to ask Vann if we shouldn't be seeking police protection instead of attending meetings with these people."

Dan got up and began to pace around the living room. "These people," he said slowly, "are my legal superiors. It's not as if I have some open-and-shut case against the vice chief or even his EA. Vann's probably going to remind us of that in no uncertain terms. So until we do have a clear case, I have to follow orders. When an Oh-ten says, 'Come see me,' an Oh-five doesn't ask, 'Gee, do I have to?' " He stopped in front of a window.

Grace could see that Dan was having a hard time believing his own theory, because it meant that a system and a profession he believed in utterly was very rotten at the very top. She went over to him.

"Look," she said. "One thing at a time. Let's go talk to Vann, see what his take is on all this. Maybe he can find a hole in it. Maybe there's another explanation for what happened last night. His people should have finished with their search of that guy Ward's house by now, so maybe he has new data. But if it all hangs together, even circumstantially, then we all three go to the Pentagon this afternoon and confront these people."

Dan sat back down and put his head in his hands, the brace sticking out like an Elizabethan ruff collar under his arms. Grace sat down beside him.

"If nothing else," she said, "the Washington system will begin to work. You know what the Navy does when there's a major scandal brewing—

they isolate the major players. This vice chief can't tell the NIS to bury this once there's been a public confrontation with the District police present."

"You're right. *If* Vann will play."

65

MALACHI AWOKE WITH a start on his couch. He could sense but not clearly see waning daylight streaming in through the balcony windows, and there were sounds of traffic out in front of the apartment building. For a moment, he could not figure out why he couldn't see, but then it all came back. He felt his face. His right eye was puffy and hot. The clear liquid that had been leaking from each corner had dried into a sugarlike crust on his cheek. There were striations of pain running along the side of his head from his right eye back toward his right ear. He had to rub his left eye to get it open, but then at least he could see. He looked at his watch and swore. Four-thirty in the afternoon. Damn it! He had lost the entire day.

He swung his legs off the couch and his right shin reminded him that all was not well down there, either. He tried to stand, but he could not put weight on his right leg. He hobbled into the bathroom to relieve himself, then turned on the mirror light to survey the damage. The right eye looked about as bad as it felt. A rolling pin. The son a bitch had done him with a rolling pin. His left eye was operational, but the panda-bear circle was even more pronounced. He sat down on the toilet seat and examined his shin. The knot was still there, and there was extensive blood bruising up and down his leg. He felt the bone area around the hit and winced, but it did not actually seem to be broken. He could still recall that blinding, nauseating pain when Navy had whacked him in the leg. It had actually hurt more than the eye—a lot more.

He gingerly washed his face and then went into the bedroom to find the makings for an eye patch, which he ended up fashioning out of two shoelaces and an oval-shaped swatch of fabric from his black windbreaker. He cut a four-inch-square patch out of a towel and used it for padding, then tied it on. The entire rig immediately fell right off. He needed some elastic. He cut the elastic waistband from a pair of undershorts and joined the two ends of the shoestrings together on the back of his head with a section of the white elastic. This time, the patch stayed in place. He took some more aspirin and then limped out to the kitchen to see if there was some ice available. He was suddenly very thirsty. He finished the half container of orange juice that was in the refrigerator, adding a dollop of Harper to the last inch of juice to get his heart going again. He made up an ice pack, using a kitchen towel and the meager pile of ice cubes in the freezer, and went back into the living room. He flopped down on the couch again, lit up a cigarette, and pulled the tape recorder over, putting the ice pack back on his leg. The patch over his eye had for some strange reason lessened the pain. Maybe it was the pressure. He had no medicine for an eye injury, nor any idea of what to buy for it. After tonight, he would head for West Virginia, maybe find some country doctor out there to work on his eye. But first, the tapes.

He examined the two tiny tape cassettes. One was still showing its clear plastic leader. The other had run all the way out. He stuck the second tape into the machine, plugged in earphones, and put it on his chest. He listened for almost thirty minutes to the sounds of what seemed like three men walking around his house, opening drawers, shifting furniture, and talking to each other about the house and the basketball championships and the new lieutenant's promotion list. There was nothing about why they were there until almost the very end of the tape, when one of the men asked about the duplex next door. It sounded as if he was speaking from the next room.

"Hey, Sarge, we gotta hit the twin next door?"

"No, I don't think so."

"Well, what's the warrant say?"

"Ain't no warrant."

There was a pause in the conversation, then the sounds of the first man coming into the room that had the microphone.

"You say there isn't a warrant here?"

"That's right, sunshine. This is a favor for Vann."

"Oh man . . ."

"Don't get your tits in a flutter, Williams. Vann looks out for people, people need to return the favor. The word around the Homicide dicks is that this is personal, off the books. He's doing it for some Navy guy. He's gonna meet with the Navy guy Monday. Needs the place tossed, see what we see. Let's just get it done and get outta here, all right?"

Williams protested some more, until the sergeant began to speculate on the joys of Anacostia patrol duty. But it was enough for Malachi. He listened to the rest of the tape, but there was nothing significant, other than that they had not appeared to find anything worthy of exclamation. The tape ran out while they were talking about the District's latest round of personnel cuts.

Malachi took off the earphones and dropped the recorder on the floor. He pulled the phone over to his lap and thought about what he was going to do. So Vann was a cop, and he was working for some Navy guy— probably moonlighting. The bastards were pulling the strings, all right. And moving right along—his house getting an unauthorized search even before the fire, and a meeting with the Navy guy, which of course meant the captain, sometime today. He looked at his watch. Probably like right now.

He shifted his body on the couch, trying to ease the pain in his leg. It was just like he'd figured—the captain was operating off the books, behind the scenes, manipulating contractors and moonlighting cops, moving in on him. Well, that would make it almost easy. The captain was still the only guy who can directly finger him for the Hardin shit. Time to tie that bleeder off. He would call the captain, tell him he was going to fold his tents and steal away into the desert night, and then propose a final meeting. Let the captain pick a place. Then pack out the barest essentials in the truck: the money, both guns—one to use, one to have after he disposed of the first—some clothes.

He knew that, after the fire, the captain might be too spooked to meet with him. But Malachi was counting on something—the captain might see opportunity in such a meeting. He had to be just about in a panic about now, even though he was getting some unofficial help. The cops would have to investigate the fire in Georgetown, and it was only a matter of time before they figured out that the guy who torched Snow's house might have a relationship to the captain, which would put an end to the moonlighting. So, from the captain's point of view, the chance to get Malachi alone, in some remote spot of his own choosing, should be enticing. Especially since Malachi intended to ask for the meet under the pretext of getting some money in return for a promise to disappear. He figured the captain would meet him, either because he would be grateful that Malachi was going to take some money and run or because he was going to try to take Malachi out and end his problem. Malachi would be able to tell a lot from the meeting place the captain proposed, but either way, he was going to ice that supercilious bastard. That would take care of *his* problem, and then he could slip away into wild and wonderful West by God Virginia.

He would make the call around 5:00 P.M. and leave the duplex phone number, which would silently forward the return call here to the apartment. He dropped the soggy towel on the rug and hobbled back out into the kitchen to get the bottle of Harper. The leg was actually a little better. He had to take it easy on the sauce, because he might have a long drive ahead of him tonight. He dismissed the notion that the captain might be waiting for him with a gun or even some help. The captain was an executive assistant, not a player. Guy like that could set a dozen ambushes for Malachi, and even with one eye and one leg, Malachi would have his ass. He should have saved some of that ice.

66

DAN, GRACE, AND Captain Vann were silent as they rode the long escalator up from the Pentagon Metro station to the concourse entrance. At five in the evening, the three of them were in lonely contrast to the steady stream of people riding the down escalator, as the Pentagon's 23,000 employees emptied the building. Grace was dressed as she had been in the morning. Dan had kept the neck brace but had changed into service dress blues, and Vann was wearing a dark suit. Dan was keeping an eye on Grace, who was looking very tired, having spent a good part of the day on the telephone with her bank, credit-card companies, and her insurance company, which had not lived up very well to its advertising. And the meeting with Vann had been difficult, as well.

Since they had to be back at the Pentagon by five o'clock, Dan had driven up to the Pentagon from Old Town and parked the car in north parking. They then took a Metro to Judiciary Square for their meeting with Vann. The trip from Vann's office to the Pentagon by car at rush hour would have taken them at least forty minutes; the Metro did it in fifteen. Vann had been late and was in a foul humor after his day of sensitivity training, and he had come into the office muttering imprecations about every variant of hyphenated Americans. He debriefed the two of them on the results of the preliminary search through Ward's town house, which had turned up nothing of particular interest.

"He's got a hidey-hole somewhere; the place was cleaned out of anything interesting, but not abandoned. My people had another look early this A.M., right after the fire, but there was no sign he'd been back. I'll have someone go back in to see if he's been back today. But I have a feeling he's still in town."

"Which means we're not out of the woods yet," Dan had said.

"That's right. What's happening on your end?"

Dan recounted his theory about who the players really were, then told Vann about the summons to see the vice chief's EA at five o'clock. Vann whistled when he heard what Malachi had said, but then he made the obvious comment about lack of evidence.

"I know," Dan said. "But you have to admit it fits together pretty well. Remember the valentine with W.T. on it? And it's why I need you to be at this meeting this afternoon—if they're getting ready to move on me, the fact that the District police are in it can block any funny business."

Vann had shuffled some papers on his desk. "The District police are only sort of in it," he said. "Technically, the Hardin case is still federal. The fire last night and what happened to you two—well, we have no evidence that any of that is tied to the Hardin case, except for what he said to Miss Snow here. But, see, this is shaping up as a conspiracy rap—and the feds will probably retain overall jurisdiction."

"But the feds who have the jurisdiction are under the thumb of the guy we think is behind it," Grace interjected. "That's been true from the start, when this same admiral took the investigation away from the NIS."

Vann acknowledged that problem. "I can go with you, but we're gonna be on thin ice. Look, I want to get these guys as badly as you do, but I know enough about the system to realize that we can also end up dropping our case into that crack between feds and locals. I've already done something I shouldn't have."

"What?" Dan asked.

"The search of his house was done without a warrant. Sunday night, actually, probably while he was waiting in your house. I made some calls after we talked to Angela, and some guys did me a favor."

"But after what he did last night, surely you have probable cause."

"Miss Snow, I don't think the courts recognize after-the-fact probable cause."

"Okay," Dan said. "But you said they didn't find anything, so there's been no evidence compromised, right? I need you at this meeting for your deterrent effect: You don't have to say anything. Just your presence ought to be enough to make them realize they can't just order me out to Alaska tonight."

"They can do that?"

"The vice chief can call up the CNO's personal airplane at Andrews and have me airborne in an hour, he wants to. Or he could greet me at his office with a squad of Marines and have me disappear into the brig at Quantico. One phone call can do that."

"Shit," Vann said. "I wish I could do that."

So Vann had agreed to come along, but Dan knew that it was going to be shaky. If the vice chief was the eminence behind all of this, he had tremendous power at his disposal. He could indeed have Marine guards waiting in his office to arrest Dan and then have him detained in a military brig anywhere in the country, at least for a while, because Dan, as an active-duty military officer, was subject to military discipline under the Uniform Code of Military Justice, the UCMJ. The code also had preferential jurisdiction over any civil court for whatever military offense they might decide to throw at him. After all, he had disobeyed direct orders to stay out of the Hardin case.

They reached the top of the escalator and went through the double glass doors into the concourse entrance, where the familiar Federal Protective Service cops, the walk-through metal detectors, and the luggage scanners were in operation, along with four very large Army military policemen in camouflage utilities. Dan swallowed hard as he walked up to the security checkpoint. Since he had a building pass, he did not have to go through the metal detectors, but the other two did. Vann identified himself to the guards as a D.C. cop, and they waved him through, but Grace had to go through the whole check. The MP's just stood there, trying not to stare too hard at Grace, but to Dan's great relief, they did not appear to be looking for him or anyone else in particular.

He escorted Grace and Vann up the ramps to the fourth floor and took them to Op-614. It was 5:20 by the time they reached the office, and Captain Summerfield was alone waiting for them. Snapper and Yeoman Jackson had secured for the day. Summerfield invited Grace and Captain Vann to sit on the couch, and Dan stood in the doorway.

"Well, boys and girls," Summerfield said, fiddling with his unlit pipe. "We are 'on call' with Captain Randall. Their lordships do not appear to be amused."

"Wonderful," Dan said. "Why did I know that already? Any idea why there are MP's at the checkpoints?"

"Bomb scare today; I think they use it as an excuse to exercise the troops."

"What exactly does the EA want to meet about?" Grace asked. Dan smiled in spite of the pit in his stomach. Grace was right on point again.

"Captain Randall remembered the name Snow when he saw the television news about the fire," Summerfield replied. "He made an educated guess about the 'friend' and called me. Asked me if Dan here was involved in the fire in Georgetown and if it had anything to do with the Hardin case. I had to say yes to both, but that that was all I knew. Hour later, I was told to get you in here this evening. Now, Dan, you want to tell me what's going down here?"

Dan hesitated. "I'm not sure if I should, Captain. How much of what I've told you already has gone straight up the chain of command here?"

Summerfield stopped fiddling with the pipe and gave Dan a studied look.

"Whatever I thought was pertinent," he said. "You have a problem with that?"

"I do if the guy responsible for one murder, possibly two, and perhaps for what happened to Grace and me last night, happens to be at the upper end of that chain."

Summerfield took a deep breath but held his temper. "Okay, you better explain that."

Dan ran through the details of what had happened last night, and then the gist of his theory about the identity of the flag officer behind the Hardin killings. Summerfield listened intently, putting his pipe down with a frown when Dan told him what he suspected about the vice chief. He began shaking his head as Dan finished.

"Admiral Torrance is a powerful, politically astute, ruthless when he has to be, highly ambitious, and very smart four-star admiral," he declared. "If

I reach real, real hard, I could maybe entertain the notion of his having a girlfriend, although I think he's much too intelligent, given what he's in line for, to do something that stupid. And besides, I know his wife, and she's a treasure. But more importantly, I cannot for the life of me get my mind around the notion that he, or any other flag officer, for that matter, would orchestrate a murder, let alone two murders."

"Four if you'd like to count us," Grace suggested.

"That reinforces my point," Summerfield said.

"I don't necessarily think *he* did—I think his EA did," Dan said, fingering his neck brace. "At best, the admiral might very well not know anything about it. He might suspect that someone has been operating on his behalf, but he can maintain his deniability. At worst, he's orchestrated the whole thing."

Summerfield thought about that as he picked up his pipe and began to load it with tobacco. Then he put it down and swung around in his chair, looking at his watch.

"Now that is possible," he said, finally, swinging back around. "Randall is as smart, ambitious, and as ruthless as his boss. He's also, in my opinion, a heartless cold fish—a purely political flag selectee if there ever was one."

"If this vice chief fella was in danger of going down in flames, would this Randall guy be affected?" Vann asked, speaking for the first time.

Summerfield looked at him. "Yes, he would. He's a captain who's been selected for rear admiral, but he's not yet officially been promoted. Sometimes that can take two years."

"So?"

"So some EAs do their job without becoming identified body and soul with their flag officer. But Randall is the other kind—the new vice, Torrance, made him his EA when I had to withdraw from the job, and he also got him selected for flag. Eldon Randall has never been bashful about wearing, hell, flaunting, his sugar daddy's four stars. Yeah, he'd be affected. You think this theory has legs, Captain?"

Vann shrugged. "It may, but evidence is in kinda short supply, and our system feeds on evidence. Lemme ask the reverse question: If the EA was guilty of all this, would his admiral go down, too?"

Summerfield nodded again. "You mean if it turned out that his EA was behind a couple of murders to *protect* the vice chief's personal reputation? Yes. Even if the vice maintained that he knew nothing about it, the scandal would at the very least end his chances to become the Chief of Naval Operations."

"Uh-huh," Vann said. "So in a way, they might both have a motive to muzzle Commander Collins here."

"Which is a pretty fair description of what they've been trying to do all along, ever since we brought the investigation back to Washington," Grace pointed out.

Summerfield nodded slowly and frowned. "Shit," he said as the phone began to ring in the outer office. Summerfield indicated for Dan to pick it up. It was one of the chief yeomen in the vice chief's office, informing him that their meeting with Rear Admiral–select Randall would be at 1745. Dan acknowledged and hung up.

"It's show time," he said, looking at his watch.

"Since this may go late, I've got to make a quick call home," Summerfield said to Dan. "You start securing the office."

Dan closed up the office while Vann and Grace waited out in the E-ring corridor and then he joined them while Summerfield finished his call. A minute later, Summerfield came out and they walked up the empty corridor toward the vice chief's office. They passed the OP-06 front office, where the EA did not appear to be in residence. When they reached the vice chief's front office, Summerfield led the way in, followed by Dan, Grace, and Captain Vann. To Dan's surprise, they found Captains Manning, the OP-06 EA, and Randall, as well as Rear Admiral Carson, OP-06B, waiting for them. The clerical staff appeared to have gone for the night, which left the administrative office suite partially darkened. The door to the admiral's inner office was closed, but light was shining through the opaque glass window. Nobody looked particularly happy to be there. Randall went right on the attack.

"Captain Summerfield," he said, pointedly ignoring Dan, "who are these people?"

Summerfield was unruffled. "This is Miss Snow, who was on the original Hardin investigation from NIS, and this is Captain Vann, from the D.C. Police Department. And of course you know Commander Collins."

Randall looked at Vann and then back at Summerfield, continuing to ignore Dan. "The D.C. police department?" he asked, going behind his desk. "This meeting was supposed to include you and Commander Collins. Why are these other two here?"

Dan was relieved to see that Summerfield was his usual unflappable self, and holding steady as Randall pressed him.

"You said this meeting was inspired by the fact that Miss Snow's house was burned down last night; if we're going to talk about that, I thought it best to hear from the people who were present when it happened, especially since it appears to involve the Hardin case."

"And this police officer?"

"This is a police *captain*. The fire last night took place in Washington, and one of the Hardins also died in Washington. There are now indications that it was not an accident, as originally believed, which is why Captain Vann is here."

"I see. Well, your first assumption is unwarranted, Captain," Randall replied, tapping a pencil impatiently on the top of his desk. "This meeting concerns Commander Collins and his direct disobedience of orders regarding the Hardin case. This is essentially going to be a preliminary hearing to determine if Commander Collins ought not go to Admiral's Mast."

"Mast!" exclaimed Dan. "You want to take *me* to mast? That's really funny, Captain. I think Captain Vann here ought to arrest *you* for complicity in a murder."

The ensuing silence was absolute, with only the distant sound of one of the trash train tractors penetrating the office. Rear Admiral Carson appeared to be stunned as he looked first at Collins and then at Randall. Randall's face had gone white.

"What did you say?" he asked in a tight voice.

Dan took a deep breath. "I think you and your boss have been covering up the real reason why both of the Hardin kids died. I think the reason you wanted the Hardin investigation handled by OpNav instead of the NIS was because you needed to control it. And when Miss Snow and I brought it back to Washington to continue the probe, I think you had us taken off the investigation so that you could hand it back to NIS, with orders to kill it, and I think that's why you have been so goddamned hell-bent for leather on making sure I didn't pursue the matter any further. Well, let me tell you something: The 'matter' pursued both Grace Snow and me last night, Captain, and while I can't prove any of this, yet, I think Captain Vann here is willing to open his own murder investigation to see if I'm right. You try to take me to mast and I'll take this little tale to the *Washington Post*. Tonight."

"What little tale is that, Commander?" a deep voice said from behind the group. Everyone turned, to find Admiral Torrance, the Vice Chief of Naval Operations, standing in the doorway to his private office. Torrance was well over six feet tall, with a massive head, wide black eyebrows over a Roman nose, weathered, ruddy skin, and a thin-lipped mouth presiding over a prominent, rugged chin. The unblinking expression of command was firmly stamped on his face, and his eyes were a piercing shade of light blue. In full uniform, he filled the doorway with his imposing presence, the mass of gold on his sleeves glittering in the semidarkened office as if imbued with its own light.

Carson, Manning, and Randall straightened automatically into positions of attention, and Dan felt his mouth go dry. Randall for once appeared to be at a total loss for words. Torrance gave each person in the room a direct look, pausing fractionally when he got to Summerfield, before ordering Randall to bring everyone into his office. They followed him into the inner office in a silent file, Summerfield bringing up the rear, with Grace just in front of him. Dan turned around once to make sure she was all right, wanting to be near her, but she seemed to be composed under Summerfield's wing.

The vice chief's inner office was thirty feet square and resembled a library study more than an office. There were two leather couches and several large upholstered chairs. Deep, plush carpeting, paneled walls, several brass lamps and other items of nautical decor, and four large walnut bookcases provided a quiet, studious atmosphere that contrasted with the four piles of three-ring binders heaped on the large mahogany desk. Dan realized that those binders were filled with hundreds of staff action papers awaiting the vice chief's perusal, and very often, decision. Dan had never been in the vice chief's office, Vice Admiral Layman's office being as high up in the chain as OP-06 action officers went.

Admiral Torrance walked behind his own desk and motioned for the rest of them to sit down. The chairs and both couches were positioned so that anyone sitting in them faced the desk. Rear Admiral Carson, the senior officer among the group called before the vice chief, cleared his throat. He looked as if he was still trying to overcome a serious shock.

"Admiral Torrance, I'm not sure how much of that you heard, but—"

Torrance put his hand up and Carson went silent. "I heard the words *murder investigation* and the *Washington Post*," he said. "Who was speaking?"

Dan stood up. "I was, Admiral. I'm Commander Collins. I work for Captain Summerfield in OP-Six-fourteen."

"You did the Hardin investigation," Torrance said. It was not a question.

Dan had the feeling he was being deliberately impaled by Torrance's direct stare. The admiral's eyes were trained on him like a battleship's optical range finder, bright, unblinking, impersonal, and with the perfect parallax of a raptor. Then the admiral shifted his attention to Grace Snow and Captain Vann.

"And you are?" he asked.

"I'm Grace Snow, formerly of the NIS," Grace said. "I assisted Commander Collins in the OpNav investigation of the Hardin incident—until it was terminated."

"And I'm Captain Moses Vann, executive assistant to the Deputy Chief of Police for Criminal Investigations, District police."

Torrance nodded slowly. Dan, still standing, was beginning to feel terribly exposed. Then Randall stood up.

"Admiral," he said, "This officer has expressed some very serious accusations concerning the Hardin case. He has also directly disobeyed my orders, conveyed to him more than once, to leave the Hardin case alone. I recommend that you do not entertain his preposterous story. Permit me to get someone from JAG down here and take this matter into appropriate disciplinary channels."

Dan could hear the phone ringing in the outer office, but apparently there was no one out there to pick it up. The other officers in the room were ignoring it. He did not know what to do. If the admiral did what his EA was recommending—and he sensed that it was the sensible thing for the four-star to do at the moment—they could bury him alive in judicial proceedings. But Torrance had his hand up again.

"I hear you, El, but I gather that I'm somehow wrapped into the commander's accusatios, so think I need to hear this. Commander?"

Dan took a deep breath and started at the baginning, when he was first tagged with the investigation. He laid out the sequence of events, the false starts, the realization that the brother and sister's deaths might be linked, and then the summary and unexplained termination of the OpNav investigation. He admitted that he and Grace had continued their explorations when asked to help by Captain Vann, adding that they had finally decided to let the NIS and the District cops work it until the phone tips came in and Vann pulled them back into it. He reminded the admiral that he had kept Summerfield informed and that he was under the impression that Summerfield was keeping the vice chief's office informed.

The admiral listened, neither contradicting nor acknowledging what Dan was saying. Dan concluded with the events of Sunday night, which provoked a few quiet exclamations from both Carson and Manning, and then got to the heart of the matter.

"I feel that someone fairly high up in the Navy is manipulating the NIS's conduct of the Hardin investigation, and is doing so to protect a flag officer from the revelation that he was having an affair with Elizabeth Hardin, whose silence may have been achieved by a murder disguised as a hit-and-run. I think that her brother, Lt. Wesley Hardin, the officer found in the battleship, had discovered who and what, and was himself killed in Philadelphia to ensure his silence."

"And you think I am this flag officer?" Torrance's face was impassive, and his voice was calm, almost reasonable. But Dan thought there was a hint of fury in it.

Dan swallowed hard again. "Based on the fact that your EA has been the principal force in pressuring me to stay away from the Hardin case, yes, sir, I do. It's either you, Captain Randall here, or someone you're both protecting."

The admiral leaned back in his chair and tented his hands under his chin. His pose obscured his lower face, leaving only those blue eyes gleaming across the room. Randall was shaking his head in a dramatic "I can't believe he's saying this" gesture. Rear Admiral Carson was looking at Summerfield in total disbelief. Grace sat upright in her chair, watching the vice chief.

The admiral stared at Dan for a few seconds and then turned his attention to Captain Vann.

"Captain Vann, have you begun a formal inquiry into this matter?"

"No, sir, we have not. Yet."

"Do you intend to?"

"We might. This guy who did Miss Snow's house Sunday night, he's not a guy who does this kind of thing on his own. We make him as one of these cleanup contractors we have here in D.C. who specialize in taking care of dirty work for the big guns in town. He's working for somebody, and it's looking to me like it's somebody high up in the Navy, like the commander here is suggesting."

"Do you have firm evidence for that theory?"

"Not yet, Admiral. But, like I said, I think we're going to start working on it."

Admiral Torrance nodded his head slowly, looking down at the desk now.

"All right, Captain Vann," he said. "Let me say this. The commander's basic premise is wrong. I had the Hardin investigation moved to OpNav for bureaucratic reasons, mostly for public-relations reasons. I did not want the NIS associated with another incident involving a battleship. When it became definite that we had a homicide, however, I changed my mind. Homicide is too important to be handled in public-relations channels. I then ordered it turned back over to the NIS, and the OpNav investigation terminated, so that we would not have two agencies getting in each other's way. You can understand that, can't you, Captain Vann?"

Dan could see what the admiral was doing even as Vann nodded. Vann was the one outsider, the one person in the room with the power to bring real trouble. If the admiral could convince Vann to back off, he could deal with Dan at his leisure. Divide and conquer. And he was powerless to do anything about it. Grace was starting to look worried; she had figured it out, too.

"And that's where it is now, Captain Vann. I think you should look into this matter. I suggest you go see the NIS. I can guarantee their full and enthusiastic cooperation. There is little question that Lieutenant Hardin was killed—the officer in the battleship, that is. I don't know anything about the other Lieutenant Hardin. I can state that I have never known her, done business with her, or even laid eyes on her. And I have not had an affair with her or any other woman other than my wife of thirty-six years. I am not stupid, Captain Vann, and the surest way for me to jeopardize my own reputation and my future in the Navy would be to have an affair with a junior officer in the Navy, especially in today's political climate. Would you not agree? The nomination of the officer who was supposed to have my job now was derailed over a sexual-harassment incident, one in which he was absolutely blameless. The merest association cost him the nomination."

Torrance then turned back to Dan. "And as for you, young man, I want you to assist Captain Vann in his inquiries. You will be his escort officer, get him into the Navy system wherever he needs to go, help him in any way you can until this matter is resolved. If you meet resistance, Captain Randall here will run interference for you. I'm doing this because you obviously and sincerely believe that I am masterminding some conspiracy here. So I want you fully involved in taking this case to its conclusion. I *know* that I'm not guilty of anything. I want you to convince yourself that I'm not guilty of anything. Now, I do think it only fair to ask that you do not make any more accusations until you can prove them. And nobody here"—his glance swept the room— "will interfere in this matter until it is concluded. Is that satisfactory, Commander? Captain Vann?"

Dan couldn't believe it, but all he could do was say, "Yes, sir." The admiral had mousetrapped him. Instead of yelling and shouting and hiding behind a phalanx of EAs and a military-discipline action, he had effectively cut Dan loose to prove his charges. If the admiral was guilty of something, Dan would have his chance to prove it, which he knew was an almost-impossible task. And if he couldn't, there was no way Dan could ever charge that there had been a cover-up. Torrance was brilliant.

"Gentlemen, and lady, it's late," Torrance concluded. "We will excuse you now."

Dan looked around. Grace, Summerfield, and Captain Vann stood up, but Rear Admiral Carson and Captains Manning and Randall remained in their places. Carson was giving Summerfield a sideways look that implied some serious heat, but Summerfield was already leading the way to the door. They filed through it, Dan leaving last, almost afraid to look behind him at the powerful men remaining behind with the vice chief. He particularly did not want to see Randall's expression, and he closed the door firmly behind him. They stood there, clustered around the EA's desk in the now-deserted front office.

"Now you know why he's a four-star," Summerfield said softly, giving them a grim smile. But Vann shrugged.

"Seems like we got a fair shot at it," he said, also keeping his voice down. "That may all be smoke-and-mirrors bullshit, but it sounds to me like we can follow the trail wherever it goes."

"What damn trail?" Dan said glumly.

"But what happens if it leads back here?" Grace asked.

"If he's the man, he's bought some time," Summerfield said. "And your reception at NIS will give you a pretty strong clue."

Dan shook his head. "I'm uneasy about the goddamned EAs; I can see Admiral Torrance keeping above the fray, but Randall—"

At that moment, a single white light flashed on at the EA's telephone console. All four of them looked at it and then back at the closed door. There were no sounds coming from the inner office. Dan looked over at Summerfield, who started to shake his head. But Grace was giving him a look that said, do it. Dan looked down at the phone. It was an EA's phone; it had a muted handset. Who are they calling? JAG? Dan reached down and put his hand over the black handset.

"Dan," Summerfield said.

Dan ignored him, giving the phone time to ring at its destination, once, twice, then the pickup. He lifted the handset and listened.

"Investigative Service, Rear Admiral Keeler's office, Captain Rennselaer speaking, sir?"

There was a sound from the inner office, and Dan hurriedly put the phone down and motioned for everyone to get out into the corridor. He closed the front office door quietly behind him and they quickly walked away down the E-ring corridor. As if by mutual agreement, no one said anything until they reached OP-614's front door.

"Well?" said Summerfield, eyeing Dan.

"Someone was calling Admiral Keeler at NIS," Dan said. "A Captain Rennselaer answered the phone."

"Rennselaer is EA to Director NIS," murmured Summerfield.

"Somebody want to tell me what's happenin' here?" Vann said.

"They put a call through to the head of the Naval Investigative Service," Grace explained. "The question is, For what reason? To warn them, or to clear the way for you to continue the investigation?"

"Probably a little of both," Summerfield said. But then he saw the expression on Dan's face. "What's the matter?"

Dan fumbled with the cipher lock to 614. A chilling thought had just struck him, and he suddenly wanted to get out of the Pentagon.

"Dan, what is it?" Grace asked.

He opened the door and then turned around to face them.

"It just occurred to me that we may have been focusing on the wrong guy. Suppose, just suppose, that the flag involved is not the vice chief, but his protégé, the director of the NIS? That the captain the goon mentioned was not Randall but Rennselaer?"

"Jesus, Dan, another theory?" said Summerfield. "Now you've got Randall running top cover here for a one-star instead of the vice chief?"

"Now wait a freakin' minute, Commander," Vann chimed in. "You enjoy gettin' your ass handed to you by these admirals? Now you want to go after another one? I think it's time to count me out for a while. I'm way the hell ahead of my procedures here."

"Let me make a phone call," Grace said. "If there's something going on over at NIS, Robby Booker will know about it."

Dan looked at Summerfield, who was shaking his head in evident exasperation. They went into the office, all except Vann.

"I'm serious, people," he said from the doorway. "I've gotta get this thing into regulation channels before it gets any more outta hand. You all are going much too fast, based on very damn little hard evidence."

Grace turned around to look at him. "If Dan is right about the NIS connection, and it's Rennselaer we're looking for, what's the only thing this guy Ward has to do to be disconnected from the Hardin killings?"

Vann blinked, then shook his head. "You're still going too fast," he said again. "You're bouncing around like some damn rubber ball here. Let me get with my people tomorrow morning and we'll get this thing set up right. I can get you protection. This murder is two years old—it ain't going anywhere. Now, who can get me out of this place?"

Dan was elected, and he left to take Captain Vann to one of the exits. Grace turned away and headed over to Snapper's desk to use the phone. Fifteen minutes later, Dan returned and went over to stand in the doorway of Captain Summerfield's office, where Summerfield was sitting on his couch for a change, his head in his hands. Across the bleak space between the E-ring and the D-ring, Dan could see a single office light shining.

"It's a good thing you're out on leave," Summerfield muttered. "Tomorrow is going to be a bad day around here. Did you see Carson's expression?"

"Yes, sir, I did. Hopefully, it will only get better after tonight."

Grace came in from using the phone as Summerfield looked up at Dan.

"Don't count on it," he was saying. "The costs in face-saving and flag officer dignity repair are going to be significant. You may want to make some preparations for a move."

"A move?"

"You don't think you're going to remain on the OpNav staff after tonight's little scene with the vice chief, do you?" Summerfield asked, looking up through his fingers. "You are going to get orders; what kind of orders, I don't know, but you are definitely going to be hurtling down the PCS pipe within about two weeks. I may be hurtling right behind you."

"And what about my being Vann's escort?"

"Like I said, two weeks. You don't come up with something really dramatic in that time, you'll—what is it, Miss Snow?"

"There's something going on at NIS. I just talked to my source over there, and he says there's been a flap on all day in the front office, with the admiral talking to some of the JAG lawyers downstairs and the EA cutting everyone off at the knees who dares even to speak to him. Robby said the admiral had left for the day, but the security guards say he's on the way back in."

"Where's Rennselaer?" Summerfield asked.

"I guess he's still there," Grace replied. "Robby said he was meeting someone."

Summerfield stood up. "Maybe the call to NIS from the vice's office has started some kind of fire," he said.

"I have visions of the Japanese embassy burning their papers on the night of December sixth," Dan said. "Grace, maybe you and I should go over there. My car's right here."

"Is that wise?" Summerfield asked. "You heard Captain Vann—he's right about getting this thing back in proper channels, and your only mandate to play is through him."

"If that bastard Rennselaer had my house burned down, with me supposedly in it, *I* don't need anybody's mandate," Grace said. "Dan, let's go."

"But there isn't a damn thing they can do tonight, except stew," Summerfield argued. "Let them panic, and then you take Vann over there in the morning after they've been sweating all night. There's another thing: Both of you ought to get off the streets until they pick up that guy Malachi Ward. Vann said they think he's still in the city."

Grace shook her head. "No. The District police might take a week to get going on this, especially after Vann reports the meeting tonight with the vice chief. I wouldn't be stunned if his bosses tell him to back off. No. I want to talk to Rennselaer, and now would be nice."

67

IT WAS FULL dark when Malachi parked the pickup truck, rigged once again with the Metro logo and flasher, in front of the large abandoned factory building that occupied the two blocks across the street from the Forge Building in the Navy Yard. The bored guard at the front gate had bought his story of a Metro bus stranded in the Navy Yard with a casual wave, and Malachi had sailed through. He backed the truck into a space between two loading docks at the front of the deserted building. The docks were to one side of two large steel doors, which were partially opened, revealing the cavernous interior of the building. He would have put it in the building except for the fact that there was a huge pile of metal scrap blocking the entrance. He checked his watch: 6:45. He stayed in the truck for a few minutes and looked around. The building was big. It appeared to be about ten stories high, two hundred feet wide, and nearly twice that long, its other end extending all the way to the river. A sign whose letters were carved into the stone lintel above the loading dock said TURRET LATHE BUILD-ING. There was no light in the building except for what was reflecting through a row of skylights from the floodlights on the power station next door. There appeared to be some very large machinery inside, but he could not make out any details.

Surprisingly, the captain had called back right away and hurriedly agreed to a meeting. He had designated the Navy Yard as the meeting place. They would meet on board the museum ship, the retired destroyer USS *Barry*, which was moored to the pier across the gun park from river end of the Forge Building. "There's no one on board at night," the captain had said, "and the main-deck hatches are all secured. There's a sliding chain-link fence and gate at the head of the pier, but you can get around it at one end. Come up the after gangway to the main deck and walk around. There's lots going on here right now, so come between seven and seven-thirty. I'll find you."

Malachi smiled in the darkness. Yeah, I'll just bet you will. Meet me on a deserted ship parked on the Anacostia River after dark. Right. Well actually, that suited Malachi just fine. He was dressed in khaki trousers, a dark red shirt, and his black windbreaker, the one with the hole in it from when he had cut out some material for his eye patch. The patch had helped; his eye, although still very sore, had stopped its broadband transmission of pain back into his brain, helped perhaps by the Harper. Malachi checked that the Browning .380 in his waistband holster was chambered, patted the Bernardelli .25 auto in his right sock, and then slipped on some black leather gloves. He was about to get out when he detected oncoming headlights. He ducked down in the front seat of the truck as a gray Navy Yard security truck cruised by. The cop driving paid no attention to him. Very good, he thought. The flasher unit makes it invisible.

He waited until the truck was out of sight before getting out. He left the keys in the ignition and shut the door quickly to stop the warning chimes. It was a cool evening, but the night air was heavy with the promise of fog from the river. He was about to set out for the gun park when the security truck came back by, so he stepped through the doors of the Turret Lathe Building. After the truck went by, he looked around. There were huge dark lumps of machinery dotting the football field–sized floor: metal presses, giant milling machines, vertical drill presses, and, in the center, the largest metal lathe he had ever seen. Suspended between its two turrets was a cylindrical gray steel mass that appeared to be more than fifty feet long from end to end. High in the overhead was a gantry crane track, with one large and one smaller crane parked in the middle of the building, their diamond-shaped hook heads positioned over the central turret lathe. In the rose quartz light reflecting through the skylights a hundred feet above his head, he could make out the larger pieces of machinery, but the floor was littered with piles of junk, scrap metal, rusting barrels, and heaps of electrical cable, all clumped indistinctly in the shadows. The entire place stank of rust, ancient oil and grease, and rotting electrical insulation. There was a blast of steam from the power plant next door that startled him back into motion.

He checked the street once more and then walked down along the side of the abandoned factory, staying in the shadows in case there were any foot patrols, although this part of the Navy Yard seemed to be deserted. He walked as quickly as his injured leg would allow, going down the length of the Turret Lathe Building, until he was even with the end of the Forge Building, its lighted windows visible across the street to his left. The entrance to the Forge Building was obscured by a small brick building whose sign identified it as the Navy Yard chapel. Beyond, he could see the slant piers along the Anacostia River and the masts of the museum ship rising over the nearest building. He slipped into a darkened doorway and watched for a few minutes, getting his one good eye night-adapted and checking again for sentries or pedestrians, but there was no one moving along the shadowy industrial street. He went one more short block and then crossed the street into the end of the gun park.

The gun park was part of the museum complex. It consisted of about two acres of ground wedged between the Forge Building and the waterfront, with one of every kind of naval gun ever manufactured in the Navy Yard on display—from a single sixty-two-foot-long sixteen-inch battleship gun to a collection of chunky black iron Civil War mortars. There was even a

World War I railroad gun, a twelve-inch naval rifle mounted on a locomotive frame, sitting on a section of track alongside a twin-armed guided-missile launcher. Across the street from the park was the destroyer, its four-hundred-foot length blocking out the lights on Bolling Air Force Base on the opposite shore of the Anacostia.

Malachi entered the park at the southwestern end, creeping silently through the shadows, moving from gun to gun, stopping and listening, and then moving again. The captain might very well be waiting here, knowing that this was the only protected approach to the ship. Finally, he reached the German U-boat conning-tower display, and he crouched down in its shadow to examine the ship across the street.

There was a single wide street running down along the entire waterfront, and it was well lighted. Directly across the street was the public entrance to the ship, which was moored to a wide concrete pier that had a tall chain-link fence mounted all the way across the foot of the pier. There was a darkened guard shack standing by a sliding gate in the fence. Malachi remembered seeing the ship museum when it was opened; there was normally a sailor in the guard shack who directed visitors down the pier to the aftermost gangway, which went up to the superstructure. Departing visitors were routed down from the forecastle area on a second gangway, past the guard shack, and back out to the street. But now the ship was darkened. Its main decks were well lighted by the streetlights along the pier, but its upper decks, being higher than the streetlights, were in shadow.

Malachi realized that there was no way he could cross that street and get to the ship without being seen by someone hiding up high in the ship. There was also no way he could get to the back of the ship and sneak aboard that way, because the piers slanted out into the river, leaving the stern of the ship sixty feet away from the waterfront bulkhead. Now if he were James Bond, he thought, he would go back down the waterfront, drop into the river, swim back to the ship, and then climb aboard over the propeller guards, although he doubted even James Bond would want to stick even a finger in the heavily polluted Anacostia River. But with only one eye and a gimp leg, he was definitely not up to Mr. Bond tonight.

He looked down the waterfront street for signs of parked cars or other surveillance, but the street and the visitors' parking lot were empty. The only signs of life were coming from the steady stream of traffic bumping over the Welsh Memorial Bridge at the near end of the Navy Yard and a row of lighted windows behind him in the Forge Building. NIS must be working late tonight.

Well, this was supposed to be a final, friendly business meeting between the contractor and his employer. Maybe not all that friendly, but it was certainly not supposed to be a shoot-out at the O.K. Corral, either. He had told the captain that he was going to leave town and disappear but that he needed five thousand in cash to pay off the people who were going to get him out of town. The captain had hesitated only for a moment, then agreed to the meeting. He said he would need to know some things before he would pay, and specifically, he needed to know what evidence a certain Miss Snow had relating to the truth behind the Hardin murders. Malachi had replied that she had one interesting bit, which he was sure the captain would find well worth the money.

So, just a final little business meeting. The thing to do was to stand up and walk across the street, slip around the end of that sliding gate, and walk up the brow of the ship, easy as you please, like he had every right to be there. Once on the ship, and assuming there hadn't been a hail of gunfire from the ship's top hampers, he would see what was possible. He figured the captain did indeed want to know what had happened in Georgetown and whether or not the people in OpNav had figured out who the great man was, so the most likely scenario was probably a "stick 'em up, don't turn around, walk straight ahead and do what I tell you" drill. Which would be fine with Malachi. The only trick would be to convince the captain to stick the gun right in his back. After that, it would be simple, a piece of cake even.

He took one last look up and down the street, then stood up and walked nonchalantly over to the fence, trying hard to minimize his limp. He did not hurry, and he kept his hands visible. And while he was counting on the captain's being the amateur that he *probably* was, the thought of a silenced .22 long rifle Colt Woodsman with a laser scope did cross his mind, raising fine beads of sweat on his forehead, despite the cool of the evening. He reached the end of the fence nearest the water and looked around again, but he did not look up at the ship. The ship's towering overhanging bow reflected little lapping sounds from under the pier, and something splashed in the trash-filled water. He grabbed the chain link and swung his body around the end, hanging briefly out over the black waters of the Anacostia. He dropped lightly back onto the pier on the other side, stumbling a little because of his leg and his one-eyed lack of depth perception. He exhaled quietly when he landed on the concrete; that would have been the place for the captain to have taken his shot. So this was going to be a "talk first, shoot second" deal. Works for me, Malachi thought as he headed for the after gangway.

DAN BANGED HIS HANDS impatiently on the steering wheel as they inched along in bumper-to-bumper traffic on the Southeast Freeway. They could see the tall, lighted stacks of the Navy Yard power plant several blocks in the distance off to their right, but they were getting nowhere due to an accident about a mile up ahead. His chin bumped on the neck brace when he had to jam on the brakes. He tugged angrily at the Velcro straps and took the brace off in frustration, pitching it into the backseat.

"Damn it!" he exclaimed. "It's seven-fifteen. Why is there all this damn traffic still out here?"

"Maybe Summerfield was right," Grace said. "The closer I get to a face-to-face confrontation with Rennselaer, the better waiting a day looks."

"No," Dan said. "I think your intuition is right about Vann and the D.C. police. His bosses are going to want to go slowly before they go tangling with someone in the Pentagon at the VCNO level. And if our man is the director of the NIS, that will complicate it even more—NIS is another police organization. If we confront Rennselaer tonight, it will increase the pressure on both of them."

"You think he's the guy?"

"I do now. The vice chief had one really strong point: He has too much to lose. Shit, you know what? We should have taken the Metro—it goes right to the Navy Yard—three stops from the Pentagon."

69

MALACHI STEPPED OFF the after brow leading up to the 01 level on the *Barry*, then passed under a large canvas awning covering the entire antisubmarine rocket-launcher deck. The tour guide's podium was secured for the night next to a closed hatch. There was an interior communications panel of some kind next to the door, with a row of small white lights across the top, but no sign of people. He could feel a faint breeze coming off the river up here now that he was out from under the windbreak created by the ship. He half-expected the ship to be creaking and moving in the current, but it was dead-silent and motionless, a testament to its four-thousand-ton displacement. He walked over to the base of the ASROC missile launcher and looked aft. There was a single steep ladder leading down to the fantail area, where the after gun mount loomed in the darkness. With the hatch into the superstructure closed up, he would have to go down to the main deck and then work his way forward. He started over toward the ladder but stopped in the shadows when he saw the Navy Yard security truck coming down the waterfront. The truck cruised by slowly, the guard's face a white blob in the driver's side window. But then it turned the corner behind the Forge Building and was gone.

Malachi knew nothing about ships, but he figured the captain would be somewhere forward and up, away from all those lights on the pier. He stepped carefully down the ladder, favoring his leg, his depth perception badly skewed by the eye patch. Long John Silver, ready to poop the mizzen-whatever, he thought as he reached the fantail area of the main deck. He stopped and looked around, but there was no sign of the captain or anyone else. The gun mount was much bigger than it looked from the pier, its rounded steel sides glinting in the streetlight. The destroyer's deck was surprisingly uneven, and it seemed to have sand painted on its surface. He walked over to the starboard side and looked up the long, narrow expanse of steel leading forward along the main deck. The port side was in full view of the pier lights, but the starboard side was entirely dark, with only the Bolling Field hangar lights a half mile across the river providing any illumination.

He realized that he was profoundly tired—tired of this stupid game, tired of all these people he had to work for, picking up after them as they scurried through their precious little tin-soldier careers. You can still walk away, Malachi. The world is probably going to fall in on these two sooner rather than later. Walk away. Go back and get in the truck and drive out of here and straight west out of town into the Blue Ridge Mountains. Even as part of his mind thought about it, the other part compelled him to start walking forward up the starboard side, trying to adjust his one good eye to the sudden darkness.

The walkway up the main deck was only three feet wide, with a five-strand bronze wire lifeline on the outboard side and the ship's deckhouse superstructure on the inboard side. He could hear the wash of the river's current against the ship's steel sides ten feet below. The river stank of mud, rotting tree branches, oil, and sewage in about equal proportions. He thought he could see *things* floating by in the current, but he did not want to know what they were. He walked two hundred feet forward, past the after deckhouse hatches, under the boat davits, past a ladder amidships going back up to the 01 level, until he came to a tunnel-like structure, just forward of a hatch leading into the ship directly below the bridge. It appeared that the tunnel, which was the same width as the main-deck walkway and about eight feet high, led out onto the forecastle area through a heavy steel door, which was closed.

Malachi stopped. The tunnel was pitch-black. He thought he could see the shapes of industrial gas bottles mounted against the river side of the tunnel. To his immediate left was a hatch marked FORWARD ATHWARTSHIP PASSAGEWAY, and under those words was a painted label enumerating the compartments accessible through that hatch: the officers' wardroom, the forward radar-equipment room, and the forward fire room. Malachi examined the hatch and saw that it was not locked. He wondered if the captain might be somewhere *inside* the ship. That would make it tough. But, no, he had said he would meet him—what was the word? Yeah, topside. That sounded like outside. He peered again into the darkened tunnel. Even with two good eyes, he would not have been able to see anything. Were the shapes along the exterior wall all gas bottles, or was someone there? He should have brought a light of some kind. He had his butane lighter, but he knew he would be night-blind the instant he fired it. Should he go inside the ship? Or forward? He put his hand on the hatch's steel actuating handle. It was cold and slightly wet to the touch. He looked up at the bridge wing two decks above him, half-expecting to see a figure up there, but there was nothing.

He took a breath and decided to go forward. Putting his right hand on the .380 in his waistband, he started forward. As the shapes on the outboard wall became visible, he saw that they *were* gas bottles, five feet high, and marked with white labels reading NITROGEN, ARGON, ACETYLENE. He stopped just inside the tunnel, trying to night-adapt his good eye. The tunnel seemed to go on another fifteen or twenty feet. He looked behind him, where he could see down the entire length of the main deck, which appeared to be bathed in daylight compared with the tunnel. He turned around again and took another step, then another. Stop. Was that someone ahead? He blinked his left eye rapidly and drew the gun. There was a figure up ahead, standing motionless against the inboard bulkhead. But there was something funny about it. The head, something funny about the head.

"That's Oscar," a familiar voice said from behind. Malachi jumped. "Don't turn around, Malachi. We're all armed here tonight. So lose the gun. Just put it down on the deck and kick it through the breaks into the river. Slowly. That's good."

Malachi knelt slightly, and with a twinge of regret, he put the Browning down on the steel deck. He was tempted to palm the .25 auto out of his sock, then decided not to. It was the captain's gun he was after, and besides, his hands were better than any gun—and quieter. He stood back up and nudged the automatic with his foot, then nudged it again until it went out a scupper hole and fell into the river with a chunky splash.

"Very good. Oscar, in case you're wondering, is a dummy. We use Oscar to practice man-overboard recoveries. He's made of kapok, so he floats. We throw him over the side and then drive the ship back to find him and pick him up. He lives up here in the weather breaks. It's a good place for dummies."

Malachi heard what sounded like the hatch opening wide behind him, and then there was a clank, as if the hatch was being latched open against the inboard superstructure bulkhead. Son of a bitch had been just *inside* that hatch. Waiting for him to go past, up into that tunnel. Had probably heard him stop.

"So now what?" Malachi asked.

"So now I tie off a loose end, Malachi," the captain said.

"You mean you don't really want to know how much *Ms.* Snow knows? You think you're going to get away with just shooting me and putting me in the river, do you? You think I haven't left some insurance out there? I mean, I know who we're all protecting here."

The captain laughed. "No you don't. Keep your hands out where I can see them, Malachi. That's good. And what I think is that you never expected me to get the drop on a pro like you. That there is no 'open this if I don't come back' letter, because you don't know anyone to leave such a letter with. You're the original lone wolf, Malachi; you've told me that a hundred times. But you've outlived your usefulness. I guess you'd outlived your usefulness when you ran that girl down two years ago. Did you mean to do that, Malachi?"

Malachi was thinking hard. He had to get the captain to come closer. Get that gun within striking range.

"She cut me," Malachi said. "When I went to warn her away from your great man. Last woman who cut me cost me my manhood. It was the least I could do."

"It was just a simple contract, Malachi. Convincingly tell the skirt to get lost. And look what happened."

The captain's voice sounded a little louder, maybe a little closer. Good. He was counting on the captain not wanting to shoot him out here, because a shot would bring the cops. Inside would be different. Had to nail that gun before he was forced inside the ship. Malachi began to take the weight off his bad leg to position his body for a turning strike. Closer, please.

"And the boy, Malachi—what really happened there? I can't see you going to Philly and doing that little job."

"I have some connections. It wasn't all that hard. They were just supposed to talk to him, too. But he got self-righteous, noisy. Didn't want to listen. Neither of them was a good listener." Closer. Definitely closer now.

"That's kind of what I imagined. Take your coat off, Malachi."

What? My coat? Oh hell *yes!* Take it off, left arm first, hold the right arm, bunch it a little, then use it as a flail. Whip it around and nail the gun. The coat would give him a three-foot reach. He began to unzip the windbreaker, easing his body to the left ever so slightly to give himself room to swing it, then shifting his weight back to the injured leg. No way around it.

"You getting cold, Captain?" he asked, saying anything to distract the man behind him as he pulled the zipper down and then started to pull his left arm clear. "Like cold feet? I think the cops are onto this little shandy, by the way. They've been through my place. Who knows what they found, hunh?"

"Who indeed, Malachi."

Malachi heard a metallic noise behind him as he began to cock his right arm, the jacket hanging free now, his left hand closing over his right hand to propel the snap properly. One chance now. Take a deep breath. Go low and whip—

And then he was down on the deck, his head ringing, his breath arrested in his chest, and his legs jerking around beneath him as if they belonged to someone else. What the hell had happened? Can't breathe. Take a breath. Chest doesn't work. Breathe, man. He hadn't heard a shot. Breathe, goddamn it. Never hear the one that gets you. What the hell—he could sense that the captain was standing practically on top of him, bending down to look at him. Something in his hand. Not a gun.

"This is a stun gun, Malachi. Shoots a little dart, trails a little titanium wire, and delivers fifteen-thousand volts. No amps, just volts. That's why I needed the jacket off, Malachi. But it does work, doesn't it? Having a little trouble catching your breath, Malachi? Give it time. And that's a terrific-looking eye you have there. A lady hit you with her purse, did she?"

The captain straightened up as Malachi strained to focus on getting that breath, getting some air, and it was coming, but just barely coming. God, it was hard, and his damn legs were still in spasm, his right shin screaming again, and the patch had come off his eye when he fell. He could feel the cool night air against his battered skin. Breathe, damn it, breathe. He felt his diaphragm move, then heard a croak escape his lips. He started to gather himself.

"Was that a little bitty breath, Malachi? I guess we're not quite there, are we?"

And then another buzzing blast hit him, knocking him back down on the steel deck as if he were a feather, his own muscles bouncing his body around, the vision in his left eye closing down to a red-rimmed circle as he fought to cling to consciousness. His ears were roaring and his right eye was suddenly blazing with pain again. His face smashed up against one of the gas bottles. Then he became dimly aware that the captain had him by his feet and was dragging him across the steel deck, and when his eye bumped on something on the deck, he slipped into a black fog, not quite fully out, but absolutely, totally helpless, the jacket dropping out of his right hand as he went over the edge into unconsciousness.

He awoke with his face pressed into what felt like oily steel, and there was a smell of fuel oil in his nostrils. His body felt like one big bruise, and there was a salty taste of blood in his mouth. The skin on his face felt raw and scraped. He tried to open his left eye, but it was not obeying. His brain dimly perceived that he was inside, inside the ship. His arms were bound behind his back, and it felt as if his feet were tied together, too, but he couldn't move them, anyway. His whole left side felt bruised and battered. And then he was moving again, being moved, sliding up what felt like planks of wood against his face, strong hands grabbing him by his belt and sliding him up an incline and then off the end of the board onto smooth steel, which had a powdery feel to it, and the smell of oil was replaced by the smell of something else. He desperately tried to open his eye, but none of his muscles would respond, and his optical nerves were jammed with whorls of red and orange and bright green. He tried to cry out, but he could manage only a long groan as more of his body slid off the end of the plank onto this strange surface. *Into* this strange surface: The sound around him had changed, and he became aware that he was *inside* something, something long, and curved. Then he felt his shoes coming off and his socks being yanked roughly down his legs and off his feet, the .25 clattering down onto a steel deck. He tried to raise his head and get that one eye open, and barely succeeded. There was light behind his head, back by his feet, his bare feet, but he could not understand what he was seeing, the round, smooth, curving surface, covered with holes, some kind of cylinder, and then another lightning bolt, this time applied to his bare feet, galvanizing his entire body into a giant convulsive leap, the top of his head hitting something very hard, tears in his eyes, both eyes. The now terribly familiar problem of breathing, the excruciatingly hard effort to make the diaphragm work, to draw even a piece of a breath.

Then a moment of silence, followed by the probing beam of a flashlight, shockingly white in his left eye, which was now opened. He tried to turn his head away from the dazzling light, but his neck was made of rubber.

"Know where you are, Malachi?"

The captain's voice. But distant, as if he was speaking down a tunnel. Wrong. This whole thing had gone very wrong. He was supposed to be headed for West Virginia now, a vision of blue-green hills and an inviting open road tantalizing his feverish brain.

"I'm not going to kill you, Malachi. But I am going to leave you. Right where you left Wesley Hardin. You're in a steam drum, Malachi. In a boiler. In a ship. In an empty ship. Nobody ever comes down here anymore, Malachi. I'm going to bolt up the cover, and I'm going to remount the lagging pad, and you are going to comtemplate your sins for a week or so until you dry up and turn to dust."

And then there was darkenss as something big and heavy shut out the light back by his feet. Only this time, his muscles did work, and Malachi began to scream.

DAN PULLED THE Suburban up in front of the Forge Building and parked in one of the spots reserved for senior officers. There were thin patches of fog drifting through the gun park out in front of the building. The downstairs windows of the building were all dark, except for the ground-floor entrance hall and a single office suite at the far-left end. Grace could see that there were many more lights on up on the second floor.

"Somebody's working late," Dan said, peering through the windshield.

"The Navy JAG Appeals Division is on the ground floor," she said. "They *never* work late. NIS has the entire second floor on this end and a piece of the ground floor at that end, where the lights are. That's the admiral's conference room." Robby was right, she thought. Something's going on.

Dan reached for his hat in the backseat.

"You going to put that brace back on?" Grace asked.

"Hell with it," he replied. "Neck's feeling a little better now."

Probably because of the brace, she thought, but she held her tongue. As they got out of the car, an elderly Federal Protective Service security guard with a familiar face came through the glass doors of the reception area, carrying a lunch pail and his jacket. He saw Dan's three stripes and saluted almost automatically.

"Evening, Commander," he said. "Miss Snow. Haven't seen you for a while."

"Lots of lights on tonight, Mr. Jansen," Grace said, remembering the man's name at the last moment. "What's going on?"

"Don't rightly know, Miss. The admiral just came back in and he looked kinda flustered."

At that moment, Grace saw Robby Booker appear in the reception area, coming toward them. He was in his shirtsleeves as he came through the glass doors.

"Hey, Miss Snow. They doin' some serious flappin' around in there. What's goin' down, anyway?"

"Hi, Robby, you'll—" Grace began, but she stopped when Dan yelled out a loud "Hey!" As she turned around, she thought she saw a figure sprinting across the end of the gun park and disappearing behind the chapel building. Dan had whirled around and was running down the steps, headed for the street.

"Son of a bitch!" he was yelling. "Grace, I'm going after him. Get the cops. Tell 'em to find us. And call Vann. Get him down here!" And then he was gone, running down the street in the direction of the industrial area, his hat flying off his head.

"Miss!" the guard said. "What's goin' on?"

"I don't know," she said, thoroughly confused. Whom had Dan seen? Why would he run after him like that? Oh hell, was it Rennselaer? Having been warned by the VCNO's office, the EA was running for it. My God, Dan had been right. She turned to the security guard.

"Can you call Yard Security? That man he's chasing is probably armed and is definitely dangerous."

"I can, but we gotta go upstairs. But what— Who—"

"I don't have time to explain. Let's get upstairs. Robby, I have to make a call."

The three of them bolted through the entrance doors and then double-timed it upstairs to the NIS reception area, the old man bringing up the rear, his lunch pail clanking against the railing. The lone desk guard, a very large woman, rose out of her chair when they burst into the NIS reception area.

"Hey," she began.

"Call Central," shouted the old man from the top of the stairs. "Get some units down to the industrial area. Armed intruder, Navy officer in pursuit. Go!"

Grace grabbed the extension phone as the desk guard got on the radio. She pushed 81 to get an outside line while fishing in her purse for Vann's card. She found it and dialed the number. C'mon, c'mon, be there. Booker stood there, obviously dying to know what the hell was going on. The phone rang over in Washington, but no one answered. She hung up after ten rings and banged the phone down in frustration. Now what?

The desk guard had made the emergency call but was now obviously trying to answer the dispatcher's question about what was going on. She looked up at Grace, but Grace wasn't seeing her, because there, in the flesh, coming down the hall, was the executive assistant to the director of the NIS, Capt. Rennselaer. She backed away from the desk in shock. Then who the hell was Dan chasing? Oh God, it had to be that man Ward, Malachi Ward. The bastard who had tortured her and burned her house down. What the hell was he doing down here in the Navy Yard? Robby had said the EA had been meeting someone. Ward had been meeting with Rennselaer! And Dan was running after him, unarmed. She whirled around and grabbed the old man's gun out of his holster and, bolting through the glass doors, ran back down the stairs, the guard's protests ringing in her ears.

DAN RAN DOWN the block, ducking between the chapel and the Forge Building. Each time his feet touched the ground, a jolt of pain whipped through his neck, but otherwise, running came naturally enough. He unbuttoned his jacket as he slid around the corner of the Forge Building and stopped. The street was poorly lighted, with only a single streetlight positioned ten feet from where he was standing. On one side of the street, to his right, was the end of the Forge Building, and one block down was the darkened end facade of the Quadrangle Building. On his left was the looming brick wall of the abandoned gun factory, the Turret Lathe Building. He eased out into the middle of the street, waiting to see if his quarry would move. Him, of all goddamned people. Then there was a wink of red light down at the corner of the Turret Lathe Building, followed by a cracking sound and something lethal slashing the air near his head. He jumped across the street and flattened himself against the Turret Lathe Building's wall. There was another red wink, and this time, the bullet tugged at his pants leg before ricocheting off the brick wall and shattering a window in the chapel. Shit! The streetlight! He was perfectly illuminated.

He scrambled back across the street, looking for a place to hide, but there was nowhere to go. He saw what looked like an arm move down at the corner of the Turret Lathe Building, and he hit the deck as another round cracked the night air, followed by more ricocheting sounds. Small-caliber weapon. His neck blazed in pain again. Then he heard a siren in the distance. The arm was gone as Dan looked up from his sprawled position in the street. He got up and headed down the street, zigzagging like a broken field runner, getting away from the damned streetlight. He kept his eyes focused on the corner of the Turret Lathe Building, but there was no further movement. He wished to hell he had a gun. The siren was getting louder; now it sounded like two sirens.

He stopped twenty feet from the corner and crouched down beside the minimal shelter of a fire hydrant. He felt as if he was in a concrete canyon, with the massive wall of the gun factory on one side and the blank brick expanse of the Quadrangle Building on the other. Around the corner, he could just see the nose of a white pickup truck juttting out from behind a loading dock. White pickup. Why was that important? He couldn't remember. He wanted to get around that corner, but what would be waiting for him when he did? He decided he had to—he was too exposed out here in the street, and his quarry could be getting clean away down the street that met the one he was on in a T-junction.

He got up and sprinted across the street to the corner of the Turret Lathe Building, where he flattened himself against the brick wall. He listened for a minute, trying to hear over the sound of his own breathing, and then he threw himself around the corner and flattened himself against the side of a loading dock. He listened for the sounds of someone above him on the dock, but there was nothing, just the two sirens that were getting a lot closer. He thought he could see flashing blue lights reflecting off the skylight windows of the building across the street. His own breathing sounded very loud in his ears. Maybe's he's gone inside. He would have heard the sirens, too, and known that anyone running down the streets of the Navy Yard would be seen.

Dan crept around to the face of the loading dock and moved to the right-front fender of the pickup truck, which he now could see was parked in a notch between two loading docks. He peered under the truck, looking for feet. Nothing. But he could see that the doors to the factory building were open. Bet my ass he's in there. You'll bet your ass big time, you go in there, a voice in his head whispered. He's got the gun, remember? At that instant, a cop car squealed into the intersection, its lights on high beam and its blue lights flashing, but as he was about to stand up and wave, the car made a screeching turn to the left and careened back up the street he had just been on. He could hear the other car somewhere in the maze of industrial buildings but couldn't see it. Shit! He made his decision.

Keeping low, he went around the front of the truck, which appeared to be a Metro truck, of all things, and sidled up to the entrance of the factory.

He stood flattened against the left-side sliding door, which appeared to be made of steel panels that were thirty feet high and mounted on tracks. There was a large mound of debris and scrap metal piled in the open doorway, but there was a walk space of sorts on one side that he could get around. He chose the other side, figuring the walk space might be targeted. He crept, bent over, across the front of the pile of debris and then bolted up over the right side of the scrap heap, tripping on something and losing his footing at the top, then sprawling down the other side into the darkness of the huge building just as another shot cracked into the pile. He rolled quickly across the floor in the darkness until he came up against a piece of machinery; then he flattened himself on the entrance side of it. He waited, listening, trying to dampen down his own breathing. Outside, the sirens were getting louder again, and this time a cop car came blasting right by the entrance to the factory and hurtled on down the street. Dan could only hope they would figure it out and start looking in the buildings soon. Starting with this one, please.

He thought he heard something move, maybe twenty feet away, and slowly turned his head. There was some light in the building, but it was all up high, and the shadows down here on the factory floor were pretty solid. Conscious of that gun, he decided not to stay in any one place for very long. He crawled on his bare hands and the tips of his toes to stay as quiet as possible. He came around the edge of the block of machinery, stopped for an instant, and then began to make his way toward the next large dark shadow about twenty feet farther into the building. He became extremely conscious of sounds then—his own breathing, the little rustling noises of rats skittering through the piles of scrap littering the floor, the deep-throated hum of the power plant fans next door, the crazy, distant siren circus going on outside, and the low sounds of the night breeze off the river whistling in the maze of girders way above his head. He reached the next machine, which appeared to be a giant drill press of some kind, and folded himself down against its base. He could see better now, and he was dismayed to realize how clear a target he had been coming through that door. The feel of the cold steel foundation of the drill press was comforting against his neck—until he felt it move.

"That's good, Daniel," a voice said above his head. Dan froze, and then he looked up. Captain Summerfield, in his dress blues, his jacket open, the gun in his right hand, and what looked like a black box of some kind in his left hand, sat above him on the operator's chair, the four gold stripes on his sleeve glinting dangerously in the gloom, his face pale but recognizable.

"I was right," Dan said. "It *was* you. Running."

"Running, yes. I suppose I'll have to get used to that now. That wasn't too bright, your running out in the open against a man with a gun like that."

"How the hell did you get here? We left you in the Pentagon and drove right over."

Summerfield smiled. "I took your beloved Metro. Fifteen minutes."

"Are you going to kill me, too?" Dan asked, trying to keep the fear out of his voice.

"Only if I have to. I really haven't killed anyone— that was all that idiot Malachi, your night visitor."

"But you instigated it."

"I guess in a way I did. Although like too many things in this town, what happened was not at all what was intended. Believe it or not, the killings were screwups—both of them."

Dan started to crawl out from under the machine to get a better look at Summerfield, but he stopped moving when the little gun came up like a snake's head. Outside, it sounded as if there were more cop cars getting into the act.

"And it wasn't the vice, was it?" Dan said. "It was NIS. Keeler. Walker T. Keeler. W.T. But the vice, Randall, Rennselaer—they were all in it, weren't they?"

Summerfield sighed and began to climb down from the operator's chair. "Rennselaer went to Randall with it, once the girl started to become a problem. That was two years ago, right after I had to leave my EA job with the previous vice chief. Randall was new, and he came to me because I had some assets left over from my OLA days that could take care of problems like that. He didn't tell the vice; Admiral Torrance would have sent Keeler home if he'd found out about the affair. Retired him in thirty days flat. But Keeler was his protégé, so the EA did what EAs do: He tried to protect both his own boss and the flag officer with the short circuit between his brain and his crank."

"By *killing* her?"

They both stopped as the sirens got closer again. Then the sirens began to wind down, leaving a galaxy of blue strobe lights flickering through the skylight windows.

"No. Ward was a contractor I had used from time to time to take care of problems when I was up in legislative liaison. He'd been recommended by a Hill staffer I knew. Keeler thought the girl was about to make a rude noise, so Ward was supposed to drop around and scare her off. That was all. Instead, she got mad and pulled a knife and apparently cut him up. He ran her over with a truck the next morning—the one parked out front, I imagine."

"Lovely. And her brother?"

"Almost the same thing, really." Summerfield sighed. He appeared to be listening for the sounds of cops out front. "The brother somehow found out about the affair, unfortunately right before the girl met her . . . accident. Came down from Philly and demanded a meeting with Rear Admiral Keeler. Rennselaer panicked and asked me to handle the meeting. The girl's death was being reported as an accident, but Rennselaer suspected that somehow it might not have been. Since my man had been sent to hush her up, it fell on me to see if we could shut the boy up, or at least divert him. We stalled him at a meeting in the Army Navy Town Club, and, once again, Ward was told to intimidate him into silence. He turned it over to some people in Philly. They mishandled it, and the boy ended up getting killed."

"Jesus. All this to protect one officer from the scandal of a senior officer–junior officer love affair?"

"A comedy of errors—or tragedy. But then there was nothing to be done, and for two years, we thought the whole thing had blown over—that is, until the kid's body was found in the *Wisconsin*. Keeler had to have known that two deaths were beyond coincidence, but there was nothing he could do about it. It was Rennselaer and Randall who cooked up the gambit of OpNav taking the investigation."

"So that part was all a prearranged little dance."

"To begin with. But once you and Miss Snow brought it back to town, the vice chief began asking questions. And once it looked to Randall that the vice might actually find out what had happened, it fell to me to eliminate the one guy who could pin this tail on all us donkeys, Malachi Ward. I took certain measures to expose him to the police, trying to make him run for it. It would have worked, too, except that you and the indomitable Miss Snow wouldn't leave it alone."

"But he implicated the vice the night he came after us! He talked about the vice's flunky."

"When it all started, I *was* the vice's EA, wasn't I? He just assumed I still was. Which brings me to business, Daniel. I can't be here when the Keystone Kops out there finally figure out which building to look in. But I need some insurance, so you're going with me. Get up."

Dan became aware that there were sounds of people outside now, the chunking of car doors, and more blue lights flickering across the ceiling—except that they were not at the front entrance. Summerfield looked over at the doors and laughed harshly.

"Rent-a-cops. They're surrounding the wrong damn building. I love it. Start walking—that way."

GRACE HAD SNATCHED the old guard's gun without a second thought and run down the stairs before any of them could even start yelling. She raced through the front door of the Forge Building, turned right, in the direction that Dan had disappeared, ran down in front of the Forge Building until she came to the chapel, and then stopped. Her heart was pounding from the sudden exertion. Who the hell was Dan chasing? It had to be that Ward character. She had been stunned to see Rennselaer coming down the hall:

Robby said he had gone to a late meeting, and they both had assumed—
except, at the edges of her mind, she thought the man running through the
gun park had been in a Navy uniform. A crack of gunfire echoed up the
street a block in front of her, and she flinched when the bullet made a
spanging noise off a brick wall. She hefted the pistol in her right hand and
examined it for the first time. It was huge. She would need two hands just
to point it. She walked rapidly down the remaining part of the block to the
corner of the Forge Building, then stopped. Now what? Stick her head
around the corner? Suddenly, that seemed an unattractive idea. Except that
Dan was down there, somewhere, and Dan did not have a gun, and the
person he was chasing obviously did. Her decision was made for her when
the front doors to the Forge Building burst open a block behind her and
the two security guards ran down the steps. The large woman saw Grace
and yelled at her to stop. Grace turned and looked back, which allowed the
guards to see the pistol. The large woman hauled her weapon out and yelled
for Grace to drop it. Grace hesitated, then stepped around the corner into
the streetlight.

The light. She was standing under a streetlight. She had to move. She
started running again, down the street, away from the Forge Building and
the cops, and across the street parallel to the Turret Lathe Building. She
slipped sideways into the next street, which separated the Forge and the
Quadrangle buildings. She never thought she would appreciate the absence
of streetlights, but she exhaled forcefully when she reached the shadows
between the two buildings and flattened herself against a wall. The Turret
Lathe Building loomed in front of her, its ten-story-high windowless brick
walls rising into a penumbra of river mist backlit by the power plant's
floodlights behind it. Where the hell were they?

Now she could hear sirens in the distance. She wanted to call out to Dan
but was afraid to. She was still holding the big pistol in both hands, and
suddenly her arms were getting tired. Great. Can't even hold the damn gun
up, she thought. She tried to remember her NIS indoctrination. Don't stand
still when the other guy has a gun. She started moving again, trying to
make herself small, proceeding down the block along the back end of the
Quadrangle Building until she reached the T-intersection between the street
she was on and the one that ran in front of the Turret Lathe Building—
which is where she saw the white pickup truck. It *was* Ward. He had
followed her in a white pickup truck. Except this one had a yellow flasher
unit on the roof. She edged down a few more yards until she could see the
front of the Turret Lathe Building; she spotted the open doors. They're in
there, she thought. The sirens were getting louder. Wait for the cops; point
them in the right direction.

A cop car came down the street between the Forge Building and the
Quadrangle Building, its lights blazing and the siren going full blast. It
slowed as it reached the intersection, and Grace started waving at them,

but then the idiots turned *left*, away from her. Goddamn it, this way, she almost yelled, but she held back, not wanting to expose her presence, in case Ward was just inside that darkened doorway across the street. With Dan. At gunpoint? Oh God, did he have Dan? A second cop car came down the street on the other side of the Quadrangle Building, sound-and-light show going full blast, screeched through the intersection, and went right on past the open doors of the Turret Lathe Building. Jesus Christ, she thought, cops everywhere, and here she was, standing on the sidewalk with a gun in her hand, waving at them, and they didn't *see* her?

She ran across the street and crouched down by the right door of the pickup truck, which was stuck between the two loading docks. The open doors were only twenty feet away. They were big doors, rising three stories into the entrance frames. She stood up slowly and looked into the pickup truck. The keys were in it, along with some small duffel bags; the butt of an automatic pistol sticking out of a side pocket of one of the bags. Ward. He had had a pistol like that in Georgetown. She was sure of it. Crouching, she crept around the front of the truck, running her left hand over the heavy steel grating, and walked very slowly over to the left side of the Turret Lathe Building entrance, the guard's cannon held out in front of her, her hands trembling with its weight. The entrance was pitch-black, with only a pile of scrap iron and cables fully illuminated in the streetlight. She nearly screamed when a dark furry shape scuttled across the loading dock, right in front of her. Then she heard more cop cars, which sounded as if they were converging on the Quadrangle Building across the street. Had they found them? Was this a false trail? She edged closer to the door, crouched down, and peered around the corner into the cavernous darkness inside. Were they in there? There was a lot of activity going on one block over. She flattened herself against the damp steel door and decided to call out Dan's name.

73

DAN STRAIGHTENED UP, turned around, and started walking, trying to see back over his shoulder, but his neck was too stiff. "You can't get clear of this, Captain," he said. "Even if you get out of the Navy Yard, there're gonna be cops all over Keeler and Rennselaer. And there's Ward."

"Ward has been, shall we say, neutralized. Without him, everyone can speculate, but if Randall and Rennselaer can hold their tongues, there will be no evidence. Now, I think this thing has about two rounds in it. It's a twenty-five-caliber Italian number. Zero stopping power. So if you get cute,

I'll put one in your brain, because I don't have ammunition to throw away. I don't want to shoot you. When I'm clear, you'll be free to go. But right now, I may need you to get through those clowns out there."

Dan tripped over some debris on the floor but regained his balance. He could not tell exactly where Summerfield was, but he knew that the captain was probably not making idle threats. Summerfield, the gun collector, the expert shot, who could probably have hit him out there on the street, even with a small-caliber pistol. He tried again to reason with the captain.

"You think if you let me go, I won't talk?" he said.

"I don't care if you do. I might be wrong, but after your little grandstand tonight in the vice's office, who'll believe you when you lash out at yet another flag officer with some preposterous, unprovable accusations? And don't count on the District cops: They're going to be behind you all the way—way behind you. You heard Vann. Go that way—toward the power plant side. Vann was freelancing, I take it. Why?"

"Wesley Hardin was his son."

Summerfield grunted but did not reply. He marched Dan carefully through the piles of debris, toward the long wall on the right side, deeper into the building, farther into the shadows. Dan started looking for a door along the shadowy wall, but there wasn't one. A chilling realization hit him: Maybe Summerfield *was* going to shoot him. Then Grace's voice called from up in the front of the building.

"Dan? Dan, are you in here? Dan, *answer me!*"

Dan turned toward her voice, saw her figure clearly silhoutted in the doorway seventy-five feet away, but then Summerfield moved to stand between him and the front door, the gun held in his right hand, his right hand cupped in his left hand, his body in professional shooter's stance. Dan could not see his face, but he was shaking his head from side to side, as if to warn Dan to keep silent.

"Dan!" she called again. "The police are here. Captain Vann's on his way. The security people heard shooting. *Answer me!*"

Two bullets left, Dan thought frantically. If he yelled now and dropped, Summerfield might fire and miss. Then he would have one round. Grace was a long way away, and one round was better than two.

"Grace, get down!" Dan yelled. As he dropped and rolled, then kept rolling, the searing heat of a .25-caliber bullet grazed his left ear as Summerfield whirled and fired. Dan rolled and scrambled, his neckbones screaming, hoping to all hell that Grace had heeded his warning. When he collided in the darkness with the base of a large machine, he froze, and listened. Now there was another cop car speeding down a street outside, then the sounds of a tire-screeching turn and brakes out front, and suddenly the car's headlights were pointed into the factory, sending a dusty beam of bright light right down the middle of the shop floor, transfixing Dan. He sat up, momentarily blinded, but then he froze, when he saw Summerfield standing to one side, not ten feet away, backlighted by the headlights. Dan started to roll, but then something hit him with the power of a locomotive and flung him back against the machine's pedestal. *The hell that thing doesn't have stopping power,* he thought wonderingly as his mind went over the edge of a wide, smooth black waterfall, the diminishing sound of gunfire echoing in the distance.

74

GRACE DROPPED DOWN on one knee when Dan yelled; she heard the shot, then realized she was probably silhouetted in the doorway. She scuttled sideways, tripping over all the junk piled around the entrance. She regained her balance as she heard a cop car coming down the side street. There were thirty seconds of rising noise from the cop car, and then it came around the corner and screeched to a halt when the driver apparently saw Grace through the doorway, its front end slewing around so that its headlights pointed directly down the center of the gun factory's floor. In the sudden blaze of white light, she saw Dan on the floor first. His face—was that blood? And then she caught sight of the tall figure standing to one side, stripes, lots of stripes—a naval officer. Who the hell *was* that? Then the tall figure pointed something at Dan, and Grace, galvanized by his move, stood up and began firing the pistol as fast as she could. The big gun bucked and roared in her hands, the muzzle flash momentarily blinding her. There was an amazing amount of gunsmoke, and she could hear heavy bullets ricocheting off the machinery. The silence when she had emptied it was almost painful to her ringing ears, and she realized her eyes were closed. When she opened them, the tall figure was gone. Then there were two cops scrambling into the building behind her, guns drawn, faces white.

"What the hell's going down here, lady?" one yelled at her. They looked as if they didn't know whom to point their weapons at.

She dropped the empty gun and headed into the building. "Snow, NIS!" she shouted over her shoulder. "Get an ambulance." The cop was yelling something back at her, but she ignored him and ran over to where Dan was lying in a crumpled heap. And then she saw all the blood: His face was covered in blood, and there was blood all over the floor. Head shot. Oh my dear God, a head shot. He was very still. She heard a noise farther down the building and caught a glimpse of a running figure all the way at the other end of the factory floor. He was headed for the far corner. One of the cops saw him, too, and yelled for him to stop.

"That's him," Grace yelled. "That's the shooter. Stop him. He's getting out the back of the building! He's killed Commander Collins!"

The cop yelled again and assumed a firing stance, but now there was nothing to shoot at. He lowered his weapon as Grace came running past him.

"Hey, lady, I need to see some ID," the cop shouted. His partner was back in the car, which was sitting in the opened doorway, calling for an ambulance. Grace never stopped; she ran right to the pickup truck. She clawed open the door, jumped in it, her mind galvanized by a white fury, started the truck in a roar, and jammed it down into gear. The big F-250 bolted out of the loading dock, laying rubber and nearly colliding with another cop car that was pulling up. Grace cranked the wheel and turned back down the street that ran along the side of the Turret Lathe Building, lights out, accelerating past a bevy of cop cars, scattering cops in every direction and knocking the taillights off one car. She reached blindly for the bag with the gun in it, never taking her eyes off the street, finding the butt with her right hand and extracting it from the bag. She had the truck halfway down the building when she saw him climbing out of a window over a door at the far corner, struggling for a moment, then dropping to the pavement in a heap, getting up, starting to run along the street, his jacket with those four stripes flying. As she veered over to his side of the street, still accelerating, she grappled with the automatic, trying to point it. Bastard had killed Dan. She took her left hand off the wheel for an instant to turn on the lights and nearly lost control of the truck. The fleeing man kept running, but then suddenly he skidded to a stop at the side of the road as if he had finally noticed the oncoming pickup truck. He raised his gun hand as Grace floored it, the engine winding flat out, the vision of Dan's bloody, lifeless face superimposed on the windshield as she focused on the motionless figure at the side of the street, the figure in the full uniform of a captain, USN. Then she recognized him: *Summerfield!*

She took her foot off the accelerator, hunting for the brake pedal, her brain not wanting to register the fact that Summerfield had stepped off the sidewalk and was calmly walking out into the path of the truck, that he had lowered his arm and was looking right at her when the truck hit him and blasted his body seventy-five feet through the air, to crash through a lighted window in the first floor of the Forge Building. Grace slammed on the brakes, skidding the truck for over a hundred feet until it finally spun around in the street in a shriek of tires and nearly turned over before rocking back on to all four tires and stalling out. She collapsed over the steering wheel, screaming Dan's name and pounding on the wheel rim with the gun until she became aware that there were cops standing all around her. A sergeant started to approach the door on the driver's side, when another cop called out.

"Careful, Danny. Jesus Christ, don't piss her off. She knocked that fucker clear into that building!"

Grace realized she was still holding on to the gun with her right hand. She took a deep breath, lowered the window, reversed the grip, and handed the gun to the sergeant, then sat back against the seat. Everyone seemed to relax when she handed the gun out, and then the sergeant was gingerly opening the door. She got out, weak-kneed, and he took her by the arm and walked her over to one of the cop cars. She reached for her identification, then realized she didn't have a purse.

"I'm Grace Ellen Snow," she said. "Formerly of the NIS. My—Commander Collins—is he . . . is he—?"

"The guy in the gun factory? The commander is gonna be okay, miss," the sergeant said. "Guy winged him in the ear, and we found a stun gun on the floor."

"In the ear? There was all that blood—"

"Yeah, well, you know ears. They're taking him to Bethesda. Now look, Miss Snow, I gotta read you your rights and all, okay? I mean, that bit with the truck, that guy stepping out in front of you that way, that may have been righteous and everything, but right now—"

"I understand. When can I see Commander Collins? I—"

"Well, first, I think we ought to go back to the NIS offices. I mean, this is gonna be complicated. Did you say *formerly* of the NIS?"

Grace slumped against the side of the cop car. There were a great number of cars and people milling around in the street now. She could tell that some of them were still unsure of who the good guys were. Then she saw a familiar face in the crowd.

"That's Capt. Moses Vann, of the D.C. police," she said, pointing. "Homicide. Please, let him through. He can help clarify this."

"Okay, but we gotta take you back to the NIS offices."

They let Vann through and he joined Grace in the cop car after identifying himself to the Navy Yard police. The sergeant drove Grace around the block to the entrance of the Forge Building, where there was a small crowd of NIS staffers and security people at the entrance. Vann didn't say anything during the short trip, but he did surreptitiously take her hand. She didn't realize how badly she was trembling. When they rounded the corner, she was surprised to see an ambulance out in front. Did they have Dan in there? They pulled nose-to-nose with the ambulance. Vann got out and gave her a hand out of the car. As she was escorted up the front steps, she saw Robby Booker and the elderly security guard on the steps. Then two other familiar figures appeared: Rear Admiral Keeler and Captain Rennselaer. Both looked as if they were in shock. The admiral had a medical orderly at his elbow, and he appeared to have some cuts on his face. Keeler paused for a moment when he caught sight of Grace, but then he walked by, stone-faced, toward a waiting staff car with Rennselaer, whose face was white with shock. They were followed out the door by Doug Englehardt, who stopped in his tracks when he saw Grace and the policemen.

"Grace, what are you doing here? Good God, are you all right? What the hell's—"

"I'm all right, Doug. Why is there an ambulance here?"

"You don't know? Of course not, how could you. But . . . well, there's been some kind of shoot-out down the block, and then, and then—" He took a deep breath. "We were all—Ames, the admiral, the EA, myself— we were all meeting in Admiral Keeler's office, about the Hardin case, when, Jesus, I don't know how to say this."

"What, for God's sakes?" She could see the cops were getting impatient.

"Well, we'd been looking out the windows at all the cop cars and had just sat back down again. Roscoe Ames and I heard what sounded like a vehicle coming up the street at high speed. The admiral was impatient to get on with the meeting, so neither of us got up to look, and then this body came flying through the windows. I mean just that: flying through the goddamned window like a rag doll. Right through the window, the venetian blinds, glass every goddamn where—the admiral even got cut. And the body—the guy was Navy. A four-striper."

"Oh," she said. "Well."

"Well? *Well!* Jesus Christ, Grace. Look, they've made a tentative iden- tification. Rennselaer said he recognized the guy, although it was kinda, uh, difficult." Englehardt swallowed. "But like I said; he was a naval officer. A captain—"

Summerfield," she finished for him. "Ronald Summerfield. I have to go inside now, Doug." Leaving Englehardt standing there with his mouth open, Grace went up the steps and into the building.

75

FOUR DAYS LATER, at just after five in the afternoon, Dan and Grace were sitting in the Potomac Boat Club lawn chairs, waiting for Moses Vann. They were watching several rowers milling about the boat landing, all of them anxious to get out on the river for the last hour of daylight. Dan was wearing his rowing togs, and Grace was wearing slacks and an old George- town sweatshirt. Dan's left ear and cheek were still bandaged. They sat in comfortable silence, worn out after days of testifying before the Navy's Article 32 hearing in the Pentagon and giving seemingly endless statements to various kinds of police.

Dan reflected on the past three days. The Chief of Naval Operations's office had moved swiftly to convene the pre-court-martial investigation and hearings after the events of Monday night in the Navy Yard. Dan's and Grace's testimony had been pivotal to untangling the conspiracy surrounding the two Hardin murders, especially with Summerfield dead and Ward in the city mental hospital. It had become clear after three days of Article 32 hearings before a military judge that Summerfield, Randall, and Rennselaer had been the key players in the conspiracy to protect Rear Admiral Keeler, although, absent any testimony to the contrary from the three captains, Keeler could not be tied directly to either of the Hardin murders. Randall, loyal EA to the last, had steadfastly maintained that he had kept everything from the vice chief, concocting the diversion of the original investigation from NIS to OpNav under the pretext of public-relations concerns strictly on his own volition.

Dan was still worried about Grace's emotional battery levels. She had gone through three days of hearings stoically, but the nights had been stormy, with sieges of crying and one more nightmarish episode of being almost hysterically ill in the middle of the night on Wednesday. Her doctor had told Dan that she was suffering from an assault of delayed stress anxiety but that with his support and presence, she should come out of it in a few weeks. The coroner's finding that Summerfield had, in effect, committed suicide in front of the truck had helped. But they both knew that it would take some time to get themselves back on an even keel.

Dan finally spotted the policeman coming through the boat shed and waved him over, indicating that he should bring one of the folding chairs. Vann walked down the lawn, shucking his suit coat as he came; it was almost hot in the gleaming late-afternoon sunlight along the river. He looked incongruous in his white shirt and tie among all the seminaked men toting shells and sculls down to the pontoon landing. The immense pistol hanging out of its shoulder rig raised some eyebrows as he came down the hill, but no one was prompted to say anything.

"So what happened to spring? This feels like summer down here," he said as he plopped down in the chair, draping his suit coat over his knees and putting his briefcase on the ground.

"You're just out of uniform," Dan replied. "Compared with July and August, this is heaven. You ought to give it a try sometime."

Vann looked around at the rowers, taking in the glossy, expensive-looking boats and then casting a dubious eye at the ramshackle club building.

"I'm too old for this vigorous exercise stuff," Vann muttered, quickly looking somewhere else when a trim and fit-looking man of at least seventy came out of the boathouse, a shiny fiberglass single balanced easily on his head. Grace and Dan grinned.

"So what did you think of the Navy's Article Thirty-two hearing process?" Dan asked.

Vann shook his head in wonderment. "I've never had a double homicide case come to closure as fast as this one," he said. "When the Navy wants to put something to bed in a hurry, they can flat ass move." He fished in his briefcase and then handed Dan a large manila envelope. "Here's your copy of my disposition report. That JAG captain said the Navy paperwork would take a couple of weeks."

"So it will stay in military jurisdiction, then?" Dan asked.

"Yup. And there ain't no volunteers downtown who want it any other way. Seems like your CNO can organize a court-martial hearing at the speed of heat, he gets him some guilty bastards in his sights."

"Randall and Rennselaer both pleading guilty?" Grace asked.

"And Keeler," Vann said.

"But not to murder?"

"No. See, the only guys directly tied to the murders were Malachi Ward and your Captain Summerfield. The captain . . . well, he's in the ground. And as for Ward, the docs up at St. Elizabeth's figure he isn't gonna come back among the mentally competent anytime soon, if ever. He's been screaming since that security watch found him in that museum ship Wednesday morning, and now they got him in diapers and twenty-four-hour restraint, with Thorazine cocktails twice a day."

"How did they find Ward?"

"Security guard found his windbreaker on the main deck, with what looked like bloodstains. He eventually organized a search of the ship, and they found him the next morning."

"I wish they'd never found him," Dan said, his face suddenly grim. "There was justice in where he ended up . . . in that ship."

Vann snorted. "Justice? Since when does justice enter into it? I'm a cop, remember? You don't talk about justice to a cop. But Ward's been useful, in his own twisted way."

"How so?" Grace asked.

"Neither of those EAs nor that Admiral Keeler fella knew what kind of shape Ward was really in after he was found in that boiler."

"And the government didn't exactly clarify it for them, did it?" Dan said.

"That JAG captain, he's a pretty fair prosecutor. What do you guys call him, trial counsel? Well, anyway, as long as Ward is alive, they all figured they'd be better off copping federal conspiracy pleas to a military judge than going to a civilian court and having that Ward guy testify under some grant of immunity. So the two EAs are both going down on conspiracy-to-murder charges and double OJ one. They'll go in for fifteen to life. The admiral has himself a civilian attorney, so we'll have to see what he does." He consulted his folder for a moment. "And the Navy threw in a charge I really love against the admiral." He snorted. "Conduct unbecoming an officer. That's rich."

Dan shook his head. "I'll bet the vice chief instigated that. It's more serious than it sounds. Conduct unbecoming is grounds for a ruling of moral turpitude. And moral turpitude is the one charge under Title Ten U.S. Code for which the admiral can be *administratively* stripped of his commission—which is to say, his pension, medical benefits, and all future veterans' benefits."

"I didn't know that," Vann said. "I thought it was just ceremonial, sort of walking the plank or something. What's gonna happen to NIS?"

"NIS? NIS is a collection of working stiffs trying to get a job done. Their boss and his EA went bad, not the troops. They'll get a new boss, and the Navy will probably change the organization's name."

"And Admiral Torrance walks free?" Grace asked.

"Not quite," Dan said. "Three days of news coverage on this whole mess means he'll never even go up for a confirmation hearing as the next CNO. It was his EA obstructing justice, and, at least administratively, his own orders to move the investigation around between NIS and OpNav. And all the flags know that Keeler was one of his crown princes. So, basically, he'll pay the price of being indistinguishable from his EA."

"Do you think he was part of it?" Grace asked Vann.

"Who the hell knows," Vann said with a sigh. "That's the old Washington question, isn't it? What did he know, and when did he know it? But a guy like that is pretty wily. Personally, I think he might have known more than he's letting on, but when he ordered you to help me get back into the investigation, he went a long way toward neutralizing any attack we could make on his personal credibility. And from what both of you have said in your statements, it looks like the EAs were the real players. But with Summerfield gone and Ward in a rubber room . . ." He shrugged.

Grace shuddered at the mention of Summerfield's name again. Dan took her hand.

"I still don't understand Summerfield's motives in all this," she said. There was a moment of silence while they watched a two-man shell make a less-than-graceful landing alongside one of the pontoons, accompanied by a great deal of rude and raucous commentary from other club members.

"I think it was the EA mentality that got him," Dan said finally. "You know, that total dedication to the promotion and preservation of their ad-miral, or whoever their principal is. Summerfield explained part of it to me awhile ago, the fact that there can be no mistakes, no ripples around the great man. This thing probably started as relatively minor damage control— you know, the old-hand EA showing the new guy how it's done in the big city. My guess is that the EAs were never going to let the vice chief find out that Keeler had even screwed up."

"You said in your statement that he had been an EA himself," Vann said.

"Yeah. That's why I think he reacted the way he did. Because of his wife's stroke, he had to take himself out of contention for flag and give up the EA job. I think he missed the action and the intensity; OP-Six-fourteen is not exactly a career-enhancing assignment for a flag-contender captain. But once the hired hand dropped them all in the septic tank, they just did what Washington horse-holders do: They hung on and hoped like hell no one would make waves; that somehow it would just go away."

"Murder never just goes away," Vann said, a bleak expression on his face.

"You lost a son," Grace said.

"A son I never really had," Vann said after a moment of reflection. "I should have done more than just talk when he said he was going to look into something about Elizabeth's death."

"You couldn't possibly have known what that was all about," Grace protested.

"That's the amazing part about it. Somebody says something like what Wesley said, and it's like that TV show I saw on PBS the other night, the one about volcanoes. These scientists are standing out on this solidified lava field, a supposedly dead one, and then they walk over to this hole in the lava, and you can look down there and see this goddamn *river* of fire flowing under their feet, going like all hell. You'd never know it was even there."

They were silent for a while, watching the Potomac and the rowers and listening to the sounds of the traffic high up on the bridge above them. Vann finally turned to Dan.

"You said you're gonna be leaving town?"

"Yeah. Summerfield was right. My continued presence on the OpNav staff is apparently unsettling to some influential people up the E-ring. They're sending me to command, though, so I can't bitch."

Vann nodded, then, glancing at Grace, asked Dan if he was going by himself.

"Never again," Dan said, squeezing Grace's hand.

"Good," Vann said. "That was my other screwup in life—walking away from Angela. I've got to do something about that, but I'm damned if I know how, or even what."

"Does she know how this all came out?"

"Yeah, but it doesn't bring her kids back, does it? But maybe she can see the road clear to being at peace about it. Maybe this time I can even help. But lemme ask you something, Commander. After all this, you gonna stay in, past your twenty, if you make captain?"

Dan paused before answering. He and Grace had spent a considerable amount of time since Monday night talking about this exact issue.

"I think I'm going to have to see what kind of Navy it is when I get back from sea duty," he said slowly. "You see, there're really two Navies: There's the fleet, and then there's the so-called Washington establishment. The fleet is mostly about taking ships to sea and keeping them and your people safe as you can while you go do what warships do. There's politics, of course, but when the sea rises up, everybody understands that politics goes overboard. Washington is mostly about the game of getting promoted. I can't answer your question right now, I guess is my real answer."

Vann nodded again, remaining silent when he realized Dan wasn't finished.

"See, the hell of it is," Dan continued, "you have to be good ashore in order to get up the ladder so that you can go back to the ships in increasingly responsible jobs—department head, executive officer, and finally command. And that's always made sense to me, because the net result of playing the political game well is that captain's chair on the bridge. After command, though, you're a relatively old man, and there are very, very few slots for admirals at sea. That's where I think the system has fallen down. We ended up World War Two with ten thousand ships and maybe five hundred admirals. Now we have fewer than four hundred ships, and over two hundred admirals. And it's not just the Navy; the other services have the same problem. Getting to stars has become such a high-stakes game in itself that people will do almost *anything* to get a shot, like these EAs did. I guess I'm going to keep going for as long as I can see a reasonable opportunity to be a naval officer. But after that . . ."

Vann smiled as he gathered up his briefcase and jacket. "After that, you'll probably hang in there till they throw you out," he said. "Just like we all do. I gotta split, guys. It's been a trip, you know that?"

"We'll let you know what the orders look like."

"Yeah, you do that."

Dan stood up and shook hands with the policeman. Grace reclaimed Dan's hand as the captain walked up toward the clubhouse.

"I wonder if he'll ever get out from under that Wesley cloud," she mused.

"If he does, it'll be because he tries to help Angela Hardin. That 'if only I had' game is a bitch when you try to play it one-handed. You are still going to marry me, right?"

She smiled and squeezed his hand. Her smile almost made the shadows under her eyes disappear. "I believe I've answered that question, Commander. About three dozen times, I think."

"Just checking," Dan said, looking back out over the glinting gray river and rubbing his bandaged ear absently. "Just checking," he said again, squeezing her hand. "Things get loose sometimes."

76

IN A DIMLY LIT, windowless room, Malachi sat on the floor, his one good eye fixed on the green steel door across the room. He was wearing a loosely fitting restraint web over hospital pajamas, but he was not in diapers. The room had a steel bed and a commode, and even a chair that was bolted to the floor. But he preferred the floor for right now. He could think better— think about getting out, think about the captain.

The dreams were better now; that was good medicine they brought him. Not as good as the Harper, but life was full of little compromises. Time enough to get back to the Harper when he got out. He had actually joked about whiskey with the orderly who brought him his two meals a day. After three weeks in here, he had started really working on making friends with the orderly. Making little deals with him: Since that first day, I've given nobody any problems, so maybe loosen the restraints one notch— just one. And yesterday, or maybe the day before—he wasn't sure—the orderly had brought a helper in and they had loosened things up a little.

The medicine made him sleep a lot, but that was all right, too. The sleep was like passing out after an all-nighter with the Harper, but without the hangover. Although that might be because they kept him on the medicine round the clock. You don't ever leave the bar, there's never a hangover. Every drunk knew that. But his victory on the restraints had been important. That first day, when they'd found him in the boiler, he'd been just a little hysterical. And then he had really lost it when they restrained him again at the hospital. They just didn't understand. But it was okay now. He knew he was safe. And he knew some other things, too, things that he would *never* tell the doctors or the police or anyone else who came to talk to him. Malachi had a plan.

He would just wait them out—weeks, months, years even. He would reinforce their preliminary conclusions: that he remembered nothing about the Hardin case, that being bolted into the boiler had seared every memory from his previous life right out of his brain. Hell, it damn near had. But he was tougher than they knew. He would be a model prisoner—excuse me, patient. No violence. Absolutely no displays of bad temper. No lunging for the momentarily unguarded door. No mashing any of the other residents into the drains at shower time. No snapping the neck bones of the younger orderlies who looked sideways at his face and whispered about the state of affairs below his belt.

None of that. He would be entirely docile. A disastrous past, a little mental trauma there, locked up in that boiler, but an entirely tranquil present. Eventually, and we'll take our time here, he would be able to converse normally. Participate in therapy, group discussions. And over time, no longer present a threat to anyone.

Eventually, they would stop worrying about him. Turn their attentions to newer, noisier casualties. He would become just another damaged box in the warehouse. Detached, peaceful, cooperative. Even friendly. Hell, maybe even a trusty. This was a public institution, and Malachi knew his civil servants. They would get lax about him, and then he would make his move. And find the captain, and his precious principal.

There were sounds of people out in the corridor. Malachi hunkered down on the floor, composed a bemused expression on his battered, one-eyed face, tested the straps again, and carefully watched the door.